MEMOIRS OF THE HUMAN WRAITHS

OMNIBUS EDITION

F.E. Feeley Jr.

Beaten Track
www.beatentrackpublishing.com

Memoirs of the Human Wraiths

Published 2019 by Beaten Track Publishing
Copyright © 2013–2019 F.E. Feeley Jr.

ISBN: 978 1 78645 321 1

Cover Concept/Designs: Roe Horvat

Beaten Track Publishing,
Burscough, Lancashire.
www.beatentrackpublishing.com

Around a campfire late at night, someone begins to tell a ghost story. Flashlights clutched in hands, we huddle close and listen with intensity, startling at the slightest sound, but we try to be brave.

This is no different.

Memoirs of the Human Wraiths, a book passed down from generation to generation, details the lives of those living on the edges of society, stalked by the darkness that awaits us all. Come see what walks the halls of Timber Manor. Step inside Jonathan's inescapable mirror. Venture to the island where promises made are enforced by a powerful curse.

Try to be brave.

CONTENTS

THE HAUNTING
OF TIMBER MANOR

While recovering from the recent loss of his parents, Daniel Donnelly receives a phone call from his estranged aunt, who turns over control of the family fortune and estate, Timber Manor. Though his father seemed guarded about the past, Daniel's need for family and curiosity compel him to visit.

Located in a secluded area of the Northwest, Timber Manor has grown silent over the years. Her halls sit empty and a thin layer of dust adorns the sheet-covered furniture. When Daniel arrives to begin repairs, strange things happen. Nightmares haunt his dreams. Memories not his own disturb his waking hours. Alive with the tragedies of the past, Timber Manor threatens to tear Daniel apart.

Sherriff Hale Davis grew up working on the manor grounds. Seeing Daniel struggle, he vows protect the young man who captured his heart, and help him solve the mystery behind the haunting and confront the past—not only to save Daniel's life, but to save his family, whose very souls hang in the balance.

PART ONE:
PICKING UP THE PIECES

THE RAIN POUNDED down on the cab of the truck, the wiper blades furiously working to no avail as my truck crept down the darkened forest road. I felt like I was driving underwater, deep in some forgotten sea. The music on the radio was barely a whisper, as I had the volume turned almost completely down; I held the steering wheel in a viselike grip, trying to see more than ten feet in front of me. The heater was cranked up on high to keep the windows from fogging up, and sweat trickled down the side of my face. I couldn't tell whether it was from the heat or from the fear tightening my gut. It was probably a combination of both.

Lightning danced across the sky, instantly followed by a peal of thunder that shook the world around me and caused me to yelp involuntarily and duck my head as I took my foot off the gas. My heart leaped into my throat as the thunder rumbled like a cranky dragon awakening from a deep slumber to find his treasure gone.

I had slowed the truck to a near crawl almost ten miles back when the torrential rains began. The two thousand or so miles from Texas had passed pretty well without incident, and I'd made very good time as I traversed hell's half acre. Now it felt like I was not moving at all, and I could barely make out the road in front of me. No cars passed me coming from the other direction, and nobody came up behind me. I was alone and isolated, as if the rest of the world had disappeared and all that existed was me and my old Chevy truck. Those thoughts didn't help the panic that was building.

Shall I pull over and wait the rain out? Or keep going until I find a gas station to pull in to?

F.E. Feeley Jr.

I didn't like the situation at all; this was how horror novels started, or some slasher movie. Some maniac wielding a knife or some other sharp weapon would come hurtling out of the woods or maybe appear at Billy Bob's gas station. You know, one of those rusted old out-of-the-way service stations no one has seen in forever.

The subject of the 1980s and 1990s horror flicks began to flash in my mind as well as each serial killer: Freddy Krueger, Jason Voorhees, Michael Myers…and who could forget the ghost-face killer in *Scream*? And of course that didn't account for the demon in *The Stand*, the ghosts in *The Shining*, or the werewolf in *Silver Bullet*. These movies were all part of my personal collection back home, their memory mocking me with sinister ease.

My throat was dry and begging for a drink; my eyes were strained and grainy from staring out into the night as rain sloshed my windshield, and my headlights peered into the darkness in a sad attempt to guide me to my destination.

How do I get myself into these situations?

A few nights ago, I'd been sitting at a campus bar with some of my friends, lamenting the end of the semester, and now here I was, wishing I were back in my dorm room surrounded by my belongings, homework, and familiarity, which were so far away. But that was before receiving the terrible news that flipped my entire world upside down.

Before that phone call, I was a college student ready to take on the world with a killer smile, a hot body, purposefully shaggy, unkempt hair, and a college degree. After the phone call, a visit to the morgue, and seven days of walking around in a stupor barely eating and hardly sleeping, unsure of what I'd signed or who I'd spoken to, I got into my truck and left it all behind me.

Now I was out in butt-fucked who-knows-where trying to reach my estranged aunt's house, where I would stay for the summer.

With one hand, I removed a Marlboro from its pack, slipped it into my mouth, and lit the end. Sweet nicotine heaven poured in as I placed my hand back on the steering wheel and thumbed

4

the window control. The burn of the drag in my lungs was the only thing on the way from Texas that reminded me I was, in fact, still alive. My head felt stuffed with cotton and my heart felt like a lead balloon. On my way, I'd eaten at fast-food joints, pissed in disgusting gas-station bathrooms (and once on the side of the freeway), and driven relentlessly from point A toward point B. Once, in Nebraska, I stopped only to get a room and passed out on the bed without taking my clothes off.

With the window rolled down midway, a deluge of rain pelted the side of my face, but like with everything else, I didn't care. My give-a-damn was fucked these days.

I put the cigarette in my right hand so it wouldn't get wet—addicts do the strangest things to get their fix. Besides, if I was going to die here in the backside of nowhere, either by a terrible car accident or a knife-wielding maniac, I was having a damn cigarette.

The rain coming through the cracked window was cool on my fevered skin, and the air, which carried the smell of the storm and the woods that surrounded me, pushed the smoke from my cigarette away with its fresh, clean fragrance. That air was sweet and again reminded me that I was, in fact, alive.

"Mr. Donnelly, can you confirm the identity of the man in front of you?"

I had stared up at the screen in the white room as a woman in a lab coat pulled away the sheet.

The city morgue smelled like antiseptic and something else. Something right underneath the smell of disinfectant. Something sticky and sweet and old that was impossible to wash off even as, hours later, I sat inside the shower with my arms wrapped around my knees. I could still smell it.

"Yes."

The man standing next to me nodded and spoke into a microphone. The woman in the white room put the sheet back and went to the next table. She pulled the second sheet back.

"And her?"

The shock of seeing her face caused me to turn mine away and squeeze my eyes shut. I nodded quickly.

"Yes?" *he prompted.*

An involuntary sob escaped my lips, but I nodded furiously and gritted my teeth against it. "Yes. Yes. It's her."

Another lightning flash lit the sky and I nearly jumped out of my seat as the world around me instantly turned a brilliant white but then disappeared. Thunder pealed again, this time closer and louder than before, and I knew the storm wasn't going to let up soon. I had to pull over or I was going to end up crashing into a tree. Game over. No law school for me.

The idea was disgustingly and seductively appealing. Suicide, I mean.

I could just hit the gas and my truck would rocket forward. I would stay on the road for a moment, maybe make Marty McFly's 88 mph before I slammed headlong into the thick trunk of a tree and ended it all. And then I wouldn't have to deal with this. I wouldn't have to go meet this lady who said she is my father's sister. I wouldn't feel like a zombie, wouldn't need to be alone in the world anymore. I could join my parents, and we could sail off into heaven together.

Or hell.

Or nothing, if the atheists are right.

My luck, all I'd do was break my legs, or snap my spine, and be in agony until someone showed up and untangled my ruined body from behind my steering wheel. Or better yet, I'd die, but because my truck caught fire and I was pinned. I'd slowly be burned to death.

I carefully pulled off to the side of the road and turned on my emergency flashers to hopefully avoid getting creamed by a passerby. Yet, somewhere deep inside, I didn't think anyone would be traveling down this road tonight.

I hoped more than anything that I was wrong.

I put the truck in park, engine running. The wiper blades slapped furiously, like a drowning man trying to hail a lifeguard at a beach. I took one last drag of my cigarette, flicked it out into the night, and rolled up my window. The left side of me was rain-soaked, and I shivered from the cool air I'd allowed in from the window, but it was soon replaced by the heat coming out of the register. I looked at the radio clock for the time, and it was only nine thirty at night. Still pretty early, but the storm cut out all ambient light except for the occasional flash of lightning. I leaned back into the seat and let the warm leather embrace my aching back as I laid my head against the headrest.

"Damn," I whispered.

I checked my phone for missed calls or messages, but there was no signal. So now I was not only stranded in the middle of nowhere, I had no way to call for help should I get attacked by Cletus the knife-wielding drifter. The rain pounded relentlessly on the cab of my truck. It began to have a lulling effect on me, and my eyes grew heavy. Trying to keep myself awake, I began to thumb through the radio stations. Not too many were available out here in the middle of butt-fucked who-knows-where, except one country music and another with a lone preacher saying, "We must have revival in this land!" I decided against both.

"This was a mistake," I said out loud as I wiped the nervous, clammy sweat from my brow.

I didn't even know this lady, and all of a sudden, she came out of the blue now that Mom and Dad were gone?

"This is nuts, Daniel," I whispered as the anxiety threatened to take over.

Lightning danced outside as if replying to my words, and the thunder shouted its amen almost instantly. Yet something caught my attention out of the corner of my eye. I thought I saw movement along the tree line as the world lit up like fire. I sat bolt upright in my seat, peering out into the rain-soaked darkness. I didn't realize I was holding my breath until my chest began to hurt and my temples began to ache. I let it out in a slow manner, as if my exhale would alert whatever ghoul or ghost or serial killer was lurking inside the shadows of those woods.

Another flash and my eyes locked on a pair of yellow eyes staring at me from the place where I saw them before. Not a ghost or a killer—a wolf.

Standing about twenty feet away, a huge, magnificent wolf was watching me with an oddly disconcerting amount of intelligence in its eyes, head hung low. Its gray-and-white fur was gorgeous and oddly dry-looking. I couldn't take my eyes off it. Instead of fading into the darkness, it began to walk forward into the headlights of my car. The beast never took its eyes off mine. Like it was staring into my soul.

My heart began to hammer and my breathing quickly picked up. My hands went back to the steering wheel and clamped down again, as white-knuckled as before. A chill passed through me, and the hairs on the back of my neck stood up straight. As if the wolf could sense my distress, it stopped and gave me a wicked grin.

"You know I can see you, don't you?" I whispered aloud. "You know I am afraid."

The wolf, in response, tilted its giant head up toward the rain and gave out a chilling howl as if to confirm that. *"Why, yes, I do know, dear boy. What do you think I'm doing here? You wanted to die? Step out of the truck, and I'll gladly make your dreams come true."*

The blood ran cold in my veins as another chill passed through me, from the top of my head to the soles of my feet, at the thought of such a grisly end. Stepping out of the truck, walking forward, the beast suddenly lunging, and its friends coming out from the trees to help it dine on a young man who tasted like sweat and cigarettes and a thousand miles of bad road.

I suddenly decided that staying alive wasn't so bad after all. But the lightning danced across the sky in giant arcs, illuminating the night, and just as fast as it had appeared, the wolf was gone.

I looked left and right into the torrential downpour but couldn't see anything. I couldn't have been paying attention, because suddenly a pair of headlights appeared behind me. Red and blue lights began to flash, and I let out a huge sigh of relief. I sat back in my seat and waited. A rap at my window, so I lowered it to find a cop in a rain slicker.

"Are you okay?"

"Yeah, yeah, I'm all right. I just pulled over to keep from getting into an accident."

The police officer was tall and fairly young—no more than thirty, I supposed. He asked for my driver's license and insurance paperwork, and I promptly handed him both. As he headed back to his patrol car to do whatever police officers do with those things, my eyes went immediately back to the front of the truck, and I suddenly wished I'd warned the officer about the wolf. Just a few minutes passed by, and then he rapped on my window again.

"Where are you headed?" he asked as he handed me back my things.

"I'm headed to my aunt's house just outside of Portland. A town called Emerson. I'm staying at her home this summer." I was going there to meet the only surviving member of my family now that both my parents were gone. I wasn't going to divulge that much information to him, though.

"You're Carol Donnelly's nephew?" His eyes grew wide and he stepped back.

"Yeah, that's my aunt." His reaction surprised me. Well, I guessed if you were a rich spinster lady who had a house large enough to be referred to as an estate, then she could have possibly achieved celebrity status, especially in a small town.

"Well, then, Danny"—my name is Daniel, and I loathed anyone calling me Danny, but I let it slide—"I'm Sheriff Davis, and I know exactly where your aunt lives. I can escort you to her house to make sure you get there all right if you'd like." The surprise left his face as he eased into a smile. I didn't want to let him go now that he was here, and the chance to be escorted safely to my destination was an offer I didn't want to pass up.

"Sure, man, that'd be great."

He nodded and pointed up the road. "It's going to be about another fifteen to twenty minutes that way. I'll drive slow and keep my lights on for you, and you follow close behind. The rain is letting up, so we shouldn't run into any trouble. I'll get you there safe and sound."

My eyes jerked up to his as he said the very last part. He was watching me intently.

It seemed like I was looking at his face for the first time. Handsome, chiseled, and defined. His nose was very prominent but not unattractive. It suited him; he almost had the look of a Roman general. His eyes were large and his lips full.

He flashed a comforting grin at me, and I couldn't help but smile back. That smile instantly disarmed me.

He's the killer, I thought. *He's going to lure you into the woods, and there he'll—*

Shut up!

"Sounds great, sure. I'll follow right behind you."

He turned and walked back toward his patrol car, and just as he said, the rain did lighten up. I looked once more at the spot where the wolf had been. Considering I was about to meet my father's sister for the first time, and the circumstances surrounding the meeting, I placed the wolf encounter in the back of my mind.

The sheriff's patrol car drove past mine with its flashers on; I put my truck in gear and followed. The woods slowly began to disappear along with the bad weather, and I couldn't help but gasp as the rolling hills opened up and the full moon hung low and heavy in the night sky. We took a few turns here and there, and soon enough a sprawling estate lay before us. The sheriff jumped out of his car, opened the gate, and motioned for me to pull forward. I slowly moved the truck toward him, hoping not to splash him with any puddles, and rolled my window down once more.

"You're going to drive up maybe a half a mile, and the road curves to the left. Now take it slow, because you're going to drive over a little covered bridge that passes over a creek, which, given the amount of rain we've had, is swollen, but just beyond that is the house. You can't miss it." He chuckled. "I called ahead. Your aunt Carol is waiting for you and was worried when she couldn't get you on your cell phone. I explained everything, so don't worry too much. Take care, Danny." He grinned.

I clenched my teeth at him calling me Danny again but disregarded it when I saw that grin once more. "Look, thank you so much. I really appreciate it."

"No problem, none at all. Your aunt is a very nice lady. She donates money every year to the sheriff's annual charity drive during the holidays. So we keep an eye out for her," he said sheepishly.

I nodded and began to drive away, then looked in the rearview mirror and saw him standing back there, watching me drive up the hill. I turned my eyes back onto the road.

I'd gotten more information from him about my aunt than I'd learned in all my twenty-three years. Mom and Dad had never mentioned her much, and when her name did get brought up, his eyes would darken and he would leave the room. Mom would look at him, annoyed, as he made his exit. For some reason my aunt and my dad did not get along.

I took the winding path across the covered bridge, and the sheriff had been right, the creek—if you could call it that—was rushing underneath quickly. But I made it across just fine, though my eyes grew large once again when I saw the house.

It was huge. There, nestled in some trees in front of me, stood a sprawling Victorian home. Instantly I felt nervous and underdressed as I wound up the paved driveway to the porte cochere. I put the truck in park and opened the door. The scent of rain-filled air slammed against me as the wind buffeted my half-soaked body, making my shirt ripple against me. My legs shook, either from nervousness, simple fatigue, or a combination of both. But they held me upright, and I was grateful as a lady, whom I assumed to be my aunt, came down the stairs of the porch. I would have known it was her wherever I saw her. The resemblance to my father left no doubt in my mind. I slammed the truck shut and jumped at the sound of it. She rounded the front of my vehicle and walked up to me. I didn't know what I should do. Hug her or shake her hand?

I was impressed by the way she was dressed and the way she carried herself. She wore a pair of black slacks and a large cashmere sweater, with a diamond brooch on her left breast. She was beautiful. Her hair was a mixture of black and gray, her clothing expensive. She was slim but not malnourished-looking. Nothing about this woman seemed weak or frail, and when she placed her hands on my upper arms and stared at me, I knew she was as sharp as a tack. I wouldn't have put her at over sixty years old.

"I have not seen you since you were in diapers." Her voice was melodious, and she looked at me in awe. "Daniel, you have grown into a fine young man."

A smile lit up her face, which was so much like my father's that I unexpectedly began to choke up. She even had his brown eyes. She wrapped her arms around me in a huge hug, despite my being wet, and I cleared my throat, fighting back emotions that threatened to surface.

She held me at arm's length again and motioned for a man who was patiently waiting on the porch.

"Thank you, Aunt Carol." My voice sounded strange to my own ears. Previous to this moment, I hadn't thought about calling her anything but Ms. Donnelly, but "Aunt" slipped out comfortably. Even though I didn't know her, her likeness to my father made her familiar.

"This is Thomas, my butler." She indicated a man who stepped out the door and came down the stairs. "He has worked for the family for many years, as did his father before him."

It wasn't until he reached me that I noticed he was like a walking mountain. Thomas's hair was as snow-white as the dress shirt he wore under his jacket. It was neatly combed back, and his uniform, tails and all, was pristine. He looked down at me with an intense stare that made me a little nervous, and then his face lit up in a smile.

"You look so much like your daddy, young man. It's good to see you again."

His voice was like a lounge singer's, whiskey-soaked and gravelly. Possibly sixty years old or so, he smelled faintly of aftershave, and my bags wouldn't give him any trouble. As a matter of fact, he looked like he could haul the truck itself upstairs. I shook his hand, mine disappearing into his, and waited for him to pull his arm back and wipe off his hand with a handkerchief or something.

In their company I felt like a drowned rat. Some poor beggar off the street coming to ask for alms. Something to be pitied. But he just grinned and patted me on the shoulder before asking where my belongings were.

Aunt Carol stood by and let us gather what I had brought with me. She took me by the arm and led me up the steps to the front door. The whole scene was overwhelming, but I let myself be taken into the massive house. The foyer was immaculate, and the house seemed to stretch into eternity from left to right and ahead. In front of us was an incredibly beautiful staircase, and Thomas climbed, carrying some of my things. My aunt took my laptop bag, and we walked up the marble steps together.

The furnishings were old—antiques—and velvet drapes hung at the windows. At the top of the staircase was the portrait of an old man, seated, with a beautiful woman standing behind him, her hand on his shoulder.

My aunt caught my stare and said, "That is your grandfather, Jim Donnelly, and your grandmother, Katherine. His father built battleships during World War II and owned a steel company called Donnelly Enterprises, most of which we still own today. Your grandfather inherited the company after his father passed away, and made money in international business. That is how this house came into being."

"Wow." I was stunned to know about all of this.

Aunt Carol laughed. "It's a lot to take in, but to be honest, Daniel, they were just two very kind people and very normal. They lived a very happy life and were much in love. Your grandmother passed away several years ago from cancer, and your grandfather just couldn't bear life without her. He followed her to heaven a few years later. You would have been ten years old at the time."

"I remember Dad and Mom talking about it, actually," I said, and immediately regretted divulging that because *talking* wasn't the right word.

Dad was distraught at grandfather's passing but pretended he didn't care. He and Mom fought about it constantly. I remember hearing them shouting from their bedroom. Aunt Carol gave my arm a sympathetic pat.

"Papa Jim and your daddy were so much alike it was scary. Headstrong and stubborn, those two argued from the moment your father was born, I think." She laughed good-naturedly and it eased my sudden bout of social awkwardness. "He wanted your father to follow in his footsteps and take part in the family business, but your dad had his own ideas."

"My dad was a Marine. Well, until he retired and opened up a business building sailboats. I guess business was in his blood." Again I felt awkward talking about him in the past tense. Since he and Mom had died, I half expected him to come out from behind a tree, or around a corner, or grab my foot in the morning to wake me up as he'd done since I'd been a kid. I'd hated when he did that—

I mentally shook myself to chase away the thoughts.

"I hear he was great at it," Carol said as she moved on. "Building boats, I mean."

I nodded. "Yeah. He was. He had customers from all over the country."

We'd always lived comfortably, but nothing like this. He'd set aside a college fund for me when I was born, and that's what I went to school on—although he never understood what a political science degree would do for me. Even as a young kid, I would read anything I could about the courts, and when I was in high school, I collected law books to read from cover to cover.

My aunt and I continued up another flight of stairs, heading to a long hallway and the room that would be mine. Thomas stood in the doorway, patiently waiting. He folded his hands in front of him, and as we approached, he stood aside to let us through.

The room Aunt Carol walked me into was incredible. The bed was a king-size canopy, which was massive, with ornate carvings etched into the frame. The furniture was beautiful and fit perfectly in a room that was at least five times the size of my dorm room back at the university. I felt like I'd walked back in time. A set of doors led out to the balcony, which overlooked the grounds in the front.

"That will be all, Thomas," Carol said. The man simply nodded and walked away. "This was your father's room when he was a boy. You have a private bathroom there off to the left, and you've already seen the balcony." I turned to her, wide-eyed, and she chuckled again, holding up her hands. "Daniel, don't be intimidated. This house has been in the family for many years, and it is as much a part of you as it is me. I hope you can feel comfortable and welcome here. When I heard of your mother and father's passing, I thought it would be good to let you know you still have some family left."

I looked at myself in the mirror over a dresser just past her: my eyes looked tired, and I didn't like the dark circles under them. My clothes were shabby and kind of just hung on me. I looked like a ragamuffin. I didn't have my father's frame, stocky and tall; I was slender. As a kid, I wasn't much into sports, but I loved to swim, and the years of doing laps had paid off. Yet now I just looked tired and worn-out. More than that, I felt worn-out. This had been a hell of a year.

Carol walked my laptop bag to the dresser and set it down.

I said, "I really appreciate you reaching out. Arranging Mom and Dad's funeral after their boating accident was surreal. Luckily, my professors had enough confidence in me to go ahead and pass me without my having to take finals. Which is a good thing, I guess. They were the last things on my mind. Dad and Mom already had most of the arrangements made, but I still had to meet with their lawyer in Texas and have them cremated like they wanted and sign paperwork." I noticed her looking at me in the mirror and wondered if I sounded as hollow to her as I did to myself.

"The authorities said the boat was lost during a storm," she whispered.

I nodded. "Dad took his sailboat out of Sabine Pass in Texas and headed to Florida. They were going to visit some old Marine friends of his near Tampa and decided to break out the sailboat early. A storm blew up, and he was able to radio in to the Coast Guard. But the mast had been struck by lightning, which caused a fire. The boat literally broke apart. They didn't have their life jackets on. Their bodies washed up—"

I stopped speaking immediately; it suddenly felt like my suitcase was standing on my chest, so I sat down on the edge of the bed. This was the first time I'd spoken about the incident, outside of the funeral viewing. The last few weeks were a blur of signatures, pats on the back, and condolences from everyone, including my schoolmates and professors.

My world, awash in vivid colors and personalities, had suddenly gone gray. And what I thought was important—my schoolwork and grades—suddenly wasn't. I reckoned I was in shock then, and still was to some degree.

But I started talking again to fill the sudden maddening silence that hung between myself and my estranged aunt. It came out rapid-fire and matter-of-fact.

"I have their house on the market now and have already sold both of their vehicles. They had more than enough in their savings to cover funeral expenses, and my tuition is still intact." I couldn't believe how easily the words just flowed out of me. "The company is now being run by Dad's best friend, Tom Barlow, and I think that was the appropriate thing to do. I don't know how to run a business like Dad, so I figured I'd rather have someone run it who can keep it afloat instead of laying off his employees."

Carol came and sat next to me and patted my hand.

I looked at her. "I am so sorry for not contacting you. I just didn't know…"

She nodded. "It's okay. You wouldn't have known how to get ahold of me anyway. I don't mean to upset you, Daniel, but once I found out where your mom and dad moved when they had you, I always kept an eye out for them."

I looked at her, confused. She continued. "I'm not a spring chicken anymore, although I don't plan on going anywhere any time soon. But I don't have any children, and all of this"—she gestured around—"is yours. You are the rightful heir to your grandfather's estate. But let's not worry about that right now. Let's get you fed and set up, and then we can talk more about these things in the morning. I can't wait to show you around the house and the property. I'll also familiarize you with the caretakers of the property, who come and go almost daily. We have a maid, Anita; you've already met Thomas, the butler; and then there is a gardening crew, a pool crew, and groundskeeper. The sheriff, Hale, checks on us daily, is a frequent visitor, and helps take care of the stables when he has time off from work."

I nodded and was about to say something when I heard a howl off in the distance. I jumped a bit. My mind returned right to a few hours prior, staring down at the wolf from inside the cab of my truck. I looked outside the window but was greeted with nothing but darkness.

My aunt said, "We have timber wolves around here. As a matter of fact, the house was named after them: Timber Manor. They usually don't start trouble, but don't wander the grounds without a pistol. You don't have to shoot at them, but the report from the gun will send them running. We've had people out here trying to trap them and relocate them, but to no avail. They seem to outsmart the trappers.

"All right, well, the kitchen downstairs is stocked with everything you can imagine. Are you hungry?"

I shook my head. "No. Thank you. I ate at some fast-food place a couple of hours ago. I'm pretty full from that."

She stood and looked down at me. "Well, if you do find yourself hungry, go downstairs and walk all the way to the back of the house. Eventually you'll reach the kitchen. If not, breakfast will be ready when you get up in the morning. Please make yourself at home, and I'm in the room on the first floor right under your room. If you need me, I'll be there. Just come knock on my door, sweetheart."

She kissed the top of my head and stood looking down at me once more. "Rest up. You've had a long day." She walked toward the door, opened it, and paused. Turning around, she said, "Welcome home, Daniel." And with that, she left and shut the door behind her.

I simply watched her go.

Carol

I HEARD THE DOOR click, and I leaned back on it, resting my hand over my heart. "Jesus, help him," I whispered, fiddling with the silver cross at my throat. "He's been through so much."

I headed back down the hallway to the staircase and stopped. Everything sat still and quiet, save for the constant ticking of the grandfather clock at the landing. I paused to look at the oil painting of Mom and Dad, thinking back over the years to why Michael left in the first place. So many bad memories flooded up from a time so long ago.

"Michael didn't leave. He was forced out," I said to the painting. "How can I tell him everything, Mother? He apparently knows nothing." The oil painting of my mother and father just smiled down on me, as if saying, "This is your show now, Carol. Do as you will."

My shoulders felt heavy and my heart fluttered momentarily, and then everything became steady again. So much heartbreak had happened inside these walls that it was hard to walk here at night. Memories stalked the halls, cold and unforgiving records of the past. Perhaps, with the workers coming tomorrow to throw open the shutters and dust out the rooms, things would feel better. Maybe a good dose of sunlight would throw some of the shadows into oblivion.

God, he looks so much like his father, I thought. His mannerisms and the way he just looked at me, as if questioning everything I said and taking time to consider before speaking. I had been almost afraid he wouldn't come.

I continued down the hallway, down the stairs, and into my room on the first floor. Flipping on the light, I walked into my bedroom, to the familiar trappings of an old lady, and fished my nightgown out of the dresser. I changed quickly and crawled into my waiting bed.

Lying back, I couldn't help but think of what had happened.

I came running from outside, just getting home from school. Thomas was busy parking the car, and as I ran up the front steps, I heard a scream.

I flung the door open and saw Christopher lying in a pool of blood on the floor at the foot of the stairs, his neck twisted at an odd angle. I uttered a strangled scream of my own and looked up to find Mother and my little brother, Michael, at the top of the stairs. He was crying in Mother's arms.

Mother had her arms wrapped around Michael's small, shaking body and rocked him. Anita, Thomas's wife, stood like a statue, staring up at Mother and Michael; she didn't move.

"Anita, fetch a doctor. Anita!" I screamed.

The maid finally snapped back into reality, looked at me as if seeing me for the first time, and ran off to call for help.

What bothered me more than anything was the look in Mother's eyes. Not horror, not sadness, but defiance, like a mother wolf protecting her pup.

***

Now Michael was a young man. I knocked on the door to his room and cracked it open a bit to peer inside. I found Michael throwing clothes into a green duffel.

"Where are you going?" I demanded.

"I have to get out of here, Carol. I can't stay anymore!" he cried, throwing in more clothes.

"You think running away from this is going to make it any better?" I asked, coming into the room, tears running down my face. "Where are you going to go? Who's going to take care of me?"

"He isn't bothering you, Carol. It's me he is after!"

Michael was crying too. He was racked with sobs and I threw my arms around him. His tears fell hot and wet onto my shoulder as his whole body shook. The fear he had felt all these years flowed out of him, angry and bitter. Mother couldn't do anything about it, and Father chose to ignore it. The house itself was killing their son.

No…not the house…

"Please promise to write. Call, and I'll come visit you," I said, holding him at arm's length.

He wiped the tears away with the palms of his hands and nodded. "I promise. I'm joining the military in the morning. I'm eighteen, and Father cannot stop me. I'll write to you, sis." He hugged me one more time. "Promise me you won't tell them where I've gone until tomorrow—swear it!"

"I swear." He headed for the door. "Wait!" I cried out. He stopped short and turned around. I took off my Saint Michael's medallion, handed it to him, and kissed him on the cheek. "For luck."

He smiled at me once more, opened the door, and once into the darkened hallway, he ran.

I felt my knees grow weak under me, and I felt myself collapse... sobbing. Not the first tears this house had heard and surely not the last...

I was happy my nephew was here and had arrived safely. Yet I had a nagging concern that I might have interrupted the boy's life. Thinking of the years gone by, I drifted off into a fitful sleep. My dreams were disturbing. Images of things, bits of old memory, faces long gone flashed before my eyes, and something a bit more sinister followed me in the shadows of my slumber.

***

Somewhere inside the house, more than simple memories began to stir.

Daniel

I FISHED OUT MY toiletries bag and walked into the bathroom. I didn't have to flip on a light switch; the motion sensor on the wall picked up my movement and lit up the room in a warm glow.

The bathroom was solid marble, save for the mirrors. The bathtub looked less like a tub and more like a Jacuzzi, and the shower was open, completely made of marble, and had two showerheads in it. The colors of the room were soft browns and white, surprisingly modern given the age of the house, and there was a small window above the toilet. The moon shone through a skylight. Fresh towels were laid out, along with washrags and soap. I reached over and turned on the taps, and both showerheads instantly kicked in with hot water. I adjusted the temperature lower—just a little under scalding—and let it run.

I stripped out of my clothes and let them fall to the floor, not bothering to fold them—they were wilted and smelled like cigarette smoke and a thousand miles of wear. In the mirror, I checked myself over and winced when I saw how thin I looked. I leaned forward and rubbed my face; stubble was starting to grow. The fatigue was still present in my green eyes, and my hair looked disheveled. I wear it shoulder length and loose, almost long enough to tie in a ponytail. I turned from the mirror, stepped into the shower, and was immediately in heaven.

The hot water flowed over my sore, aching muscles, and I just let it pour over me. I leaned into the wall at my side, folded my arms together, and rested my eyes for a moment. Visions of the funeral home, the throngs of people who'd come to pay their condolences, and spreading my parents' ashes out into the Gulf of Mexico flooded my mind. My friends' concerned faces— especially my roommate, Jeff, who'd never left my side during the whole ordeal—shuffled through my thoughts.

My heart swelled and a sob escaped my lips. I shook myself. "Stop it!"

Angrily I reached for the soap and lathered myself down. I couldn't afford to lose control of myself now. Besides, what was the point? Pain had kept me fueled across the country, and it would get me through this crisis. My friends, associates, and life were back in Texas, but it was going to be put on hold for now. At least until the end of the summer—and after that, who knew? Now here I was, in a house that would rival the Biltmore Estate, and me its Anderson Cooper. *Shit.* I towel-dried, wrapped it around my waist, and walked into my bedroom to dress. When I opened the suitcase where my jeans and T-shirts were, another reminder slapped me in the face.

Unlike my father, I'd never joined the Marines, but everyone folded their clothes the same way. Mom had done laundry for Dad over the years, and when I wanted to help, she passed along her knowledge of the way things were done. I had never broken the habit.

I fished out a pair of underwear and slipped them on. The bed looked incredibly inviting, and I was so tired. As I pulled the covers back, I could smell the fresh linens and fabric softener, and I knew the bedclothes had been washed recently. I slipped into the cool sheets and laid my head on the pillow. Thinking about the trip up here, I lay there a moment. The wolf instantly flashed into my mind, then Sheriff Davis. I grinned at the memory of his smile and, while focusing on that, drifted off to sleep.

Out in the woods, I stood on the road where I'd been stranded a few hours before, my bare feet planted on the asphalt of the highway.

I glanced around to the tree line, but something was off about it. The trees were misshapen and twisted, the branches reaching toward the heavens leafless. They sent their fingerlike limbs out and covered the road like a canopy. I looked back down to find Timber Manor awaiting me at the end of the road, so I started walking toward it.

"Go back," I heard behind me.

I stopped and turned. Nothing there. I turned around and continued walking.

"Go back," the voice said again.

There was something familiar about it. I glanced back—nothing but the open road behind me. As I turned back, I was greeted by my father.

"Go back!" he screamed.

I jerked awake and sat up in bed, my heart pounding furiously. Sweat had gathered above my brow, and I wiped it with the back of my hand as I tried to catch my breath.

Outside, thunder rolled in the distance, and as I lay back down, I listened to the rumble, hoping it would lull me back to sleep.

Eventually, it did.

Carol

*E*XTRAVAGANT, LARGE, ORNATE, and *breathtaking* were words used to describe this house in many magazines over the years, from *People Magazine* and *Luxury Home*, as well as several back copies of *Forbes Magazine*. Rightly so. Made of stone, brick, and wood, she stood grand as her wings stretched from right to left and her spire reached for the sky. Windows cascaded throughout the house, allowing plenty of sunlight to find its way inside. Her alabaster coloring was warm and inviting, and although she was intimidating to look at, inside she felt like a home. The furniture was antique, but not in a cold, sterile way. No, the chair cushions were thick, plush, and welcoming. Her floors were solid wood, save for the marble foyer just inside the front door. The rooms, many of which had been closed off over the years, were receiving special attention by the handymen and maids I'd hired to spruce her up.

As a young girl, I would ride my bike up and down the long corridors when the constant Oregon rain would drive my siblings and me indoors. With pigtails in my hair, Michael and I would tear through the hallways or play hide-and-seek in various rooms, ripping past the maids, who laughed and dodged the children.

Momma and Daddy gave us free rein to build forts and have sleepovers, swim in the pool, and if accompanied by Daddy or Thomas's daddy—because of the wolves—we would ride horses over the fields. It was a good life here. Until the darkness came, when things changed. But I won't think about that. Not now. Right now I have a house to prepare.

The house sat on fifty-three acres of private property that butted up to national forest, four acres of which was always mowed and maintained, surrounding the house and stables. When the sun was out, the six-bedroom, six-and-a-half-bathroom Timber Manor looked like a giant white stone set in the midst of a sea of green. It hadn't changed much over the years, except for the stables Father built me when I was a girl and the renovation of the servants' quarters in the back. It was home. It was my home. And now it was Daniel's if he wanted it.

As I wandered about dictating to various workmen, I felt pride well up in my heart at seeing the house begin to sparkle like a new penny. The rooms were being dusted and vacuumed, the linens washed or replaced. Windows were thrown open to let the summer air creep into the home, bringing with it the smell of freshly cut grass, dew, and roses. In the upstairs hallways, green carpet stretched the length of the house, dark and inlaid with golden threads in little fleur-de-lis. The walls were adorned with portraits of a happy family shown on all manner of special occasions, as well as various other pieces of artwork. The marble foyer shone like glass now, as the workers had buffed and waxed its sandstone-colored surface. Large bouquets of fresh flowers filled each grand bathroom. New candles in silver candelabras replaced the old wax candles in the library and on top of fireplaces. Chimney sweeps had cleaned out the flues, removing old soot and birds' nests.

Timber Manor was waking from a deep slumber. I stood watching the goings-on in my house, directing the temporary hires, and I thought about Daniel, asleep upstairs. This was his home now. He was the last of the Donnellys, and he was going to see what this house looked like when they chased away all the shadows and the dust.

I walked through the back-patio door and stood looking out over the back property. Down a small path that eventually led to the stables was the servants' quarters where Thomas and Anita lived separate from my home. Several years back, they'd insisted they be allowed to live near me, and I had renovated the whole building to their liking. I appreciated their constant companionship.

Beyond that was the pool house, an enclosed and heated structure my father had built to give them something to do in the predominantly cool months.

After speaking with Daniel on the phone about competitive swimming back home, I'd gone ahead and had the pool house cleaned out, the water drained from the Olympic-length pool, and the walls scrubbed down. Now water was filling her up at this very minute. Money, I knew, wasn't an object for me—never had been my entire life, thanks to the awesome financial planning of Papa Jim and his daddy all those years ago, and to my own piloting skills concerning the various interests of my company.

It would also never be something for Daniel to worry about now that the legacy would pass to him. Anita and Thomas had arrived earlier than their normal time, half in anticipation of Anita meeting the Donnelly heir and half to help me manage the throng of people wandering about the house on assignment. There was still a great deal happening. Servants polished silver and cleaned crystal, and men armed with Windex attacked the windows with expert ease. A carpenter pointed out that minor repairs had to be done, but all that could wait for the boy to wake up.

He was here, inside this house, and that thought made my heart warm.

Speaking of warm, I wandered over to the side of the house and peered out into the rose garden to see workers busy about the grounds. The smell of flowers and freshly cut grass flowed in through the windows on the summer breeze, and I inhaled deeply, pleased with the work going on. Gardeners were trimming the bushes and cleaning up the pathways that led throughout the vast stretch of colorful blooms that had been Mother's favorite pastime.

Supervision is such hard work, I thought, and laughed as zero-turn lawn mowers and Weed eaters droned in the early-morning sunlight. Thomas and Anita occasionally appeared with questions from the workers, and I answered them plainly enough.

Marcie, the interior decorator I had used to redo some of the large bathrooms, had shown up an hour earlier to help me with the drapes and other linens that had become moth-eaten from years of neglect. Once I told her what I wanted, she nodded and set her crew to work without another word.

Another crew was sent to the basement to retrieve old boxes of Mother's fine china, which would be cleaned and put out for use, and still another was out in the conservatory cleaning up the dead flora and replacing old and broken pots. The project reminded me of a resurrection of sorts.

Again my mind turned to Daniel and how worn he'd looked when he arrived the prior night. Thinking about our brief conversation, my heart thumped against my chest. I was anxious to show off his home to him, should he decide to stay. That gave me pause for a moment.

What if he decides this is too much for him? What if he packs up, bids me adieu, and goes home to Texas?

"That would be his choice, and I'll cross that bridge when we get there," I said to nobody but myself.

At the sound of my voice, a worker stopped with an inquisitive look on his face, but I smiled and waved him away. I knew what I would do now; I had it prearranged. All assets of Donnelly Enterprises would be liquidated; the house would be sold…

"…And that, as they say, will be that," I muttered, this time out of earshot of people.

However, even though that would be an option, I couldn't possibly be forthcoming with it.

With a wave of my hand, I dismissed the idea he would leave. Of course, he'd stay. Who wouldn't? He was about to be a millionaire several times over either way. That didn't bother me in the slightest.

The resemblance to Michael was so surreal I had to keep mentally shaking myself, reminding myself he wasn't Michael at all. I was also anxious to know how much he knew of his family, and I was prepared to understand should the answer be "very little."

His father had kept him away, for good reason. Yet he was gone now too, and so was his wife. Poor Daniel was alone in the world and entirely too young for the decisions and the burden he'd had to face. I'd had my lawyers call his family's firm to let them know they were keeping an eye on the transfer of his father's estate and to make it very clear that any shenanigans would be dealt with swiftly. Their response, given the size of the firm that represented me, was amicable, and they promised to make sure everything moved quickly and efficiently. I even made arrangements for his father's house to be purchased by a branch of the company to ensure that, should Daniel decide not to stay here, he would have a cushion to fall back on.

"You're interfering," I scolded myself aloud but easily dismissed all that, given the boy's situation.

Another worker stopped and asked what I'd just said, but this time, instead of answering him, I simply turned and walked to another part of the house.

Isn't anyone allowed to talk to themselves uninterrupted anymore? I thought to myself as I made my way back to the front of the house. I knew I was being rude, but I couldn't help myself—I was on pins and needles. The future was uncertain before me, it was uncertain before Daniel, and Timber Manor hung in the balance. The idea of this old house being sold off as a hotel, or left abandoned, or worse yet, torn down, made me sick to my stomach. Sure, a lot of bad things had happened here, but there'd been a lot of good too. I was proud of my home and my family, and I would show Daniel what being a Donnelly really meant.

"Surely that thing is gone now. I haven't seen anything in years," I wondered aloud to myself once more, banishing its memory as soon as I thought of it.

It was gone.

No one should be without family. I would be here for the boy to make up for my inability to be there for his father. Now I was just waiting for him to come down and greet the day.

Daniel

I AWOKE STIFF AND sore but rested. Lying in bed staring up at the ceiling, it took me a moment or two to get my bearings.

I wasn't home in Texas anymore; I was in Oregon. Out in the middle of nowhere with what sounded like a battalion of people underneath my bed, hammering away on an estate I was an heir to. I groaned and threw the covers back before wandering into the bathroom, where I took a brief shower, hoping to wash the sleep away. I dried off, dressed, and stood in the middle of my new bedroom, nervous about going down and greeting the people. I walked to the door a couple of times and hesitated, only to go back and sit on the bed, staring at the door as if a monster waited on the other side of it. Or perhaps only a flood of information I wasn't ready to process, things about people I never knew—about a part of my dad I never knew, a whole other life he'd lived that I hadn't been privy to.

Sure, the Donnellys had always existed on the periphery, and over the years I'd wondered why they simply didn't show up, or call, or send cards or something. I figured they were, perhaps, just rich and snotty, and that was why Dad didn't want anything to do with them. But Carol had reached out immediately after Mom and Dad's deaths and wanted to get to know me, wanted me to come to the family home. And now...

"She said this is my home."

Last night she hadn't seemed snotty at all; she was, in fact, very gracious and kind.

"What were you afraid of, Dad?" I wondered aloud as the noise from downstairs carried up through the hallway.

I rolled my eyes and steeled myself against the idea I didn't belong here and headed downstairs to find my aunt Carol. On my way down, I marveled at the sheer size of the house. It was cavernous, and the effect made me feel kind of small and foreign.

Like I was an intruder on a past that could have been, that should have been, but wasn't. Dad had always made enough money for us to live on—we never really wanted for anything, especially after he opened his sailboat business—but this was wealth on a whole other level.

Downstairs I found men carrying heavy furniture in and out of the house and people mopping floors and dusting busts and wooden railings till they shined. My aunt was outside on the patio, dictating to several people where she wanted the furniture set up and placed. Two men carrying a bookcase out of one of the rooms nearly bowled me over.

"Good morning, Mr. Donnelly. I am Anita, your aunt's cook. Well, I guess your cook now. May I interest you in some breakfast?"

I jumped at the sound of her voice and turned to see an elderly woman dressed prim and proper awaiting my answer. She wore her hair back in a severe bun, and unlike my aunt, Anita was rail thin. Her eyes were large and warm as she watched me.

"Thank you, Anita. I...uh, yeah, that would be great." I nodded.

"Eggs, sausage, and hash browns for you, then?" She smiled.

"That would be amazing." My stomach growled in agreement. I was starving. And really thankful for her kindness.

"Coming right up. And, sir...?"

"Hmmm?" I asked, trying to pat my growling stomach into submission.

"It is good to see you again."

With that, she turned and disappeared back into the kitchen.

"You too..." I whispered in confusion, but she was too far away to hear me.

My aunt came in from the patio door and greeted me with a smile and a kiss on the cheek. "When I went and visited your father and mother, Ms. Anita went as well. You'd just been born. Anita is Thomas's wife. She changed your diapers once or twice."

Of course she looked amazing. She wore a pair of tan pants and a white blouse that buttoned in front. She was gorgeous and honestly could have given Jane Fonda a run for her money in the category of women who look great after fifty.

"How did you sleep?" she inquired with a smile and a hopeful light in her pretty eyes.

How did she never marry? I asked myself. I wasn't going to tell her about my romp in dreamland with a wolf, so I lied. "Great! Fell right to sleep."

"Good!" She took my arm and began to walk with me. "I haven't had this many people here working in a long time. But because this is a special occasion, I have called them in to sweep through the house and the grounds, and clean it up and clean it out. A lot of the rooms in this home do not get used, but I wanted you to see them as they should be. This is, after all, going to be your home, should you want it." She smiled at me. "Here, let me show you around."

She took me on the grand tour of the house, which had so many rooms I forgot to count them. There was a library, a billiard room, and a conservatory complete with a fountain, tables and chairs, and what looked to be a swimming pool on the other side of the glass. The formal dining room was just as ornate as the rest of the house. A large twelve-person table sat dead center in a room decorated with sconces and candles and a giant chandelier over the dining area. Pictures of my deceased grandfather and grandmother hung on the wall, snapshots of some of their adventures. Also pictures of Carol and of course my father. I stopped, picked one up, and saw a very happy man in a tennis shirt and shorts, grinning back at me. His handsome face had no lines of age, and his hair was longer than I had ever seen it in my life, not streaked with gray.

My aunt said softly, "You have your mother's build, but you look so much like your father, it startled me when you first got out of your truck."

I inhaled a deep breath, set the picture down, and looked at her. "Mom always said that too. She said I had his eyes."

Carol reached over and wrapped an arm around my waist. I instantly felt emotion trying to break through my careful restraint, so I cleared my throat and shook my head and averted my eyes.

Other pictures hung there too: oil paintings of what must have been distant relatives, and I focused on them. To break the mood, I laughed and asked if there were any secret passages I should know about.

"My goodness, no! Although you would think there would be in a house this size."

Carol walked on and I followed, completely dumbfounded by everything I saw. It was like stepping back in time to a different era when antique furniture, large vases, oriental rugs, and grandfather clocks were common.

A music room, complete with a baby grand piano and plenty of dance floor, should anyone feel the urge, boasted a stocked bar in the corner. The room was brightly lit, with floor-to-ceiling windows that looked out on the west side of the property, over a rose garden in full bloom. Like the rest of the house, mahogany and chestnut paneling covered the walls, and the floors were hardwood. "This house once bustled with life. Grand parties were thrown by my grandfather and grandmother, and anyone who was anyone came. Your grandmother and grandfather continued the tradition. Greta Garbo, J. Edgar Hoover, as well as Tolson, Nancy and Ronald Reagan, to name a few, all danced in this very room. When your grandmother and grandfather were alive, they would have huge summer parties and invite friends they met on their travels. There was always music and laughter. Oh, don't get me wrong, it's seen its share of hard times and sadness. A place this big and this old has a lot of memories built into her walls. But Timber Manor is solid. She's a good home."

She led me back to the front of the house, where Sheriff Davis stood in the doorway. At the sight of him, my heart jump-started.

"Carol! You called out the army?" He laughed as he dodged several people carrying out what looked to be a rolled-up oriental rug on their shoulders.

"Just doing some spring cleaning a few months late, Hale!" She snickered.

The sheriff leaned down, gave her a peck on the cheek, and looked up at me. "Hello, Danny!"

I resisted the urge to throw the ornate vase on the table nearest me at his head.

God, he looks good.

He wasn't dressed in his uniform, but in a pair of jeans, boots, and a flannel shirt; the fabric stretched across his wide shoulders. His hair, which I hadn't seen the night before, was black, and his face was perfect save for a scar near his upper lip. Of course, his hair was cut short for the job, but not completely flat-topped. His green eyes were alight with good humor as he folded his arms and leaned back onto the doorframe.

I could climb that.

He flashed me his megawatt grin again, and again I let it go. I really hadn't paid too much attention to him the night before, but now I was glad to see him. "Got the day off, Sheriff?"

"Yup. Saturdays and Sundays are my days off, usually, but I figured I could take an additional Friday off. That's when I come up here to take care of the stables for your aunt. Have you seen them yet?"

Hale

THERE HE STOOD, the new heir to the Donnelly estate and Timber Manor. His eyes were as big as saucers, and as he stood there next to his aunt, the discomfort just rolled off him in waves. He would put his hands in his pockets, look at his aunt, look at the floor, and then glance around the foyer over and over again. I felt sorry for him. He looked incredibly uncomfortable.

Now, don't get me wrong, the kid was tall and good-looking, *very* good-looking as a matter of fact, and his clothes were fashionable for his age. Today he wore a pair of ragged blue jeans and a button-down pearl-snap shirt with some wild designs on it. Both his ears were pierced, adorned with small silver hoops, and his brown hair was wavy and thick, hanging well past his ears. His lips were full, his skin was flawless with just a trace of stubble, and his eyes…his eyes were beautiful. The color, a mixture of deep green and gray, like the ocean after a storm, was complemented by long lashes.

Carol mentioned something to Danny about there being a very large swimming pool connected to the conservatory, and Danny's eyes lit up, as did his face as he smiled. That smile…

"Don't you, Hale?"

My mind snapped back, and both Carol and Danny stared at me. I shifted my feet and smiled back at them. Danny had an odd expression on his face, and I'm sure I was busted just from staring at him.

"Yes. Wait—what?" I asked, trying not to sound too lost and failing miserably. Heat flashed through my body, and I was shocked at it and embarrassed by the way Daniel's gaze seemed to pinpoint my little secret.

The triumphant smirk on his lips didn't help matters much. And for now, he seemed to relax as he folded his arms over his chest.

Carol, however, was none the wiser. "I was explaining to Danny that you and your dad both worked on the property and that you take care of the stables now."

"Yeah. Sure do. Every weekend and sometimes during the week," I managed to choke out. "Have you seen the stables yet?" I asked in a panic, reverting to my former question, hoping to draw attention away from my embarrassment.

"No. I was just given the tour of the house," Danny said, still with an inquisitive expression.

"Breakfast is ready."

Anita had materialized from out of nowhere, causing both of us to jump.

Carol said, "Hale, please stay for breakfast, and then why don't you show Daniel out to the stables and the rest of the grounds?"

I patted my stomach and grinned at Carol's nephew. "You don't have to ask me twice. Sure, I'll show Danny around. There's plenty to see."

He led the way to the kitchen, and I followed.

Daniel

I CONSIDERED MYSELF TALL at six two, but Hale had at least two inches and fifty pounds on me. I caught him staring at me while Carol was talking. His eyes were so intense that it caused my heart to stutter for a moment. Could he be into me? His whole body tensed up when I caught him, and his face turned a bit pink.

The coloring of his cheeks gave me some satisfaction. I don't know why. But I felt some power in the surprise of it. The past few weeks had been chaos, a whirlwind of unpredictability. And here was some guy checking me out. There was something in me that wanted as much attention as this man was willing to give—and possibly a whole lot more. And I knew if I wasn't careful, I'd give it to him. That truth unsettled me as I instantly became aware I was hungry, and not simply for the meal Anita had cooked for us.

We made our way into the kitchen. I was again stunned at how beautiful it was. The floor was brown-and-white stone and there was a big island in the center. Plenty of windows let the morning light shine through, illuminating the room and making it glitter. Everything was modern and updated. And although it was a large purse that had created it, like the rest of the house, it didn't feel untouchable. It was homelike and welcoming. As Carol led us to a breakfast nook, a place she insisted she, Thomas, and Anita always took their meals instead of the dining room, I was happy to see just a regular old table whose pale wood looked well used and plain.

We sat down to eat, and I just about inhaled everything on my plate. I was mopping up egg yolk when I finally raised my head. Everyone at the table was staring at me in wonder. I swallowed what was in my mouth, grinned sheepishly, and set my fork down, embarrassed.

"Sorry," I muttered.

Carol laughed. "Not at all! I think it's just the fresh air. Honey, I've heard of starving college students before, but I've never seen one in action. Don't you worry. There's more where that came from."

Anita, who'd been standing by the table with a skillet in her hand and an inquisitive look in her eye, offered me another helping. I nodded and took some more bacon off the platter in front of me. This time I ate more slowly. Carol and Hale talked about the town and the summer tourists who came to camp and swim in some of the mountain lakes. I watched Anita move from the stove to the sink and back again, and listened halfheartedly to Carol and Hale, and to Thomas instructing movers in the back of the house. The kitchen was beautiful: open, sunlit, and spacious. The range was huge, with a giant vent above it. The refrigerator was massive as well, and a pantry nearby opened up to the dining room.

"The workers who are here today aren't normally around. I just figured I'd get everything dusted off and shining so Daniel can see what the house really looks like. As you know, Hale, I keep most of the house closed off, and everything that isn't in use is draped over with a dustcover. I didn't want him coming into what could easily be mistaken for a haunted house," Carol explained to Hale.

Anita turned sharply to look at Carol, and the look she shot her was one of disapproval. Yet she didn't say anything and went back to scrubbing the breakfast pans. My eyebrow went up at that, and I was about to ask Carol about the possibilities of ghosts being around when Hale spoke first.

"So, you ready to see the grounds?" He smiled across the table at me.

I'd finished my plate and sat back, satiated. I nodded, thanking God he hadn't called me by that pet name.

"Well, come on, then, Danny. Let's get you out there."

I rolled my eyes and got up, thinking, *Never mind.*

***

We walked out of the back door and stepped out into a beautiful morning. The sun was warm against my skin, and the grounds were certainly busy. But despite the warmth of the sun, the wind was still cool, and my shirt whipped around my body as it had last night. The sound of lawn mowers running and Weed eaters weeding abounded.

We were on a patio where workers busily removed leaves, twigs, and other debris. A swimming pool was currently filling with fresh water. It would be a great place to do laps. I made a mental note of that and figured catching some rays wouldn't be an altogether bad idea.

The smell of the freshly cut grass enshrouded us, as well as pine from the nearby tree line and roses from the garden not too far off. Hale walked by my side the entire time, and I was acutely aware of his presence.

I stopped to take another look at the house and shook my head.

"It's something, isn't it?" he said.

I cast him a look. "This house is bigger than some of the buildings at my school. But it's beautiful."

It really was. Last night the house had been impressive as it stood dark against the night sky, but I'd been tired and hadn't really paid much attention to it. In the sunshine it was breathtaking. Painted mostly white, with black wrought iron all over the place, it was very elegant. The windows reflected the sun, and the grounds were vast and immaculate. The detail and the architecture were fantastic, like something out of a book or a dream.

I looked back at Hale and caught him staring at me again.

He averted his eyes. "The groundskeeper has a truck over here behind the shed. We can use it to go down to the stables, or we can walk."

"Honestly, I'd like to walk it. I need to stretch my legs, especially after that huge breakfast I inhaled."

"I was going to lecture you on the virtues of chewing, but I thought better of it." Hale smirked.

I couldn't help but laugh. "I'd been eating fast food for the past couple of days. It was nice to have something that didn't come precooked, prewrapped, and a precursor to a heart attack."

Hale grinned and looked at me again with color in his cheeks. His hands were in his back pockets. He was a study in contradictions: he was strong—that was visible—but there was a softness too in the way he looked at me and in his smile as his lips stretched across his teeth. Lips I was sure would be warm and—

Dude, stop! Why not just bang him on the patio out in front of everyone!

Clearing my throat, I walked past him. We started down the path between the house and the stables, stopping every few minutes for Hale to point out this or that detail. Woods surrounded the property and stretched for miles all around. Except for the small town of Emerson off to the east, the house sat alone in the landscape. He talked constantly about the grounds, and as I understood it, he knew the place like the back of his hand.

He told me that most of his childhood he'd spent here with his father, who had been the handyman until his death a few years ago. Since then, Hale had started taking over some of the responsibilities, but he mainly took care of Aunt Carol's horses.

I liked his company very much. His mannerisms were smooth and his smile was quick. The way he carried himself was self-assured without being cocky. He had that all-American, apple pie, and "gosh darn, I burned the muffins" quality about him. Every time he smiled, it did something to my heart—to say nothing about my loins. I smiled as he chatted on, then stopped midsentence when he caught me grinning at him.

"What?" he asked, chuckling.

"You know I'm never going to remember all this," I said unapologetically.

"Yeah, I guess it's quite a lot, but you'll get to know it good enough, I guess," he said matter-of-factly. "So tell me about yourself."

I considered that for a moment. "What do you want to know?"

"What do you want to tell me?" he replied, chuckling.

Man, don't play with me.

"Well, there isn't much to tell, really. I was a military brat and traveled most my life with my parents. My dad was a Marine since he was eighteen, and my mother was a schoolteacher. He retired almost ten years ago and started building and selling sailboats. He was really good at it."

The land had now gone from manicured lawn to taller grasses. We were heading uphill, and the day was growing slightly warmer. Yet, after having been in Texas during the summer, it felt sort of chilly to me. It might have been eighty-five degrees or so, but the wind was nice and cool, caressing our sweaty brows, which were damp from the walk. The smell of earth and rainwater permeated my senses, and I felt myself waking up from a weeklong fugue state. I was both exhilarated and terrified at the same time. My nerves were raw.

"Carol said he and your mother died recently," Hale muttered. "I'm sorry to hear that."

I nodded quickly, biting my cheek and staring at the ground as we walked. "Yeah, about two months ago... It's been a roller-coaster ride, for sure. I thought handling their estate was a big deal. Then I get blown away with...with this."

"Yeah. I imagine it's a big surprise to know you now have more money than you can spend in a lifetime," he said.

We continued our walk, each lost in our own thoughts. Finally I asked, "So, is the place haunted?"

Hale stopped dead in his tracks. I turned to him with a smile that quickly died. His eyes had clouded over and he just looked at me.

"Yes, it is," he said.

I waited for him to smile. He didn't. "C'mon," I scoffed.

That would be a great distraction, I knew, so I hoped he would tell me something terrible and frightening. Anything that would take away from thinking about my parents' deaths.

"Look, I'm not going to lie to you about anything, Danny. This place does have a reputation." He shoved his hands in his pockets and shrugged. "I don't know how much your aunt has told you yet, but…this house has seen its fair share of tragedies. Now, I don't know if it's haunted per se, but…weird stuff has a tendency to happen."

I threw my head back and laughed. "Really? Like what?"

He didn't join in. "I come and check on your aunt regularly. Some nights I'll actually come and stay the night here at the house with her so she isn't alone. Now, if I hadn't spent so much time here myself, I would be reacting just like you, but…" He sighed.

"I really shouldn't be getting into this," he murmured. "You just see things. Weird things sometimes that just don't make any sense, ya know? A shadow will pass by you out of the corner of your eye, or you'll walk into a cold spot. I've seen things move around on their own or heard a voice behind me, and when I turn to look, no one's there. It's just—listen to me. You just get a case of the creeps."

The sincerity in his voice surprised me. "What else, Hale?"

"There have been a few accidents. Look, your aunt is going to kill me if she finds out that I said anything to you about this, but I would rather have it come from me than Anita. She means well, but I think she's more fascinated by it than anything else."

Just then a cool breeze blew across the grounds and sent a shiver up my spine. We started walking again.

Hale explained to me that my aunt had never married. "She was a beauty, your aunt Carol. Still is. All the men in town would fall all over themselves to have a chance to marry her. Some liked her for her money; others were just captured by her beauty. She fell for a realtor in town by the name of Mark Gibson, and everyone was sure they would get married. This was before I was born. Mark was handsome and successful and loved by everyone. The local newspapers had a field day when they caught him and your aunt on the town together, and everyone was just counting the days until they said, 'I do.'"

I listened to him intently. "Go on."

Hale stopped and picked up a tree branch, stripped off the leafy twigs with his hands, and used it as a walking stick. He seemed to be considering what he was going to say. Struggling with it. Perhaps searching for the right words. Finally, down apiece, he started to speak again.

"One night there was an emergency call placed from the house. It was your aunt. She was hysterical. My uncle Robert, who was the sheriff at the time, rode out to the house and found Carol running down the driveway to meet him, waving her arms and screaming. My uncle and she ran back into the house to find Mark had fallen down the main staircase and his neck was broken. It looked like an accident, but according to her, he had been pushed."

"By who?" I asked.

"Nobody knows. But that isn't the weird part. When the coroner autopsied the body, they discovered that his neck had indeed been broken, but not from the fall. It had happened prior to the fall, and his body just fell. And the other thing was, apparently, Mark was going to propose to your aunt that night, but he never got the chance. Her ring was found jammed down his throat."

"Sweet Jesus." I stopped. "Where did the investigation go from there?"

"Where could it go? Carol is a strong woman, but unless she had been high on LSD or PCP, there was no way she could have done that to Mark. It's just not physically possible. Besides, Anita gave a statement that Mark had arrived early to surprise your aunt, but she hadn't returned home yet. So Anita met him at the door and showed him in, and according to her, he was going to freshen up before Carol returned. She headed back to the kitchen to finish supper and came out when she heard Carol screaming a few minutes later."

"What about Thomas?" I asked. "He's huge."

"Thomas had gone to pick Carol up from the airport. She'd been away for a business meeting in Chicago. Now, I know what you're going to say. This leaves Anita alone with Mark. Anita is smaller than Carol. No, whoever broke his neck was strong, very strong."

We'd reached the stables. My mind was racing with this new information. I was shocked and a little unnerved, and felt bad for my aunt. As Hale opened the doors to the barn, I stood back, and then we walked in. The heat inside the horse stables was quite a bit more intense than outside. My aunt had only two horses now, but the stables were built to house many more.

The two stood in stalls side by side and were happy to see us. One, a chestnut gelding, whinnied and shook his head. Hale said his name was Thunder. The other was Apple, a rescue horse Carol had taken in a year or so ago and nursed back to health. Apple, whose white color stood in stark contrast to Thunder's red, whinnied when she noticed us.

"Thunder, you can ride. He's spirited and loves to run. Apple, on the other hand, is not able to run. Her leg was badly hurt. Some rejects really mistreated her, but Carol took her in and has been nursing her. She's doing really well." Hale had stopped to pet Thunder, but Apple put her head into his stall to be loved on too.

"Jealous thing, you." Hale laughed and nuzzled her nose. She started sniffing his pockets, and he backed up. "Oh, you think I brought something for you, do ya?"

Hale reached into his pocket and produced a few carrot sticks wrapped in a sandwich baggie. Then he shared them between the two horses. They munched happily on their treats, their tails swishing back and forth. Apple leaned into Hale's hand, sniffing and hoping for more. He ran his hand over her beautiful face, stroking behind her ear.

I walked up to Thunder, who looked at me suspiciously but calmed down once I started to pet his nose. "They're so gentle," I said.

Even though I'd spent several years in Texas, I'd never had the opportunity to be around horses. I had always been at school, busy living my life.

"Yes, they're gentle creatures. Powerful, and you can get hurt if you're not careful, but otherwise, yes…they're kind." Hale was watching me as I petted Thunder.

He was petting Apple when I asked, a little matter-of-factly, "Do you always stare at people, Hale?"

A surprised look came over his face, and then he started to stammer. "I didn't realize I was. I—sorry..." He turned to Apple and started to brush her.

I took a brush off the side of the stall and started brushing Thunder the way he was brushing the other horse. We kept that up, working in silence for quite a while. I did just fine—Hale told me so and was even impressed when I didn't try to walk behind Thunder.

I laughed. "I've seen enough John Wayne movies to not make that amateur mistake, bud."

We fed the horses some oats, cleaned up their stalls, and put down some fresh hay for them from the loft above us. "Not too bad for someone who's never handled horses before."

"Thank ya very much," I said in my best Elvis voice.

Once the stalls were clean, we stepped out and dusted ourselves off. Something was bothering me, and I asked, "How did the medical examiner know his neck was broken before the fall?"

Hale nodded. "Good question. They knew because Mark never tried to stop the fall. When someone pitches forward or falls backward, it's instinctive for them to try to brace themselves. There was no bruising or anything that would indicate that type of fall."

"Wow," I whispered. "But Mark could have fainted for some reason and fallen. Then he wouldn't brace himself."

Hale nodded. "It's a possibility."

"But you think it was snapped on purpose. But by who? An intruder? What's the motive? Robbery? Or was it a ghoooost?" I teased.

Hale shook his head. "Look, I'm not saying anything about ghosts or goblins. All I am saying is freaky stuff happens in that house. So you have to be careful," he replied, a little chilly.

Me busting him staring at me and calling him on it might have embarrassed him a bit. I felt like a jerk about it, but I didn't like being eyeballed, either by someone who was curious about me as a person, or if he couldn't help himself because he was a cop. I started to apologize, and as if on cue, thunder rolled in the distance.

We both jumped. I looked up at Hale and he looked at me, and we started laughing. It felt good. The tension eased. We stood there looking a little embarrassed that we'd startled.

There was a slop sink that had a bar of soap above it and a water hose for a faucet. We stopped to wash our hands and fill up the horses' water trough. Hale was standing next to me, lathering his hands and rinsing them off, and I noticed there wasn't a wedding ring on his finger.

"So it's your turn. Tell me about you," I asked.

"Well, I grew up in town and have lived here all my life. My mom, like yours, was a schoolteacher, and my dad worked on the property. The Donnellys paid him pretty well, and your grandfather and my dad got along great. Mom still teaches at the local high school and volunteers at our library down on Main Street. Dad passed away a few years ago, though." He dried his hands on some paper towels, which he then promptly tossed into a wastebasket.

I grabbed some towels and did the same. "I'm sorry about your dad," I said.

"Yeah, he was a good guy. But he was pretty sick in the end, so it was expected. Cancer in the belly kind of moves quickly and does a lot of damage. So...his end came as a blessing. Unlike what happened to your parents, I'm sure."

His words hit me like a bullet train, and before I knew it, my eyes misted up, a lump formed in my throat, and my breath was gone. The emotions hit me hard and fast. I put a hand over my eyes to shield them, and with the other, I braced myself against the wall of the barn. A groan escaped my lips.

Fuck, don't cry now, I thought. *Fight it back. Swallow it down. Not here. Not here!*

But the wear and tear of the past few months, the last few days on the road, a terrible night's sleep, and being cast into a new life all conspired to bring me down.

Suddenly I was no longer standing in the midst of a barn. The horses were gone, Hale was gone, Oregon was gone, as well as Timber Manor. I was standing outside of my classroom with a police officer who'd come to speak to me, I was back in the morgue looking at my parents' bodies through a monitor on the wall, I was standing alone in my parents' house looking around at a life that had been cut away from me.

All their stuff had been right where they'd left it, and it remained there until I hired a moving company to come in and pack it away in storage. Then I was in the funeral home, a pink affair that smelled obnoxiously like dead flowers and had tinny, piped gospel music playing over the speakers above my head, receiving the handshakes, frowns, and mutterings from friends and associates as they said the same thing over and over again.

"I'm sorry."

"Daniel, we're so sorry."

"So sorry, dude."

"Daniel, this is your aunt Carol. Honey, I'm so sorry."

"Danny, are you okay?"

The heat of the tears that slid down my face scalded me in their descent. And I was completely powerless to stop them. The way the emotion came charging out of me was like someone who'd gotten too drunk on their preferred poison, knew beyond the fog of drunkenness that they were going to throw it all back up, and simply acknowledged the inevitable. As if my heart was saying, "Yup, you've reached your limit. You're going to cry now."

And I did.

God, I did.

I wept, perched over a slop sink as my body heaved out all the grief and disbelief of the past few weeks that I'd bottled and fermented inside myself, and all I could do was hang on.

Hale

*D*AMMIT, I THOUGHT. "I shouldn't have said that, Danny. I'm sorry." I pulled his hands away from his face. He stared at me like someone who'd just witnessed a murder. I guess the shock of everything suddenly decided to hit him all at once, and I stood there watching this kid, whose whole life had just been uprooted, start to crumple right in front of me. I watched him fight it back, blinking rapidly and clenching his fists, but the dam was about to break.

Fuck, Danny, you're breaking my heart, I thought.

I stepped into him and wrapped my arms around him, and he began to sob. His whole body shook from the force of pent-up emotions. It was a full-out sob—even now, Danny was trying to restrain both himself and the flood, but all attempts failed.

I ran my hands up and down his back and through his hair. "Cry it out, Danny. It's okay."

"They're gone. They are really gone!"

Disbelief and heartbreak poured out onto my shoulder as we slid to the floor. I rocked him back and forth with his head buried in my shoulder, his arms wrapped around my chest.

My heart ached for him as he let loose. How long had he been holding on to all this? *Too long*, I figured, and now he was surrounded by virtual strangers. Probably scared to death.

I held him close and let him do what he needed to. I was surprised and shamed by my reaction to this: at once horrified at the tears, concerned for his well-being, and secretly in heaven at having this young man holding on to me like a life preserver in rough waters. He smelled amazing; he felt better. And there was something to it that warmed my heart. The way he'd looked at me earlier, as though if I weren't careful, he'd devour me whole. As if he knew how attractive he was.

My shoulder was wet with his tears; his cheek pressed against my shoulder as we sat entwined together. I didn't care. I loved it—I was melting right into the floorboards of the barn. I knew people out there didn't believe in insta-love, and I didn't very much believe in love at first sight either. I mean, I'd had a couple of trysts. Who hadn't? Fumbling, tumbling, get naked quick, get what you needed, get dressed, and get gone. Gay men had a tendency toward that. It was the way of the world for us. Romance often came after, if at all. And sometimes, if the sex was good, it kept people together who shouldn't have been, and relationships then ended in disaster. That's why I focused on my work. Threw myself into the day-to-day activities of securing the safety of the residents of a small town.

Not to say I wasn't attracted to Danny. Fuck, no. I totally was. Since I'd seen him last night on the side of the road, with his window rolled down and looking terribly lost, then looking up at me, grateful I was there, I'd felt it. And all last night as I'd lain in bed, staring up at my ceiling, I'd counted down the minutes before the sun rose, so that I could dress and make my way to Timber Manor to see him again.

No, it had been electric. Instant. *Thunderous*, now that I mention it. And to have him in my arms now, regardless of the reason—I wasn't mad at the fates for it.

That's kinda fucked-up, Hale, I thought to myself and winced. Let me clarify. I wasn't happy his parents were dead. I...uh...

Why do I even bother to think things? I should just stick to carrying a big gun and intimidating speeders into slowing down.

Danny calmed down and raised his head. His cheeks were pink with embarrassment as he cleared his throat. "Ah, fuck." He wiped the remaining tears off with the palms of his hands. "I'm sorry... I just..." His lower lip trembled.

"You've been through quite a bit in a short amount of time, Danny."

We were sitting very close together; I rubbed my hand up and down his back. He looked at me, and the volume of his sorrow was overwhelming. His hair had fallen in his face; his eyes were puffy and red.

He laid his head down on my shoulder, and I wrapped my arm around him and dragged him even closer to me. I leaned back against the wall, and he rested there. I was shocked—not only by the tears he'd shed but by the easy comfort between us.

We sat there for a little while, just he and I staring down the barn and listening to the thunder. I was soaking up and enjoying how tenderhearted he was, charmed by it a little as well. He acted tough, but beneath all of it was someone who'd just suffered a tragedy. It tugged at my heart, but I shoved the feelings back in their place.

This is no time to start hitting on a person, I reminded myself. *You're a cop; you should know better.*

Danny was attractive, but looks could be deceiving. I hoped he didn't end up being a jerk, especially to his aunt. I doubted it, though.

He suddenly stiffened—I could feel him under my arm—and he sat up straight. I think the swiftness of the moment kind of hit him too, and he turned to give me a sheepish smile.

"Sorry," he said, his cheeks red and blotchy.

"I bet you say that to all the guys." I grinned and he laughed, rolling his eyes.

"Yes, I usually burst into tears around handsome men because that in no way makes me look neurotic."

I laughed and let a few minutes pass as he gathered himself together. "So, handsome, huh?" I responded.

You're pathetic.

Shut up.

Why don't you just go hit on people at a funeral. Or better yet, at the scene of an accident? Ask them, "Hey, come here often?"

I was pleased at that moment for human beings' lack of telepathic ability.

Danny swallowed hard and looked a bit nervous.

"Look, it's cool. I'm gay, but if you're not, it's totally—"

Loser.

Danny stopped me. "No, I am too. It's just…well, you know I don't really know you, and…*pfft*." He blew long strands of hair out of his eyes and then, when that didn't work, brushed them aside. "I have no experience at this. I mean, I have experience…I just. Well. Fuck, shit, baseball," he said and rolled his eyes.

"It isn't a job interview."

"I would hope not, given my string of expletives," he said, smiling.

"Hey, Tourette's is a real condition. I'm an equal-opportunity flirt."

Danny burst out laughing. "You're sick in the head."

It was my turn to laugh. The thunder rumbled above our heads again and Danny looked up at the roof.

"It's really pretty here. Even in this barn. It's kind of homey," Danny said softly.

I looked up and followed his gaze. In the shafts of sunlight coming in through the windows, dust motes floated gently in the air like little dancers. As we sat in the shadows and watched in silence, save for the occasional shuffle of a horse's hooves, we were quiet for a time.

He smiled and leaned back into me. I accepted it and wrapped my arm around his shoulders.

There was something innocent and sweet about him, brazenly truthful and honest. I liked that. I liked him.

"I don't want to go to bed with you right away."

Yep, brazen *is the word.*

"No?" I asked, looking down at the top of his head. "I thought we'd go up in the loft and have a roll in the hay."

He snorted and slapped my chest. "I've thought about it. Thought about it the moment I saw you. Thought about it when you led me down here and away from the rest of the house."

"Me too. What? Wait! My intentions were pure."

"As the driven snow."

"I'm serious."

Danny laughed and squeezed me. He tilted his head up and looked at me. "That would be really confusing right now."

I leaned in and kissed the end of his nose. "I know. You've got a lot to deal with. I want to be a safe place for you, if you'd like."

Danny snorted. "Is that what they call it these days?"

I feigned shock. "Scout's honor."

"I thought you were a cop."

I grinned. "Cop's honor, then."

He leaned in and kissed the side of my mouth. My heart jumped into my throat, and it was everything I could do not to try for more.

As he pulled away, he must have seen my stunned expression. "I'll let you know when I'm ready for more."

"I'll be waiting for that moment."

"I know. Wow, this is just a bit much," he said and stood up.

"No pressure. Let's be friends. I'd like that," I said, standing up and dusting myself off.

"Me too. I'd like that too," he said with a grin.

"Okay, then, friend, let's get you back to your aunt."

We headed out of the stables, and I watched as the clouds gathered on the horizon. *Ah, Oregon*, I thought.

"Oregon gets a lot of rain. You cool with that?"

"It rains a lot where I'm from too. I lived about twenty minutes from the Gulf of Mexico, and we had occasional tropical storms and hurricanes," he said.

"Was that what killed your family?" I hadn't heard of a named storm yet this season.

He shook his head. "It was just a freak storm," he said softly.

We continued walking back to Timber Manor as the air began to chill. But I didn't feel cold. My insides were all sort of warm and fuzzy.

Daniel

I THOUGHT ABOUT WHAT had just transpired in the stables and smiled to myself. In high school and college, I'd had a few girlfriends, but relationships were fleeting and we usually ended up in the friends category. I realized I was gay, or figured that I was, but I never really had an opportunity to get out and explore my feelings. I was always buried in my work. Sure, there had been a few good-looking guys on campus, and I was never a saint. Some nights I found myself studying the joys of anatomy and physiology with a male nursing student or some random hookup at a bar, but after that, I was back to my studies.

I'd been a man on a mission. That was before the worst day of my then-sheltered life. Now I had been thrust, no pun intended, into a brand-new reality, and I was a stranger in a strange land. No way would Dad have allowed me to cross the country alone, to come to his childhood home. He'd kept us away. Kept us protected. Kept us safe.

I felt a twinge in my heart for him. I missed him. I was fucking devastated by his and Mom's deaths, but I was embarrassed by my emotional outburst with Hale. In the midst of it all, his sexuality and mine were the only commonalities I could find in this sudden upheaval I called a life. Sure, Carol was my aunt. But our relationship was as distant as the one between Hale and I had been until just a few moments ago. Should it go too fast, as some relationships go with gay people, it would be kerosene on an already-burning fire of uncertainty, and the result would be disaster. And while I was not picking out china patterns in my head concerning Hale, it was nice to have him around.

I had a feeling I would need a distraction in the weeks and months to come.

Now, without even putting forth any conscious effort, I felt Hale reach for my hand, and I surprised myself by letting him hold it. Now there I was, traversing the back forty of an estate with a handsome, tall, dark, and very tender man, and it felt right. My heart was thudding in my chest as his fingers intertwined with mine. I glanced over at him quickly and considered what I knew about him, or what I thought I knew about him, and chewed on that information as we slowly headed back to the house.

He was solid, built like a tree, but he didn't seem at all self-absorbed or intimidating now. Sure, he was a bit older, but I didn't mind that. It wasn't as though we were separated by a decade, but I could tell by his eyes that he was mature. I mean, he was a town sheriff, after all, so I was sure he'd seen his fair share of rough things. Even in a small town, bad things can happen, and probably to really good people.

Like freak accidents, I thought with a twinge of melancholy.

The world around me felt surreal, and being there now was like being transported to someone else's life: nothing was familiar. *Yet, the hardest roads are the ones that lead to something good*, I said to myself.

I just didn't feel much like hiking down that path. Like any kid, I wanted the difficult path to instantly be gone and replaced with the old, familiar winding road that had been my life. I wanted my mom and dad back.

I looked up into the sky and noticed it getting dark pretty quick.

Hale followed my gaze and said, "We still have a few minutes. Looks like it will be here before too long, though."

We were walking close together. His hand was warm and callused but comforting, and he squeezed mine occasionally. I think he sensed my thoughts, and I smiled to myself. It was one of those perfect moments where nothing had to be said. Circumstances were throwing us together. And while that wasn't exactly a romance novel beginning, I'd take it.

The family land stretched out in front of us, and the sun pierced the clouds to cast its bright light on the grounds in different places. But the sun was fighting a losing battle. The storm clouds were full, thick, and heavy with rain. Thunder rumbled hard, and lightning streaked across the sky.

"Welcome to the Northwest, Danny," Hale said. "Like I said, it rains quite a bit around here."

"So I've noticed."

"The winters are beautiful, though. Snow covers everything, and there are nights, especially on this property, when the moon is full and the clouds have all passed on, and it's like the snow is on fire. Like it gives off its own light and it looks bright enough, almost like daytime. Nights like that, I'll ride Thunder for hours."

He pointed to a wide-open area that ran all the way up to the house.

I followed his pointing finger, looked beyond it to the tree line, and stopped when I thought I saw a pair of yellow eyes staring at me. The hairs on the back of my neck stood straight up.

"What is it?" Hale asked.

"Nothing." I relaxed slowly and turned my head to him. "I was just imagining the scene you were describing."

We continued walking hand in hand until we were visible from the house. We quickly undid our intertwined fingers, but we didn't walk far apart. I didn't think I wanted to be apart from him at all. Hale was sturdy and handsome, and his body felt like a redwood underneath his clothing; I snickered at where my mind took that one.

Hale had turned to me, a question in his eyes, when the skies opened up and poured buckets down on top of our heads. The wind picked up, and even though the day had been warm, the water was chilly, stinging us on our faces where it touched us. I laughed, although the rain was soaking me to the bone.

Hell of a cold shower, God, thanks.

Hale laughed too, and we took off across the property to the house. We started at a slow jog, but it quickly turned into a race.

I won, by the way.

Carol

S O ALL HE has to do is sign these papers?"
I sat across from Mr. Martin Lahey, the family attorney. One of them, anyway. His beady eyes shifted nervously left and right, and my heart went out to him. He brought out a handkerchief and occasionally dabbed at his upper lip and his forehead, then nodded as he looked around him, fidgeting.

We were sitting in Papa Jim's office. The rain pounded on the windowpane, and when the thunder rumbled, Martin's eyes would grow wide, and it was everything he could do to keep himself seated. He looked ready to bolt.

The firm Martin ran was actually paid by a larger firm in Portland that handled our business assets. It was good to have a local face, regardless of how terrified he was to be in the house.

"This is the updated version of the will you requested. Everything: all assets, businesses, stocks, this…house… everything will be left to Daniel in the event of your passing. Also, medical power of attorney is given to him in case you were to be incapacitated, and of course he would have the ability to direct your care from that point on. Carol, are you sure you want to grant him that kind of authority? Perhaps Anita—" he started, but I cut him off.

"Anita and Thomas will be left with enough to make them very comfortable should Daniel decide to sell the residence or terminate them for whatever reason. The McCabes have been with this family for a very long time, but Daniel has the right to make his own decisions on that matter. In regard to my health, once Daniel has been…told…of my condition, I would still trust family to make the decision over even our housekeepers," I explained.

I picked up the pen my father used to use and began to sign in the appropriate places and initial where Martin told me to.

"Have you told him everything?" Martin asked, sitting back in his leather chair.

The gloom from the outside and the soft lighting in the room made him look sickly yellow. Or perhaps it wasn't the light at all. Martin had never liked being in this house, even when Papa Jim was alive. I hated to see him so uncomfortable, but given the circumstances, it was better that these papers be signed immediately. I didn't want to run the risk of something going wrong, because the time was coming. Daniel had to know about his family and about my health.

"No. I wanted him to settle down for a few days, get familiar with the house, but I guess I had better talk to him as soon as possible. He has every right to know. He needs to know everything." I sat back in Papa Jim's chair, remembering the days I would come in here running and squealing. He would pick me up and spin me around in the air. He was a huge man, tough—so tough that he'd never miss his chance to give me a whisker burn. I absently ran my fingers over my cheek. Time was so fleeting...

Martin wiped his brow. "I think that would be the right thing. As soon as he signs, I can file these and all other paperwork as necessary." He cleared his throat. "One more thing, Carol. I am not going to be representing the family anymore. I—my wife and I are retiring, and I-I think it's..." he stammered, nervously wiping his lip and forehead.

"It's okay, Martin, don't worry. You don't have to spare my feelings. This house has always scared you."

He started to protest and I raised my hand. "Martin...it's okay. It has and still does scare me. I just haven't left all these years because...well, because it wasn't always this way. It was once a place of warmth and laughter. Then things grew cold after... after—"

After Michael was born. Christopher, my eldest brother, hated him, and it showed at a young age. Mother tried to ignore it, yet she started to see bruises on Michael's fat little legs and arms. She was sure, as was I, that Christopher was the one doing it. They looked like pinches.

Christopher was about ten when Michael was born, and very jealous. But it went far deeper than that. Sometimes I came home to find my dolls beheaded, and Christopher would protest, saying, when I confronted him, he didn't do it. Yet when I told Mother, she would simply chide him. When she turned her back, he would grin at me, evilly. He was tall and gangly, very blond, with the palest blue eyes. Asleep he looked like an angel, but when he was awake, he was the devil himself.

Christopher's hatred for his brother was something he could barely contain. The ironic thing was that Michael loved him and over the years always tried to please him. Yet Christopher rebuffed his attempts to be friendly.

Those were the easier times. On occasion, Christopher would try to seriously hurt him. He was calculating and cold and never showed remorse. He would jump out and scare Michael, or lock him in a closet with the lights off, leaving Michael banging on the doors and screaming the whole time. Poor Michael would go into a panic and wail and try to claw his way out. Sometimes he would soil his pants...

I snapped to when Martin leaned across the desk, a look of concern on his face. "I'm fine, Martin, please."

Suddenly there was a great deal of commotion going on downstairs. Laughter rang through the house, a thud and then a yelp—my heart stopped for a second. Then even harder laughter and a good-natured *ow!* My heart warmed to hear those things as Martin and I rose to find what all the noise was about.

I thought Martin was at my heels as I discovered two very soaked, very out-of-breath young men. Hale and Daniel were both laughing, with Hale trying to pick Daniel up off the floor. He wasn't doing a very good job of it, and his shoes kept skidding along the marble foyer floor. Anita was fussing over them, but the gales of laughter kept rolling. Daniel had his hand over his stomach, laughing so hard his face was beet red. Hale wasn't much better, as he could barely stand.

I stood there smiling, leaning against the stair rail, watching the two of them. The sound of laughter was like sunshine bursting through on a gloomy day, and I basked in it. I cleared my throat and they both looked up at me and settled down a bit.

Anita had already grabbed the mop, and Daniel took it from her.

"We made the mess, Anita, and we'll clean up after ourselves." He smiled up at me, and my heart couldn't help but leap for joy—he looked so much like Michael. "Hello, Aunt Carol, sorry about the mess we're making."

"Not at all, not at all!" I laughed, coming down the rest of the stairs. "It's good to see you both didn't get zapped by lightning. A little water isn't going to ruin anything."

"Supper is almost ready, Carol," Anita said. She stood there staring at the mop in Daniel's hand, as if her best friend had just been taken from her. Surely she didn't know what to make of Daniel taking the chore upon himself. "You two are going to catch your death playing in the rain like that," she chided, but that was where the seriousness in her tone died. She too was enjoying the sight of the two drowned boys.

"How was your tour, Daniel?" I asked.

"Oh, it was great. I saw the pond, and then we saw the tennis courts, the pool, and the stables. Your horses are awesome," he said as he squeezed the contents of the mop into a bucket.

Anita left and came back with two large towels.

He continued. "And the land is so huge, and it's gorgeous. And hard to run across when it's pouring!"

I smiled. "I'm glad you liked it."

"Carol, will Mr. Lahey be joining us for dinner?" Anita asked, handing the boys the towels.

"Martin? No, he"—I turned, expecting him to be by my side—"isn't," I finished.

He would never sit in that office by himself. Fear gripped my heart, and it was everything I could do not to run up the stairs to find him. Hale and Daniel, sensing my distress, followed close at my heels. As I walked to the office, which was almost across from Daniel's room, I saw the door ajar. We all approached almost on top of each other, and I reached out to open it. We stood there looking in as the door swung wide to reveal the office.

There sat Martin in the seat, papers clenched in his right hand. He was facing the desk, where I'd sat during our conversation, and the back of his chair was to us.

I spoke tentatively. "Martin?" He didn't move. "Martin?" I said more nervously but quite a bit louder.

He didn't respond.

I felt Hale's hands on me, holding me back. Then he walked cautiously around the chair to face Martin and my worst fear was confirmed. The look on Hale's face was of shock and fear. His eyes grew wide and I couldn't restrain myself anymore.

Daniel and I both rushed around to see what he was staring at.

Martin was clutching the documents with his right hand but clutching his chest with the left. His heart must have given out on him. There was nothing we could do to save him.

Yet that wasn't the most disturbing thing. His face held a look of sheer terror. His eyes were wide and staring, his mouth agape, his face as white as a sheet.

Daniel whispered, "My God," and Hale leaned in to feel for a pulse.

There was none. Immediately, Hale lifted Martin's body off the chair and lowered him to the floor to perform CPR. He gave up after a few minutes; he must have known it was a futile gesture.

Hale grabbed the phone off the cradle on Papa Jim's desk and dialed 911. He gave the operator his badge number and asked immediately for an ambulance and the coroner. He also asked that someone head over to the Lahey residence and notify Martin's wife. When he put the phone down, it was a little harder than perhaps he intended, and we all jumped.

Daniel had a troubled look on his face and was shaking his head. I reached out for him.

"He was the family attorney. He came over to draw up some paperwork for me. I shouldn't have left him in this room alone." I felt the tears grow hot at the back of my eyes.

Hale came to my side. "It's okay, Carol. Let's just see what the coroner says."

I shook my head. "He was terrified of this place, Hale. I knew it. I just didn't think anything could happen like this."

Hale led me out of the room, and Daniel followed, but Mr. Martin Lahey, who was ready to retire, went nowhere. He and his wife had intended to take a trip across America in their new Winnebago.

The man who had been terrified to death now stared out with sightless eyes, waiting for his last time to leave Timber Manor.

Daniel

WE WALKED OUT of the room and waited in the kitchen in silence for the emergency vehicles to show up. It felt like an eternity. Carol was white as a sheet, and she sat silently with her hands around a coffee mug. Hale and I sat next to her.

Hale spoke to her and tried to comfort her. Occasionally our eyes met, and I couldn't help but feel he believed what he was telling her about the suddenness of heart attacks, how heavy Martin was, his age, and the unpredictability of bad health, despite our earlier conversation. And Carol nodded and patted his hand while Anita chimed in on occasion. But I was creeped out by the whole thing. Especially with the look on his face. However, I kept quiet.

Thomas, however, sat stoically, unspeaking.

When the knock came on the front door, Thomas got up and answered it, only to return quickly with a couple of uniformed officers and the coroner.

Instantly, Hale switched over to sheriff mode and took care of the situation. He started barking orders and gave a statement to the coroner, an elderly man who no doubt had more days behind him than in front.

One of Hale's deputies showed up and informed him that someone was sitting with Mrs. Lahey until her daughter arrived from Portland.

While Hale was away in the other room with the coroner, I sat next to Carol and held her hand.

After some time, once everyone was gone, Hale came back into the kitchen and told us that he'd handle the case. Anita and Thomas had gone for the night to their little two-story on the property, and supper was put away. No one felt much like eating, anyway.

"I am staying over tonight, Carol," Hale said.

His voice snapped her back to reality—she had been staring far and away—and she patted his hand and nodded.

The papers Martin had been grasping so hard were laid out on the table, but none of us spoke of them.

Carol sighed. "Daniel, I wanted to take you into town tomorrow and show you around, but instead I think you and Hale should go and explore. He can show you the sights of Emerson. I'm so sorry you had to see that, Daniel." She looked at Hale and me and then wearily stood up, thumbing her silver cross. "Say a prayer tonight, fellas. I'm exhausted, so I'm headed to bed." She kissed us both on top of the head and made her way down the hall toward her room on the first floor.

"What a way to end a Friday night," I murmured, still feeling sort of sick. Death seemed to be hanging around me lately. And to be honest, I was quite tired of its icy hand on the back of my neck.

"Yeah. No kidding." Hale leaned back and looked at me. "I'm soaked, I'm cold, and I'm exhausted."

He was, too; his clothes were matted to his body, as were mine. And it wasn't helping matters much that my underwear was riding up my ass and starting to chafe. Perhaps that was the cold hand of death I was feeling—it wasn't on my neck, it was gripping me by the balls.

I stood up and nodded toward the door. "Come on. I have some pajamas you can use." I walked out of the kitchen, down the hallway, and up the stairs. I couldn't help but look into the office where Martin had been, and shuddered. The coroner hypothesized that Mr. Lahey had suffered a massive heart attack and died in seconds, but of course nothing would be definitive until an autopsy was performed.

I shook my head and entered my room. Hale was at my heels as I flipped on the light and went over to my suitcases. I fished out a pair of pajama bottoms—my friend, Amanda, gave me them for Christmas—for me, and my university sweatpants for Hale. Hale began to strip off his soaked shirt. He got the flannel off just fine, but when it came to the T-shirt he wore underneath, he ran into trouble. I laughed as he struggled.

Midway through he said, "I'm stuck."

I walked over to him, and on the way admired the body underneath. I resisted the urge to rub my hands over his stomach, which was flat and muscular and disappeared into his jeans in a V. He had a happy trail that disappeared underneath as well, and I wanted more than anything to drop his trousers and take him to heaven right there. But I fought that urge with everything I had in me and reached up and plucked off his sodden T-shirt, which had caught on his broad shoulders. I tossed it away, and as I stood inches from him, he reached forward and unbuttoned my own shirt.

I stared into his eyes as each pearl snap was released, then turned as he pulled it down my arms. He discarded my shirt on the floor, on top of his. I smiled and placed a hand on his right pec, which, of course, he made bounce under my palm while wearing a smug grin.

"Stop it," I whispered.

I really didn't want him to. My cock was burning my cold thigh as it pressed there, rigid and demanding attention. What I wanted him to do was strip me naked, take me over to the four-poster bed, and make me say his name, backward, forward, and in Swahili.

Instead he drew me to him, and the warmth of his body felt amazing against mine. His hands ran up and down my back, stopping to rest, finally, at the small of my back. We stood cheek to cheek, and I inhaled deeply of him.

"You feel good," he murmured into my ear.

I chuckled. "You smell good."

We pulled apart, and Hale held me at arm's length.

I stuttered, "I don't even know where...how..."

"I think we can figure that out," he replied, and I snorted and laughed at that. "I wasn't talking about that," he said, his eyes mocking me. "You have a dirty mind."

"Like every twenty-three-year-old male alive, I'm sure."

"Wow, you're twenty-three?"

I furrowed my brow. "Yeah. You can't be much older."

"I'm twenty-eight."

"Not that much older."

"No, I guess not."

I reached over and grabbed the waistband of his jeans and pulled him closer, staring into his eyes as I did so. I watched them glaze over. "Well, these days I feel like twenty-three going on seventy."

"You don't feel seventy to me. Would I be taking advantage of you then? I mean, gay or not, I feel sort of roguish."

I snorted. "Boyfriend, friends with benefits, paramours, fuck buddies..."

Hale feigned shock. "Such language."

It was my turn to laugh.

"We don't need to label anything. We know what it means, but I think people have a nasty habit of overemphasizing a title. I do, however, want to take it slow. I'm dying to do things to you that I can't spell. However, I'm going to sleep on that couch tonight. If you don't mind, that is," Hale said with a gentle smile.

"I don't mind at all." I gathered a few large blankets out of the chest at the foot of the bed and spread them out on the couch for Hale. Then I turned, walking into the bathroom. "I'm going to get changed in here."

He looked at me and said, "And I'll get changed out here." He laughed, and so did I.

Once I'd changed, teeth brushed, I heard him holler, "I'm dressed!"

I chuckled to myself and stepped into the bedroom. There he lay, covered up to his waist in a comforter, his chest bare, looking positively adorable. I smiled and walked over to kneel next to him.

He looked at me and rubbed my bare arm as I rested my head on the chest I'd admired from the doorway. He slipped his arms around me and held me tight for a second. "Get over in that bed, mister," he said, letting me go.

"'Kay." I kissed him quickly on the lips, wandered back to my bed, and climbed in. He gazed over at me from across the room, and I clicked the light off. "Good night," I said tentatively.

"Good night, Danny."

I expected to be awake all night, extremely aware of the presence in my bedroom of a half-naked man who was having the same thoughts about me as I was having about him. But my eyes got heavy immediately as I sank into the bed and got warm in the comforter.

Despite the grisly ending of the evening, as I drifted off to sleep, I felt a warmth in my chest that was appreciation for having someone to watch over me.

I was running, furiously pounding the ground with my bare feet as I tried to get away. The night winds screamed around me; the skies overhead were filled with fast-moving clouds that hid the moonlight momentarily, only for the moon to peek out again. My feet pounded upon the soft earth as I tried to put as much distance as possible between me and my pursuer. My breath came out in giant bursts of moist air as I ducked and dodged tree branches.

The wolf behind me was catching up. Once I reached the clearing of the woods and saw the house resting just yards away, I felt a new burst of energy. I leaped from the shadows and into the moonlight in a race to home.

A call from behind me and the sounds of crashing echoed in the woods.

I ran past shrubs and through the wet grass, which made me slide occasionally. I silently prayed I wouldn't lose my footing. My breath was coming out as vapor as I ran for my life.

The house was closer now, but still too far away. I'm not going to make it, *I thought.*

I was close to the rose garden now, near the back door, when he walked out. The figure stepped into the moonlit night and smiled at me, but the amount of hatred that rolled off him stopped me in my tracks. He was unnaturally tall, twisted, and horrible. His pale skin was sunken and his eyes were huge. His teeth were long and pointed, his fingers warped, long, and thin. I was more afraid of him than of what was chasing me.

From fear of this unnatural thing, I started to backpedal and slid down on my backside. My wrist popped at the force of the impact.

He started to laugh, and the blood in my veins ran cold. He held up a finger and beckoned me to come to him.

"Danny, come inside the house. Come inside, Danny."

His voice was as horrible as his face. Thin, high-pitched, and raspy, like an adolescent's voice, in a way, but the dust of decades seemed to have dried it out and raised it an octave. I shivered as he spoke. The house was now the last place I wanted to be.

His eyes were dead, soulless pits that threatened damnation. The smile on his lips made me want to scream.

I'd started to get up and run in the other direction when the wolves arrived.

Two of them leaped over me and landed in front. The eyes of the terrible man, filled with animosity, suddenly showed fear as the wolves lowered themselves to attack.

The creature let out an earth-shattering scream, forcing me to cover my ears, and then it was gone...

"Danny! Danny, wake up!"

Hale's voice dragged me from my nightmare, and I found him hovering over me as I lay on the floor, sweating and tangled up in my blankets. Apparently, these dreams were something else, or sometime in the middle of the night my bed had ejected me onto the floor.

"Jesus, are you okay?" He knelt down and helped me to my feet.

I was shaking and breathing heavily; my knees felt weak under me. "Yeah... I think so."

I sat down on the bed, placed my head in my hands, and tried to control my breathing. I felt the mattress dip as Hale sat down next to me. He rubbed my back and picked up my blankets as my heartbeat slowed and my breathing returned to normal.

"I heard you talking in your sleep. You were mumbling a name over and over again, and then you started screaming."

"What name was I saying?"

"Michael."

"That's my dad's name."

"Yeah, I know. Did you have a dream about him?"

"No, actually, it was about wolves and this *thing*. It was terrible, Hale. God, its eyes alone..." My voice trailed off and I shuddered. I looked over at the clock on the wall: three fifteen. It felt like the dream had lasted all night, but we'd only been asleep for a few hours.

"It was just a dream, but damn, Danny, I thought someone was trying to hurt you. Scared me," he muttered.

"Sorry." I felt foolish about what had happened. Outside, a wolf bayed, and others soon joined it. I jumped at the sound and stood up.

"What is it?"

I didn't answer, didn't really know what to say as I walked from the bed over to the balcony door to look out. It was blustery outside, and the branches whipped in the wind as the wolves continued to cry. I shivered as I watched the moonlight appear and disappear in rapid succession as I gazed at the tree line. At one point I could have sworn I saw a pair of yellow eyes looking up at me.

I shivered, suddenly cold from sweat.

But Hale was quick to come up behind me, and he placed his hands on my arms and ran them up and down. "Are you okay?"

I could feel his chest at my back as I leaned into him. The warmth of his body felt great against my own as he kissed the top of my head. I took his hands and wrapped them around my waist. He kissed my shoulder, and I leaned my cheek against his. "Am I okay? No. But I will be eventually, I suppose."

"Is there anything I can do?"

"Sleep in the bed with me tonight?"

He turned me and wrapped me in his arms. I laid my head on his shoulder and closed my eyes. The world turned around us, the wind whipped through the trees, and the wolves padded somewhere out there in the night.

"I won't let the boogeyman get you," he said in my ear, and I smiled and pulled back to look at him.

"I believe you."

"Come on. Let's get you back to bed."

I nodded and gave the night one last gaze before he led me by the hand.

This was night number two of these fucked-up dreams, and as I climbed in, I apologized for waking him.

"Nothing to be sorry about, not at all," he said as he spread the covers over me. He walked over to the other side of the bed and climbed in, then made a come-here motion with his hands. So I obliged. I laid my head on his chest, and he drew the covers over us and up to my chin. I laughed and looked up.

"What?" he whispered, leaning close and kissing my nose.

"You gonna be my dream catcher?" I raised a hand to run it down his handsome face. My hand reached his chin before he took it in his and kissed my knuckles. The intimacy was strange, yet wanted and exhilarating. He felt so good beside me. And it wasn't long before I became so tired I couldn't keep my eyes open.

With my ear pressed against his chest, I could hear the beating of his heart. It was a steady rhythm, strong and true. A wonderful sign of life. The arms around me were equally as strong. I ran a hand across his chest and felt the powerful muscles underneath.

"Yes. I'll keep the nightmares away," he said.

I wanted to believe him. God, I wanted to believe him. But I had a feeling it wasn't going to be that easy.

With the steady beating of his heart, and the slow steadiness of his breathing, I drifted off to sleep.

Thankfully, I didn't dream again that night.

It

THE WITCHING HOUR came upon the Donnelly house and found it quiet. The hallways of the grand home where children once played were silent as the grave, the stillness only broken by the ticking of the grandfather clock on the landing and the occasional call of a wolf to her mate from nearby. Papa Jim and Katherine smiled down from their painting as if that moment in time caught on canvas would lord over the house and keep her inhabitants safe.

Shadows stretched long and foreboding as the moon cast its silver glow through the windows of Timber Manor. And from those shadows, It emerged. Slowly at first, there was a darkening of the shadows of the grandfather clock, the banister, a Queen Anne chair, and a small table in the foyer where Carol kept a vase of roses from her garden. The shadows seemed to pour out of hidden places and begin to move. As black as oil, the shadows climbed the walls and the stairs, then began to drip from the high ceilings until the darkness gathered together within a pool of moonglow. The slick mass began to swirl counterclockwise and bulge upward.

Like darkness itself giving birth, a head emerged. A shock of white hair; then thin shoulders; a horrible, elongated face; and black holes as dark and deep as pitch. Unnaturally long arms hung at Its side. Its hands were huge, the fingers so long they began to curl in at the tips. Standing at Its full height, shrouded in black cloth, It was disgustingly waiflike and twisted in the back, Its bony hips jutting to the sides. As It hovered over the spot where It had emerged, Its talon-like feet, curled inward like Its fingers, hung suspended in the air.

It stayed there staring at the canvas for quite some time, a smile playing on Its lips. The statues of saints and the cherubs carved into the wooden banisters seemed to scream at the sight of it. Had someone been there to witness its emergence from the abyss, they would have seen the saints and cherubs turn their heads away in mortal terror.

Its form hovered over the spot where It had died, cast from Its human body into this incorporeal shape.

It once had a name, a heartbeat, but over time most of those memories had faded away. Had It gone to the pearly gates of heaven or the farthest pit of hell, It would never have aged; It would have maintained its identity. Yet here, on this plane, It grew older, and with time, what shred of humanity It once possessed had gone.

Yet *she* was still here, Carol—the sister. And the men. Daniel, the one with his father's face, slept in the room that once belonged to Michael.

The house heard It whisper his name over and over again.

They'd tried to forget It. Banished It—*banished It*—from their minds. Their lives had gone on while It stood there watching, aging right along with them but unable to interact, save for a few things like moving chairs and throwing the odd dish around. Sometimes, if It shouted loud enough, they paused as if they heard a whisper, but soon moved on, leaving It to grow angrier as they grew happier with him/It gone.

All but Michael. He'd remembered. *He/It* remembered. And with each passing thought, It gathered strength. It emerged from the veil and watched the young man grow up with the family that should have been Its and Its alone—*his* mother, *his* father.

Michael had replaced him. It had watched the smiles, the hugs, the interactions of a family glad he was gone.

But Michael hadn't been able to stop thinking about him, thinking about what had happened to him. And at night he'd dreamed of him. All those thoughts had brought It forward, farther into the physical world, and once again he'd had his way.

It was still able to play with Michael, though. Michael couldn't forget.

After all, Michael had been at the mercy of the creature when It was still human. But Michael ran away, never to return. Even when their father lay dying. And he never came back.

It stared at the portrait of Papa Jim and Katherine. The whites of their eyes seemed a little wider than usual, and their grins stretched a bit thinner, as if they too were staring down in horror.

Perhaps they were.

They should, It thought. *I would be alive if it hadn't been for that bitch. I was human before she and her husband snuffed my life out.*

The last thing It remembered before It died was the triumphant look on her face. The look of satisfaction on her face as she held Michael in her arms. The disgust, the horror, as she looked at It.

Well, It had played with her in return, on her deathbed. She'd screamed Its name and tried to hide her face while her husband stood helplessly by her side. It had tormented her from the shadows of her room as Its infection seeped into her bones.

"*Bitch*," It whispered with all Its strength.

It immediately felt the loss of the energy it had taken just to speak that single word. It began to waver, from a solid form to see-through, as moonlight began to filter through its twisted body. It still stared upward at the face of the two who'd taken It from this life. The looks on their faces were triumphant, haughty.

Her expression was just as it had been when she took Its life away and exiled it to this state. Now she and her mate walked the grounds, banished from the house, unable to come inside, unable to interfere this time. Victims of the same curse that held It here. The house was Its territory, and now that doors had been reopened, dust stirred up and memories resurfacing, It was growing stronger.

It was nothing but a memory. A simple memory.

But sometimes memories were all you needed to create a revenant.

He, the boy, was here now. Carol would have to tell him. And when she did—

Outside, a wolf howled a warning to It to stay away, but It just laughed. He was doomed to walk these halls, and they were doomed to walk the grounds. As long as the boy was in here, he belonged to It.

It just had to get him to open that last door. It stared at the portrait of those who had forgotten It. Before It dissipated in the moonlight, It vowed to have Its revenge.

Hale

D ANNY DOZED OFF quickly and lay there with his head on my chest, his arm slung over me. I lay there for quite some time thinking about the events of the evening.

Well, that was until Danny murmured and snuggled down closer. I stroked him from the base of his neck to the small of his back and felt myself melting. Into what, I wasn't sure. But it felt like our fates intertwined.

Having grown up underneath the shadow of Timber Manor, I knew the property inside and out. I knew the family. They'd taken care of us and us of them over the years. And now I wondered what Carol would think about me being in bed with her nephew. A twinge of guilt hit me in the chest at the thought of her disapproval. But as Danny shifted in bed and placed his hand on my chest, that guilt quickly dissipated. Danny had, in some ways, inherited me right along with everything.

That idea made me frown. I wasn't property; I wasn't a slave. But as Danny lay next to me, his body pressed against my right side, I knew that wasn't exactly the truth. I thought back on the men I'd dated, the men I'd taken to bed with me. My lack of interest in more than a tumble in the sheets or their lack of understanding of my sometimes-long hours prevented those relationships from having any staying power whatsoever. It required a vulnerability I didn't think I possessed. But with this man lying across my chest, I found myself more than naked underneath him. If I didn't get up, walk out of that bedroom door, and let Danny and Carol figure out their lives themselves, there would be no escape for me this time.

I looked at my clothes lying damp on the floor, then at the man sleeping in my arms.

I smiled to myself as I closed my eyes.

Daniel

DAYS PASSED UNEVENTFULLY as Carol filled me in on the papers the lawyer had drawn up and the businesses that belonged to—well, me, I suppose. I signed my name on dotted lines here and there and became owner, along with Carol, of the house and all the Donnelly assets. I was now a multimillionaire several times over, but I didn't feel any different. I didn't know what to do with that large sum of money and a house so massive, and trying to think about it made me oddly claustrophobic.

Carol seemed strained over the death of her lawyer friend—understandably—and I just felt like I was in the way. Hale visited as often as he could, and on the nights he couldn't, my phone would light up with calls or texts. Our conversations lasted hours, and I was grateful for them. He left me with limited time to be lonely, kept me engaged in talk that wasn't as strenuous as getting to know a lost relative.

Subjects ranged from favorite colors, music, philosophy, art, movies...anything you can possibly imagine. We discovered we both liked rock and roll, Chinese food, and the History Channel. He was a Leo, and I explained that I was an Aries—not that I knew what the hell that meant or put any stock in astrology, but it was something to talk about. We would talk late into the evening, and I fell asleep on him a time or two, to my horror. The next morning there would be a text confirming that he didn't mind. He would apologize for keeping me up so late. In turn, I told him that of course I didn't mind either.

He became a sweet spot, a light in all the confusion and strain these days could carry with them. Our friendship quickly grew.

Carol noticed how close we were becoming, and I openly and honestly talked about it. She listened without judgment, and it was pretty much a nonissue with her. She inquired about whether or not my parents had known about my sexuality, and I simply shrugged and responded that I didn't know. I'd really had no time to explore it outside of the bedroom, and I felt terrible because I could never tell them. That realization made me sad. My parents had been pretty progressive, and although Dad had been in the military, he hadn't been a bigot or narrow-minded in any way. Hell, when they gave me "the talk," they mentioned that sometimes people of the same sex fell in love with each other. I was raised to accept people as they were and never as what I thought they should be.

Although I wished my parents were here to meet Hale, I knew that had it not been for their passing, I would never have had the pleasure of meeting him.

Our nights were busy between Carol, Hale, and me. We would watch movies and laugh together, or he and I would stay up late at night watching videos of our favorite musicians on my laptop. He had great taste in music and was a fan of old and new music alike. Every day it seemed that we found more and more in common with each other.

I hated seeing him leave on nights that he absolutely had to, and loved having him stay. He was always the perfect gentleman, and when things got too hot and heavy, he would pull away.

"I want to make sure we're doing this right," he would whisper in my ear as our bodies trembled with desire for each other. He quit insisting on sleeping on the couch in my room, though, and sometimes we would fall asleep in each other's arms after having been up half the night, talking.

Sometimes he snored, but I didn't care. Just by being close, Hale made me feel better. His arms were solid; he would wrap them around me and the world would simply have to stay away.

Truth be told, though, there were days when the clouds would gather and I would start missing my family. I felt like I hadn't had time to really mourn them, and I would be surprised by the amount of emotion that came bubbling to the surface at times like that. Sometimes I would have to excuse myself from a phone conference with business partners or conversations with Carol, and go and sit alone in a corner somewhere so I could catch my breath.

Today, four weeks since I'd first arrived here, we took the horses out to exercise them while the rain was, at that moment, letting up on us.

A week ago, Hale had given me a crash course on riding, but he always secured my saddle, stayed very close to me, and kept the horse on a rope, which he held in case Thunder spooked and bolted.

The sky was bright blue, and the sun shone down upon us, but I felt clouded over, distant, and it sucked. I wanted to enjoy the day, but fatigue was eating at me. As were the dreams I kept having. They were frightening, but they didn't happen all the time. If I made it past three thirty in the morning, I would be fine. It was just that some nights I would find myself clawing at the carpet, facedown or wrapped up in a sheet, yelling at someone who wasn't there. After I woke, the dreams faded from memory, and I could only recall bits and pieces of them. I knew the general theme was that the wolves kept trying to keep me away from the house and away from...him.

That monster with the deadly black eyes and high-pitched voice—the one that stalked the house—was what they were trying to protect me from.

But that wasn't the only odd thing going on in Timber Manor.

I couldn't get over the fact that sometimes I thought I was being watched. Periodically I found myself alone in my room, in the library—on days when it rained, which it did more than not—in the kitchen, or even in the bathroom taking a shower, and then I felt eyes on me. The hairs on my arms and neck would stand up. Late at night, when I made my way to my room, I would sometimes have to force myself to complete the journey. As I stood at the end of the hallway and looked down it, I could swear the house had expanded. The length of hallway had somehow doubled. On more than one occasion I barreled down to my room and slammed the door shut behind me.

I didn't bring those things up to Carol or Hale. Most of the time, like now, when the sun was out, I forced myself to forget about it.

"Danny, you're being awful quiet," Hale said.

We sat perched upon our horses as they walked through the open field near the stables. The sun was warm today, bright and friendly, the air perfumed with the scent of grass, dirt, and last night's rainfall. Hale had brought along a horse named Harley for him to ride, and we had set out early that morning to work in the stables. Harley was going to be the newest addition, company for Apple and Thunder.

I glanced over at him and gave him a half smile. "I'm just enjoying the morning," I said.

That was a damn lie, but I hoped it was convincing enough. Hale stepped his horse closer to mine and reached out to rub my back. *He has to be the most tactile human being in history*, I thought. Not that I minded; I didn't. I enjoyed the attention he gave me.

A month had passed since we'd first met, and our relationship seemed to be growing stronger through each passing day. I thought about the first night he'd slept in my bed and how he looked early the next day, tired but attentive, and my smile brightened. When he came around, I felt this insane angst in my chest, like I was cresting the hill of a roller coaster or standing in an elevator going down way too fast.

The electricity seemed to roll higher and higher between us. Yet this house and its grounds was an even deeper mystery than my newfound affection for the local sheriff. And every day he was here made it harder to see him go. Not that I minded watching him walk away. That butt was a sight to behold.

I had spent one day last week with Carol going through old pictures of the family and of my father. I really did look like him when he was my age. She asked me questions about this and that, and I answered them as best I could. I asked her questions as well, and she kindly returned the favor. However, things were still a little strained between us. It was probably more me than her, and

F.E. FEELEY JR.

how getting familiar with everything took its toll on my mind. The forced emotional strain of trying to figure each other out made us both tired, and as she retired to her room one afternoon, I went outside for some air.

The day was beautiful, a welcome break from the rain, and I found myself walking in the rose garden. All manner of roses were on display, alive and blooming. Throughout the garden, stone statues of various saints silently stood guard, as did wolves, gargoyles, and the occasional cherub. The paths through the roses were made of brick. My boots clicked as I walked slowly, strolling among the fat blooms, their fragrance enveloping me. I can't say that my mind was on anything in particular, but I was lonely. Not lonely for Hale, but lonely for the familiar: Mom, Dad, and my life back home.

I took a seat on a bench that faced the conservatory; then I heard a rustling sound behind me, off to my right. I turned and arched my back a little to see what had made the noise—and stopped cold. A wolf stood between the rose garden and the wood line a few hundred feet away.

His massive body moved with his breathing, and his eyes fixed on mine.

It's the same wolf I saw on the road on my way here, I thought.

He panted and grinned his canine grin, and my heart leaped into my throat.

"Shit, what do I do?"

My thoughts screamed warnings in my head, and my body wanted to react as adrenaline shot through me. If I ran, the wolf would easily intercept me before I could get to the house. Yet if I stayed, I was sure to fall to whatever fate had planned for me.

With my heart in my throat and my legs shaking, I slowly stood. I wiped my sweaty palms on my jeans, but the wolf just stood there staring at me. I moved a leg to take a step toward the house. In response to my movement, the wolf hung his head and a low, menacing growl escaped his lips. I pulled my foot back and he stopped. I tried once more and he did it again, letting me know he didn't approve of my moving in that direction. I pulled my foot back once more; once more he calmed down.

Curiosity, the thing that killed the cat, was responsible for my next move.

I took a step toward the wolf, and to my surprise he whimpered and began to wag his tail. I was about to take a step farther when a gunshot rang out. The wolf, spooked, darted back to the tree line, regarded me one final time, and then disappeared from view.

I turned my head to see where the sound had come from, and there stood Hale in his uniform. "Danny! Are you okay?"

I yelled over that yeah, I was fine, and turned my head back to the tree line. I felt a pang of guilt for the wolf having been scared away. The sadness that crept into me surprised me. For a while, I'd forgotten about my loneliness.

That was only one of the interesting things happening at Timber Manor.

The night before last, however, nearly sent me packing. Hale had been working a double shift. I lay awake and was about to turn off the light after another texting marathon with the handsome man I was growing quite fond of. As I reached for the bedside lamp, I heard footsteps coming down the hallway. It was probably Carol, and I waited to hear a knock at my door.

The footsteps stopped right outside my room. Several heartbeats passed, and I felt the hair on my arms stand up. By leaning up against the headboard, I was able to see the crack under the door, but I couldn't see a shadow that would indicate someone was standing there.

Creepy, I thought.

I looked back at my phone and read the good-night message—the third one, actually, but who was counting?—when I heard footsteps again. They were retreating down the hallway, so I climbed out of bed and walked over to the door to listen.

As if the phantom walker knew I was there, the steps picked up speed and turned into a full-out run heading away from my room and to the stairwell. I jerked the door open and peered down the low-lit hallway. Nothing but darkness greeted me at the other end of the house. Everything was quiet, save for the grandfather clock tick-ticking in the foyer downstairs. A draft swept through, chilly on my bare arms, and I shivered a bit. Absently I rubbed my arms and shifted on my bare feet. Finally, I shrugged and turned back into my room.

"*Daaaaaaannnnnyyyyyyyy.*"

I stopped dead and turned toward the voice. It was high-pitched, almost feminine. And it had come from the direction the footsteps had retreated.

I couldn't swallow, couldn't move. *Is it just my imagination?*

"Who's there?"

No one replied. Nothing stirred. I stood there staring into the darkness for what seemed like forever.

As I was about to turn back into my room, something whispered in my ear. "*Danny.*"

I screamed and flung myself into the room, shutting the door and making sure to click the lock, just in case. I nearly jumped across the room and back into bed, moving so fast, and stared at the door. Shaking, I could hardly breathe. I picked up the phone and read Hale's last message as thunder began to rumble outside.

I wish he were here.

I had a seriously bad case of the creeps. My sleep was fitful for the rest of the night, and morning took forever to arrive. One good thing was that I would be able to tell Hale about these peculiar things without feeling as if I should be in a hug-me jacket and a padded cell. Hale would frown and nod and listen. *Good cop.*

I wanted to pack my stuff and leave. Just pack it all away and disappear over the horizon. But I'd been too afraid to move that night, and in the morning when I greeted Carol, Anita, and Thomas, I felt guilty at the idea of leaving them here alone.

Yet now, sitting astride Thunder, with the sunlight soaking into my skin and my boyfriend/friend/kissing partner next to me, all of that seemed to melt away as if it were a dream.

Hale was my distraction from the chaos and oddball things that were happening here. Usually he never prodded me, didn't try to dig, but let the conversation happen easily, without pressure.

He did prod me on the voice. Asking what it sounded like, where I'd heard it, whether I saw anything. I told him I was going to stop talking about it unless he was going to show up with Buffy Summers, Egon Spengler, or Sam and Dean Winchester.

He stared at me for a minute, confused.

"*Buffy*? *Ghostbu*—do you even watch television?"

"I like to read."

"Okay, then, Sookie Stackhouse, Harry Blackstone, Dick Hallorann?"

"…Nonfiction?"

"Oh, fuck a duck. Never mind." I laughed and made a decision right then and there to start ordering things off Amazon. Over the next few weeks, I was sure, Carol would be astounded with the boxes that appeared on the doorstep.

I liked him. A lot. I just hoped the feelings I had for him were mutual and frowned at that thought. The romance seemed easy, uncomplicated, and organic. Hale didn't have to tell me how he felt—I could feel it in the way he looked at me, spoke to me, and stayed near me at all times. He was just there. As sturdy as a tree. Except that trees didn't hug you, or talk to you, or kiss you, or place their hand on your lower back as you walked, or ask about your day, or—

No, he was definitely better than a tree.

He was Hale: smart, funny, sexy, sweet.

And he was mine.

Yeah, there was no way I was leaving.

Hale

DANNY WAS LOST in thought, so I let him be.

I honestly have to say that I was thinking quite a bit too. I'd taken some time this week to stop by the old high school. There was someone I needed to see. I stepped into the air-conditioned hallways of Emerson High School and walked down the familiar corridors I'd traveled as a kid. My uniform was damp from the rain, and my rubber-soled shoes squeaked as I walked on the polished linoleum floors. The rain had begun to fall as I darted across the parking lot to the building, not long after school had let out for the weekend.

The smell of disinfectant and old paper filled my nose as I walked along, squeaking as I went. I became incredibly self-conscious about the sound: it was as loud as cannon fire in the empty building. But no matter how much I slowed down, I sounded like Dale Earnhardt Jr. burning rubber. So I sped up and tried not to bust my ass when rounding a corner.

I came to an intersection and went right, past the cafeteria and down the science portion of the school, wiping the dampness off my brow onto the leg of my trousers as I approached the stairs. I went up a flight.

School had been out for about an hour, but it was customary for my mom to stay a bit later grading homework or tests. I needed to talk to her. I found her classroom, knocked, and poked my head in. "Hey, Mom."

She set down a paper she was grading and looked at me in surprise. "Hale Wayne Davis, you startled me. Come on in, son."

She stood up from her desk and walked to me. I hugged her and kissed her cheek. Mom resumed her seat, and I found one in front of her to sit at. She looked like the quintessential teacher. Her graying hair was done up in a bun, and her thick-rimmed glasses even had a chain attached. Right then they were perched on her nose, and she looked at me through them.

"How ya been, Ma?"

"Oh, I'm fine. These students are dumb as ever. I swear, son, every year it gets worse."

She grinned at me and I laughed. Mom didn't have any dumb kids. She taught honors classes, and her students won awards. The slowest student in her class was sure to get As in regular classes.

"How 'bout you?" she asked. She folded her hands and set them down on the desk in front of her.

"Just came to talk is all." I felt the knots in my stomach clench and unclench over what I was about to tell her. She sat patiently, waiting for me to begin, so I acted like a big boy and let it flow. I started from the beginning. I told her about Carol and how she had contacted her nephew, about Daniel and how he had lost his parents. When it came time to discuss the odd events at Timber Manor, I omitted them and concentrated on discussing my time up there and how close Danny and I were becoming.

"You really care for him." It was a statement and not a question.

Outside, rain pattered on the windows and the sky was steely gray. Under her gaze, I felt the same color, but I had to let her know.

"I like him, Mom. I like him a lot." I'd served almost ten years as a police officer and been in some precarious situations, but no one intimidated me more than Mom did.

She sat back and considered me for a long time and finally said, "Hale Wayne Davis, I have a question for you."

"Yes, ma'am?"

"Are you happy?"

"Yes, I am."

"Does he feel the same way about you?" she asked.

I nodded. "Yeah, I think so."

She stood up from behind her desk and came and sat next to me. We faced each other.

"Your father and I raised you to be the best person you can be. You were a great kid, more than a parent could ask for. You got good grades, never broke any laws, and were on the science team... What I mean to say is, we were very proud of you, son. If Danny is going to be a part of your life, then I'm happy for the both of you. I really am."

I nodded, feeling a bit bashful.

"There is one request I have," she said, leaning forward.

"What's that, Ma?"

"Bring him by to meet your old mother." She laughed.

"You're not old, Mom." I grinned.

"Bullshit. These kids are outsmarting me nowadays." She stood up and walked back to her desk. I looked around and saw posters of Bill Nye the Science Guy, the periodic table of elements, a replica of a skeleton, plastic models of organs, and microscopes. "Remember when you were in this class?"

"Sure do." I remembered catching hell from other students for the amount of homework she handed out. As if that was *my* fault.

I watched Mom walk over to one of the models, a human heart, the kind where you can open up the chambers and look at the inside. She picked up the model, turned around, and began to talk.

"I remember Michael. It's terrible what happened to him and his wife. And poor Danny. I can't imagine what that must be like. And Carol...that poor woman has been through so much through the years..."

"What do you remember about them?"

Mom sighed and regarded me with sad eyes. "Well, Michael was in your Aunt Betty's ninth grade class. I had already graduated but was attending university and doing my internship here. He was a handsome young man. Really kind and a little shy, but he was popular with everyone, the ladies especially. They fawned over him. He was the star quarterback, you know. Well, he did really well in school, but I do remember he hated the thought of going home. Betty came to me one night at home and mentioned it to me. We wondered if maybe things were not right there."

I was curious now. "Go on."

She set the model back down and crossed her arms over her chest.

"Oh well, there had always been rumors about the Donnellys and the passing of their eldest son. Christopher, I think his name was. Some say his father murdered him, but everyone who remembered the incident knew what the papers had said about it being an accident. But Michael always was first to be here in the morning and the last to go home. He was involved in as many extracurricular activities as he could possibly be involved in. Yet when he up and left, no one was really surprised."

I listened intently to what she had to say. In a small town like Emerson, it's hard to remove rumor from fact, especially with a prominent family. Yet Michael had left, and now Danny was here. I wondered if maybe Danny was in some kind of danger.

That's stupid, I thought. But I couldn't shake the nagging feeling.

"What do you remember about Carol?"

"Carol and I were in the same graduating class. She started in the tenth grade and was just as sweet as Michael and just as loved. But she seemed sad. When her brother left and her mother died, she left university to take care of her dad. And when he passed, she kind of withdrew from social circles and stayed at the house. When she did travel, it was just to the businesses she owns in the state, nothing more...er, listen to me. I'm talking like I know her daily planner."

I looked at her and checked my watch. "It's six o'clock, Mom. Can I walk you to your car?"

She said yes and I did so. The rain had slowed down, but a fine mist floated in the air. I watched her get in and drive away, and stayed until her taillights disappeared. Then I turned to my cruiser, checked my text messages, and headed to Timber Manor. I wanted to see Danny.

That was Tuesday of this week, and it had made me reaffirm my dedication to taking care of him.

Now the sun moved through the sky, thunder rumbled in the distance, and the wind began to pick up a little. We set off for the stables to put the horses away, brush them down, feed them, and lock them safe and secure in their stalls.

I watched Danny work. His body flexing under his clothing turned me on, and I couldn't help but stare. I shook my head and returned to work. Our nights together were incredible, and I hated the mornings when I had to leave him. Sometimes he would be curled up in his comforter, deep in sleep, mumbling nonsense words, and I would have already gotten up, showered, and dressed. So I would sit down next to him on the bed, rub his chest or move the hair out of his face, and he would wake up just long enough for me to kiss him good-bye.

I hated leaving him there alone. Carol kept him company most of the time, but it wasn't her I was worried about. There were odd occurrences that seemed to be happening with increasing frequency: cold spots, shadows moving at the corners of your eyes, feelings of being watched—and then there were Danny's nightmares. I didn't know if they were connected, but I had a nagging suspicion they were.

That really pissed me off, by the way. How do you arrest something you can't see? How do you pummel something that isn't really there?

And how do you help the one you love who is caught under its power?

Later on in the evening, we sat down to dinner with Carol, Thomas, and Anita. The conversation was light and we bantered about this and that. Danny, who'd been lost in thought most of the day, seemed to perk up and chat right along with everyone. I sat across from him, and we stole glances at each other as often as possible.

Carol was leaving in the morning to head to Portland and would be gone for the week, she told us. We all nodded, and Danny looked relieved when she said he didn't have to go. I could tell he was tired of traveling to the city to meet members of the boards of companies the family still owned. Carol's schedule was always busy, and she handled the reins of business very well. Danny, on the other hand, looked like someone who was lost in the shuffle. He'd get it eventually; he was smart. But I did wonder if that would have been the life he would pick for himself. The Donnelly legacy, or the continuation of it, would hang on his decisions now.

After dinner, we retired to the library with Danny's laptop, as I helped him look over more papers he had to sign, date, and initial.

He was taking his lumps in stride and doing amazingly well, finding his way through the mess, and I watched him as he worked. Most of the papers that had been drawn up by the recently deceased Martin Lahey were signed, but a few remained. And Danny read every single word on every single page.

I was leaning on the lounger, with Danny lying up against me, my arm wrapped around him. He had tied his hair—which had grown some in the few weeks he'd been here—back with a rubber band. We'd both kicked off our socks and shoes for comfort. Danny thumbed through the documents, underlining places he felt were important to remember, and I teased him about his ability to understand the jargon.

"I *am* prelaw," he said, taking a break and laying the myriad of papers he'd replaced his laptop with. Instead of watching more television, Danny closed his eyes and leaned against me for a few quiet moments.

Which was a blessing. If I had to watch one more episode of *Buffy the Vampire Slayer*—ah, who was I kidding? I would have bleached my hair to look like Spike's if Danny asked me to.

Night had fallen, and the winds outside had not settled down. The wolves that stalked the property were also restless, and they howled. Every time they did so, Danny would raise his head from my shoulder and listen as if they were talking directly to him. It was something I watched with quiet interest as his eyebrows would furrow. Silently, and apparently done with his break, he picked up his papers once more and continued. He would lean forward, sign, date, and initial in places that he had to, then settle back next to me to read more.

I didn't mind. I wasn't bored. Just being with him, in moments like that when time always seemed to fast-forward itself, was something I'd grown to love.

Before too long I knew I had to go. I had work in the morning, and 5:00 a.m. came early.

Carol poked her head in the sliding door, and we both looked over at her. "Daniel, there are still going to be some workers throughout the house while I'm gone. They already know what they have to do, so they shouldn't bother you too much."

Daniel stood up with the paperwork and walked it over to her. "This is all signed. I hope I got everything," he said as he handed it over.

She took the papers and smiled at him, tucking them under her arm. "Good. Then it's settled. You are now a homeowner." She grabbed his hand and patted it.

I watched them both from my place on the floor and couldn't help but smile. He was indeed going to stay.

Carol continued. "If you need anything, I'll have my cell on me. Thomas and Anita are going with me. Do you think you two can manage while we're gone?" She looked at me and winked, and I felt my face flush.

"Sure," I replied. "As a matter of fact, I'm thinking about showing Danny the town. The carnival is here for the Fourth of July, and the tourists are everywhere. What do you say?" I asked him.

"Sounds great. And don't worry, Aunt Carol. I can cook, and I promise not to burn the house down." He leaned in and kissed her cheek as she laughed.

"Good. I'll be gone probably before you two get up in the morning, so you boys take care." With that, she walked out, and Danny slid the door closed behind her.

He walked back over to me and snuggled up as we listened to the wind howl.

"Taking me to the fair?" he asked, turning his head toward me.

"Sure. I'll even buy you some cotton candy."

He smiled, and I leaned in for a kiss. His mouth met mine, warm and inviting. He sat up straighter to lean into me, and I wrapped my arms around his body and dragged him closer. We ravaged each other's mouths, and the heat between us threatened to consume our bodies. He ran his hands up my chest, held my face with one hand, and with the other trailed his fingers through my hair. I reached over, lifted him, and sat him in my lap, and as the passion intensified between us, I leaned into his neck and moaned. My lips hurt from the intensity of our kissing. We both were breathing heavily, and he held my head close to him. My pulse raced through my whole body, and every nerve felt on edge. I wanted him so badly, but I was determined to take it slow. To do things right.

Dammit, stupid standards.

He sat back from me and I stared up at his face, so handsome, and those lips, so kissable.

"I gotta get going soon," I said.

"I know. I know." He sighed and stood up; I had to adjust myself quickly. He reached for his laptop, turned it off, and unplugged it. "I'll walk you out."

I stood up. We walked toward the door. Danny set his laptop down on the desk, and before I knew it, he pitched forward and fell hard. As he fell, he braced himself with his hands, but when he rolled over, he was holding his wrist and scooting back from the desk with a confused look on his face.

I leaned down to help him up, but he wasn't budging. His gaze was fixed under the desk, where there was nothing but a lamp cord plugged into the wall.

The wind outside howled, and the wolves howled with it.

The look on his face disturbed me, and I said, "There is nothing there, Danny."

But the evidence on his ankle belied my words. Five distinctive red scratches were present along the foot, as if someone had grabbed it.

"I didn't stumble on anything," he said. "Something tripped me."

I was going to reiterate that nothing was there, but the scratches defied anything I could have said. Finally I got him to his feet. He dusted himself off, and we headed out of the library, shutting the door behind us.

It

B ENEATH THE DESK, It lay exhausted.

The amount of energy it took to interact with the physical world to that degree left It powerless as It lay prone on the floor giggling to Itself remembering how It would once torment Carol. When It was alive.

With all the activity in the house lately, It had begun to gain strength. As the dust stirred and doors opened, when things were moved and Carol began to remember It, It grew stronger.

The boy had fallen flat and hurt himself. Not badly, but enough to satisfy It. More would come later.

The revenant had watched them in the library, their disgusting affections and their intimacy. It also watched as that bitch came in and took the papers Danny gave her. Her time was coming too.

Now It slid under the door of the library and up the stairs, unseen. It hesitated outside Carol's room and listened as she finished her packing. She was thinking about It when It/he was alive. It was being remembered, and It laughed silently to itself, feeling the energy of those memories slowly empower It.

Outside, the wolves howled, their spirits rife with fear and anger. They worried about *him*, what It would do to him, and they were right to. It would do everything in Its power to drive the boy mad and then kill him.

It floated up, back to the foyer and the spot on the floor that had made It, then up the stairs and finally to the place where It hid.

To wait.

Daniel

HALE REFUSED TO be convinced that I was going to be okay. After I promised him I would call if I needed anything, he left reluctantly. I stood outside and watched as his taillights disappeared around the bend. I didn't want him to go, but I forced myself to be okay with it. My ankle throbbed where the scratches were, and the entire incident plagued my mind.

The wind was still whipping around outside, the leaves rustled at an almost-roar, and my clothes whipped against my body. Again I thought about leaving. But where would I go? School was out for spring, it was way too late to register for summer classes, and if by chance the house was being haunted, what kind of person would I be if I left Carol here alone?

I sighed deeply, my breath white plumes in front of me in the cool evening air, turned to walk back to the house, and stopped dead in my tracks.

Two feet in front of me, between me and the house, was the wolf. He was sitting on his haunches and staring at me. I hadn't heard him approach. I still didn't carry a pistol around when I went outside. Now I regretted the decision.

"*Daniel.*"

The wind seemed to whisper my name. I looked around and was greeted with nothing but darkness. That voice was different from the one I'd heard in the house. It sounded like...almost like...

Moonlight filtered through the clouds, but everything was dark. I turned my attention back to the wolf, my pulse racing.

"*Daaaaaaaniel.*"

That time I knew I'd heard it. It seemed to come from all around me, as if drifting on the winds that pummeled the night. Chills cascaded up and down my back. It was a man's voice. It was...

"Dad?" I called.

The wolf growled and began to back away from the house. It turned and ran out into the night.

"*Daaaaanielll*," the voice called again.

The front door opened and Carol stepped out, wrapped in a robe. "What are you doing out here by yourself?"

I looked at her, dumbfounded, and finally shook myself. "I just walked Hale out. I...I'm on my way in."

I started up the steps and paused to take one last look around the grounds. My heart was breaking. There I stood. Between becoming the heir to a fortune, having so many new people in my life, meeting Hale, and my curiosity about the wolves, I'd been feeling a lot of things recently. Yet all I could feel, at this moment, was how bad I missed my mom and dad.

Walking into the house, I clasped the last gift my father ever gave me.

Carol

DANIEL LOOKED SO downtrodden when he came up the stairs that I almost missed what he was holding. He turned and shut the door behind him, and I nearly cried out as I reached for the medallion.

He looked at me, confused, and then smiled sadly. "It was my dad's."

Tears welled up in my eyes. "I know."

He looked unsure for a second, as if I were going to ask for it back.

"You gave this to him," he said in wonder. It was a statement, not a question. Michael must have mentioned it to him before he died.

I wiped away the tears and smiled. "Yes. Your father was a few years younger than you are when I did. I haven't seen this in so long."

We walked out of the foyer and into the kitchen, where I poured us each a cup of coffee, and then we settled down at the kitchen table.

"How did you come to have this?" I asked, pointing to the chain. I really didn't mind. Actually, I thought it was beautiful that Michael would pass it on to his son.

Daniel took a drink from his coffee and wrapped his hands around the mug. "We were in the swimming pool, and Dad was holding me up in the water, trying to teach me how to swim..."

Daniel

Then

*K*ICK YOUR FEET, *Danny, and pull with your arms."*
I laughed and squealed, splashing in the water and having a
ball. Dad was leaning over me, giving me instructions, but I was
too busy soaking him to really care.

"All right, son. I'm going to let you go now. Try to swim to the
other side."

He slid his hands out from underneath me, and instead
of swimming to the point he indicated, I immediately went
underwater. Instantly he reached down and brought me back to
the surface as I coughed and wiped water out of my eyes. He held
me close to him and laughed, chiding me to listen to him next time,
and that was when my gaze caught the medallion, its golden face
reflecting the sun into my eyes.

***

And then

People stood and cheered as the general dismissed the throng
of Marines who had just come back from the Iraq War.

Mom had my hand, and when we spotted Dad, we started
running. At eight years old, I could run faster than Mom. Dad cut
away from the other Marines, and as he saw me, he ran toward
us. I raised my arms in the air as he knelt down and leaned in to
swoop me up. The chain fell out of his shirt along with his dog
tags, and suddenly I was up in the air, my arms around his sun-
darkened neck.

***

And then

"Danny?"

His voice drifted up the stairs. I stood, surrounded by what used to be my room. The remaining boxes were taped shut, with "Danny's dorm" written on them. I was going over the room one last time, making sure I didn't leave anything behind. The bed had been stripped, the dresser emptied, with the only things remaining being my pictures and pennants on the walls.

High school was over. I'd graduated salutatorian, and summer was winding down. School, my freshman year at the local university, was about to begin. As a swimmer, I had received a full ride and was very excited about being out of the house.

Dad, however, had been a handful about the whole issue. Yet he'd finally come around when I explained he really didn't have much of a choice. The day had come.

"Danny?"

Dad's voice interrupted my thoughts, and I turned to see him standing in the doorway. Time had aged him: he was a little rounder in the gut than he had been, and gray had crept into his hair. He leaned there, arms crossed over his chest—which was where the aging had stopped. Dad was built like a tree trunk, and he was still powerfully strong. His forties looked good on him. Hell, they looked good on Mom too, who was at the moment directing the movers with my things.

"Yeah, Dad?" I asked.

"Been wanting to talk to you," he said.

"Look, Dad, I'm not going that far away, and I'll be home on weekends to do my—"

He cut me off with a wave of his hand. "No, it's not about that. Here, sit down for a second." He motioned to the few remaining boxes that were filled with books. We sat down.

He scooted closer to me. "I know these past few years have been trying—you know, living here. But I never meant to shelter you or deny you from having any fun. Believe it or not, I was your age once. I just wanted to keep you safe," he explained.

"Dad, I know," I replied, feeling a little guilty over the hell I'd given him.

We were always a bit combustible, prone to drive each other crazy. Mom played the peacekeeper between us, yet sometimes even she'd get frustrated, which meant both of us were in the doghouse. "You're as bullheaded as your father," she'd shoot at me when our arguments got too heated.

Dad reached around his neck and unclasped the gold chain. He reached for my hand and placed the chain on the palm, closing my fingers over it with his own. His eyes were wet, and I felt a lump forming in my throat. I opened my hand, and the Saint Michael medallion I'd been so fascinated with was now mine.

I looked back up at him, at his weathered face.

"You're all grown up now, and I know I can't always be there to protect you. So I want you to have this. It was given to me by my sister, Carol, when I left home, and I want you to have it...for luck. Your mom and I are so proud of you. I love you, son."

I was speechless, and I reached over and hugged the man who'd always had the strength to lift me in the air when I was a kid. "I love you too, Dad."

Carol

"MOM SAID THAT, even as an infant, when Dad would feed me or hold me, I always went for this chain."

Daniel held it in his fingers and tucked it in his shirt. His face was flushed and his eyes emotional. The boy missed his father so much I felt it deep within myself. All the weight of the world seemed placed on his shoulders, and I hated myself for my part of that. Perhaps I should have let him be and just had everything changed over to his name in my will.

Nonsense, I thought, *he's a Donnelly*. Besides, Hale would have never come into his life, and his parents' deaths couldn't be undone, anyway.

"Are you okay being here with me?" I asked. "With all of this…" I motioned around me.

"Yes, Aunt Carol, of course. I don't mean to sound like a burden," he said meekly.

"Daniel, you're not a burden. Not at all. I was just hoping that I haven't made things worse for you." I reached across the table for his hand, and he held mine in his own.

"No! God, I don't know where I would have gone or what I would have done. I mean, here I feel like I have something to focus on. I just really…really miss my mom and dad." His face crumpled and his lower lip trembled as his eyes filled with tears. "It's just…if I stop for too long…I can't help but think of them." His voice hitched and he covered his face as he began to cry.

I stood up from where I was sitting and came around the table. I wrapped my arms around him and brought him to me as he let loose a torrent of sobs. As my own eyes misted over, I rocked with him and whispered nonsense things. Eventually his tears began to taper off, and he cleared his throat and sat up.

I wiped my own tears away now, understanding exactly what the boy was feeling. I had lost Mom and Dad not far apart from each other. Living alone in this massive house made me feel like it could swallow me whole sometimes, but Thomas and Anita made it bearable. This poor fella had been cast into the unknown and was struggling to make the best of it. I admired how brave he was.

He calmed himself and laughed. "Shit. I have a bad habit of that lately. Sorry."

"It's totally fine." I laughed. "Sometimes a good cry resets the brain. Kicks out the cobwebs and drains the poison that gets built up in there. It's good to let it go. I know, how about some ice cream?" I stood.

His eyes lit up. "Okay."

He laughed, and that was how we ended our evening. Talking about the past, about growing up, our connection grew stronger, as aunt and nephew, over banana splits. Sometimes barriers come down on their own, and sometimes they have to be torn down. Regardless of how, it's usually a better thing for them to come down so we can see each other for who we really are, warts and all.

That's when we're at our most human.

Daniel

I HAD BID AUNT Carol good night and was about to climb the stairs to my bedroom when a knock sounded on the front door.

It's nearly midnight, I thought as I hurried over and swung the door open.

There stood Hale, face drawn, with a bag slung over his shoulder. I stepped aside to let him in.

He turned on me as I closed the door. "You didn't answer your texts! Then I tried to call and you didn't answer."

He looked so worried and was so wound up, his eyes wide, watching me. Anger was storming around in those eyes, brewing like an oncoming storm.

I leaned back into the door and folded my arms over my chest. Hale wore a pair of sweatpants, running shoes, and a T-shirt, and looked absolutely amazing. His muscles bulged from under his shirt, and his pants hugged him in all the right places.

He's worried about you, Danny, I told myself.

I walked over to him and placed my hands in my back pockets. Standing close, I let my brow furrow, trying to look as mad as I could. His anger was replaced with a bit of confusion at my sudden aggressive stance, and he was really blown away when I reached for his head and pulled him into a long and very passionate kiss. He let the bag slide to the floor and wrapped his arms around me. I could taste the toothpaste he'd just used; he smelled like a fresh shower and aftershave.

I stepped back from our kiss, and the shock on his face made me laugh. "You know, I could kiss you like that forever."

Hale's facial muscles clenched and unclenched. When he spoke, his voice took on a huskier tone as he reached out and pulled me to him. "I'd let you."

He kissed me again, and then, hand in hand, we walked upstairs.

When we reached the bedroom, I took his bag and set it down in the chair as he sat on the edge of his bed to remove his shoes. Once there, and when the shoes were out of the way, I climbed in his lap and pressed close to him. I got up on my knees and looked down.

"Hey…" I cupped his face with my hands.

"Hey back."

"Did you miss me?"

He hesitated and narrowed his eyes before saying proudly, "Not one bit."

I laughed and kissed him gently on the mouth, then pulled back. "What about now?"

Desire ignited in his eyes, as well as a little mischief. "Nope."

I kissed him again, deeper. Tasting his mouth, I let my hands wander to his chest and felt the hardness of his pecs underneath my touch. I darted my tongue out to taste him and was greeted with his own. A low moan escaped his lips. I sat back then and removed my shirt. His hands slid up my back and then lower down to my ass, where they lingered.

"What about now?"

He grinned and chuckled. "Danny, what's gotten into you?"

I slid my hands down his flanks and reached for his T-shirt. His arms went up as I pulled it off. Desire was now rocketing through my body at the sight and feel of him. I returned my hands to his chest, where I ran my thumbs across his nipples until they stood erect. With my heart hammering in my chest, I kissed him again.

He grabbed two fistfuls of my ass and ground me to him.

"I want you to get into me."

In a flash I was lifted up in the air and turned over until Hale lay between my legs. His eyes searched mine intently as his hands ran up my body, up my arms, and held my own hands fast.

I was on fire.

"Okay, I missed you," he said finally as he lowered his face inches from mine. His beautiful eyes watched me. "I miss you every time I walk out of that door. My days drag on like molasses in February. I count the minutes until I can set my eyes upon you again. When I'm gone, I think about you, Danny."

The intensity of what he was saying surprised me. And then, on the other hand, it didn't. What I had wanted—mindless, simple sex—wasn't going to be achieved right then, and I felt ashamed for wanting it like I did. Well, maybe not ashamed, he's fucking hot. I felt somewhat inconsiderate. I hadn't known his feelings for me were that intense. "Are you falling in love with me?"

Hale kissed me then, slow and passionate. After letting my hands go, he wrapped his own around my back and rolled us over until I was on top of him. I sat up on his hips, bracing myself on his chest. "What do you need me to be for you right now?"

"Wow. I have choices?"

Hale inhaled deeply. "Losing your parents wasn't a choice. Being saddled with a legacy that you didn't know existed wasn't a choice. While I work here, and have, and will continue to do so as long as you'll have me, I don't want you to think you inherited a boyfriend you can't break up with, right along with it. So yes, you most certainly do have a choice."

His words made me feel funny inside. Funny good, not funny bad. And in those words I heard the answer to my question. *He loves me.*

I scooted down his body and lay on top of him, my head on his chest. His heart beat underneath me, and I felt the rise and fall of his breathing. His fingers gently caressed my back as sleep tugged me down.

"I need you to keep doing what you're doing," I murmured.

Hale kissed the top of my head and rolled me onto my side. Then he grabbed the blankets and pulled them over us.

Within ten minutes max, I was asleep in his arms.

***

"So, you gonna be ready for me to pick you up after I get off of work?" Hale asked as he got dressed.

The bag he'd carried in last night had been stuffed with his gear, and he'd run out this morning to retrieve his uniform, left hanging in the backseat of his truck. From the bed, I watched him get dressed and admired his body. I glanced at the clock; it read 5:00 a.m.

"Yeah. What time are you going to be getting off?" I asked.

The bed felt empty without him, so I decided to get up too. I threw back the covers and stood up, stretching.

He smiled, walked over to me, and wrapped his arms around me. I wrapped mine around him and snuggled close.

He dropped a quick kiss on my lips. "Around five or so. Is that okay? I'll go get changed and come and get you. What are you going to do today?"

He cradled my head next to his as he held me. I ran my hands up his chest and rubbed it, making my way up to his shoulders, loving the feel of the muscles there. I felt guilty last night for coming on like a horny teenager. But damn…

"Hmmm? Oh well, there are some workers coming to do repair work throughout the house. Carol said they knew what they were doing, so…I guess I'll just read or go for a swim. I'm not sure. Come on, you're gonna be late."

I ran into the bathroom to brush away my dragon's breath and nearly jumped out of my skin when I saw my face in the mirror. My hair was a mess! I had bed head. I ran my fingers through it so it would lie down, just as Hale walked in, saw what I was doing, and laughed.

"What?" I asked innocently.

"You snore and sometimes talk in your sleep. Either way, don't worry about how you look in the mornings. It's my favorite time to see you."

"Aww." Looking at him in the mirror, I laughed. He wore a bashful smile. "You must be exhausted. What time did we fall asleep?"

Hale folded his arms and leaned on the bathroom doorframe. "It was after one." I turned, wincing. He laughed and shook his head. "I'll be all right. I'll take a nap in the office if I have to."

We walked out of the bathroom. I threw on a pair of jeans and a T-shirt and walked him downstairs. Carol, Thomas, and Anita were all in the kitchen as we wandered in there, and I caught Anita and Carol exchanging knowing looks. Thomas, however, just kept reading the paper.

"Good morning, you two," Carol said. "You're up awful early."

"Hey, Carol, Anita, Thomas," Hale said as he headed over to fill a thermos with coffee.

I walked over and pecked both Anita and Carol on the cheek. "Morning," I said, looking at Carol with a grin.

She winked back at me.

"See you at five?" I asked Hale as he readied to leave.

"Yup, I'll be here." He leaned in and daringly kissed me a good smack right on the lips in front of the family, turned to bid everyone a good day, and walked out.

"When did he come back?" Carol asked, looking amused.

"Last night, right after you went to bed," I said, a bit embarrassed. Anita and Carol both snickered like schoolgirls over their coffee. "When you and I were down here talking last night, he couldn't get ahold of me either by text or calling, since we were in here talking. So he showed up."

"Awww," both ladies said in unison.

I laughed and grabbed my own coffee. "I know, right?" I took my place next to them.

Anita said, "You guys have been spending a lot of time together." She elbowed Carol, who just grinned at me.

"Yeah, he's pretty great."

Thomas lowered his paper and looked at the rest of us. "I, for one, am happy you two are getting on as well as you are. Hale is a great guy. These two biddies over here talk about it all the time."

Anita threw her balled-up paper towel at him. "We do not! Hush, old man. Oh, Carol, look. We have to go."

I just laughed. "Thank you, Thomas."

All three of them stood up and gathered their things, which had been sitting in the kitchen. Thomas went to get the car, and Carol and Anita both wished me well and to have a good week. Carol reminded me that her phone was on should I need anything, and promised to call me on mine when they got to Portland.

I walked them to the door and made sure I locked it behind them.

Today is going to be a good day, I said to myself as I headed back upstairs for a quick shower before the workers showed up.

***

I was nervous about being left in the house alone, but the first knock came promptly at 9:00 a.m., and before noon, projects were going on all around the house. A foreman came in, introduced himself as Dale Parrish, and let me know he would handle the crew, and if I needed anything, to come see him. I said sure, have at it, and decided to go lie out by the pool—the noise in the house was driving me crazy.

As I changed into a pair of swim trunks, I remembered to grab my cell phone. I took off my Saint Michael's medallion and placed it on the nightstand, grabbed a book, my iPod, and a pair of sunglasses, and headed outside.

The weather was warmer than it had been, and I laid my stuff by the side of the pool and put my foot in the water to test it.

"Jeebus, it's cold!" I laughed to myself, walked over to the diving board, and jumped in.

Holy shit, I thought but quickly swam a couple of laps to warm myself up.

After that, I took to the water quickly. Back and forth I swam, and my muscles, which had been stiff, started to ease up as tension flowed out of me. I swam a multitude of laps and finally climbed out of the water when my body shook with exertion.

I laid my towel next to the pool and put on my sunglasses. The sun felt great on my skin, and thankfully, I tan and not burn. Yet I reminded myself not to be out there too long.

Between dips in the pool to cool myself, answering Hale's texts, and thumbing through my iPod, the morning drew on. I finally put on a T-shirt to cover my body from the sun, feeling satisfied from the rays I'd received, and just lay there on the towel, enjoying the day. I wasn't in that damn house, the birds were singing, and the skies were cloudless.

Around midday, however, the foreman, Dale, came out to the pool area. I was gathering up my things to go in when he walked over.

"Mr. Donnelly, we have a slight problem," he said.

Dammit. "What's wrong?" I asked.

My arms were full of things, and I followed him into the house. We walked up the stairs, and after I laid my things down, he explained to me what had happened. Apparently they'd been working on some crown molding in the hallway of the second floor, and one of the workers hadn't been watching what he was doing.

Dale walked me down the hallway off to the right of the staircase. The only time I had been down that way was when Carol had given me the tour on the day I arrived.

"James was moving his ladder, and a corner of it caught the wall. It gouged out a section of drywall—put a pretty big dent in it, actually."

I was confused. "Is that a major problem?"

"Well, no, not really. Yet there's something I think you need to see." We walked to where other workers had gathered, putting their hands over a hole in the wall and talking to each other.

"That's the spot right there." Dale pointed to the hole in the upper part of the wall.

"Dude, put your hand over that spot. The air coming out of there is ice-cold." A tall, blond-haired guy turned his head to look at me.

I walked over to where the worker stood, and as he moved his hand away, I reached up.

He was right. It was frigid.

"Air conditioner?" I asked, looking back at Dale.

He shook his head. "Those run through vents. I don't know what's behind this wall, but listen. It's hollow here." He knocked on the wall close to the hole and then moved across the hall and knocked on the wall behind me to show me the difference. It was hollow by the hole, like there was some kind of space there.

"Huh" was all I could manage. "I don't know, guys. Patch it up, and I'll mention it to Carol. I can't figure it out either. I'm new here," I said, laughing.

All the guys laughed, and Dale promised to take care of it. I told him not to paint it, though; I wanted to show it to Carol and didn't want to forget where the space was. Dale agreed and went about his business.

Before too long I had gone and showered. The day was dragging on by then, and I dressed and ate lunch. Dale came back and told me he would be available to sand down and paint the repaired area after I told my aunt. I thanked him, and the workers left.

I was curious about it and decided to walk back down the hall. The new plaster covered the hole and was drying solid, already turning chalky white. The house was quiet save for the ticking of the grandfather clock down the hall. *Why would anyone cover up something like that?* I asked myself. I knocked on the wall just under the newly plastered section to hear the hollowness. *Hmmm,* I thought. *Weird.*

The hallway lights flickered for a second and came back on, then went off and on in quick succession. All I could hear was my own breathing, and I was about to turn to go back when I heard knocking from the other side of the wall.

One, two, three, repeating the same rhythm I had used. My skin began to crawl, and I backed away, my heart pounding in my chest.

The lights flickered once more and stayed on.

I bit the inside of my mouth, hard, and stepped forward again.

I knocked three more times. However, I did it slowly, deliberately waiting a breath between each knock, and then I backed away from the wall.

The lights didn't flicker this time. Not once. I exhaled slowly and was about to leave—

Knock. Hesitation. *Knock.* Hesitation.

I stepped forward in wonder once more.

BOOM!

Outside, a wolf called, and before I knew it, I was halfway down the hallway heading back to my bedroom.

I'd broken into a sprint. My stomach clenched and my fight-or-flight kicked into high gear. Adrenaline pulsed through me, my brain told me to flee—but I wouldn't. I gritted my teeth and slowed down.

Back in the living room, I waited for Hale to show up as I sat watching TV. I kept an eye on the door of the living area and tried to convince myself that I was being a wuss, that there was nothing to be afraid of.

The hours seemed to drag; finally, Hale showed up.

I began to relax, but when he asked (as he often did) if I was ready to get out of there, he was surprised when I enthusiastically said yes.

Hale

T HE QUAINT LITTLE town of Emerson was something out of a Norman Rockwell painting.

Emerson, tucked inside the mountains of Oregon, far away from the business of Portland, had a sleepy quality to it. Antique stores, mom-and-pop markets, boutiques, candy stores, knickknack peddlers...all manner of storefronts lined Main Street. It was neither poor nor rich, its citizenry as eclectic as the stores along the road through town. The houses of Emerson lined up one by one in pretty rows, with mowed lawns, sprinkler systems, and patio furniture. Some flew American flags on their porches as the city readied itself for the annual Fourth of July celebration.

In the town square, red-white-and-blue bunting was on display as city workers rigged it to anything that would stand still. The local high school band was practicing, marching through town playing off-key while the band director tried to get them to pay attention to him. In the park, mothers with strollers greeted each other, and children squealed and chased one another around. Their families talked over bottles of beer and barbecue pits. Politics, football, 401(k)s, and the economy were highlights of the discussions.

Other families filled vans and station wagons with their beach towels, bags of clothing, and suntan oil, heading on their way to the lakes to celebrate there, and still others pulled boats full of coolers and fishing tackle behind souped-up trucks, ready to set sail.

In the parking lot of the SaveMore, the Rampton Brothers' Carnival had set up shop. The smell of cotton candy, popcorn, and deep-fried batter filled the air with the aroma of sticky sweetness. Screaming teenagers, loud music, and the voices of barkers calling out to the crowds, enticing them to their stands, seemed all over the place. The air was filled with joy and celebration, and I couldn't help but smile as Danny and I wandered through the crowds of people.

He had been quiet all the way to town, but as soon as he saw the rides, his face lit up. He nearly dragged me through the ticket booth as he looked all around him.

The sun hung heavy and hot in the sky. Evening was coming on quickly, but the fun was just beginning. We stopped at various booths and checked out their wares. Some sold cheap junk jewelry, and others sold bits of art that were really well done. Danny's arm brushed mine as we walked and talked, pointing to this and that.

Children with painted faces ran screaming between us, causing us to dive sideways. Butterflies and fairy wings were on the girls' faces, Spider-Man and Batman on the boys'. All of them, however, carried sparklers or large candy-coated sticks of who-knows-what.

The warm breeze felt good on our skin as we passed booth after booth.

"Hey, you. Yeah, you! Step right up and test your strength! Come on now. Step right up," a barker hollered at me. The man stood at one of those thermometer-shaped wooden boards that had a spring-loaded lever at the bottom and a bell at the top. I looked at Danny and grinned, and we walked over to the guy.

"How much?" I asked.

"Two bucks for the medium prizes and four for the large ones," he said.

Danny laughed, and I followed his gaze to the assortment of prizes. Large koala bears, monkeys, flamingos, and other stuffed animals adorned a screen behind the man. I handed him a five, and he made change for me. I gave the dollar to Danny, who looked at me with amusement in his eyes.

I winked at him, then took the mallet from the vendor and stepped up to the line. I raised the oversized hammer above my head and brought it down with all my strength.

Danny laughed and cheered when he heard the *ding*.

I handed the mallet back to the man.

"What'll it be, sir?"

I pointed to a brown bear. The man handed it over and looked between Danny and me with a smirk. I handed the bear over to Danny, who turned beet red as we walked away. The look on his face was bashful, but he accepted the bear without arguing.

"So, what are you going to name him?" I asked.

"I'll hug him and squeeze him and call him George," Danny said, laughing, after a thoughtful moment.

"George, huh? How about we give the bear away and you take me home. I'll let you love and squeeze me too, ya know?" I looked over at him, dressed in a pair of blue-and-white board shorts and a tank top. I could tell he had lain out in the sun today, as his skin was a little darker, tinted a bit red. His slender, muscled body looked amazing in the fading light. The cloth of his tank top stretched against his chest, and his toned arms were loose and wrapped around his bear. The shorts hugged him in all the right places, and I caught women checking him out. Occasionally I would see a man glance over and linger on him for a while, but they looked away when I smiled at them.

I felt that pleasant discomfort, that deep-down redirection of blood flow surge through my body as Danny said, "I'm keeping my bear. But I'll take you home and squeeze and love you too."

He reached for my hand and transferred the bear into his other arm, and we walked through the crowds like that. I didn't care what people thought. I was the sheriff in this town, and Emerson was pretty progressive. Thank goodness I was appointed and not elected, but right then I didn't care about that either. All that mattered to me was the man walking next to me.

My day at work had been blessedly slow. No accidents, a couple of tickets, and a fight between two neighbors had been all that had gone on. I had paperwork to do, of course, but by lunchtime that was out of the way. I shut the door to my office, propped my feet up on the desk, and fell right to sleep.

My secretary, Doris, knocked on the door and woke me up at four thirty. I nearly tipped out of my chair.

She laughed as I pretended I was awake. "You know, I've worked for you for—what? Five years now?"

I straightened some papers and pretended to look for something. "That's right."

"You've been kind of distracted lately."

"Oh?"

She laughed. "Who is she?"

I sat back. "What makes you think there's someone?"

"Honey, I was born at night. It wasn't last night, however."

I inhaled deeply. I would be picking Danny up in a few minutes and escorting him to the carnival. People would see us. People would talk. And I didn't want to hide him. I wasn't ashamed of him, I wasn't ashamed of myself.

"There is someone," *I said standing up and pushing my chair in.*

Doris smiled sweetly and peered at me over her glasses. The sweet lady attended the First Methodist Church of Emerson, sang in the choir, and volunteered at an animal shelter on the weekends.

"His name is Daniel Donnelly," *I said and waited for hell to break loose.*

Doris's smile dropped for a second, and then she stepped inside and closed the door behind her.

Here it comes.

She walked around the desk to where I was standing and placed her hand on my arm. I tensed and wondered if she was going to offer her resignation on the spot. Instead, she leaned up and kissed me on the cheek.

"Like I said, I wasn't born last night, sugar. I have four children, Hale. A mother always knows. I just wanted to give you the opportunity to tell me yourself. He's a lucky guy."

I grinned, relieved, and nodded. "I think it's me that lucked out, Doris."

"That's Carol Donnelly's nephew, then?"

"Yes."

Doris nodded grimly. "That family needs a bright ray of sunshine, Hale. And they found him. You taking him to the fair?"

"I'm on my way now."

"Good. Go have fun. Be safe," she added.

"I will. Call if you need anything." I made my way to the door, turned the handle, and opened the door.

Doris spoke up. "Hale?" I turned my head and raised my eyebrows. "I'm proud of you."

Now that I was walking through the heart of the town with Danny's hand in mine, so was I.

Daniel

I LOVE HIM.
The realization hit me like a ton of bricks as we walked through the crowds. I nearly stopped right then and there. I watched him pick up that mallet, turn and wink and me, and then slam it down as hard as he could. When the bell dinged, I found myself extremely proud of him. And kind of turned on.

And the bear...oh my, cute! When he handed that to me, I thought I was going to die. I had this tingly feeling in my guts, and from head to toe, as I walked with his hand in mine. And every time he looked over at me with that twinkle in his eyes, I'd smile. And then he'd smile right back. And I'd smile harder and look away.

Yes, ma'am. I'd like two tickets to cloud nine, please. No, make it three. I need one for the bear.

Night was falling fast upon us as the stars came out, lights from the rides flashed, and music rang out over the lot. There was every kind of ride imaginable: Tilt-A-Whirls, Gravitrons, merry-go-rounds, a double Ferris wheel, teacup rides, Kamikazes, and a multitude of other rides that spun you around in circles or tossed you ass over tittleberry in an attempt to get you to scream and upchuck the hot dogs, cotton candy, popcorn, deep-fried chicken, and french fries the vendors sold you. There was even a ride that tossed you up in the air at ungodly speeds.

As we walked by this last ride, the car was unloading; a woman was laughing as she had to half carry her poor husband, who'd passed out on the ride.

I walked hand in hand with Hale through the people, and some of them looked and whispered, but I didn't care. I felt safe, empowered, and a little goofy carrying that bear around with me, but that was cute, what Hale had done, so I dealt with it.

The night was filled with magic, and the cares that had infested my day fled before the sights and smells of a town celebrating and reveling around us.

***

We laughed and talked more, and he did buy me cotton candy as he'd promised, and we shared it as we traded George back and forth. We'd almost reached the end of the thoroughfare when I spotted her. Well, when she and I spotted each other. People were milling about us, walking and talking, screaming and laughing, yet our eyes locked and the world faded away.

She was sitting in front of a tent, with the name *Francine the Amazing* written in yellow letters above her head. On the table in front of where she sat was a cheap crystal ball. Her mocha skin was flawless, and as I stared at her, I could never have guessed her age. Her hair was done in dreadlocks, piled on top of her head, and decorated with what looked like gold coins. She ignored the people walking by, as did I.

She sat forward in her chair, arms propped up by her elbows on the table, her head resting on her fists. Her eyes bored into me, at me, and through me. Before I knew what I was doing, I walked over to the table and sat opposite her. Her dress was cut low at the top, exposing slender shoulders and a full bosom. The dress itself was full, and she seemed to be from a time long past. Her beauty was otherworldly, and the energy coming off her was like ocean waves. I was her shore.

Suddenly Timber Manor came to my mind, along with the noises, the wolves, and the nightmares. I wanted to tell this lady everything. About my parent's deaths. How I came to be here. The man at my side and the way I felt about him. There was a magnetism about her and I was caught in her orbit.

She sat back and stared at me with her honey-colored eyes. She was beautiful. Ethereal and otherworldly.

Hale sat next to me, looked at her, and looked at me. He sat back and folded his arms over his chest, and I knew right away he didn't like being there. The lady's feline eyes regarded me as she sat in her chair. Finally, she spoke. Her thick Creole accent rolled off her tongue as she scooted the crystal ball aside.

"I have not seen someone as touched by the spirit world as you in a very long time. Your heart is broken, and you have a heavy burden on your shoulders, don't you, boy?" she asked.

Her words pierced me deep inside, and I nodded, my pulse slamming in my ears.

She reached over the table for my hand. I gave it to her without knowing I was going to do so.

She opened my palm and ran her hands down it. "Now, I can tell you lies that others like to hear, give you the lines people expect from me. Lies about love, fortune, travel, and future children, that make people feel better about their lives. But I won't do that to you. I won't tell you that you will live a long life, get married, and have children. I will speak the truth if you'll hear me, boy. Or should I call you Daniel?"

The use of my name shocked me and I instinctively pulled my hand back. "Yes," I said thickly.

Patrons walked by, and cheers and cries of delight filled the night behind us, but where we sat, the world had gone still.

She continued, "Well, then, you must know this. Our spirits, our essence, our souls are eternal. These bodies of flesh and bone carry who we are inside of them. It is the way nature allows us to experience life, love, and pain. Our bodies allow our souls to mature, like a cocoon allows a caterpillar to transform into a butterfly."

She smiled at me and then continued. "Right now, your souls are intertwined." She looked over at Hale, who seemed to have relaxed a little and was sitting forward, listening. "I can see them hovering over the both of you right now. Dancing, changing, and touching...experiencing each other. That is what this earthly realm is for. And what the both of you have is beautiful."

She leaned forward in her chair and faced me alone. "When we touch each other, we leave parts of our souls upon the other. Like fingerprints upon glass, this experiencing is how our souls learn, and this knowledge we carry with us beyond this place.

When we depart this plane, we carry our souls on to higher places, new realities, taking with us everything we've learned in this life. This is our mutual destiny as human beings."

She sat back, placed her hands on her lips, and looked at us both. We couldn't help ourselves, and we sat forward, listening intently. "Yet sometimes, when a soul becomes infected, when it is touched by lowly things, or when the soul itself has rotted and lost its ability to feel, it warps the vessel that carries it. Should it die, it leaves a stain upon the world around it, and the soul becomes chained to the places it used to know in life. Many people speak of ghosts and specters, and this is how they originate.

"You both have been touched by this infection. I can see it as plain as the noses on your handsome faces, Daniel. It is really concentrated on you. Your life and your essence are in danger."

"What do you mean?" Hale's voice was cynical.

"Spirits of all origins walk among us all the time. Some of them never come into contact with us—they have their own realities—yet the ones who were human often do. They are usually lost, confused, bitter, and, most of the time, angry. When those who remembered them pass away, they lose their substance, and their ability to manifest, to touch us. Yet every once in a while, something can stir these things up. Do you understand?"

I shook my head. "No, not completely."

"Think of it this way, Daniel. They say that the sense of smell is the most powerful sense we have. Perhaps the smell of a perfume may trigger a memory long forgotten. This is how spirits maintain themselves in this realm—they have to be remembered. Right now, whether you know it or not, you're running into spirits who are trying to interact with you. However, luckily for you, they're not all malevolent."

A chill cascaded down my back and I absentmindedly rubbed my arms. The night wind had turned cooler. Hale reached for my hand, and I stood with him. She watched us as we got up.

"You people are scam artists! How dare you—"

Her laughter pealed through his critique. "I am not fortune-telling, Sheriff Davis, and you don't have to fear anything from me. But you had better guard your lover." She looked from Hale to me.

"Not all the spirits that have touched you are evil. Some are lighter. I can see their imprint on you. They will fight for you, Danny, when the time is ready. But you have to welcome them in." She stood, reached inside her dress, and pulled out a pack of cigarettes. "Don't be afraid of the wolves at your door." She lit a Parliament, inhaled, and exhaled the smoke. "If you want to talk again, I'll be here."

And with that, Hale and I walked away into the crowd. The whole time, however, I could feel her eyes on my back.

Francine

THEY WALKED AWAY as I smoked the rest of my Parliament. I exhaled the plumes of smoke and crushed the butt under my heel on the concrete of the midway, closed my eyes, and reached out to touch Daniel's thoughts with my own. I knew where he was going and what little time they had left.

The fair was winding down for the night as custodians began sweeping spilled popcorn and empty cups into their mobile trash cans. I ensured that I wouldn't be bothered further as I clicked off my overhead light and stepped inside my tent.

I was disturbed at what I saw on that boy. His lover had been touched by it too, but not as badly as Daniel, whose aura looked horribly bruised by signs of contact with a malignant spirit. Hale's affection and care for him was one of the things preventing Daniel from succumbing, becoming sick; Hale was like a doctor treating an infection with a mild antibiotic. I knew in my heart that someone else lived in that home and wondered about their health, as malignant energies can have a negative effect on those around them. I feared the worst.

I turned on a lantern I kept at a small table. Upon it lay my book. The large book, its leather still shiny even after all these years, was my cross to carry. *Memoirs of the Human Wraiths*, its title inscribed into the binding like a brand. And like a brand, it looked burned on. Standing before it, I reached for an inkwell with my right hand while my left passed over the tome. The cover flipped open, and pages began to riffle as if with an invisible hand.

Once a blank page appeared, I tipped the inkwell sideways and let a small amount of its contents pour onto the page. Instead of a blotch of black ink staining the paper, the book absorbed it. I set the well back down and waited. Of course, I'd known they were coming. The ancient book told me.

"Will they be able to fight this on their own? Can they do this without intervention?" I asked as I leaned over, my hands pressed against the table.

I didn't have to wait long. It wasn't a prolonged explanation in a series of paragraphs—it wasn't even a sentence. One word. The script, in a handwriting not my own, pressed itself upward onto the page.

No

So they would succumb to the spirits in their world if I didn't do something about it. I picked up the inkwell again and poured a little on another page. As before, the ink was absorbed.

"What kind of spirit am I dealing with? A poltergeist? A shade? A wraith?"

Each had their nuances, with different methods to deal with them.

This time two words emerged and my heart nearly dropped into my shoes.

A Revenant

"Shit."

I should have known that. Prolonged exposure to them, just like any carcinogen or high-voltage power line, could cause any number of illnesses and result in death. If they didn't outright kill you themselves. Now that I had seen Daniel and felt his aura, it wouldn't be hard to track him down again. I closed the book and picked it up, holding it to my breast as I exhaled. "Well, Francine, there's no rest for the weary. It's time to go to work," I said.

I stepped out of the tent and went to look for my boss.

Daniel

WE WERE IN the parking lot, getting ready to pull away, when Hale looked over at me. "That lady is full of shit," he said.
"I don't know."
"You can't possibly believe that garbage!"
I looked at him. "I'm not sure what to believe." And I began to tell him what had transpired after the foreman had shown me that space in the wall.

Hale's face went from skeptical to listening to disbelief and confusion. George was sitting between us as we weaved in and out of traffic.

"Where are we going?" I asked.
"Back to your place," he said. "Why?"
"Because I would like to go to your house tonight, if you don't mind." I looked over to him and he smiled and grabbed my hand.

We drove through most of Emerson, and as the night fell heavily on the sleeping town, we pulled into the driveway of 7314 West Pinochle Street.

This is more like it, I thought, as my gaze fell upon the house.

It was a modest two-story bungalow with a huge front porch complete with a swing. The lawn, like many of its neighbors, was mowed, and flowers grew in pots and along the porch. As we walked up the stairs, Hale grabbed my hand and held it. With the other hand, he unlocked the door, and we stepped in.

The house was clean but well furnished, the floors carpeted, and a stairway climbed up to the second floor. One of the things I noticed right away was the large number of books in shelves, piled on counters, and tucked in wherever there was space. To the left of the entryway sat the living room, with a large bay window that overlooked the front yard.

Hale walked through to the kitchen, and I followed him. There, the appliances had been cleaned to perfection, although they were not all new, and the floor was made up of cream-colored linoleum. The refrigerator hummed, and a clock on the wall ticked away the seconds as I stood watching him put his keys in a jar upon the counter and check the locks on the back door. I couldn't help but smile as he looked at me.

"What?" he asked.

"I think your home is wonderful."

He smiled and grabbed my waist. "It's not Timber Manor, but it's home."

"No, it isn't. That place is too much house lately. This...this is just right."

He grabbed my hand, and we proceeded up to the second floor, to his bedroom. He stepped in and switched on the light, and a ceiling fan began to turn. I headed off to the left, to his bathroom, as Hale sat down at the foot of his bed.

I turned the light on and started the shower running hot and fast. As I reached back to shut the door, hands grabbed my hips.

Hale

I SHUT THE DOOR behind us. Steam was filling the room and fogging up the mirrors.

Danny had walked in ahead of me, and I watched him strip out of his clothes. His beautiful body took my breath away. He stepped into the shower and closed the curtain behind him. His muscular back ended at a round ass—perfection. Light brown hair covered his long legs, but the rest of him was smooth. I quickly stripped out of my clothes and followed him.

My mouth was dry and my loins ached. I was not hiding the fact either, as my engorged cock stood out in front of me. I pulled back the curtain to find Danny had begun to lather himself up. I stepped in behind him and turned him to face me. His eyes were wide as his gaze moved down my body. He shakily reached out and put his hand on my side. The hot water cascaded over both of us now. I pulled him to me, and he rested a hand on my pec. When our bodies met, passion erupted, so hot it threatened to burn the house to the ground.

My mouth was instantly on his, tasting, testing, exploring; our tongues lashed and fought with each other. I let my hands roam his body and travel as far as I could reach. His firm muscles molded to my hands as I went downward. I reached around, cupped his ass, and brought his groin to mine, and he broke the kiss and leaned his head back, moaning. Our cocks stood snug against each other as we touched, tasted, and teased with our mouths. I reached down and slid my hand over his erection, and as we kissed, slowly worked my grip back and forth over his solid flesh.

"Hale...slow down," he panted.

I stopped, wanting this to last. Instead I grabbed for the shower gel and a rag and bathed him. Down his arms, down his chest and belly, down his legs I scrubbed, turning him to do the back as well. After I turned him, he braced himself against the shower-curtain rod and hung on. I brought the rag up and washed the backs of his legs, his ass, the whole procedure intimate, private, and loving. He stepped into the water, rinsed himself completely, turned, and then took the rag from me.

His hands shook as they traveled the length of my body, and I watched him. First he paid attention to my chest, and then my shoulders, down my arms, and my belly. I wasn't smooth like him, and the foam lathered into the hair on my torso. He motioned for me to turn, and he washed my back, down the backs of my arms, to my waist. The rag moved downward, and he knelt to wash my ass and the backs of my legs. "Turn."

As I did, he reached for my cock, looked up at me, and took me into his mouth. The sensation nearly outdid me, and I had to grab hold of the shower rod to steady my shaky knees. Then I reached down and raised him up, turned off the water, and stepped out.

A small closet contained towels, and I pulled out two, wrapped myself in one, and dried Danny off with the other. We walked back into the bedroom and made our way to the bed.

We slid in between the sheets, and soon our passion rekindled. He rolled me over on my back and climbed on top of me. I sat up, wrapping my arms around him, our kiss unbroken. I ached for release and thought that if this lasted much longer, I would lose my mind. I didn't care; I was hungry for him. I'd tasted him, and I could never have enough. I rolled him over on his back, gently laying him down, and slid down his perfect body.

His stomach was flat, and I kissed his belly button and all the way down, grabbing his cock in my hand. He moaned and writhed under me as I took him in my mouth. He thrust upward, running his hands through my hair. I stopped, raised myself up, and kissed him, with our bodies wrapped around each other.

I reached into the nightstand, retrieved a bottle of lubricant, and put some on my hands. He watched me as I lowered myself back to his waist and his erection. I rubbed some lubricant on my cock and then lowered my mouth back onto his, then slowly worked a finger into his ass. Daniel moaned his approval.

I sat back on my haunches and watched him as I worked two fingers slowly in and out. When I thought he was ready, I positioned myself over him, and he nodded.

As I slid into him, he gasped at first, winced a bit, and his eyes grew wide. I leaned in, fully inside his ass, and he wrapped his legs around me. I kissed him, and he returned it hungrily.

"Are you okay?" I asked.

"Yeah—oh my…yeah."

Slowly I began to rock with him, sliding in and out. He felt so amazing, and I moved gently at first.

Then our pace began to pick up. His hands went immediately to his cock, and he jerked himself in time with my thrusts. Before too long he arched his back and cried out as he came. I followed close behind, feeling my body tense up and release deep inside him. We crashed together and seemed to fall into oblivion as I lay on top of him, both of us breathing heavily, sweaty and sticky. Finally I rolled off and lay next to him.

"I've been missing out on that?" he asked, looking at me.

I laughed and scooted him closer.

He snuggled on my chest as we both calmed down. "I love you, Hale," he said, stroking my bare chest.

Those three words I'd longed to hear had finally come to me. "I love you too, Danny," I whispered, running my hand up and down his back.

Before too long, Danny's breathing became slower and deeper.

I thought back on what the woman had said at the fair. If our souls were as she described, then mine belonged to the man in my arms.

Tonight we'd touched, our bodies and our souls, and I knew that things had changed and would continue to change for us. Daniel and I had crossed the divide between friends and lovers a few weeks back. Now our love had become a full-fledged commitment, and as I drifted off to sleep, I knew I would do whatever it took to keep it alive.

PART TWO:
CONVERSATIONS
ABOUT DEAD THINGS

Daniel

THE WEEK UNTIL my aunt returned went by quickly.
After the night of the fair, Hale and I went back to town for
the Fourth of July concert and fireworks in the park. Crowds of
people in lawn chairs, many toting coolers and wearing flip-flops,
gathered in the city park to watch the display of artillery that lit
up the night sky at dusk.

Earlier in the day, Hale had invited his mother to meet us for
lunch, and she was so pleased to meet me, I blushed. She sweetly
expressed her condolences for the loss of my parents, and I
thanked her, but the rest of the conversation was casual and fun.

Ms. Davis entertained me with stories of Hale as a child, and
I listened with a grin on my face. My big, bad cop boyfriend used
to be in the glee club. Nice. She also joined us for the evening
festivities, and I found out that Hale and his mother knew just
about everyone in town.

When I was introduced as Hale's boyfriend, most people took
the news graciously. When they found out I was Carol Donnelly's
nephew, they were all the more kind to me. I met the mayor, most
of the city council, the public defender, and a judge and his wife.
The minute they were gone, I couldn't recall their names, but hey,
whatever.

The fireworks display was awesome as we sat there upon a
blanket spread out on the lawn, among the people. Hale's mother

sat in a lawn chair, and we chatted until we could no longer hear above the explosions of red, white, and blue fireworks. Afterward we walked her to her car, shuffling through the crowds of people and through the parking lot.

As we reached Ms. Davis's Honda and she was about to get in, she hugged her son and then hugged me as well. "It was so great to meet you, Daniel. Don't you be a stranger."

I promised I wouldn't, and Hale and I watched her pull out into traffic and head home.

We smiled, walked to my truck, and climbed in. I dreaded the thought of returning to Timber Manor, but I didn't want to leave it empty for too long. Yet, even with the mysterious goings-on in the joint, I could cope. Nothing could bring me down from this high. I had my reservations, sure, but with as much as I had lost in the past few months, it felt good to score one for happiness.

Hale volunteered to stay at Timber Manor for the rest of the week, and I gladly accepted. Besides, the thought of not being around him now felt weird. We drove back to Timber Manor that night, with the radio blasting and us singing away to old '80s rock, sunburnt and happy.

As soon as I turned into the driveway and the house came into view, our moods calmed down a bit. The house stretched out against her grounds, and her dark windows seemed to watch us driving up.

Hale put his hand on my bare leg and squeezed it for confidence.

We put the truck in park, walked up the stairs, and let ourselves in to be greeted with quietness. Everything seemed in fine order, so we looked at each other and then took our stuff upstairs to my room. It all seemed just fine that night.

I showed Hale the section of wall that had been plastered over and told him again about the noises I'd heard. He thumped on the wall, same as I had.

Nothing happened. No flickering lights, no knocking, no cold spots, so we made a quick snack in the kitchen and retired to my room to watch movies.

Once in there, as we got ready for bed, I noticed my Saint Michael's medallion wasn't on the nightstand where I'd left it. I moved the stand out, checked under the bed, in the bedcovers, but it wasn't there. It made me sad and a little anxious.

"When is the last time you saw it?" Hale asked.

"I took it off before I went down to the pool the other day. I didn't want to ruin it. Now it's gone," I said, exasperated.

"You don't think anyone came in here and took it while you were down there, do ya?" Hale asked, hunting around the room with me, looking for my missing chain.

"My laptop is still here, and so is my iPod. Nothing else has been moved."

"Aw, Danny, I'm sure it will turn up somewhere," he said hopefully.

I wasn't so sure. Something didn't seem right about the whole thing, and while we watched the movie—Michael Bay's *Pearl Harbor*—my mind kept drifting back to the medallion. I felt sad and disappointed that I had been careless with it, and mentally kicked myself for not simply keeping it on me. We made it through a good chunk of the movie, discussing why we thought Josh Hartnett and Kate Beckinsale made the best couple.

However, we didn't make it till the end. As we grew close, got warm, and our bodies relaxed, we both drifted off to sleep as the Doolittle Raid invaded Tokyo.

"Daniel?

Daniel!"

My eyes shot open and I sat up in bed. I looked next to me. Hale was sound asleep.

Who's calling my name?

I slipped out from under the covers and walked to the balcony door, opened it, and stepped out into the night. The wind was chilly, blowing steadily against my naked chest, and the concrete that made up the balcony was cold under my feet.

"Daniel," a voice called up from the grounds below me, and I peered over the edge.

There stood my father in his Marine fatigues. He wasn't as old as he'd been when he died. Younger, much younger—probably not much older than I was now. He was waving his hands above his head, trying to get my attention.

"Dad?" I blinked twice, trying to focus on the figure below me, and leaned farther over, placing my hands on the railing for support. "Dad!" I called out.

He stopped waving, and I could see a smile break out on his face as he looked up at me.

My heart swelled at the sight of him. I called out again, waving both my arms. "Dad! Don't move. Don't move. I'll come down."

I was so happy. Overjoyed.

His face turned serious as he yelled back up at me. "You have to get out of that house, son! He's in there, and he's going to try and hurt you. You have to get out."

"Who's here, Dad?"

"Son, you have to listen to me. You have to get out. Get Carol, get Hale, and get out!"

"Dad, who are you talking about?"

"Christopher! Please, son, get out! Wait...no—no!"

His face contorted in fear. I spun around to look at what had caught his eye, and there it stood.

Between me and the door stood that same disfigured monster I'd seen before. The black holes it had for eyes were wide, and its grin stretched disgustingly, as if it was extremely pleased to see me. Before I could scream in terror, it raised its face, which contorted angrily, shot out its hands, and pushed me, hard. I tried to grab for the railing but failed.

Suddenly, I was tumbling...tumbling...

"No!" I screamed, sitting up in bed.

The light came on as Hale turned to me. "Are you okay?"

I jumped out of bed, ran over to the balcony doors, swung them open, and stepped out. The sound of thunder rumbling off in the distance periodically interrupted the night. I looked over the railing, trying to stare down into the darkness. My father would be standing down there, beckoning to me.

All I saw was grass stretching out into the woods.

A hand landed on my shoulder and I screamed and spun around, hands raised in fists.

Hale backed away. "It's just me, Danny. What the hell?" He looked confused and a little scared. His wide eyes regarded me with concern.

I bent over and put my hands on my knees, trying to catch my breath. Shaking and suddenly very pissed off, I raised my head to look at Hale. "I want to know who the fuck Christopher is," I said through gritted teeth.

Hale's eyes widened. "Who told you about him? Did your aunt?"

I shook my head. "Never mind who told me. Who is he?"

"Danny, I'm not the one you need to ask—"

"So help me God—"

"That's really for your aunt to discuss—"

"Goddammit, who is he!"

Hale sighed. "Come back into the bedroom."

I stepped back into the warm room, and Hale latched the door behind us. I walked over to the bed and sat down.

Hale, wearing nothing but a pair of boxer briefs, pulled up a chair in front of me. "Have you talked to your aunt about the reason your father left?" he asked, taking my hands.

"No. I figured he hated it here and just wanted to go."

"Well, he did hate it here, but for a good reason," Hale replied. "Look, Danny, Christopher was your father's older brother."

I opened my mouth to inquire further, but he held up his hand. "The rest is for your aunt Carol to tell you. Do you understand?"

"No, I don't understand! What the hell is the big secret? I didn't know Carol until she called, so what's with this Christopher guy?" I asked angrily.

"He died, Danny. He fell down the stairs to the foyer. That's all I know, honest."

I sighed. Hale looked grief-stricken that I was upset, and the look on his face was killing me. "Fine. But Carol has a lot of questions ready for her when she gets back," I said, sliding into bed.

Hale sighed and moved the chair back to its original place near the wall. The look on his face was unreadable as he climbed in next to me.

I was furious, and when Hale wrapped his arm around me, I stiffened.

"You're angry with me."

"I *am* angry at getting jerked around. You tell me this place is haunted. My aunt's lawyer dies here, Carol tells me nothing herself except that I'm a fucking bajillionaire, and neither one of you wants to tell me what exactly is going on. What else have I inherited?"

"I was hoping your aunt would disclose some of Timber Manor's less-than-stellar history. I didn't think it was my place."

Finally, I relaxed. I took his hand and wrapped it around my waist. "You're loyal to Carol. I understand that, I guess."

"I'm loyal to you too."

"I know."

There was a moment's hesitation, and Hale asked, "Do you want to tell me about your nightmare?"

The vision of my father sprang into my mind's eye. His smile. The way he looked was like when Mom and I met him after his deployment. My eyes swam. "I dreamed of my father and the monster that chased him away."

Outside, the wolves were howling. Their mournful song filled my heart to the point where it overflowed onto the pillow.

Hale tightened his arms around me and tried to calm me down, but it wasn't too long before my own cries rose up to meet theirs.

It

RIGHT OUTSIDE DANIEL'S bedroom door, the shadows grew darker and began to move.

All along the corridor, the shadows converged like a giant tsunami, and instead of hiding in spaces beyond the light of the moon, they pulled away from the walls and slapped down silently in the center of the hallway.

Like a silent river, the darkness began to flow toward its master. Its name had been spoken, and somewhere deep inside the house, the revenant raised Its head.

Carol

THE MORNING DAWNED dismal and gray. The clouds above were bloated and the color of a battleship.

The trip back from Portland wore me out, much as the doctor's words had. Cancer. Stage IV. It was in my bones. It was in my blood. And it was in my pancreas.

The doctor suggested I try a place in Norway that was experimenting with a new procedure, but I held up my hands and shook my head. The cancer was eating away at my bones now, and I knew it was only a matter of time. It had started a few years ago, and we had fought it into remission once, but the cancer was back with a vengeance.

"How long do I have?" I asked the oncologist, a beautiful Middle Eastern woman named Dr. Noor.

We sat in her office, I in my chair in front of her, with Anita and Thomas at my side. They held my hands, and Anita wept silently into her handkerchief. Thomas's face was stony and unreadable.

I'd known this day was coming. The doctor sighed and sat back in her chair, my folder spread out on her desk. She looked truly sympathetic, and it showed in her beautiful almond-shaped eyes as she said, "Maybe six months. With more chemotherapy, maybe a year."

I nodded and thanked her for her time. We cut the trip short. I canceled the meetings I had with some distributors and headed back home. It was the night of the fifth when we got back, and Hale and Daniel were watching television when I walked in the door.

Daniel came out into the foyer to greet us and took our bags. He looked shocked to see us back so soon and inquired about our trip. I gave some sort of trivial answer to his inquiry, and he regarded me coolly.

Something is wrong, I thought.

Anita and Thomas both said good night and headed back home. Anita promised to arrive bright and early the next day. After a bit of pleasant conversation—mostly one-sided, for Danny's answers seemed a bit cool—I finally asked what was wrong.

What he said next about knocked me out of my chair.

"Who is Christopher, Aunt Carol?"

I stared at Hale. He threw his hands up in a gesture that said "It wasn't me" and took his seat next to Danny.

One thing about the Donnellys is that we have no poker face at all and you can tell when we're pissed off. It was written all over Daniel's face. His eyes were alight with it, and I felt like I could wilt under his gaze.

I sat back in my chair. "Please, not tonight."

He went to protest and I held up a hand. "Please, Daniel, not tonight. Tomorrow morning would be better. Ask me in the morning and I'll gladly—"

I stopped suddenly. Something was wrong. There was a strange feel to the air, almost like it was charged. The crystal bowl sitting on the kitchen table began to wobble, slowly at first, and then it picked up its pace. Everyone jumped up and backed away from the table, staring at the bowl. Then it suddenly stopped.

This isn't over, I thought.

Above our heads, the sound of running feet made us all look up. The footfalls were heavy and headed toward the landing of the stairs.

"What the hell?" Hale pulled Daniel back toward him and motioned for me to get away from the doorway.

We all backed up toward the sink. I counted my heartbeats as they thudded against my breast. Daniel and Hale stood in front of me as if to block me from an unseen assailant.

We stood on trembling legs, waiting for something to happen. One second, two seconds, three…silence. It was almost deafening.

Hale took a step forward, cautiously staring out into the darkness. The kitchen door had been propped open, and as he approached it, it slammed shut with a bang. Hale stumbled backward and nearly fell, but Danny caught him under his arms and helped him regain his footing. The air in the room slowly returned to normal, and we collectively exhaled.

On trembling legs, I walked forward. One step, two, three, until I reached the kitchen door and pulled it open again. I waited as Hale walked up behind me and tried to pull me back, but I resisted, shrugging my shoulder out from under his hand. I turned my head to see both Hale and Danny moving to turn me out of the way. Instead of fighting them, I relented and let them get ahead of me. It would have been funny had we not been so scared.

We walked cloistered together in a huddle, moving almost as a single entity, anticipating something terrible happening at any moment. But as the seconds ticked by, we were greeted with nothing but silence.

"What the hell was that?" Danny asked, turning on me.

He was afraid; I hated myself for it. "I'm not sure. I have an idea, but I'm not sure." When Danny opened his mouth to inquire further, I raised my hand. "Please, in the morning. Tonight we'll sleep in the library."

Hale agreed and ran upstairs to grab a few quilts and a change of clothes for them.

As the boys settled down, I lay awake thinking about what I had just gotten my nephew involved in. My heart hurt for him, as I was pretty sure things were about to get a lot worse. I knew then and there how wrong I had been not to tell him everything. When the sun came up, I would.

Right then I was so exhausted. So sad at the news I'd received. I would tell him, but in the dark, the words just wouldn't come. I slept fitfully, dreams tormenting me as the wolves howled their displeasure.

***

The next morning I awoke, dressed, and made my way to the kitchen for coffee. On my way I heard laughter and someone trying to shush it.

Knowing Thomas and Anita did not get on that way, I wasn't surprised to come upon Hale and Daniel at the table, speaking in hushed tones and exchanging light touches, and I paused.

What an interesting turn of events, I thought to myself.

I hadn't known Hale was gay. I'd had no idea that Daniel was either. And I really hadn't known that they would find each other. They'd become lovers.

I was jealous of them. Jealous of their life, of their love. And I was ashamed of that jealousy. Oh, how I longed for the days when Mark had touched my hands like that and smiled at me with forever written in his eyes. Yet those days were long gone; the house had made sure of that. They would need each other when I told them all that must be said.

I cleared my throat as I walked in, and they leaned back and away from each other. They still had their nightclothes on, and while Danny sat there looking bashful, Hale, like a gentleman, fetched me a cup of coffee.

I checked my watch—only 6:00 a.m. Anita would be on her way shortly to start breakfast. Thomas would not be joining her today, as Sunday was his day to attend church. At the kitchen table, I sat down across from Danny and reached for his hand. His hair was mussed and he was blushing a little bit.

"You know how much you look like your father?" I asked.

Daniel smiled longingly. There was something in his eyes, something far more than simple sadness at missing his father. Something had happened.

Something. The house had done something, and all the hopes that whatever had lingered in this house was long gone dashed against the rocks of the sorrow I saw in Daniel's eyes.

He said, "Mom would say the same thing to me sometimes. When Dad would be on one of his long deployments, she would be doing dishes or something and look over to see what I was doing. Sometimes she would just stop and stare. I'd catch her looking, and she'd smile and ask the same question you did."

"You had a happy life, didn't you?" I looked deep into eyes that were so familiar to me.

He nodded. "We had our ups and downs, sure, but yeah, it was happy." His voice had grown thick, and Hale, who'd sat down next to him, ran a hand over his back for support.

"Tell me about your life, Daniel. Tell me about your father, my Michael."

"Dad was a tough guy and a Marine to the core. He was strong, and when I was little and would get underfoot, he would pick me up with one hand, put me on his back, and keep on walking through the house. Nothing scared my dad. He worked long hours, and sometimes when he went on deployment, we didn't see him for months. Mom hated those times. We would be left at base housing when he was away, and those days would drag on forever. Those were the only times Mom would be a little short-tempered and more emotional, but Dad would eventually come home and we would be a family again."

He sat back and then continued. "Dad was prompt, determined, and sometimes rough on the outside, but he was never mean to Mom and me. He was very protective over us, like he was always worried something was going to happen to us. When he was away, he made Mom stay in contact with the other wives so he could check up on us if we missed his call. Yet when it came to me, he was even more protective. It almost made him crazy if something would happen while I was at school or at home. I remember I fell off my bike one time and had to get stitches. Mom was home with me, and Dad was at work. Well, she took me to the hospital on base, and when Dad got there, he paced and paced and kept checking up on me to make sure I was okay. I never understood that. He treated me like I was made of glass. Like I could disappear into the air."

I frowned at what he was telling me, knowing where that protectiveness came from and the reason behind it. I let him continue.

"When I was a teenager, he and I never got along at all. I thought he was smothering me, and my friends were scared of him. Some of the friends that I had, though, stuck around, and when Dad got to know them, he calmed down. But…his reaction to me wanting to go out—to a park, to a movie, to the mall to hang out with friends—was over-the-top. It wasn't 'typical dad' behavior. He lorded over me. Even though Mom kept saying he wanted to keep me safe, I was drowning. Our personalities clashed many times, and I must have driven him crazy. I was a good student, but I couldn't wait to get out of that house.

"It was after we quit moving around the world so much that things got that way between us. When we were always on the go, spending a few years here or a few there, I wasn't in a place long enough to really get to know my surroundings."

I nodded encouragingly for him to go on.

"Yet there were times he would lighten up and we'd tinker in the garage together. That Silverado that is parked outside—Dad and I bought it when I was a senior in high school, and we rebuilt it over the summer before I went to college. That thing is a beast, but I would never trade it for anything. Also, Dad and I both loved rock and roll. Old stuff, ya know? Queen, Bad Company, Boston, and we would always have it blasting in the garage while we worked. Dad couldn't sing to save his life, although he tried, and Mom would laugh at him. She could really sing, and sounded like Patsy Cline.

"Now that they're gone, I really regret the times he and I would fight. I would trade my life for one day with them back. I didn't really know how good I had it."

His eyes misted up, and he clenched his jaw to keep himself together, but a tear escaped and ran down his face. Hale sat there watching him, close, never moving away.

I patted his hand, leaning over the table. "I know, baby. Even though you argued, that doesn't mean you two didn't love each other. Quite the opposite is true.

"Danny, did your father ever talk about his life here?"

Daniel shook his head and frowned. "Never. It was a conversation Mom and I knew to avoid. Dad wouldn't get mad or anything, but it was like he would withdraw into himself and disappear. Sometimes he would go into his room and not come out for a few hours. I guess when Grandpa passed away, Mom tried to convince him to come back here, but he wouldn't do it.

"I remember that night too. Mom had gone to bed, and I got up to get a glass of water, and Dad was sitting in the kitchen, alone in the dark. He was rocking back and forth with his face in his hands, crying so hard his shoulders shook."

Daniel

I SAW HIM SITTING *there, still wearing his work pants and T-shirt. I'd just turned ten two days ago, and the rest of my birthday cake was sitting on a plate on the table, getting too hard to eat. Sometimes Mom cried when Dad was gone on a mission, but I'd never seen my dad cry before.*

It broke my heart and scared me a little.

His hair was very short, and he was built like a barn. His arms were muscular, and his face had begun to look leathery from being out in the sun all the time. His eyes were deep-set, and he always seemed to have a frown on his face. Yet, there he sat, two hundred pounds of devil dog, weeping.

"Dad?" I said, putting my hand on his shoulder.

His head spun toward me; his eyes were bloodshot and swollen. The grief he felt was etched all over his face.

I couldn't help myself. Seeing him like that sort of scared me. I wrapped my arms around his neck, and he grabbed me up, just like when I was little, and sat me in his lap. I knew what had happened. Grandpa, a man I'd never met, had passed away.

Mom had received a phone call, and earlier that evening I'd heard them shouting about it in the bedroom.

"You have to go back! What is wrong with you?" Mom had demanded.

"I am not going back into that damned house! Never again am I setting foot in there, with or without the two of you!" he'd said.

I looked up at him. "Grandpa is in heaven now?"

Dad smiled, though his face was still soaked from crying, and he nodded.

I remember holding his face in my hands and looking into a pair of eyes that were like my own. And for once, I saw a man I had so often regarded as a superhero become a mere mortal. I stopped being afraid of his tears. In a strange way, they comforted me. It meant he was like me. So I did what he would when I got upset. I hugged him once more and said, "It's going to be okay. I promise."

Carol

H E LOVED ALL of you. He just wouldn't budge on the issue.
I never understood that. I mean, with them passing the
way they did, as hard as it was, I had to go through the motions
of doing everything that needed to be done funeral-wise.
Everything. I had to go to the morgue, identify the bodies, speak
with the funeral director, buy the caskets, and pick out their
clothes. Looking back, there was something final about the whole
thing. As much as my heart wanted it to be true, when I saw their
caskets lowered into the ground, I knew they no longer existed
in the world. There was a finality to it. I said good-bye. I can't
imagine not being able to say good-bye."

Daniel's face was a picture of misery. I was about to say
something when I heard the back door open, and I looked up.

Anita walked in, carrying a few bags. She cast me a look and
I nodded to her. In silent communication, she understood what
I was about to do. She went to the coffeepot and poured herself a
cup, lit the stove, and started breakfast. Soon she would sit down
and speak her mind as well.

"You need some help, Anita?" Hale asked, always the
gentleman.

Daniel will be just fine, Carol. Hale is a good man.

Anita looked at him, at me, and finally over at Daniel. She
shook her head. "No, baby. You sit right down there and listen
to this too. There are things she'll say that you don't even know
about. Don't mind me. I'll be coming over there shortly."

"Daniel, there is good reason why your father never wanted
to come back to this house," I said. "And now I am going to tell
you why."

Daniel

A NITA SET PLATES of eggs, bacon, and sausage on the table, along with a large jug of orange juice and the coffeepot. She poured herself a cup, sat down next to Carol, and squeezed her hand.

Hale winked at me and then looked back at Carol, waiting for her to begin. I felt a knot gathering in my stomach, but I couldn't help but be curious about what she was going to tell us. Anita seemed to know a great deal already and was there to support Carol in telling her tale.

Carol began. "Your father was a wonderful child and a very sweet man, Daniel. That's the first thing I want you to understand. As a little boy, he always seemed to be the center of attention and would capture the heart of anyone he came into contact with. I was eight when he was born. Mom and Dad had him a little later than they had the rest of their children, but it was a joy to have him. When he was born, there was so much happiness in this house that these walls could barely contain it."

Her eyes stared off into yesterday, and she wrapped her hands around her coffee mug, a smile tugging at her lips. "See, Michael was special. He was born premature, and the doctors didn't think he would make it. Our mother had a very rough pregnancy with him and was bedridden the last few months prior to him being born. Nurses would come and take care of her during her pregnancy, and doctors were called quite often, sometimes in the middle of the night. Papa Jim was very much beside himself and spent hours at her bedside, tending to her. When she had Michael, he was almost two months early. It was a very difficult delivery for both mother and baby. Yet, thank the saints, they both pulled through.

"Your grandparents' friends came from all over to celebrate his birth. As a businessman, Papa Jim was very influential, but also very much loved for the work he did, not only in opening mills and employing thousands of people, but also for the charity he and your grandma Katherine founded and were a part of. They were very kind and generous people, so naturally people gravitated toward them. No one had a bad thing to say about them, you understand. Your grandfather was on many committees and part of so many organizations that at the parties they would throw here at the house, you could barely fit anyone else in here. Oh, but those gatherings were something else, lavish and festive, and your grandparents spared no expense. I wish you could have known them."

She sighed, and her eyes grew dark. She leaned forward a little more as if she was afraid of the house hearing what she was about to say. "Your father had a brother. His name was Christopher, and he was older than I. When Michael was born, he had just turned eleven, and he was Michael's polar opposite. Christopher was mean, withdrawn, and very sneaky. It was more than that, really. Your uncle Christopher was evil, and he liked to hurt people, especially your father."

Carol looked sad, and she took a drink of her coffee to moisten her throat before speaking again.

"When it was just Christopher and I, I was his target for the longest time. He would fight with me and be downright mean. Sometimes he would hide things from me, like toys or a book I was reading, or he would pull my hair when no one was watching. As he got older, he would do other things to torment and scare me. He would jump out of closets and make me scream, or he would hide under furniture, and as I walked by, he would grab my ankles and make me fall. Anita caught him doing it once and spanked him good for it."

Carol looked at Anita, who nodded.

Hale shot me a glance.

Carol spoke again. "Christopher got even with her. Anita and Thomas have lived on the property for years. Anita had a cat she loved very much. Sable was her name, wasn't it?" Anita nodded. "Yes, Sable. Anyway, one night when Anita returned home, she found Sable dead at the front stoop of the house. Her whole body had been broken; she'd been beaten to death. Of course Anita couldn't have proved it—and I didn't learn about this until much later—but she knew who'd done it. Thomas, from that point on, never left her alone in a room with Christopher, and nothing was mentioned to your grandparents.

"Christopher and I received private tutoring, and the tutors that I had would stay here and work with me without a problem. The ones Christopher had would never stay because he ran them off. He would do mean things to them as well, and they couldn't handle him. The only one your uncle was afraid of was Papa Jim. I think more than anyone, Papa Jim was aware of what Christopher was and what he was capable of."

Carol's face became stony, and her eyes grew cold.

"Your grandmother was also wary of Christopher and, like Thomas, would never leave the baby around him for too long. Once she caught Christopher pinching Michael on the legs and making him cry. Papa Jim spanked him really bad for that one, but it didn't do much good. While we were growing up, and as Michael got bigger, Christopher would do very mean things to him. He was always trying to hurt your father. Papa Jim would intercede and stop it, as would your grandmother, but Christopher found ways around them. The odd thing was, as was your father's nature, he loved Christopher and always tried to please him. This made him an easier target for Christopher's plans to manipulate or hurt him."

Carol shook her head and started to cry. I was caught up in the story. She wiped her eyes, and Anita spoke up.

"Daniel, this is very hard on Carol. These things haven't been spoken of in years, but she is telling you the truth. Sometimes Christopher would hurt your father badly, and not all of it was physical. The children of this house had free rein, and that included playing in the attic. They were forbidden to go into the wine cellar down in the basement, but the rest of the house was open to them.

"One night your grandmother couldn't find Michael. She asked Christopher, and he said he didn't know. Well, after a while your mother grew frantic. The whole house was turned upside down to find your brother, and no one could locate him. Christopher refused to say anything."

Anita wiped her eyes. "Downstairs, there is the wine cellar and a root cellar that no one had gone into for years. That's where Thomas and I eventually found him. Michael was alive but nearly comatose. It was dark in there, and he was too small to reach the light. He had beaten on the door, and his little hands were bloody from his attempts to get out. He was barely conscious, and his voice was completely gone, and he had soiled himself. Thomas carried him up from the basement, and your parents, who were searching other parts of the house, came running when I screamed for them. Jim took him from Thomas and tried to get him to speak…"

Carol

*H*IS BODY WAS *limp, but his eyes were huge. His face was white as a sheet. The smell of feces and urine rolled off him so strongly that I had to cover my nose. Mother was screaming and crying, saying, "He's dead! Oh, he's gone." She kept calling his name over and over.*

"Thomas, sit her down! Katherine, he's okay, he's alive. Michael! Michael! Who put you down there? You know you're not supposed to be in there!" Daddy said as he knelt on the floor with Michael and tried to get him to open his eyes and speak.

Michael just clung to him and refused to be put down. He couldn't speak anymore, but he raised his hand and pointed toward the hallway that led out of the kitchen to the front of the house. There, standing with his arms folded, looking angry and defiant, was Christopher.

"You little monster! You leave your hands off my baby!" Katherine grabbed Michael up and swooped past all of them, heading upstairs.

Thomas grabbed Anita, who kept crossing herself, and led her out the back door of the house.

Daddy didn't even see me standing off to the side, but I watched. His breathing was ragged and his face had gone as white as the dress shirt he was wearing. In two short strides, he grabbed Christopher up by his collar, spun, and pinned him to the wall. Christopher's face changed from shock to fear and finally back to smug arrogance.

Daddy clenched his fist and unclenched it and spoke between gritted teeth. "If you hurt my child again—my wife or your sister again—I'll kill you. Do you understand me, you little shit? I don't know who you are, but you're no son of mine. Don't get comfortable. I'm going to find a place for you to go, away from here, and you'll never come back."

He let him drop and Christopher fell to the floor with a thud, but he stared at Daddy as if he were some kind of creature he'd found under a rock. Daddy must have noticed that too, and before I knew what was happening, Christopher went flying across the room and hit the back door. Daddy had backhanded him hard— Christopher had hit the door with a crash. He got up and faced Daddy, blood running down his nose, and there was murder in his eyes.

I grabbed Daddy's hand. "Come on, Dad, let's go check on Michael."

Daddy looked down at me and then at Christopher once more, and we headed out of the kitchen.

Daniel

C AROL HAD GROWN pale. Anita fetched her another cup of coffee.

"Dad didn't want anyone left alone with Christopher, except for Thomas or himself. He had given explicit orders to Thomas that he was to use whatever means necessary to restrain his eldest son should he get out of hand. Thomas, who hated the boy anyway for terrifying his wife, simply agreed."

My mind was reeling. I was terrified to hear more, but I couldn't help myself. I glanced over at Hale, who looked shocked and confused. Our eyes locked, and I could tell that some of this information was new to him as well. Outside, the rain had moved back into the area and cast the breakfast table into gloom. Bushes brushed and scratched against the window, and thunder rolled in the distance. Our plates of food had gone cold, most of them left untouched, and Anita quickly cleared them away. She returned to the table with more coffee, offering it around.

Carol continued. "Dad stopped the tutors from coming over, and Mom and Dad enrolled me in the public school in town. Christopher was only allowed to come out of his room for food—which he ate alone, save for either Dad or Thomas—and bathroom breaks, escorted by either one of them. Mom and Dad had someone come in, a psychiatrist, to talk to Christopher, and he told Dad that he was very mentally disturbed and possibly psychotic, but because of Christopher's age, he couldn't make that diagnosis. When asked what they should do, the psychiatrist suggested he be institutionalized. Mother asked if he would ever get better, and the doctor said no. I remember this because what the doctor had to say was for everyone's ears. Christopher was dangerous and could possibly hurt any one of us. We had to stay away from him."

She sighed deeply. Her age was showing now. Her beauty seemed to have diminished with the story, and fatigue set in.

"It was two weeks later when Christopher was killed. Dad had gone into his room the night after the doctor had left and explained to Christopher that he was going to be taken to a hospital for treatment. Christopher screamed in rage and tried to hurt Dad, but he was easily able to restrain him. I remember how haggard and tired Dad looked through those days. He loved Christopher, and for a long time tried to ignore his bad behavior and explain it by him being a kid. Now that the truth had come out, it hurt Dad very much to have to place him in a hospital he might never come out of.

"As I was saying, two weeks passed by, and Christopher had grown quiet. I only saw him as he was heading to eat and go to the bathroom. I never felt safe with him out into the house itself, but he had to eat and, well…"

She shrugged. "One afternoon the worst happened. Thomas had retrieved me from school and was parking the car. He had dropped me off in front of the door because, like it often does here in Oregon, it was pouring down rain. I heard a scream and came running in the door, and I saw Daddy upstairs hurling Christopher over the banister. He hit the floor of the foyer and his neck snapped. He was dead."

I shuddered at that image and felt sick to my stomach. "Oh— oh my God." I put my hand over my mouth.

Carol waited a second, like she was catching her breath, and then went on. "Dad had gone to get Christopher from his room to eat lunch. Well, Christopher had taken his bedframe apart and pulled off one of the supports that held it. When Dad opened the door, Christopher swung and hit him in the head hard enough to nearly knock him out. Michael was playing with his trucks on the second floor while Mom was busy in Dad's office getting all of Christopher's shot records, birth certificate, and other papers together for him to go to the hospital. Well, Christopher came charging down the other wing of the house—he had spotted Michael playing there.

"Michael looked up and saw Christopher coming toward him and cried out for Mom. Well, naturally she came running and found Christopher with that bedpost raised over his head. He was going to kill Michael. Mom couldn't get to her sons fast enough, and she screamed. Suddenly, Christopher rose up in the air. Dad had lifted him up, and he went sailing over the banister and onto the marble floor below. At least, that is how Mom told the story."

Carol stopped. She looked exhausted.

Anita spoke up. "I saw it happen. That bad boy was going to hurt Michael. Your daddy did the only thing he could." She wrapped her arms around Carol, and the older woman groaned in horror and wept.

I looked over at Hale, whose face had gone two shades of gray. He had crossed his arms across his chest, and he wore the expression I had seen the night he pulled me over. He looked like a cop who'd just heard a confession.

Hale turned to look at me, and I shook my head. This wasn't over; I tried to tell him with my eyes. His eyes softened as he understood. He unfolded his hands and placed them back in his lap.

I reached for one under the table and held it. I had a gut feeling the story wasn't over. "The story doesn't end there, does it?" I asked. My mind went back to the noises, the banging, the nightmares, the wolves, the feelings of being watched. I was reeling.

"No!" Carol sobbed.

Anita said, "The police came, and when everything was explained, they left after taking our statements. No charges were filed. Mercifully, the papers and the police accepted the explanation that it was a freak accident, and the family was left in peace. For a while, anyway. Little Michael had nightmares for a long time afterward, but outside of that, he was doing just fine. Jim and Katherine decided that Christopher's name was never to be mentioned again. They didn't even have a funeral for him. All of his pictures were taken down and boxed up, and his room has never been opened since that day. He was buried on the property with nothing more than a stone cross for a headstone. They didn't even put his information on it."

"He was forgotten," I said.

Anita nodded.

Carol had quit crying and sat staring out of the window behind me. The weather hadn't let up, and rain sloshed against the window. It was fitting for the story being told and for the atmosphere of the kitchen.

The back door opened and Thomas walked in wearing his Sunday best. Anita stood and went to her husband, and they embraced. When she whispered something in his ear, he looked over at me. His face set, and he looked pretty grim. He moved to Carol. Anita took her seat on Carol's right, and Thomas sat on her left. This was her family, her support, her comfort, her protection. My heart warmed knowing that, and I stored it away in my memory.

Carol, rejuvenated by the sight of Thomas, spoke. "Ten years passed without incident. Michael was a happy child once again, and the family was whole. All aspects of Christopher were wiped away, and no one even spoke his name. I had graduated high school in town, and Michael was now in the tenth grade. He was so handsome, and the girls fawned all over him. He was popular and had the gift of gab. His grades weren't the best, but it wasn't because he was stupid. He was bored. Restless and more artistic than he let on, fun loving and very compassionate, he was the life of the party.

"Then Mother fell ill. She had abdominal cancer, and it spread quickly. Dad had hospice nurses come in to take care of her until she passed. Michael was heartbroken. At the very end, Mom began to lose touch with reality. She would scream that Christopher was in the room with her or that he was following Michael around. We thought that speech was a result of the morphine until things began to happen. Michael with bruises on his arms and legs... like someone had been pinching him in his sleep."

A chill cascaded down my back, and the hairs on my arms stood on end. The room seemed charged with energy now, electrical and pulsing around us. But still Carol continued.

"Then one night Michael came tearing out of his room because someone was in there with him. He felt like he was being watched, and when he went into the bathroom, he saw a man looking at him from inside his mirror. That wasn't the only incident either. At night you could hear laughter or talking, and no one would be there. You felt like you were being watched as you took a shower or stood in a room alone. It wasn't all the time, and it seemed to be more pronounced during certain times and would cease altogether at others.

"Michael went through high school and spent most of his time outside the house. When he had to be home, he would have his best friend, Morris, over to stay with him. Morris Collins still lives down in town with his wife, Jenna, and he would swear on a stack of Bibles that what I am telling you is true.

"When Michael was home, he would withdraw, but the moment the front door shut behind him and he stepped out into the grounds, he was fine. Daddy was aging faster by the day now that his wife was gone, and I quit school at the local university to take care of him and Michael. One night, Michael came to me in the library, and while we sat there talking, me on a chaise lounge and him in a chair opposite me, I finally saw it.

"Behind him, this figure...it was disgusting to look at: tall, white-haired, and gaunt. I had never been so scared in my life, but I knew instantly who it was. Michael saw the look on my face, and I thought he was going to faint."

The fire popped in the fireplace, and a log slid in the grate, sending sparks up the chimney. I was lying there reading my favorite book, Pride and Prejudice, *when I heard a knock at the door. I looked up. Michael poked his head in and smiled at me. I loved my brother more than anything in life and was always happy to see him smile.*

"Hey, sis, can I come in?"

153

"*Of course, Michael, come on in. I was just rereading this book. I swear Mom and Dad designed this house after Pemberley.*" I laughed.

He took the book as I held it outstretched, saw Jane Austen's name, and laughed, pulling up a chair. His long hair fell in his eyes, and he brushed it out of his face as he sat. "*Yeah, I think they did. Mom loved this book too.*" He thumbed the well-worn binding. "*There is something I want to tell you,*" he said, handing the book back to me.

"*What is it?*"

"*I am joining the Marines. Dad is furious about it, but I think it would be a good choice for me.*"

I set the blanket on my knees aside. "*That's a pretty big deal, Michael. Are you sure?*"

He nodded. "*Yeah. I'm not happy here. Too much weird stuff goes on. I feel like I'm haunted.*"

"*Have you thought about university? The family business?*"

He sat back and narrowed his eyes. "*Now you're sounding like Dad.*"

I held up my hands. "*I know. I'm sorry. I'm worried is all.*"

"*You are the worrier in the family.*"

I smiled. "*Yeah, that's me.*"

"*What about you? Are you going to return to college?*"

I shook my head. "*Dad needs me.*"

"*Carol, you have your own life to lead. It's the seventies. You don't have to be bound to this cold and dismal place. Dad's a grown man.*"

I took Michael's hand. "*Christopher's memory hasn't left you. We tried to abandon him for your sake. We tried to ignore the goings-on here, Michael. For your sake and for our sanity. But you're in misery. I see that. Just do me a favor.*"

"*What's that?*"

"*Tear off your rearview mirror and don't look back.*"

"*Carol?*"

"*Michael, listen to me. I—*"

The warmth in the room suddenly disappeared and the light in the fireplace I'd been reading by began to wane. I felt eyes on me as the hairs on the back of my neck began to stand.

Michael, seeing my distress, began to stand as well. "Where's Dad?"

"He's not here. He's in Portland," I whispered.

"Carol, you're white as a sheet."

"You need to get out of here."

The flames went out with a huff as cinders flew up the chimney, leaving us in total darkness. The darkness seemed to seethe as it deepened, as if the room itself was breathing. I grabbed for Michael's hand. We stood there on trembling knees, unable to move.

"Miiiiiiiichaellll."

The voice came from everywhere and nowhere all at once. A chill ran through my body that nearly stilled my heart.

"Michael, you have to get out of here," I said urgently, tugging his arm.

He was staring past me, over my head, into the darkness that had overtaken the rest of the room. His face was a mask of terror, of absolute horror. My heart hammered so hard in my chest I felt like it would burst. My throat constricted, and my mouth was so dry that it felt like cotton had been stuffed in there. Slowly I turned my head toward the darkness. I trembled as I turned, terrified of what I was going to see.

It emerged from the shadows, Its long white face distended and horrible. Standing unnaturally tall and thin, It grinned at me. Its fingers were long, disgusting things, like white snakes held stiff on bony hands. Enshrouded in total darkness, Its twisted body hung suspended. I was either about to scream, or to faint dead away.

It grew fast and seemed to encompass the entire wall. Turning Its gaze between Michael and myself, Its grin turned down into a snarl as It approached. And instead of fleeing in fear, a bubbling rage took hold in my gut. Despite my fear, despite its horrible visage, I didn't step back. I stepped forward.

Outside, the wolves howled.

I spoke. "Christopher—"

With the mention of Its name, It turned Its attention back to me and shrieked in delight, so loud the floor shook. But I wasn't finished. "—you coward. You disgustingly wretched being. Is this your fate? To linger here among the shadows? You won't even give him peace in death?"

"Carol, what are you doing?"

I ignored Michael and stepped forward again. "You're powerless. You are nothing. We forgot you. We buried you. No headstone, no service. This house has been wiped clean of you and still you linger. GET OUT!"

It shrieked again, this time in rage.

Michael grabbed me and put me behind him. It pointed a long finger at him—and suddenly disappeared. All at once warmth rushed through the room and replaced the freezing cold. The fire reignited, and we were left staring at the portrait of a wolf that father had commissioned years ago. Its white face stared out at us as the wolves outside howled their lonely song.

Hale

C AROL HAD BEEN speaking for so long, but she was surely reaching the end of the story.

"The next day, your father joined the military, and just like that, he was gone. I only saw him one more time afterward, and that was when you were very, very small. He walked out on the life that he'd lived here and shut the door.

"That is why he never came back, Daniel."

I looked across the table at the woman I'd known for years and at the two people flanking her. They were as serious about this apparition as they were about what caused it.

Carol's description of the ghost scared me because of the nightmares Daniel had. My heart was pounding in my head, my hands had turned clammy, and I could feel sweat pooling under my armpits.

I believe her.

My God, I believed her...

Daniel

I WAS STUNNED INTO silence. The rain sloshed on the kitchen windows, and the mood around the table was somber. I looked at Hale, who had his arms folded over his chest and his face pointed down.

This is a nightmare, I thought.

My father was tortured as a child by a psychotic sociopath, and even when his brother died, the torture continued from beyond the grave. My thoughts went back to the night at the fair with Hale and the seer who'd talked about our souls. If Christopher was still here, then how far would he go to harm us? The thought made me shudder a bit, and I absently rubbed my arms. The family had tried to cover up all existence of Christopher. Yet how far had they gone to do that? My mind wandered back to the other day and what the contractors had discovered in the upstairs hallway.

"There is one more thing, Daniel…" Carol's face was taut; her fatigue showed in her eyes.

"Carol," Anita started, but she was cut off as my aunt raised her hand.

"He needs to know, Anita. Daniel, I'm sick," she said.

I shook my head. "You're sick? You're…*oh*." I sat back in my chair, my breath escaping me. *She's terminally ill.* "Cancer?"

She nodded. It all made sense now: the urgency to get me up here, the drawing up of the wills I'd signed right away, the familiarization with all the companies and assets. My aunt was dying and didn't want to risk the family fortune and legacy.

"When were you going to tell me this?" I could feel the anger rising in my body, but I kept my voice calm.

"I had to know for sure, Danny. That's why I went to Portland. I had a doctor's appointment with my oncologist," she explained, but I was beyond listening.

I stood up. "Look, this is too much. Jesus." I glanced around the table at the faces staring back at me. I was furious, and I needed to step out. My face was burning; my teeth were set on edge.

My dad had been chased out of this house by a psychotic brother, and they'd tried to hide the fact that Christopher existed. "You lied to me. I believed you. When my parents died, a benevolent aunt swoops out of nowhere with riches she wants to extend to me, only I find out she's dying and has to pass it on. I'm trapped here now that she is dying, in a house that's haunted by memories and a—what? A ghost? Is that what you're telling me? That what I've been experiencing in here is a ghost? A ghost of a kid your father murdered because he tortured my dad and scared him so bad it affected him the rest of his life? I...I...I... I treated him like shit before he died because of the way he hovered over me.

"I thought there was something wrong with him, and I couldn't figure out why he was so protective of me and Mom. And all along, I treated him like shit."

Thomas stood up. "Young man, I think—"

"Can it, old man! Let me tell you one thing, Carol. I have a story too."

"You said you were going with us." Dad's voice was angry.

I held the phone to my head as I packed his old duffel bag. "You said I was going with you, Dad. I didn't say anything."

I looked around the dorm room, grabbed a pair of blue jeans that were lying on the floor, and stuffed them in the bag.

"We've made this trip every year since you were a kid."

"And you'll make it again just fine without me."

"Well, what are you going to do?"

"I'm going to Austin with some friends. We're going to float the Guadalupe. It's summer. I have finals, and I need a break. I've earned it. And a road trip to deliver the boat you made, to sit and listen to you and your friends reminisce about the glory days of the Marine Corps, doesn't sound like much of one."

"And what friends are these?"

I stopped packing and rolled my eyes. "The ones I've made at school. James, Beth, Rodney, Shonda, and Mike. There's a bunch of us going."

"You didn't ask me whether or not you can go."

"I don't live under your roof anymore, Dad. I don't need your permission."

"Oh, is that right? You're fine with me footing the bill for school, but you don't need me to tell you what to do."

I became furious. "Speaking of which, that scholarship came through. I no longer need your money. So no, I don't need you to pay for that either. So no, I don't need you to tell me what to do."

"Don't you take that truck—"

"It's in my name."

"The insurance isn't."

I bent over and picked up my wallet, which had fallen out when I picked up the jeans. I opened it up and withdrew my Allstate card. "That's funny. The insurance card here says it is. That's another bill you don't have to worry about."

"So that's it."

I nodded. "Yeah, that's it."

"So our plan to use the Silverado to haul it with is also gone. It's the only truck big enough."

I sighed. "The yacht is moored at Sabine Pass. Sail it to Florida. You've done that before. And you won't have I-10 traffic to deal with."

"Okay. Fine. That's it. But I gotta tell ya what, Daniel. Don't ever call here asking for goddamn help again. Go have fun with your friends. I can't believe I've raised such an inconsiderate asshole."

"Inconsiderate? Wow, Pot, my name's Kettle. And as far as asshole goes, well, fuck you. That's as far as that goes. I'm not the one who insists on living people's lives for them. There's a reason why I moved out. It was to get away from you. But you'd know all about that, wouldn't you?" I yelled into the phone.

And then I killed the line.

"That was the last thing I said to him before he left, the last time I talked to him. If I had just gone with them like he'd planned, they'd still be here. They'd still be alive. But I was an inconsiderate asshole. At least I come by it honestly enough." I turned to go.

Carol reached out and tried to stop me. She looked distraught, but I didn't care. "Danny, please…"

"Please what, Carol? You can't bury the past. Don't you understand? You spent your lives ignoring what was happening around you, and now you want to pass this on to me? This is insanity!" I shook my head, disgusted.

I leaned across the table at the three of them sitting there. My teeth were chattering with rage. "If I'd known a tenth of any of this, I wouldn't have been so goddamn mean to him."

Hale tried to calm me down. "Danny—"

"No! Goddammit! Stop calling me Danny! My name is *Daniel*. You knew about Christopher, and you chose not to tell me. You're just as bad as she is. I don't want anything to do with any of it. This house. Anything in it. Or any of you."

Hale recoiled as if slapped.

I turned from the kitchen and stalked down the hallway, grabbed a jacket from the hook on the wall near the door, and headed outside. The day was steel-gray and cooler. I wrapped the jacket around me and walked out into the grounds. Rain was falling lightly, and it soaked my hair and face as I headed down the property. Walking fast, nearly running, I found a trail into the woods and ducked in there. Footstep after footstep, brushing tree limbs out of my way, walking farther and farther into the woods. I stepped over a fallen log, swatting away no-see-ums, and the anger slowly seeped out of me.

All that was left was exhaustion.

I looked around at where I'd gotten and was actually quite taken with it. The woods were green, and the trees varied from pine to elm to others I didn't recognize. Moss grew up their sides, and the branches hung low, dripping water to the ground below. The earth was soft under my feet, and the air smelled of pine.

I wrapped my jacket tighter around me and followed the path that took me down a steep grade and into a small valley. At the bottom, a creek ran the length of the valley, spilling out into a pond, I figured. There, a large chunk of rock jutted up from the ground, and I decided to take a rest. The woods were filled with all the sounds you could imagine, and I sat there for a while, listening.

I was wrong to leave like that, I thought, regret blooming in my chest. *I shouldn't have said what I did.*

"Aw, fuck it." I leaned over, plucked a few pebbles off the ground, and started skipping them across the water.

"No, do it like this, buddy," Dad said.

We stood on the shore of Lake Michigan. The sun was setting, and fireflies danced in the air. It was summertime. Dad had rented a cabin near Mackinaw City. I threw the rocks over my head, and they hit the water with a plop *and sank out of sight.*

Dad stood in his shorts and T-shirt, laughing at me, and I grinned up at him. He leaned to the side a little, clasping the pebble between his thumb and forefinger, turned his wrist to the right, and flicked the stone. One, two, three, four, and on the fifth skip it sank beneath the darkening waters.

I was twelve years old, but Dad was still my hero. Seagulls danced in the air, and sanderlings ran across the sand looking for minnows; they dodged the water coming in and out. We had spent the past few days on a sailboat Dad had built for a customer, a close friend of his, and Mom and I had been happy to tag along for the sail.

Dad leaned down and maneuvered me so he could assist in my throw. He placed another smooth rock in my hand. I pinched it in my fingers as he'd shown me, and we swung. One, two, and plop! *Mom and Dad cheered. Not as far as Dad could do it, but it was a start.*

"I miss you guys," I said as I flung another pebble into the water.

One, two, three, four, and it sank on the fifth skip. I sighed heavily and got to my feet.

I had to go back into that house and eat crow. I didn't want to. I wanted to stay right here on the banks of the creek and listen to the honesty of the forest around me. No secrets. No lies. No hidden lives.

That was when I heard the growling.

I spun around where I stood. Three wolves were standing at the top of the incline that led to the creek. I froze in place. All three of them were staring at me, but only one moved. His massive body came down the side of that incline with expert ease while the other two just sat there staring at me. My heart was in my throat.

How stupid of me, I thought.

I'd been so angry I hadn't paid attention to the fact that I'd just walked into woods that were infested with wolves. And, of course, I wasn't carrying anything to protect myself.

I didn't dare make any sudden movements or yell out. Sweat trickled down the back of my head, onto my neck, and down my spine. I stank of fear, and the animal knew it.

He padded closer to me, sniffing the air around me, and all I could do was tremble. I sat back down on the rock as my knees, which had almost been knocking together, gave out. The wolf didn't stop walking forward. Instead it came nose to nose with me.

I could smell his fur and feel the heat coming off his body. His yellow eyes peered into mine, staring deep within me.

Suddenly he jumped, tumbling me backward off the rock. I hit my head on the ground, and the world around me exploded in stars and finally turned black.

***

Whispers. My head was full of them. I could hear them all around me. It sounded like a million bees buzzing in my head.

Daniel. Daniel. Daniel, they said.

I sat up, groggy, nauseated, and soaking wet. The world was dark around me, the ground underneath me soggy, and my fingers sank into wet mud, leaves, and debris.

Daniel. Daniel. Daniel.

My head felt heavy, and I reached back and felt a lump on the back of it that was tender to my touch. When I pulled my hand away, it was covered in blood. I tried to stand, but my legs were so shaky I stumbled and went to my knees. Wave after wave of nausea came and went, and I gasped for breath. I gagged and groaned from my stomach clenching so hard.

Daniel. Get up. Daniel, get up.

The whispers raged on the breeze.

I stumbled to my feet, swayed, and focused on a figure standing in front of me.

I saw the boots first, tied above the ankle, and then my gaze moved up to a pair of camouflage trousers, a T-shirt, a pair of dog tags, and the smiling face I could never forget.

"Dad," I mumbled.

A light shone from him and seemed to illuminate the forest where he stood. This was the younger version of my father, the man I'd known as a child. Two other figures flanked him, and I recognized them from the oil painting hanging over the staircase of Timber Manor. My grandfather and grandmother stood with my father, and each shone with that same light. The family resemblance was so strong. I felt tears well up in my eyes, and I reached out a hand and stumbled forward.

I couldn't manage to get close enough to touch him, and his eyes grew sad, but his smile stayed the same. I lowered my hand and stared in wonder. "Dad," I cried out again.

"Hello, son."

"What are you doing here?" I asked. "You're dead."

Daniel. Daniel. Daniel. Daniel. The whispers kept coming from all around me. I stared straight ahead, not daring to take my eyes off him.

"Listen to me, son. You have to leave that house. It isn't safe there. He's coming for you. He wants to hurt you." My father's face turned serious, the same look he gave me when he meant business.

I whispered, "Christopher."

"I knew he'd figure it out," my grandmother said, smiling triumphantly.

"Of course he did. He's a Donnelly," replied my grandfather.

"He is imprisoned in the walls of that house, Daniel. His soul is locked in there. Look." My father pointed behind me.

I turned my head, and instead of seeing trees, I saw a segment of the house. Walls were formed out of thin air on both sides, and in the center, a door.

Yet there was something wrong with it. Thick black tendrils reached through cracks in the door, slid down the walls, pulsing like arteries infused with the blood from a dead heart. An infection, poisonous and spreading. And with every pulse, it split the cracks in the door, a millimeter at a time.

"He grows more powerful by the day, Daniel. It isn't safe there. You must leave."

I turned my head back and faced my dad. His eyes were filled with worry, as were my grandparents'.

Daniel. Daniel. Daniel.

"I don't understand. Dad, why are you three here? Where's Mom?"

"Your mother moved on. She can't be here." My dad looked sad, and my grandfather put a hand on his shoulder.

"Moved on... Dad? Dad!" The figures began to fade slowly.

"Get out, son, leave this place."

"Don't go, Dad! Please...don't gooooo," I sobbed, reaching forward.

Daniel. Daniel. Daniel.

***

My eyes snapped open to a darkened forest and pouring-down rain. I was shivering so hard my teeth were chattering. In front of me was one lone wolf, sitting on his haunches, staring at me. My throat hurt and so did the back of my head.

A fever had begun inside me. I felt like I was on fire, and my whole body ached.

The wolf stood and started walking up the incline. He turned his massive head and stared at me for a second, then tilted his head back in a solemn howl.

He wants me to follow him, I thought.

I took a step forward, and the beast climbed a bit higher. In the distance I heard voices calling my name; it sounded like Hale and Thomas. I walked over to the incline and started up the path, and the wolf scampered a few feet in front of me, turned, and waited to make sure I was following. My legs felt like rubber and the nausea returned with a vengeance. I had to stop at one point as bile rose from my stomach and I spilled what little I had eaten that day on the ground.

Yet the wolf never left my sight. Patiently he waited until I could walk a little farther. Down the path we went until I could see flashlights, and I walked toward them.

"*Daniel!*" Hale yelled.

Yellow beams pierced the woods. I followed the sound of his voice.

The wolf had gone.

Hale

D ANIEL!" I YELLED, my voice cracking as panic began to set in.

Hours had passed since he'd stormed out of the kitchen in a fury. Carol had been beside herself in grief. Anita had done her best to calm her, but to no avail.

"He hates me. Oh my God, I've chased him away!" she sobbed into the arms of the older woman.

Thomas stood silent, gray-faced, and patted her shoulder.

"He doesn't hate you, Carol," Anita said, stroking Carol's hair as she cradled her. "He just has to go blow off some steam. This is a lot for a young person to have to digest all in the matter of a few weeks. He'll come back. You'll see."

I was angry myself. Angry *at* myself for not telling Daniel everything I knew, angry at Carol for keeping this secret from me. And I was angry at Daniel for what he'd said to me.

I waited for him to come back. I waited with the words I was going to say to him when he did. And I waited to give him a piece of my mind and to tell him that yes, he was indeed an inconsiderate asshole.

Except he didn't come back. We all figured he'd taken the truck for a drive, but when I stepped out to run to my vehicle, I saw the truck standing where we had parked it the night before, next to mine. I ran out and placed my hand on the hood of the truck—it was cold to the touch. He hadn't taken it anywhere.

So I checked his room, and when I couldn't find him, we began to search the house and the grounds in a panic.

Nothing.

I ran to the stables, thinking that perhaps he'd ducked in there and fallen asleep in the loft, as we had done one summer day. I startled the horses when I flung the door open with a bang, and was disappointed by what I found.

Then I went back to the house, calling out for everyone to come and meet me in the foyer. So we all donned rain gear and grabbed flashlights and headed out into the grounds to see if we could track him down.

I kept thinking of him falling prey to a pack of wolves. Images of a bloody and broken Daniel filled my thoughts, and I tried everything I could to keep those thoughts away.

The sun had begun to set, and with no trace of Daniel, I called the office and requested a squad car and dogs. Now three of my officers were here, along with a K9 unit that had picked up his scent. We followed, calling Daniel's name the whole time.

My heart thudded hard against my chest, and adrenaline was pumping through my body. Desperation was trying to claw its way out of my guts, and I would have leveled every tree until I found him.

Yet it was he who found us.

As we approached the tree line to the right of the house, Danny came stumbling out, barely able to walk. He was soaking wet, pale as a sheet, and mumbling incoherently.

We all rushed over to him, and I caught him before he fell. I lowered him gently, holding his head in my hands, and was disturbed to find that when I pulled my hand away, it was bright red with Daniel's blood.

Danny's voice was hoarse, his eyes rolling wildly. "Dad. Come back. Come back," he pleaded.

He was burning up.

"Oh my God, Anita! Fetch the doctor!" Carol cried, falling to her knees at his side.

"No, we have to call an ambulance. He has a concussion," I yelled over my shoulder.

Officer Lewis, one of my deputies, keyed his mic and called for assistance. I ripped open my jacket and wrapped it around Danny—the inside was warm and dry—and picked him up in my arms. I was scared; his whole body seemed to burn me where our flesh touched.

We raced back to the house to wait for the ambulance, which, on this side of an emergency, felt like it took forever. Meanwhile, Daniel kept saying his father's name over and over again and telling us to "Stay away from the door!"

"He's delirious." I laid him on the kitchen table. "Bring me some blankets!" I barked at anyone who would listen, and it was Carol who returned with a patch quilt. I wrapped him up in it. My heart was breaking, and I felt helpless as I watched my lover slowly growing still. "Danny, don't leave me, baby. Stay with me. C'mon, stay with me."

My voice, hoarse from crying out his name, sounded foreign to my own ears. I rubbed his cold hands with mine, trying to warm them up. It was odd; as the fever racked his body, his hands were like ice.

"Goddammit! Where are they?" I yelled at Officer Lewis, who keyed his mic again.

"They're pulling in now!" Thomas yelled from the foyer. He held the door open, watching for the yellow-and-white ambulance to arrive.

Instead of waiting for them to come into the house, I picked Daniel up in my arms again and carried him outside to greet the two paramedics, who were pulling a stretcher out of the back of the vehicle.

Daniel had fallen quiet as we emerged into darkness broken only by the flash of red lights from the ambulance.

"I've got a concussion victim here—there's a large gash at the back of his head. He's also been exposed to the elements for quite a while, and he's running a fever," I rattled off as I laid him out on the stretcher.

The paramedic opened Daniel's eyes and checked them with a penlight, confirming the concussion.

"How long has he been out?" the paramedic, Bradley, asked.

Bradley was tall and lanky, with blond hair, a young guy, but very good at his job. He'd been a paramedic for many years already, starting off volunteering and making his way up. I had worked several accidents and crime scenes with him, and I thanked God it was Bradley who had shown up.

"He's been talking incoherently for a few minutes. We just found him. He's been quiet for less than a minute."

They strapped him into the stretcher. Bradley and his female partner, Bridget, lifted him up and rolled him inside. I went to climb in back, but Bradley stopped me.

"Hale, only immediate family members can ride back here," he said.

"I'm the goddamn sheriff, and I am his boyfr—fuck!" I yelled in anger and frustration, stepping back down. The health information privacy rules had suddenly taken over. I turned to Carol. "Get in there. I'll follow you in my truck." I asked Bradley, "Where are you taking him?"

"Saint Elizabeth in Emerson. They can handle this," he said. "I'm calling ahead now."

Carol stepped into the vehicle and sat down as Bradley got to work. The last thing I saw before they closed the door was him starting an IV in Danny's arm.

Thomas and Anita followed me to my truck, and as I pulled open my door, I felt Thomas's hand on my shoulder.

"Give me the keys, son. You're in no shape to drive."

I was going to protest, but by the look on his face, he meant business. So I walked around to the other side of the truck and opened the passenger door for Anita. She climbed in and sat in the middle, and I jumped in next to her. We headed off on the twenty-minute trip to Saint Elizabeth Memorial Hospital in Emerson.

It would be the longest twenty minutes of my life.

Daniel

I SURFACED SLOWLY, A level at a time, and the first thing I noticed was that I was thirsty. As I ascended into consciousness, I became aware of other things: the smell of antiseptic, a chill in the air, a pillow beneath me, and a bandage wrapped around my head.

I swallowed. My throat was so dry I could almost hear it click, and my mouth tasted like cotton. I hurt all over—not anything excruciating, but dull and throbbing, and I had to fight to remain awake. Sleep wanted to drag me downward into blissful oblivion.

A constant *beep, beep, beep* noise pierced the fog of my semi-awakened state. My eyes opened to a darkened room. I was in a hospital bed, sitting up slightly. I looked down at my wrist. An IV line wrapped around it, and as I turned my hand, I saw the needle buried in a vein. On my index finger, a little clamp with a red light led to the machine that kept beeping at me.

My head felt heavy, and my eyes wanted to close. Sleep kept trying to entice me back into the abyss, but I fought against it.

I licked my lips; they were as dry as the inside of my mouth. I turned my head to the right and saw Hale, seated in a chair next to my bed, sleeping with his hand on my leg and his head on the bed. His breathing was slow and steady. I looked to my left, out the window at the darkness beyond the glass; I was not on the ground floor. I turned my attention back to Hale and raised my hand, placed it on his head, and stroked his hair. He mumbled something, and I tried to call out his name, but all I could manage was an inaudible whisper. I kept rubbing his short-cropped hair. My heart filled up with love for him, and he jerked upward, staring at me.

"You're awake," he said simply. He stood up from the bed and walked to the door. "He's awake!" he yelled.

In seconds, Carol, Thomas, Anita, and a nurse named Jalinda—according to her name tag—came into the room. Carol immediately headed for my bedside, and the nurse walked to the other side. Carol leaned down, kissed my brow, and touched my face.

"You scared us for a second, you sweet boy," she whispered.

Her eyes misted over, and I reached up, took her hand, and gave it a gentle squeeze. I think she had forgiven me for my outburst at her kitchen table the other...er, whenever that happened, that had led me to be here.

The nurse smiled. "Yes, you were actively fighting our antibiotics for a while there, handsome. We're glad you decided to cut it out and let them do their job."

I smiled the best I could, and she winked at me. Thomas and Anita stood at the foot of the bed, and both of them smiled down at me. Anita was wiping her eyes as her husband rubbed her shoulder.

The nurse asked, "Danny, have you been feeling under the weather at all? Flu symptoms or anything?"

Her use of the nickname made me wince and then look over at Hale apologetically. I didn't mind his pet name for me; I'd actually gotten used to it. Earlier, I'd just used it as an excuse to lash out, and now I felt like a total jerk.

I shook my head.

"Hmm. Well, your lab results came back, and it seems that your immune system has been fighting something for a little bit. We didn't see anything serious, but just try to take it easy over the next week or so. We are going to send you home with some more antibiotics to help fight off infection. Remember to take them all," she said as she leaned in to fluff my pillow and then check my arm with the IV attachment. "Can I get you anything else?"

"Water?" I asked.

Aunt Carol looked at the nurse for permission.

Jalinda nodded. "That's fine. But drink it slow. Don't want you choking yourself on ice cubes, and the antibiotics may cause a little nausea, so we don't want you throwing up either. If you do, I have something in my bag of tricks for that too, so let me know." She checked my IV bag and my chart. "Glad to have you back," she said as she left the room.

She closed the door behind her. Hale, who'd stepped out of her way, now stood back in front of the door, his arms folded across his chest.

Carol handed me a cup of cold water, and I did as the nurse told me, sipping a little bit at a time. Heaven. It hit my stomach like a ton of bricks, though, just as Jalinda had said it might, and I took it easy. So I laid my head back against the pillow, exhausted from the exertion of just sitting up.

Carol beckoned Thomas and Anita and motioned to the door. Hale stepped aside for them to pass, and again, when the door shut, he stood in front of it, watching me as if I would disappear any second.

"Hey" was all I could manage to say. What do you say in moments like this?

Hale walked over to the chair next to my bed and sat down. He looked rough, still in his pajama bottoms, a T-shirt, and a jacket. His eyes were bloodshot and tired-looking, with dark circles under them.

"Hey," he replied.

He reached for my hand, and I intertwined my fingers with his.

"How long have I been here?" I asked. God, my throat hurt.

"This is your second evening. You've been asleep almost thirty hours. Danny, I thought we... They had a hard time bringing your fever down... The doctor... Danny..."

My handsome man sat there for a while looking like an airplane crash survivor, wide-eyed and panic-stricken, his voice cracking. Then his face crumpled and he began to cry. It wasn't a quiet cry either. Sobs racked his body as he leaned over the chair and placed his head on my stomach. He wrapped his arms around my body and held me fast to him.

I was shocked. "Oh, Hale, don't. Oh, baby, please don't." My voice cracked with emotion as I sat up and pulled him to me.

His arms went around my neck as he cried. His tears fell hot and wet on my skin.

"They couldn't get your fever down," he sobbed into my stomach. "I thought I was going to lose you."

"Baby, I ain't goin' anywhere" was all I could say over and over again as I rubbed his back. If I'd doubted his love for me prior to this, doubt just leaped out of my hospital room window and died a horrible, splattered death on the concrete below. *I hope no one's standing under it*, I thought rather hysterically. "Shh, it's okay."

His sobs eased off, and he shook as he inhaled a breath and raised his head. I reached up and wiped the remaining tears from his eyes as he smiled.

"I love you," I said. "Come here."

"I love you," he responded and stood up.

I kissed his sweet face. He cleared his throat and sat back. He exhaled a breath and wiped his eyes. His unshaven face was red and patchy from crying, his eyes were still misted over, and I fell in love with him all over again.

"You had a concussion that was pretty bad. You also managed to catch some sort of bug while you were out in the woods. By the condition of your clothing, it looked like you had decided to take a nap up to your neck in mud. What the hell happened out there?" he asked me.

"Jesus. Hale, it was my fault. I took off not thinking. I was so pissed off that I didn't realize how stupid that decision was. There was this embankment that led down to a creek—which I think runs to the pond, by the way—and I just sat there on this rock for a bit, skipping stones. I just had to cool off, ya know? I was on my way back when a pack of wolves knocked me out."

"Fuck, Danny, you know you can't just wander into—wait, they did what?"

"One of the wolves knocked me out." I reached behind my head; it was still sore from where I hit the ground.

"Wolves don't knock people out, Danny. This is Oregon, not New York. I suppose New York wolves may do that and take your wallet, but the ones out here, if they catch you out, we'd be lucky to find a shoe or something they couldn't digest." He looked at me like I was crazy.

"No. These didn't eat me. When I came to, one had stayed behind and walked me out of the woods. I followed him," I said defensively. The story even sounded absurd to my own ears.

"You must have hit your head harder than we thought," Hale replied.

"Dammit, Hale, no—listen to me." I recounted the entire events of the night prior, and Hale listened attentively. When I got to the part about my dad, I started to cry again. Hale's eyes grew wide, but he didn't say anything. When I got to the part about the door, he looked confused.

"So there was a door in the middle of the woods?" he asked.

"No, no, the door is in the house somewhere. They just showed it to me," I replied, feeling helpless.

"How did they do that?"

"Meh… I…how the hell should I know? I think if they had the ability to talk to me, then I guess that isn't too far out of their abilities either." I huffed. I felt like a kid trying to explain to my parent that I saw Ms. Jones, the cat lady, abducted by aliens. "Will you stop being a cop for a second and consider everything? The haunting in the house, the stuff Francine, the seer lady at the fair, said, and the fact that you love me and I'm not crazy?"

"Sorry, cop questioning is a habit. You're right. But he said your mom had moved on," Hale said, bringing up a very good point.

"Yeah, he looked distraught about it too. What if he's trapped on the grounds like Christopher is trapped in the house?"

"Who said anyone is trapped in the house? You think this is a ghost?"

"What did you tell me about that house when I first moved here?"

"At Timber Manor, anything is possible."

I shot him a look and he relented. When I reached for his hand, he took mine and held it.

"I'm so sorry about what I said to you," I said. "I didn't mean a word of it. Can you forgive me?"

Hale sighed. "I love you. Of course I forgive you."

"You can call me Danny."

He smiled. "I planned on it."

I chuckled. "Good."

I thought about the house for a while, and the prospect of it bothered me. My dad had told me to get away, to leave, but if he was chained to that place like Christopher and unable to move on, would he fall prey to the same fate Francine had described: would he age himself into oblivion and just cease to exist? The thought troubled me, and I didn't like the possibility of the answer being yes.

***

That night the hospital staff moved another bed inside the hospital room and scooted it close so Hale could stay with me.

Jalinda, the redheaded nurse with the sassy personality, periodically came in to check on me but didn't come in again that night.

The next morning, Dr. McKee walked in and cleared me to go home, with strict orders to take it easy. I was grateful to hear it. As she was leaving at the end of her shift, Jalinda poked her head in one last time to tell me not to go playing in the woods alone at night again. Hale and I both laughed, and I promised not to.

We were pulling out of the hospital parking lot, awaiting the traffic to die down so we could get on the road, when I caught a glimpse of gold coins in a woman's hair.

"Hale, stop the truck."

He put on the parking brake and I jumped out on the sidewalk and looked around. There was no one there—certainly no one with golden coins in her hair. I looked everywhere; then, shaking my head, I got back in the truck and we drove home.

Carol, Thomas, and Anita were all waiting for me to return home and greeted me when I walked in the door. The library had been converted into a makeshift bedroom, and Hale wouldn't leave my side. My thoughts went to Carol and the cancer that was eating her up inside, and I felt like a real jerk for her fussing over me as much as she did.

Carol and I were alone in the library, me propped up on pillows surfing Netflix for the next movie to watch, when I apologized for my outburst.

"Never mind that, Danny. You were right. I should have told you. To be honest with you, there are several things I should have put out in the open immediately when we met. It was...you had just lost your parents, and I was hoping for the right time," she said as she sat down on the bed next to me.

"I know. It all came at me so fast. I overloaded," I tried to explain.

"You're just a kid. You may be able to die in a war, vote, and drink yourself silly at twenty-three, but Daniel, everything you've been through in the past few months has been enough to drive anyone around the bend. I'm proud you've been able to hold up as well as you did. Yet you are a Donnelly, after all," she said proudly.

My mind instantly went back to the conversation I'd had with my dead family members. I decided to keep a lid on that part for a while.

So much for open and honest communication, I chided myself. Instead I asked, "How has the house been?"

She looked at me and frowned a bit. "Honestly, it's been quiet. We haven't experienced anything, but then again, we've all been really too distracted to think about Chris—"

I shot my hand up. "Don't say his name, Aunt Carol." She looked at me curiously but nodded. "I'm sorry you're sick," I said timidly.

She chuckled. "Honey, I'm not sick. I'm dying. Oh, don't look like that. These things happen, Daniel. Death is as much a part of life as living is. Besides, I have it on good authority that there's more to life than just this place," she said, bringing out her silver cross.

"My parents weren't particularly religious. *Protestant* is all that's on Dad's dog tags," I said, reaching over to check out her symbol of faith.

"Well, we weren't brought up any particular religion in this household. Your grandparents were pretty educated people and very practical. It wasn't until Chr—after *he* died and I was a teenager that I started going to Mass with some girls from school. There was a young priest there by the name of John, who would sit and talk to me about faith and God. I liked him a lot. He was the perfect mixture of religion and education, not like some of those kooks you see on TV. He gave me that Saint Michael's medallion that I gave your father," she said.

"Does he still work here?" I asked, curious.

She shook her head. "No. He joined the Jesuit order and was sent on a mission to help the poor in South America. The last I heard, he had become a cardinal and was now presiding over the archdiocese. Oh, but I was able to talk to him about everything, and he listened and always gave sound advice. We still keep in touch through e-mails and the like, and I'll get an occasional card during the holidays," she whispered, tucking the chain back inside her shirt.

Hale walked in with a fistful of flowers wrapped in cellophane, and Carol grinned as he handed them to me. I smiled and blushed.

God, love can make you feel funny, I thought.

The flowers were beautiful, bright yellows and oranges, and I melted. Carol offered to take them and put them in some water, and she left us alone in the library.

Hale sat down next to me. "How you feeling?" he asked.

He was dressed in a pair of jeans and a T-shirt, looking all kinds of adorable. I sat forward and planted my mouth on his, then scooted up into his lap and kissed him passionately, running my hands up and down his back. The muscles underneath his shirt bunched as he wrapped his arms around me, holding me tight. I loved the smell of him, soap and aftershave; I loved the feel of him, solid and warm; and the taste of him, sweet and salty.

I broke the kiss and rested my forehead against his. Breathing heavily, I held the back of his head with my hands.

"That good, huh?" he asked, chuckling and slightly out of breath.

I nodded. "I love you."

"I love you."

"We're sleeping upstairs tonight," I said, snickering, as I laid my head on his shoulder.

He laughed. "Oh, are we now?"

"Yup. You're lucky there are people awake, otherwise I'd have my way with you right now," I said, sitting back and looking into his lovely eyes. My body ached for him, and judging from the bulge pushing back against me, he was in the same predicament.

"You're incorrigible." He laughed.

"No, I'm horny, is what I am," I said, laughing, sliding off him and standing up to stretch. I was restless, and it had already been a day or so of being cooped up. I was sick of it.

He looked up at me from the mattress and grinned. "I like that in a guy."

"Oh, I bet."

To be honest, since my excursion in the woods and seeing how much this man cared for me, I couldn't stand taking my eyes off him. His movements, his words, his touch—everything seemed so important for me to take notice of and acknowledge.

***

Later on, I stepped into the bathroom, took one look in the mirror, and almost freaked. I looked like five miles of bad road.

No, I thought, *you look like you got lost in the woods and were in a hospital for two days.*

My face was unshaven and my hair stuck to my head. My clothes were limp and hung on me. All I had to do was put my arms in the air, shuffle forward, and make loud groaning noises for the perfect zombie impression. After a shower, a shave, and brushing my teeth and hair, I felt human again and joined the family for more TV time.

After dinner, Hale and I turned in early and I kept my promise.

It started off gently at first, but the passion ignited a sense of urgency in us, and the emotion of the past couple of days came roaring to the surface and exploded between us. Our clothes came off easily, and we slid into bed, the sheets cool underneath our superheated bodies. Hands explored each other as we touched, teased, and tasted, our hands finding each other's as they intertwined and grasped. We rolled over and over in the bed, kissing passionately, until finally Hale ended up flat on his back. I was on top of him, holding myself up on my arms as I teased his lips.

Hale's hands moved to my ass, kneading the muscles, making me groan. I slowly kissed down from his lips to his chin. He let go of me so I could maneuver down, and I guided his hands to rest over his head before I continued my journey down his neck to his chest. I buried my face in the fur there and flicked my tongue across one nipple, teasing, sucking, nibbling, and making him groan before I turned my attention to the other.

His body shook with desire as I lowered myself farther, kissing his flat stomach, feeling the muscles clench as my lips touched him. I kissed past his navel and down to his groin. In one fell swoop, I took him in my mouth and he arched his back, crying out. My hands were on his thighs as I paid attention to him, and I relished the feel of them trembling in my hands. Hale called out my name as he arched his back again, driving himself into my mouth. He tried to sit up, and I stopped him, gently pushing him back down to the bed.

I reached into his bag for the bottle of lubricant he'd brought with him, opened the cap, and poured out enough to stroke him and prepare me. As I put some on his fingers and straddled his hips, moving his fingers to my ass, he sat up. I held on to his shoulders as he slipped one digit in, then two, making me ready. As I felt myself open to him, I groaned with pleasure.

When I felt enough time had gone by, I laid him back down. Never taking my eyes off his, I took his shaft in my hand, placed it to my ass, and guided him in. His head snapped back onto the pillow as he slowly worked his way into me. He pushed, and I returned the push until finally I sat down completely on him, my cock hard and rigid as I began to ride. His eyes were huge, full of passion and hunger, and I loved that it was me he starved for.

We both groaned in pleasure. The feel of him inside me, threatening to spill me off the cliff of the mounting desire building in me, had me aching for release. As I rode he met me thrust for thrust, and I braced myself on his chest.

"Baby, I'm going to come," he groaned, pistoning faster and faster.

I grabbed my cock and stroked in rhythm with him, my orgasm also imminent. My muscles flexed and relaxed again and again, driving me wild.

He grabbed me and flipped me over on the bed, pushing himself farther into me and driving his face down into my neck. With a shout and a whimper, he let go, and I met him as we tumbled off the peak of passion together: sweaty, shaking, and satiated. He rolled off me and lay on his back, breathing heavily.

He turned his head to me. "God, I love you," he said simply.

I started to laugh. He looked incredulously at me and then joined in.

"I love you too. I do, Hale. I don't know how I could have gotten through any of this without you," I admitted. "Please, don't go anywhere."

He rolled over on his side, leaned in, and kissed my nose. "I ain't goin' anywhere, baby. You're stuck with me."

I grinned and snuggled into his arms, resting my head on his chest.

In a singsong voice, he whispered to me as I slipped into the waiting arms of sleep. "Oh, Danny boy, the pipes, the pipes are calling. From glen to glen, and down the mountainside. The summer's gone, and all the flowers are dying. 'Tis you, 'tis you must go, and I must bide."

Love kept the monsters away that night.

***

I woke up in the early morning as gray light fell across me. Lying on my side, I felt Hale's arms wrapped around me, holding me tight, and I could feel him breathing slow and deep. I basked in the warmth of the moment, ran my hand down his strong bicep to his forearm, and clasped his fingers to pull his hand to my mouth. My body was so relaxed, and I silently wished that time would freeze and I could experience this forever.

The lovemaking from last night was even better than our first time, I thought.

Lovemaking. That was a new concept to me. Before, sex was for fun. A roll in the hay. Stress relief.

Grateful to the fates that had led me to this place, I considered our relationship and the man sleeping next to me.

Admittedly the haunting scared me, but it angered me as well. I hated that Christopher had the power over my father that he did, even in death. I hated the fact that Carol's life had been chained here, and now that she was sick, she would probably end her days here.

I also thought about what had happened in the woods. It hadn't been a hallucination, nor was it fever induced. Dad's distraught appearance at the mention of my mother and the vision he showed me of the door was something I could never have conceived of on my own.

But where was the door? The hallway had looked like it was aboveground, like any of the doors in the house, so which one was it?

Hale mumbled in his sleep and snuggled closer to me. I kissed his knuckles gently and murmured, "I love you."

"Mmmm, I love you," he said in a sleepy voice as he pulled me closer to him, closer to his strong chest and the beat of his heart, and I let him. "Good morning, baby."

"Good morning." I rolled over to face him.

His face was half-buried in the pillow, but his eyes were open and he was looking at me. I loved him like this: with his face scruffy and his hair, which was starting to get longer, standing up all over the place. His kissable lips and long eyelashes made him beautiful, and I loved looking at him. *Perfect.*

I reached out and ran my hands across his chest as he closed his eyes and smiled. "Is the fair still in town?" I asked.

"No. It should be in Portland by now. They only stay about a week in each place and then move on. Why do you ask?"

"Damn. I was hoping to go down and see that woman again."

Hale looked at me for a moment, quiet. "You really think she can help?"

"I don't really know. Dad wants me to leave this place. He said so. But, Hale, I can't leave him here, leave my grandparents here to just haunt these grounds. That's…that's…cowardly. I couldn't live with myself knowing they were here."

"How do you know they're trapped?" He moved a strand of hair out of my eyes.

"I just have a feeling. I mean, I asked him about Mom, and the look on his face was terrible. He misses her, and I don't think he can follow her. At least not yet."

"That has to be terrible." Hale winced. "That would hurt me too."

I smiled, kissed him lightly on the lips, and slid out of bed. I walked over to my duffel bag and reached inside until I felt the thin metal tags I was looking for, then pulled them out and looked at them. My dad's dog tags dangled as I untwisted the chain and slipped them over my head, the metal cold on my skin at first.

This will have to do for now, I thought.

Hale followed me out of bed, and we dressed, washed up, and walked downstairs to greet the morning.

Carol

THE COFFEE WAS steaming in the cup in my hands as I sat reading the morning paper. The boys came walking into the kitchen and sought the coffeepot as Anita worked over the stove. They were happy, and I was happy for them.

Hale had been so worried about Daniel when he disappeared, and I had no doubt in my mind that he loved my nephew. The world certainly was a different place from when I was young. Sure, gay people had always existed, and those obnoxious people who tried to interfere or even hurt them were an anathema, but I didn't worry about them. Hale would die to protect Daniel; I knew that in my heart. He watched Daniel's every move, stayed close to him, and the look in his eyes when Daniel walked in the room secured that assurance for me.

I loved that kid. I loved that Michael had escaped this place and led a happy life and created a son as remarkable as this one.

My body hurt. I ached deep inside everywhere. Before too long, I would have to have hospice come in. The cancer was eating me alive and the medication the doctors prescribed for the pain was only enough to stave off the worst of it. But I was oddly at peace.

I missed my mother, I missed my father, and more than ever, I missed Michael. Now the fresh face of the hope of the Donnelly fortune stood in my kitchen. The youth, the promise, and hope for the continuation of the bloodline. His sexuality was of no concern. Should the two men find themselves settled, perhaps one day they would find a child to adopt, or maybe pay a surrogate to bear a child for them.

There were far more days behind me than ahead of me, and I was thankful for that. I would face my death, not cower in fear of it, but greet it as one would greet an old friend.

I couldn't help but remember the first time I laid eyes on this beautiful boy. My heart broke as I remembered the last time I'd seen my Michael. My dear, sweet brother who I often pray for late at night before I fall asleep.

He squealed and giggled as I bounced him on my knee, and Anita and I both cooed over him.

Michael and Sarah sat on the couch across the room from us, smiling and holding hands. Thomas, Anita, and I had traveled to North Carolina to meet my new nephew after a surprise phone call from Michael.

Now Michael sat proudly, beaming across the room from me as I held his son, Daniel, in my lap. Their little home was quaint and full of love, and Sarah was just as pretty as a picture.

This was also my first time meeting my brother's new wife. She was a beautiful woman, blue-eyed and raven-haired. Michael explained that he met her right out of boot camp when he graduated. Sarah had been working on an art degree and waiting tables at a local restaurant in North Carolina when Michael walked in one day. She was used to the recruits from Camp Pendleton coming and going in her town, immune to the advances of the men looking for a bit of skirt, but she quickly found out Michael was different.

As we sat there, I listened to her tell her story.

"Oh, he looked like a devil dog, all right." She gave him a sly glance, with a teasing smile on her lips. "Tall, dark, and handsome in his dress uniform, hair cut in a high-and-tight, green eyes, and a smile that lit up the world. He came into my restaurant one evening and sat at my table. Then he came back, and he came back, and he came back. Sometimes he would bring a book, sit and read until I got off shift, and then walk me home. He finally convinced me to go out on a date with him. We were married six months later." She placed her hand on Michael's knee, and I looked at the modest little diamond on her wedding finger. "He can be so stubborn."

I laughed, knowing that was the truth. My brother was handsome, yet I had never seen him looking so sharp. His long hair was gone, the baby fat on his face all but vanished. His shoulders were square and he puffed out his chest proudly. He'd grown up. He was a man now, and he and his wife looked wonderful together. They were happy, and I was happy for them.

That evening we sat out on the front porch. Thomas and Anita were still in the kitchen, talking with Sarah and playing with the baby. Sunset had come, and the evening breeze was light and fragrant. I was so thankful to see him after so long, but as the evening wore on, I knew the conversation we were about to have was unavoidable. It broke my heart.

"Your dad is sick," I said, rocking in the swing alongside him. Michael looked at me but didn't say anything, so I continued. "The doctors say that his dementia is getting worse. We have a nurse living at the house around the clock now. After Mom died, he just never fully recovered."

"I can't go back there," he said simply. "I won't."

"Michael, you wouldn't have to stay long—"

"Absolutely not." His voice had grown icy. "I escaped that place. You should have too."

"How was I supposed to? Mom got cancer and then you left. Was I supposed to leave Dad there by himself?" Bitterness was creeping into my voice.

"I don't know what you should have done. But get out of there, get married, have kids. That house is rotten from the inside out. I don't care how quiet it's been. It's still there. He's still there, and I am not exposing my family to it. My son," he said angrily.

I shook my head in disbelief. "You were there for your mother's funeral. You won't be there for Dad's? Your father is dying, Michael," I said, trying to plead with him.

"I wasn't strong enough to handle that house then," he said quietly.

"And now?"

"Look, Carol, it was good of you to come. But let's drop this. I am not going back into that house, and that's final."

I nodded. It was final.

Anita and Thomas came out onto the porch, and we stood up. I hugged my brother good-bye and then hugged my sister-in-law, *who looked shocked at our sudden departure. Michael stayed stoic and placed a hand on his wife's shoulder. The baby had been laid down for sleep.*

We both promised to call, and Michael told me I was more than welcome to come and visit. All three of us got into the car.

As Michael waved good-bye to us, standing next to his wife on their front porch all those years ago, it was the last time I would see my brother alive.

Now that I looked at Daniel, I saw so much of his father in him. Yet he didn't have his build. He was more graceful, thin and tall like his mother.

The boys both came and sat down with me, and we talked lightly as Anita served us breakfast. We ate and discussed our plans for this rainy Saturday. My stomach burned—a result of either the cancer or the medication, I wasn't sure which—but I ignored it as best I could. I had an appointment to speak to a hospice specialist this coming Monday.

Sleep was a rare thing for me these days. I watched the two of them banter back and forth and saw Anita smile to herself. Things were going to be okay on this end, perhaps. Thunder began to roll outside as the rain started pounding on the windowpane.

"Danny, I have one more form for you to sign," I said cautiously. He looked up from his plate and nodded. "Okay."

"It's a medical—"

"Power of attorney. I thought you might have made one. Sure, I'll sign it." He smiled over at me, and I couldn't help but return his smile. He knew what I was asking him to do, and I knew he had the courage to do it.

Hale watched our silent communication, then lowered his head and stared down at his plate, paying attention to his breakfast.

The lights above the table began to flicker—one, two, three— then held dark for a second and came back on. Daniel dropped his fork and stared up. Outside, the wolves howled and he jumped at the noise, his eyes wide. Hale placed a hand on his shoulder, and they exchanged a glance I'd seen before.

I asked, "Danny, besides the other night, have you noticed any odd things happening?" He looked at me with a little trepidation in his eyes. "It's okay," I said.

"Shit, Aunt Carol." He sighed and began. "Sometimes there are footsteps. Noises. Feelings of being watched, bad dreams. I swear I was tripped in the library the other night—"

I cut him off. "Something grabbed your leg?"

His eyes widened and he nodded. "Yeah, and I pitched forward."

"It is starting again, then." I sat back in my chair as Anita crossed herself. The lights flickered again—one, two, three—and stayed on. "Christopher," I whispered.

Thunder rumbled out in the night, and lightning flashed as if to confirm my words.

"How bad was it when my dad was here?" Danny asked.

"Your grandfather wanted no part of acknowledging that his house was haunted…"

Michael came stumbling out of his room one night, screaming my name. "Carol! Carol!" each cry more urgent than the one before.

Father and I were in the family room watching television, and when we heard Michael's voice, we looked at each other and took off for the stairs. As we rounded the corner, we spotted Michael coming down, white as a sheet and shaking.

"Michael, what's wrong?" asked Dad.

Trembling, Michael sat down on the third step from the bottom, wrapped his arms around his knees, and lowered his head into his arms.

I sat next to him and placed my hand on his shoulder. He raised his head and looked at me. His eyes were tortured, and it broke my heart. Although he was a teenager, he looked so hopeless and small, and his lower lip trembled. "What is it, Michael?" I asked, smoothing his hair back. I had a bad feeling I knew what it was.

"He was in the mirror, Carol, the one on top of the dresser. I was getting out my pajamas and looked up. He was behind me in the mirror. His face is all messed up, and he looks raggedy and old, but God, his eyes. They were black and empty. But it was him, Carol."

There were times in the beginning, when he started complaining about things like this, that I would chide him, thinking he wasn't serious. Yet, as I started experiencing things too, I did all I could to try and comfort him. I'd heard doors opening and closing on their own, seen shadows move along a wall, felt cold spots or like I was being watched. The worst of it focused on Michael, though. Yet, even as we talked about these things, we'd made a pact to not tell Papa Jim about it. But now he'd heard.

"What are you talking about? Who was in the mirror?" Dad asked, concerned.

Michael turned his pleading eyes to me, and with a heavy heart, I spoke the words he couldn't.

"Dad, since Mom got sick, Michael has been seeing—no. We've both been experiencing some strange goings-on," I said tentatively.

"Strange like how?"

I sighed heavily, already knowing where this was going. "Strange *things. Things* that would leave us to conclude the house is haunted."

He snorted in disbelief.

"Dad, it's true!" Michael pleaded.

"Haunted by who?" Dad asked.

Michael hesitated for a second and then stared at the floor. "Christopher," he said gravely.

The lights flickered. Thunder shook the house so loudly that Michael and I leaped into each other's arms.

Dad's face had turned red in fury. "Don't you dare say his name! I dealt with him a long time ago. You saw it happen." He turned his gaze toward me. I thought I was going to wilt under it. "And as for you, young lady, I expected more from you. Why are you feeding into this?"

I glared back at him defiantly. "Because I've seen things myself."

"You've seen Christopher yourself?" he asked skeptically as he crossed his arms over his chest.

"Well, not exactly… But there are the footsteps, the pinches on Michael's arms. I've been tripped on a couple of occasions. When I look, there's nothing there. It's all stuff that Christopher used to do."

"Both of you are out of your minds! What kind of sick joke are you playing at?"

Michael's head shot up, and he raised his arms and pulled his sleeves down to reveal the bruises: dark, multicolored, some fresh, some healing with that sickly yellow tint to them on the soft underpart of his flesh. "Does this look like a joke to you?" he asked angrily.

"Wha—I don't know where you got those, but you two had better knock this off or I'll—"

"Or you'll what?" Michael cut him off. "Ignore it? Oh, you've done a good job at that so far. As a matter of fact, you're great at it," he sneered.

"How dare you—" Dad began, but stopped when Michael stood up, fists clenched and trembling.

This time Michael's tremors were not from fear but from anger, and he took a step closer and leaned in to his father. "How dare I what? Tell the truth? Dad, has it ever occurred to you that I'm never home? Do you wonder about that? Are you even paying attention to that? You're so caught up in your business, I'm sure this place could burn down around you and you wouldn't notice."

"Michael, stop!" I stood up and got between the two of them. Dad had balled up his fists and taken a step forward into the fray, and I tried to push them apart. "Dad, stop it!" I yelled.

My hands were placed on their chests, but they were easily overpowering me to get in each other's faces.

"You saw Mom when she was sick. You heard what she said. She saw him too," Michael said through clenched teeth.

"Your mother was dying from cancer and out of her mind on morphine. And don't bring her into this, or I'll—"

"You'll what now, Dad? Wait till it's too late to do anything about it and then toss me over a balcony too? And then what? Pretend I never existed? You're a terrible father."

The words shocked me, and Dad and I stared at him. I looked at Dad, expecting a swinging fist, but Dad's face had turned pale and he seemed to deflate.

Michael nodded. "I see how this is going to be. Don't worry. You can return to your office, your payroll, your files, and your money. I can take care of myself."

Michael turned and headed up the stairs. I stood there as his door slammed shut. Speechless, I turned to Dad, whose face was unreadable.

As hell broke loose outside and a lone wolf howled in the night, Dad turned and left me standing there in the foyer. I went back into the room, sat there in the dim light, and cried into my hands.

"Jesus," Danny whispered, but his face grew stony and his eyes flashed. "When the workers were here, they accidently poked a hole in the wall upstairs with their ladder. Dale Parrish, the foreman, came and got me and showed me. He had me place my hand above the opening, and we couldn't figure out why it was so cold. With everything going on, I just forgot to tell you."

The blood in my veins became rivers of ice. "Where at, Daniel?"

"Upstairs, down the hallway on the other side."

"Show me." I stood up from the table.

We all walked out of the kitchen and up the stairs together. I hated going to that part of the house and usually avoided it. It was where Christopher's old room had been: the room Daddy had sealed up after Christopher died. Just as I feared, the patch of new plaster that covered the hole the contractors had made was right in front of the door to Christopher's old bedroom. All that separated us from it was a sheet of plaster. I explained that to the boys.

"I stood here after everyone had left and did this." Danny leaned forward and rapped on the wall three times. The air around us was charged, and gooseflesh broke out on my arms. "I stood here for a second, and all of a sudden, I felt like I was being watched, like now. And then I heard the knock repeat itself from behind the door. I know it sounds crazy."

I turned to him. "No, it doesn't, Daniel. Not at all."

Danny said, "Hale, this might be the door from my...vision."

"Could be," he concurred.

"Vision?" I asked.

Danny recounted what he'd seen in the woods, and I stared at him with rapt attention. He told me about the nightmares he'd had, about the wolves, and what his father had told him and shown him. I was floored by what I was hearing, but it all made sense.

After Mark died, I'd tried to convince myself that it had been an accident, but I'd never brought another person into this home until now. Not anyone I loved romantically. I didn't trust the house. I didn't know what would have happened should I have let myself fall for someone else. I couldn't bear the thought of them dying the way Mark had. I mean sure, Anita and Thomas were here, but they had been all along.

I said, "You know, Daniel, perhaps your...father...is right. Perhaps you should just leave this place. I mean, things have become more active since you've been here, and I can't bear the thought of something bad happening to you."

"No," he said stonily.

"But—"

"No. This son of a bitch tortured my father in life and in death. If Dad is trapped here along with your parents, it will be only a matter of time before he claims you as well. You'll be damned to this place, just like them. We have to do something." Fire burned in his eyes.

"Like what?" I asked.

Danny turned to Hale. "I've been thinking about that, actually. Is it possible to contact the local Portland police and have them go find Francine at the carnival?"

Hale nodded. "Yeah, but what are we going to tell them?"

"Tell them that there's an emergency back here in Emerson and that her...services are requested. See if she'll come."

Hale nodded. "I have a friend with the Portland PD. Sergeant Melissa Jones and I went to the academy together. She'll wonder why I'm asking, but psychics have been used in criminal cases before. I'll just, you know, embellish a little."

"Wait—who is Francine?" I asked.

Danny looked painfully at me. "Uh, she's a medium of sorts, Aunt Carol. But she seemed to know what she was talking about. Right now, it's the only avenue I can think of to help us. I mean, before we start calling out priests for a full-on exorcism, which I'm not sure would work, maybe she can help us figure it out."

Hale looked at me. "I don't really know if Danny is right on this or not, but where else do we turn?"

I said, "Well, Daniel, this is your home now. If you think her presence would help us, then, by all means, have her come."

"Hale?" Danny asked, looking at him.

"I'm on it."

Hale went down the hallway toward Daniel's room, and Danny and I walked back downstairs together.

Hale

Thank you. I'll be waiting for your call." I hung up the phone.

The local PD had seemed skeptical about the request, but I'd done them a few favors over the years, so their lieutenant granted the plea.

I stood outside on the front stoop, watching the rain coming down. Daniel came out of the door and stood beside me. Thunder rolled and lightning danced in the sky above us, and he slid his arm into mine.

I said, "They're going to try and get into contact with her. I made arrangements to have her transported down here if she agrees to it. Danny, are you sure we're doing the right thing?"

"No. I'm not sure if this is the right thing. But I do know we can't sit back and do nothing and let all hell break loose, and I refuse to run away," he said, turning me to him.

The fire in his eyes was hot and he clenched his jaw. I grinned to myself.

"What?" he asked.

"You're sexy when you're angry."

For a second he looked at me as if I were crazy, and then we both broke into laughter.

"Do you think she'll come?" he asked.

I shrugged. "I don't really know, Danny. But I think we may have a good chance. If not, I can go down and find a local parish priest. Although for an exorcism, I think they need to do some extensive background checks. Or somebody better start speaking in tongues or something."

He snickered. "Well, it's not a demon we're dealing with. What we are in fact dealing with is the spirit of someone who was psychotic. I wonder what would have happened had he been allowed to grow up."

"You said your father mentioned Christopher looked old and raggedy. Why isn't he that young kid anymore? His spirit, I mean."

"I think that may have something to do with what Francine referred to as the *infection*. Dad and my grandparents looked the same. Hell, Dad looked younger, so I'm not so sure about that."

The rain continued to pour down in buckets as the thunder rumbled again and lighting lit the sky.

Danny paced back and forth, popping his neck and rolling his shoulders. He looked like a boxer getting ready for a fight. I could see the anxiety on his face and the tension in his back as he stood ramrod straight.

"I feel like a swim," he said suddenly. "I'm all worked up and needing to do something with myself. Want to come and count laps for me? It would be a great way to kill some time."

"You're damn right I'm going, buster. After what Carol told us in the house, don't be surprised if I never leave your side again."

Danny walked over and kissed me. "Promise?"

"Promise."

"Okay, then."

We headed into the house.

***

I had to say I was impressed by the way he looked in a Speedo.

We were standing in Danny's room. He quickly changed his clothing and grabbed his swimming gear. It was everything I could do not to reach out and snatch him up. Danny's body was amazing. His physique was something to behold: the muscles were smooth and long from years of swimming, not bulky like a weight lifter's. Yet I had no doubt in my mind that when it came down to it, he was pretty strong. His shoulders were square and his waist thin; his abdominal muscles could be clearly seen.

Danny said, "I feel like if I don't get back to doing this regularly, I'm going to look like the Pillsbury Doughboy." I tossed my head back and laughed. "What?"

I sat on the edge of the bed, with my arms folded across my chest, admiring the view. "Do swimmers really shave their hair?"

"Yes. Legs, chest, arms, anything that slows them down in the water and keeps them from critical seconds. I'm not shaving today, as you see. But I am going to put this on." He produced a swim cap and a pair of goggles. Over that, he pulled on a pair of sweatpants and a shirt.

We padded downstairs into the empty kitchen, out the back door of the house, and dashed through the rain to the pool building. The smell of chlorine was intense and burned my nose, and it was very humid inside. The pool was massive and stretched almost the entire length of the building it sat in, with multiple lanes and a diving board on one side. Little markers along the edge of the pool told the depth of the water, starting at three feet and down to twelve at the deep end. The water was crystal clear and looked inviting; I thought about skinny-dipping in here one night with Danny and smiled to myself.

I took a seat on a chair and pulled out my cell phone, slid the Android open, and found my clock. "Want me to time you?"

He started slipping off his sweatpants. "Sure." He stepped out of them, then folded and placed them on the ground, along with a towel he had brought with him. Then he took off his shirt, folded it, and placed it neatly on top of the other things. Danny pulled his hair up, put on his cap and his goggles, then began a series of stretches to limber up his body. Finally he walked over to the deep end of the pool.

He smiled over at me, and I waved back at him.

"Tell me when," I said.

"'Kay. Ready, set—" He stood on the side of the pool and took the right posture. "—*go!*" And he leaped into the water.

I started the timer and sat back and watched. Arm over arm, breathe in, stroke, breathe out, stroke, get to the end of the pool. Dive, flip, spin, kick out, arm over arm again. One lap, two, three…I was impressed. He sliced through the water effortlessly: twelve laps, thirteen, fourteen, turning this way and that as he went.

I worked out often, kept myself in shape because of my job, but this would wear my ass out in no time flat. Twenty-seven, twenty-eight, twenty-nine… *Good Lord, how many laps can this guy do?*

I followed him down to the shallow end of the pool.

The lighting in the pool house, while bright, didn't fully keep the gloom of the day away. Rain splattered against the high windows of the long building. The room was heated and thick with humidity as chlorine permeated the air. Watching him swim was having a calming effect on me.

Danny was strong. Stronger than most would be in his situation. I felt myself waxing poetic…

I felt both overjoyed and scared to death at the same time when it came to him. When I looked in his eyes, I saw my future laid out before me in a spectrum of infinite possibilities, each of them wonderful and intimidating: Who would we be? Would we stay here? Would we move? Would there be children? A large family or a small one? What would Christmases be like? Should I get a different job? Could he live with a cop?

Will he marry me?

I swallowed hard at that thought as Danny made his way back down the pool.

Married. Marriage. Me. I'd never thought that would be in my future, never considered it before. At night when he rolled over on his side to sleep, I'd listen to him gently snore, watch the rise and fall of his chest in wonder. In the morning when I awoke, his face was so serene. And when his eyelashes fluttered open and he saw me, he would smile and my heart rate would kick higher. It had been so easy to love him. I slid right into my role.

Will it always be this way?

I don't know the answers to any of those questions. And that was where the terror lay. I was a man about my own business before Daniel showed up, accepting sex when it was there, forgetting about it when it wasn't. I had a town to take care of and my work at Timber Manor.

What if it didn't work out? What if I lost him? What if this house hurt him irreparably? What if he finally threw his hands up and left? What then? What would I do? Now that I'd been touched by love, would it be so easy to erase his fingerprints on my heart?

I didn't know.

I groaned inwardly at the idea of him going somewhere I couldn't follow. And it was at that very thought that the lights in the pool house flickered.

Thunder was rolling in the distance, so I chalked it up to the storm.

Then the lights flickered a second time, a third. I was sure the power was going to go out as Danny reached the other end of the pool, flipped, and started to make his way back.

It was the fourth flicker that changed my mind about the storm. The lights went out for a heartbeat, and when they came back on, I saw it.

At the deep end of the pool.

At first I thought it was a sewage backup. The filter at that end was pouring dirty black water into the pool. Luckily, Daniel had flipped again and was heading back this way. I was about to warn him of the nasty stuff when all of a sudden it began to rise up out of the water. And I saw it for what it was.

First the head emerged, a shock of white hair, and then a long, thin, distorted face. The lights in the pool house were flickering rapidly as my breath caught in my chest.

But it was the eyes—the void where the eyes should have been—that moved me into action. I leaped into the pool and waded toward Danny as he made his way back to the shallow end. I reached down, grabbed him under the arms, and yanked him up.

Danny shouted in fear and tried to jerk away from me, and in the process clocked me hard against the temple. The world swam, and I nearly collapsed into the pool before Danny grabbed me. He straightened me up. I stared past him at the figure starting to close the distance between us.

"Hale, what the fuck!"

"*Christopher.*"

Danny's head turned and he screamed.

Christopher had risen to his full height. The lights in the pool house were flashing faster now as the creature let out a shriek that almost stopped my heart. Danny began to shove me backward, and I turned and trudged through the water until we reached the edge, where we both climbed out. The figure was still advancing, unimpeded by the water; It hovered over the pool.

Danny grabbed his sweats and pulled me toward the door. I was getting my bearings again as we pushed the door to go outside.

It wouldn't budge.

"Did you lock it?" he asked.

"I didn't touch the damn thing."

Danny grabbed the lock but it wouldn't turn.

"Danny—"

The door didn't budge.

"*Daaaaaaaaaannyyyyyy,*" the creature shrieked.

Danny spun his head to look at It. "Hale, kick out the glass!"

He didn't have to tell me twice, and I used him to hold me steady. With all my might, I drove my heel through the glass door. It shattered into a thousand pieces and cold air and rain blasted in. I grabbed Danny, threw him over my shoulder to avoid his feet getting cut up, and jumped out of the pool building and into the pouring rain.

Daniel

HALE SET ME down in the wet grass, and I stumbled on shaky knees and slid onto my back. My heart was in my throat. I landed hard on my elbow and pain shot up through my arm. Hale grabbed me and lifted me to my feet. Thunder rolled and wind whipped through the trees. Hale looked panic-stricken as we piloted our way through the rain to the back of the house. I stopped dead when I saw a wolf between the door and where we were. She was pacing, then growling and then pawing at the ground.

"She isn't going to let us in," Hale said.

"She knows what's in there." I stepped forward.

"Danny, don't," he warned, but I put up my hand.

I took a few tentative steps toward the wolf; she watched me. I walked forward, clutching my soaking-wet clothing under my arm, and knelt down a foot or two away from the gray-and-white animal. She growled low and bared her teeth, her gaze never leaving me. She sniffed the air around me and took a step forward, her tail tucked between her legs. She approached slowly, and I stretched out my hand. My throat constricted and my hand shook; water dripped off my fingertips.

If she wants a chunk out of me, I've just become a Happy Meal on legs.

When she nuzzled my hand and stepped into my touch, I was very much surprised.

"My God," Hale said. The amazement in his voice was audible.

The wolf regarded him and then looked back at me. She raised her head to the sky and let out a howl that was both chilling and awesome at the same time.

From the tree line, a response came: one howl, then two. I turned my head in the direction of the howls and smiled to myself. The wolf took off, running past me and down into the woods. I stood up and put on my rain-soaked clothes.

"Where are you going?" Hale asked.

I nodded toward the woods. "I think she was sent here to get me."

"You're not going by yourself this time," he said.

I smiled at him. "I'm glad you said that. Come on."

Barefoot and soaked to the bone, we took off at a slow jog toward the sound of the wolves. We hit the tree line and slowed a little, waiting. When we heard the next howl, we took off jogging again, our breaths coming out in bursts of vapor. The rain pounded down, but the wind had been cut off by the surrounding trees.

I followed the path I had taken down to the creek, with Hale at my heels. When I reached the downgrade that led to the flowing water, I stopped, surprised. Sitting on the large rock where I had been not so long ago was Francine. She was surrounded by the three wolves, but they were not menacing her. They simply sat there staring at her and her at them; she had a smile on her face. Her hair was adorned with those golden coins, and her dress was loose and flowing and seemed untouched by the rain. She turned her head toward us and, with a wave, signaled us to come down. Around her, the sunlight poured down on the spot where she stood.

I turned to Hale, whose eyes were wide with wonder. I couldn't help but smile. We navigated down the embankment, sliding mostly on our butts to keep from pitching forward, and landed on the bottom. The wolves simply turned their heads and looked at what we were doing.

As we walked toward Francine, she smiled and turned to us. "Heard you boys were looking for me." Her French-Creole accent was as thick and rich as the soil under our feet.

"How did you know that? Did your bosses call you, letting you know?" Hale asked.

She turned her head up to the sky and laughed. "Those men are not my bosses, no. I did not hear from them. Let's just say a little wolf told me. Come, sit," she instructed.

We looked at each other and then walked toward her. The three wolves took steps back to allow us to sit down in front of her, like schoolchildren looking up to their teacher.

Given the events of the past couple of months, the oddity of her simply being there really didn't feel out of place. The rain had tapered off and was tap-tap-tapping the heavy leaves of the trees. The creek babbled across its bed, the water streaming over smooth stones, clear and clean, as it headed to the pond. The ground underneath us was soaked, but given the current state of our clothing, a wet butt wasn't much of a worry. The overall feeling of the moment was serene, gentle almost, as Hale sat close to me under the watchful eye of Francine.

"Spirits walk all over these grounds, Danny," she said, looking directly at me. "I see you've recently figured out who they are." A smile tugged her lips.

I raised my hand to the spot on my head where I'd fallen, thinking about when I was knocked unconscious.

"It was the only way they could communicate with you," she said as if reading my thoughts.

I believed she had been and, again, readily accepted it as true.

She continued. "When we sleep, we are the closest to the spirit world that we will ever be in this life. It is an altered state of consciousness. Different peoples from all over the world have found ways to reach the spirit world through meditation, ceremony, or the use of various drugs in religious practices. It is usually effective, but in this case, what the spirits did worked as well. You don't seem the type to use peyote." She slapped her knee and laughed.

"Oh, you sweet, sweet boy," she said. Staring at me, she reached down and stroked the side of my face. Her hand was warm and dry against my wet skin.

I smiled at her touch. It was motherly, comforting, and her skin smelled of cocoa butter and something more flowery, perhaps jasmine.

She turned her attention to Hale, who was watching her as closely as I was. His expression wasn't as solid, as stony, as it had been at the carnival. He sat with his legs up and his arms wrapped around his knees. He looked so much like a little boy, his warm eyes regarding her, that my heart warmed in my chest. His defenses were down—for now, anyway.

"As for you, Hale Davis, I see you have come into contact with that world as well." Her voice had taken a cooler quality, but not toward Hale, rather toward what he had seen recently. She reached out again, but this time she didn't touch anyone. She hovered her fingers over him with her right hand, then with her left, and did the same over me. Closing her eyes, she took a deep breath.

"Yes, it's written all over you. Spirits like that leave marks, impressions, and I can smell its stink. You cannot be around that stuff for too long, otherwise it infects you, makes you sick."

Hale looked at me, and we both said her name in unison. "Carol."

"Ah, the daughter." Her gaze turned to the wolves. They simply panted and looked back at her, sitting on their haunches. "What's wrong with…? Ah, cancer. I see." She nodded solemnly. "Yeah, long-term exposure could do it, all right."

"You make it sound like it's radiation or something," Hale said.

She turned her attention to him and nodded. "Sometimes spirits can be so malignant they infect and affect everything they come into contact with. Remember me telling you at the fair that souls touch? Over time, exposure to malignant ones, even in small doses, can make you very sick. They are not a good thing at all. The only thing worse than those spirits are demons. No, what you have is definitely human."

"Demons are real?" I asked.

She smiled at me: the teacher, the mentor, the friend. "All things are real, Danny. Demons, spirits, angels, ghosts, poltergeists, and many other things that do not even have names."

The rain had stopped entirely, the clouds overhead breaking up as the sun poked through, sending rays of light down to where we sat.

"These spirits, like the one in your house, not only affect people, they affect things. For instance, the house itself is not untouched by its influence. You have to be careful of that. As it grows powerful, it will have control of that house."

"Why is he doing this to us?" I asked.

"All he feels is pure hatred. He hates you, your life, and your love, everything about you, and wants to influence and even destroy it. In life, Christopher's soul was broken, rotted. What you're seeing now is the festered mess that he has become. It's aged him and turned him into a representation of the monster he was. In life he trapped your father behind closed doors. Now he has done it again with those who pass away. Instead of letting them travel on, he seized them, cursing them to walk here for eternity. Christopher is not just a spirit. He's a revenant."

Hale looked confused. "A revenant?"

Francine nodded and leaned back on her rock. "A revenant is the ghostly equivalent of a vampire. In Latin the word is *reveniens*, in French *revenir*, meaning 'to come back.' The Gaelic people referred to them as *neamh mairbh*. Often, when people in the Middle Ages were executed unjustly, their revenants would come back and exact revenge on their killers and their families.

"When your grandfather killed Christopher, his hatred was so intense for your father and his family that he cursed them in death. And when he did so, he damned your family to walk as beasts on the grounds. When they were alive and remembered him, he tormented them. When everyone who was alive forgot, or in the instance of your aunt Carol, buried him away in her mind, his powers dwindled. But the spirits, however, remained."

"Now that I'm here and we've talked about him," I said, "he's come back into his full strength?"

Francine smiled sadly. "Not quite to his full strength. But he's getting close. You saw what he did in the pool house. Had you stayed, he could have hurt you terribly."

I turned and looked at the three wolves behind me. "This? This is my father, grandmother, and grandfather?" Francine nodded. "Why wolves?"

Hale shrugged. "The house was named after the timber wolves that are in these hills."

Francine chuckled. "Good guess. But it's more complicated than that. Danny, many Native Americans believe that the wolf symbolizes courage, strength, and loyalty."

She took a deep breath before she went on.

"We often believe that when one society is conquered, everything about that society is wiped away. Or that's what the Christians thought throughout the ages. But it isn't true. Old rules, old laws, old faiths have put their mark on this world, and their power remains. When your grandfather named this estate, the wolf became a totem. A symbol. And it's the old laws, the old faiths, that have kept them in this place as protectors. While they are bound to the grounds of the house, Christopher cannot leave the house."

Hale looked behind him. "Danny, look," he said, nudging me. I followed his gaze. My grandfather, grandmother, and my father were all in human form. Sitting on their knees, with their hands resting gently on their thighs, they stared up into the golden shafts of sunlight that lit their faces. Their eyes were wide and in them was something akin to rapture. Pure joy.

I stood up and walked toward them on trembling legs. They were not entirely solid. The sunlight shone through them and there were no shadows behind. I knelt down next to my father's side. I was overcome with joy. "Dad? Dad! Can you hear me?"

My father didn't move. He just kept staring up. My heart was hammering in my chest as I raised my hand to touch him, but just as I suspected, my fingers slid through.

I turned my head to Francine. "Why can't they hear me?"

She tilted her head. "They can in a way, my darling. They hear everything. But what they're listening to is much more powerful than your voice. It's overwhelming them."

I shook my head in confusion.

She smiled. "They're enraptured in the light, Daniel. It holds within it a song only the soul can hear. They've been kept here too long. They want to go home."

As I turned my gaze back to my father's face, her words shook me and something dawned on me. "My mother's not here."

"Sarah never set foot on the property nor inside Timber Manor. She's gone on."

"Sarah," my father sighed sadly.

I bit my lip, fighting back tears. "He misses her."

"Of course he does. Their souls were joined for a very long time. He's missing a part of himself."

"Danny, maybe we should get you out of here. Get you away from Christopher," Hale said.

"Yeah? Well, what happens to them if they stay this way? And what about Carol? She's dying."

Francine's eyes narrowed. She crossed her legs and leaned forward, placing her hands in her lap. "If you leave this place, Carol dies. That's inevitable whether you go or stay, at this point. But just as inevitably, she joins them here, and after a while— maybe years after you die—they will simply cease to exist, no one here to remember them. That is what will happen. They will disappear into oblivion, boy, and Christopher along with them.

"Should you stay, however, your fate will be like theirs."

"This is bullshit," I said angrily.

"Then what do you suggest?" she retorted.

I looked over at Hale, the love of my life. His warm gaze fell on mine, his hair falling over his forehead now, after months of not being cut. He regarded me with such love and trust and gave me such strength, I knew what I had to do. "We fight," I said, still looking at him.

Francine sat back on her stone chair and clapped her hands together.

"You can't fight him, Danny. He can kill you," Hale said.

"Is that true?" I asked her.

"*Oui, mon ami.* That is a truth. He can snuff your life out should he get powerful enough. Should he escape his confines and bring the house completely under his control."

"Can I fight him?" I asked point-blank.

"Boy, you can do anything you want to do. You want to fight him? You sure can. You can destroy him as well. But you'll have to lure him out of that room. You'll have to set him loose upon that house. Once that happens, all hell will break loose."

"I don't mean to be rude," Hale said, "given the present company, but how can I see these people? I mean, I don't think I'm unconscious, and I don't remember smoking peyote before coming down here."

Francine laughed again. "I am a medium. A rather powerful medium, and that means spirits tend to seek me out. I can see them for what they are, and in turn it gives them substance. That is why I cannot come into the house yet, Danny," she said sadly. "I would inadvertently make Christopher more powerful than he already is. He is already manifesting himself to a degree, is he not?"

I nodded. So, we were on our own in this.

Hale spoke again. "So, you, Francine? You're a medium. You seem to know a lot about this stuff."

"What's your point, Sheriff?"

"My point is, what are you doing here? Do you wander around helping people fight ghosts?"

Francine nodded and gave him a thoughtful frown, narrowing her eyes. "Yes. To be quite frank, that's exactly what I do. Why? Do you require references?"

"How do we deal with him?" I asked, shooting Hale a stop-it glance.

"You have to lure him to the spot where he died. His essence is locked up in that room, but he is most vulnerable over the spot where he died. Once there, you must open the doors of the house and invite the other three here in. They will hear you, and they will come. Only they can combat him. You must get out of the way. Get out of the house. These three should be able to handle him and cast him into oblivion. Then, and only then, will this end and will they be set free."

Fear crept up inside me. "Can't I just burn the house to the ground?"

Francine shook her head vehemently. "All that will do will be to unleash him on the world. It would unchain him from the house. The world is bad enough without a spirit like that roaming around free. It would also damn your family, for sure. They can't move on unless his grip on them is broken."

"Daniel," my father said in a whisper that was just audible.

I whipped my head back around. "Dad? Dad, I'm here."

He didn't respond, just kept staring upward into the light filtering through the trees. Clouds began to roll back in, and as the shadows swept through the forest, I was dismayed to see the trio began to fade. When the sunlight disappeared, the ground in front of me was barren.

"Where did they go?" I cried.

In the distance a wolf howled. I felt a hand on my shoulder and looked up to see Francine standing above me.

"They're always here, Daniel. Always."

Hale crawled over and wrapped me in his arms. "If you want to fight, we'll fight."

"I love you, Hale. And I want to fight."

He nodded and hugged me. "Francine? What do we do?"

I absorbed the comfort of his arms. His cheek pressed against my own; his heart pressed against my heart. A myriad of emotions hurtled through me, caught me in a hurricane. I was terrified at the thought of facing that thing, but I was brokenhearted for my father bound here without my mother. I felt sick knowing Carol was going to join them sooner rather than later.

But Hale loved me. I could feel that love surrounding me. He was my eye in the storm. And it would be in that space where I would make my stand.

I tried to gather as much of Hale's energy into me as I could. I wouldn't break, I wouldn't bend. If I could make it through this, it would be worth it in the end. If we held through this, I would love him for the rest of my life.

Francine spoke to Hale first. "Christopher expels a great amount of energy to interact with the physical world. It's very difficult for souls to manifest themselves here." She turned to me. "Same goes with your family, Daniel. I am certain you are safe for now. I need to do some work of my own to prepare for our confrontation. It'll be an exorcism of sorts."

Hale and I broke our embrace and got to our feet.

She walked over to where I stood and took me by the shoulders. "Danny. I am so proud of you for fighting back. I know you're scared. But evil, even evil as deep and as powerful as your uncle Christopher's, trembles in the light. And our job is to turn a spotlight on it. We'll free your family. But a word of caution to you both: this isn't going to be easy. There'll be danger, you can guarantee. I need you both to be strong. To hang on to each other."

Hale nodded and reached for my hand. I took his, and he squeezed.

Francine nodded. "Good. Now, walk an old lady back to her car. I have something to give you."

We made our way out of the little valley and up the slope on the opposite side of the creek, with Francine leading the way. Hale and I walked hand in hand, occasionally glancing at each other. He, like me, was covered head to toe in mud, but to me he'd never looked more beautiful in his life. He looked at me as if he was thinking the same thing, and on the way pulled me closer to him. We continued the stroll with an arm slung around each other.

Hale leaned in when we were almost there and whispered, "My underwear is chafing."

I burst into laughter and looked up at him. "You're sick in the head."

He grinned. "Yeah. Do you like that in a guy?"

I laughed and kissed his cheek. We made our way to the road and Francine's car.

She walked to her trunk and opened it. "There are a few herbs I need to pick up for this to work." Inside was a woven basket with several jars containing different herbs, all labeled with plain white stickers and simple black writing. I was familiar with some of the names, such as basil, clove, mistletoe, and rosemary. Others I didn't know, like vervain, Solomon's seal, asafetida, and dragon's blood. She rummaged around in her trunk, brought out two small empty sachets, and handed one each to Hale and I. Then she opened three jars and added a little bit of their contents to each sachet. I got a good whiff of lavender.

"Now pull those tabs tight and keep those with you," she instructed.

"What is this for?" Hale asked.

"It keeps the nightmares away. Place them under your pillow. It should give you some peace from Christopher. But it may not last long. He grows stronger by the hour. That's why I must hurry. There are a number of ingredients I have to get together for Danny to withstand this fight. Are you two going to be okay?"

We both nodded and placed the sachets in our pockets.

"So you are a witch," Hale said.

Francine shook her head and laughed and looked him square in the eye. "Honey, do you randomly accuse people of things?" She looked over at me and placed a hand on her hip. "He's a charmer, this one."

"Only when his underwear is chafing," I replied, elbowing him.

Hale turned bright red.

Francine narrowed her eyes and looked him up and down. "I don't have anything in my trunk for that. You may want to have that taken care of."

I laughed, then asked, "So, witches are bad?"

"A witch would have skinned you both before you knew what was going on, hung you from a tree, disemboweled you, eaten your innards, and bathed in your blood. They're not very nice.

Well, most of them aren't very nice. There are others, though. Children of the dawn who are fairly safe to associate with, or Wiccans, who are fair. But a real witch? Perish the thought."

Hale shook his head. "I can't believe witches are real. What about vampires? Like the bloodsucking kind."

"Hale," I said, giving him a look.

"Yes. They're very rare. But vampires are real. Werewolves, skinwalkers, banshees, pookas, angels, and so on."

Hale looked impressed. "Just like *Buffy*."

Francine looked at me. "What's a Buffy?"

"It's a… Never mind," I muttered.

"I am a medium. However, I have picked up a few tricks over the years that may help us." She slammed the trunk shut and fished out her keys, looked over to Hale, and smiled as she opened the driver's door. "Besides, handsome, this is a car, not a broom."

And with that, she pulled away and drove down the road toward Portland.

We stood there watching her go, and I wondered if we would ever see her again. Then Hale and I walked, hand in hand, back to the house that felt less like a home and more like a prison.

Francine

I LEFT THE BOYS to walk home in the afternoon rain. The car hummed past others as I wound my way to the freeway, up the ramp toward Portland. Time was of the essence.

Daniel was in trouble and the clock was ticking. I prayed that my little concoction would be enough to keep Christopher away from them until I returned. I changed lanes and sped past a truck hauling a trailer. My windshield wipers sloshed off the rain thrown up by the Dodge on my left. The road sign on the right advised me that my destination was three hundred miles up the road, so I settled in for the drive.

After meeting Daniel and Hale at the fairgrounds, I'd gone to my boss, Mr. Gunter—a dear, sweet friend of mine—and explained my need to take some time off. I met with him in his trailer filled with furniture and signs for the fair, which was also his office. He greeted me with a smile, as did his wife, Norah, and they ushered me in from the rain.

After brief pleasantries and some of Norah's homemade brownies and coffee, I told him of my need to take some time off work.

Mr. Alan Gunter was in charge of all the booths in the park and knew of my abilities—well, my real abilities, anyway—and my desire to help people. After all, it was I who had helped him when his wife had delved too far into the occult. She'd become fond of talking to a spirit named Lazarus on her Ouija board. Lazarus ended up not being a human spirit after all but actually a lemur, an ancient Roman spirit of mischief and despair. Once summoned, it had caused a bunch of misfortunes and accidents on the midway, and it was only after I confronted it that the spirit detached itself from her and drifted away. The whole affair had been pretty messy, but everyone ended up all right. Except for Lazarus, who'd been banished into the abyss.

From that day forward, whenever I ran across a special case like Daniel's, Mr. Gunter would go and clear my brief absence with the owner.

I didn't need the job for the money. The owners of the carnival were not my bosses in the sense that they held this position over me. I rented space on their midway and paid them a portion of what I made. Having a company to work for that traversed the continent from one end to another made my mission in life easier.

It was a funny sort of arrangement because it's been a funny sort of life. I've a doctorate degree to my name and the finances to not work again and still leave more than enough behind. The carnies kept me company between projects, and it was always nice to use my gifts in the background as we traversed the freeways and backroads of America. Many of the souls I've encountered would have been listed as unsolved murders, suicides, or missing persons.

"Got a job to do, do ya?" Mr. Gunter asked.

"Yes, Alan. It's a case I have to take."

Norah crossed herself.

It was a funny thing how religious people got when they tampered around with things they shouldn't. I didn't mind, however. People make mistakes, and things can change quickly. I explained it would only be for a few days and I would be leaving that night. He promised he would have everything taken care of, and when I came back, my job would be right where I'd left it. Although I would have to travel to California to meet up with them, I told them I understood and took my leave.

Now I was speeding toward Portland. My mind went back to the days when I'd discovered my abilities.

On my thirteenth birthday, I was sitting in the living room with my two older siblings, playing a board game, when Father walked in, proud as a peacock, and handed me a long box with a bright yellow ribbon. I was so excited I tore away the ribbon and opened the box.

Staring back at me was a beautiful porcelain doll cushioned by tissue paper. I could tell just by looking at it that it was incredibly expensive.

"A keepsake, darling. You're old enough to start collecting things you like. I saw you staring at the ones at Hudson's when we went to Detroit during Christmas last year."

I looked at him. "Where did you get this one?"

"From a man I met in Baton Rouge. He had a shop, and when I told him it was your birthday, he said he had just the thing for me. He went into the back of his shop and came out with this, and he told me to give it directly to you."

My mother had come in from the kitchen and stood by her husband as he proudly beamed down at me, hoping to catch my surprise and approval.

Oh, how I hated to disappoint him.

I'd immediately seen a greenish glow emanating from the doll. The sight of it made me sick to my stomach. My two older sisters stood up to see what I had received, and they both fawned over it, telling Daddy how beautiful it was. Yet I refused to touch it, and I wondered who that man he met in Baton Rouge really was.

"What's the matter, baby? Don't you like it?" Daddy's kind eyes looked a little hurt.

I didn't know what to say.

"Answer your father, Francine," Momma scolded, wiping her hands on her apron.

I could feel the power emanating from the doll, and it made my skin crawl. I couldn't bring myself to touch it, not to mention the thought of picking it up…

"Momma, can I talk to you for a second?" I placed the box gently beside me and stood up, grabbed Momma's hand, and led her into an adjacent bedroom.

"What is it, Francine? What has gotten into you?" she asked.

I peeked out from around her, through the doorway, and watched as Daddy picked up the doll to inspect it. My heart broke at that when his shoulders slumped. He had worked long and hard to save up enough money to buy the doll. Still, Momma had to know.

"Momma, I think we need to take that doll to Granny Celine," I whispered. "There's something wrong with it."

"Francine, that's nonsense. You're just thirteen. Wha—?"

She stopped midsentence. Shock registered in her eyes. Without another word, she ran into the living room and snatched the doll away from my sisters. I followed her as she pulled Daddy off to the side to whisper in his ear.

His eyes grew wide, and he nodded vigorously. Not long after, Momma threw the doll into the trunk of our car, and off we sped to my Great-Grand-Mère Celine's house.

***

During segregation, life in Louisiana wasn't great for blacks. To be honest, it was slavery without the clasp of manacles. The chains had become invisible, but the weight of them still stooped the shoulders of those who lived underneath its auspices. However, all folks in town, white or black, gave my family a wide berth, especially my great-grandmother Celine Decoudreau, our family matriarch. She was deeply respected by those who knew her and deeply feared by those who had mistakenly crossed her family in some way.

Rumors abounded, the whispers of old women as they sat on their porch swings, gossiping about things they knew nothing of. One of the most predominant stories was that Granny Celine practiced voodoo. I'd asked her about it once when we had stopped over for a visit. I expected to get a rap on the knuckles from her cane, but she just cackled, delighted with the question.

"No, child, voodoo is bad mojo. I am a Christian woman. I just use the abilities that God gave me. We Decoudreau women are gifted," she said as she happily rocked in her chair, her rheumy gaze fixed on me. "You'll see."

That evening, when my mother pulled up in front of her house, Granny was already waiting for us on her porch, rocking away as we got out and walked up. Mother retrieved the package from the trunk, took me by the hand, and marched me up the sidewalk.

Granny stopped rocking, grabbed her cane, and pointed it at Momma. "You leave that package there on the ground, young lady. Do not bring that filth onto my porch."

We both stopped dead in our tracks and looked at each other. Mother simply threw the package on the ground and absently wiped her hands on her coat. I gasped and looked at Granny with wide eyes. She knew there was something wrong with it, just as I did.

"Bring that baby to me, Delphine."

Momma looked down at me, swallowed hard, and ushered me forward again. I walked up to Granny's porch as I had done a thousand times before, but now my knees shook. Momma followed close behind, wringing her hands.

Granny barked at her, "Calm down, girl!"

The old woman grabbed my hands in hers and closed her eyes. Her creased face, brown and soft with age, became still for a second as she ceased rocking. I was terrified of what she was going to tell me, but I dared not say so—her cane wasn't that far away.

Breathless moments passed as both Momma and I waited. Finally, a bright smile broke out on her face and she let my hands go. She turned her head to Momma. "Has her period started?"

"Momma..."

"That doll has Cunja. A curse, Delphine, and she saw it! Has she started?"

Momma nodded. It was true; I'd started a month earlier.

Grand-Mère sat back in her rocking chair, nodding. "She is of age now, Delphine. She is a woman. And yes, she has the touch."

The years I'd traversed from that point in my life came back to me in a slow narrative as I made my way through the state. It was a precious thing, something I was proud of. The grandmother I'd feared my whole young life became a teacher and a friend. A confidante. As my powers—for that was what they were—matured, her guidance was strict but not unkind. She taught me about my family, who came from the western shores of Africa and the Caribbean on one side, another side from France, and the final part was Native American.

I had begun to see shadows move. Spirits pressed against the veil that separates life and death. I saw colors hovering above people, their auras in different shades and hues. I saw illness in some and death close by in others. My grandmother taught me small charms, potions, minor magic that would keep me safe from the world. She tempered my curiosity with evening Christian prayers and the saying of the Rosary.

My family wasn't particularly religious, so I inquired about the prayers Granny said in the evenings.

She said, "There are trails of people who've lost their minds when they walked in between worlds, Franny. God has kept me steady throughout my life. Never use your power for personal gain, never use it for vanity or to ensnare a lover. Ever.

"Your blood runs hot, with tribal blood as old as life itself. You are the daughter of the four corners of this earth, and in your blood you carry the memories of these people. That is where your powers come from: the old ways. And if you aren't careful, that heat can overwhelm you."

"How do I keep myself under control?"

My grandmother stared out into her yard. The sun was beginning to go down, and she was silent for a while. "You make yourself a servant of man. You help them. You help those who wander too close to the veil. When, without your help, they would step perilously into the void, you step in."

"Like Dr. King says?"

She turned her white eyes toward me and regarded me silently. "Yes, my dear. Just like Dr. King says."

I chewed on that for a little while. How could I help people? Who would ask for it? When would it be time? The country we lived in was flirting with madness. Church bombings, lynchings, fire bombings, and cross burnings were happening all across the country as America was caught up in the throes of civil discord.

Creatures lurked in the distance behind crowds of cops and dogs. White people screamed at those walking into newly desegregated schools, creatures of shadow that scared even my grandmother.

"Demons," she said and crossed herself.

"Like in the Bible?"

She nodded. "The very same."

"What are they doing here?"

She inhaled slowly. "Eating. They feed off this: the discord, fear, and hate."

Even though the fear was of certain whites, those Celine referred to as "po' white trash," who hurt people who looked like me, there were "white folks," those marching arm in arm with people who looked like me. It was the po' white trash we had to watch out for.

Grand-Mère Celine had been born into slavery, raised on a sugarcane plantation south of Baton Rouge, and freed after the Civil War. She'd married my grandfather Laurent Dauphin, but she'd never taken his last name, and he died after my mother and Uncle Pierre were born. She was a Decoudreau woman, and she didn't scare easily.

But these demons scared her.

"Those people don't understand what they're doing. The monsters their hate is feeding are slowly eating them away."

"Are they what I help keep people safe from?"

"These things, and others like them. Can you handle that, chère? Your life will be a lot different than perhaps the one you had planned for y'self."

"If there are things out there in the dark waiting to take people away, then yes. I can handle it."

Celine beamed with pride and looked away for a moment. Uncle Pierre winked at me.

"How do I help people? Will they ask me for it?"

Celine looked over at Uncle Pierre.

Daddy didn't like him. Referred to him disgustedly as "the queer" when he was talking about him to Momma. I once asked Daddy what queer *meant, and he told me I was too young to understand. But Momma pulled me aside one day when I'd told her Pierre and*

I had gone to run errands for Celine and I'd had fun. We'd stopped at the soda shop, and he'd bought me a chocolate shake that I'd sipped on while he played the jukebox.

Momma wanted to know where we went and how long we'd been gone. I'd told her it hadn't been more than a couple of hours.

"Don't tell your father."

I shook my head. "Why not?"

Momma pursed her lips and didn't say a word. Impatient with her, I reached forward, touched her hand, and looked her directly in the eye. An image flashed in front of my mind of Pierre kissing another man, and I was taken aback. But there was something in Pierre's eyes when he looked at this other man that wasn't dissimilar to what I saw when Daddy kissed Momma. While the image was confusing, and a memory Momma had experienced perhaps by walking in on them, I didn't understand what was wrong...

Except for the man he was kissing was white. That was the only real unusual thing I could put my finger on.

Momma was instantly angry and slapped my hand away. "I don't ever want you doing that to me," she spat.

"Your mother does it all the time! As a matter of fact, Pierre, her, and I all have conversations without saying a word."

Momma whirled around with her hand up as if to slap me. I backed up two steps and shook my head as anger bubbled up inside me. "That would be a terrible idea."

Momma's jaw dropped and she too stepped back.

I was packed up once again—this time with all my belongings—and delivered to Celine's front door. When it opened, Celine ordered me and Uncle Pierre to take my stuff back to the room she'd made up for me even before I showed up. From the back of the house, I could hear my father yelling at her and Celine shouting right back. And as I stood there on trembling legs and completely dissolved into tears, Uncle Pierre hugged me and wiped my face.

"Ma chère, do not cry. You are special. Unique. And they are not. They do not understand what it's like to be you."

I wiped my eyes with the backs of my hands and looked up at him. He was handsome. Devastatingly gorgeous now that I really

thought about it. He was what Momma referred to as "high yellow,"
and even though I'd seen handsome men in my life, both black and
white, he was ethereal. Beautiful would be the appropriate word.
Uncle Pierre always dressed his finest, and now that I knew what I
knew, I watched when we went out. Both men and women, black,
white, Hispanic, and otherwise, would stop and look at him. He
knew it too.

"Momma has a memory of you. You're different as well.
Different like me and Celine, but different in your own right. True?"

He smirked a little. "You saw that, did you?"

I nodded as he knelt down in front of me. "Let me give you a
little bit of advice, Franny. Peeking into people's minds sometimes
upsets them. And sometimes you'll find that when you do it, you
see things that upset you. Things you wished you'd never known. I
learned that from a young age. Only look in on what you've been
given permission to look in on."

I nodded. "Who was that man? Do you love him?"

Pierre smiled sadly and placed his hand on my cheek. "One day,
Francine, I'll tell you all about it. But let's wait till you're a little
older, huh?"

"Okay."

Now that we were back on the porch, I saw the silent exchange
between Pierre and Grand-Mère Celine, a conversation I wasn't
privy to. Eventually, Pierre stood up and walked in the house.
Grand-Mère stayed quiet until he returned and announced that
everything was ready. Then she stood slowly and motioned for me
to follow her.

I did. And was formally introduced to the book I would carry
after she passed away.

Mémoires des spectres humains was its title when the book was
in her possession. Once it became mine, the cover changed itself
to read *Memoirs of the Human Wraiths*.

It was there, in the room where the book was kept under lock
and key, that I learned of our legacy. And it was then, once she

explained to me the story of how we came to be, who had created the book, and why, that the real training began.

The years had flown by. From the tumult of the civil rights movement, through the women's revolution of the seventies, the rise of the Moral Majority in the eighties, the Clinton era, and then the events of 9/11 during the Bush presidency, I had worked behind the scenes to protect people from the dark.

I was old. I didn't look it, but that didn't matter. I felt it, deep inside me, and despite the book's power, I would one day have to pass it on. Despite having more lovers than I could count, none produced children, as the doctors said I was never to have them. So I would have to pick a successor.

My mind drifted back to Hale and Daniel. Neither of them was suitable. Neither had enough psychic ability to be trained to use and protect this book. They were just two more faces in the long line of people I worked to protect. Two more clients. Two more souls in over their heads.

I thought about the revenant, then. The creature held captive by the sins of his father.

I had to hurry. I just prayed they would be safe until I returned.

Hale

T HE ENTIRE SITUATION was surreal, ethereal. The ground where we had sat felt like holy ground of some sort. I had never experienced that in any way, shape, or form in my life. I thought I'd seen beautiful things—Oregon itself was spectacularly breathtaking from one end of the state to the other. But this had been different.

Francine's image and the way she dressed, which had been appropriate for the carnival, took on a completely different air. What had been gaudy and loud became serenely appropriate in the midst of the sun-dappled wood. She looked like the high priestess of some forgotten religion.

But it didn't mean I wasn't struggling with what was happening.

And then there were the wolves. Their predatory beauty was something to behold at a distance. Their song something that caused my heart to stop in my chest. But to see three of them up close like that, within touching distance...

But they weren't like other wolves.

No. They'd been ghosts. Or wolves possessed by ghosts.

It was making my head hurt.

"Should we tell Carol about all of this?" I asked as we stomped back through the woods.

"Tell her what? That unless I get rid of her psychopathic-ghost-killer-uncle-revenant thingy, when she dies she's doomed to walk the grounds with her brother and parents until I die and forget them?"

"A simple no would have been sufficient."

Danny stopped in his tracks, turned to look at me, and winced. "I am so sorry. You're right. This whole thing has me freaked out."

"I know what you mean."

"Thank you for standing by me. I mean that, Hale. Most guys would have cut and run after I snotted all over you in the barn the first day we met."

"Second day, and you didn't 'snot all over me.' You were vulnerable. You needed a moment, and I was glad I was there." I cupped his face in my hands. "I still am."

"Thank you."

I kissed him gently and wrapped an arm around his waist as we continued on.

As a police officer, I have arrested drug dealers, murderers, and rapists, and stood up for the citizens of Emerson in every legal capacity I could. Now Danny was about to take on a dead man who was trying to destroy him and his family, and I felt powerless. Nothing in my training, my years on the force, could prepare me for something like that, but as I looked at Danny, his jaw set, his muscles tense, and his eyes hot, I knew that, no matter what, we were walking head-on into the supernatural.

I had always considered myself a practical man until I met Danny. Along with changing my life, he had changed my mind. I was a student of science. Sure, I'd heard stories about the house, had always gotten weird feelings there, and even warned Danny in the beginning when he asked. But never had anything manifested itself to this degree.

The stories that were told to me as a child around a campfire, or that I'd read in books, now dripped off the pages and ran rampant in Timber Manor. With the affirmation from Francine that there was life existing in the seen and the unseen, my worldview, my life view, and my spiritual view were in a state of flux. I didn't know what to think about it all, but I knew one thing: whatever happened, I'd stand with Danny.

His ability to accept these things staggered me and left me in awe. His fierce determination, his loyalty to his family, his willingness to put his life on the line to save his father's very soul swelled my chest and made me very proud of him. So many things could go wrong in this endeavor; so much could fall apart. I could lose Danny, but there was no talking him out of what he was about to do. His mind was made up, and who was I to interfere?

For the first time, I realized what loss of control felt like. But I should have known it would come to this. For when you fall in love, what control do you have, anyway? What force is more capable than love to build a man or break him? What could make him walk proudly among his peers, fearless in their eyes, or make him crawl broken, alone, and confused?

You're waxing poetic again, I thought to myself.

Yeah, well, if you don't like it, you can fuck right off. Do not pass Go and do not collect two hundred dollars.

The feeling in my heart was exquisite. I both adored and feared the man walking next to me. I would walk straight into hell with him. And I might be forced to crawl out alone.

It was that in-between feeling, that uncertainty, that kept my pulse up and, to be honest, was making me extraordinarily horny. I wanted him. I wanted him here in the middle of nothing. I wanted him in the bed. I wanted to bury myself in him and make him feel both the pleasure and the pain that I felt. And I wanted him to give it back to me. I wanted to make him feel my love, and I wanted to feel his.

I could feel my face heat as the thought embarrassed me.

Danny looked over, moved his hand down to my ass, and gave it a pat.

We walked back up from the creek bed alone. The sun, which had come out temporarily to soak us in its golden light, was now gone behind a steel-gray sky. The wind had picked back up again, and we ducked low, moving swiftly toward the house. We were still soaked to the bone, and I was becoming a wee bit chilly when we finally reached the back door of the house.

It was quiet. I silently thanked God for that—an entity I'd never really taken too much stock in, but now, who knows?

We quietly went up the stairs to Danny's bedroom and slipped into a hot shower together. The water heated our bodies as we soaped up and rinsed off.

When we went back into the bedroom, we made love, slow and easy. This time I gave it up.

"Are you sure?" Danny asked as I rolled him on top and opened my legs for him.

"It's been a long time…"

He reached for the lube and stretched me slowly before he slipped himself in. And with slow, deliberate thrusts, he moved. His body tensed and relaxed, tensed and relaxed as he grabbed for the headboard with one hand and drew my head up off the pillow to kiss him. There was pleasure and there was pain, both of which rolled through my body as the thunder rolled through the countryside. With each thrust of his hips, I pushed back.

I grasped my cock in one hand to keep from coming too soon, and with the other hand held on to his ass and squeezed it. "Damn, boy, you feel good," I grunted as his pace picked up.

His eyes rolled. "Not as good as this feels."

"Do you like that?"

"Yeah."

"Is it tight for you?"

"So good, baby," he said, looking down at me.

Then he did something that surprised me: he grabbed my legs, opened them up into a V shape, and really began to drive it home. The molten heat of friction caused my eyes to roll back in my head. I began to jerk myself off.

"Oh baby…" he moaned.

I opened my eyes and with a grunt sat up on my elbows, and we locked eyes. Sweat was pouring down my face. "Give it to me, Danny. Everything. Your pain. Your fear. Don't hold back. I can take it."

He stilled for a second before resuming, then let go of my left leg as his hand went behind my head and cradled it. "You can take it?"

"Every bit of it," I grunted back.

He was in control. He was the one with the power. I had to trust it. Trust him.

"Yeah?"

"Yeah."

His gaze softened. "I love you."

"I love you," I panted.

"I'm not going to last…"

"Let go."

I worked myself over in a frenzy, attempting to catch up to him. Pleasure rippled through me in wave upon wave as I felt the orgasm coming on.

Danny was grunting now, moving faster, more erratically, and with a shout, we both came. His back arched as he thrust himself inside, and I grabbed the covers. I shot all over my chest. The world tilted and spun, and I fell back exhausted onto the bed.

Daniel slid out and away and collapsed next to me, breathing as heavily as I was. He leaned up on his elbows and kissed my lips and looked at me. I couldn't move. He reached up and brushed the hair out of my eyes. "What inspired that?"

I looked away for a moment, out into the night sky, before returning my gaze to him. "I needed to be vulnerable," I admitted quietly.

I felt uncertain for a moment as Danny's eyes went wide. Then understanding passed through them; he smiled gently and kissed me again. "Hey. Be vulnerable with me any time you like."

Danny pulled the blankets up and wrapped us both in them before turning me over on my side. He slid up next to me and wrapped his arm around me.

I've always been the holder in the relationships I'd had. The top, so to speak. But as my eyes grew heavy and the miles I'd put on these tires just from today crashed into me like a wave on a shore, I quickly slipped into the world of dreams.

I went easily, willingly, knowing I'd been rocked safe in the arms of love.

It

3:00 a.m.

DEEP IN THE bowels of the house, darkness deepened to a midnight black. Shadows came alive. Like the rush of a river, each darkened corner shot blackness out from itself and down. From behind chairs, radiators, and down walls, the dark mass bolted through the corridor, heading to the part of the house where Danny had heard the knocking.

Had anyone been in the way, they would have been overtaken by the darkness, and just as a riptide may carry someone out to sea, this pit of nothing would have taken their soul far from the mortal world. But now the shadow gathered, rose up, and with a *slam* crashed into the wall below the contractors' plaster fix.

With a peal as loud as thunder, the wall tore itself from baseboard to crown molding. A crack formed in the center. The shadows split apart as ice-cold air burst forth and flooded the corridor. The frigid air and the shadows converged on each other, intertwining and writhing in some profane act as the lights in the hallway flickered on.

The light surged until one by one the bulbs began to explode in their sconces, sending flames licking upward before fading out in a whoosh of air.

The creature that was once Christopher rose up out of the shadows and the freezing atmosphere.

Outside, the wolves howled relentlessly.

"She wants to be rid of me," the revenant said as It landed solidly on Its feet.

The darkness spread around those feet as if lying prostrate before its master.

"We can't have that, now, can we?" It said as power coursed through It.

The woman's presence did make him stronger. A hell of a lot stronger than she'd known. "And she left them all alone…"

Closer to the house, the wolves howled futilely outside. Closer, but too far away.

Christopher laughed. "That's right, Michael. She left your boy alooooooooone. We should do something about that."

And just as quickly as It appeared, the white-haired, white-faced devil melted back into the shadows.

Hale

I WOKE WITH A start. But I wasn't sure what had startled me. A noise?

I listened closely, sitting up in bed, my heart pounding in my ears. Outside, the wolves were howling repeatedly, and I wondered if that hadn't been it. Wiping the sleep from my eyes, I sat up for a moment and looked over at Danny, sleeping with his arm thrown over his eyes.

He was snoring happily away. I couldn't help but smile. Finally content that I hadn't heard anything, I lay back down. Danny rolled over and murmured in his sleep, and I closed my arms around him. His head was resting on my chest now, his hand over my heart. My eyes started to grow heavy as I ran my fingers up and down his back.

Thump!

My eyes shot open, and I held my breath for a second. Something was wrong. The air in the room felt different, and my nerves were wide-awake.

Thump!

The noise came from the hallway. I slid out of bed, gently so as not to wake Danny, and reached for my pajama bottoms. I put them on and slowly walked to the door.

Thump!

It sounded like footsteps, one after another, like someone stomping down the corridor.

Thump!

I reached for the door handle and quietly opened it, peering out of the crack between the door and the jamb. The hallway was dark save for the dim lights along the wall.

I opened the door farther, struggling to calm my breathing as the hairs on the back of my neck stood up. I couldn't see anything moving at all, so I stepped out a bit farther.

Nothing is out there, I thought to myself.

I padded down into the hallway, walking down toward the foyer. The grandfather clock ticked and tocked itself along. The air in the house was chilly, and gooseflesh formed on my arms. My bare feet were being tortured as I stepped out onto the marble landing near the stairs, but I saw nothing.

Thump!

I jumped and backed up to the wall. It was coming from behind me, down at the other end of the hall. I stared down there and saw nothing but darkness.

Wait, that wasn't right...it was *blackness.* Solid. I couldn't see anything beyond a certain point, and the longer I looked, the more the darkness seemed to writhe as if it were alive.

Thump!

It was coming closer.

Thump! Thump!

Then I realized I'd left the bedroom door open. *Oh my God,* Danny!

I took off running toward the door, and the mysterious footfalls did the same, approaching the door from the other end of the hallway.

Thump!-Thump!-Thump!

I reached the door first and dove inside, throwing it shut behind me. I landed on the carpet, rolled, and braced my feet against the door. Something hit the wood with a powerful *boom!* that vibrated up my legs from the sheer force.

"Hale. What the fu—?"

Danny had sat up in bed, but he stopped when he heard the footfalls retreating back down the hallway.

Thump! Thump! Thump!

I was sweating; the stench of my fear filled my nostrils. Breathing heavily, I stood up on shaky legs and turned to look at a much-disheveled, wide-eyed Danny.

"Was it him?" he asked.

I swallowed hard and nodded. "He was trying to lure me out of here so he could come in."

It almost worked.

I scolded myself silently for being that stupid. Christopher wanted Danny, and he needed to get me out of the way as he had done to Carol's fiancé. He wanted them for his playthings the way a cat longs for a mouse. I locked the door behind me and walked over to our clothes, which lay discarded on the floor. Rummaging through pockets, I brought out both sachets, handed one to Danny, and placed the other under my pillow.

The last thing I needed was Danny having a dream and going wandering through the house. It killed me that I had to go to work in the morning, but my responsibilities had to be taken care of, even if that meant leaving Danny.

"Oh my God." Danny jumped out of the bed. He virtually threw his clothes on.

"What?"

"Hale!"

"What!"

"*Carol!*"

He ran out of the door.

Carol

THE NOISES UPSTAIRS woke me with a start, and before I got out of bed, it began to shake.

I leaped out, my knees threatening to buckle underneath me, and charged for the door. It wouldn't budge.

The air around me was thick and oppressive, and as I turned back to stare at my bed—now literally jumping up and down on the floor as if a wild animal were underneath it—I heard a scream and realized it was me.

I pinned myself against the door as the bed came to a rest, but whatever was happening wasn't over yet. As a tsunami gathers up the ocean to throw it against the shore, so was the atmosphere in my room. Suddenly pictures all around me flew off walls, the glass shattered in their frames, and I rushed to the center of the room. I pulled on the chain of the light overhead. The room was momentarily cast in the bulb's luminescence before it popped and shattered as both bulb and fixture tore away from the wall and rained down on the room.

I tried the door again, frantic.

This time it swung open, sending me flailing back into the mess of broken glass toward...toward...

I grabbed the bedframe and kept myself from moving, the muscles in my arms straining under the pressure of the hurricane that had just erupted. *It* was here; he was here. And with that thought, I pushed myself forward as hard as I could, stumbled, and hit the wall outside my room with my full weight. I spun around to see glass fragments, dust, and broken pieces of masonry start to form into a person.

My God, those eyes!

I screamed again and stumbled down the hallway. My nightgown tried to hinder my strides, and I gathered it at the sides and lifted it up to free my legs and feet, which were bleeding.

"Get away from me, Christopher! Get away!"

Wolves howled outside, their cries so loud it sounded like they were at the front door. As I shot through the hallway into the foyer, I wasn't the least bit surprised to find a wolf standing near the glass window, barking and leaping at it.

"Carol... Carol"—the monster behind me whispered my name—"come play with me, Carol."

The blood in my veins turned to ice water, and I spun to run upstairs.

"Daniel! Daniel! It's him! Daniel!" I screamed as I took the stairs one at a time. Almost at the top now, my feet cut, bleeding, and painful, my stomach burning where the cancer had begun to spread—but I had never in my life wanted to live so badly.

"Carol! Carol!"

I could hear Daniel's and Hale's footfalls as they rushed to me. But it was too late.

To my horror, the black mass emerged from the downstairs hallway, took flight, and cut me off from reaching the boys, who had come into view. The look on Hale's face was one of terror; Danny's was rage. I turned my head up to look at the beast standing in front of me.

His black eyes were pools of death and destruction, his body misshapen, his fingers disgustingly elongated. He looked like Death itself.

"Stay away from her, you son of a bitch!" Danny bellowed, trying to struggle out of Hale's grip on him. "Stay away from her! Carol! Run, goddammit, run!"

The fear and anger in his face broke my heart, and I would have done what he asked, but it was too late. The creature turned its head to them and, with a laugh, reached out and pushed me backward.

"*Nooooo!*" I heard Daniel scream as I fell.

I hit the marble stairs. First, my back broke. Inside, my ribs punctured a lung. Then I rolled, and my leg broke from the cancer that had hollowed me out.

And finally, my neck snapped.

The last thing I knew before merciful darkness consumed me was the oil painting of my parents at the top of the stairs, smiling down.

Outside, the wolves still howled.

Daniel

"No!" MY VOICE cracked as I struggled to get Hale's arms from around me.

We stumbled to the floor in a tangled heap as the figure floating above the head of the stairs faded into nothingness. I felt like I was losing my mind. The smile on its face was mocking, and its dead eyes regarded me with hatred and disdain.

She's dead. She's dead. Oh God.

I bucked underneath Hale's weight, calling out her name. "Carol! Carol! Goddammit, let me go! Carol!" I sobbed and finally broke free from his restraint and was up on my feet. I turned the corner to head down the stairs and got about halfway before I saw her body lying lifeless and broken. Her eyes were staring up at me, past me, to the wall behind, but there was no light in them; her neck was angled awkwardly. I rushed forward and came to rest next to her.

"Don't touch her, Danny," Hale said.

He finally made it down, huffing and puffing, and pulled me away. Her hair was tied up in a bun, black-and-gray, her silver cross hung from her neck off to the side, and I began to shake. Hale knelt and wrapped his arms around me to shield me from the sight, but I fought him off and stood up.

"Why did you stop me? I could have—why did you stop me!" I demanded, fists clenched.

"You could have what? Ended up like her? Danny, no. There was nothing you could do. We were too late," he said calmly. The sorrow in his gaze, however, broke my heart. "Jesus, we have to get you out of here," Hale said, standing up. He walked over to the phone on the table and picked up the receiver. Hale dialed what I assumed was the police and reported the incident. He gave his badge number and asked for the morgue to send someone out. I had a sense of déjà vu with this and groaned, putting my head in my hands. He hung up the phone.

"Call Thomas and Anita. Let them know what's happening," I said brokenly.

He nodded and picked up the receiver again as I stood up, walked to the front door, and opened it. Standing outside in the rain, about a hundred yards away near the tree line, were the wolves.

Four of them.

They turned and walked back into the trees. I sighed, leaning against the doorframe. Thunder rolled and lightning danced on the horizon. The smell of rain was heavy in the air.

"They're on their way. Anita was so distraught she dropped the phone twice. Thomas had to finish the conversation." Hale's voice made me jump. "Sorry."

"It's okay. I think with all the energy Christopher just used, the house will be quiet for a while."

"Maybe, but I am not going to take that risk. Until we come back to...to—well, you know—I don't want you in here by yourself," he said, turning me toward him. "You're going to come and stay with me."

I nodded, thinking about what all had to be done: funeral arrangements, calling a minister... *And here we go again. I'm getting to be a pro with this*, I thought.

"This is two deaths in less than six months, Hale. How do we explain this?"

I looked past Carol's broken body on the floor toward her bedroom. Bloody footprints led down the hallway to her room. I walked alongside them, making sure to avoid disturbing anything that could be evidence. I flipped on the hallway light and peered inside.

It was a disaster. Her bed was torn apart; so was all her furniture. It looked like someone in a state of rage had destroyed the room.

Someone did, I reminded myself. *Christopher.*

Hale whistled low, opening the door farther. Glass and other debris were piled up in the center of the room, and the light fixture above it hung by a few exposed wires, dark and cold.

I shivered as I thought about Carol's last few moments of life. She must have been so afraid. We backed out of the room. Red-and-blue flashing lights were coming up the driveway now, followed by the whine of an ambulance siren. Hale instructed me to go with him outside, to look as bereaved as possible, and he would handle the rest. I didn't have to act at all. My heart was broken; I'd just lost the last remaining family member I had. I was the last Donnelly alive.

I glanced over at the clock, and it read 3:20 a.m. Before I stepped out the door, it occurred to me that all of this had happened approximately at 3:00 a.m....the Witching Hour.

Hale

DANNY WAS ASLEEP in the passenger seat of the truck as I drove down to Emerson. My nerves were shot.

I should have packed them both up and left with them. Brought them to my house. I should have made sure they were safe. Carol's dead. Carol's dead. It's my fault.

I steered the car with my left hand and wiped the tears away with the right.

She would be alive now.

I was sick to my stomach. I had known her for years. She'd been very kind to my father and me. Always there when we wanted to talk, invited us in for supper when Mom was out of town. She'd been like an aunt to me.

How could I have been so careless?

I looked over at Danny, whose head was resting against the driver's side window.

How can I let him go through with this? Francine said we would be all right. She said we should have time before she got back.

The officer who had shown up took my statement as well as Danny's and photographed the scene.

"Bad luck here, huh, Hale?" he asked as he snapped pictures on his camera.

"You can say that again," I replied cautiously.

"Terrible thing for someone to die like this. Especially someone who has so much money. Your friend must be taking this hard," he said suspiciously.

"Get off it, Roger. He didn't kill his aunt. There's no motive. He'd already signed all the paperwork making him sole owner of this house, and he has access to everything Carol did. He would gain nothing from her death," I said flatly.

The deputy sniffed his reply and kept shooting pictures.

Finally, the coroner lifted Carol's broken body and put her on a stretcher that had been lined with a bag. He zipped the woman in it and rolled her out into the night past Danny, who looked like he was going to be sick, and Anita, who cried softly into the arms of her husband, Thomas.

"Well, perhaps he didn't. So, you're saying it was an accident?" Roger asked, putting away his camera.

"Yes. There is no other explanation for it, other than her having cancer. I think she freaked out about it tonight. She knew it was terminal. It somehow struck her, and she just lost it. She slipped on her own bloody feet," I said, feeling guilty for lying about the poor woman they'd just rolled out, the woman I had known most of my life.

Yet I couldn't tell him that the ghost of her brother had decided to end her life. I just thanked God in heaven that she hadn't suffered—not through this, not through the cancer.

"Alrighty, then. I'll go back to the station and start writing this up. Thanks for the extra paperwork tonight," Roger said and headed out the door. "See ya in the morning."

"See ya." I stepped outside with them and Danny, who looked like a ghost himself, wrapped in a blanket to shield him from the cold.

Anita and Thomas were standing by his side. I looked at Anita.

"I know how close you two were. I am so sorry," I said.

"It was him, wasn't it?" she asked. "Christopher. It was him that did this to her."

"Yeah, it was," I admitted.

She nodded and started to cry again.

Her husband put his arm around his frail wife's shoulders. He looked worn and drawn, tired and sad all at the same time. He spoke slowly. "I knew that boy had something wrong with him about the time he learned to speak. Now, all these years later, he still has control over this family and this house. It's a damn shame." His voice was husky with age and emotion.

"I want you two to get a hotel room for the time being. It's not safe anymore on these grounds," I ordered.

Thomas nodded. "I already have a bag in the car."

"It won't be dangerous here for long" came the reply from Danny.

Anita and Thomas looked confused, but I simply waved it off. I turned and went inside to collect Danny's clothing and a few of my personal items, threw them in a bag, grabbed my truck keys and Danny's house keys, and rejoined the group near the entrance. I explained that Danny would be staying with me and that no one should be in the house alone for a while. Anita nodded and promised me she wouldn't return until Danny did.

With that, we parted ways. Danny climbed into the passenger seat, and I climbed into the driver's side, started her up, and followed Anita and Thomas down the driveway into the night.

Danny fell fast asleep next to me, leaning his head against the window of the truck. I'd retrieved the sachets from underneath our pillows, and while Danny slept, I slid one into his coat pocket.

As I pulled into the driveway, I turned off my headlights and looked over at his sleeping form. The days ahead of us were going to be rough, and my heart went out to him. Raindrops fell lightly on the windshield of the truck and coated the glass, distorting visibility and making everything outside look odd and misshapen. That was what this new world felt like to me: everything out of sync and distorted, and what was once familiar wasn't any longer. The only anchor I had was snoring softly as he fogged up the window.

"I love you so much, Daniel. I'll die to keep you safe," I said.

I killed the ignition and sat there for a moment. Already, the sky was starting to lighten. Work was going to suck today, but I wanted Danny to sleep in, safe and sound in my bed.

I made a mental note to call my mother as soon as it was daylight and have her come and check in on him.

Sometimes that anchor was all you had to hold on to. I woke him up, got him out, and walked him up the steps. Then I opened the door and shut it behind us.

Francine

B Y THE TIME I reached my destination, the shop was closed, so I took a motel room close by and slept that night, fitfully, my dreams filled with dread and loathing.

I woke up at around three in the morning after a nightmare about the death of a woman. Daniel and Hale had been in the dream, and I feared the worst. I reached out my mind and touched Daniel's. There I felt grief, and my heart broke for the poor boy. I was pleased, however, to discover his mate had the good sense to get him out of that house, and so I was able to fall back asleep before the sun came up.

The next morning dawned sunny and cool, and I checked the book to make sure I'd been correct and not just dreaming.

There it was in black and white. I sighed and shook my head before checking out of the motel room.

I drove down to the storefront of Crystals, Herbs, and Sage and let myself in.

The doorbell jingled, announcing my entrance as I stepped inside. The smells of incense, musty books, and coffee greeted me, and I smiled.

Thank God for capitalism.

I let my gaze roam around the room at bookshelves filled with every imaginable tome dedicated to the arts of herbology and magic. Littered around the store were couches and little bistro tables where couples sat and drank coffee and visited with each other. I hadn't taken two steps inside when a familiar voice called out from the back room behind the counter, and then her footfalls approached.

"Welcome to Crystals, Herbs, and—Franny!"

The middle-aged woman came rushing out from behind the counter, her blonde-and-white hair pinned haphazardly on her head. Marybeth Lawrence, a dear friend of mine these many years, wrapped her arms around me, and I wrapped mine around her. She stepped back, her lovely heart-shaped face flushed with happiness.

Marybeth and I had a long history that spanned more than thirty years.

"How are you, my darling? What a surprise!"

"I'm good, Marybeth. You look amazing." Her aura, a bright orange, glowed healthily about her, and I smiled.

"Bullshit. I'm getting old. But you, Francine, I swear you haven't aged a day. It's that Creole blood, I'm sure. Come in, come in! Sam, Francine is here!" She guided me to a small table in front of her counter.

Marybeth's professor husband, Sam, came out of the back room, his gray hair a mess and bifocals perched on the end of his nose. He came out from behind the counter and embraced me, smelling of pipe tobacco and cologne.

"Hello, Sam. It's good to see you," I said.

Sam was a great guy. I had once objected to Marybeth dating him since he was a literature professor, afraid he would always be Romeo searching for his next Juliet. I didn't want her to be Juliet number thirty-three. But I discovered he broke the stereotype of the ascot-wearing bard and was actually a decent human being.

"Same here, Franny. How are you?" he asked.

His aura was bright blue and just as healthy as his wife's. I said a silent prayer of thanks for my two friends. "Busy these days. The store looks great." I had met them while I had been attending Georgetown University, where I had saved Marybeth's life.

Sam was a young professor then—an adjunct, if I remember correctly—and Marybeth was a major in women's studies and liberal arts. I recognized her aura before I ever said hello. She was a daughter of nature: a Wiccan. A day walker. She and I hit it off immediately, and the three of us—Marybeth, Sam, and I— became fast friends. She was a gifted herbologist and a natural potion creator, and she sold her own creations to the student population for a little bit of cash.

"I really love your hair. It's groovy," Marybeth said as she peered over her armload of books.

She was dressed in an olive-green, flowery skirt and white blouse. Her thick-rimmed glasses perched on her delicate nose. A spattering of freckles wound their way underneath the glasses to alight upon her slightly rosy cheeks. Her auburn hair, thick and curly, flowed like waves down to her shoulder.

The hair she was talking about framed my face like a halo. I was in the midst of my rebellious streak and had adorned it with gold coins. I knew I could do both: save the world from its darkest elements and be a liberated woman.

The seventies were in full swing. Women were now marching in their own revolution, and here I was. Far away from the Deep South and the shadows of Jim Crow, far from my family and the mysticism that surrounded that part of the country.

I stood in one of the most prestigious schools in the country, in Washington, DC, and I had every right to be where I was. The scholarships from the NAACP—the National Association for the Advancement of Colored People—the United Negro College Fund, and the National Urban League didn't hurt either. I was happy to be away. Happy to be gone from the shadow world I'd walked in while my Grand-Mère had been alive, to walk in the light of day in sunlight and reason. And I was there to grasp reason by the ears and hang on as tight as I could.

I stared at this little mouse of a child, a foot and a half shorter than my nearly six-foot frame, her aura as orange as the freckles on her face. I also sensed about her some of the same gifts I had. She was psychic. The first one outside of my family whom I'd ever met.

Laughing, I said, "Of all the things you could have said to me when you walked up, it was my hair that won out?"

She blushed a deep scarlet and buried her face a little in her books. "Forgive me. I've never met anyone like me before."

So she *is* aware.

"What gifts do you possess?" I whispered to her.

My curiosity was overwhelming my common sense not to talk about these things in public, and I couldn't help myself. Grand-

Mère hadn't mentioned what I should do if I ever met someone else like me. I mean, I always knew they'd be out there, but I didn't know it would be in the form of a petite white girl from Maryland.

"From what I've gathered, I'm a clairsentient—I know things by touching them. I can feel emotions."

"From what you've gathered…?"

"What I've researched, I mean."

"You mean you've had no formal training?"

She perked up at that. "You've been trained?"

"Well, yes. My grandmother taught me."

"Oh, that must have been nice. A grandmother…"

Before I even learned her name, I learned she had been orphaned at birth and raised in an orphanage. She'd hidden all her talents since a young age.

Marybeth and I went to a local pub and talked the night away. She was the first friend I'd met in a world I was boldly walking into but deathly afraid of.

We became fast friends, and then sisters.

"Thank you," Sam said.

Marybeth served us coffee and pastries and sat down next to me. We spent a few minutes catching up, but the urgency of why I was there took over the conversation. I hated bringing *him* up, as it would destroy the festive mood, but I had no other choice.

"Marybeth, do you remember Nathan?" I asked tentatively.

Her eyes widened with shock at the sudden shift in our conversation, then darkened as she set her jaw. "Yes, I remember him," she said coolly.

I knew this was an incredibly sore subject for her.

"Wasn't he the guy who—?" Sam started and stopped as Marybeth rapidly nodded. He exhaled a deep "Oh my…" took off his glasses, and started wiping the lenses.

"Well, I have a situation."

"Another werewolf." She'd gone slightly pale.

I shook my head fervently. "No, not this time. A young man by the name of Daniel is in trouble. It's a revenant—"

She held up her hand, stood, and walked to the door. For whatever reason everyone in the store had gotten up and left, so she flipped the Open sign over to Closed, locked the door, and came back, then waved me on to finish saying what I had come to tell her.

And Marybeth listened with rapt attention to every single detail.

***

"That poor kid. And you said his aunt died last night? That the revenant got her? Sam, can you believe it?" she asked as naturally and with the same amount of sympathy as if I'd told her Carol had died of her cancer.

It truly was wonderful to have friends to talk to who understood your life; it was normal to her.

Her husband sighed. "Thirty years ago I'd have called the hospital and had you both committed for just a third of what was said here at this table. However, being married to you, Marybeth, and with you as a friend, Francine, and having gone through what we all went through together, tells me that I should believe whatever you say, dear."

Marybeth patted his cheek. "You're a good man. Isn't he a good man?" she asked, turning to me.

I laughed. "He sure is."

Satisfied, Marybeth asked, "So, what do you need from me, toots?"

"I need some ingredients for a banishing charm. Dragon's blood, five-finger grass, sulfur—"

"Lye, monkshood root, lily of the valley, cemetery dirt, and vervain. Got it."

She got up and headed into the back room, where I could hear her yelling about Native American influences on the land, how revenants dated back thousands of years, and how much she'd like to visit South Florida over the winter because she was worried she was getting arthritis in her knees.

"She knows her stuff. That's our Marybeth." I sighed.

"Oh yeah, she certainly does," Sam replied.

"How's she getting on, really?"

He sighed and took off his glasses. "I worry about her. She misses him. Especially this time of year."

"She chose you, Sam."

"You don't think she settled for someone safe?"

I snorted. "As opposed to the one who may have one day eaten her? I think yes, she did choose someone safer. But 'settle'? Sam, come on. You're not a bad guy."

"Nathan wasn't a bad guy either, Franny. It wasn't his fault he was…like he was."

I nodded sadly. "I know. But there's no cure for lycanthropy." I sat back all of a sudden and groaned. "The wolves…"

"Franny…"

"Sam, I didn't think."

"I'll get her through it. It'll be okay."

It wasn't too long before Marybeth emerged with two sachets full of material and a bundle of sage, and she sat back down, handing the materials to me with a beaming smile. Her eyes shimmered, but she held her ground.

"If he died in the house, you're going to have to pour this over the site of his death and the site of the place he resided in. His bedroom would be perfect. The wolves—er, his family should be fine after that."

She looked at us and picked up on the solemnness in the room. "What is this…? Ah. For the millionth time, Sam, I love you. Francine, tell him I love him."

I turned my head. "Sam, she loves you."

"I know."

Marybeth added, "And that was a long time ago."

I stayed silent but Sam nodded. "I know."

"We couldn't save him. He was a good guy. He was such a good guy," she said, breath hitching in her throat. Her face began to crumple.

I stood, as did Sam, but Marybeth held up her hands. "No. Stop it! I'm fine. Besides, their issue is not lycanthropy. It's a totally different reason. Go on, now."

"All right. What is this for, the sage?" I picked it up curiously.

"That is blessed sage. You're dealing with old Indian magic. Gives it a little extra kick for banishment and purging. Should do the trick. When things start to happen, light it," she explained.

I nodded. Uncle Pierre would have loved Marybeth. Herbs had been his specialty. He had passed away in the arms of his lover almost a decade ago, back home in Louisiana. They had lived almost forty years together. I reminded myself silently to call Charles, his partner, and check up on him. So much time had gone by, but as with Marybeth, it didn't mean that it had healed all wounds. I hugged them both and explained that I had to go.

They graciously understood. I gathered the belongings to myself and asked Marybeth, "How much do I owe you, sister?"

She waved me off with a grin. "It's on the house. No, really, go help those boys. But promise you'll come back and visit soon. And bring the book; I want to read all about it." She put her arm around her husband's back.

Sam held her and smiled at me as I made my way to the door. I really loved these two human beings.

As I walked out the door and into the afternoon sunlight, I promised Marybeth I would return.

Storm clouds were gathering again on the horizon as I pulled a U-turn and headed back to the freeway, now armed with everything we would need to put the wheels in motion. I just prayed we wouldn't get crushed under the weight of them when things really got rolling.

Daniel

T HE NEXT FEW days were long. Just like before, I found myself taking care of funeral arrangements and hating every goddamn minute of it. And like my parents' deaths, it was a morbid ritual of going down to the morgue, signing the release forms, and having the funeral home come by and pick up her body after the doctor certified her cause of death.

This time, however, I wasn't doing it alone. Hale was with me every single step of the way.

Carol's death amounted to the death of a celebrity in these parts, and I met hordes of people who wished to express their condolences. Many of them had been affected in some way by money and support from the Donnelly family.

Her law firm in Portland called me right away and sent a young probate lawyer to Hale's house to go over the will with me and to introduce himself as my new attorney. His name was Brian Lockheed, and he was kind enough to go over what Carol had wished for her funeral. I followed everything to a T and thanked God she had taken care of all this prior to her death.

Carol's funeral was on a Wednesday. It was cold and rainy; the sky was steel-gray and bloated, but that didn't keep the mourners away. Oh no, they were there in droves at the church where Carol had gone as a young girl.

Money and fame were powerful things, and word had reached deep inside the Catholic Church. Cardinal John, the friend she'd made as a young girl, flew in to celebrate Mass for her. I was grateful for that.

I sat at the front of the church, alongside Hale, Anita, Thomas, and Hale's mother as the Rosary was said, and then I stood up to give a eulogy. As I approached the lectern to say pleasant words about the deceased for the second time that year, I was taken aback at the vast sea of faces looking up to me. Recovering quickly, I looked out at the crowd of people gathered there and began.

"There are four people in this room who I know. Four people who've become fixtures in my life, to one degree or another, over the past five months since I came to Emerson. The fifth person was Carol Donnelly.

"I feel rather strange standing up here, eulogizing her to you. I think the roles should be reversed. I should sit down and have each one of you come up one by one to tell me a little bit about her. I can't tell you about Carol's life growing up, what she was like as a young woman. You see, I didn't know anything about her until the day my father, Michael Donnelly, and my mother, Sarah, passed away. They died in a boating accident, and I was set adrift."

I smiled, although I felt a lump in my throat and saw my vision blur.

"But I didn't drift long. My aunt Carol came out of nowhere and brought me here to Emerson. She told me that family is everything. She taught me who my grandparents were and told me about a part of my father I never knew. She loved her parents, Papa Jim and Katherine. She loved my father, Michael. And while it's heartbreaking for me to stand here in front of you as we say good-bye to her, I have it on really good authority that she's with them now. Thank you, all, for listening."

I quickly took my seat.

The rest of the service was beautiful, as were the flowers. Hale never left my side as we departed the church and went on to Emerson Cemetery, where the family had their own mausoleum. My father's name had also been listed there. The cardinal said another prayer, and we slid Carol's casket into the wall next to her parents.

All I had to do was go out into the woods to see her again, but the whole process of life being taken away so suddenly was what really brought me to the realization that our situation was special; very few people had the opportunity to interact with family members who had passed. Soon, however, that would change. It was time to end this nightmare once and for all.

After the service, the cardinal met with me and took me into an office to talk. Hale said he would be outside waiting for me. I nodded.

The cardinal was a slight man with short dark hair with gray running through it, but he was bright and his intelligence rolled off him in waves. Inside the office he motioned for me to sit in a chair in front of the desk that he leaned against.

I sat, feeling tired and worn.

"I knew your aunt a long time ago, Daniel. She and I have kept in contact over the years," he said. "She was a good woman. I am so sorry for your loss."

"Thank you," I whispered. I was exhausted, and my replies to people were becoming so painfully automatic that should someone have accused Carol of being a cannibal hooker from Mars who stole the life out of everyone she met, I fear I would have replied with the same polite thank-you.

"Her death wasn't natural, was it?" he asked.

I jerked my head up. He had my attention now. I stared at him for a moment before I shook my head. "No. She was killed by a ghost."

He took a deep breath and sat back on the desk, crossed himself, then folded his hands neatly in his lap. "Have you been going to Mass?" he asked.

"I'm not Catholic. I am not religious at all, to be honest with you. But I'm not prepared to let her death go unanswered. I intend that justice be done in regards to my aunt," I said, surprised at the anger in my voice.

"What *do* you intend to do?" He watched me carefully.

"I intend to take one from Saint Michael the archangel and fight this thing back through the gates of hell," I said, meeting his curious gaze.

"Then I will say a Mass for you. I knew your aunt was facing some darkness when she came to talk to me as a young girl.

I worried that it was demonic, but it wasn't, was it? It was her brother," he said flatly.

I nodded. "I'm so tired," I said, placing my head in my hands.

"God knows how tired you are, but the fight is just beginning. Here, take this. And good luck to ya."

I looked up from my hands to see a gold chain hanging in front of me, the medallion an exact replica of the one my father had, and I felt something burn inside of me. For the first time, I believed I was going to win this fight.

I placed the chain around my neck alongside my dad's dog tags and smiled.

Cardinal John said if I ever needed anything, he could be reached day or night at the number listed on the card he gave me. I thanked him for his time, but before I could go, he stopped me.

"Daniel?" I turned around and looked at him. "One more thing. Carol was a dear friend of mine."

I nodded, feeling sympathy for his loss. "I know, Your Eminence."

"Just do me a favor, would ya?"

I straightened up and cleared my throat. "Sure. Name it."

"Make sure that son of a bitch goes down."

I snorted. "You got it."

He winked at me. Giving him one last smile and nod, I left and met Hale in the truck.

That night sleep came in fits and starts. After lovemaking that was slow and passionate and much needed, I lay in the arms of my slumbering lover.

Hale woke up several times to reach out and pull me closer to him, and I was grateful for it. His strength gave me strength, and I prayed silently that come what may I would not fail in my task of both keeping my lover alive and setting my family free from the memories that held them captive.

Hale

T HE DAY AFTER Carol's funeral, I received a phone call from Francine, telling us to meet her at the same spot in the woods where we had met before.

As we drove to Timber Manor, Danny and I were both nervous. When we finally pulled into the driveway, the journey felt like it had taken forever. It was a perfect day for a haunting: the skies were dark with storm clouds and the air chilly and heavy with rain. We walked down the path to the creek bed, and I was surprised to find Francine sat alone this time. As we made our way down the hill to her, she looked up and smiled.

"The Hour of Grace is upon us, gentlemen."

"The hour of what?" I asked.

"Grace," Danny said. "The Hour of Grace: the time Christ died, 3:00 p.m."

"Very good, Danny. Spirits this malignant are usually more powerful during the Witching Hour." Francine stood and held out her hands, one to each of us, and we took them. "This is going to be very difficult, but it is what we have to do for your family, Danny, and for you. Hale, should you feel the need to back out, then now is the time."

"There's no way that's happening," I retorted.

"Then know that from this point forward, your life is in real danger. Christopher isn't going to make this easy. He is going to try to hurt the both of you." She handed me two black sachets full of herbs.

"What's this?" I asked.

"Two separate concoctions. One contains mandrake root, morning glory, monkshood, St.-John's-wort, black pepper, and a few other things. The other has dragon's blood, five-finger grass, sulfur, lye, monkshood root, lily of the valley, cemetery dirt, and vervain. Basically, it's going to weaken Christopher and start to dislodge him from this reality. Once inside the house, the first bag must go into the place he dwelled in life—his bedroom—and the other in the place he died. Once that is done, his grip on this physical reality will loosen long enough for us to expel him."

She turned her attention to Danny. "*You* have to expel him. Carol is gone now, and you are the master of the house. You must do most of the work. Hale is going to be with me in the foyer, where Christopher died. You have to go and pour the contents of this on the floor of his room. When you've done that, Hale and I can pour the contents of ours onto the floor where he died. Do you understand?"

Danny nodded, and I opened my mouth to protest about not going with him.

"Hale, you could end up being a distraction," she interrupted. "Danny needs to focus on what he is doing, and that is getting rid of Christopher. His family has gone ahead of us to take their places near the front door. Danny, you're going to have to lure Christopher downstairs and over to the spot where he died. From there you have to invite your family in. Remember, it's your house, and you have to let him know this.

"Are you boys ready?"

I felt sick to my stomach. My nerves were jumping all over the place, and my body was tense. I looked over at Danny, who played with the strings of his sachet as if to make sure they weren't too tight. I thought of something else we'd need. "Danny, there's a sledgehammer in the shed behind the house. We'll take it with us. You'll have to knock down that wall to get inside the room and pour that out."

"Won't Christopher stop me?" he asked Francine.

"Hopefully he won't know what's happening until it's too late. But he has surprised us before. This is the moment of truth, gentlemen. We either go in swinging or we don't go in at all."

"I'm ready," Danny said.

"Me too," I said.

"Good. Good. May angels watch over us, for we are about to descend into the ninth level of hell. Let's go."

She turned and started up the hill, and we followed, hand in hand.

Daniel

W E EXITED THE woods, and as we approached Timber Manor, the house grew larger with each footstep. With its white paint on the exterior, its glorious expansion left and right, its many windows washed till they glinted in the dying daylight, the house no longer had the welcoming presence it did the first time I laid eyes on it. It loomed in front of us, threateningly.

The windows were now eyes that stared at us as we made our way toward it. Its deep-set porch no longer felt like the place to spend a lazy summer afternoon reading; it now looked more like the mouth of a beast. The latticework above no longer seemed decorative; it now felt like teeth. I half expected the house to grin at me before contorting into the face of Christopher himself. Timber Manor was no longer the Donnelly estate; it belonged to its master now despite what Francine said. Despite what Carol said. Despite the paperwork I signed. Christopher made it dirty. It now felt menacing, unclean, and unholy.

After a quick detour to the shed at the back of the house, the sledgehammer in my hand felt good. With each step we took, I gave the handle a gentle squeeze.

As we made our way onto the front lawn, four wolves broke from around the side of the house and padded their way beside us. I looked to my left and saw them walking shoulder to shoulder, their napes bristled and their heads slung low.

We reached the front steps. The wolves stopped, and we walked up to the door.

Francine turned and addressed us. "Okay. Here we go. Danny, remember, spill the contents onto the floor and then run like hell. We'll be waiting for you."

I nodded nervously and took a step forward.

Hale grabbed my hand and turned me to face him. "I love you," he said.

I could see the fear on his face and hear it in his voice. I looked deep into the eyes of my lover and set my hammer down on the ground. I grabbed his face and kissed him hard, desperately holding him close to me. I wanted to remember the way he tasted, the way he felt, knowing I might never feel him again. "I love you," I told him. "One soul touching. One soul, baby."

"One soul," he confirmed. "Come back to me."

"I ain't going anywhere, handsome. Francine, take care of my man."

"You got it, sugar. We'll be right here," she said, smiling. She rolled up her sleeves like a boxer getting ready to take on a heavyweight champion.

We entered the house and stepped into the foyer. Inside it was as dark and quiet as a tomb. The air was chillier than outside; I could see my breath puffing out in front of me. Yes, this was his home now.

"Danny, are you sure you can do this?" Francine asked.

I turned my head and looked out the door at the four wolves watching me with canine grins on their faces. "Yeah. I got this."

I hefted the hammer over my shoulder and let it rest there. My sachet I gripped with my left hand, and then headed up the stairs. At the top, I looked back over my shoulder and blew both of them a kiss.

Hale looked like he wanted to die, wringing his hands as I set off down the hallway.

The air was thick and opaque, and I felt like I was swimming underwater again.

One step, breathe in. Second step, exhale.

Come on, Danny.

I walked the unfamiliar hallway, looking for the spot I'd been shown weeks earlier. As I went, with my heart slamming in my chest and my nerves wound tight as piano wire, I heard movement—or rather, scraping noises. I looked behind me.

Every picture frame on the wall tilted toward me as if pointing to my location. The lights flickered a bit, and I swear the air grew even cooler. I finally reached the spot where the workers had plastered the wall, only to find the plaster they'd used lying broken on the floor. A black hole yawned in its place and a crack ran from floor to ceiling.

"Daddy! Daddy?" I cried, sitting up in bed.

My father burst through the bedroom door and stood there in his pajama bottoms and T-shirt. "What is it, Daniel?" he asked, coming to the side of my bed. "Did you have a nightmare?"

I nodded, my lower lip trembling. He chuckled, and I scooted over as he sat down beside me.

"Wanna talk about it?" he asked, his eyes tired and red from having been asleep himself.

"There's a monster in the closet."

"Oh, there is, is there?"

He stood up and I nodded.

In a loud and booming voice, he announced, "If there is a monster in my son's closet, I'm gonna tear you to shreds. Do you understand?"

He stalked his way to the closet door, looked back at me, and winked. I couldn't help but giggle. Daddy flung the door open real fast and stepped to the side, peering in. He looked back at me. My eyes were wide as saucers. Then he reached inside and turned on the light, and of course there were no monsters to be found.

Daddy turned out the light and shut the door. "Could he be under the bed?" he asked.

I giggled and nodded, all the fear gone because my daddy had shown up.

"If there is a monster under the bed, I'm gonna tear you to shreds!" He dove to the floor, flipping the covers up over me, and I roared with laughter. Then he poked his head up and grinned at me. Had there been a monster, it would have run in fear of my big, bad dad. Marines scared monsters, he explained. Hell, had there been a monster in any kid's closet or under their bed on the whole block, they'd just checked out.

"No monsters there either, buddy," he said, laughing too. He sat down beside me on the bed and looked serious. "You gonna be okay?" he asked.

I nodded.

"Checking for monsters again, Michael?" Mom stood in the doorway, her hair all messy.

"Sure am, pretty lady."

"Sure am, pretty lady," I mimicked, and they laughed.

"Well, you tell those monsters not to mess with my handsome men or they will have to deal with me," Mom said as she turned and walked down the hallway.

"Now, that would scare even me, buddy," Dad said, his eyes big as he tucked me back under my blankets and handed me George, my stuffed bear.

My eyes were already growing heavy, and I knew I would always be safe as long as my dad was around.

I raised the sledgehammer behind me like a baseball player would his bat. "This one's for you, Dad," I said and swung with all my might.

Hale

I HEARD THE SLEDGEHAMMER hit.
Again. And then again.

"I'm through!" came Danny's voice from upstairs.

Francine crossed herself and I found myself doing the same thing. Suddenly Timber Manor shook around us. It groaned deep and low as if in pain and trembled under our feet as the sound of snapping wood cracked from distant parts of the house.

To my right was a radiator, and it began to clank. I was about to walk closer to it when the house seemed to heave upward once, hard, and then down. The sound of windows shattering echoed throughout the house.

I lost my footing, as did Francine, and we pitched over sideways, with plaster dust and glass raining on our heads. The chandelier in the foyer bounced on its chain and the lights flickered. The house groaned and shuddered; the oil painting of Danny's grandparents dislodged itself from the wall and crashed to the floor.

"Jesus Christ," I muttered.

"He's infected the whole house, Hale, look!"

Darkness poured out of every corner of the room. At first I thought it was some kind of sewage. But as it hit the ground, there was no splash, no splatter. The blackness poured down from corners of the foyer, gathering on the floor, and then began to pool around and encircle us.

"Francine, what is that?"

"It's ectoplasm! Don't let it touch you! That's what made Carol so sick." She shot her arm out to back me up behind her.

Francine reached inside her bag and produced a bundle of dried sticks tied together with red thread, and a lighter. She lit the tops of the bundle and the herbs immediately filled the foyer with a pleasant odor. Instantly the ectoplasm reacted and began to back away from the source of the sweet smoke. Even along the walls, the viscous black material arched to escape the touch of whatever she was burning.

"Sage," she explained and began to walk around the foyer with it, bathing everything in its perfumed smoke.

"Danny! Are you all right?" I yelled as loud as I could.

"I'm fine," he shouted back.

The blackness pooled at the foot of the stairs began to writhe and suddenly pull upward. The figure of a man quickly formed from it, and from the top, the black ectoplasm pulled away, leaving behind a figure with a shock of white hair and merciless black pits for eyes.

"Christopher…" I muttered.

It shrieked with fury at the sound of Its name and Francine and I had to cover our ears. The house trembled and pitched before It shot up the stairs in a boiling black mass.

Francine, her burning sage held out in front of her like a sword, kept her other hand on my chest. The thing watched us for a second and then shot down the hallway.

"*Danny*! He's coming!" I yelled, panic taking me along for the ride.

"Easy, Hale. He's got this."

"Francine!"

"*Be still!*"

As the lion approached Daniel in its den, I could only hope and pray.

The house rattled around us. Cracks formed along the walls, and floorboards buckled. The groans and creaks, the sounds of tearing plaster, began to pick up all around us. If we didn't get out soon, we'd be crushed to death.

Daniel

INSIDE THE BEDROOM of my dead uncle, I was tossed to the floor as the house pitched and rolled like an ocean liner on an angry sea.

I was surprised at what I saw. The room reminded me of the legends of the ill-fated Roanoke colony, where the inhabitants disappeared, leaving everything behind as though someone was about to return to the place. Christopher's bed, missing a leg, leaned over on one corner. The dresser held toys and knickknacks that longed to be played with. There was a laundry basket with extra blankets laid inside and a closet with the door propped open, revealing clothes hung up on wire hangers.

I was in a child's room, a child's room that had been long forgotten. The layer of dust on everything lay thick and untouched.

Something caught my eye. On top of the bed was a gold medallion—*my* gold medallion—and I grabbed it and stuffed it in my pocket.

I turned to the doorway and caught sight of him standing out in the hallway, watching me. *Christopher.*

A boiling black mass surrounded the horrid figure I had seen in my nightmares, and my heart almost stopped. The thing was pissed. Those eyes, which had always been hate-filled, watched me with even more anger than before. The chain at my neck began to burn against my skin, and I reached down into my pocket for the sachet.

That was when It rushed me.

It pushed me back against the wall with a powerful blow, forcing the air from my lungs. Its hands were on me and my skin froze at the contact. I screamed in agony, my flesh becoming frostbitten at his touch, and It screamed in rage and tossed me across the room. I hit the opposite wall and fell forward. My vision swam before me, and the room tilted as I clung to consciousness.

It watched me from the other side of the room and began to speak. "You're just like your father. A coward. And to beat it all, you're a disgusting queer. I've watched you and your lover. I've watched you as you took it up the can and begged for more. You think your daddy would be proud of you? You little queer. I bet you scream louder than he did when I used to hurt him. I hurt him baaaad, Danny. Real, real bad."

Anger and disgust boiled in my gut. I stood on trembling knees, blood dripping from a gash on the side of my head. "Hey, Uncle Christopher, why don't you go outside and play a game of hide and go fuck yourself?"

With an enraged roar, It slammed me up against the wall by my throat. With all the strength I could muster, I thrust the satchel inside him. As my hand passed through his form, the burning sensation was almost too great to bear. But I tilted the bag and watched as what I remembered being dust, twigs, herbs, and who-knows-what-else turned into particles of fire as they ignited inside him.

A tortured scream rang out of him, and I pulled my injured hand back. He faded in and out of reality, screaming and trying to brush away the fire, and I knew that was my cue. I dove right on top of the bed and vaulted past him and out into the hallway.

The house pitched again, more violently than before. I stumbled forward, trying to keep my feet under me. The snapping of wood and crumbling foundations sounded all around me as the floor trembled underfoot. Huge chunks of masonry fell. Throwing my hands over my head, I was quick enough to shield myself from a patch that broke away from the ceiling, but it hit my already-injured arm.

But I didn't stop running. If anything, I poured on more speed, screaming Hale's name as I made my way down the hall.

The masonry behind me crumbled as It crashed into the walls in hot pursuit. Bits of plaster, debris, and other bits of house that exploded hit me as whole sections of wall disappeared in his attempt to catch me. Glass shattered, tables were knocked away, and the floors underneath me heaved as I made my way as fast as I could to the staircase.

As I cleared the corner, Hale and Francine were there. I managed to bolt down the first two steps before I was picked up from behind and turned around.

I kicked as hard as I could to break Christopher's hold on me. Suddenly I knew what it was going to do. It turned me around to face It, Its horrible eyes watching me as It grinned in triumph.

I screamed into its face. "This is my house, Christopher! You rotten son of a bitch! This is my house! *Get out!*"

This is it, I'm going over the landing.

Hale was yelling my name and Christopher had tensed up to throw me...when he started screaming again.

Surprised, I dropped, not over the railing, but on the floor, awkwardly, on my ankle, which snapped under my weight. I looked up again; he was brushing what looked like snowflakes made of fire off him. I turned my head. Hale held the empty bag over the spot where Christopher had died, and Francine had the door wide open. Christopher fell backward, his spirit flashing in and out of reality again, and I decided to boogie. I lunged forward down the stairs on my hands and knees, the marble bruising the shit out of me. No way was I getting thrown down to break my neck.

Christopher, *It*, screamed in fury that shook the entire house, which was crumbling faster than ever. I was almost down, and I knew It was coming again. I clawed my way on hands and knees, bleeding, down the stairs, as the specter whipped down and slammed into Francine, picking her up by her hair and smashing her into Hale. They fell in a heap on the floor and were pushed back up against the wall.

The boiling black mass now hovered over me as I lay where it had died the first time. "Danny Boy. Who's gonna help you now, Danny Boy?" he mocked as he floated above me, bent over at the waist and leering. The pits of darkness in his eyes were horrible to look at, but I jutted my chin out in defiance.

"My dad is gonna kick your ass! *Daaad? Carol? Grandpa? Grandma? Come in!*"

Christopher recoiled and raised his head. I turned mine as well toward the door as the first of the four wolves launched itself inside the house. As each wolf crossed the threshold, their four legs turned to two. Michael was the first inside, followed quickly by Papa Jim, Katherine, and finally, Carol. Their bodies were ethereal and filled with so much light I was forced to look away, but not before I saw my father step forward, fists clenched.

"Get the hell away from my son!" Michael shouted.

Jim was the first to attack, and Christopher fought back. Their spirits slammed against walls, the ceiling, the floor, accompanied by screams of rage and pain. Plaster splintered and exploded where they hit, sending debris flying through the foyer.

I rolled over on my stomach and low-crawled to where Hale, Francine, and I could huddle together in a corner, our arms above our heads, trying to deflect pieces of plaster from hitting us. I watched from underneath the crook of my elbow. Christopher knocked his father to the ground and was about to leap on top of him when his mother hit him from the side.

"You tried to kill my baby!" She screamed in rage and the two of them flew up stairs, rolling along the steps, and shot down the hall, accompanied by crashes and explosions. The disintegrating house shook with the sheer force of the impacts. I felt the tremors underneath me.

Hale noticed it too and shouted, "This house is going to shake apart. Danny, we have to get out of here!"

"I know!"

Katherine and her son came screaming back into the foyer. Christopher had his mother by the neck and tossed her next to her husband on the floor. Their energies were being consumed trying to defeat him, but Christopher didn't look like he was tiring at all.

All that changed when Dad stepped up to the plate. Fear crossed Christopher's face. Dad charged him, hands outstretched and fingers drawn into claws. Christopher backpedaled, trying to fight him off, but to no avail. Dad fought him furiously and appeared to be starting to overpower him when Christopher pushed back. It regained Its composure and slammed Dad up against the wall, clawing gouges out of my dad as he howled in pain.

I had no idea I was charging across the floor of the foyer, ignoring my ankle, until I leaped upon Christopher's back. I figured I would go right through them, but I felt a solid mass under me. He felt cold, and the smell coming off him was nauseating, like rotted flesh and rancid meat. I didn't care; I slid an arm around Its neck. Bracing it with my other arm, I wrapped my legs around Its midsection and started beating It with my fists, aiming for the head and neck.

Roaring in rage, It tried to buck me, but I held on. I was hurting It, and I continued to pound away.

"Daniel, no!" my father's voice rang out.

Christopher let him go and flung himself and me back against the opposite wall. I hit hard and saw stars. As I started to lose my grip, I slid down to the floor. Christopher turned, his elongated fingers in claws, and he was about to take a slash out of me when the gunshots rang out.

I turned my head to Hale, who was standing above Francine, his legs spread and his service revolver out. Francine was desperately trying to reignite her sage.

Crack! Crack! Crack! as Hale fired.

The bullets tore through Christopher, sending plumes of black smoke into the air, but of course it didn't faze him. In a flash, he was in front of Hale, lifting him up by his chin and wrapping his hand around the base of Hale's throat.

I realized what he was doing—he was going to snap Hale's neck. I immediately surged back onto my feet and tried to reach him.

As Hale's face turned purple and his eyes bulged, Christopher laughed.

The laughter turned to a high-pitched scream. Christopher tossed Hale backward out of the front door.

Francine had ignited the sage and was standing now. She had buried the cluster of sticks inside Christopher's belly. Her eyes were wide with wonder as Christopher stumbled backward, hands clasped over the sage as a dying person might hold a dagger embedded in their flesh. He floated backward up the stairs, his eyes huge.

"Don't let him get back into that room!" Francine screamed.

From where she was standing, she couldn't see what I could. My aunt stood at the top of the stairs, and as the others were recovering and collecting their strength, it was Carol who attacked next. When he turned, she smiled at him and leaped.

Carol flung them both down the stairs. Marble exploded as they hit the foyer floor. The chandelier above them shook, broke loose, and crashed onto what was left of the floor, sending shards of crystal flying about the room. All the living ducked their heads again in fear of being impaled.

Hale had managed to crawl and was making his way toward me, alongside Francine. We went back to huddling in the corner. But the tide of the battle was turning. The sage must have weakened Christopher significantly, and he struggled under Carol and Dad's force. Soon Jim and Katherine reentered the fight, all four of them battling fiercely. The house they'd built swayed and shuddered around them. Masonry fell, walls split, the staircase collapsed.

Finally, Christopher dragged his weakened form over to the spot where he'd been killed.

Each family member stood on one side of him: north, east, south, and west. The boiling black cloud was drenched in a white light so pure it was hard to look at. Christopher screamed in agony, so loud I had to cover my ears to keep from going insane. His body was simply fading away into nothingness; it wouldn't matter if he was remembered, he was being forced out of this world. Forever, this time. As he melted into oblivion, a shock wave of light dispersed from ground zero, flooded throughout the house, and was gone.

The house groaned once, real loud, and before I knew it, Hale had me up in the air and over his shoulder as he and Francine bolted out of the house. Behind us, as if Timber Manor were nothing more than hollow bones, what remained of the house caved inward with a terrible, thundering crash. The shock wave pitched us all forward into the mud and debris.

Hale and Francine landed face-first, and I lay upon my back as rain fell on my face. I saw stars from the impact. The world around me started to go dark.

"Danny! Danny!"

Slaps on my face; I opened my eyes to see both Hale and Francine over me. Hale looked panic-stricken and pale as a ghost; poor Francine was covered head to toe in mud.

I sat bolt upright, shoving them both out of the way. "They're gone now, huh?"

Looking back at Timber Manor, we could see the spire had started to sag. Instead of pointing straight up into the sky, it looked as if it was melting into the house, now pointing west. I looked at Francine, who looked as distressed as I felt. She watched the house for a second, and then her eyes drifted back to mine. A bright smile reappeared.

I repeated the question that burned in my thoughts. "Are they gone?"

"Not yet, we aren't" came the reply from behind us.

I looked over my shoulder to see my family standing side by side in the rain. Carol and Daddy smiled at me, as did my grandmother and grandfather. And my God, they looked solid. They *were* solid. The rain fell on them, and I could see it.

Dad walked toward me, and I launched myself upward and forward, hopping on one foot, sobbing as my arms reached for him. He was solid, all right. He picked me up and swung me around before gently putting me back down.

"I am so sorry. I am so sorry," I wept as I wrapped my arms around him and buried my head into his shoulder.

"Sorry? What are you sorry for?"

I sobbed into his shoulder. "I let you and Mom die. I should have gone with you. I should have driven down with you both. It's my fault. This is all my fault."

"No. No, no, no, no. Daniel, look at me. Look at me," Dad said, putting me at arm's length. "There is no fault to be assigned, son. You did what other kids your age do. If anyone was to blame, it was me. I shouldn't have lorded over you, should never have kept you from this place. From Carol, from your family, from who you are and what you would eventually become. A strong young man. I tried to shield you from it because *I* was scared of him. You've done what I never could have. You stood up for your old man. I am so proud of you." He stared into my eyes and wrapped his arms around me again. I clung to him for dear life, knowing I would have to say good-bye again.

Over his shoulder, Papa Jim, Katherine, and Carol approached. Their bodies, which had once been solid, became luminescent again as they neared.

"You were so brave, Daniel," Katherine said.

"Of course he's brave. He's a Donnelly," Papa Jim replied.

Dad let me go. He backed away as Carol walked up.

"I knew you'd stand up for us," she said. "I love you, Danny."

"I love you too, Aunt Carol."

I felt a steadying hand on my back and turned to see Hale and Francine.

"Hale, take care of my son," Michael said as he joined the other three spirits.

I could see right through all of them now; I leaned hard on Hale for support.

"Yes, sir."

"Daniel...? Are you going to be okay?"

"Yeah, Dad. I'm going to be fine. Go find Mom."

His face lit up again with that faraway look of longing. "Sarah." He looked back at me. "I'll always be near you, son. I love you."

I wiped my face with the backs of my hands. "I love you. All of you."

Their departure wasn't as dramatic as Christopher's had been. They were there for a second, and then they slowly faded away, with Dad and Carol waving the entire time.

Their presence was replaced with the steady rainfall of an early-autumn evening in Oregon.

Hale

I WATCHED DANNY AS he slept. The injuries he'd sustained from the collapse of the house were severe enough to land him in the hospital for observation.

The same doctor and the same nurse from before came by and made their rounds. Danny's right foot and his right arm had been cast, and just as before, a mild infection had set in and made things more complicated than they should have been. Another round of antibiotics, and the fever that came on fast and heavy dissipated within a few hours, leaving Danny spent. As before, I was sick to my stomach with the idea of losing him.

"It's the house, Hale," Francine said. "Combined with how powerful Christopher became, had Danny been exposed to it much longer, the results would have been worse. However, Christopher's gone now. The infection is gone too. He should make a full recovery." She stood behind me with her hand upon my shoulder and patted me one more time before making her way to the door.

As she opened it, I turned to her. "Are you leaving?"

She looked from me to Danny and back. "*Oui, mon ami.* I have to be going now. I made a promise to an old girlfriend in Portland to visit her and her husband when this was over. She's going to want to hear all about this. It'll do me some good to tell it, and it'll do her good to hear it."

I stood up and walked over to her. "How do I ever repay you?"

She laughed deep down in her soul. "Sugar, don't you worry about that. This is my job."

"Aw, come on, Francine. Let me do something for you."

She smiled and patted my face. Then a quizzical look overtook her features. "Very well, then. When what is to happen happens, send me an invitation."

I shook my head. "I don't understand."

She winked at me. "You will. I trust you know how to find me."

And with that, she walked out of the room and shut the door behind her. I was standing there staring at the door for a moment, trying to figure out that last bit, when I heard Danny's voice from behind me.

"We have to stop meeting like this. People will talk."

I spun around and saw him looking at me with a crooked grin. I felt relief flood through me again, as well as the urge to hide my face in my hands and cry.

"Oh no you don't. Not again. Come here," Danny laughed as he motioned for me with the cast on his arm.

So I lowered my head and did as I was told, taking my seat beside his bed. Leaning over, I kissed his lips. Once we parted, he raised his hand and brushed his fingers across my face.

"Is there anything I can get you? Do for you? Do you need anything?"

"Yeah."

"What is it? I can call Jalinda right now."

"Jalinda can't help me."

I paused for a moment and then checked my watch. "Well, it's only seven. Stuff is still open. I can run out if you need something."

Danny shook his head again. "Can't find it out there either."

I laughed. "Then what do you want?"

He shifted over in his bed and grabbed hold of my hand with his. The intensity of his gaze caught me by surprise. "Will you marry me?"

"What?"

"I want you to marry me. I want you to be a permanent part of my life. I want you to be my family. I want to have a family with you, Hale."

When what is to happen happens, send me an invitation.

I ran a hand through his hair and looked into Danny's beautiful eyes as his gaze searched mine for an answer. I couldn't imagine a world without him. A life without him, now. When I watched him drive away the first night I met him, I knew somewhere deep down that my life was about to change. And it had. For the better.

While I now believed in ghosts, demons, and psychics, which I had to admit to myself rocked the entire foundation of what I believed to be true, as I stared down at the man in the bed before me, I had to admit to myself one more thing. I believed in the overwhelming and oftentimes terrifying power of love and its ability to set souls free.

I wanted to feel what that was like.

"Yes, Daniel Donnelly," I said, leaning in and lowering myself to stare into his eyes. I took his chin in my hand, traced his lips with the pad of my thumb, and saw my future written in his gaze.

"I will marry you."

OBJECTS IN THE REARVIEW MIRROR

Their new home on Frederick Street in Clay Center, Kansas, was supposed to give writer Jonathan David and his husband, clinical psychologist Dr. Eddie Dorman, an opportunity to enjoy married life. Jonathan has just released his first major bestseller, and he hopes to finally escape his traumatic past and find the quiet existence he has always craved. Eddie has taken a job at the Kansas State University psychology department, and they intend to begin anew.

They have barely settled in when the nightmare begins. Noises, disembodied voices, and mysterious apparitions make Jonathan's life hell. Part of the house has decided to bare its teeth, show its jagged edges, and bring back the worst of Jonathan's past. At first, Eddie cannot perceive the spectral events and fears for his husband's sanity. When he's also affected by the haunting, he's unsure of what to do but refuses to be beaten.

Together, they seek a way to fight the forces trying to tear them apart. The world is a frightening place, but confronting their fears plunges Jonathan and Eddie into absolute horror.

PROLOGUE

A LAN PEMBERLY WOKE up slowly, his head throbbing, and when he opened his eyes, he shut them again quickly as the fragile morning light in the room assaulted his senses. That was the first round of trying to figure out where he was. His mouth tasted like yesterday's news, and his body ached. He coughed once, twice, three times, hard and raspy; his abdominal muscles cramped in protest. He placed one arm over his stomach in an attempt to soothe it as he rolled over onto his side. He reopened his eyes to the unfamiliar room; the stench of sweat, booze, and old sex lingered in the dusty, humid air.

Next to him, someone groaned and buried themselves deeper into the blankets. Alan froze, racking his brain as to who it was and how Alan had come to be there. Then it all came back to him in a rush: he had been at a bar in San Francisco, drinking away his pain after his split with Tommy and the realization that the one who was supposed to love him more than anything, more than anyone, had cheated, and so Alan had gone out to find a cold bottle to drown his miseries. Their relationship had ended in a heated argument of accusations, both sides blaming the other for their shortfalls, and then the worst had happened, the death knell, the final nail in the coffin of their relationship: Tommy had struck him in the face. Even knowing what Alan had been through, Tommy had lost his temper and hit him, hard. Alan hadn't uttered another word. He'd simply grabbed some clothes, a bag, some money and his checkbook off his dresser, and left. Now, as he scanned the unfamiliar room, looking for his clothes, he remembered how he had gotten there. He'd wandered the streets of the city, having left the apartment he and Tommy shared, and had found himself standing outside the bar that Tommy had started to frequent regularly while Alan was at work. In the misty darkness, he'd stared at the flashing yellow sign that read "The Copa" for what felt like hours as men wandered into the place, staring at him as they passed by.

Alan took stock of his current situation. The three years he'd spent in California hadn't been good to him. His runaway love had run away from him, and now he was near broke and in bed with a man whose name escaped him. Oh, but the older man was a sweet-talker and had filled his ears with every word he wished Tommy had said. He had been so sympathetic, kind, and gentle, and the normally strong defenses Alan had to rebuff men's advances crumbled at his feet. He'd ended up following the stranger back to this place. It looked like an office, and the bed was a hideaway pulled down from the wall. The brown paneling was stained dark, and there were several framed certificates on the wall along with pictures that Alan couldn't quite bring into focus. He sat up as quietly as he could. His head was spinning, forcing him to shut his eyes once more and take a couple of deep breaths. As his head and stomach settled, no longer threatening to dispose of the alcohol he had consumed the night before, he pulled the thin blanket off his middle and stood up. The cool air in the room chilled his naked body.

Outside, someone was walking down the hallway toward the door. He froze. The footsteps drew nearer and nearer until he could see an outline in the heavily frosted glass where the shadow of the person paused, tried the handle of the office door, and discovered it locked. Alan was terrified they were going to knock, or worse, simply unlock the door, but he exhaled as they continued on. However, that and the groan coming from the person in the bed next to him was enough to motivate him. The salt-and-pepper-haired man rolled over and muttered something, casting one arm over his eyes. Alan's groin filled at the sight of him. He was muscular, furry, with chiseled features and sturdy, long, muscular legs. Memories flooded back from the night before, and Alan now remembered them stumbling in here in the dark, laughing and whispering, Alan a little drunker than he should have been. Ed…that was his name. Or was it David? The man had poured them another drink and brought it over to him as Alan had taken a seat on the couch.

"I can't believe your boyfriend would cheat on someone as beautiful as you," he'd said, brushing his fingers against Alan's as Alan reached for the drink. Alan had taken a sip, and it had burned all the way down into the pit of his stomach. But with that gentle touch, just the way Tommy used to, he'd yearned, ached to be held and to hold. And that was how it began. There hadn't been any more talking before the clothes came off, and Alan and David… Ed…whoever, had been a tangle of limbs, kisses, and passion so hot, it nearly slew them as they fell over the edge and into oblivion. Alan had been so sure of the moment, and it had felt so good and so right, but now he was disheveled, exhausted, and uncertain.

He found his clothes on the hardwood floor that creaked with his every step, causing him to try to tread lightly as he picked up his shirt and slipped it on over his bare shoulders. He found his underwear next and slid them on, trying to move quickly and quietly. He found his pants and picked those up as well, wincing as change fell out of the pockets and spilled noisily onto the floor. He would have ignored the coins had he not needed every last penny he had, and he hurriedly picked them up and put them back in his pocket.

"Meh…um…zzzzzz" was the only sound he heard from the bed as he slid his pants on. He located his shoes on opposite sides of the room. As he picked up one, he licked his lips. They were still sore from the other man's whiskered face. He smiled to himself as he went looking for his socks. Maybe there was something here? Maybe more to it than a one-night stand? *Maybe I don't have to return home after all? I could just go visit Dad, and me and David…or…whomever could really get to know one another when I got back. We could…* The thoughts continued to parade in his mind as he rounded the corner of the desk, having found his sock discarded on a picture frame. He grabbed it quickly and was about to walk away but hesitated and picked up the photograph. His heart dropped into his stomach. It was a family portrait. David...or Ed...was standing with a beautiful woman with brown hair swept into an updo, and a child of no more than seven years old, who grinned at the camera with his two front teeth missing.

"Jesus," Alan whispered in shock. He set the picture frame down again as ice water ran through his veins. He found a nameplate on the desk that read "David Edward, Esq." Well, at least he had been honest about his name, even if Alan could hardly get it right. He grabbed the sock, then found the other one, his mind spinning as the last bit of his broken heart cracked and crumbled to the floor. Tears welled up in his eyes as he sat down in the wooden chair in front of the desk and slid on his socks and shoes. His bag. Where was his bag? He looked around the room and found it near the bed. He walked over to it, no longer bothering to be quiet. He didn't care.

He opened the zipper and checked his clothes and his wallet before zipping it back up and standing. He realized David had sat up in the bed and was watching him with a grin on his face. God, he was handsome, but the smile made Alan feel sick to his stomach. Did he grin like that when he looked at his wife?

"Just gonna sneak out of here without saying good-bye?" David asked, his voice sleepy and sexy low.

"I have to be going. I have a plane to catch in a couple of hours," Alan said, slipping his bag over his shoulder. He hadn't made the reservations yet, knowing it would drain his bank account, but he didn't care. He just wanted to go home.

"Aww, come on. Stay. I'll take you to breakfast," David said, uncovering his loins and displaying a large and throbbing erection. Alan swallowed thickly, nausea sweeping through him and turning him cold. He walked over to David.

"I have a better idea," Alan said huskily, leaning down and lightly kissing David on the lips before sliding his hand over David's erection. He cupped it in his hand.

"Hmmm. What's that?" David asked with a low groan as he arched his hips upward and his breathing become ragged.

Alan kissed the side of his mouth, his right cheek, and worked his way back to his ear. He took David's earlobe in his mouth and lightly bit down, causing the man to groan with pleasure. "I'll take a rain check on breakfast, but I think you should go ahead and take your wife and little boy. I'm sure they would prefer your company more than I would," he said coolly, and then he stood up and backed away. David looked at him in shock.

"The fuck do you know about my family, you little trick?" he asked standing up, his erection deflating by the second.

"Not much, except they have a father and husband who doesn't have balls big enough to do the right thing by them. Your wife is beautiful, and that's a great-lookin' kid. Why don't you stop this and go home and act like a real father instead of being out late at night turning 'tricks,' as you say. Most families appreciate that," Alan said.

"You don't know shit!" the man said, red-faced either from fury or embarrassment, or perhaps a little bit of both. He was making a mad rush to get dressed, throwing things around, his erection now shrunk to a flaccid state as he looked for his clothes.

"I know enough to understand how heartbroken your wife would be if she were to catch you here with another man," Alan said. As he turned to leave, he put his hand on the doorknob and grasped it.

"I love my wife" came the reply, hollow and sounding guilty, and Alan stopped.

"Not enough, apparently," Alan replied over his shoulder and walked out the door, then shut it behind him. As soon as he did, he knew what he had to do. He had to admit defeat and go home.

***

Alan leaned against the office door to catch his breath before starting out. His heart hurt, his head hurt, and his body had that used-up feeling from a night of carnal knowledge. Shuddering at what he had done, he set off down the hallway and became more ashamed of himself with every footstep. He was almost broke, homeless, without a vehicle since Tommy had sold it, and afraid to make the phone call to his father's house. He'd been left in horrible circumstances after his mother died. His father had lost control and become a full-fledged alcoholic. He'd beaten Alan on a regular basis. It had been a horrific time in both their lives, as the man Alan had once admired turned dangerous and inconsolable. After Alan left Kansas, he never thought he'd hear from his father again, until almost a year later, when a stranger had knocked on his door. Tommy had been at work, and Alan had just woken up. He'd been shuffling off to the kitchen to make a cup of coffee when the knock came.

Clad in pajamas, hair sticking up all over the place, Alan answered the door and came face-to-face with the man he would meet with several times over the next couple of years. He swung the door open and was greeted by a man in a blue suit and sunglasses.

"Alan Pemberly?" the man asked.

"Yes, that's me," Alan said, naturally suspicious of someone knowing his name without the luxury of an introduction.

The man fished out his wallet and displayed his credentials: Christopher Wells, Private Investigator. Alan's heart skipped a beat.

"Can I help you?" Alan asked, shocked and uncertain as to what a private investigator would want with him.

"Actually, yes. I was hired to look for you. Your father procured my services, and he wishes..." Before he could finish his sentence, Alan slammed the door in the man's face and threw the dead bolt. His throat constricted in panic as he backed away.

"Alan. Your father sends a message," the man yelled through the door. "I'm putting it in your mail slot. It has my phone number and his. I'll be going now," the man said, and then, sure enough, a yellow envelope was shoved through the mail slot.

"You tell that no good son of a bitch to leave me alone, do you understand? Go away!" Alan screamed. Christopher never replied, and after a while, Alan approached the door cautiously to look out. His doorstep was empty. He reached down and plucked the yellow envelope up, stormed into the kitchen, and threw it away. Later that night, after making love to Tommy, Alan got up and made his way into the kitchen. He dug through the trash and found the envelope. After wiping some grease off, he stared at it for what seemed like an eternity. He sat down at his kitchen table and slid a window open. After lighting a cigarette, he thumbed the envelope to break the seal and pulled out a letter.

Dear Alan,

I have sat here at my desk on occasion to write you, on several occasions, for the past six months, ever since Wells told me he knew where you were. I have started, stopped, thrown away, and restarted letter after letter, trying to think of what to say to you. The only thing I can say is how sorry I am. I know that doesn't make up for the things I did and said to you. I know I can't take those things back, and as I sit in this empty house, sober for the first time in more than five years, the silence is deafening. So I am not going to try and explain to you why I let myself become the monster that I was. Instead, I hope to explain to you the steps I've taken to get better. First of all, I entered a twelve-step program. I am sober. I go to meetings at the local Methodist church I attend in Clay Center. The minister stopped by the house one day, and he told me about an outpatient program through the hospital in Junction City. I entered rehab and did a three-month stint there. The withdrawal was terrible, and I thought I was going to die. I wanted to. As I sobered up, the realization of what I had done nearly drove me mad and made me want to drink that much more. I should have protected you. I should have been there for you. I lost a wife, but you lost your mother, and I am sorry.

These are my sins against you: I hit you. I screamed at you. I called you names. I blamed you for the death of your mother. I blamed you for my own misery. I made you cry. I made you afraid of me. I made you hate me.

One of my steps is to apologize to those I have wronged, but I plead with you to understand it is more than just that. I want to be your father again. I want to be your dad again. I know I don't deserve it. I know I am not worthy of it. And if that isn't possible, I would like to ask that you forgive me. I am not the man I used to be. I am the man I was before the bottle. I am the man who held you as an infant, who got up in the middle of the night to feed, and change, and burp you. I am the man who taught you how to ride your bicycle. I am the man who dropped you off at school and picked you up. I am the man who held your momma's hand as she held yours, and we walked together as a family. That is who I am now. I am sorry it took you leaving me here alone in my own vomit for me to realize this. You were and always will be my proudest accomplishment.

Your loving father,

Mark Pemberly

P.S. The home number is still the same.

Alan shook as he read those words, his eyes clouding over and a sob escaping his lips. His anger toward the man and Alan's desire for him to be in his life brought both infinite hope and eternal torment. Since he had arrived in California, he'd dreaded that one day he would get a phone call that his father had drunk himself to death, or worse, had killed someone on his way home from the bar. He laid his head in his arms. Sitting alone at the kitchen table, he wept, wanting more than ever the comfort of the man he had once known. He called his dad the next day.

As the weeks flowed into months, and months turned to a year and then two, father and son tentatively began to reform a very fragile relationship. But Tommy was resistant, even detrimental, to the reconnection.

"You're going to go back into the wolf's den after you escaped?" Tommy ranted at him one evening when Alan tried to talk to him about it.

"He's sober, Tommy. I've talked to his minister, the neighbors, everyone we knew together, and they all say the same thing. They brag about him and how well he is doing. It's just a visit, for crying out loud. Why is this a problem?" Alan asked, throwing his hands up.

"He hurt you repeatedly. What if he isn't sober, just hiding it well? You'll think everything is fine, and when you move back, he'll fall off the wagon and start back over again. He doesn't like the fact that you're gay and with me, and he'll never treat you the way you should be treated," Tommy said angrily. They were talking over dinner at a local diner, whispering back and forth.

"I'm not moving back there, Tommy. I think a visit wouldn't be a bad idea. I mean, he is doing everything he can to show that he wants to reconnect. He even told me to bring you along, that he wants to talk to you as well," Alan said.

"He wants to take you away from me," Tommy said, shaking his head. "He's going to tell me to get lost is what he is going to say. I don't trust him and you shouldn't either."

"He can't take me away from you. I'm over eighteen now; there is nothing he can do. Come on, Tommy, it's been almost three years," Alan pleaded. The rest of the conversation didn't go well at all, and they drove home in silence. Over the days and months ahead, Alan realized he had traded one abusive relationship for another. He walked away when Tommy finally struck him and landed him in the mess he was in right now.

He resolutely pushed those memories of that time away and continued down the hall, passing different types of offices, most of which had the same frosted glass covered with black bold letters. As he rounded the corner, he saw a cleaning lady dressed in a blue uniform bent over a mop. She straightened up, looked at him curiously, and nodded politely as he approached. He gave her a brief smile as he passed her, but she stopped him.

"It's Saturday, son. The elevators are down for the weekend. The stairs are back the other way," she said, pointing behind him with a bony finger.

"Oh. Thank you," he said and turned on his heels.

"It's fine, mister. Had to tell a crying woman earlier about it. It was like she didn't hear me. Finally went back the other way, though," she said as he walked away, but Alan wasn't paying much attention. He was too busy with the desire to get out of the building as fast as he could.

Instead he stopped, turned around, and asked, "There wouldn't be a phone in this building, would there?"

"Yup. Down in the lobby. Keep on going down the hallway, take a right and then a left, and the lobby stairs are there. Tell the guard Nessa said to let you out when you're done. He won't mind," she said with a smile and a wink.

"Thank you," Alan said.

"Sho 'nuff, baby. Just be careful outside. The weather is nasty," she said and returned to her mopping.

Eventually, Alan found the staircase that led down to the lobby—the same one the married man had brought him up the night before, he realized as the fog started to lift in his mind—and quickly slipped down until he reached the ground floor. He opened the door leading to the lobby, feeling a whoosh of air hit him. The area smelled of pine cleaner and lemon. It was brilliantly lit, and as Alan walked into the large space, he looked up at the fresco painted on the ceiling. When the gravelly voice of a man called to him, he jumped.

"Can I help you, young man?"

Alan brought his startled gaze down to meet that of the older man, who had turned around behind a desk and was staring at him. His white hair was perfectly combed and his uniform was sharp.

"Oh. Sorry. Hi. I ran into Nessa upstairs, and she said I could use the phone," Alan said nervously. "If that's okay."

The man grunted and pointed to a few private booths on one side of the lobby. Alan quickly walked toward them. The first was out of order, but it wasn't until the guard pointed it out that Alan noticed the sign in black and white hanging on the doorknob. Embarrassed, he went to the next one and pulled the sliding door open, stepped in, and shut it behind him. He was so nervous, he stared at the phone like it was a snake. *Why don't you go home and try to work it out with Tommy?* he asked himself quietly. *Maybe he's right. Maybe this is a mistake.*

He reached for the phone, picked it up, and set it back down several times before putting it to his ear. The dial tone hummed as he searched his pocket for change. He threw a few dimes in the slot and then dialed quickly before closing his eyes and holding his breath.

One ring. Two. Three. After the disheartening fourth ring, he was about to hang up when his father's voice came through the static.

"Hello?"

Alan hesitated.

"Hello?"

"Dad?" Alan asked meekly.

"Hey, boy," his father said, seeming happy to hear from him. "How are you?"

"Oh…well…pretty rotten," Alan said as he began to choke up.

"What's wrong?" Dad asked, sounding concerned.

"Aw, Dad, I'm a mess. I've made a mess of myself out here. Tommy and I split up, and I don't have a place to live. I don't think I can make it anymore," Alan said thickly, tears trickling down his face. It was silent on the other end, and Alan asked the question he had feared the answer to.

"Dad…can I come home?" he asked.

His father didn't hesitate. "Yes. Where are you?"

"Downtown San Francisco. I've got enough money, I think, for an airplane ticket," Alan said.

"Okay. Get to the airport and buy it. If you don't have enough, call me back and I'll wire it to you. Don't worry about a thing. As a matter of fact, call me when you get to the airport, and I'll have the ticket waiting. I'll call them as soon as we get off the phone," Mark said rapidly.

Alan heard his recliner shut. He envisioned his father in the living room, now standing there, twirling the phone cord in his hand. "Dad, I..." Alan said and hesitated. His lower lip trembled, and he felt worn out but hopeful this all was going to end soon.

"What is it?" Mark asked.

He wanted to say "I love you," but the words wouldn't come. There would be time enough for that later. Right now, he had to get out of here and get to the airport. He should have enough for a taxi.

"I can't wait to see you," Alan said and heard his father sigh.

"Me neither, son. All right, get to the airport, and I'll have the ticket ready. Call when you get there," he said happily.

"Okay. I'm on my way now," Alan said. "Bye, Dad."

"Bye, Alan," his dad said, and Alan hung up.

He turned and stepped out of the booth. The lobby was abandoned, the guard having left his post behind the desk. Alan looked at the front door and decided against trying to use it and instead, pulled his bag up, tucked his head down, and headed for the stairwell to go out the back door. Since the guard seemed to have stepped out, he didn't want to wait for him to get back to unlock the front. His heart was racing, and his feet were a little lighter. He walked back through the lobby, through the doors, to a back entrance of the building. Nessa had been right—it was nasty-looking weather out there. As he pushed the door open, the damn wet December weather slapped him on the face, and he blinked as rain blew in at him.

The back door opened on an empty alleyway. Alan walked down a set of cement steps and headed toward the street. His sneaker-clad feet sloshed in the puddles as he made his way forward at almost a run to hail a taxi. As he broke free of the building, he heard shouting coming from his right and froze.

David and the woman he'd seen in the photo were screaming at each other inside a pearl-colored Mercedes; he could hear them even though the windows were shut. She was in the driver's seat, shaking her head, mascara running down her face, making her look like an insane clown, and David was in the passenger's seat, gesturing emphatically as he yelled at her. Alan's heart leaped into his throat when David turned forward and their eyes met. He stopped talking and gesturing long enough to catch his wife's attention.

She pointed at Alan and looked at David with a shocked look of horror on her face, and then threw her hands up in disgust. Bingo. David had just gotten outed and was now on the defensive end of her slapping and punching him. Alan smirked as she whaled on her husband, before he turned his head and raised a hand to hail an oncoming taxi.

The woman screamed, but it was too late. Tires screeched on wet pavement as the Mercedes sped toward Alan. There was a moment when he saw the horror in David's eyes. He felt the impact as the car hit him, and suddenly he was hurtling up over the hood, onto the windshield, over the top, and down the other side. Alan's head hit the pavement with such force, the world faded in and out for a second. He was immersed in red light as the brakes of the car that hit him were stomped. Pain seared through Alan as he tried to raise his head off the pavement. Blood ran from his nose and mouth, and he barely registered the screams of people telling the woman she had hit someone and to stop.

As Alan lifted his head, he caught sight of the woman staring at him in her rearview mirror. The cold satisfaction in her insane clown eyes made him shiver. *If you only knew I stood up to your husband for you and your kid*, Alan thought as the red lights of her brakes turned white. He'd ceased to be a person and had simply become an object of disdain and disgust. He closed his eyes once more as the sound of squealing tires and screaming pedestrians filled the air...

***

On Frederick Street, in Clay Center, Kansas, in the house he'd once loved, in a familiar room, in a familiar bed that hadn't been slept in for almost three years, Alan opened his eyes to the sound of a gunshot…and then the nightmare began.

CHAPTER 1

2013

T HE KANSAS STATE line had been crossed about an hour
earlier, and I-70 stretched on forever in front of Jonathan
David as his Dodge tore through the plains state at eighty miles
an hour. The window was down, and the warm summer wind
blew in, bathing his sweat-soaked body. The air conditioner was
on the fritz again and gave off only strange noises rather than
cool air. He shut it off and reached down beside him, blindly
grabbing for the pack of Marlboro Lights he had sitting in the
center console. He lit one up, inhaling deeply before exhaling a
plume of bluish-gray smoke through his nostrils and mouth. The
tendrils of smoke got caught on the wind and whipped past his
face and out into the fiery glow of a quickly approaching evening
as darkness descended like ink across the eastern expanse of
prairie sky. He smiled to himself; he was going home, back to
the familiar, back to where he'd been happy. Well, he had never
really ever been happy in his life, but this was the closest he had
ever come.

As he looked out over the darkened plains that whipped past
him as his forty-thousand-dollar jukebox on wheels plowed the
black-top roads, he thought, *You aren't in Detroit no more.* He
hated that place, the city of empty and broken dreams, where
one could find himself staring down death either by gangbangers
with murder in their eyes or by the prostitutes with the forced
sway of their hips, offering their poisonous wares while their
pimps looked on, salivating over the money their golden girls
would hand over at the end of their shifts. Drive-by shootings,
fire bombings…a place where residents looked forward to winter,

because criminals, like the rest of the wild animals in the world, seemed to hibernate in the deep depression of the cold months. Summer was hell, as the heat poured over the concrete jungle that time had forgotten, drug dealers, disgruntled teenagers, and dangerous cops prowling the neighborhoods like jackals ready to pick off the weakest among the populace.

There, his private Vietnam remained among the broken cracks of sidewalks that hadn't ever been repaired. He occasionally looked up the house of his childhood on Google Maps, like a sorcerer scrying through a crystal ball. He would do it late at night, while his lover slept, looking with sick fascination at the house that had once been meticulously cared for, but now had boarded windows and a screen door barely hanging on to its frame. Those that weren't boarded up remained curtainless and hollow, like a corpse that had lost its eyes during the process of decomposition.

He had dreamed of standing outside the house armed with a Molotov cocktail he would ignite and send hurling into the living-room window and then watch as the flames engulfed the house slowly. But that dream would turn to a nightmare as the house began to scream in agony, along with the spirits and memories and pieces of him left there. He had been to war long before he joined the Army after that horrible day on September 11, 2001. As a matter of fact, resting in the arms of those in his command, he had, for the first time in his life, known peace even in the midst of all the insanity happening around him. But Kansas had been different. It had been gentle with him, almost nurturing to him when he'd come here to Fort Riley almost eight years ago.

He worried he was chasing a memory, that the most positive four years of his life had faded into the recesses of time, like castles built of clouds, easily swept away with the wind of change and now someone else's to look upon as they lay in the grass looking up toward the heavens. But he was willing to risk it, to risk everything, like Roland of Gilead looking for his beloved tower, like Gollum searching for his precious, this lonely soul plowing through the countryside as night closed in on the midnight hour, seeking peace not knowing, and like the other two, not caring what the price might be. He leaned back in his seat and rested his head on the headrest and stretched his weary body a little.

Unlike Detroit, there was no urban sprawl to be seen in any direction out here. Exactly the opposite was true. The only thing sprawling along I-70 were the open fields rolling along on the hills that rolled out from Missouri and into Kansas.

The east side of Kansas wasn't as flat as the west side was, past Salina. Fort Riley had been built strategically around rolling hills that looked out over the prairies of the plains state. Perhaps it was the contrast that fascinated him, the fact that Kansas was not what he was used to, that made him want to be there. It seemed he would do anything to make his life exactly opposite of the life he had been born into. Sure, they had Topeka, the state capital, but that was an urban oasis in the middle of nowhere, a place they could visit long enough for Jonathan to get sick of and then be able to leave. He loved that idea.

While he drove onward, rock and roll blared out of the speakers from a CD mix he had made before hitting the road. He had hit random on his stereo to make sure he wouldn't know what was coming on next. He liked the thrill of the drums, the squeal of the electric guitar, and the occasional drama of the piano played heavy.

He imagined himself standing in front of thousands of people singing his heart out to them—a little fantasy he played in his head as he sang along with the tracks. The CD player in his dash had seen almost as many miles as the Durango had. He looked in his rearview mirror for telltale signs of lights on the freeway behind him, perhaps a cop car out looking to pop someone, but there was nothing there but his past. He smirked, took another drag of his vice, and with his thumb, pushed the rearview mirror up so he couldn't stare at it.

Foreigner was telling him it always felt like the first time, and Jonathan David thumped the steering wheel as he put distance between himself and everything he was leaving behind. Every minute, every mile marker, every turn of his wheels meant he was closer to freedom—a never-ending search. Yet, this was a first for him. Returning to a place was not his style—quite the contrary, in fact. Jonathan loved new places and new faces. He loved fresh starts and had made plenty of them now that he was in his early thirties. So many faces he had once looked upon were removed from his life by time and, now, by distance. He missed them. He loved them, in fact, but he couldn't stay. He thought they'd probably known that from the moment they'd met.

The track quit playing and the truck was suddenly quiet save for the engine and the sound of the wind. Jonathan inhaled deeply, the sweet smell of grass wet with summer dew filling his lungs as he drove the familiar road. For being on the road almost thirty-six hours, stopping only to refuel, sleep, and eat, he felt pretty good. He had enough caffeine in his system to power a small industrial plant, and the half-smoked carton of cigarettes kept him from chewing his fingernails, a bad habit of his. The trip to meet with his publisher in Texas had been well worth the drive, since he loathed flying.

The next track started up, and the familiar opening bars brought his mood down a little, as it usually did, but instead of skipping it, he leaned forward and cranked the volume up louder. It was fitting, really, this melancholy song that was so familiar to him. It had been an anthem for him for most of his life. Ever since his sister had given him his first CD, he had played the album over and over again. Listening to it late at night while the rest of the house slept, the lyrics empowered him, and the piano called to him like an angel calling him from some distant portal. Tonight, he was traveling back through a portal he'd never thought he would ever return through. As the sun finally set in the western sky, and the deep blues and purples of the night took over, the anthem played out over the speakers: *The skies were pure and the fields were green, the sun was brighter than it's ever been…*

He listened in reverence as Meat Loaf sang, his high voice pounding out along with Jim Steinman's piano. Each note stirred a dusty memory, dry as sand, and sent them swirling, waiting in line to pass over the always active movie screen that was his mind, a constant production with endless scenes from his life. As he mouthed the words, and his cigarette burned down closer to his long, thin fingers, his thoughts went back to places he had been... *We got in trouble but we sure got around...* His throat turned as arid as bones that had just been rattled, having never been buried deep enough. Six feet, eight feet, twelve feet, it really didn't matter—they always found their way up and out. He smirked thinking about it. Trisha Yearwood had a song called "The Song Remembers When," and nothing was truer than those words. Especially tonight, right now, as he rocketed toward his destination.

The crescendo of the song was coming up, and as Jim pounded away at the piano toward the end, Jonathan shivered in his seat. A cold chill cascaded through him and down the length of his T-shirt, soaked in the back from a cool sweat. The cherry on his cigarette was now down to the point where it was burning his knuckles, and he let it burn. He was dying to feel something, and as always, pain would suffice. "Objects in the rearview mirror may appear closer than they are." The track ended, but Jonathan was so lost in thought that when his phone rang beside him, he jumped and jerked the Dodge to the right ever so slightly. Correcting the vehicle and calming his beating heart, he reached for the Droid and saw who was calling. His mood lifted as he slid his thumb expertly across the face of the device and answered.

"City Morgue. You stab 'em, we slab 'em," he said, suddenly realizing how parched his throat was.

"Hey, handsome. You gonna get here sometime this century or what?" Eddie asked.

"Yeah, yeah, I am on my way. I just crossed the state line. It's another two hours between here and Topeka, and another two hours from there to Clay Center." Jonathan yawned. "Sorry."

"I didn't catch that last part," Eddie said.

"It'll be another two and a half hours or so. I should make it in about ten o'clock. You getting settled in all right there?" Jonathan asked as he fished another cigarette out of the pack and lit up.

"Yeah, the movers were a big help. They set everything where I needed it, so I've just been going through boxes and unpacking everything. By the way, I picked us up some Chinese food in Manhattan earlier today, in case you're hungry when you get in."

He loved hearing Eddie's voice on the phone; it always soothed his nerves. "Sounds good. In what condition did you find the house?" he asked curiously.

"Tip-top shape. The lady, Betty...was that her name? Yeah. She met me at the front door with the key and the deed in hand. We did a last walk-through, and she said she could call someone if anything was out of place or not up to our standards, but it was immaculate. They did exactly as we asked," he said.

"That's what happens when you pay for a house with cash," Jonathan said.

"Hmmm, must be great to be a big-time writer," Eddie teased.

"Hey, you're married to a big-time writer," Jonathan shot back jokingly. Actually, he wasn't a big-time anything. He'd written a book. Juuuust one, as he liked to say, but it had paid off well. As a matter of fact, *Sands of Time* was still on the *New York Times* best sellers list and had done miracles for the young couple. They'd paid off their student-loan debt, as well as other minor nicks on their credit, and it had opened up a world of possibilities for both of them. So the slow track they had planned for themselves because of financial restrictions had suddenly been speeded up. In a flurry, they had moved out of Eddie's parents' house and run off to Vermont to be married.

"I know. And I can't wait for him to be home so I can kiss his face," he purred. Eddie, or Dr. Edward Dorman, PhD, as he was known to his peers and students, was the new clinical psychology teacher at Kansas State University in Manhattan. After reading about a job opening for the position from their website, Eddie had mentioned it to Jonathan over coffee one morning as they sat in a café in Boston. It was like a thunderbolt from heaven had come down and struck Jonathan on the spot.

"I can't wait either, babe," Jonathan said. He wasn't twenty-one anymore, he was thirty, bugger it all, and these long drives put wear and tear on his butt and legs. However, he was used to it because of his time in the Army. He'd already had to remove his wallet to keep his right butt cheek from going numb.

"So, how fast ya going?" Eddie asked.

"Oh, a hundred or so," Jonathan said. He looked down at the speedometer and let up on the gas when he saw himself creeping near eighty-five.

"Seriously," Eddie said, anxiety in his voice, just at the edges.

"I'm doing eighty, there isn't a cop in sight, and I-70 is as clear as a highway could be," Jonathan replied, trying to quell Eddie's fears.

"That's a little fast," Eddie said.

"I know, but the sooner I get home, the sooner I can shower. Remind me tomorrow that I need to have the truck detailed, too, and get an oil change," Jonathan said.

"Just be careful, eh?" Eddie said.

"I promise."

"Okay. I love you."

"I love you too," Jonathan said, and then he hung up the phone. He placed it on the seat next to him, put his cigarette back in his mouth, and took a drag. *Those will kill you someday*, an annoying voice nagged in the back of his head. He exhaled slowly, coughing at the end of it.

"Not today," he replied aloud and changed the CD. Tina Turner began to sing about steamy windows in her recent, and possibly last, live album. The crowd roared with delight, and Jonathan smiled as he cranked up the volume and readjusted the rearview mirror so he could see behind him once more. The fears and demons were exorcised from his mind, at least for now. They would return in short order, just as they always did, but for now, he rolled on down the highway with Anna Mae, the young girl from Nutbush, as he made his way home.

CHAPTER 2

I T HAD TAKEN some phone calls and a lot of time talking, e-mailing, more talking, inspections, text messages, a flight out, an interview, a signed contract, and a good-sized cashier's check before the deal had been done. They had a home and a fresh new start. Well, newish and fresher. Their relationship had been through its share of storms since its infancy, and Jonathan feared this might be the last-ditch effort to save the ship before she finally went under.

Jonathan had been stationed at Fort Riley from 2002 to 2005 and had fallen in love with the countryside. Those had been the happiest days of his life, although he'd never been sure if it had been the place or the people that had made him so happy. But for Eddie, having a full-time teaching slot and a tenure-track position was heaven for a new PhD, and it finally pulled him out of that post-doctorate crap he'd had to deal with for the past two years. Working on research for others wasn't what he'd planned on doing for the entirety of his career.

At ten fifteen on the nose, Jonathan drove up Sixth Street to Frederick Street and turned left, then went up a tiny incline. He pulled in front of the white colonial house on his right-hand side. He expertly guided the truck into a space and killed the engine, engaged the parking brake, and sat there for a second staring into the brightly lit living room. He could see Eddie through the windows, going through a box on their new dining-room table. He smiled to himself as he realized Eddie was singing along to something and shaking his butt slightly to the rhythm. He leaned his head back and watched him a second longer.

Finally, he opened the driver's side door and climbed out, his shoes finally hitting pavement after several grueling hours on the road. His legs tingled and his knees were stiff as he straightened and stretched his arms above his head, grabbing on to thin air. His head swam as he took a minute to get used to being in the upright position, and then he shut the door and clicked the alarm, arming it against any roaming small-town Kansas ninja robbers who might possibly be out.

Jonathan looked at their new home. The old colonial had been built in 1914 and was one of the oldest houses in the little city of Clay Center. The previous owners had taken good care of the place, according to the Realtor, and it showed. The house was painted white, and each window had shutters that were gray. It had a deep-set front porch, also white on the frame and gray on the steps and decking. It sprawled healthy and strong, its foundation firm, its roof solid, and its walls sturdy. As Jonathan walked up the concrete pathway, he stopped midway to soak it all in, thankful he was here now, instead of back where he'd started. He smiled to himself and continued on.

Slowly, he snuck up the stairs and stood by the screen door watching the man inside, who was holding two picture frames in his hands, his head going back and forth between them. Eddie was shorter than Jonathan by almost five inches, but he fit perfectly in his arms, something Jonathan loved more than anything. He admired the handsome dark-haired man, whose skin, every inch of his body, was so familiar to Jonathan he could describe it to an artist line by line.

"Hey there, handsome, may I have a cup of sugar?" Jonathan asked.

Eddie nearly dropped both things in his hands as he jumped and spun around. "Creeping Jesus Christ, Jonathan! You scared the shit out of me!" said his blue-eyed lover. But his face broke into a smile anyway at the sight of him.

Jonathan laughed and tried to open the wooden door, but it wouldn't budge. Eddie smirked and set the pictures down before slowly walking toward the door, eyebrows raised.

"I don't know, Mr. Strange Man. We have sugar, but you see, my husband is really the jealous type. He would be very angry if I were to let some random sexy daddy man into his house," he said, getting close to the screen.

"Oh yeah?" Jonathan asked, resting an arm on the doorframe.

"Uh-huh," Eddie said.

"Well, how about we not tell your husband, and we keep our torrid love affair a secret between us," Jonathan said sexily.

"Hmmm," Eddie said and then laughed, unlocked the screen, and opened the door.

Jonathan stepped inside and swept the man into his arms, holding him close. He buried his nose in the soft flesh between Eddie's neck and shoulder, smelling the scent of the man he loved. Eddie wrapped his arms around Jonathan's strong shoulders and laughed as he was picked up easily off the floor.

"God, I've missed you," Jonathan said, planting a kiss on Eddie's mouth.

"Mmm. Missed you too," Eddie replied when he was finally able to break away. He laid his head on Jonathan's chest for a moment as they stood there, their anxieties mutually drifting down through to their feet and outward into the solid foundation of the earth, to disappear below, leaving them both relieved and momentarily satisfied.

Jonathan looked around and was pleasantly surprised to see that most of the unpacking had been done, except for a box here and there. Eddie had been right: the house had been cleaned immaculately, and everything smelled fresh and new. Some of the wallpaper was outdated and needed to come down, and they had talked about all of that when they saw pictures of the place, but they were actually excited to be able to do it over the summer. It would be at least a month or two before Eddie would have to start worrying about turning in curricula for his classes, and Jonathan's agent knew they were getting settled in, so she had promised to stay off his ass for the time being. His book had been a shot in the dark for the company, but it had paid off well for both parties involved. Still, his agent wasn't pushy and always answered his frantic e-mails and phone calls when something struck him—anytime, day or night.

Jonathan was as much in love with the inside of the house as he was with the outside. The house boasted over three thousand square feet, with high ten-foot ceilings that created a massive open space begging to be filled with memories. The rooms were huge, with crown molding that lined the top and baseboards the bottom. The handrail going up the stairs was carved wood that was polished and well maintained, and they had a glass chandelier that hung over the dining-room table where Eddie stood after he led Jonathan back into the room to see what he had accomplished.

"So, what do you think?" Eddie asked.

"I think you've been a busy little bee," Jonathan said admiringly as he pulled his husband back so he could look into his deep-blue eyes.

"Awww, shucks, it was nothin'," he said with a grin. Jonathan knew better. Their combined books alone made up most of what people moved with, and he noticed all of them had been put on their shelves in alphabetical order, as Eddie's minor OCD demanded.

"Bullshit," Jonathan said.

"Actually, you have your own packing to undo. There are several rooms upstairs that I don't have anything in yet, and I wanted you to be able to choose your workspace. I know we decided on one room, but that was through pictures. So I figured, why not let you go up there and decide for yourself?" he said.

"I get to pick my own room! Awwww, man…sweet!" Jonathan said, and he took off up the carpeted stairs. He misstepped, as his legs were still tired from the trip, and would have landed on his whoopsy daisy if Eddie hadn't been right behind him, preventing him from falling. Both laughed and continued up the stairs at a reasonable pace so neither of them would end up in the emergency room. They climbed the remaining fifteen steps or so, and as they reached the top, Jonathan noticed it was quite a bit warmer than on the first floor.

"The air conditioner works, right?" he asked as he landed on the top step and turned his head to see Eddie reaching for his butt. He twisted his hips and backed up, wagging a finger at him.

"*Ne touche pas à la marchandise*," he said, laughing.

Eddie laughed too. "Yeah, the AC is fine, but it cooled off quite a bit this evening, and even with all the cleaning they did, the house still has a musty old-house smell. It isn't unpleasant, but it was a bit stuffy in here this morning. I've been trying to let it air out all day."

"Ah, okay. That makes sense," Jonathan said as he rounded the corner. He saw their bedroom, everything in its place, the door ajar. At the end of the hallway were three doors—one on the left side, one in the middle, and one on the right. Eddie stood at the top of the stairs and looked at Jonathan expectantly.

"Go on. Take your pick, handsome, and we can move the stuff in the morning," he said, shooing Jonathan down the hall.

"Which door shall it be? Ah, we'll try this one," Jonathan said, pushing it open and flipping on the light. The room was barely more than a closet with a tiny window. *Work in here and you'll be apeshit and bananas inside a week. More space, writer man, more space*, the annoying voice said.

"No shit," he whispered.

"What?" Eddie asked.

"I said, too small. This room," Jonathan said. "How about this one?" he asked as he opened the second door. He flipped on the light and was awash in a sea of pinkish rose-colored wallpaper.

"Yeah, I've dubbed this the Pepto-Bismol room and declared it the first to be redone. It has potential," Eddie said, laughing. It really did. It was large and airy, and two big windows looked out onto the backyard below. He could work in here. He checked for an air vent and was pleased when he saw it above his head.

"Get some heavy drapes or curtains in here and that way it stays cool. You should be set," Eddie said. He had come down the hallway and now stood in the doorway.

Jonathan stood in the center of the room with his hands on his hips, nodding. "Yeah, but the wallpaper has got to go," he said. "Who lived here before us? Aunt Bee from Mayberry?"

"No. It was two sisters, Sarah and Martha. They were in their mideighties when they sold the place and moved to a retirement community in Manhattan," Eddie said as Jonathan walked out.

Jonathan shot Eddie an inquisitive look. "How do you know that?"

"Realtor lady. Her skirt was as pink as the room, by the way. So was her lipstick," Eddie said, rolling his eyes and stepping back out of the way so Jonathan could shut the door.

"Ooh. Nice. Mary Kay much?" he asked.

"Oh yeah. I was surprised not to see a pink Cadillac parked out front." They both laughed as they made their way toward the stairs again.

"Hey, aren't you going to check out the last room, just in case? It's just as big in there, and it has large windows on the side, but the walls are white," Eddie said with shrug.

Jonathan stopped and smiled. "Sure." What he wanted to do was go downstairs, eat, then shower, screw his husband's brains out, and pass out, but he humored him. He stepped back up on the landing and ran his hand across Eddie's solid belly as he headed for the third and final door. He reached out as he approached but stopped suddenly, just short of the knob.

It felt like he had stepped into a freezer. A jolt like lightning passed through him, and he shivered hard.

"What is it?" Eddie asked, but to Jonathan, he sounded like he was a million miles away. He stared at the doorknob and with everything he had, forced himself to open it. The doorknob turned under his hand, and he swung the door open. Another jolt passed through him, this time hard enough to force him to close his eyes from the sudden pressure of it. He felt as if he were in an elevator descending too fast. Jonathan nearly fell to his knees before he caught himself. He raised his head and opened his eyes as sweat started to prickle at his hairline. A shiver cascaded down his back. He raised his head to look into the room and suddenly felt like he was being watched, although he saw nothing in there but bare walls.

Eddie tugged at his arm, turning him around. "Oh my God, Jonathan, you're as white as a sheet. What happened?" he exclaimed.

Jonathan, whose head was spinning and who suddenly felt nauseous, leaned along the wall to catch his breath. His legs threatened to buckle underneath him. "I dunno."

Eddie looked past him suspiciously into the room as he kept his hands on his husband's trembling body, holding him against the wall. There was nothing there, just empty walls and a single white light hanging in the center of the room.

"You look like you saw a ghost," Eddie said.

Bingo, hot stuff, the annoying voice in Jonathan's head said. That lone voice, derived of pain, which both lauded and criticized, threatened and adored. Well, maybe not a ghost, but something. "No. No, I just…the drive caught up to me all of a sudden. I'm fine," Jonathan said with a faint smile. *Where did that come from?* he asked himself. He felt sick to his stomach, and his mouth was as dry as the desert.

"Are you sure?" Eddie asked, keeping one hand on Jonathan's side.

"Yeah. I just need some food and some lovin'," Jonathan said as he pulled Eddie closer.

"Well, those things I can provide," Eddie said, staring into his eyes.

Jonathan wondered if Eddie knew he was full of shit. Something had just freaked him out. Eddie turned off the bedroom light and shut the door behind him before walking with Jonathan down the stairs.

CHAPTER 3

JONATHAN STOOD UNDERNEATH the hot shower with his hands resting on either side of the showerhead. The water cascaded down his naked body, running over the lines and ridges of his muscled back, down his butt and his legs. They had gone back downstairs to the kitchen, where Jonathan had taken a seat at the table and Eddie had reheated the Chinese food for him. He ate the noodles and beef slowly as the nausea wore off while he thought about what had just occurred upstairs. Eddie talked about plans for putting in a garden in the backyard and things they would have to pick up from the local hardware store in the morning. He stopped talking when Jonathan stopped responding with even grunts and nods.

"Hey, space cadet? You pickin' up any of this?" he asked, as he leaned against the counter, a ceramic mug in one hand and the other on his hip. He was watching Jonathan with curious and concerned eyes.

Jonathan looked up. "Huh? Oh, yeah. We can rent a tiller for the yard if that's what you want to do. It would save on vegetable shopping in the fall."

"Mmm-hmm. What else is going on in that brain of yours?" Eddie asked, sitting next to him on a stool at the island.

"You think you'll be happy here?" Jonathan asked. He sat back from slouching over his plate and rubbed Eddie's back, not wanting to mention what had happened to him upstairs.

Eddie smiled, contented. "Yeah. You know why?"

Jonathan raised his head and smiled as Eddie leaned in for a kiss. Their lips met, and Jonathan turned to cup his husband's face as they explored each other with their mouths. Desire swept

301

all the feelings of anxiety out of him as he lowered his hands and grabbed Eddie's legs and pulled him into his lap. He was careful not to send them both spilling over backward on the stool. He broke the kiss, and both men sat back.

"Why is that?" Jonathan asked, slightly out of breath.

Eddie leaned in and kissed him on the tip of his nose. "Because you're here. I can go anywhere, be anywhere, as long as you're there with me," he said breathlessly. There were many miles riding on those words—the many ups and downs the duo had already been through giving depth to those words—and Jonathan loved him for it.

Jonathan felt the length of his manhood straining against his pant leg in response. It was funny, what love did to one's sex life. *First, it's all hormones and physical touch and exploration, hot and explosive, and then when love shows up, it becomes a slow burn. God, I love this man.* He turned in his seat, and Eddie wrapped his legs around Jonathan's waist as they kissed again. Jonathan touched Eddie's chest and squeezed, feeling the muscles there. Eddie moaned into the kiss and let Jonathan lift him as he stood. Jonathan was mindful of the plate of food as he swiped the rest of the island clean with his forearm and laid Eddie back on the counter.

"What are you doing?" He laughed as Jonathan kissed down his neck.

"Christening our new house," Jonathan murmured between kisses as he lifted Eddie's T-shirt. Eddie moaned and arched his back as the material slid upward, then raised his neck and arms so Jonathan could pull it off completely. Eddie sat up and pulled Jonathan's shirt off. He pulled him closer, wrapping his legs around Jonathan's waist. The passion between the two lovers mounted as they whispered heated words to each other, their bodies colliding to become one. As clothes were discarded, Jonathan placed them on the floor of the kitchen as a makeshift bed. He laid Eddie down underneath him, then pressed his naked body against Eddie's, their desire for each other met as Jonathan entered his lover. It ended in an explosion that left them gasping for breath and lying side by side on the floor, hot, sweaty, and content.

Jonathan smiled as he leaned against the wall of the shower, the long miles, grit, soap, sweat, the smell of sex, and the taste of his lover washed down the drain as his skin reddened from the heat. He stepped once more underneath the water to let it run through his hair and then bent over and turned the nozzle off. He pulled the sliding glass door of the shower open and reached for the towel Eddie had hung on the bar for him. He patted the dampness on his face away before wrapping the towel around his waist and stepping out. The bathroom door was open a crack, and he could see the steam hovering in the air, cascading into the bedroom, where Eddie was asleep. Jonathan walked to the sink and wiped away the fog that had gathered on the mirror. He stood there for a second and looked at himself. Thirty years had come and gone since his birth, and the past ten years had certainly put miles on him, but he'd held tight to his good looks, even if he did have a few lines here and there.

He stood for another minute staring, not in admiration, but in wonder. He was alive, he was here, his feet on the cold tile floor of the bathroom in the house he and his husband owned together, in defiance of the odds that had been stacked against him. For all intents and purposes, he should have been dead a long time ago, wasted under the pressure of a foul beginning and a misspent youth, but here he was, breathing, feeling, together with Eddie, and it amazed him. Luck. Persistence. Something other than what he felt he'd earned had brought him here.

He opened the door to see Eddie sprawled across the bed, snoring happily. Tears pricked the back of his eyes as he watched him, his lover, running around somewhere in dreamland. It was not luck, or persistence; it was salvation. But for how long? *You can't run away forever*, the annoying voice chided him. Jonathan wrapped a mental hand around its throat and warned it that if it spoke again, he would choke the life out of it. In fear, the voice quieted.

Jonathan and Eddie had met at college, two souls wandering around the world of academics, trying to forge a path for themselves. Jonathan had noticed him a few times, moving quickly through the corridors of different buildings. Eddie had had a cell phone permanently attached to his ear as he disappeared in the crowd, leaving Jonathan simply watching after him.

Now here he was, lying in the bed they had bought together. Jonathan was just about to step into the bedroom when something cold brushed against his naked torso, like a breath of winter wind, causing the hairs on his arms to stand erect. His testicles pulled upward as if he'd been splashed with a bucket of ice water. With his back lit from the hallway light, Jonathan could have sworn he could see his breath in the two seconds the arctic temperatures surrounded him.

Then, as suddenly as it started, the room returned to its normal temperature. "What the fuck?" he whispered as he tried to figure out what had just happened. The air conditioner wasn't on yet, and the bedroom window was open to allow the cool night air in. He raised his head and saw the ceiling fan turning at a good pace but no explanation as to what had caused the burst of cold air.

He stood there for a few more minutes, nerves on edge, his gut churning, but as he calmed down, fatigue set in. His mind, so used to being hypervigilant, ground to a halt, and his eyes grew heavy. *You're just tired, old man*, the voice said cautiously, almost tenderly. It was a sympathetic change from its usual chastisement, the voice born as a key to his own survival of abuse. He nodded and walked over to the right side of the bed, unwrapped his towel, and pulled the blankets back. Naked, he climbed into bed with Eddie, who had rolled over on his side, muttering something into the pillow before falling back under sleep's spell. Jonathan snickered and pulled the covers up as he snuggled up to his lover's underwear-clad bottom. He waited patiently for Eddie to bring the sleep wagon around and fling the door open for him to jump in. Within minutes, despite what he had just felt, he was flying through dreams with his lover at his side.

***

Eddie jerked awake suddenly, sitting straight up in bed, heart thudding against his chest and his eyes wide open. He didn't know what had awakened him, but he was sure he had heard running or heavy footfalls. He waited for the pounding in his ears to calm down so he could hear properly. He looked past Jonathan's sleeping form to the doorway, where he was certain he would find someone standing, but his gaze fell upon nothing but the yellowish glow of the hallway light. *It's new-house noises*, he thought rationally. *You're just not familiar with the place yet, and you're edgy.* Eddie lay back on the bed and sighed. He was too sleepy to get up. Jonathan had been right. He had busted his ass as soon as he'd gotten there earlier that morning to finish getting the place situated and aired out as he worked alongside the movers to bring in the few things they owned. He was about to drift back to sleep when a thought occurred to him.

He was certain he had shut the bedroom door before he had fallen asleep. Maybe Jonathan had opened it, headed downstairs for something, and simply left it that way? He didn't know, but he brought his hands up to his eyes and tried to wipe the sleep away from them. He was so tired, and he ached from all the work he had done, and instead of showering with his husband, he had simply put his underwear back on after their lovemaking and fallen quickly to sleep. He turned his head toward the sleeping man beside him and smiled.

Jonathan's right arm was tossed over his eyes, and he was snoring quietly, mouth agape, his naked chest moving slowly up and down. Eddie watched him for a second, loving the sight of his furry body, tattooed arms, and strong jaw. The Kansas State University marching band could walk through the bedroom while he was sleeping playing Fleetwood Mac's "Tusk," and it wouldn't wake him.

"My hero," Eddie said sleepily, and leaned over to kiss him where his belly and chest met.

He sat back up and decided to get up for some water and, with a groan, threw his legs over the side of the bed and stood. He had to adjust his erection to keep it from poking outward in an uncomfortable fashion. He grabbed for his blue fuzzy robe and wrapped it around him as he walked out the bedroom door and down the stairs. He stopped for a second, thinking he'd heard something, and listened. His ears pricked at the sound of glasses or dishes being jarred downstairs in the kitchen. He turned toward the top of the stairs and questioned whether he should wake Jonathan, but decided against it.

"I'm not going to be that spouse," he muttered and decided to go at it alone.

He snuck down quickly to the bottom stair and grabbed one of Jonathan's baseball bats, which was leaning up against the wall. They always kept one handy in the umbrella stand for home invasions and persistent proselytizers. He made his way through the hallway to the room where the noise had come from, arguing with himself all the while.

What if it's a burglar? he asked himself.

In the kitchen? the rational side countered.

Sure. They have to start somewhere, he argued.

Well, then, they have to be pretty hard up, because we have nothing in there besides a few plates and drinking glasses, and even they don't match, he concluded.

He was still searching for a comeback as adrenaline pumped through him. Even though he reasoned against someone being in the house, it still left a pit of apprehension in his gut that burned and churned.

He held the baseball bat behind his shoulder like a real player, ready to knock the head off any unwelcome intruder who had made their way into his new home. His mouth was dry, and his pulse raced in his veins as he approached the room.

He entered the darkened kitchen, then reached in, flicking on the light on the left side of the wall. He hoped the light would momentarily blind whoever was there. As it came on, he readied the bat, but he was greeted with nothing but emptiness. Relief flooded through him instantly, and he put the bat down. There was no way out of the room except past him or out the back door.

"Shit," he said, laughing as he walked to the door to make sure it was secure. It was. It wouldn't budge a millimeter as he pushed or pulled on it. Then something caught his eye. One of the cabinet doors was standing wide open; the cabinet where, hours before, he had placed all the drinking glasses and coffee mugs.

"Huh," he said.

He skirted around the island and studied the door for a moment, swinging it back and forth. It wasn't loose, and when he closed it three quarters of the way, it shut and caught on the magnet. He pulled it open, feeling the magnet give way as he applied a good tug to it. He shut it once more and turned, drawing his eyebrows together in mild annoyance. He made his way over to the refrigerator and opened it, revealing mostly empty shelves save for a case of water he had thrown in on the bottom, beer, and tea. He reached in and grabbed a bottle, untwisted the cap, and put it to his lips. He took three long swallows, feeling the cold water flowing down into his gut, before he put the cap back on and shut the door.

The adrenaline that had been so hot and heavy in his veins felt like it had just disappeared into the ether as he calmed down. He yawned and looked around the kitchen of his new house, smiling to himself. They were finally homeowners, and their place was beautiful. They would have to go shopping to buy furniture together. They'd left Michigan with all they owned, but it could have filled a single room in the new house. Now they were on their way to domestic bliss. Eddie smirked at that thought as he yawned once more and remembered he'd left his warm bed upstairs. He suddenly wanted more than anything to get back to it and his snoozing husband. He was halfway down the hall when the hairs on the back of his neck stood up. Eddie froze.

He felt like he was being watched. *You were just in there*, his mind insisted. *There's nothing there.* He was sure any moment a hand would wrap itself over his mouth and drag him back, and Jonathan would awaken to find no trace of him. He whirled around and stared into the blackness of the kitchen before forcibly marching forward until he reached the light switch. He flicked the light on, revealing the kitchen was just as he'd left it: empty. He gathered his robe around him and flicked the light back off. This time, he took off for the stairs, taking them two at a time. Once he reached their room, he shut the door behind him and shucked his robe before sliding under the covers next to Jonathan, who had rolled over onto his side. He pulled the covers up to his chin and listened. *Stop it, Eddie*, he tried to reason with himself. The thought-stopping method he had successfully used to treat certain patients who suffered from intrusive thoughts failed to work for him that night. Seconds turned to minutes, then minutes to an hour, before his eyelids grew heavy. Jonathan turning over in bed and wrapping his arm around Eddie's chest finally allowed Eddie to relax and slip back under the waves of unconsciousness. But his sleep was disturbed and restless as images of empty hallways and unopened doors disturbed his dreams.

Downstairs in the dark kitchen, the clock Eddie put up on the wall ticked relentlessly for several minutes and was the only noise to be heard until, with a soft click, the kitchen cabinet door popped open again.

CHAPTER 4

GOOD MORNING, K-STATE fans! This is your host, John Bates, on Kansas's home for rock 'n' roll, playing a great tune from 1980. Here are the Eagles and 'Seven Bridges Road'!" the alarm clock shouted, and suddenly the sunlit bedroom was filled with the four-part harmony of the old song.

Jonathan woke first with a smile on his face, his voice cracking as he sang the song quietly into his pillow. He stretched, holding the pillow tight against him as he did, and opened his eyes. He stared at the face of the clock that brought the heavenly music out of its speaker. *It's 8:00 a.m. What a way to start the day*, he thought as he moved to sit up.

An arm came out of nowhere and pulled him back down. "Uh-uh, mister. I get at least to the end of this song to hold onto you," Eddie said as he pulled Jonathan closer to him, still sounding sleepy.

Jonathan let himself be dragged across the bed into the muscular arms of his man and smiled. Eddie kissed the back of his neck and held him there. Jonathan felt the warm sunlight on his back and smelled the morning dew as it evaporated outside. He breathed in deeply and sighed contentedly. He was surprised at how well he had slept during the night; usually new places made him edgy. But last night, after he'd climbed into bed, he'd been out for the count, and his dreams had been light and nonsensical.

The song ended and the radio announcer came back on. Jonathan reached over and shut the alarm off before rolling over on his back, drawing Eddie into his arms. He rested his head on Jonathan's chest as Jonathan played with his hair.

"Morning, baby," Eddie murmured, still facing down, apparently not wanting to inundate his lover with his morning dragon breath.

"Morning," Jonathan said and kissed the top of his head.

"Sleep good?" Eddie asked.

"Like the dead," Jonathan replied, staring up at the ceiling fan.

Eddie snorted and snuggled closer. He pressed his erection against Jonathan's side. Usually that would entice Jonathan to playful morning lovin', but not right now. His bladder was full and screaming at him.

"Gotta pee, babe," he said, detaching his husband and rolling out of bed. His feet hit the carpet and with a push, he headed to the bathroom to do his business. Once he was done, he stepped out to see Eddie getting dressed in raggedy work clothes, looking half-awake.

When he saw Jonathan standing there, he grinned. "Yay! More unpacking and work to do today!" he said, feigning sheer joy. Jonathan chuckled and nodded, then walked to his dresser drawers and opened them, pulling out cut-off shorts and an old T-shirt. He put on a pair of underwear, slid the shorts on over his hips, and fastened them.

"You want some coffee?" Jonathan asked, leaving his shirt off for a minute.

"Yeah. I need to brush my teeth, but I'll be down in a second," Eddie said, heading to the bathroom. As he passed by, Jonathan snapped his T-shirt at Eddie's ass and made him jump. Eddie laughed as he ran into the bathroom and shut the door behind him. Jonathan chuckled and, still bare-chested, walked down the stairs and turned down the hallway to the kitchen. The first thing he noticed was that all of the kitchen chairs had been pulled away from the table and pushed against the walls. He stood there for a second, wracking his brain on whether they had been like this the night before, but then he simply shrugged it off and scooted them back in. The second thing he noticed was that one of the kitchen cabinet doors was open, the one with the coffee mugs and glasses, which all looked a little closer to the edge than what they should be.

"Huh," he said aloud and wondered if Eddie had gotten up in the middle of the night, opened it, and forgot to close it. He decided not to say anything and simply slid them back where they had been and shut the cabinet door. That was when he saw the baseball bat leaning against the kitchen wall near the door. *Wonder if he got the jitters last night?* the annoying voice asked. Jonathan had never felt him move. He made a noncommittal sound.

It took him a second to orientate himself with the new kitchen layout, as some of the things had been put away and others were waiting their turn. However, knowing his husband's love of coffee, he knew the coffeepot, coffee, and filters would be at the ready, and where he found one item, he found them all. He walked over to the sink, put the empty pot underneath the faucet, turned it on, and stood there while the pot filled. From this vantage point, he could see into the next-door neighbor's backyard. The sight of a blonde woman, her wispy hair white in some spots, donning a pair of slick yellow gloves and then walking over to her rose garden, pulling a small wagon behind her, made him smile. He turned off the tap, picked up the pot, drained off the excess water, and then froze. The cabinet door was open again.

Jonathan shook his head and closed it again before pouring the water into the reservoir for the coffeemaker, then turned the machine on. Reaching up, he opened and shut the cabinet several times. The catch was magnetic, and unless you gave it a good tug, it stuck.

"Whatcha doin'?" Eddie asked, causing Jonathan to nearly jump out of his skin. He whirled around to see his husband standing near the refrigerator.

"Jesus, babe. Make some noise when you enter the damn room. You nearly gave me a heart attack," Jonathan said, clutching his chest and laughing.

Eddie leaned against the refrigerator and stared past Jonathan to the kitchen cabinets behind him. He narrowed his eyes and crossed his arms over his chest.

"What's wrong?" Jonathan asked. Eddie shook his head, walked over to the wall, retrieved the baseball bat, and handed it to Jonathan, who looked at him inquisitively. Eddie just smiled sweetly and shrugged.

"What's wrong with the cabinet?" Eddie asked.

"Ah, nothing. Just keeps popping open on its own," Jonathan said nonchalantly. He went to the backdoor and stared out into the big yard. "Are we going to pick up that tiller for the garden? Babe?"

Eddie was still eyeballing the cabinet, and when he spoke, he looked like Jonathan had called him out of a stupor.

"Yeah. Yeah, that sounds good," Eddie said, tearing his gaze away from the kitchen cabinet to meet Jonathan's.

"Good. Well, how about some breakfast?" he asked. "What have we got?"

Eddie laughed. Jonathan raised the bat and looked at Eddie, who shrugged and rolled his eyes, signaling him not to ask. Jonathan set it back down and opened the pantry door, revealing a box of instant oatmeal that had made the journey all the way from Michigan. Thank goodness it was peaches-and cream-flavored and not regular instant oatmeal that required milk and brown sugar to make it edible.

"I love this yard. I'm thinking vegetables and flowers and bags of mulch… Nah, scratch that. No mulch. You have to rake that shit up in the spring. I didn't realize how big the backyard was going to be. Maybe we can get a pool," Jonathan said, leaning against the doorway, looking out.

"Inground or aboveground?" Eddie asked. He walked over to the stove and turned the igniter around until it clicked and the flame kicked on. He put the teakettle on to boil for the oatmeal.

"Well, it gets really hot during the summer, and there is nothing worse than getting into a pool of tepid water, so I would think an inground pool would do. What do you think?" he asked, still leaning against the door.

Eddie retrieved two bowls and spoons and set them down beside each other. "I don't know; it's up to you. I think a pool would be very nice, and we don't have any large trees out in the back, so we don't have to worry too much about leaves," he said. He walked over to Jonathan and slid his arm around his waist, and Jonathan pulled Eddie against him. The backyard was very large—at least a half-acre—and Jonathan mentally jotted down "riding lawn mower" onto the "to buy" list.

The kettle began to whistle, and Eddie walked over to the stove to turn off the flame. He shook the packets, then dumped the contents into each bowl and poured the boiling water into them. He stirred the oatmeal before walking out to sit on the back patio. There was a little bit of ledge for them to park their butts on as they sat in the morning sun to have their breakfast. The older lady Jonathan had noticed earlier waved at them, and they politely waved back.

"I think a vegetable garden in the far back would be our best bet. It gets full sun, and we don't have to worry about drainage. The back rises up a little farther as you go back," Eddie said between mouthfuls.

"I see that. It slopes up. Which is fine, I guess, if we put the pool over in the center and then extend this patio out, maybe have a gazebo or something we can sit under to hide from the sun, have a barbeque grill, yeah...I think that would look great," Jonathan said. Eddie looked over at the woman, admiring her roses, and Jonathan quickly wiped away his tears. Too many long roads had brought him here, full circle, to a place where he had once been happy, and now he prayed silently it was a sign of good things to come. He hesitated for a minute, as a lump in his throat formed, threatening to break his voice.

"...with the running of water pipes underneath the ground out to the gardens. I don't think it would cost much. What do you think?" Eddie said, turning his head back to Jonathan and cocking his head to the side, looking at him inquisitively. "Are you okay?" he asked, and Jonathan nodded.

"I love you," Jonathan said as he leaned in for a slow and tender kiss.

Once it broke, Eddie reached up and moved the hair out of Jonathan's eyes. "It's a new start, babe. We're going to be just fine," Eddie said and placed a kiss to the tip of Jonathan's nose, then pulled his face back a few inches.

"Yeah. I think so too," Jonathan said as Eddie rested his head on Jonathan's shoulder. Jonathan closed his eyes and inhaled a steadying breath. The air was sweet with late-spring scents floating about in the summer sunshine. The smell of dew and flowers, mixed with the heady fragrance of the sunbaked earth, infiltrated his nostrils as he drew it in deep, feeling it penetrate right into his soul. He exhaled slowly, contentedly, and soaked up the sunshine on his skin. They sat that way for a good twenty minutes or so, both lost in their happy nonthoughts, before Eddie finally stirred.

"Before we go out today and burn a hole in our savings, I've written down the possible colors to be used in each room, along with the trim. I'd like you to take a look at it and see if we can't come to an agreement on them," Eddie said.

"Meh, that's your job. I trust you. Just nothing pink, for God's sake," Jonathan said.

"Why is that my job?" Eddie asked, wide-eyed.

"Well, you know more about that shit than I do. I mean, I want to paint my own room blue and that's all right, but the rest of the house I leave in your capable hands," Jonathan said with a "please forgive me, don't make me sleep on the couch for insulting you" grin.

Eddie shook his head. "You are such a man." He chuckled, and Jonathan looked down at his bulging crotch.

"Last I checked, I was," he said, laughing, and Eddie rolled his eyes.

"Well, come on, Don Juan. Let's go over it real quick, and then we'll head out," Eddie said, standing and holding out his hand.

Jonathan took it and stood. They carried the remnants of their breakfast inside and placed them in the sink.

They spent nearly an hour going over what Eddie thought would be good colors once they removed the antiquated wallpaper. He'd chosen light and airy tones for each room that would make them feel larger and complement the natural hardwood floors. He suggested buying an oriental rug for the dining room to keep the chill off it in the winter. For the living room, which was carpeted, small rugs and a runner could keep feet from dirtying up the beige-colored floor covering. Jonathan nodded and gave his approval on all things, trying to stay focused. He so desperately wanted to go play in other places. It was all he could do to keep his ADD in check and not start thinking about video games, the lottery, the wedgie he was suffering from at the moment, or what they were having for lunch.

"So what do you think?" Eddie asked. Jonathan nodded and tried his best to feign interest. He gave a rather overenthusiastic, "Yeah." Eddie snorted and shot him a sideways glance before elbowing him in the ribs.

"Aww, come on, babe. It's great. You have a better eye for this stuff than me," Jonathan said.

"All right. You ready? Eddie asked.

"Yeah, let me go change. I look like a porn star in these shorts." And with that, he took off.

***

Eddie stayed behind, watching Jonathan's denim-clad butt bound up the stairs before wandering back into the kitchen. He picked up the baseball bat with the intention of putting it back in the umbrella stand, but stopped short of doing so. He felt safer with it in here and set it down once more. The cabinet door was shut, and he said a silent prayer of thanks as he walked over and locked the back door. He poured himself a cup of black coffee and shut the machine off. Jonathan refused to drink coffee and instead was a Mountain Dew junkie. Eddie knew they would be stopping by the gas station on their way to town. He went back into the foyer to wait for Jonathan, who reappeared a moment later in a pair of cargo shorts and a white T-shirt with the words, "Go Rock Yourself" written in black letters across the front. God, he was smokin' hot.

"Ready?" Jonathan asked, car keys in hand.

"After you," Eddie said, and the pair walked out the front door, Eddie locking it behind them.

The Kansas summer sun beamed down as they jumped into Jonathan's beloved blue Durango—Jonathan's baby—and started the engine. They rolled the windows down as soon as they got in and set off on their adventure.

***

Inside the house on Frederick Street, all was quiet until the boys turned the corner. Then all hell broke loose. The pantry door flung open and then shut. The lights in the kitchen and the hallway turned on and off. The basement doorknob shook as if someone on the other side was trying to get out, and the chairs around the dinner table pulled outward, lined themselves against the wall, and then put themselves back before going completely still. The only sound in the house was the clock ticking on the wall and the painful cry of a child who sounded lost, lonely, and in torment.

CHAPTER 5

THE BACK ROAD, K-18, took Jonathan's breath away, just as it had the first time he'd driven the route. Unlike the never-ending rolling hills of I-70, this little state road showed him the wonders of the beautiful state. The little beauties were the old state roads that wound through tiny towns from Clay Center to Topeka, should anyone want to go that far, and cut through the college town of Manhattan. The sky was robin's-egg blue with dots of puffy white clouds traveling lazily in the sky. The fields were green and happy, having had plenty to drink during the winter thaw. Jonathan thanked God that neither he nor Eddie had allergy problems as they drove with the windows down and the air cooling their sun-warmed bodies. During their trip, they pointed different things out to each other and oohed and aahed as they passed ranches high up on the plains in one direction, or when they hit Manhattan and saw the rolling hills and suburban sprawl before them. Some things had changed, but not much; most had stayed the same.

When Jonathan had first broached the topic of moving back to Kansas, Eddie wouldn't even listen to him. That was before Eddie found his dream job waiting vacant for him to fill it. As if by divine providence, something Jonathan smirked at when mentioned, Eddie pulled up the job posting through a cursory web search. Afterward, he was easier to convince. However, the argument to even consider the move was a doozy.

"What's in Kansas? It's flat… It's frickin' Kansas, for cryin' out loud," he'd said at one point.

But as they drove past adorable little houses with their purple K-State flags waving proudly, Eddie was talking in rapid nonstop babble. He was excited, and Jonathan was pleased as they rolled through the town and stopped at the hardware store on McCall Road.

They spent a great deal of time, and a great deal of money, rifling through color wheels and buying paint. The woman at the counter was more than helpful, yet watched curiously as the two men went back and forth on what colors should go where and why. The older, more portly woman—Della, according to her name tag—with pink lipstick and abnormally red hair stacked on top of her head, watched as they loaded up her counter with paint cans, sticks, brushes, a five-gallon bucket, and paint trays.

"You boys doin' some paintin', huh?" she asked, her red face even redder as she hoisted cans down to her side of the counter. She took the color schemes they asked for and operated the machine that added color and shook the bejesus out of the cans. She bent over the side, her rather large bottom going up into the air as she did, and Jonathan caught Eddie's gaze with a mischievous wink as he raised his right palm as if he was going to give it a good smack. He lowered it in time for Eddie to give him the glare of death and the woman to turn around. Jonathan instead ran the hand through his hair as if he was adjusting the sunglasses on his head.

"Yes, we are painting quite a bit. We just bought a house in Clay Center and are redoing it," Eddie explained.

"Ah. So, are you guys going to 'flip' it and resell?" she asked expectantly with a strange look in her eye.

Jonathan caught it first. "Nope. We just got married in Vermont and have decided to nest here. I'm a writer, and Eddie here is a professor," he said with a proud grin.

Della's eyes nearly bugged out of their sockets when the word "married" passed Jonathan's lips. "Oh," she said curtly.

She turned back to the paint buckets and what ensued was twenty minutes of uncomfortable silence as she finished up, and they lifted the materials into their buggy. She rang up their totals and said in an annoyed voice, "That will be $354.17."

Jonathan turned to Eddie. "Do you have the card?"

He shook his head. "Nope. You do."

"If his name is on the card, he is going to have to run it," the woman said, somewhat smugly. Something in her eyes belied the smile on her lips.

From across the counter, Jonathan could almost hear the screaming rage between her ears cursing them for who they were and what they were doing here. Her eyes, deep set in her piggish face, watched them both like a hawk that had spotted a wounded mouse in a field. The only saving grace Jonathan perceived was that this woman would probably be terminated if she were to express her opinion, and she didn't want to risk that. Oh, but Jonathan wished she would, wished she would unload her God-fearin', red-blooded, all-American opinion all over the counter. He silently prayed to a being he had long since stopped believing in that she would, because he had a string of retorts waiting for her. Like two predators sizing each other up, like two nations with nuclear weapons, they waged a silent cold war as Eddie watched them.

Jonathan retrieved his wallet and pulled out the blue bank card. "We're on a joint account. You know, living that gay agenda," he said in the same tone and swiped his card. The register fed out their receipt, and the woman handed it over.

The woman's face puckered. Eddie shook his head and wordlessly berated his husband, but he also wanted to laugh. The woman looked like she had taken a shot of pure lemon juice, and as far as he was concerned, she deserved it.

"Have a nice day," Jonathan said, as he and Eddie walked out the door.

"I don't know why you do shit like that," Eddie said, half laughing as they strolled out of the store. "It makes us look bad."

"No. It doesn't make us look bad. It makes us look human," Jonathan said as they headed into the parking lot.

"We're in a conservative state, Jon. What did you expect?" Eddie asked. They made their way to the truck parked down by the garden center.

"I don't expect much out of people, but I don't pretend to be something I am not. At least that woman in there was offensive to my face and not behind my back as we walked away. I respect her for that, but you see, I gave her unspoken opinion a dose of my unspoken opinion. She doesn't like gay people, and I don't like bigots. Gay people are no better than that woman in there, but they are no worse either," Jonathan said, hitting the button on his key fob that opened the back of the Durango. They started to unload their items.

That's Jonathan, Eddie thought. *Outspoken to a point where he is almost offensive; he is brutally honest and sometimes crass.* But the man loading several cans of paint into his truck was the man Eddie loved more than anything. As Eddie stood by and watched the muscles work under Jonathan's shirt as he hoisted can after can, he couldn't help but remember the way Jonathan had been and the miles he'd personally traveled to get to where he was now.

"Now, let's go back in the garden center and get your tiller and some plants," Jonathan said happily, shutting the lid. Eddie put his arm around Jonathan's waist as they walked together toward the fenced-in area where blooms and foliage were lined up in perfect little rows. Eddie thought about that as they walked. Why couldn't people be more like plants? No emotional baggage, no opinions, no dogma; they just wanted one thing in all the world— to put their roots down in fertile soil and have the opportunity to reach for the sky.

They spent nearly as much money in the garden center as they had inside the hardware store, and by the time they finished loading the tiller, flats of flowers and vegetables, and rose bushes into the back of the Durango, Jonathan had a hard time seeing out his window. But that was okay, he wasn't driving backward, he said, making Eddie laugh. The Kansas sun was high in the sky, and both men were feeling hunger gnawing at their bellies as they drove through downtown Manhattan and back to the state road toward home.

***

They pulled up to the house at about two o'clock that afternoon, full from a Sonic drive-in order. Eddie went up the front steps and opened the door, then propped it open with a box so they could haul their treasures inside. Together, they pulled everything out of the truck and took items either inside the house or around the back to be used in the garden. Jonathan was placing the paint cans into their respective rooms when he heard a female voice call through the house.

"Hello?"

Eddie was still out back, and Jonathan narrowed his eyes at the intrusion. Curious, he made his way to the front door, where he saw his neighbor standing next to the propped-open screen door. She was peering inside and holding what looked like a pie in her hands.

"Hi," Jonathan said.

"Hi. My name is Maggie Stooksbury. I live right next door. I just wanted to come over and welcome you two to the neighborhood," she said pleasantly.

Eddie had come in and was wiping his hands on his jeans. He caught the end of her comment.

"Oh, thank you so much," Jonathan said and went to take the pie from her but hesitated. She had oven mitts on and turned slightly to keep it out of his reach.

"I just pulled it out of the oven, dear. My momma used to do this when she was still alive and a neighbor moved in. It was a tradition of hers to have a pie cooling on a windowsill in a new home; it's supposed to bring good luck and good memories," she said with a wink.

Jonathan guessed her to be about fifty-five, maybe sixty years old, her blonde hair turning white in some areas. She was tall and thin, and the pants she wore only went to midcalf. Her top was white and had a little yellow floral print on it.

"How thoughtful," said Eddie with a smile. "Won't you come in? The kitchen is back this way, and we happen to have a free windowsill."

"Yes, please. Come in," Jonathan said. "Sorry about the mess—we're getting ready to paint the inside."

The woman stepped in and rolled her eyes at Jonathan's statement. "Think nothing of it, dear," she said and followed Eddie into the kitchen. Jonathan pulled the box away from the door and closed the screen to keep bugs out. *And strangers from walking in*, the annoying voice said. Jonathan shook his head in defiance of that thought. She was just being neighborly. When he got to the kitchen, Eddie had pulled the window up, and Maggie placed the pie on the sill and made sure it was secure.

"Can I offer you something to drink?" Eddie asked, opening the refrigerator.

"Tea would be perfect," she said, taking off her blue oven mitts. Eddie hesitated as he reached for the cabinet where they kept the glasses. The door was shut this time, but he tossed a look at Jonathan, who had pulled out a stool for Maggie to sit at the island. Jonathan winked at him and gave a slight shake of his head that basically meant, "See? Nothing to worry about."

"I haven't been in this house for years, and not much has changed. You guys plan on remodeling it?" she asked, taking the glass Eddie offered.

"Not a whole remodel, no. We love the layout. We're just stripping the wallpaper and painting," Jonathan said. Eddie handed him a beer out of the fridge, and he used his T-shirt to twist the top off.

"How long have you lived here?" Eddie asked, sitting at the island next to Jonathan.

"My entire life, save for the time away at school. I'm a professor at K-State," she said.

Eddie's eyes grew big. "I am as well. Or, rather, I start this fall. What department are you in?"

"I teach English literature," she said, getting excited. "What department are you in?"

"Psychology. I was hired to—"

"You're Dr. Dorman?" she asked, sounding pleasantly shocked. Eddie stuttered for a moment before she reached across the table. "Small world! I was talking to Susan Bates, another professor from that department, and she was telling me they had hired someone. I just didn't expect you to be my neighbor," she said, patting his hand.

"Yeah. Dr. Bates is who I interviewed with," Eddie said.

"Well, you'll be pleased to know that she loved you, and so did the board," Maggie said with a wink.

Eddie exhaled a big sigh. "That's a relief. I was nervous," he said, laughing.

"Not to worry, now. You're on tenure track, aren't you?" she asked.

"Yes, as a matter of fact. We don't plan on moving anytime soon, and K-State looks wonderful. The campus is beautiful."

"Oh, it really is, and so full of life. You'll see when fall comes around. Manhattan fills up with people coming and going. I just can't get over you being chair of a department, let alone a clinician. You're so young!" she exclaimed.

"I'm thirty-one!" Eddie said good-naturedly.

"Psssh. Darlin', I'm fifty-seven. You're young. Well, isn't this something?" she said, and then she turned to Jonathan, who had been listening to the conversation like a spectator would watch a tennis match.

"What do you do?" she asked.

"I am a bum," Jonathan said coyly and took another draw of his beer. Maggie looked uncertainly at Eddie, who rolled his eyes.

"Jonathan is a writer. He just finished his first novel a year ago. *Sands of Time*," Eddie said, patting his husband's bicep.

Maggie's eyes grew very large then. "I have seen your book on the *Times*' list. You're Jonathan David? Well, my, my, my, what a day!" she said, laughing. "I can't believe this. You must come and talk to one of my classes sometime."

"I would love that," Jonathan said. He was really starting to like her. She seemed upbeat and full of life.

"I'll let you know my schedule, then," she said. "And I'll buy a copy of your book right away."

"Well, thank you. I appreciate that," he replied graciously. "I promise to autograph it."

"Would you like to see what we're going to do?" Eddie asked, eyebrows up and tone welcoming.

"I would love that."

Starting in the kitchen, they used the color samples they had to describe what they would do to the stark white cabinets and walls. She listened intently, nodding and oohing and aahing as they laid the sea-foam-green tile against the wall. From there, they passed into the dining room and did the same, explaining they would pull down the faded yellow wallpaper and paint the room a deep-maroon color to bring out the dark wood stain of the floors and the dining-room table.

They repeated this for every room in the house, and as they did so, realized how much work they had in store for them. She seemed fascinated and kept saying how excited she was to have the house well taken care of. Jonathan made a point to watch her as they described everything, wondering if she had clued in to the fact they were a couple. He was pleased to conclude that if she did, she didn't seem to care. But something about the way she looked around disturbed him a little. As they passed from one part of the house to another, she glanced warily from side to side, and she would peer into a room before walking in, as if she expected something or someone to be there. Finally, they made their way back downstairs, with Eddie in the lead, talking a mile a minute. Jonathan could tell he was taking quickly to Maggie, and it made him smile.

"...and that is it, really. I think later on we might replace the carpet upstairs and here in the living room, but even that doesn't look to be in too bad a shape," Eddie said.

"Well, I certainly think that what you all intend to do will be lovely. I am sure Mrs. Pemberly would look down from heaven and be pleased," she said as the trio returned to the kitchen.

"Was she one of the ol...er...elderly ladies who owned the house before us, Eddie?" Jonathan asked, and Eddie shook his head.

"No, dear. Those were two old schoolteachers who taught at the elementary school. Those two old biddies moved away to a retirement home, I think," Maggie said as she retook her seat. Jonathan grabbed another beer, thinking this lady likely wasn't going anywhere anytime soon.

"The Pemberlys were the previous owners of the house. Helen, Mark, and young Alan. Tragic story, really. But that was more than forty years ago," she said dismissively, her gaze wandering upward as she gave a dramatic shake of the head. Eddie and

Jonathan cast each other a look. *She's dying to tell it to us*, Eddie's look said.

Jonathan rolled his eyes and nodded once. *Yup.*

"Maggie, that pie should be cool by now. How about we get a slice of it?" Eddie said encouragingly.

"I'll get the plates," she said and turned back toward the cabinets. Both men grinned at each other as Eddie plucked the pie from the windowsill. It was still warm but cool enough it wouldn't fall apart as they tried to cut into it.

"So...the Pemberlys?" Jonathan inquired.

Maggie returned with three small dessert plates, a gift from Eddie's parents on their wedding day, and a knife. She placed them on the table and began to tell her story.

"I was just a young woman when I first met Helen and Mark. They moved in here when they first married. They were from New York originally, and Mark was stationed at Fort Riley as an Army officer, although I can't recall his rank. Anyway, they were a lovely couple; she was just as pretty as they came. Chestnut-brown hair, always fashionable, always well-dressed and mannered, very genteel, and very feminine. And her husband was a handsome devil, and everyone who knew them knew how much they loved each other. They had a romance that lasted for years even after their first and only child, Alan, was born.

"Their little family did very well, and Alan grew up with two adoring parents. That is, until his mother was diagnosed with cervical cancer, and you know, back then..." Maggie shook her head sadly as the boys leaned closer to listen.

"...they just didn't have the same technology they do today. It progressed slowly, and there were times that she went into remission. I remember Mr. Pemberly would bring his wife out to sit on the porch in the spring sunshine, her head wrapped in a scarf. Her hair was gone, but her lovely face never lost its beauty," she said as she took a bite of apple pie.

"What happened to her?" Eddie asked.

Maggie sighed and gave the boys a sympathetic glance. "She eventually passed away, bless her heart. It had been a struggle."

Jonathan furrowed his brow at that and reached over to rub Eddie's shoulder absentmindedly. Eddie reached his hand up to touch Jonathan's.

"That's terrible," Jonathan said somberly.

"Yes. Bad things happen to good people," she agreed, and the three of them finished their pie in silence; the only sound was the clinking of forks on plates. Eddie was the one who finally asked the burning question in both his and Jonathan's minds.

"What happened to Mr. Pemberly and...Alan, did you say?" Eddie asked.

"Well, that is an even sadder story. You see, Alan wasn't an outstanding student or exceptional at sports. As a matter of fact, when he was a little boy, he was a bit overweight and rather spoiled. But when his momma got sick, the boy had to grow up quickly. Too quickly, folks around here say. His daddy started to drink and sometimes drank heavily. When Helen became bedridden, Mark retired from the Army and started working down at Clarks Granary here in town. Those two big silos you see as you come in off K-18. That is when Alan just seemed to bloom at school. His grades, involvement in sports and other activities escalated. The teachers were shocked, but I wasn't. I knew exactly what was going on. He was hiding from his father, from his home. Even his behavior changed. He was afraid to get into trouble."

Jonathan looked out the window at the sun. The world seemed bright and warm. But the longer Maggie talked, the cooler Jonathan felt, until his arms were covered in gooseflesh. The air in the kitchen turned frigid as he idly rubbed his arms. He looked at Eddie, who was sitting forward, chin in his right hand, staring at Maggie as she told her story. Neither he nor she seemed to be affected in the slightest by the drop in temperature.

"Momma would come over and do her best to tend to Helen, who was in constant pain, and her husband, drunk as he was, was always very gentle with her. Momma said she thought Mark got it into his head that somehow, some way, he had something to do with her being sick. He changed, gradually, and when Helen died, he went right over the edge. Mark became a full-blown fall-down drunk," Maggie said with emphasis. Suddenly the kitchen cabinet, the one containing all the glasses and coffee mugs, popped open, and all three of them jumped on their stools.

"Either way. It was a bad ending for both of them," Maggie said gingerly, obviously hoping to end the conversation quickly.

"The kid. What happened to the kid?" Jonathan insisted.

"Honey, let's drop the story. It really…" Eddie started to say, but Jonathan shot him a look. Eddie stopped speaking. Jonathan knew where this story was headed. Something inside him felt the gravitas and the veritas in the tone of Maggie's voice. It was there, just below the surface of her words. Maggie shot a worried glance at Eddie but then continued. Eddie's fears were realized, and it broke his heart to hear the rest of it.

"Like I said, Alan grew up quickly. His mom was sick, and so was his father. When she died, Mark did nothing but work every day and every night. It was terrible. When he was home, we could hear the kid crying and him yelling. The jubilant child was gone. Sometimes we would call the police, and they would haul Mark off to jail to sleep it off, but it was on the weekends that it got really out of control. My father interceded several times. He and Momma talked about taking Alan in and raising him too, but they couldn't afford the extra mouth, and they doubted Mark would allow that to happen. They hoped, and I know this is going to sound terrible, but he became so bad they hoped he would simply drink himself to death, and maybe then…" She trailed off. "Look, I've taken up too much of your day. I am going to head home. It was really nice to meet you two. I hope we get to see a lot more of each other."

Eddie placed a hand on Jonathan's underneath the island. His husband's hands were sweaty and they shook, but Jonathan's control was admirable. From the chest up, you couldn't even tell how tormented he was. He smiled and stood up.

"Let us walk you out," Eddie said, and Maggie smiled graciously at them as they waited for her to walk past them into the dining room to the front of the house.

They waved good-bye at the front door and watched as she went inside her house before they spoke a word to each other. Eddie sighed as Jonathan walked back through the house and opened up one of the boxes on the table that still needed to be unpacked. Most of it was junk: scented candles and Glade plug-in things along with other odds and ends. He started slamming them down on the table's hard surface. Eddie walked up behind him and slid his arms around him. He laid his palms against Jonathan's pecs and pressed his chest against Jonathan's back. Under his hand, he could feel Jonathan's heart hammering away against his rib cage.

"It was a long time ago, babe. There was nothing they could do," Eddie said, trying to calm him down.

"Yeah. I know. I know," Jonathan said, trying to play it off and brush it aside. But Eddie knew better. He felt him trembling under his touch. Eddie held on tighter. He leaned his head against Jonathan's back and prayed for peace as tremors shook his husband from head to toe. His prayers were answered as they began to subside. When Jonathan pulled in one long deep breath and slowly let it out, like Eddie had taught him, Eddie knew the crisis was over.

"It's okay, babe. You're going to be okay," he whispered to him.

"It's the same ol' bullshit story, isn't it, though?" Jonathan whispered, but Eddie wasn't sure if he was speaking to him or to the objects in his rearview mirror, an analogy used by the two of them to talk about his past. Eddie knew his husband's kryptonite, the green energy used to take his Superman to his knees, and he hated it.

"Yeah, babe. It's the same old bullshit," Eddie replied. They stood there together for a while as the sun shone through the dining-room window and warmed their backs. The taller, stronger man trembled deep inside and the smaller of the two used every cell of his body to hold them together.

CHAPTER 6

T HE EVENING FELL steadily upon them, turning the blue skies into fiery displays of reds, blues, and dark violet as the sun dipped below the western horizon and the stars came out of their hiding place to dot the night sky. A cooler wind, a nighttime wind, floated across the plains, lifting pollen off prairie flowers and tenderly spreading it out around the great state of Kansas, like a kiss upon the face of a sleeping child. The stars winked down like diamonds from the vast mine of the heavens, thick and numerous. The trees, their leaves green and thick and healthy, swayed in the perfumed air and rustled whispered secrets down the streets of Clay Center.

In the distance, a storm produced lightning that could be seen from where Jonathan stood, smoking his third cigarette. He leaned against the wooden post of the front porch and listened to the crickets chirping while he thought back on the days when he had been here before. Young and stupid, he thought as he took another drag. This produced a chuckle and a snort as he exhaled the gray smoke into the air, where it tumbled and disappeared. The storm was still hours away, but Jonathan could smell its sweetness on the air, and it served to soothe his aching heart and put his soul at ease. If heaven were real, it would be a place like this, he thought to himself. He waited for a snarky response from the annoying voice in his head, but he thought it must have turned in early tonight or was just being careful not to poke the bear.

Their evening had ended earlier than they had planned. As Eddie dried a bowl with a dishtowel, he watched his husband on the front porch from his vantage point in the archway that separated the kitchen from the dining room. After Maggie's unannounced visit, the seemingly endless bundle of nervous energy that usually consumed Jonathan had been unplugged, leaving him melancholy and quiet. Eddie knew not to push him during times like these, and instead quietly suggested a trip to the grocery store to fill up the pantry and the refrigerator.

As he had many times before, Eddie took the helm and guided his beloved through the motions of shopping and dinner. The cooking process, like his writing, was cathartic and therapeutic in many ways, and like always during the process, Jonathan perked up and came back to him a little at a time. But moments like the one they'd had earlier, after their neighbor had left, exhausted Jonathan and left him feeling beaten up.

Eddie wondered if Jonathan would ever achieve the happiness he sought. From his point of view, his husband always seemed to be searching for an answer, a place, or a theme to bring him peace of mind. Many would say wanderlust propelled him forward, and to some extent, they would be right, but his lover wasn't wandering toward something in the hopes of finding new and exciting things; he was wandering away from something that followed him like a shadow attached to his feet, always there, always just a step behind him. Eddie wondered where it put him in the grand scheme of things, and when they first met, it had been a fearful thing for him. Now, when Jonathan disappeared into himself like he did, Eddie didn't fret so much. He had the power to pull himself out of it, and for now, that was good enough.

The heat of the day that had permeated the house was chased away by the cool evening air coming through the windows. It wasn't as hot as Texas this time of year, where Eddie had grown up, which was a nice change, but Jonathan had warned him that the summers could roast even here. Still, it wasn't the heat he was worried about. He remembered one conversation in particular.

"Kansas has tornadoes," Eddie had protested as they lay in bed one late night in Michigan.

"You have hurricanes down in your part of Southeast Texas, and those spawn tornadoes," Jonathan countered. He was propped up on an arm next to Eddie. The house was quiet save for the ticking of the clock in the other room.

"Honey, I don't know…" Eddie stated.

"I just thought it was beautiful, is all," Jonathan said. "I was happy there."

Eddie looked at him with hurt-filled eyes. "Don't I make you happy?" he quietly asked his lover. And then he chided himself and changed his expression, but not before Jonathan saw it.

"I didn't mean it that way," Jonathan said.

"I know. But, my love, no matter where you go, there you'll be," Eddie said.

Jonathan nodded and lay back in bed. "Oh, how I know that to be the truth."

Eddie knew this was the place where they would make their final stand. As Jonathan tossed his cigarette butt into the street, turned, and then walked into the house, the truth of those words sank their teeth into the flesh of Eddie's soul. However this worked out, however this ended, good or bad, it would be here. He ducked back into the kitchen and placed the bowl he had been drying for the past fifteen minutes in the cabinet where it belonged. The kitchen was clean and the night was growing later. Sleep crept along the edges of his brain, begging to be listened to.

"I think we can get started on everything else in the morning," Jonathan said from the archway of the dining room.

"Yeah. I think so too. Which room do you want to begin in?" Eddie asked.

"I dunno. I think we can work on peeling the wallpaper off the walls first and then paint," Jonathan said, putting his hands inside the front pocket of his hoodie.

"Sure," Eddie said, and Jonathan nodded, looking down at his bare feet. "Hey. Why don't we start with your office? Get you back behind your computer and get you writing again?"

Jonathan lifted his head. "Sounds like a plan. I think I am going to go sit outside for a little while longer. I'll come up to bed soon," he said as he crossed the kitchen and kissed Eddie on the forehead.

Eddie closed his eyes and leaned into Jonathan's strong body. Jonathan placed his chin on Eddie's head and held him close. Eddie could smell a hint of the cologne he wore mixed in with the smoke and sweat.

Jonathan let go and walked over to the fridge, pulled out another beer, popped the top, and put it up to his lips.

Thump.

Eddie started to say something, but stopped short when the noise came again.

Thump.

They both raised their gazes to the ceiling as Jonathan walked over to the wall for his baseball bat. He didn't believe in owning guns, and he figured this would give him more pleasure without all the cleanup necessary in dispatching someone with a firearm. He wrapped his hand around the base of the bat as they both listened intently, hearts beating.

Thump. Thump. Thump. It sounded like someone heavy walking across the floor above their heads.

Their gazes locked, and Jonathan mouthed, *Someone is upstairs.*

Eddie nodded and reached for his cell phone, which was plugged in on the counter. The two of them moved from the kitchen to the staircase. They had both been standing in view of the front door and knew there was no way someone had simply walked in. As silently as they could, they made their way up. Jonathan led with the bat over his shoulder, and Eddie followed, having already tapped 911 into the phone. He waited to press the Send button, wanting to make sure it wasn't a squirrel or a raccoon first. He didn't want the embarrassment of having the police show up because of a furry home invader.

They crept up a stair at a time and were nearly at the top when they heard the sound of footsteps again. Whoever it was was coming toward them from the back room. Jonathan pushed himself farther, feeling a burning sensation in his gut as his trembling legs fought to hold him up. The three steps to the landing were the most difficult three steps either of them had ever taken. One, breathe, two, hesitate, breathe, three, and they were there. The first thing they noticed was that all four doors were shut, including their bedroom door. Jonathan pressed his hand against Eddie's stomach as a sign to stay put as he approached the bedroom. Eddie stood watching, ready to hit the Send button.

The door swung open to a dark room. Eddie's nerves were on high alert, his heart hammered hard in his chest, his mouth was dry, and his palms were sweaty. Jonathan walked in.

"Jon—" Eddie began, but he was silenced when his husband turned around and held up his hand, signaling him to be quiet. He shut his mouth with a click but kept his gaze glued to what Jonathan was doing. Jonathan disappeared into the dark and, from somewhere inside, clicked on a light. Eddie breathed a sigh of relief when Jonathan came walking back out giving him a shrug.

Thump. Thump. Thump. The sound came from one of the empty rooms down the hall. The feeling of relief Eddie had felt suddenly vanished like smoke, making him tense up again. Jonathan rolled his eyes. He was getting sick of this. Instead of creeping down the hallway like he had up the stairs, he charged down the hallway and Eddie chased after him. Jonathan flung the door of the room on the left open. Nothing. He reached out and swung the middle door open. Nothing. Finally, he grabbed for the last door and hesitated. Instead of turning the knob, he pressed his ear to the door.

"What is it?" Eddie whispered.

"Shhh," Jonathan said.

Eddie leaned closer to the door and listened with Jonathan. Jonathan motioned for him to back up before turning the knob and trying to push the door open. As it started to swing inward, it hit something and stopped. Eddie jumped back. The room was empty, or it should have been. Surprised, Jonathan let go of the handle, and the door swung shut and slammed hard in his face with a loud bang. Jonathan backed up a step and then grabbed the knob again. This time it wouldn't turn.

"Whoever the fuck is in there, I'm coming in to beat your ass!" Jonathan said, and he twisted the knob with all his might. Whatever or whoever was on the other side was struggling to keep Jonathan out. Eddie brought his phone up to call for help but discovered that it was inexplicably dead. Jonathan struggled with the door and finally lost his temper. He backed up a few steps, dropped the bat, and charged the door with his shoulder. Instead of meeting resistance he had expected, the door burst open and slammed against the wall. Luckily, Eddie had been hot on his heels and kept him from going headfirst through the closed window directly across from the door. To their surprise, the room was empty.

"You gotta be fucking kidding me!" Jonathan said, looking around the bare room. He immediately went over and checked the windows to see if any had been recently opened. They were all locked from the inside.

"What the fuck?" Eddie asked.

"I don't know. All I do know is that someone was on the other side of this door, holding it shut," Jonathan said, a vein in his forehead pulsing with each heartbeat. He was pissed. Eddie knew that there was one thing Jonathan didn't like, and that was to be scared, especially in his own home. He stalked the room, looking for some way for someone to crawl out: an attic entrance, a loose panel in the wall, something, but there was nothing.

"Where could they have gone?" Eddie asked. "There is no way out of here except for the windows and those are locked!"

"I know!" Jonathan said, shooting him an impatient look, hands on hips, fuming.

"That's fucking weird," Eddie said. "What's weirder is that my phone had a full charge. I was about to call the cops and then suddenly, look, the battery is wiped out," he said, holding up his Android phone. The battery light flashed red repeatedly, and then the phone shut down again. Jonathan stared at Eddie for a second, then shook his head and began to whistle the *Twilight Zone* theme.

"No shit, right?" Eddie asked. He had been ready for an intruder, ready to jump in there and call the cops and cheer Jonathan on as he beat the shit out of the intruder while screaming at the police to hurry to save the poor bastard's life. But now that the incident had gone from scary to freaky, Eddie felt uneasy. "Creeped out" would be the right term.

"Maybe the door just caught on something," Jonathan said, opening and then shutting the door. It swung freely with him handling it, nothing obstructing its path.

"A door doesn't push back when caught on something," Eddie said, knowing he was playing the role of Captain Obvious. Jonathan shot him a look. "Sorry," Eddie said.

"It's all right. I know what you're saying. Dammit, I was just sure there was someone in here," Jonathan said as he fidgeted with the doorknob. His bursting into the room had split the frame, and now the latch wouldn't catch completely.

"Eh...fuck it," Jonathan said, as he walked back down the hallway, leaving Eddie watching him go. Eddie had started to follow when he stepped into what felt like an arctic night. He would have called to Jonathan, but the breath froze in his throat and he went rigid. He lifted his hand, reaching for Jonathan, who had turned into their bedroom. He managed a squeak before his voice failed him. The sensation passed quickly and left him staggering forward, shivering and rubbing his arms.

Jonathan backed out of the room, shut the door, and nearly ran right into Eddie. He saw the look on his face and grabbed him by the arms.

"What's wrong?" he asked.

"I just...walked into a cold spot... Jesus, I couldn't breathe," Eddie said, his arms still covered in gooseflesh.

***

The little blue station wagon stuttered at the stop sign and threatened to stall, but Jonathan's dad kept tapping on the gas, having enough sense about him to do so, even though he was yelling and screaming. His father was staring in the rearview mirror at his brother, who had gotten in trouble for running around inside of the church this sunny summer evening. They'd spent many days there through the week, and Jonathan and his two younger brothers were easily bored, but then again, most of the time Jonathan sympathized with them.

"You aren't supposed to run around in there!" his dad yelled.

"I'm sorry!" the middle brother, Roger, said.

Dad turned his attention to Jonathan, as he was the oldest boy and sitting in the front seat, which made him an easy target. Jonathan did his best to ignore it and was staring out the window as they drove through the desolate area of Detroit, near the train tracks. Even though his eyes were averted, he could feel the pressure in the car mounting and his father's eyes on him.

"Why weren't you watching them?" he asked.

"I was talking with my friends," Jonathan explained. He hated being his brothers' keeper. The church was a converted bar: the congregation had replaced sin with Sunday school, and its fledgling membership was tiny. Everyone knew everyone else. He didn't think the boys could get into too much trouble.

Jonathan fought this dream, for he knew it for what it was: another old dusty reel, objects in the mirror from long ago, yet so close to him in his mind, a scar that wouldn't quite heal. He had lived it—his father yelling at his brother about something else in the backseat—but Jonathan wasn't paying attention. Something was different about this dream. Something was wrong, out of place. As the car came to a stop again, at a red light this time, Jonathan's gaze locked onto eyes from a young man standing at the corner. He didn't look like he had been waiting to cross at the light, otherwise he would have at that moment. Instead, he stared directly into the car as if he was there to witness something.

Jonathan's mind snapped back to what was happening inside the car when he heard his brother cry out after being struck by his father, who had reached into the backseat. It was too late to do anything about it as his father brought his hand forward and struck him in the back of the head.

"Hey!" Jonathan cried out in dismay.

"Hey?" his father asked, outraged at Jonathan's reaction. *Yeah. Hey, you fuck. Keep your goddamn hands to yourself.* A thought Jonathan didn't dare vocalize. But he might as well have, for the blows that rained down on top of him. Jonathan put his hands up around his head, trying to block the blows from his father. Pain shot through his back, causing him to yelp and tear up, filling him with hatred. He turned once more to the window, and he saw the blond-haired young man look in with sympathy, and again, Jonathan was struck with the sensation that this wasn't right. The light turned green, and through his vision, now distorted by tears of rage and pain, they drove off, leaving the man to sadly watch the car go by.

His father must have felt a pang of guilt not because he had seen the man witnessing the abuse but from guilt further down than that, for the last thing his father said before they left that road was, "Don't tell your mother." Of course he wouldn't—he had been afraid to do so. Afraid of what would happen to him. But later on, when he finally did, it fell on deaf ears. The truth would then become another buried bone, a constant voice telling he would never be good enough.

***

Jonathan jerked awake, breathing hard and shaking, tears rolling down his face, and he quietly wept for what felt like an eternity. Eddie murmured in his sleep and pressed his face closer to Jonathan's chest, disturbed by the sudden jerking motions of his lover. But he hadn't roused yet, so Jonathan tried to calm down and bury the memory back in its place. He took in a ragged breath and let it out slowly. He hadn't had that dream in a while and figured Maggie's story from earlier had brought it fresh into his mind. He lay there watching the ceiling fan twirl and twirl, letting it have a hypnotic effect, making him sleepy again. He wondered about the man he'd seen in his dream, and before he knew it, he'd fallen back under the weight of unconsciousness. This time, thankfully, nobody was there to torture him.

CHAPTER 7

THE STORM JONATHAN had seen in the distance had swept downward into Clay Center, bringing cooler air with it and soaking the parched earth with much needed moisture. When they woke up in the morning, although it was steely gray and raining, the house was stifling hot and too humid to get any painting done. So by midafternoon, when the sun had broken out hot and was high in the air, they took the party outside and decided to put in a garden now that the soil was nice and loosened up. It also gave them a chance to shut all the windows, turn on the central air, and cool everything down on the inside.

The previous owners had left a few pots here and there, but most of the yard was grass. They sat down with a piece of paper and a pencil and sketched out how they wanted the yard to look. With that, it was off to the races.

Two hours later, they had dug and tilled quite a bit of yard and moved the sod to fill the bare and low spots. The soil was muddy from the rain the night before, but not as soaking wet as they thought it would be, so they opened several bags of garden soil, manure, and peat moss and worked it into the ground with the tiller. Before long, both of them had their shirts off, were sweating profusely, and had dirt up to their elbows.

Slowly and steadily, they put the vegetable garden in. Corn in the back, and then they planted peppers, squash, zucchini, tomatoes, green beans, and okra in neat rows one right after another. They remembered to put an occasional marigold in between the rows to keep the bugs away. Once that was done, they moved on to planting the flower gardens, filling the backyard with petunias, peonies, snapdragons, and other annuals that would die at first frost. They planted hostas in shaded areas and roses in the middle of the yard and in elevated beds, in which they laid cedar mulch to keep the roots from drying out.

While they worked, they laughed and chased each other around the yard with the garden hose, which kept them from overheating. Occasionally, they would pick up the hose and drink from it, the water tasting coppery but cold and refreshing. The sun beat on their shoulders as they labored with the earth, pulling out rocks, broken bottle tops, and other debris.

Jonathan's mood lifted. He was enjoying the labor and the feeling of getting down and dirty. He didn't tell Eddie about his dream the previous night. Instead, they talked about where the best spots to plant their treasures and whether they should have picked up bug spray while they were at the garden center.

Maggie came outside with a tray full of lemonade and chicken-salad sandwiches and invited them over for lunch. They looked at each other and hopped the fence into her yard. They sat, sipping and eating with dirty hands and happy stomachs while Maggie gave them gardening advice. After lunch, she went inside to retrieve a bottle of sunblock and insisted they put it on. She was worried about how sunburned they were going to be. Both of them would thank her later, seeing with horror how red their skin was in the mirror later that evening, but for now, they were content with their work.

"We still have the front to do," Eddie said, feeling his muscles cooling off and growing tight.

"Wanna get it done tonight?" Jonathan asked with a grin on his face.

"Sure," Eddie said. He didn't want to. He wanted to keep sitting under Maggie's umbrella and out of the sunshine, but he knew he needed to get the work finished. So, even though his legs protested as he stood up, he reached out and took his husband's hand and pulled him to his feet.

"Why don't you let me help you out?" Maggie asked. The boys looked at each other and fervently nodded. So the three set off, Maggie going out her side gate and the two men hopping back over the fence and dragging the tiller to work on the front beds. Maggie and Eddie teamed up together to plant in the spots that Jonathan tilled up. Maggie had brought a few hanging baskets, and they placed them on hooks that were drilled into the porch ceiling while Jonathan made sure they were even from down below. The sun was setting, and a cooler wind blew down the street. It chilled the sweat on Jonathan's body as he crouched down, his back to the tree.

A car driving down the street caught his attention, and his throat dried up and a winter wind cascaded through him, chilling his insides. It seemed to happen in slow motion. The beat-up blue Ford Escort station wagon rolled past him, and his testicles drew up and his stomach cramped. *It can't be the same one. It can't be,* Jonathan thought disbelievingly, begging, pleading with himself. For whatever reason, he couldn't see through the windows, they seemed oddly fogged up, but his heart nearly stopped as it passed by him and he focused on the license plate. It was blue, and before he lost consciousness, he read the white letters across the top. The plate said, "Michigan."

***

"Is this on here right, Jonathan?" Eddie asked over his shoulder, holding up the hanging basket. Maggie, who had been having a great time talking with Eddie as they worked, told him in a steely voice to turn around and pay attention to Jonathan. What he saw made his heart drop.

Jonathan was watching a car, an old blue station wagon, driving by. He was swaying unsteadily on his feet.

He's going down, Eddie thought as he ran off the porch.

"Jonathan!" he called, slowing as he approached him. His husband turned around in time for Eddie to see how deathly pale he was, his eyes wild, bugging out of their sockets. His mouth was moving and he was shaking his head, and as Eddie reached for him, Jonathan's eyes rolled up until only the whites showed, and his knees buckled. Eddie grabbed him underneath his arms and pulled him toward the porch. Maggie was hot on Eddie's heels, fanning Jonathan with her large hat. Eddie sat down on the grass and cradled the bigger man in his arms.

"Should I call 911?" Maggie asked frantically.

"I don't know. Jonathan. Jonathan!" he shouted, slapping him lightly on the cheek. Eddie was scared to death. Heatstroke was the first thing he considered, but Jonathan's face was starting to regain its color.

His eyes fluttered open, and Eddie about passed out himself with relief. "Hey, you, going somewhere?" he asked, his voice breaking.

"What...what happened?" Jonathan asked, looking confused.

"Babe, you just passed out," Eddie said as Jonathan reached up, wiping his mouth with the back of his hand. He sat up and hung his head.

"It's the heat of the day, it will get you every time," Maggie said in a singsong voice. Eddie figured she was right, it could have been the heat, but something in Jonathan's eyes bothered him. They looked distant, and something lingered underneath the surface. But Jonathan eventually nodded and cracked a smile, shrugging off the incident.

"I'm sure you're right. My vision swam for a second. I'm fine, just help me up. I don't want the whole neighborhood to see me," he said, chuckling, and with Eddie and Maggie on each side of him, he stood up with shaky knees. He took a step, but his knees buckled. Eddie was beside him in a flash, wrapped the bigger man's arms over his shoulders, and helped him up the stairs. Once they reached the porch, Maggie ran ahead of them and opened up the door to allow them to go inside. They were assaulted by a blast of air-conditioning that caused Eddie to shiver.

"Why don't you run him a cool bath, and let's get his body temperature down," Maggie suggested.

Eddie nodded and sat Jonathan on the couch. Jonathan sank back and exhaled slowly, his hands shaking. *Babe, what's going on with you?* Eddie wondered as he turned toward the stairs as Maggie went into the kitchen. His thoughts were interrupted when Maggie let out a huge gasp and stumbled back against the wall. Eddie shot into the kitchen to see what all the fuss was about and couldn't believe his eyes as he caught up with her.

"Oh my God," whispered Eddie as he walked further into the kitchen.

All the cabinet doors stood wide open, revealing cleared-out shelves. Every glass, plate, and piece of cutlery was stacked up on the island in an impossible balancing act of shining silverware and china.

"What is it?" Jonathan called from the other room. Eddie dropped his gaze to Maggie's and shook his head, silently begging her not to say anything. She looked as pale as Jonathan had when he passed out, but she nodded and turned to go back into the living room.

"Oh, it's nothing, dear. I got more sunshine than I should have, as well. Eddie is going to get us something to drink," she said, and Eddie silently thanked her for not getting Jonathan worked up worse than he already was. Moving quickly and as quietly as he could, he grabbed a stool and slowly pulled apart the small mountain of dinnerware and restacked it on the counter. He had to be careful not to send the whole thing tumbling, and even though nervous energy coursed through him, he was able to do it more quickly than he'd thought he would. Luckily, he was able to finish the task without making much noise. He was scared shitless, first of all because of this, but also because he knew how Jonathan would react to it.

"Honey, what's taking so long in here?" Jonathan asked, coming back into the kitchen with Maggie right behind him. Her eyes were large and apologetic when she and Eddie locked glances, and then she looked relieved at how fast he had cleared the mess up.

"Nothing. I just…got distracted in thought, is all," he said, his words sounding hollow and unconvincing even to himself. Jonathan looked at him strangely.

"I think I am going to take that bath."

Eddie moved to go to him, but Jonathan held up his hand. "I'm fine now, really; stay here with Maggie, babe. I'm good. I'll use the upstairs bath and call if I need anything," he said as he turned on his heel and walked out.

Eddie was a little hurt by his husband's abruptness and felt guilty for lying to him. When Jonathan had disappeared up the stairs, Maggie walked to the island and sat down on the stool. "What in God's name was that, Eddie?" she asked in a hushed tone.

"I don't know. I just…I don't know," he said, feeling defeated.

***

The man fell to his knees, the air having been knocked from his lungs, and the world threatened to disappear around him. He had difficulty breathing as the policeman's words sank in, and he tried to scream in defiance: *No. No. No. No. No!* But the words lodged there as his mouth opened and closed like a dummy on the lap of his ventriloquist. The room tilted and turned like it had so many times before when he had been on benders and needed to crawl to the bathroom and wrap himself around a toilet.

He looked up from his place on the floor in the living room of the house he and his family had shared for years. Now he would live here alone. The eyes in the picture on the mantel stared out into the room and down upon him, mocking him, reminding him of what had been and what was no longer: him, with his arms wrapped around his family—his beautiful wife, with her chestnut-brown hair and wide white smile, and his blond-haired son. They looked so happy. Someone screamed in the room, and it took him a moment to realize the peal of grief and rage had come from his own throat. It burned and strained before finally breaking, the sound tapering off as he ran out of oxygen.

He inhaled again and let off another horrible, heart-rending cry as tears broke free and poured down his face. He shook, racked with sobs. His mind was reeling as he stood up on uncertain feet, grabbed the photograph, and pulled it down. His son. His beautiful, loving son, smiling at him from behind the glass in a pair of jeans, a white shirt, and a tie, a cowlick causing the back of his hair to stand up, was gone. The memory of his wife trying everything to get it to lie down that day assaulted him. The cowlick defied gravity and all of his wife's attempts at fixing it. As the memory flashed through his mind, the realization that his son, who had been eight years old in this picture, existed no more.

"You were so gentle," the man said, rocking back and forth, weeping. "I'm so sorry, boy. Daddy's so sorry." But there was no one in the house to hear him. The police officer who had come with the news had told him and turned his back to him as soon as the words were out of his mouth. It was evident the officer was disgusted with him, as well he should have been. He had arrested him enough times in the past for being intoxicated.

"Mr. Pemberly, I regret to have to inform you that the San Francisco police have confirmed that the body they found was that of your son. They are making arrangements to have his remains shipped back here for burial," he'd said, his words icy and cold, and then he'd turned and walked away. And just like that, Mark's world shattered. Everything he had done to clean himself up and find his son had been for nothing. His son was lying dead in a coroner's ice cabinet, awaiting transport back to Kansas.

He moved the portrait out of the way quickly, dropping to his knees, as the contents of his stomach came up on the floor in front of him. Gagging again, wave after wave of nausea pulled his insides out. Tears rolled down his face, but he managed to stumble to his feet; saliva hung from his mouth in a long string. He wiped at it with the back of his hand, his mind roaring and his throat begging for water, but his mind begged for whiskey. He shook his head, denying both urges. He'd promised Alan he would never touch another drop of booze if Alan would just come home, and he had kept his promise. And even though his boy was gone now, he wouldn't break it.

He stumbled forward, walked into the kitchen, and immediately went over to the cabinet where he had once kept his liquor bottles. It was bare now, save for a few coffee mugs and drinking glasses. He pointed the picture at the empty space before him.

"See, Alan? See? Daddy kept his promise," he cried. He turned, leaning against the cabinet as sobs shook him. He hugged the picture and again moved through the house. He passed the puddle of vomit. Sidestepping it, he made his way to the stairs and ran up, stumbling and almost falling as he climbed to the second floor. He pushed open his son's bedroom door. It banged against the wall as he turned the lights on. Everything was in its place. Nothing had changed since the boy had fled three years ago, after Mark came home from the bar drunk as a skunk. The boy had finally fought back and made it out the window.

"Oh God," Mark said as the memory assaulted him. His sobs subsided, and his mind cleared as he tore his gaze away from the wall of pennants and trophies. Most of them had been earned after his mom got sick. The boy had poured himself into everything outside the house, and he had excelled.

Mark calmly walked down the hall into his own bedroom, where he kept a pistol in the nightstand by the bed. He sat down, withdrew the revolver, and opened the chamber. He never kept it loaded out of fear of an accident, but now he loaded it with purpose. Deliberately he placed round after round into the chamber, spun it, and slapped it in place. He took the picture and walked it into the bathroom he had remodeled at his wife's insistence. He shut the door behind him. The light bounced off the white tile and assaulted his eyes to the point that he had to blink a couple of times, black dots dancing in front of him. The little blue flowers across the top of the tile had been his wife's choice, handpicked from dozens of patterns. His beautiful Helen, nothing more than old dusty bones in the ground now.

He placed the picture on the back of the toilet tank. The three figures smiled naively back at him like they didn't know what he was about to do. He looked at his face in the mirror and the horror of what he saw before him made him cry out weakly. The eyes were the same; the red lines of the capillaries that had burst from years of drinking were barely visible in the face red from crying. But his blue eyes were the same, the same eyes his son had. He raised the revolver and placed the barrel of it in his mouth. He closed his eyes. *I'll see you in a few minutes, son. I'll come to you,* he thought, mistakenly. He counted to three and pulled the trigger, decorating the white tile in brain matter and blood.

***

The door swung open to the white-tiled room. Jonathan was stepping in when all of a sudden, his ears rang as if he had heard a loud noise. He put his dirt-stained hand on the sink to steady himself and shook his head. It took a second to wear off as Jonathan proceeded to the tub and drew himself a bath, then stripped out of his clothes and discarded them on the floor.

Shhhh, never mind what you saw out there today; it was just objects in the rearview mirror, the annoying voice in his head said gently, trying desperately to relax him and keep him from shaking himself apart. Even that annoying voice occasionally showed a vested interest in keeping him from toppling over the edge. That same voice, which usually criticized him and reminded him of his failures, would surprise him occasionally and do something nice. Jonathan did his best to listen to it as he slid his sore and overheated body into the high claw-foot tub, now filled with tepid water. He lay back, resting his head on the rim as he stared up at the white tile with faded blue flowers and wondered whose delicate hands had put up something so perfectly.

CHAPTER 8

WHILE JONATHAN WAS upstairs in the tub, Maggie and Eddie went out front to finish up and put everything away. Evening was falling quickly as they gathered everything, and while Eddie stared at the yard, it dawned on him how much they had gotten done. It also occurred to him that, in the process of making the yard produce what they wanted it to, the earth had to be scarred and beaten up. He'd always hated the process of ripping a yard apart—tossing dirt around and making it ragged, in turmoil, and in a state of upheaval. But eventually, roots would take hold, and the rain and the sun would tamp everything and lay it down again as the fruits of their labor began to bear themselves proudly.

His heart ached for Jonathan, and he knew in some way his lover's mind was like this garden, in a constant state of upheaval. Time had shown him how to bear beautiful things, such as the book he had written that had won critical acclaim and led them to find this place. Eddie's only fear was the ground would never be quite stable enough to sustain them both. He silently toiled with this as he and Maggie closed up the shed in the backyard and dusted themselves off.

Maggie, apparently sensing his silent distress, reached over, laying a gentle hand on his sunburned arm. When he turned to look at her, he found no judgment in her eyes, only a well of sympathy that made a lump form in his throat. He turned away to hide the tears that threatened to spill over. Wiping a dusty, sweaty hand over his face, he smelled the richness of the earth and saltiness of his skin as he took in a ragged breath. Maggie didn't move her hand; if anything, her hold on his bicep strengthened, and he patted it with his own.

"Something tells me that out of the two of you, it is you who feels the weight of holding things together," she said kindly, like she had looked into his soul.

He shrugged. "We both feel it, I think. Just in different ways. Jonathan is...well, he's Jonathan. Sometimes here with me, sometimes a million miles away," Eddie said as they made their way back through the yard and out the side gate, walking slowly.

"His hair is a little long, and he's not clean-shaven, but he carries himself like a soldier," Maggie observed.

Eddie smiled. With age comes wisdom, and this lady had her fair share. "He actually served right here at Fort Riley for a few years," Eddie said. "Was in a chemical company, deployed in support of Operation Iraqi Freedom."

"Those boys are coming home pretty upset. It's not as bad for them as it was for the soldiers during Vietnam, thank goodness, but it's still pretty tough," she said solemnly as they made their way around the front porch, where they sat down on the top step.

"He talks about his time there. He loved it. When I've worked with soldiers returning from the battlefield, they are proud of their service but they really don't show much affection for the institution. They love their comrades in arms, but Jonathan never served in combat. He loved the Army. Sure, it was tough, but I think it probably saved his life. Actually, knowing what little I know, it did," Eddie said.

"Home life?" Maggie asked, and Eddie nodded. Just then, the front door opened and a cleaner and more relaxed Jonathan came outside. Eddie and Maggie stopped talking.

"Maggie, I am going to make a steak stir-fry. Since the damsel rescued the dude, the least he can do is cook her dinner," Jonathan said with a chuckle. He had changed into a pair of light cotton shorts and a white T-shirt. He brought a cold beer out and handed it off to Eddie, who took it gratefully.

"Yes, please stay," Eddie said before taking a draw on the ice-cold drink.

"Well, I'd be happy to, sweetheart. I have some sweet rolls next door that I'll go grab to go with it," she said and departed quickly, heading home. Jonathan sat down next to Eddie and kissed him on the nose.

"You okay?" Eddie asked.

"Yeah, babe. It's just been a hectic couple of days," Jonathan said, reaching out to rub his partner's muscular back.

"Yeah, and you're no spring chicken anymore," Eddie teased, and then he laughed when Jonathan feigned shock and offense.

"I'm just your old man now, huh?" Jonathan asked. Eddie smirked and took another draw on his beer. Jonathan did the same. There were a thousand questions, a thousand fears parading back and forth in Eddie's mind, never mind the odd things happening around them now in this new house. Eddie wanted so badly to open his heart up and tell Jonathan he was afraid, afraid of this new place, of leaving him alone here while he went to work, of losing him.

"I love you, Jonathan," Eddie said as Jonathan looked at him inquisitively, seeing the questions in those lovely blue eyes.

"I love you too, sweetheart. What's on your mi—," Jonathan was interrupted by Maggie as she reappeared holding a pan full of sweet rolls.

"Here we go!" she said cheerfully.

They would have to be okay with talking later.

***

Laughter rolled through the house, Maggie's wine-induced cackling making the boys laugh harder as they sat around the dining-room table over bowls of steak stir-fry and rice. Eddie had been chilling two bottles of white wine for a few days and broke them out to lift everyone's spirits. It worked. Maggie's spirits were higher than everyone else's as they traded stories back and forth.

"...he blew a hole right through the back door," Maggie said, laughing so hard tears were streaming down her face and she was having a hard time continuing.

"That poor boy," Eddie said, snickering and staring wide-eyed at Jonathan, who was laughing hard as well.

"Oh...oh...it was only salt pellets...but he learned never to try to be that romantic again," she said, wiping her face. She had been regaling them with the story of her as a young girl and the love-struck suitor she had married three years later. Her daddy hadn't liked him, and when he found the young man outside her window one night with a guitar, trying his best to croon to Maggie, the man took offense. Maggie took another sip of her wine and nearly choked on it as she started to laugh again. Her face was flushed from the alcohol and good humor.

"We've not had anything that dramatic," Eddie said, taking a bite of food and chuckling too.

"Oh, come on, we've had our moments," Jonathan said, rolling his eyes.

"How did you two meet?" she asked, elbow on the table and her head held up by the cup of her hand.

"We were attending the same university. Here comes this handsome, well-dressed man talking a good mess about the virtues of the Republican Party. I called bullshit," Eddie said.

Jonathan nodded and his face warmed with embarrassment. "Yeah. It was love at first sight from that moment on," he said, laughing. "He's been calling bullshit ever since," he teased.

"Sounds like any other relationship I've ever come across." She leaned in and elbowed Eddie gently. "I called bullshit with my Richard all the time."

Eddie smiled. "How long were you married?"

Maggie sighed and took another sip of her wine. "We had twenty-four years before he passed. He had a massive heart attack three years ago."

"I'm so sorry," Jonathan said, the mood of the room cooling off a little.

"Oh...I am too. We had a wonderful time. Doctors said it was stress," she said somberly. And then, with a mischievous wink of her eye, she said, "He was a Republican too."

It was still for a second before everyone burst into laughter once more. Finally, they focused on eating and finished their dinner before working together to clean the kitchen. They retired to the front porch with their glasses and sat down on the steps, enjoying the cool of the evening. Eddie had gone up to shower quickly before they started dinner, and now, their sun-kissed bodies were tender under their shirts, as the soap had tightened their skin.

"You boys are going to have to get furniture for out here; an old lady's backside can only take so much," Maggie said, sitting next to the duo. She closed her eyes as the sweet wind blew by.

"You know, I was going to go out in the morning and take care of that while Jonathan starts stripping the wallpaper. I have to pick some other stuff up, so I wouldn't mind the company," Eddie said.

"That would be great. Can we stop by the grocery store? Since you boys are going to be working all day in the house, I can make my famous fried chicken so you don't have to worry about cooking," she said, turning her gaze to them.

Jonathan really liked the lady and how sweet she was. "You don't have to do that, Maggie."

"Hush. I don't have many opportunities to cook. That is, if I'm not imposing," she said.

Eddie looked at Jonathan, who looked pleasantly surprised. "Hey, not at all," Jonathan said.

"Then it's settled," she said. And so it was. The boys had made a new friend in their new place and happily chatted with her late into the night.

***

"There were no complaints by the former tenants in the house, then?" Eddie asked as he and Maggie drove through Manhattan in hopes of finding the furniture store on Pillsbury Drive. They were in his Sonata, windows rolled up and the air conditioner on. It was hot and muggy, the forecast calling for a chance of severe storms that afternoon. It made Eddie nervous and kept him watching the sky. They had left Jonathan at home, at his insistence, to start taking down the wallpaper. Maggie had shown him how to peel it back using a steam cleaner and a little vinegar, so Jonathan had laid down some drop cloths, opened up the windows, cranked on his radio, and set to work. Eddie figured he would be fine in the house as long as he was distracted.

"No. The two old ladies who lived there ten years never said anything, and before them, the house sat vacant for a long time. Nobody would buy it because of, well, its history. The real-estate agency wouldn't let it fall into disrepair, though. People came and went, and the yard was kept up, but the only trouble was when the Pemberlys lived there. God love 'em," Maggie said, looking out of her window.

"What ever happened to Alan and...Mark, was it?" Eddie asked, steering his car down the street the patio place was supposed to be on, and he hit the brakes when they would have passed it, had Maggie not pointed it out quickly with a tap on the window. He pulled into the open parking lot and onto the gravel. People were wandering around the outside, women wearing light tops and short pants accompanied by their jeans-clad husbands and towheaded children. A few of them had on large hats or sunglasses. The white rock of the gravel lot forced Eddie to pull his sunglasses down from atop his head as he got out of the car. The air was heavy, but he was glad to be out. He was excited about getting a swing for the porch, and this place promised it would deliver for free.

"Maggie? Alan and Mark?" Eddie reminded her as she walked around the car to join him as they made their way through the throng of people.

"Yeah, I remember, Eddie. I just...let's wait till we get back in the car, huh?" she asked, motioning with her head at the people who walked close by, browsing the patio tables, loungers, and other lawn decorations. Eddie nodded, and they walked side by side, the gravel crunching underneath their feet.

They were approached by a tall, lithe, sandy-haired young man wearing a green polo shirt tucked into his jeans and a giant smile on his handsome face. He couldn't have been more than twenty years old, Eddie thought.

"Hey, there. Welcome to Patios and More. I'm Ted. Can I help you with anything?" he asked.

"Hi, Ted. I'm Eddie. We're looking for a porch swing and some patio furniture for a back deck," Eddie explained with a grin to match the salesman's. He was impressed by his friendliness, and the muscles underneath his shirt weren't bad either. His chest was wide and his hips narrow. He instructed them to follow him before turning on his heel, which allowed Eddie a view of his denim-clad butt.

Maggie stood on her tiptoes and whispered in Eddie's ear, "Gotta love farm boys." She snickered and elbowed him in the ribs playfully. They both laughed and happily followed Ted as he led them to the back, where several wooden swings were on display.

"These swings here could be used for either a stand-alone swing or you could attach them to hooks in the ceiling of the porch and use them as a porch swing," Ted explained. There were five different variations to look at, and Eddie and Maggie tried them all before deciding on one that was most comfortable and fit the dimensions of the space they had to work with. Ted stood by patiently as the duo talked between themselves and finally made their decision. He wrote the model type down on a pad of paper he pulled from his back pocket and with a pencil that had been behind his ear.

"What's your best seller when it comes to patio furniture, Ted?" Eddie asked as Ted finished writing and placed the pad back in his pocket.

They were walking with the young man over to another display when Eddie heard the first roll of thunder. He looked at the horizon, and there in the distance, moving quickly toward them, was a mass of bluish-gray clouds. Lightning arced upward across the bloated angry mass and forked out before a low rumble of thunder accompanied it. Maggie followed his gaze as a cool breeze brushed past them.

"We still have time, but it's moving fast. We need to hurry," she said. Ted, having noticed the weather change, quickly described the various sets they had. The clouds were moving in faster and the wind starting to kick up a little dust, which kept the trio occupied wiping their eyes. Eddie finally settled on a set and gave his card to the young man for him to run. The boy took off, running inside a little storefront, and came back quickly with a receipt for Eddie to sign. He took down their address and told them since the weather was about to turn bad, they would deliver it to him the next day.

Almost a thousand dollars later, Eddie and Maggie spilled themselves back into the car and rolled the widows down. The sun had baked the interior of the vehicle, and it was stifling hot. Careful not to mow over other people dashing toward their own vehicles, Eddie guided the car out of the lot and back onto the street. The car cooled once again, and they rolled the windows up and sat back for the ride to Clay Center. Eddie was feeling pretty good about his purchase and thinking Jonathan would love it when Maggie splashed cold water on him.

"They died," she said, as they made their turn back onto the state road that led them back home.

"Huh?" Eddie asked.

"Alan and his father, Mark. That poor family," Maggie said, shaking her blonde-and-white hair. She was staring out the window as they rolled slowly out of the city toward the open prairie.

"Mark killed his son?" Eddie asked, thunderstruck.

"No. Nothing like that. Alan's death was an accident. Mark's death was intentional. You see, after Alan left, Mark realized what he had done and sobered up. Daddy sat round the clock with him for two evenings as the man went through the shakes, before talking him into going to the hospital for real treatment. It was horrible, but he made it through to the other side. He started going to church at the First Presbyterian Congregation down the road, started attending AA meetings, and completely turned his life around. He looked for Alan right away, hired a private investigator, and finally found his phone number. The boy had moved to San Francisco.

"Alan wouldn't take his calls, wouldn't call back, wouldn't have anything to do with Mark at all, but his dad never gave up. One night Mark came tearing out of the house, shouting with joy. We were all sitting on the porch that afternoon, and the man stumbled over. Daddy thought he was drunk. He wasn't, he just couldn't hold himself up straight, he was crying so hard. Alan had called and told his daddy he was on his way home. Oh…I'll never forget that night. My daddy held the man as he wept in his arms. Wasn't a dry eye on the porch that day, I tell ya," Maggie said as she wiped at her eyes and fished out a wad of tissues.

"Wow. What happened?" Eddie asked, feeling dread settle in as the sky in front of him turned a bruised color with the clouds rolling in. They were thick and unhappy and pregnant with moisture. In the distance, lightning danced off the ground. The storm would hit before they got home, Eddie was sure.

"A terrible accident. Fate. A cruel God. I don't know. We never got the whole story, but Alan had gotten himself into some trouble there in California and tried to flee. He didn't make it very far before it caught up with him. Anyway, he was run over leaving an office building in downtown San Francisco. I had gotten off shift working at the grocery store and had just walked in the door when I heard the gunshot from next door. I ran upstairs to wake Daddy up…and…it was horrible. Mark had killed himself in the upstairs bathroom. His wife and now his son. Daddy found him, and in all my years, I had never seen him like that. He was a mess. He had always had high hopes for Mark and was happy Alan was coming home. He never spoke of it again as long as he lived."

"Jesus," Eddie whispered as lightning flashed overhead and thunder rolled. The clouds opened up and openly wept upon the earth below, as if the heartbreaking story Maggie told had drifted up into the heavens.

**

355

Jonathan wiped the sweat out of his eyes as he stood back from the wall. The steam cleaner was helping tremendously, but it made the rooms so unbearably humid he had to pull a box fan with him into every room. The walls underneath the paper were plaster, which made the process of removing it easier, and for that he was thankful. He had rubbed them down with warm vinegar water to loosen the glue before he came back through and used the steamer to help with the rest of the paper. He was upstairs now, in the center room with the god-awful pink wallpaper, most of which now lay at his feet. He was pretty pleased with himself thus far, although his hands were waterlogged and smelled like they had been soaked in salad dressing.

Elton John sang out from the portable MP3 player at his feet about the virtues of fighting on a Saturday night. Jonathan belted along and moved his hips with the rhythm as he admired his work. Outside, the sunlight had been replaced by gloomy darkness and the smell of rain came whipping through the turning blades of the fan in the window. He'd had a productive morning and had most of the wallpaper peeled down and crumpled into balls on the floor. He'd picked up the wand of the steam cleaner to attack the last wall when he noticed he was out of water.

"Well, shit," Jonathan muttered, and he turned the machine off to extract the empty tank. He'd walked into the bathroom to refill it in the tub when a thunderclap sounded so loudly, he nearly jumped out of his skin. He backpedaled and sat down on the toilet seat with the bucket in his lap. The lights flickered hard but stayed on as Jonathan laughed at himself and stood back up to fill the container. He placed it in the tub and turned on the hot water as thunder rolled again. He had forgotten what it was like to live in Kansas, where the thunder sounded like Thor sitting astride the peak of your roof, pounding away with his hammer. He laughed at how jumpy he was, and as his heart slowed to a normal beat, he turned the hot water off and carried the bucket back into the room he was finishing.

Kings of Leon kicked into high gear, and Jonathan sang along as he put the bucket in the steamer and clicked it into place. He picked up the wand again and raised it to the wall, and he was getting ready to turn it on when his cell phone rang.

"Dammit." He set the wand down and took off down the hall to his bedroom, where his cell phone was plugged in. He rounded the bed and looked at the caller ID. It was Beth West, his agent. He picked up the phone and answered it. "Hey, Beth. What's up?" he asked as he put the phone to his ear.

"Just calling to check in and see how you're getting settled. How's the new place?" she asked, her voice bubbly, as always. He could envision her, sitting in her office, feet up, cord wrapped around her fingers and her blonde hair held up in a clip on top of her head.

Jonathan shut the door partway to block out the music from the other room.

"Oh, it's great. We've got everything moved in, and now we're working on getting the house repainted and everything. How are you?" he asked.

"Oh, good, sweetie. Everything here is fine. Although, I have to tell ya, I'm getting constant e-mails from anxious readers wanting to know when the next novel is going to be out," she said, and there it was.

It hadn't taken too long for this to come up. Jonathan grinned. With the moving and promotion for the first book, he hadn't had time to sit down at his PC and write.

"Well, let them know I have an idea already waiting," he said. It was a lie. Since the book deal, he hadn't had time to think. As a matter of fact, with his newfound fame, the book signings, the meetings with his agency, and everything else that had come along with it, he hadn't had time to think. Jonathan had hoped moving to Kansas, back to a place with such fond memories, would provide a much needed balance.

"Well, don't rush," she said, and Jonathan interpreted that as, "Don't wait too long to get your butt in gear."

"I won't. I have a few rooms that need painting before I can sit down again. I'll let you know when I've started another WIP, and then I'll disappear into my work, so you can take all my calls," he said, laughing. The MP3 player stopped midsong, but Jonathan barely noticed as he sat down on the edge of the bed and rested his chin in his hand and his elbow on his knee, holding the phone to his ear with the other hand.

"Your sales are still running strong, and we have a few interviews we would like you to do, a few blogs entries we would like you to write, and a few readings you could do. We can set them up in Kansas City or Topeka, which would give you a lot of good exposure in the Midwest. Eventually we would like you to tour, but that can wait until you're settled in. How's Eddie?" she asked.

"Oh, good. He's out right now picking up patio furniture with our new neighbor, who's sort of adopted us," Jonathan said.

Creak.

"Well, look at that—you two are already making friends," she said.

Creak.

Jonathan's ears pricked up. Something was wrong. All of a sudden, the air felt funny. The hairs on his arms stood up as Beth kept talking. He put the phone down to his chest so he could listen better. It sounded like it was coming from the stairs. Suddenly, he was frozen to the bed.

Creak. Creak. Creak.

"Jonathan, are you there? Jonathan?" Beth said, her voice muffled by his chest. He hit the end button, silencing her voice in case she could be heard. He did everything he could do to hold his breath steady as he stood on two very shaky legs. He looked around the room for a weapon, and there, like the sword in Arthur's stone, the Louisville Slugger waited patiently for its master. When he saw it, Jonathan darted quickly to the other side of the door, shoved his phone in his pocket, and stood there waiting. The footsteps were getting closer. They were on the landing now. Jonathan edged closer to the crack in between the door and the frame so he could peer out and jumped back as soon as he saw a thin young man with blond hair walking past.

He waited for the footfalls to continue down the hall before he swung the door open, baseball bat raised, and charged down the hall like a knight…only to find no one there. He looked in all three rooms, throwing each door open, but nothing.

"The fuck?" he said aloud. There was no way the man could have gotten down the stairs again; he would have had to walk past Jonathan again. Thunder rolled heavily once again as lightning danced outside. Downstairs, the front door opened, and Jonathan whirled around and charged down the stairs, frightening Eddie and Maggie.

"Jonathan, what the hell?" Eddie said as he backed up against the wall at the sight of Jonathan's raised bat and angry face.

"Did you see someone outside?" he demanded.

"What? No. It's pouring outside," Eddie protested as Jonathan shot past him and Maggie and tore out to the front porch to look for himself. Eddie was right, it was pouring, but Jonathan ran down the front steps to the sidewalk so he could look down both sides of the street. Empty. Warm rain poured over his head, soaking him from head to toe and pushing the salty sweat that had dried on his forehead into his eyes. He rubbed at them, trying to stop the burning. He shook his head and stood there a few more moments, feeling stupid and wondering if he was losing his mind.

CHAPTER 9

D INNER WAS A quiet affair. After Eddie had convinced Jonathan to come in out of the rain, Jonathan was both angry and embarrassed by what Eddie and Maggie had seen. He apologized to both of them, but they assured him it was all right. But to Eddie, it was far from all right. He was worried about Jonathan. His husband seemed on edge, nervous, and pensive, and the fact that he thought he saw someone bothered Eddie even more.

Once Jonathan had come back in, he had stormed up the stairs and turned on some heavy metal while he angrily tore away at the last wall of the room he had been working on. Eddie worked around him, picking up the paper that had been discarded on the floor and dodging Jonathan as he stepped right and left with the wand. Eddie waited for him to open up and talk, but his mood was as stormy as the weather, so Eddie had gone to rejoin Maggie, who had stayed downstairs to cook. She had tried to excuse herself, worried she was imposing, but Eddie asked her to stay.

"Is he all right?" she asked worriedly.

"I don't honestly know," Eddie said, munching on a carrot stick as she battered the chicken and placed it in the cast-iron skillet.

"He said he saw a blond kid walk by the door. He seemed rather convinced about it," she said.

"Yeah, that's what bothers me," he replied quietly.

"The two women who lived her before never complained about anything like that. Is it possible the house is...you know... haunted?" she suggested, removing one chicken breast from the skillet to a plate and then adding another to the hot grease.

"Haunted…like, by ghosts?" he asked. She shot him an annoyed look and he laughed. "Ghosts? No. I think that—"

"You think what? That Jonathan is simply seeing things? I would think a haunting is less damning than someone hallucinating," she said rather stiffly. Eddie was shocked to hear her abrupt tone.

"I'm not saying he is seeing things, I'm just suggesting he might be a little tired and stressed out. The move could be affecting him negatively, is all. Jonathan…he's a little…prone to cracking under too much stress. We try to keep it to a minimum," Eddie said. "What I mean to say is, he hasn't fully developed his coping mechanisms to certain kinds of stressors."

Maggie looked at him and arched an eyebrow. "He is prone to cracking under stress? He looks fine to me."

"It's just…he has a hard time sometimes. It's like the world gets too big for him. He's brilliant, funny, but he's been beaten up pretty badly before, and he holds it together as best he can." Eddie peered out into the hall to make sure his husband wasn't eavesdropping. Eddie would have been devastated if his husband busted him talking about this.

"That's quite a bit for you to handle," Maggie said as she took the chicken piece out of the oil and added another. "How bad was his home life? I know you mentioned something about it the other day."

"Pretty awful. He is a child-abuse survivor," Eddie said. Maggie nodded solemnly. "Sometimes he goes for long stretches where he's fine. Operates well in social circles; he's the life of the party and can run circles around me. A perfect extrovert. It's like he feeds off the energy of other people. Then, sometimes he just reverts to being an introvert and becomes melancholy and distances himself away from people." Eddie shook his head. "I'm sorry. I shouldn't be unloading on you like this. It's just, I feel like I can trust you, is all. I haven't spoken about this to anyone."

"That's perfectly all right. I won't tell a soul what you're telling me," she said, patting his hand. "When did he start writing? I got the book, by the way. It's pretty damn good." Maggie turned away from the stove, picked up a pot of freshly snapped green beans and onions, and placed it on the stove. Eddie honestly couldn't wait to eat.

"Well, he's always been a writer. His papers for school were very good sometimes, depending on how 'into them' he was. He can't do math to save his life," Eddie said, laughing. Maggie smiled and finished frying the pieces she had before moving them over to a cookie sheet and placing them in the oven.

"So, the abusers. Alcoholics? Drug addicts?" she asked with a sympathetic look in her eyes.

Eddie shook his head. "No. Stone-cold sober. They did it all in God's name." Maggie placed a hand over her heart as her eyes grew wide in shock. Eddie nodded as the music ended and a new song began.

"Sexual?" Maggie asked cautiously.

"No," Eddie said emphatically. "It was physical, emotional, and mental. Nothing sexual. At least, I don't think there was. He has denied anything like that. But if you ever hear us talking about 'objects in the rearview mirror,' or 'rearview-mirror stuff,' he's talking about that."

"Oh," she said. "I don't get the reference."

"It's from the very first CD I got as a kid," Jonathan said. Eddie swung his head around and saw Jonathan standing with his arms folded over his chest, staring at the floor. "My sister gave me an album by Meat Loaf, and that song has always spoken to me. If you ever hear it, you'll understand why. Well, at least now you will."

"Oh my God, Jonathan, I'm so—"

"Nothing to be sorry about, babe. I have nothing to hide," he said coolly. Eddie's face burned with embarrassment and shame. "Dinner smells great. Is it almost done?"

He walked over to the stove and peeked in the pot, inhaling deeply.

Eddie stood there, his heart beating hard. He was so upset, he wanted to cry. He felt like he had violated Jonathan's trust.

"How long did it go on?" Maggie asked bravely. Jonathan turned and looked at her, meeting her eye to eye. Countless minutes passed as she fearlessly kept his gaze. He was the first to drop his. She walked forward and did something that touched Eddie's heart. She reached out and placed her hand on the side of Jonathan's face. He raised his gaze once more, and there it was—the hurt and uncertainty that had always scared Eddie. But Maggie bravely held him there.

"You sweet, sweet boy. God bless the child who suffers," she said kindly, and Eddie watched, fascinated. He had never seen Jonathan get this vulnerable with anyone other than him.

"I'm not sure there is a God," Jonathan whispered.

"Don't worry about that right now. Come on, let's eat," Maggie said.

***

Jonathan stood in the shower and let the hot water run over him. The sweat from the day rinsed off him as the hot water made his skin pink. He braced his hands on opposite sides of the sprayer and let the water fall. Like the rain working its way into the soil to bring life to it, the water in the shower worked to relieve the tension in his muscular back, allowing him to relax. He had been furious at Eddie, but that had dissipated, diffused by the kind woman's words. She hadn't brought judgment, hadn't looked at him like he was a freak, and hadn't seemed afraid of what Eddie had told her. She'd taken it in stride. He had walked in on Eddie explaining their code words for the abuse and had stopped to listen.

He wondered when it would end, when it would eventually get better. He had been to therapists, talked about it with them, talked about it with close friends, talked about it with his siblings, and sometimes he could get by like that. Then other times, the poison built up too quickly and made him sick again. It could bring him to the brink of madness and break his heart and make him afraid of the world again. It made him want to be reckless, drink excessively, find a drug dealer, find a stranger whom he didn't have to care about, anything that would give him the ability to leave his tormented mind for a little while. But that had all changed when Eddie showed up. Eddie didn't ask anything of him, didn't demand anything from him—he let Jonathan come to him and be vulnerable when he felt like he couldn't hang on.

Tonight was going to be one of those nights. He felt exposed, raw, and frustrated. He turned off the water and towel-dried, making sure to get every square inch of him. He hung up the towel on a hook behind the bathroom door and walked naked to the bedroom. Eddie wasn't there, so he went to the room he had been working on. Eddie was there, admiring his work. The white had been painted over, and the walls were drying.

"You did good work in here—" Eddie stopped short when he saw Jonathan was naked and semiaroused. They stared at each other for what felt like an eternity to Jonathan, as he lost his breath in anticipation.

"Will you make love to me?" Jonathan asked, his heart pounding hard in his chest. His defenses were down, and he needed Eddie more than ever. To cover him, to be inside him and to watch over him, to let Jonathan go and fall, knowing he would be caught safely in the arms of his husband. Not waiting for a response, hoping love and desire would pull Eddie after him, he walked back down the hall and into the bedroom, where he climbed onto the bed and slid against the cool sheets. Moments later, he was greeted with the feeling of Eddie sliding in on top of him, naked. Eddie rubbed his chest against Jonathan's bare back as he laid his weight down on top of him. Eddie ran his hands up Jonathan's shoulders to his arms to intertwine their fingers together.

He could feel Eddie's arousal at the cleft of his ass, hard, thick, and pulsing. Jonathan stretched against Eddie as Eddie turned his head and closed his mouth over Jonathan's. They touched, tasted, and teased in passionate hunger as Eddie slid his hand down Jonathan's face, to his neck and down his chest as far as he could go before the bed stopped his exploratory advance. Every muscle begged to be touched, every inch of Jonathan's skin hummed as the blood rushed from the farthest distances in his body to the organ tissue between his legs that pushed against the mattress. He relished the feeling of his husband on top of him, strong and purpose driven. Knowing he hungered for him turned Jonathan on all the more, as his body begged to be the focus of his desire.

Eddie braced himself against the mattress, raised himself, as Jonathan turned over. Jonathan stared up into Eddie's eyes. He ran his hands down Eddie's furry chest and reached between their bodies to hold his lover as Eddie's eyes rolled back in his head and he groaned soft and low. Jonathan turned his head and reached inside the drawer near the bed to pull out a bottle of lube. Eddie took it from him, knowing what Jonathan needed and what he wanted. Jonathan leaned back and absently stroked himself as he felt a hand on his bottom and a finger sliding gently inside of him as he arched his back. One finger became two as he moaned and clutched the pillows around his head.

"I'm ready," Jonathan panted and opened his eyes. He saw the intensity of passion in his lover's eyes and felt him pressing against him. The moment when Eddie slid in, gently, Jonathan whimpered his name over and over until he was filled completely. Eddie grabbed Jonathan's right leg and raised it over his shoulder as he slowly began to move back and forth gently in the age-old rhythm of love. He reached down and grabbed his lover's swollen cock, and as he stroked him internally, he stroked him externally in time with his thrusts, causing Jonathan to moan and cry out.

"Oh, God. Don't stop. Please don't ever stop." He raised his hips to meet his lover's thrusts.

"Never, baby. You feel so good," Eddie whispered hotly. The passion burned between them, hot, sticky, and slow, causing perspiration to break out on Jonathan's forehead.

"Please. Roll over, roll me over," Jonathan said.

Eddie ended up on his back with Jonathan on top. Jonathan grabbed the headboard and positioned his feet parallel with Eddie's hips to give himself maximum leverage as he used his body to pleasure them both. Jonathan's mind shut down; he was just a mass of nerve endings and breathless pleasure as Eddie put his hands on his hips to help guide him up and down. The feeling of being taken over soared through him. The act of letting go and letting his mind disappear took over and propelled them into the inevitable fumble toward ecstasy. He was safe in his lover's arms.

"Babe. Oh. Jonathan. My God. I'm not going to make it, babe. I'm gonna…oh, I'm going to… Arrrgh," Eddie cried out, bucking his hips against Jonathan.

"Do it, babe. Do it," Jonathan panted, meeting him as they flew over the edge together. Exhausted, he leaned forward and kissed his lover on the mouth, then rolled off to lie next to him, panting for breath. Both were sweating and gasping as Jonathan turned over and placed his head on Eddie's chest. His heart beat strong and true against his rib cage as fatigue pulled at the edges of his mind.

"Please don't ever let me go," Jonathan whispered.

Eddie wrapped his arms around him and drew him closer.

"Never. Hey. Look at me," Eddie said. Jonathan tilted his head up, and Eddie gave him a gentle smile. "Never. I'll always be here."

Jonathan smiled back and laid his head back down, praying Eddie was telling the truth.

***

"Let me go!"

Jonathan gasped as his senses were assaulted by a quick awakening. He was standing inside the front door of the home he used to live in as a kid. It was all the same: the pictures on the wall, the furniture draped in covers, the TV, everything. He looked down at himself and found that he was clothed in the same pair of sweatpants he'd put on before he went to sleep.

"This is a dream," he said to himself. "Wake up. Wake up."

"You'll take this or you'll take my fist" came the angry retort. Jonathan jerked and blinked rapidly at the realization that he also knew when this was. He surged forward to the room on the left but stopped dead when his mother wandered around the corner. She didn't see him, didn't hesitate, just walked calmly to the bedroom, where the other voices were coming from. She did stop at the doorway to the bedroom, though, and smirk.

"Beat the hell out of him!" she said. "Serves you right for hanging down the street with those whores! Smoking cigarettes!" She was referring to the girls Jonathan was friends with. They were his only friends. Both girls' parents smoked and the houses were saturated with the smell. He had never smoked before, but when he'd continually been screamed at over it, he'd figured what the hell?

Jonathan continued walking forward and fearfully peered around the corner into the bedroom he had occupied for a couple of years before he and his family had moved. What he saw both broke his heart and enraged him. There he was, or rather, the sixteen-year-old version of himself. The fat, acne-scarred, greasy-faced version of himself afraid of the man who held a wooden board about the length of his forearm and brought it down several times across the kid's back and ass.

"Leave him alone!" the older Jonathan screamed in the face of his father. The man didn't flinch, instead sneered and brought it down harder as the kid screamed and cried. Jonathan looked at his sixteen-year-old self and screamed.

"Fight back! He's a pussy! He'll cave if you put him on his ass! Fight back!" he cried as he watched the young man being tortured. Jonathan cried out in dismay as tears rolled down his face. The father raised his baton once more, and Jonathan locked his gaze on it, stepping forward, trying to intercede and wrench it from his hands, but to no avail. To Jonathan's surprise it simply passed through his body as if he wasn't there and landed on the backside of the boy crying out in pain.

Jonathan whirled around, shaking, confused, and angry. "Oh God! Wake me up!" he cried out, his voice cracking. His mother was there, the fifteen-year-old memory as accurate as anything he could remember. The screams of his younger self being tormented made him gag. Pure panic, rage, and fear burst inside him and made him want to cower in the corner and beg for mercy. But one glance at the woman who stood in the doorway filled him with murderous contempt. Jonathan stalked away from the scene toward her and got in her face.

"Stop him. Stop him! He's your son! Stop him, you bitch! He's a good boy! He's not done anything wrong! Stop him!" When she wouldn't respond, he raised his fist and swung as hard as he could, his hand passing unencumbered through her so he stumbled forward and crashed silently into the wall, sobbing in frustration and fear. He could still hear the boy's harsh weeping, his voice hoarse now. The bruises would last for weeks. They would hurt, burn, as the pummeled flesh struggled to repair itself.

Grief and despair filled him at not being able to intercede. He was reliving the nightmare. He thought his mind was finally going to shake loose as a hand came down on his shoulder. Startled, he looked up to see that same blond man looking down at him with sympathy. Then suddenly, everything was different. The house he knew was gone and replaced with the house he lived in now. But not exactly. The wallpaper was back, and Jonathan looked around as the blond boy beckoned him to follow.

"Who are you?" Jonathan asked dumbly, but the boy's eyes grew frantic, and he waved his hands for him to stop. The boy stood there, eyes wide and a finger over his lips, as if he were listening. Jonathan went still. Finally, the young man motioned for him to follow. They walked into Jonathan's bedroom, but it too was different. Rather than his lover sleeping in bed and their own trappings, the walls were adorned with things a normal teenager would have.

The boy pointed to the floor, and in a voice that sounded far away, said just two words: "Help me."

"Help you. Who are you?" Jonathan asked, stepping forward. The door behind him kicked open and the blond boy screamed and ran for the window. Jonathan whirled around in time to see a middle-aged man built like a linebacker with a huge beer gut stalk forward out of the hallway. The smell of liquor saturated his breath, and at first, Jonathan thought he too couldn't see him, but he was mistaken. The man in fact saw him plainly and screamed in his face. *"Get out!"*

Then everything went black.

***

Eddie woke with a start as a clap of thunder rocked the house. The first thing he realized was that the bed was empty and the bedroom door stood wide open. He figured Jonathan had wandered off to the bathroom or downstairs for a drink.

Eddie moved his hand across Jonathan's side of the bed, and to his dismay, it was cold. Something screamed in his head, *Go find your man*! Eddie jumped out the bed and dashed naked to the bedroom door and into the hallway. It was dark save for a few nightlights that dotted the baseboards. Eddie took the stairs two at a time as his heart pounded in his chest. He missed the last step and nearly took his own feet out from under him, but caught his balance at the last minute and plunged through the dark house.

Jonathan wasn't in the living room, the dining room, or the sitting room off to the side. Something was wrong; Eddie could feel it. It was causing the hairs on his arms to stand up. He opened the hall bathroom. Nothing. He was resisting the urge to scream out Jonathan's name, afraid to startle him, when he noticed the kitchen light on. Breathing a sigh of relief, he followed the hallway down and pushed the door open. When he peered inside the room, the words he'd been about to say died on his tongue, and his heart nearly stopped.

All the furniture had been pushed to the center of the room and stacked on top of each other from floor to ceiling. All the cabinet doors were open wide, and the room was stifling hot because all of the stove burners were on high. But that wasn't the worst part, nor the most shocking. Standing in the corner of the room, staring blankly into the kitchen, was Jonathan. The look on his face terrified Eddie.

Jonathan's face was slack and his head tilted to the side, his eyes wide and staring as he stood there in the corner, facing out, rocking back and forth on his heels. Eddie rushed forward and stopped as if he'd hit a brick wall. He gagged as the heavy scent of urine hit him right across the face. The heat wasn't making it any better, so he quickly sidestepped and shut off the burners, then ran to the window and threw it open. The stench and the heat of the room seemed to be sucked out of the window quickly as the breeze flew through it and rain fell on the windowsill. Eddie whirled around and swallowed thickly, readied himself, and approached Jonathan. He reached out and gently touched Jonathan's bare arm. He was surprised to find it cold.

"Baby," he whispered gently. "Baaaaaaby," he said again, just as he did when he roused Jonathan from sleep. He reached up and stroked his lover's cheek.

"Baaaaaaby," he said a third time, just as tender, and the pupils in Jonathan's eyes constricted. Jonathan blinked once, twice, three times, and then he took in a breath as if being awakened from a deep sleep.

"Wha...? Eddie?" Jonathan asked, looking confused.

"Yeah, baby, I'm here," Eddie said. Jonathan shook his head and looked at him, then at the kitchen, and then back at him. He tried to form words, his mouth opening and shutting. Then he caught sight of the furniture and the cabinets, and his eyes grew wide.

"Eddie!" he cried out in disbelief. He went to take a step forward and stopped. It broke Eddie's heart when Jonathan realized the front of his sweatpants was wet. His eyes filled with horror, and he looked so forlorn and helpless Eddie had to fight back the urge to rush forward. He knew moving too quickly might trigger a startle response. So he placed a hand on Jonathan's arm and kept eye contact with him. In a soothing and calm voice, he encouraged him to walk out of the kitchen.

They moved past the furniture and Jonathan turned his head. "The cabinets are open again," he said absently.

Eddie stopped and looked at him, his curiosity and fear getting the better of him. "Jonathan, look at me," he said. Jonathan looked fearful and remorseful. Eddie hesitated and then forced the words out. "What happened here?" he asked.

Jonathan stood silent for a moment, considering. His eyes were wild. "Rearview-mirror stuff, babe. I went through it. I went through the mirror, and I got lost."

CHAPTER 10

T HE NEXT FEW weeks passed without incident, but Eddie watched Jonathan like a hawk. They finished painting the house and doing minor repairs. They bought, arranged, and rearranged furniture until they got it just right.

At first, Eddie fretted over the events from that horrible night, but Jonathan didn't seem to remember any of it. Eddie had led him upstairs to the bathroom, helped him strip out of his sopping wet sweatpants, and run a hot tub. Jonathan had let Eddie bathe him and tuck him into bed, and then he'd fallen fast asleep and hadn't moved a muscle. Eddie knew that for certain because he'd stayed up all night watching him. When the sun began to rise, Eddie had finally let himself fall asleep, and the two slept in. After that, nothing odd happened at all, and Jonathan took no more nocturnal strolls to rearrange furniture in the kitchen.

Eddie brushed it off as a case of sleepwalking and let it go. He didn't want to bring it back up to Jonathan, who he feared would be more embarrassed than worried. But Eddie still occasionally would startle awake at night, worried that Jonathan had wandered off, only to find him snoring steadily in his sleep. The only oddity that remained was the tendency of the same damn cabinet door to be wide open.

But as scary as that night had been, Jonathan seemed to regain his cheerful composure and eventually tackled his study one morning. He had painted the walls a very light blue with white trim and had hung white lace curtains to allow plenty of light. On the desk, Jonathan placed a lamp and pictures of the two of them together. He reassembled his beloved PC and attached the printer, then plugged everything into a power strip. As Jonathan worked, Eddie snuck to the closet in the hall, pulled out a large brown package, and brought it into the study.

"Hey, Mr. Writer Man," he said, tucking the package behind his back. Jonathan raised his head and smiled, cocking it to the side.

"What's that?" he asked.

"Mmmmm, a prize," Eddie said and moved the large brown paper-wrapped gift from around his back.

"A prize. Was I in a contest?" Jonathan asked.

"Yup," Eddie replied and leaned in for a kiss.

"What was it?" Jonathan asked.

Eddie smirked and winked at him. "Husband of the year. Go on, now, open it. Tell me what you think," he said, shooing him back.

Jonathan sat down at his chair and undid the twine that held it together. Then he pulled the paper down, and as a big grin broke out over his face, Eddie knew he had done something good.

"Babe. I love it," Jonathan said in a touched whisper. Eddie had taken his book cover, blown it up to poster-sized, and then framed it. "Sands of Time" was written in bold golden letters over a blue sky, and Jonathan's name written in blue over the sand.

"Yeah?" Eddie asked.

"Yeah," Jonathan said. He walked over to the wall beside his desk. He held it up. "What do you think?"

"I think it's perfect," Eddie said with his arms folded. Jonathan turned his head, his eyes wide and searching. Eddie reiterated, "Yeah, perfect."

With the room finished, Jonathan sat down and went through countless e-mails that had clogged up his in-box while he had been disconnected from the world. This left Eddie free to go and set up his own office in one of the other rooms. He hung up his degrees and set up his laptop and other office supplies before starting the long process of getting his curriculum down for the fall. His classes, as well as his appointment book, had already filled up. He spent a few hours on the phone with textbook distributers, ordering the overly priced reprints that always made him wince when he handed out his syllabus to his students. Six hundred dollars for three books? He hated to use the word, but "insane" was the only one he could use to describe the obnoxious cost his students would have to incur.

***

One afternoon Jonathan appeared at his door, chewing his bottom lip and looking slightly worried.

"What's wrong?" Eddie asked, his heart skipping a beat.

"That yard of ours is getting out of hand. We don't have a mower," he said with a roll of his eyes.

"We've spent so much freaking money already," Eddie said, sitting back in his chair, exasperated.

Jonathan shrugged and looked down at his bare feet. "Welcome to the world of home ownership, I guess. But this should be the last thing we need to buy for a while. Everything else is new; we just…forgot a mower and edger. Besides," Jonathan said as he sat down on the edge of his desk and crossed his legs, "it'll give us a chance to get out."

"Manhattan?" Eddie asked, opening Jonathan's legs. Jonathan scooted forward and Eddie sat back as he straddled his lap. Jonathan gave a noncommittal sound at the suggestion.

"Nah. Let's just go to Junction City and look for one there. We can pick up dinner and bring it home so I don't have to cook," Jonathan said, staring into Eddie's eyes.

Eddie put his hands on Jonathan's ass and pulled him closer. He loved to feel Jonathan's muscular legs and loved how beautiful his man was. "What do you want for dinner?"

"Dunno. But I can tell you what I want for dessert," Jonathan said with a smirk, and then he leaned in and kissed his husband slowly and passionately.

"Careful. We might not make it down there," Eddie panted as the kiss broke.

Jonathan laughed and stood up, adjusting himself. "Come on, it'll be fun," he said and held out a hand.

Eddie took it, and off they went.

***

Jonathan was shocked at how much Junction City had grown since he had been there last. As a soldier at Fort Riley in his early twenties, he had been a reckless young man, hitting the bars as often as possible, spending copious amounts of money, and running all over Kansas in one great whirlwind. He'd frequented Junction City to eat and hang out with friends, but the city hadn't had much to offer then. Now, it was a booming little burg, and as he and Eddie walked hand in hand down Main Street, they looked into the antique stores, army surplus, and other novelty places that had sprung up in the years since he'd left. They stopped at a hardware store and purchased their mower and edger, put it in the back of the Durango, and decided to take in what the little city had to offer.

Eddie stopped in front of the antique furniture store, one of three they had passed, and peered inside the dusty window. There was a dim light on inside the vast display room, and they could see someone sitting at a counter in the back of the store. The sign said "Open," and Jonathan shrugged when Eddie asked, "What about this place?"

Eddie pushed the door and stepped into the cool, dry air of the building. He looked around. A bell tinkled as they walked in, and an older mountain of a man looked up from his magazine at the counter. He waved at them and smiled. Furniture was on display, some of it in great condition and other pieces looking like they were barely holding together. Rugs of all sizes were either laid down flat or rolled up against the brick wall on one side of store. Rarely would they find a complete set of something, but besides that, most of the things were mismatched and old and the prices were steep. Portraits and pictures hung on the walls and were stacked on top of each other. Oil paintings of landscapes, beautiful women, rugged cowboys, a castle in the moonlight, and various other subjects littered the room, as well as lamps of every shape and color. Some were made of iron, others of wood, some of cheap ceramic.

"Wow, look at these end tables, Jonathan," Eddie said, admiring two pieces of furniture he had knelt down to look at. When Jonathan didn't respond, he looked up to find his man digging in a box of old records.

"Hey. They have Zeppelin, Joplin, AC/DC, Journey, and, holy crap, babe, they've got a Beatles' *Yellow Submarine* album," Jonathan said with a grin, holding up an ancient cardboard sleeve and showing it to Eddie. He looked like a kid in a candy store, and Eddie smirked at the expression on his face.

"We have those and plenty more. I have boxes in the back full of records like this," the man's booming voice came as he walked across the dusty, creaky wooden floors of the shop. Both guys turned to look as he lumbered forth. His salt-and-pepper hair matched the beard around his wide grin as he hobbled with a slight limp. He was dressed in a long-sleeved red-and-blue plaid shirt haphazardly tucked into a pair of carpenter jeans. Eddie and Jonathan stood when he came over. Eddie held out his hand and wasn't surprised when his own all but disappeared into the meaty fist of the shop owner.

"Name's Jonah Pilot," the man said gruffly.

"Eddie Dorman. This is my partner, Jonathan David. This store is incredible," Eddie said as he let go of his hand.

"Ah, thank ya. My sweet Molly Anne ran her for several years, and now that she's gone, I just can't bring myself to close it up. Most days I just sit here watchin' the world go by. Once in a while I'll get a customer, but then there are days..." His voice trailed off in a watery whisper, which tugged at Eddie's heartstrings. The man was lonely for his Molly Anne, whom Eddie figured must have been his wife. "Anyway..." he said, clearing his throat, "you like these pieces? I've had 'em for a bit, I could clean them up for ya if you'd like. No extra charge."

"I think they're amazing, and I'll take them just as they are," Eddie said. "But I don't see a price tag on them anywhere."

"Meh," the man said dismissively with a wave of his big beefy paw. "Fifty dollars for the both of them, and they are yours. Anything I find and restore, I don't charge much for. They were someone's junk. But stuff I make myself, like that bedframe over yonder, I usually charge a bit more, put my heart 'n' soul into it," he said, pointing to a headboard and baseboard leaning against the wall. Eddie stepped over some odds and ends on the floor and went over to take a look at them.

"These here?" Eddie asked in surprise. The pieces were gorgeous. The frames were for a queen-size bed and made of solid oak with a cherry finish. An image of a herd of wild horses in full gallop had been carved into the face of the headboard with so much detail that it looked as if they could leap right from the wood.

"Jonathan," Eddie whispered. "Look at this...Jonathan!" His husband had wandered away from the box of records and was now kneeling in front of an old jukebox.

The older man laughed loud and deep when he followed Eddie's gaze over to Jonathan, who was staring inside the thing like a sorceress might stare into her crystal ball. "That there is a 1980s remake of the old Wurlitzer 'Bubbler.' It can play both records and those CD things," he said, shuffling over. Jonathan turned his head and stood up, looking at the man like he was Santa Claus.

"It works?" he asked in wonder.

"Ahhh, yeah. Of course it works. I don't keep junk here, young man," the man said as he leaned over to plug the machine in. It lit up immediately, and a track began to play. Music blared out of the speaker, and Jonathan's face lit up with a grin so wide it threatened to split his face. *Uh-oh*, Eddie thought. The old man turned something in the back and the volume decreased right away to a level where one could hear one's self think.

"How much for this?" Jonathan asked. The old man looked at him and shook his head. "I have no idea, honestly. It was given to me as a gift when a bar in Manhattan went up in flames. I restored it, like everything else in here. So…aw, hell, give me two thousand, and she's yours."

"Where in hell are we going to put that in the house, Jonathan?" Eddie asked impatiently, and Jonathan shot him a look that said, "Aww, come on." Eddie shrugged and motioned for him to come over. Jonathan excused himself, and Jonah walked back behind his counter, where he waited patiently, giving them enough space to argue. He had an amused look on his face as he turned his attention back to his magazine.

"What?" Jonathan asked innocently.

"We're going through the money faster than I'd like, Jonathan. You said the lawn mower was going to be the last thing," Eddie said, reminding him.

"Awww, come on, babe. That's a steal. Two thousand for a piece of history like that?" Jonathan countered.

"A piece of history? It was made in the eighties. That's thirty years old. That makes *you* a piece of history. And besides, you're not going to take advantage of him like that and only give him two thousand," Eddie said, miffed.

"Look, fine. If I give him three thousand, will you be happy?" Jonathan asked, giving him his most adorable puppy-dog eyes, and Eddie felt his resolve slipping. Where Eddie was frugal and watchful, Jonathan was a compulsive spender. If he wanted it, he usually got it.

"When will you play the damn thing? It's huge." Eddie said.

"Well, I can plug my CDs and records into it," Jonathan said hopefully.

"All right. On one condition. We don't buy anything else for a few months outside of the necessities we need to survive, and I get to put some of my music on it," Eddie said, giving way.

Jonathan brightened. God, Eddie loved seeing him smile. Jonathan was going through a hard time right now, and the distance between those smiles was increasing. Eddie was really worried about him and what the house was doing to him. All his training told him it wasn't the house but Jonathan's memories catching up with him. Inanimate objects were powerless. But at

Eddie's core, deep in the recesses of his instincts, he felt there was something amiss, a feeling he didn't like. When the sun was out and the birds were singing, the possibility of living in a haunted house got chased away by the golden rays. But when the sun set over the horizon, those shadows crept back in and possibilities became an endless sea of the unknown that shook Eddie to the core and made a mockery of everything he had ever learned.

Maggie had been right to chastise him. Would it be better for Jonathan's strange behavior to be explained by paranormal phenomenon or by a breakdown in his psyche? He didn't like either scenario. He wasn't exactly convinced the strange events were either one or the other, but he didn't know where to begin researching. He had spent several years in labs, in the classroom, in clinical settings counseling people with problems that ranged from eating disorders to anxiety issues to psychosis and neurological problems. He knew how to keep an upset person calm, how to defuse an intense situation, and how to talk people down from suicidal ideations, but this was out of his league. Topical research had led him to various "paranormal research" groups and to psychics and mediums. None of it really made any sense to him at all, and it was speculative at best. Their evidence consisted of audiotapes filled with static, grainy photographs, and unreliable eyewitness accounts. Given the nature of the phenomenon or the supposed hauntings, it would be impossible to scientifically test the likelihood of paranormal activity, because anything considered metaphysical simply hovered outside of science's purview. All Eddie knew was that he loved his man and was scared for him. Yet right now, Jonathan was still holding on to his permission to purchase the Bubbler as if any second Eddie would change his mind, as if it was his only care in the world.

"All right. Go ahead," Eddie sighed. Jonathan gave him a look of triumph, about-faced, and marched up to the counter where Jonah was waiting. Eddie stood there watching him, and was shocked to see him stop in midstride, run back, grab Eddie's end tables, grin at him apologetically for forgetting them, and dash back to the counter. Eddie took his time walking back up, detouring to other parts of the store where he thought about what he had been doing as of late.

Jonathan rejected almost anything having to do with spirituality. He rejected it with such a visceral reaction that Eddie hated it being brought up in company or even when they talked about it.

"I've had enough bogeyman Jesus and holy-rolling dime nutter bags to last me a lifetime, thanks," he had said once when Eddie tentatively broached the subject of finding a place of worship for them. When pressed about it, he got angry. "You want to go to church, go. You want to join a convent, smoke peyote, join a cult, coven, or a Baptist church, go for it! I'm not going." And that was the end of that discussion. He would have to let Jonathan's issues take their course and see how far things got before Jonathan stumbled into any danger. Besides, how bad could it get?

***

He ran from the window when he saw the car pull up. Dinner was made and on the table, the house was clean, and the dishes he'd used to cook with were put away. His homework was done and the yard work was finished. The young man mentally went through his checklist. The car door slammed and the nervous sweat began. *Please don't be drunk. Please. God, I'll do anything. Get me out of this nightmare. This perpetual cycle that never ends. It's always the same*, the young man silently prayed as he waited at the dinner table. The heavy footfalls on the stairs were steady. A good sign. The young man breathed a sigh of relief, which was cut short when the front door slammed against the wall.

"*Hey!*" his father yelled.

On shaky legs, the boy got up and walked into the living room. "Yes?" he asked.

"Why didn't you roll the hose up after you used it?" the man bellowed, kicking off his boots.

The boy's heart sank. He'd missed something. Shit. "I'll do it right now," the young man answered, and he tried to wedge his way past his father, who was filling most of the doorway. The sickly sweet smell of liquor was on his breath, and the last bit of hope for a quiet night died. He tried to squeeze through, but his father brought his hand up and hit him in the back of the head sending him into the door. He hit his nose and blood immediately started to flow as his eyes teared up. He reached blindly for the latch so he could get out. He couldn't find it.

"You're bleeding all over the goddamn floor!"

Alan raised his head, his father was right, he was bleeding all down his face, and when he looked down found that he had bled on his shirt, his shoes, and now blood dripped at his feet. The snap in his brain was almost audible.

Alan braced himself against the screen door to give him as much leverage as possible as he brought his elbow back against his father's face, hitting him dead in the face. He was rewarded with the sound of a sickening crunch as his father's nose broke. The man stumbled back as Alan wiped the moisture from his eyes, clearing his vision so he could see what he had done.

His father was bent over, gagging, holding his hand over his face. Blood oozed from between his fingers as Alan walked over to him and knelt down, coming eye level with him. His rage burned inside of him, a fire so hot it turned his insides into ash.

"You son of a bitch, you broke my nose," Mark cried out, gagging and coughing on the blood. He dropped his lunch box and the lid broke open, revealing a half-empty bottle of Jack Daniels.

Alan grabbed it and held it up so his father could see it. "Sixteen ounces. This is all you're worth these days. It's rotted you from the inside. I'm glad Mom's dead so she can't see you like this. And as for me? I'm out of here. I'm going to let you soak in your misery." He threw the bottle against the living-room wall, where it shattered and rained glass fragments.

"Go on! Go to your faggot lover! You and him can butt fuck each other until you both go to hell!" the man screamed, staggering to his feet.

Alan didn't flinch from the hate-filled words. He laughed mockingly. "Condemnation from a drunken child abuser? Oh, the irony. If I'm going to hell, Daddy, Tommy and I will be sure to reserve a seat for you," he said coldly and walked around the man to head for the stairs. He had something he had to get out of the floorboards in his room, a container filled with cash that he had stashed away for the time he grew strong enough to break the chains that held him to this place.

His father grabbed his lunch bucket and charged the young man. He grabbed his foot on the stairwell, sending Alan pitching forward. The young man kicked out with all of his might, connecting with his father's chest. Mark fell flailing backward out the front door and down the front steps. Alan turned and ran, laughing, up the stairs and tore toward his room. Adrenaline flowed through him as he hit the landing, yet something caught his attention. He turned his head and looked through a window as a large blue truck pulled up to the curb and two men got out. *This isn't right. This isn't how this goes*, Alan thought, hearing his father's scream of rage as he ran up the stairs. The two men were carrying several bags and walking up his driveway toward the front door. He was out of time. He dove through his doorway into his bedroom. It was too late to grab what he'd come for. Tommy was waiting for him, had told him to come when things got to be too much, and they'd leave for California together.

His father was on the landing now, and Alan turned and dove through the open window, grabbing for the nearest tree branch. He shimmied down the large oak until his feet hit the ground. He saw his sweet neighbor looking over her back fence, her blonde hair tied up in a ponytail.

"Take care, Maggie. I'm out of here!" he said, half laughing and half crying. He raised a hand to her, and she simply waved back.

"Come back here, you son of a bitch queer! *Come back here!*" his father cried from the window. He was trying to climb out, and Alan silently wished he would tumble out and break his neck on the ground below. But he didn't have the nerve to stand there and watch. He took off through his backyard, over the fence toward freedom.

"Fuck you, you old bastard! See you in HELL!" Alan screamed with elated joy as his feet took him far, far away.

***

"Eddie, put the table down. There is someone in the house," Jonathan shouted as he took off for the front door. They had just pulled up with lunch, having changed their minds on dinner, and several bags filled with albums that the owner of the store had given to him for making such a large purchase. He reached the porch in a few quick strides and struggled to put the key in the lock and turn it because his hands were shaking so badly. Finally, the key turned and Jonathan flung the door open. The first thing to hit him was a smell of liquor that made his eyes water.

"Ugh...it smells like a brewery in here," Eddie said, walking in and covering his nose.

"You check the back of the house. I'm going upstairs," Jonathan said, dashing up the stairs.

Eddie rushed to the dining room, which he found empty. He moved through the side door to the kitchen; the cabinet doors were open. He ran for the back door and tried the knob; it didn't budge.

He was about to close all the cabinet doors when Jonathan burst into the room. "Anything?" he asked.

"No. Locked. You?" Eddie asked.

"Nothing. Not a goddamn thing. That liquor smell is gone too. Come check it out," Jonathan said, walking out of the kitchen. Eddie shut the cabinets and nearly ran out to the living room to join him.

"Maybe it was just the lighting," Eddie suggested looking at Jonathan, who was violently shaking his head back and forth.

"No. I saw him. The curtain upstairs moved, and he looked right at me. There was something familiar about him," Jonathan said as they stood by the stairs.

"Hello?" Maggie called from outside. They looked at each other and stepped out of the house. She was standing next to the table and bags they had thrown down in their rush to get inside.

"Hey, Maggie. You didn't see anyone in or around the house, did you?" Jonathan asked, blood pounding in his temples.

The blonde woman shook her head. "No. I've been out in my backyard all morning. I didn't hear anything, either." Jonathan looked at her gardening gloves, black with soil, and walked over to kiss her on the cheek.

"It's all right. How are you?" Jonathan asked.

"I'm good, sweetheart, how are you?" she asked.

"I'm all right. We got some new end tables, and you wouldn't believe what I bought today," Jonathan said with a grin.

"What's that?" she asked, amused and blushing from the peck on the cheek.

Eddie walked up and kissed the other side of her face. "A jukebox," he said.

Maggie's eyes grew wide, and she laughed. "My goodness. You opening a sock hop?"

Both boys laughed and went to pick up their belongings from the yard. They'd started back toward the house when Eddie called over his shoulder, "Care to come in for some lemonade?"

"Sure. That sounds lovely," she said as they made their way inside.

Jonathan set his bag down in the front and turned to take the table from Eddie. Eddie went to grab the other one from the back of the Durango. A few minutes later, Jonathan joined them in the kitchen as Eddie was catching Maggie up on what Jonathan thought he'd seen. Maggie turned as he walked into the kitchen and asked, "Did you get a good look at him?"

"Yeah. He looked right at me. Medium height, about five seven or so. Thin, with blond hair," Jonathan said as he took a drink.

Maggie went white as a sheet and raised a hand to her mouth in shock as her eyes widened as large as saucers.

"What is it, Maggie?" Eddie asked. He set his glass down and reached across the table.

"You just described Alan," she said breathlessly.

Jonathan nodded. "Yeah. I kinda figured that." He took a swig of his lemonade and then set it down. "Listen, you don't have a picture of him or anything, do you?"

She nodded. "I do. We got a picture of all three of them when things were good, and Daddy snapped one of Alan when he was older. I would have to dig them out of some photo albums, but that shouldn't take too long."

"Okay. Just whenever you get the chance. No rush. I'm just curious to actually see him," Jonathan said, sitting back.

"This is extraordinary," Eddie said, putting his head on his forehead. "Babe, are you sure you just didn't just see a glare of sunlight or something?"

Jonathan looked at him. "You've said yourself you've walked into cold spots, you noticed the cabinet doors standing open, you've heard the footsteps…what else do you need to know?"

"Yeah…but…" Eddie started to protest.

"Then there were the dishes stacked up in a tower," Maggie said, looking down at her lemonade and then back up as Eddie glared at her.

"What dishes?" Jonathan asked.

Eddie opened and shut his mouth as he tried to figure out what he was going to say. Maggie reached across the table and took his hand, speaking for him.

"The day you had your…dizzy spell outside, when we brought you inside and sat you down on the couch, he went to get you a glass of water, remember?" Jonathan nodded, so she continued. "Well, all of the dishes from the cabinets were stacked one on top of the other on the island. He didn't tell you because you were already upset," she said, trying to smooth it over.

"Yeah, he tries to do that from time to time," Jonathan said stiffly. Regardless of whether it was meant to protect him, he hated that Eddie treated him as if he were a fragile piece of glass. His blood pressure spiked and his temper started to boil. He glared at Eddie for an explanation.

"I just didn't want to upset you," Eddie said, exasperated.

"No? So the next time I walk into something and think I'm going crazy, I'll just assume that, yes, I'm losing my shit?" Jonathan asked, his face heating. "Look, the reason I knew what the kid looked like is because I dreamed about him, and then, that day I passed out, it wasn't from the heat. I saw my father's blue station wagon drive by the house. It didn't look like the one he had, it didn't resemble the one he had, it was the exact fucking one I dreamed of the night before."

"What?" Eddie asked, shocked. Maggie straightened up too and cocked her head to the side.

"A couple of weeks ago it happened, as well. I had a dream. Well, I think it was a dream. It was more like a memory. But I was in the house in Detroit, and my father... It was right before I left home, and he was there. That blond kid. And a few weeks prior, it was the same thing. Another dream about being inside that blue station wagon, and we stopped at a stop sign, but something that wasn't there before was Alan. That kid, standing at the sign, looking at me as if he had witnessed the whole thing," Jonathan said, his voice becoming shrill as he started to shake.

Maggie had gone pale and had her hand at her throat. Eddie stood up, came around the island, and put his hand on Jonathan's arm. He stared him in the eyes.

"It's okay. It's all right. It isn't happening now. You're right here," Eddie said, his voice very cool and his words punctuated as he emphasized each word. His eyes looked distant and there was something in them Jonathan didn't like. He had gone into professional mode. He wasn't Eddie his husband, he became Dr. Dorman, clinical PhD.

"I know. Babe. I know. I ain't crazy," Jonathan said, starting to choke up as frustration and fear roared through his mind.

"I think we need to get you in to talk to someone," Eddie said, and Jonathan pulled away.

"Why? So they can use their powers of whatever to have me declared crazy?"

"No one thinks you're crazy, Jonathan," Eddie said, trying to calm him down.

"Bullshit. You're both looking at me like I've lost my mind," Jonathan yelled.

"No, we're not, dear," Maggie said. "But you seem really stressed out."

"Yeah, well, if you think I am going to let one of your headshrinkers give me medication that makes me so oblivious to the world that I don't know my ass from a hole in the ground, forget it," he growled and stormed out the back door. Eddie reached for his cell phone.

CHAPTER 11

EDDIE WALKED PURPOSEFULLY across the campus at Kansas State University, having parked his car in the faculty lot. The near empty campus had a few people milling about the sprawling lawns and walkways, relaxing in the sunshine or hurrying to a summer class. The buildings were beautiful and had an old-world style with their turrets and castle-like structures. The sidewalks were clean of litter, the gardens manicured, and the lawn recently mowed—the scent of freshly cut grass lingered in the warm summer breeze. Apparently, there had been a tornado in this city a couple of years prior, but as Eddie looked around, he saw no telltale signs of it anywhere. Yet he felt as though there was a tornado doing damage in his heart as he worried about Jonathan. His wish that this would be a fresh start for them was being ripped apart by the F5 of reality setting in. The reality as thus: either their house was haunted, or his husband was having a psychotic break and Eddie was being swept up in it.

The other night had ended badly. Jonathan had refused to talk to him, and Maggie left pretty shaken up. Eddie had tried to go outside to talk to his husband, but was given the cold shoulder as Jonathan angrily put the lawn mower together and did everything he could do to avoid coming inside and talking to him. He even mowed the lawn...twice. When he'd finally come in, Jonathan would just look at him, open his mouth soundlessly, shake his head, and walk away, leaving Eddie at one point sobbing on the stairwell. His heart had crumbled in his chest as their hopes were dashed upon the rocks of his despair, and then suddenly, he'd stopped crying as a white-hot rage tore through him. Jonathan was getting ready to step into the shower when Eddie busted through the door.

"Stop right there, you son of a bitch," Eddie said with clenched teeth and balled up fists as Jonathan turned around to look at him.

"Excuse me?" Jonathan said as he withdrew his foot from the shower stall. He crossed his arms over his naked chest and glowered.

"You know what? I'm not a violent person, but I swear to God I could kick your teeth in right now. How dare you? How dare you storm off and accuse me of wanting what's bad for you? I've fought our entire relationship to keep us together, and you just turn a flip hand to that?" Eddie said, outraged.

Jonathan opened his mouth to speak, but Eddie couldn't stop. "Do you think I want to have you declared mentally unstable, or have to deal with the fact that you are possibly having a psychotic break? You think that's a walk in the park for me?"

"I'm not sick!" Jonathan yelled back, stepping closer, his eyes flashing dangerously.

"Then let me get you some help. Let me take you to a clinic and have them run some tests. If they come back negative, then we will pursue other avenues—" Eddie pleaded, trying to talk sense into him, but he was cut off.

"What avenues? Hospitalization? Medication?" Jonathan asked, narrowing his eyes. The room was getting steamy from the hot water pouring into the empty shower.

"I don't know. I've treated every form of mental illness possible, and if I were to get your symptomology across my desk, I would diagnose you as having schizophrenia. Auditory and visual hallucinations are an immediate diagnosis—"

"They're not hallucinations, Eddie. You've experienced them yourself," Jonathan countered.

"There are too many cases where someone has been too close to a person with these symptoms, and they start experiencing them as well," Eddie said.

Jonathan threw his head back in surprise and hurt. "Too close?"

"I don't mean it like that," Eddie protested.

"You most certainly do. You think I'm schizophrenic. There is no way in hell I am going to a hospital and being put on medication. If you think so, you're the one who's out of his mind," Jonathan said. He turned and walked toward the shower.

"I can have you committed," Eddie said coolly. Jonathan whirled around, his eyes wide in shock but soon narrowing as he leaned close to Eddie's face. A dangerous smile formed on his lips and a fire burned bright in his eyes.

"No, you can't. Our marriage is valid in the Northeast, but not here," Jonathan said icily between clenched teeth. He had just drawn a line, and he dared Eddie to cross it.

Eddie hadn't even been thinking about spousal rights. He had more or less been hinting toward him being a licensed psychologist in the state of Kansas, but Jonathan's words hit him dead in the chest. Eddie brought his hand to his own chest because he could have sworn his heart stopped beating in that moment. He hadn't meant to throw his credentials at Jonathan, and he knew he had bullied past the line with that, but Jonathan's words stung him.

Jonathan must have realized what he had said, because his gaze softened and he dropped his arms to his sides. "I'm not crazy. I'm not... Sure, I've had some past issues with post-traumatic stress, issues with child abuse and general anxiety, but so what? Does that make me a candidate for lithium?"

"What if I just had your physiology tested to rule out a biological explanation?" Eddie asked, starting to relax.

"What do you mean?" Jonathan asked warily.

"Schizophrenia is usually caused by striations in the brain. It's an abnormality in the prefrontal cortex, which basically causes mixed signals. Some people hallucinate, others hear things, and some people suffer from what is known as 'word salad.' They speak jumbled words incoherently. Let's rule that out," Eddie said, moving forward. He placed his hands on the hips of his lover, who was struggling to look away.

"Look at me, Jonathan. I love you. You're everything to me. I'll give everything up—the house, my job, everything—just to make sure you're okay. Just work with me..." Eddie started choking up and had to clear his throat, but an errant tear slid down. "I'm here for you. Let me make sure that the physical world isn't trying to upset you before we start playing around with what we can't see. Please."

Jonathan searched his eyes and finally nodded. "Then what do we do?"

"I don't care. Let me rule out the worst-case scenario. I'll do everything I can to make sure you're safe, and if it is medical, I'll be here to deal with that too."

"Yeah, but what if it isn't? What if the house truly is haunted?" Jonathan asked.

"Then we'll get a priest, a shaman, move out, or I'll burn the joint down myself. I'm not losing you, do you understand me?" Eddie asked as he pressed his fingers into the flesh of Jonathan's waist. "Besides, I don't give a fuck where my legal status dictates I have husband rights. I am your husband here, there, and this side of heaven, and if anyone or anything thinks they are taking you away from me, I'll fight back, and I'll bring with me all the powers of hell." Then he buried his face in Jonathan's chest and wept as Jonathan wrapped his arms around him.

***

Now, as Eddie walked across the campus toward the psychology building, he checked his watch. He had an appointment to make at the clinic, and one of the lead doctors was meeting him in his new office. He would be on time, but just barely. The Franklin building was in front of him, and he picked up his pace. He strode up the walk and made it to the front door as a student was coming out with headphones on her ears and her head down looking at her iPod. She would have run into him had he not opened the door and stepped to the side to let her walk past. Eddie shook his head and stepped into the artificially cooled building, feeling his sweaty dress shirt begin to cool and dry. The building smelled of old books and some kind of lemony cleaning agent. The sound of his work shoes tapping against the hard concrete floors echoed down the empty hallways. He climbed two flights of stairs until he reached the offices for his department. Dr. Joey Hill was standing by the door in his lab coat, checking his watch.

"Sorry I'm late," Eddie said as he came up and extended his hand.

"No, not at all. You're right on time," said the sandy-haired man, smiling warmly and shaking Eddie's hand firmly.

"Come on in. Sorry in advance about the boxes. I have yet to set up the office," Eddie said, unlocking the door and then swinging it open. "Just move that one off the seat," he said, pointing to the chair in front of his desk as he walked around and sat down.

"Sure, Dr. Dorman," Dr. Hill said as he moved the box and sat down.

"Please, call me Eddie."

"Then, please, call me Joey," the young doctor said, crossing his legs. Eddie leaned forward and folded his hands, placing them on the desk, intertwining his fingers to keep from fidgeting.

"All right, Joey. Then I guess we can get right down to it, then. I need to order a sleep study for a patient. I want also to order an fMRI," Eddie said.

"Okay, sure, that's no problem. Who's the patient?" he asked.

"Well, Joey. It's my husband," Eddie said cautiously. He expected an immediate denial over ethical reasons, and Joey would have been right to deny him.

"What's going on with him?" Joey asked, adjusting the glasses on his nose.

"I know that me asking this breaks ethical rules, but he has generalized anxiety disorder, and he's a veteran, and I just want to make sure that everything is going all right up there," Eddie said, lying to the young man and feeling bad about it, especially when the doctor narrowed his eyes.

Joey sat up straighter and gave Eddie a friendly smile. "Look, why don't we start this off the right way. You're right, it's highly unethical, but what the clinic doesn't know won't hurt it. However, I am not ordering an fMRI on someone with generalized anxiety disorder. If there is a problem, as a sitting clinician, I have no problem helping. But do me a favor—don't blow smoke up my ass. You don't need a real-time imaging scanner of the brain for an anxiety disorder."

Eddie's face burned in embarrassment, and it took him a minute to gather up the strength to say this, but finally he shrugged and decided to let it fly. "You know what? I'm willing to risk it all, what the hell?" he said, laughing. "Okay, so here it is. Either my husband is schizophrenic, his hallucinations are affecting me personally, and I'm losing my shit right along with him, or my house is haunted."

Joey's face didn't register anything for a moment. He sat quietly across from him with a slightly bemused look on his face, hands folded in his lap, before he asked, "Are you serious?"

"I am as serious as a bulimic on a binge," Eddie responded.

"Well, now you're talking. I knew you wouldn't frivolously use our equipment. Dr. Dorman, I respect your work. I've read your research. I disagree with your views of narcissism but that's for another time. If you say there is a problem, well, there is a problem. What's going on?" Joey asked. Eddie had underestimated the young man, and although his reaction surprised Eddie, he wasn't disappointed.

Eddie slowly walked out the events of the past few months and talked about everything that had gone on since they'd moved there. Joey's eyes grew wider as he listened and nodded during rather climactic parts, like a child listening to a fireside story. When Eddie finished, he sat back in his chair and let what he'd told the younger man sink in.

"That's incredible. Your husband's the author, right? My wife loves his book, by the way," Joey said.

"Yeah, that's him," Eddie said, unsure where this was going. He couldn't believe what he was hearing.

"Well, I gotta admit this is one extraordinary story. I was expecting that you wanted to use the machine because you didn't want word getting out of the possibility of him being sick," Joey said. Eddie could have kicked himself for that. He could have invoked professional courtesy, but he was not accustomed to lying to anyone about anything.

"We can set up the sleep study and the fMRI scan. That shouldn't be a problem. I can conduct the sleep study myself, so as to not draw attention to him. If he does happen to have the physiological components or the physiological striations, I won't say anything to anyone, but I will advise that you seek an outside psychologist to handle that," Joey said writing a note down in a pad of paper he pulled from his coat. Eddie couldn't believe his luck. Could the tide be changing? He'd feared he would have to sneak Jonathan in as someone he didn't know or try to pay a hospital cash to keep quiet about the testing.

"Dr. Dorman, I can have this taken care of, no problem. I won't mention anything else, including the haunting, but there is a favor I must ask."

Eddie sat back to listen to his demand.

***

Jonathan sat at his computer, staring at the open word-processing document that stared right back at him. It was driving him crazy. Every sentence he put in he deleted, every little theme that ran around his head he chastised himself for. His mind, which usually rock-and-rolled with different ideas for books, was empty, mocking him. He clicked his mouse on another document behind the blank one—a document that held little bits of his past.

Almost every night, the nightmares came, and Jonathan was feeling more on edge than he ever had. He would awaken shaking and sweating. He would look over at his sleeping husband before getting up and stumbling to his office to sit down in front of his computer. He'd started typing out the nightmares he was having while they were fresh in his mind, to go back and read later. While he sat there staring at a blank document, his mind drifted back to those writings. There were several pages now, disorganized, grammatically wrong, some words misspelled. He'd written in the dark with blurry eyes. He read through them, his chest pulling tight as he recounted his past on the page.

So many wasted years, so much pain in just a few pages that made him feel like that kid he'd left in the rearview mirror all those years ago. Jonathan sighed and sat back and thought about Eddie. The only reason Eddie had left him here alone was the fact that the jukebox was supposed to be delivered today at noon, and Jonathan swore on a stack of Bibles he would be okay. He'd promised if anything strange did occur, he would simply go out on the front porch and wait for Eddie to return from his appointment at the school. Jonathan had gone with him a few times over the past week to help him take boxes to his office. The argument they'd had a few days ago still lingered in his mind, and he felt guilty for minimizing their marriage. Eddie seemed a bit quieter now, and that broke Jonathan's heart.

Exhausted from the physical toll on his mind and body, he closed his eyes for a second, trying to ward off the headache trying to set in as he rocked back and forth in his computer chair. He ran his fingers across his scalp, a habit he used to keep himself calm. Slow deep breaths, in and out and in and out...

Creak.

He paused his breathing and went still, sure he had heard something. He counted heartbeats, squeezing his eyes shut a little tighter as the hairs on his arms stood up.

Creak, creak, creak.

It sounded like footsteps coming down the hallway; Jonathan felt his face flush and his scalp tingle.

Open your eyes, Jonathan. Open them. There is nothing there.

He shook his head, his heart plummeting to his stomach. Sweat broke out on his forehead as shivers shot through him. *Open your eyes now!* the annoying voice screamed, and he did with a sharp inhale expecting to see that same blond-haired kid staring at him from the other side of his desk. Alas, there was nothing there. He exhaled quickly, his heart still thudding. The adrenaline that triggered the fight-or-flight response still hummed under his skin and caused his hands to tremble as he held on to the top of the desk, the sweat under his hands slick against the surface. Jonathan chuckled and relaxed behind the desk again, letting the anxiety flow out of him.

Tick. Tick. Tick. Tick. Tick. Tick. Tick.

The sound of the keyboard caused him to open his eyes in disbelief. Jonathan quickly scooted his chair away from the desk.

"The fuck?" he asked the empty room. He stared at the keyboard as the letters pressed themselves down faster and faster. He shot his attention upward at the screen.

Help. Please. Alone with him. Stuck. Lost. Help me. Help him. Help me. Help him. Help me...

Jonathan stood slowly as the words "help me" flowed repeatedly down the monitor and across page after page. Panic set in.

"Please, please stop," he whispered. The keys stopped clicking, and the words ceased scrolling down the screen. Jonathan swallowed thickly and tried scooting farther away but bumped into his filing cabinet. He braced his hand on the side of it and eyed the distance to the doorway.

"God, I'm losing my mind," he said, closing his eyes and trying to slow his breathing. The clicking noise started again. He opened his eyes in a flash.

No. No. No. No. No. No. No. No. No. No. No. No. No.

"Stop!" he cried out. What did that mean? That he wasn't losing his mind? Jonathan dared to take a step closer. The command prompt flashed at him impatiently as he neared the desk. It was chilly here, chillier than the rest of the room, and he shivered. He asked, "Who are you?"

The command prompt kept flashing at him, as if it didn't understand the question. Was it over? Had the spirit exhausted itself? Was he alone again? Jonathan didn't know. He called out to the empty room once more. "Do you have a name?"

Alan. Alan. Alan. Alan. Help me please. Help me. Wait. Oh no...

"What? Oh no. Oh no...what?" Jonathan cried out, staring at the screen, his hands level with the monitor.

He's home.

The front door slammed, causing Jonathan to start. He walked around the edge of the desk and out on the landing. The curtains on the door were swaying back and forth from the force of the door, but no one was there.

"Eddie? Babe?" Jonathan called out. No one replied. He stood there for a second before he began to descend the stairs. *Go outside and wait for Eddie*, the annoying voice pleaded with him.

"Why? So he can say I'm losing it and lock me up?" he asked aloud. He smirked as the voice failed to respond. As he made his way toward the kitchen, he heard a cabinet open. He stopped and listened for a second before plunging into the room, swinging the door wide with a bang as it hit the wall. Sure enough, the same cabinet door stood gaping, although the rest of the room remained undisturbed.

Angrily, he crossed the kitchen and slammed the cabinet door hard enough to sound like a shot and pop back open. The blood pumped in his temples as he spun around and bellowed.

"I don't give a fuck what happened to either of you. Why you're here. Why you died. Why you're still in this house. But let me make something very clear: this is my house, and you're an unwelcome—" Jonathan didn't have a chance to finish his sentence before all the cabinet doors popped open at the same time, and their contents spilled out onto the floor. Plates and glasses hit and shattered against the linoleum floor, sending shards of glass airborne. Jonathan yelped and covered his face in time to feel bits of glass cutting into the backs of his hands. Pots and pans shook and spilled out, clattering and banging as they went. The pantry and refrigerator door burst forth and their contents shifted forward, pouring out onto the floor. Bottles of beer exploded and foamed, and brown liquid sprayed the room.

Jonathan lowered his hands shakily to his side when he felt a presence right in front of him. He smelled it before he sensed it. The stench of liquor being breathed into his face was enough to make him gag. It was accompanied by a foul aroma much like rotted meat, and Jonathan's eyes watered. He tried to turn his head to the side, but his jaw was grasped by the unseen force, fingers like ice on his skin.

"Mine" came a disembodied voice. Suddenly, Jonathan was lifted off his feet into the air. Icy fingers closed around his throat, and he thrashed to break loose of the grip. He couldn't breathe. As hard as he tried, he couldn't make contact with anything, including his invisible assailant.

Black spots began to swim in his vision as he drifted toward unconsciousness. *You're going to die*, the annoying voice said, and Jonathan knew it spoke the truth. Eddie's face snapped into his thoughts as he slipped further, and he knew how heartbroken he would be. That was all it took. Something popped in his brain and a surge of power seared through him.

"Ahhhhhhhhh!" The spirit cried out in pain.

Debris on the floor began to shake and thump. The silverware and shards of glass tinkled across the linoleum floor before they started to levitate. The fingers loosened their hold on Jonathan, allowing him to take precious air into his aching lungs. The debris swirled up and around faster and faster as the pain in Jonathan's head increased. It felt as though his brain was on fire as tears clouded his vision and then dripped freely down his face. The fingers steadily lost their grip around his throat and then let go completely.

Jonathan fell to the floor in a heap, gasping air past his bruised throat and into his lungs. Glass cut into his hands as he tried to climb to his feet. His rubbery legs buckled underneath him before he lost consciousness.

***

Eddie was just arriving in Clay Center when his phone blew up with text messages. He reached across the dashboard and grabbed for it, waiting to slide it open until he reached the first red light. They all came from Jonathan. Eddie's heart stopped. Dozens of the same message, repeated over and over again. They came so quickly that the alert hadn't finished chiming before the next message rang in.

Home... Home... Home... Home... Home... Home... Home... Home... Home... Home... Home... Home...

"What the fuck?" Eddie heard the car behind him honk. He looked up and noticed the light had turned green. Instead of slowly accelerating to the thirty-five miles an hour indicated on the sign, he mashed his foot to the floor, his Sonata pushing forward as he tore through town leaving rubber marks on the road behind him. He shot past building after building, before speeding past a gas station where a squad car was sitting. His guts tightened when he glanced at the rearview mirror and saw it pull out after him, lights on and sirens blaring.

He wove in and out of traffic as he rocketed down the main street. Traffic remained light and no one hit him as he flew toward Frederick Street. He slammed on the brakes and spun hard left, tearing up the small incline before whipping into the parking spot behind Jonah's big truck, the jukebox still sitting in the bed. Jonah was on the porch, waving frantically at Eddie as he threw the car into park and flung the driver's side door open. He forgot his belt was still attached, and it pulled him back down as he tried to get out.

"Goddammit!" Eddie screamed. He clumsily found the release and flung the belt sideways. He heard a voice demand he stop where he was, but Eddie ignored her and ran to the porch and up the stairs, screaming at Jonah, "Where is he?"

"In the kitchen. I've never seen anything like this. You have to help him. Oh my God. You have to help him," Jonah said, his voice shaking and his face pale. Maggie was running down her front porch stairs, calling Eddie's name. He barely registered it as he flung the front door open and raced inside. He could smell trouble before he laid eyes on it. The pungent odor of booze and rotten meat hit him in the face as he crashed through the house toward the kitchen, calling Jonathan's name.

When he reached the kitchen, he stopped dead in his tracks and let out a scream that came from the depths of his soul. It was chaos—everything was absolutely destroyed, and everything they owned was either shattered or twisted into indiscernible shapes. Knives, forks, and spoons were in little piles, manipulated and bent into metal balls. Glass plates that had been shattered were now pieced together in mismatched shapes and colors. The glasses and cups were the same.

The cop, Maggie, and Jonah were shouting behind him, but Eddie ignored them. All he could focus on was Jonathan. He was sitting on the floor, his head to the right, his eyes rolled back and his jaw cocked to the side at an odd angle. Above him, scrawled in red liquid across the white cabinet doors, were two words: "Help us."

"Oh my God" came the unfamiliar female voice, but Eddie ignored her as he got down on all fours and slowly crept forward. He called Jonathan's name. This wasn't like anything he had ever seen before, and he very much regretted having left Jonathan home alone.

"Babe. It's Eddie. Listen to me, babe. Listen to my voice," Eddie said, getting closer. He reached out and touched the hand of his lover, noticing how badly cut up it was. Blood had gathered on the floor under the palms of his limp hands.

"Babe! It's Eddie! Listen to me, babe. Listen to my voice," Jonathan shouted, his voice so loud everyone jumped back a few inches. His mouth went slack again.

"This is Officer Riley. I need an ambulance at 4554 Frederick Road. Have an unresponsive patient. How copy, over?" the police officer said. Eddie tried to touch Jonathan again, but Jonathan recoiled as if he had been shocked.

"Jonathan. Are you in the mirror again?" Eddie asked.

"What's wrong with him?" Maggie asked, but Eddie put up a hand to silence her.

"Jonathan?" Eddie asked, trying to coax him back to the here and now.

"Mirror? Alan is in the mirror. His daddy is in the mirror," Jonathan barked. His eyes shut and his head nodded forward. Eddie was about to reach forward again when Jonathan's head jerked upward. His eyes had almost returned to normal, save for the left one that was blood red, and he blinked several times. This time Eddie glimpsed bruises around his neck as he sat up straight.

"Eddie?" he croaked. His eyes were wide and scared, and when he spoke, he grasped his bruised throat.

"Ugh…ow. Eddie?"

Eddie scooted closer to him, feeling sharp pieces of glass embed themselves in his knees. He didn't care. He didn't talk because he couldn't trust his own voice as tears thickened in his throat. Jonathan opened his arms and Eddie pulled him close. They wrapped their arms around each other.

"My throat hurts," Jonathan whispered in Eddie's ear.

"I know, baby. I know. It's okay. We're going to take care of everything," Eddie said as Officer Riley knelt next to them. She caught Jonathan's attention, but her presence seemed to confuse him.

"Hi," he said simply.

"Hey, there, handsome. How you feelin'?" she asked. The gentleness in her voice caused Eddie to choke up. It felt good to have a little authority here, someone who at least thought they were in control.

"My throat," Jonathan said again, cupping his hands around it.

"I see that. Who did that to you?" she asked.

He looked at Eddie and shook his head. "I don't know."

Officer Riley surveyed the room and picked up one of the twisted utensils and showed it to Jonathan.

"Did you do this?" she asked. Jonathan shook his head with vigor. The look on his face was not that of a grown man but rather a scared child. His eyes were wide and he was as white as a sheet.

Eddie doubted anyone could have done it—no one with normal strength, anyway. They would need a vise and a pair of pliers, and still probably couldn't have made them perfectly round.

"Did someone in here do it?" she asked.

Maggie, white as a sheet, was standing next to Jonah, who looked as confused as Eddie felt.

"Nobody was home but me," Jonathan said, voice cracking.

"Okay. All right," she said comfortingly. "Well, the ambulance is on its way here, and we're going to go have you checked out and have those bruises looked at," she said, standing up.

"Mr...?" she asked, looking down at Eddie.

"Dr. Edward Dorman."

"Dr. Dorman, we need to talk," she said, coolly sizing him up. He nodded and told her he would answer any questions she might have once the ambulance showed up. But first, he went upstairs and opened the safe. Prior to moving to Kansas, they had contacted a lawyer in Manhattan to draw up power-of-attorney paperwork for the both of them, since their marriage license was void inside the state. He returned to the kitchen as the police officer and Jonah tried to help Jonathan to his feet. Before long, there was a knock at the door and two paramedics walked in. It took Officer Riley directing their attention to Jonathan before they snapped into work mode and started to check him out.

While they did, Eddie motioned for Officer Riley to walk out to the front porch with him. Before he could speak, she started.

"Look, I'm willing to overlook you driving like a bat out of hell if you explain to me what is going on in this house. I've been on the force ten years and have never seen anything like that," she said impatiently. "Is he on drugs?"

"No, ma'am. No drugs," Eddie said.

"You said you were a doctor. A doctor of what?" she asked, folding her arms over her chest.

"I am a clinical psychologist. Jonathan is my husband. We moved here a few months ago."

"Has anything like this happened before?"

Eddie shook his head. "No. This just recently started happening."

"Look, how do I know you're telling me the truth? That you two aren't hyped up on anything?" she asked.

"You're more than welcome to run whatever tests you would like and search this house from top to bottom. I assure you, you will find nothing illegal. My husband is suffering from some sort of breakdown or...something."

"A breakdown. You mean he is becoming psychotic?" she asked.

Suddenly the gravitas of those words hit Eddie dead in the face. It was everything he had been implying to Jonathan for some time now, but now that he was hearing it for himself from a complete stranger, an authority figure, it sounded like the worst thing anyone could say about anyone else. Instead of saying yes, he skirted the issue.

"I just recently scheduled him for a psych evaluation at a clinic for sleep studies and an fMRI. He's a veteran of war," Eddie said, lowering his voice as if to explain away the unusual behavior. He hoped she would understand what he was implying.

Her eyes registered understanding. "Ah. I see. What about those two?" she asked, nodding toward the inside of the house.

"Maggie is our next-door neighbor, and the big older man, that's Jonah. He owns an antique shop in Junction City. He was delivering a jukebox to the house today," Eddie said, fatigue starting to set in.

"So, Dr. Dorman, what would you like me to do?" she asked, her voice warming a little.

"I would ask that you use discretion in regard to Jonathan when you write up your incident report. He's a writer, and if anyone catches wind of this, they'll be all over him like flies on shit. I don't think the rest of the neighbors have figured out who he is, but they will in time," Eddie said.

"Look, I'll make you a deal. I'm not going to mention this to anyone today. However, I will be coming by frequently to check on you two and to see how he is progressing. Just do me a favor: don't make me have to use the law. I want you both safe, you hear?" she asked.

Eddie breathed a sigh of relief and nodded. He held out his hand, and she offered hers to shake. She made her way down the stairs, and Eddie went back into the house to find out what the hell was going on in their little world. As he moved through the house, the medics said Jonathan should be fine, and he was refusing to go to the hospital for further examination. Eddie knew he was scared, not only of what had happened, but what would happen to him if a doctor heard this story.

"That's fine. I'll keep an eye out for him," Eddie said. They had moved Jonathan to a chair brought in from the dining room, and he was resting his head in his hands. Jonah had kindly knelt down and was trying to comfort him when Eddie came in. Maggie was standing by with wide eyes and trembling hands, listening to the large man trying to soothe Jonathan.

"Maggie. Do you have a camera?" Eddie asked.

She nodded, lowering her hands and clearing her throat. "I have a digital one."

Eddie walked over to her and took her by the arms. She jerked her head up and stared at him, her fear and anxiety over Jonathan evident. "What's wrong with him?" she asked.

Eddie shook his head. "I don't know. But I want you to go and get your camera and take pictures of the kitchen, okay?" he asked calmly. She nodded and quickly left.

Eddie knelt at Jonathan's side and placed a hand on his lover's back. "Jonathan? Babe?" Eddie whispered calmly. Jonah watched Eddie like a hawk. He could feel the older man's eyes on him.

Jonathan raised his grief-stricken face, still wet from tears and etched with misery. It pierced Eddie's heart like a dagger. Their gazes met, and Jonathan's lower lip trembled.

"What's happening to me, Eddie?" Jonathan asked. He began to cry in earnest. His face crumpled as he leaned on Eddie's broad shoulder. Eddie felt tears in his eyes as he held his lover in his arms and rocked him gently. Jonathan sobbed like a child.

"I don't know, sweetheart. But I promise you, help is on the way," he said. "You just hang tight to me, okay? I'll never let you go, so don't you let go. Okay?" He felt Jonathan nod quickly, and the dam broke open for him as well. His greatest fear—losing his husband—surfaced and broke over the shoulder of the man he loved. Eddie buried his face against Jonathan's neck. He felt a large hand pat his. He'd forgotten Jonah was still there. Eddie jerked his head up to see the older man standing up painfully. He looked down at Eddie and winked. Eddie mouthed the words "thank you," and Jonah simply nodded and left them in peace.

CHAPTER 12

J ESUS, MARY, AND Joseph," Joey whispered as he made his way into the kitchen, stepping carefully through the mess. "Lisa, are you getting this?" he asked, pointing at the mound of bent silverware. His intern, whose camera was clicking away, didn't acknowledge him. She put her camera down and picked up a spoon that had been twisted into a spiral. The windows were open to allow the noxious odor to be swept away, but the food was stored in a bag on the counter for future examination.

"'Help us'? Who is 'us'?" Joey asked, turning to Eddie, who had been about to speak when another man walked through the kitchen. He was tall, maybe in his late forties, and had wire spectacles and a rather strong frame. Eddie shot a look at Joey, who greeted the man as he came in.

"Ah. Dr. Spencer. Thanks for coming on such short notice," Joey said, moving forward to shake the man's hand. "Eddie, this is Dr. Paul Spencer from the sociology department. Dr. Spencer, this is Dr. Dorman, our new clinician." Eddie shook the man's hand as well, his grip solid and firm.

"Please, just call me Paul. Nice to meet you. Is it all right if I call you Eddie?" he asked, the timbre of his voice soothing and calm.

"Of course. Thank you for coming. Joey, when did you call him? Not that I'm not grateful. We need all the help we can get."

Joey looked a little embarrassed by the thought of possibly overstepping his bounds. "I called him as soon as you called me. Dr. Spenc...Paul, here, is the head of the paranormal research group at the university. He was the gentleman I sought out after our conversation the other day. Dr. Spencer is a believer in the afterlife and avid 'ghost hunter.'"

"Oh. I'm sorry. Forgive me for being rude, Paul. I didn't make the connection," Eddie said apologetically.

"No trouble at all. My students and I are used to it. Some in our profession balk at the thought of giving credence to the world of the paranormal," he said with a smirk. "Eddie, I also know the sensitivity concerning your husband's career. I can guarantee that my students and I will use absolute discretion in this case. But I must ask that you do the same," Paul said, looking Eddie square in the eye. Eddie recoiled a little from the thought of the media catching wind of this and the circus that could possibly result.

"Of course. Look, Jonathan can't handle much more stress. I have to ask you for your professional word that you will try to avoid pushing him any further," Eddie asked.

Paul nodded and said, "You got it. Where is your husband right now, Eddie?"

"Next door with Maggie and Jonah. He's resting."

"Okay. I'd like to talk to him in a little bit and take pictures of the bruises so we can have them on file," Paul said. "Joey told me a bit of what was happening here, and that you think it may not be what you originally thought it was. Paranoid schizophrenia, wasn't that what you were leaning toward? Tell me. Why are you changing your mind?"

Eddie folded his arms defensively and looked at Joey. He was insulted right away by the new man's questions, but for the sake of his husband, he dropped the posture and addressed Paul as plainly as he could.

"Because I was afraid of what it could be if it was out of my professional scope. My pride got in the way. I figured I could protect him by having him subjected to tests and a doctor's scrutiny. But the truth is...fuck...I think the house is haunted," Eddie said, his face burning with embarrassment. "I think the house is haunted, and I think somehow Jonathan is the center of it," he said sadly, his defenses crashing to the ground. He wiped his face with his hands. "This flies in the face of everything I have ever learned to be the truth."

Paul nodded. "Well. Let's see what we can do," he said, putting a hand on Eddie's shoulder to comfort him.

***

Jonathan took little sips of water and winced at the pain in his throat. It felt like he had swallowed razorblades. The ice cubes clinked against the side of the glass as his hands trembled. His head raged with pain, and as Maggie made her way out of her bedroom into her kitchen, where Jonathan sat with Jonah, she handed him four aspirin and helped him as he swallowed them one by one. Then Maggie gently removed the glass from his grip and set it on the table.

"You really should have someone look at those bruises," she said gently, but firmly.

Jonathan shook his head. "Not without Eddie," he whispered. "I won't go without Eddie." Every word had to be forced out past his bruised larynx, stumbling out of his mouth. He looked around her pristine kitchen and noticed that, other than the newer stove, refrigerator, and a dishwasher, it looked like it hadn't been updated in twenty years. The table he sat at was oak, thick and sturdy, a matching chair hugging Jonathan's butt comfortably, which he was grateful for. His back was pretty bruised up too, he could feel it, but he wasn't inclined to say anything about it. He felt like he had made enough of a mess of things already. He couldn't remember, though, what had happened. He remembered walking into the kitchen, and then, after that, nothing. Everything else was a blur.

"You all right, son?" Jonah asked. He had been watching Jonathan like a hawk with a mixture of curiosity and worry. Jonathan nodded. He wasn't, though. He was scared. What if Eddie was right? What if he was simply succumbing to some awful mental illness that would steal him away? What kind of life would that be for Eddie? What kind of husband could he be? *Well, one thing is for certain: you're going to stop fighting him when he says you need treatment,* the annoying voice told him. He silently nodded again, knowing if that didn't work, he would make sure Eddie wouldn't have to take care of an invalid. He refused to live that way.

The back door opened and Eddie came in, followed by two men Jonathan had never seen before. *Well, here they are,* the annoying voice said. *Now, don't fight them when they take you to the hospital.* Jonathan couldn't help it as his breathing became more rapid, and his palms started to sweat. His chest tightened and a feeling of loneliness and despair washed over him. He put his head down once more.

Eddie knelt and gently took his hands, bringing them to his lips. Jonathan raised his head a bit so he could look him in the eyes.

"Is it time to go to the nuthouse now?" he asked sadly, simply, like a lost child. Eddie's gaze softened, and he placed one of Jonathan's hands on each side of his face and held them there as he closed his eyes. What he said surprised Jonathan very much.

"My big, strong, brave, brave man. No. We're not taking you to the hospital, my love. Sick people go to the hospital. You're not sick," he said

Jonathan was shocked and confused. "What do you mean? I'm a schizophrenic, right? Don't I have to go to the hospital for that?" he said, his voice hoarse.

"Jonathan, I was wrong. Do you hear me? I was wrong, and I am so very sorry," Eddie said. "Can you forgive me?"

Confusion set in as Jonathan held his lover's face. "What do you mean?"

"Jonathan, I'm Dr. Paul Spencer, head of sociology at Kansas State University. I am also the founder of a group of academics and students who study cases of paranormal phenomena. Eddie believes your house is indeed haunted. He has given me the rundown of everything that has happened since you two moved in, and with your permission, we would like to interview you and start a proper investigation of the premises."

Jonathan looked from Eddie to Paul and then back to Eddie. "What's he talking about?"

"Were going ghost-hunting," Eddie said with a sad smile.

"Well, it's not that simple, actually. Jonathan, my team and I would like to investigate the house for any evidence of this phenomenon," Paul said, putting his hands in his pockets. "To create a controlled environment, we need to borrow the house for seven days. We're going to bring in all kinds of electronic gear to monitor for temperature changes, UV changes, shifts in electromagnetic fields; we're going to bring in cameras, digital recorders, the whole works," Paul said, pulling up a chair and setting it in front of Jonathan.

"You mean I'm not going to the hospital after all?" Jonathan asked hopefully, looking back at Eddie.

"No, babe. No. I cancelled those appointments with Dr. Joey here." Eddie indicated the other man, who stood uncomfortably behind Eddie.

"Wait. Wait on that, Eddie," Paul said. "Instead of cancelling them, why don't you go through with them?"

Eddie swiveled on his feet and looked at Paul, holding onto Jonathan's bare leg for support. "I thought you agreed with me that it isn't a mental-health issue." Feeling Jonathan tense up under his hand, he squeezed Jonathan's knee to keep him calm.

"I do agree with you, and I don't think it is. But from what I've gathered and from what you've told me, this seems to be centered around him. I would like to see what the tests might tell us. I doubt we're going to see anything wrong with the structure of the brain, but let's give it a shot. That is, if all parties involved are willing?" he said, addressing Joey.

"Sure. I don't see why not. We could get started tonight, if you'd like. However, we'll make arrangements for you to be there, Eddie. Since this has gone completely down a different rabbit trail, I could use your help in setting up and monitoring the equipment," Joey said with a hopeful look on his face.

Eddie turned to Jonathan. "What do you think? Wanna go hang out for a few days at my job? It's totally up to—"

"Why not just leave the house? Sell it? Or walk away from it?" Jonathan asked.

Paul reached into his coat pocket, pulled out one of the twisted spoons, and showed it to Jonathan. "Because whatever did this was damn powerful, and I don't think anyone here could have pulled it off. Now, either we're dealing with a powerful spirit or a powerful medium, and if it's the latter, you might never find peace anywhere, even if you did put this place in your rearview mirror."

Jonathan cocked his head at this and sat quietly for a moment until he remembered something. "Objects in the rearview mirror may appear closer than they are," he whispered, leaning forward. "Eddie, the computer upstairs. My computer. Before I blacked out. Alan was talking to me."

"What do you mean, talking to you?" Paul asked, sitting forward.

"My keyboard. He was typing out a message to me," Jonathan said.

"What did he say?"

"Basically repeating the same things over and over again."

"Like the messages you were texting me before I got home?" Eddie asked.

"I didn't send you any messages," Jonathan replied, confused.

Eddie fished his cell out of his pocket and pulled up the texts he had received earlier. He flipped the phone around so Jonathan could see. "The texts came from your phone, babe," Eddie said.

Paul stood up. "Jonathan, would you show me the computer? Eddie, would you get his phone for me, please, and let's have a look?"

And so they did. Eddie retrieved Jonathan's phone from the bedroom as the others, including Jonah and Maggie, made their way into Jonathan's office. Paul didn't give Jonathan any time to activate his computer or to manipulate anything and wiggled the mouse. When the screen woke up, the Word document was still there, and so were the words.

"My God," Paul said, astounded, as he leaned forward to read the content of the message. "You didn't do this?" he asked, addressing Jonathan.

"What? No! Why would I do something like that?"

"People do strange things for attention, possible publicity and fame. Look at the Lutz family in Amityville."

Jonathan's face grew red with anger. "Look, pal, if you think that I like the notion of having a Stephen King novel playing out in my house, you're crazier than..." he said, pointing a finger at Paul, but Eddie stepped between them.

"Look at this, Paul. Here's my phone with the incoming texts that brought me to the house. They register Jonathan's number. Now here is Jonathan's phone. Nothing." Eddie handed the man both handsets and maneuvered himself in between Jonathan and Paul.

Paul looked as shocked as Eddie felt at the revelation, and then he nodded. "Oh yeah. This is stuff people like me dream of. Mr. David, I am going to have my crew come in tonight and set up. They won't be told about any of the happenings around here. We'll clean up the kitchen and use Lisa's pictures to catalogue the event and also take a few pictures of your neck." He thoughtfully adjusted his glasses. "Guys, I think if all this is true, we may have a real...measurable...physical science inside this house," he said excitedly to a room of people who either couldn't care less or who were afraid of that truth.

***

Eddie walked down the hall and into the bedroom, where Jonathan was packing a bag for them while Paul took everyone downstairs to the kitchen to clean it up and to interview Maggie, who had come back next door with Jonah and agreed to help out however she could. Eddie shut the door and locked it behind him as he stepped into the dimly lit room. Jonathan was shoving clothes into a black suitcase along with toiletries and a laptop. Eddie knew he was angry; the tension was rolling off him in waves. Eddie placed his hands on Jonathan's shoulders and gently dug into the muscles. He could feel the knots there, taut like wires stretched across a desert highway. Jonathan stopped packing and hung his head as Eddie worked slowly and carefully. Eventually Eddie stopped and ran his hands from the man's shoulders down his arms to reach for his hands. He intertwined their fingers, and Jonathan responded with an encouraging squeeze.

"I always thought I would one day outrun him. I always thought if I put him in my rearview mirror and keep the pedal to the floor, the past couldn't possibly keep up. I figured it weighed so much and was so cumbersome, it would slow itself down. But that isn't the way of it, is it? It's found a way to touch me once more," Jonathan said miserably, his voice cracking as it was forced from his damaged throat. Eddie remained silent and let Jonathan finish talking. Jonathan held Eddie's fingers in his hands and wrapped his arms around himself, pulling Eddie in against his back, where his lover rested his head on Jonathan's back.

"But I guess no matter where you go, there you are. We've been through hell already, fighting to stay together, and now of all things, of all the craziest things in the world to happen, we wander right into hell again," Jonathan said thickly. Eddie turned his head to see the soft evening sunlight dance through the window and upon it, fine dust particles floating in the air as the sunset sky took on darker blue tones. Eddie rested his hands on the tight and muscular chest of his husband and turned his head to rest the other side of his face against his powerful back.

"I'd rather spend every day of my life in hell with you than a single day in heaven with you nowhere to be found," Eddie said and stood up straighter, turning Jonathan around. His lover was staring at the floor, a white T-shirt crumpled in his hands, and it was only when Eddie raised Jonathan's chin so his eyes met his own, did Jonathan finally look up. "Don't give up on us yet. We've been through a lot, which means we know how to handle the hard times." Eddie grinned. "Besides, this can't be a Stephen King novel: we're in the Midwest, not a sleepy New England town," he said, laughing.

Jonathan rolled his eyes. "Then you've never read *The Stand* or *The Dark Tower.*"

"Regardless, this is real life, Jonathan. You and me, and I feel I contributed to your life of running away from the problem. I let you drag me here because there isn't a place in the world I would rather be than wherever you go. Perhaps this is our chance to take our stand. Maybe this is a way for you to finally confront the dark shadows of your past and drag them kicking and screaming into daylight, which is the best cure. No more rearview-mirror stuff. Let's do away with them once and for all."

Jonathan's eyes misted over, and one tear slipped past and slid down his cheek before Eddie caught it and brushed it away with his thumb. "You're not weak, Jonathan. You've just been fighting for too long," he said, cupping his sweet face and leaning in for a gentle kiss. "I love you, Jonathan."

"I love you too. But what about the blackouts? I wake up and there is chaos all around me. How do I deal with that?" his husband replied.

"As you've dealt with your own abuse, as you've dealt with life, as we deal with everything when its gets hard like this: one step at a time," Eddie said, backing up. He was about to turn and head toward the door when his heel caught on something, and he stumbled backward and nearly fell on his ass.

"What the fuck?" he asked, catching himself on the footboard of the bed. A piece of floor was sticking up because the weight of the bed had cracked it in two. "Aw, dammit, all this and we're gonna have to do the floors. Wait, what are you doing?"

Jonathan's face had suddenly gone slack, pale, and then he surged forward and scooted the bed over. "He said it was under the floor. Look under the floor. That's what he said," Jonathan said. He knelt where the board had resettled and used his finger to pry not only that one up, but the one beside it as well.

"Who said?" Eddie asked, kneeling beside him.

Jonathan raised his head and stared at him in the eye. "Alan."

***

Eddie carefully eased his hand into the hole and felt around. His eyes grew big when his fingers collided with something cool. He wrapped his hand around what felt like a jar and pulled it out. Sure enough, it was a mason jar filled with what looked like cash. It was coated in dust. He blew on it and dusted it off with his hand. Black letters in shaky pencil on a faded white label read "Alan Pemberly's Sekrit Stashh."

"What else is in there?" Jonathan asked, awestruck. He reached into the hole. "I don't feel anything else. Oh, wait. It's…" He pulled his hand out, clutching what looked like an old photo album. It, too, was covered in a layer of thick dust, and Jonathan used his forearm to brush it away. "Wow. Look at this, babe," he said after clearing his sore throat. He opened the front cover and a piece of white paper slipped out.

"What's this?" Eddie asked, picking up the paper. It had been folded once long ways and then again in half from the other direction. Eddie gently began to unfold it.

Jonathan set the book aside and scooted over till he was next to Eddie. It had grown dark in the room, and Jonathan reached over to the end table and clicked the light on and moved back. Eddie tilted the paper up to the glow so he could read it while Jonathan waited impatiently. He watched Eddie's face turn from wonder to sadness.

"What is it, babe?" Jonathan asked, reaching for it.

Eddie pulled away. "Almost done. Awwww, babe. This breaks my heart. Listen to this: 'Dear God, my name is Alan, and I am seven years old. Mrs. Collins, Momma's nurse, said you had taken her home to be with you today because she had cancer. When I asked her where heaven was, she pointed upward and said you lived in the sky. That's good. Mamma loved going with Daddy on his airplane rides in the Army. Tell my momma that I love her and will miss her a lot. Daddy misses her a lot too, but he doesn't say anything much anymore. But I know he does. He doesn't talk to me much either. I asked Mrs. Collins why, and she said it was because Daddy was suffering from the broken heart.

She says that people who have the broken heart can't see very well, and two broken hearts can't see each other at all. She says I have to try and not have a broken heart so my daddy can one day find me again. I'll try, but I am sad too that Momma is living with you now. Daddy just stares at the picture of Momma and drinks a lot. I hope you can make my daddy better from the broken heart. Sincerely, Alan Pemberly,'" Eddie finished and dropped his hand to his leg.

***

They finished packing their bag and started down the stairs. Outside, a large van had pulled up with "Tom's Plumbing Service" written in yellow letters on the side. A collection of people were sitting in their living room, awaiting their arrival. The group consisted of Joey, who was quietly talking to Maggie and jotting down whatever she said, and Dr. Spencer, who was instructing not only his group of students how things were to be set up, but Jonah as well, who was listening with fascination. He kept looking at Maggie, who was casting glances his way as well. Eddie elbowed Jonathan when he saw this and gave him a knowing look as they descended the staircase with their suitcase and treasures.

"Hey, we found something I think you may be interested in, Paul. Check this out," Eddie said as he came into the room. Many different people were there now, and so were boxes filled with equipment that members of the group were rifling through. Paul looked over from where he was standing with Maggie and nodded toward the kitchen. Eddie remembered then that Paul had said he didn't want to contaminate the perspective of his "ghost hunters," so all the information of the goings-on in the house would be restricted to those who already knew. The more Eddie talked to him, the more he respected the man. He might be involved in a ridiculous hobby, but at least he was professional about it.

Maggie, Joey, and Jonah filed into the kitchen, and Maggie was the first to address what Eddie had in his hands. "My God,

I haven't seen this in years. Where did you find it?" she asked, reaching out for the album. Eddie handed it to her, and she gently took it from him and opened it. The letter Eddie had read to Jonathan lay open at the front, and Maggie began to choke up as she read it.

"Oh, Alan," she said, sniffing loudly. "Oh, you poor little boy, I remember the day he wrote this. I helped him. He was just a small kid at the time, and I was thirteen or fourteen. I told him if he kept it with him in his book of pictures, God would know it was important and would read about it when he was asleep," she said, delicately tracing an old finger down the worn yellow page.

"It was stashed under a floorboard upstairs. I nearly broke my neck tripping over the broken floorboard. It was in there along with this," Jonathan said, producing the jar of money from behind his back.

Maggie saw the jar and laughed hard and loud. "He was probably the most frugal kid you ever met. Every time he lost a tooth or got money, or if he hit my father up for a dollar once in a while, he never spent it. He would have been an incredible investment banker if...well, you know...if... Oh goodness," she said, covering her face and crying. "He was such a little stinker when he was little, but he was always smiles and crooked teeth," she said, lowering her hands and reaching for the letter once more.

"Are you okay?" Jonah asked, placing a hand on her shoulder. She looked slightly shocked for a minute, and then her face turned a little red, perhaps embarrassed by Jonah's show of affection. She sniffed once, wiped at her eyes with her blouse sleeve, and cleared her throat.

"Yes. I'm fine. You know, a couple of years after Alan left, his father, Mark, who had sobered up by then, had a hard time holding a pen due to some early onset arthritis, so he asked me to come over one evening, and I wrote as he dictated the letter to me in the living room. You know, I actually have that letter, or rather, a copy of it, in my cabinet at home. The private investigator Mark hired to find Alan asked for several copies just in case one of them were to get lost or delivered to the wrong Alan. Would you like me to go get it?" she asked, looking up at everyone.

"Actually, Maggie, perhaps you should hold on to these things while we're gone. Keep them in a safe place, and we'll look at the other letter when we get back. With all the shuffling around and chaos, I don't want them accidentally destroyed. Will you do that for me?" Eddie asked.

"Oh, of course," she said, taking the book and the jar and holding them close.

"Hey, Joey?" Eddie asked. "You ready to head to the clinic?"

"Yes. We have a room ready for Jonathan, and Lisa, here, will be joining us to help out. We'll start with the fMRI and then from there go into the sleep study. We have two beds side by side in there. We want to make this as normal as possible for the both of you, and Jonathan may feel more relaxed sleeping next to you than with you staring at him through the window," Joey said, and Eddie and Jonathan nodded.

"Hey, Paul, don't let any member of your team walk alone in the house, huh? Just in case I am not the epicenter of this thing, I couldn't bear the thought of someone getting hurt. Make them work in teams," Jonathan said lowering the neckline of his T-shirt and arching his head back so everyone in the kitchen could get a good look at the finger-shaped bruises around his neck.

"Good point," Paul said admiring the bluish-black bruises. "I've asked Joey to reduce the three days to two should the activity of the house die out and we don't pick up anything. Whether we run into some high-level activity or no activity at all, we will keep you both apprised of the situation," Paul said. "Also, if you notice the whip outside, we disguised one of our vans to keep folks from being attracted to what's going on. As far as some people will be concerned, you had a severe plumbing issue and had to leave for a couple of days and—" He was interrupted as the cabinet door in the kitchen opened slowly, deliberately, until it stood wide, bare of all glasses, which had been destroyed hours earlier. Everyone watched it happen in silence and wonder.

"Did you all see that?" Lisa asked nervously.

Jonathan laughed. "Yeah, that's nothing. Believe me. That's just the beginning."

***

He rushed to the window upstairs to stare out at the man walking away, ushered out by his lover, negative energy swirling around him and his mind in a perpetual fog of anger, pain, and betrayal.

Good! Go! How dare you come into my home and declare it yours! This is mine! the man thought with enough force to cause the lights in the hallway to flicker. The smell of booze and sweat and vomit and pain and rage and despair permeated the empty spaces around him as he watched them pull away. *Who was he? Where had he come from?* Mark wondered. His punishment wasn't over. He must continue his penance. This was his hell, his damnation, and every night he must die for his transgressions. Every night he would feel the bullet tear through the back of his head into his skull to decorate the wall behind him.

All this queer had done was bring confusion. Thoughts of salvation. *He tried to trick me, drag me away from my hell into a deeper one*, he thought, gritting his teeth and clenching his fists in anger. He hadn't meant to hurt the man, but he'd been so angry he could barely contain himself. Just like with Alan... Alan...his poor son, who he had worked to bring home to be part of a family, was now eternally gone, and all that remained to torture him was the never-ending routine and reminders of the terrible things he'd done. He would beat him, Alan would fight back, then run away, and Mark would hear about his death from the unfeeling policeman who would show up at the door, which would lead Mark to put a bullet through his head. Over and over and over and over...

Yet this man had brought something different. Mark would catch a whiff of something not right sometimes. His ears would prick at the sound of Alan desperately trying to call him... *No!* It was lies! It was deceiving! He was a demon of some sort, come to test him. If not, how did he fight back? What power did he possess to send Mark hurtling toward the wall when he had nearly throttled the life out of him? *How dare he fight back? This is* my house*!*

The blue truck started up and pulled away from the curb as Mark began to lose substance, and there was satisfaction in returning to the void. He must finish his penance; he must make amends to whatever creature had put him here to pay for his sins. He must do it for his beloved son. Alan. Alan. Alan. *My son.* The downstairs was filled with people now, but they were not like this Jonathan. They didn't have his abilities, and Mark would be able to go on without them bothering him. *I must pay. I must pay. I must...*

The lights that had been flickering on and off flickered once more and then turned off as the man disappeared and left the hallway empty.

***

"This is incredible," Joey said, leaning over the machine with a notepad and pen in his hand.

"What? What is it?" Eddie asked, walking into the room. He had been downstairs in the room below the observation window, preparing Jonathan for bed. They had given him a dose of melatonin and a glass of water after a doctor came in, looked at the bruises on his neck, and declared him fine. Jonathan was worn out already, and within minutes was fast asleep while Eddie sat with him. Like they promised, they had pulled a bed in next to Jonathan's, and Eddie would join him later, but for now, after getting a text from Joey, he had gotten up and returned to the room set up to keep an eye on Jonathan as he slept through the night.

"Well, his fMRI looks normal in all parts of the brain. We aren't picking up any signs of hallucinations. He isn't hearing anything at the moment or seeing anything at the moment because he's asleep, but check this out," Joey said, pointing to the screen. "All of this is normal as he is starting to move into REM sleep. All except this. Look at his frontal lobe, the prefrontal cortex. Check that out and tell me what you see," Joey said, moving his rolling chair aside so Eddie could lean down.

"Holy shit. His prefrontal cortex is lit up like a Christmas tree," Eddie said with wonder, brushing hair out of his eyes.

"Exactly. He's heading to sleep, and there is a good deal of frontal-lobe activity in everyone, but this is off the charts. We know from basic neuropsychology there will always be activity in the brain—the signals that are sent through are no different than those that are sent when you are awake. Now, I took the liberty in cross-referencing this information with an EEG, so we'll have to keep an eye on him."

Eddie leaned forward to look at the EEG as well as the monitor keeping tabs on Jonathan's vital statistics. His heart rate was slowing down, his breathing becoming deeper; everything indicated he was sleeping, yet his brain was still high-functioning. "What is going on with you, babe?" he asked as he stood up, then walked to the window to look down on his husband's sleeping form. He brought a hand to his mouth as he leaned on the windowpane and watched him for the next hour or so.

***

Jonathan stood outside the house on Frederick Street. It was the home he and Eddie lived in, but the time was all wrong. The oak tree in their front yard was too small, maybe a few decades old, and not as high and as thick as it should be. The wooden front porch was also different. Instead of the dark-brown stain, it was painted an ugly gray-green color. The front door was changed as well—it was thick wood with a glass inlay almost the size of the door itself. Jonathan looked around at the rest of the street, confused and a little worried. *What's going on?*

Suddenly the front door opened and a wheelchair came rolling out with a fragile-looking woman sitting inside it. "Inside it" wouldn't have been an appropriate way to describe it had she not looked so frail and drawn-in. The seat of the wheelchair seemed to consume her little body as she leaned to the right. Her head was wrapped in a beautiful scarf of warm tones—reds, oranges, yellows, and browns glared in contrast to her pale skin and the faded nightgown and robe around her tiny shoulders. The woman was wheeled completely out the door, and he was surprised to see a very young Maggie pushing her and moving oh so gently. She pushed the sick woman to a swing, put the brakes on, and walked around to help the woman delicately to her feet. Jonathan wanted to help her, fearing the lady would lose her balance, hit the porch, and shatter into a million irreparable pieces. That was when he discovered he couldn't move. He couldn't lift his arms, nor cry out, try as he might. He was stuck in one position, his arms pinned to his sides by an unseen force, and the only thing he could do was move his head.

The duo on the porch didn't seem to notice him either, even though he was standing in plain view. Movement at the periphery of his vision caught his attention, and he saw a yellow school bus bounce down the street and stop in front of the house. A red stop sign popped from the side of the bus as the airbrakes hissed. The door opened, and a young, round, red-faced little boy bounded off, his yellow-blond hair sticking up in the back from a cowlick. He wore a green backpack that slammed against his chunky self as he clung to the white handle of his blue lunch box with a fat fist.

"Hi, Momma!" he cried happily as he made his way up the walk past Jonathan, whom he didn't even glance at, pulling up his britches as he raised a foot to go up the first step.

"Hi, baby!" she cried out, sitting forward happily with a grin so beautiful it broke Jonathan's heart. "What did you learn in school today?"

"Oh, nothing. Just the same old boring stuff. But Robert Chastain got in trouble for pulling Suzie Shoemaker's hair and had to stand in the corner! And Suzie, Suzie got in trouble because she called Robert a turd head," he said, out of breath from climbing those steps quickly.

"Well, that wasn't very nice, now was it? Come give me a hug," she said, holding her arms out for him. The little boy handed the lunch box to Maggie, who took it with a smile and pulled the wheelchair out of the way so Alan could get through. As bumbling and heavy on his feet as he was, Alan gently leaned in and gave his mom a big hug that brought tears to Jonathan's eyes. *This little boy won't have her for too much longer,* he thought.

"Shit," someone whispered to his left, and he turned to see the much older version of Alan standing not too far off. Their gazes met and locked, and the older Alan raised a finger and pointed in the same direction the school bus had come from. When he turned his head once more, the same beat-up old car Jonathan saw outside of his house came driving up the road and parked. *No! What the hell? This isn't right.*

He tried to move again but couldn't. He wanted to run away, hide behind the older Alan, anything but see who came climbing out of the car. He even tried to close his eyes but couldn't do that either. Eventually the car parked, and to Jonathan's relief, his father wasn't the one climbing out. It was another man—it was Mark, dressed in old Class A dress military uniform. He slammed the door shut and walked around the front of the car and up the sidewalk. Just like young Alan had, Mark moved past him and didn't see him there. But Jonathan noticed something: the handsome father smelled faintly of booze, and it made Jonathan's stomach clench.

Jonathan whipped his head back to the older Alan, who had ceased looking at Jonathan and was staring longingly at the scene on the porch. Jonathan turned back once more to witness the scene before him. The older man cleared the porch faster than his young son had, and on lithe feet. Maggie had set the wheelchair off to the other side of the porch and was sitting down on the swing with Alan between them.

"Hi, Daddy!" Alan called.

"Hello, son!" Mark replied and leaned down to kiss his wife on the cheek. "How ya feelin', beautiful?" he asked as he sat on the banister of the porch.

"With my hands, handsome. How do you feel?" she said with that same pretty smile. Mark laughed and shook his head. The mother looked at Maggie and asked, "Honey, would you take

Alan inside and feed him his supper and get him started on his homework? I'll have Mark bring me in," she said sweetly.

"Sure, Mrs. Pemberly. Come on, Alan," young Maggie said as she stood up.

"Awww, Mooooooom," Alan protested.

"Go on, Alan. Go on, get it done now and out of the way so you can play all evening. Get," she said patiently, her voice thinning at the end of the sentence.

"Oh, all right, fine," Alan said, and with his head bowed in defeat and Maggie following him, he headed inside. Mrs. Pemberly waited until he was out of earshot to turn her attention quickly to Mark.

"You promised me you'd stop drinking," she said calmly.

"I did," he protested.

"You're a liar. I may be half in the grave, but dammit, I can still smell," she hissed.

"Don't talk like that. The doctors—" She raised a hand wearily.

"The doctors don't know squat. They keep pumping me full of morphine and the radiation isn't working, Mark. I'm dying. Now, you have to get ahold of yourself before I go. Alan needs you," she said, leaning forward, and she tried to take his hand. He jerked away and stood up. She immediately looked hurt.

"How can you talk like that? How do you know what is going to happen?" Mark asked, raising his voice.

His wife closed her eyes, sat back, and mumbled something.

"What?" Mark asked, wiping his upper lip.

"I can feel it, Mark," she said and opened her eyes. "I'm dying and nothing is going to change that. But I need you to promise me you'll be strong for that little boy in there. He's going to need you," she said plainly.

"He is going to need his mother. What am I to do with him? Hell, if you hadn't had him perhaps you wouldn't even be...oh shit. Alan. *Alan!*" Mark yelled. What he hadn't noticed was that Alan had come to the door, cracked it open to listen, and had caught the whole conversation. The door slammed, and the last thing Jonathan saw through the glass was his fat little legs trying to climb the stairs quickly...and then everything went black.

***

"Jesus fucking Christ, Eddie. Look at this!" Joey called to Eddie, who had started dozing in a chair. He jerked awake immediately, nearly toppling out of his chair.

"Wuzzat? What?" Eddie asked, standing up and rubbing his eyes with the heels of his hands.

"Come here, dude, you gotta see this," Joey said, his eyes wide and his face pale. Eddie rushed over to the monitor and stared at it for a second before he realized what he was seeing.

"That's impossible. Recalibrate the machine," Eddie said sternly. The monitor showed that Jonathan's entire brain was lit up all over the place at the same time.

"I did. Three times," Joey said.

"Then the fMRI is fucked—" Eddie began.

"It isn't fucked," Joey countered, talking over him.

"It has to be, because this isn't humanly possible," Eddie said, temper flaring.

"Don't you think I know that!?" Joey said defensively and just as sternly. "Look at the EEG. His vitals are up too."

Eddie looked at the readings from the EEG, and yes, Joey was right—the brain waves were off the chart. "I am going to go wake him up," he said, but Joey grabbed his arm.

"Wait. Why don't you wait. Sure, these levels are incredible, and, yes, his vitals are up, but let's wait this out," he said, and then he let go and went over to the observation window. Eddie followed him and looked down to see Jonathan still sound asleep. The tech was sitting there, having dozed off, her head lolling to the side.

"What's going on with him?" Eddie asked worriedly. Joey put his hand on his shoulder, trying to comfort him.

"I don't know, man" was all he could say. "He's in a REM cycle, so let's wait to see what happens."

Eddie wanted more than anything to wake Jonathan up, throw him in the Durango, and take him anywhere he wanted to go and put this place in the rearview mirror.

***

The blackness didn't last. As a matter of fact, it lightened up as quickly as it had gone dark. But the scene had changed. He was standing in the kitchen now, this time with older Alan near his side. In front of them, sitting quietly and unmoving in their respective chairs, staring at the steaming piles of food on their table, were young Alan and his father. Mark wasn't in uniform anymore and was dressed in a pair of plaid pajama pants and a thin white T-shirt that didn't hide the bulge of his stomach. Both looked miserable and brokenhearted. On the counter, countless pies, cards, flowers, casserole dishes, and other odds and ends overflowed. Neither one of them made a move to start eating, not even the young, plump Alan, whose face was as pale and drawn as his father's. Mark spoke first.

"Alan, you need to eat," he said quietly.

"Why? You're not," Alan said back, just as hushed.

Mark raised his head, and they looked at each other. Alan began to cry, and Mark pushed back from the table and opened his arms.

"Come here, boy," he said as he started to weep as well. Jonathan looked at the older Alan, whose face glistened with tears.

The child jumped up from his place at the table and ran into his father's waiting arms. "I miss Momma!" he cried into his father's chest. The sound of his voice was muffled in Mark's embrace as the man wrapped his arms around his shaking son. He placed his chin on the boy's head and in a tear-soaked voice, "I miss her too." For several minutes both of them cried through this bout of grief, clinging to each other for dear life, young Alan's blond head lost in the arms of his father.

Older Alan reached out, as if to try and touch them. His face was a picture of anguish and grief as he wept openly for the two of them. Eventually realizing what he was doing or understanding his action was futile, he lowered his arm to his side. Their tears had run dry for the most part when they parted, and Mark held his son at arms' length.

"Go wash your face and get ready for bed. I'll clean this up, and I'll be up in a minute to check on you. We'll get through this, boy. Your momma's in heaven, but we'll get through this. Okay?" he said, looking his son square in the eye. The little boy nodded and left the room, leaving his father sitting there, wiping the top of his mouth. After making sure Alan was gone, Mark stood up and, instead of reaching for the untouched plates, leaned over to look down the hall once more. Satisfied he was unwatched, he walked over to the white cabinet Jonathan and Eddie used for glasses and mugs and opened it.

Jonathan shook his head, knowing what he was going for. And he was right. When Mark closed the door, he had a bourbon bottle in his hand, and he unscrewed the top and put it to his lips. He hesitated, and that gave Jonathan hope. But those hopes were dashed when he tipped his head back and took three or four hard, long swallows of the amber liquid. He lowered the bottle, now significantly more empty than before, shivered as he exhaled, and screwed the lid back on. He placed the bottle back in the cabinet and shut the door. Then everything turned black again.

Like before, it didn't last long. Yet this time, when the light came, it wasn't a gentle scene before him. This time, the light brought with it a harshness that surprised Jonathan.

"Get the fuck down here!" he heard an angry man shout. His gaze fell on a larger Mark Pemberly. His expansive gut hung over his blue jeans and the sleeves of his plaid shirt were rolled up over his biceps. Upon closer examination, his face was bloated and the telltale signs of alcoholism were etched across his nose and cheeks. He was standing in the foyer, and a much older and thinner Alan came down the stairs and stopped short of his father's reach.

"What's wrong?" the boy asked, his voice as flat and lifeless as could be. He kept his gaze on his feet. Jonathan saw the shadow of a bruise on his face.

"I said get down here," Mark said between clenched teeth.

Alan took one hesitant step forward, and Mark reached out, grabbed his arm, and pulled him down harshly until he was leering in Alan's face. Alan turned his head to avoid the reek of booze that rolled off him and made a disgusted sound. That was the wrong thing to do, as Mark lifted his hand lightning quick and slapped him across the face. Alan yelped and landed on the stairs, covering his cheek with his hand, and what surprised Jonathan was the lack of surprise in his eyes. They looked hollowed out and empty.

"You disrespectful little shit. How dare you tell the neighbors what happens inside this house!" Mark bellowed angrily as he stood over him, fists clenched. Jonathan prayed silently for Alan to keep quiet. No such luck.

"I didn't have to tell them anything. They can hear us. They can hear you in your drunken rages," Alan shot back coldly, slowly lowering his hand and raising his chin defiantly.

"You need to learn some respect," Mark spat.

"As soon as you earn it," Alan retorted. Jonathan closed his eyes and heard Alan cry out in pain. His own disgust and fear kept him from looking as the sound of fists coming down echoed throughout the room.

***

Eddie was halfway down the stairs, heading toward the room in the clinic where his husband slept, when he heard the tech scream in fear. His heart jolted, and he launched himself down the stairwell, skipping four stairs, and landed on the concrete floor. He dashed to the stairwell door, flung it open and took off to the room that housed Jonathan and the tech. She was screaming and calling for Joey and Eddie to help her. He reached the door, threw it open, and saw the tech lying on the ground, nursing her head. Jonathan stood at the back wall, his back to the door.

Joey burst through the door next as Eddie helped the tech to her feet. "What happened?" Joey asked her.

"He sat...no, 'sat' is the wrong word. He rose up like Dracula. He didn't move a muscle, just was suddenly standing at the edge of the bed. He reached for my pen and dug into his arm with it, and when I tried to stop him, he hit me," she said with her hand on her forehead. Eddie turned to Joey for confirmation, and he nodded.

"I saw it happen. Suddenly his vitals spiked, and I jumped up and...saw it happen. Jesus, Eddie," he said, taking his assistant's arm and guiding her to the bed so she could sit. Eddie watched him lead her away and slowly walked toward Jonathan, who kept reaching for his left arm and writing on the wall with one finger.

"Jonathan?" Eddie asked gently. His legs were shaking and so was his voice.

Jonathan didn't respond, so Eddie cautiously advanced and moved right so he could see what was happening. To his horror, he saw blood dripping down Jonathan's arm, and when he caught sight of the message on the wall, he inhaled sharply. It was scrawled in blood, the same message that had been on the cabinets.

HELP US

"Jonathan. Tell me. Tell me what I have to do to help you," Eddie said, touching the shoulder of his beloved. Jonathan stopped moving at that moment, his face contorted in pain and his eyes rolled up, his jaw slack. He lowered his arms to his sides and stared at Eddie with the whites of his eyes, a sight that chilled Eddie to the bone. He was silent for a moment, and then his jaw clicked shut so harshly it made Eddie jump, only to open again.

"You don't know shit about my family, you little trick," he said in a voice that wasn't his own.

"Faggot," he said, this time a different voice than the first.

"I miss my mommy," he said in a childlike tone.

"Daddy's sorry, son. I stopped drinking. I swear. Oh God," he said in a tone full of despair. Jonathan was moving forward now.

Eddie was shaking so badly with fear, he could hardly stand. His mind reeled as he shook Jonathan. The voices kept changing, as well as his facial expressions, and that terrified Eddie.

"Baby, stop!" Eddie yelled as he began to cry.

Jonathan started shaking his head and his knees buckled, taking both him and Eddie to the ground.

"You're in the mirror, babe. Come back," Eddie yelled.

Jonathan blinked once, twice, and finally, his eyes rolled down, and he locked his gaze on Eddie as he held him in his arms. "Help us," Jonathan whispered before he closed his eyes and collapsed against Eddie.

CHAPTER 13

THE HOT SUMMER morning air was heavy, thick, and weighed the world down and made Eddie's shirt stick to him. He pulled out Jonathan's cigarettes, lit one up, and inhaled deeply. He held the carcinogenic smoke in his chest and let it out slowly. Since he'd never smoked a cigarette in his life, the nicotine made the world tilt and roll, but he didn't care. He simply closed his eyes and let the sensation pass as sweat dripped down his collar, then his neck, to soak the wilted T-shirt that was damp at his shoulders anyway. The campus was dead on this Saturday morning. He leaned against the clinic wall and took another drag. The events of last night ran through his mind, and fear of the unknown gnawed at him. The air was stifling as he took another drag of the Marlboro Light and exhaled the bluish-gray smoke into the thick air, where it disappeared into oblivion. He glanced down at the cigarette and chuckled. Eddie always lectured Jonathan on his bad habit, and Jonathan usually rolled his eyes and told him no one got out of life alive. It all had to end someday. And as he stood there, he realized there was something incredibly comforting in the act that sort of said "fuck you" to fate, God, and his biology, and dictated to them that he was, at least for a brief few minutes, the one holding the reins of his runaway world.

He launched himself off the wall and decided to go for a walk instead of standing in one spot baking. He had been in the air-conditioning so long his insides felt frozen, and although the heat was oppressive, it felt good on his bones. He moved down the walk, head tilted to the side to avoid the glaring sunlight that mocked him and everything he was trying to do to help his lover. He walked past several buildings as he traversed the campus

430

along the white walkway that mirrored the sunlight up at him, making him wince. He finished his cigarette and tossed it angrily into an empty parking lot as he journeyed farther and farther away from his lover. Joey had assured him he would be fine while Eddie was outside and promised to call if anything happened. They had managed to wake up Jonathan after his episode and stitched up his arm, but he'd seemed so exhausted, Eddie hadn't bothered trying to talk to him and simply let him lie back down. As soon as Jonathan's head hit the pillow, he was out.

His phone rang in his pocket, and his heart jumped into his throat. He reached for it, saw it was Maggie, and slid the call open.

"Hello?" he answered, placing his phone to his ear and his back to the wind.

"Eddie. It's Maggie. I've got Dr. Spencer here with me. He wants to talk to you. Is that okay?" she asked.

"Yeah, Maggie. That's okay. Put him on," Eddie said as he switched ears to hear better.

"Dr. Dorman? This is Dr. Spencer. We had an incredible night over here," he said. "We've had a bit of excitement."

***

Jonathan opened his eyes and sat up. He felt the electrodes on his forehead trying to pull him down, but he reached up and started prying those off one at a time and casting them aside. Joey entered in the room, asking him not to take them off.

"Bugger that. Where's Eddie?" Jonathan asked, removing the last of the sensors and standing up next to the bed. His head swam for a second, and he had to put a hand out and steady himself, but it passed quickly.

"He stepped out for some air. Jonathan, you're not well. Why don't you…?" Joey tried reaching for him, but Jonathan felt infuriated by his weakness and swiped his arms away.

"I'm done with this. Where are my clothes?" he asked, trying to get his bearings. There was the luggage, the one bag they had brought with them, and Jonathan walked to it and unzipped the top of it. He ripped off his T-shirt, grabbed a fresh one, and changed into it. The tech, who was watching from upstairs turned her back as Jonathan pulled his sweatpants down and stood bareassed on the observation floor. He found a pair of cargo shorts, stepped into them, and pulled them up.

The door opened. Eddie came in carrying his cell phone and looking shocked to see Jonathan up and about.

"Babe. What are you doing? Are you okay?" Eddie asked, walking over.

"Yeah. I'm good. Eddie, I remember everything except for this. What is this?" He held up his bandaged arm.

"You cut yourself with the tech's pen and wrote that message on the wall," Eddie said, pointing with his phone.

Jonathan read what he had written and somberly nodded. "Oh," he said, slipping on a pair of sandals. He gave Eddie a bashful look along with a wistful smile. He noticed Eddie had the Droid in his hand.

"Who was on the phone?" Jonathan asked.

"Well, it was Dr. Spencer. Apparently we weren't the only ones who experienced excitement last night," Eddie said.

"What happened?" Jonathan asked, zipping the suitcase.

"Apparently what he calls some low-level paranormal phenomenon, and then about the same time you started…well… doing what you were doing, all hell broke loose in the house. They have it on tape," Eddie said. "They want us to come back and take a look. Are you up to it?"

"Yeah. Let's get the hell out of here. Joey, thank you for your time, but I no longer require your services," Jonathan said, grabbing the bag and hoisting it. He went to the door with Eddie by his side. Jonathan pushed open the door, stepped out into the hallway, and reached for Eddie's hand, holding it as they made their way to his baby, his ride, his escape. This time they wouldn't be running from anything.

The heat was ferocious, but a cool breeze that had pierced the sunburned air to touch their bodies as they made their way across the campus caused Jonathan to stop and look at the horizon. There they were, in the far distance: the dark clouds of a summer storm, pulsing with lightning. Jonathan closed his eyes, and as he felt another waft of cool breeze float past him, he squeezed Eddie's hand.

"What did you see, Jonathan?" Eddie asked softly.

Jonathan opened his eyes and turned to look at his lover. "I saw his pain and I felt my own. Alan is trying to find an end to all of this. He's trapped in the rearview mirror of his life."

"So his father tortures him even in death?" Eddie asked, shivering with the thought.

"Yes and no," Jonathan said. "But I don't think the father knows it. He's too wrapped up in his own grief to realize what he's doing and so is Alan." He was silent for a moment before adding, "There is something else in there with them."

"Something else?" Eddie asked.

Jonathan's face was ashen and serious. "It's the beast in all of this, in all of us. It feeds on them. Lies to them. It's manifested itself to such a degree that they can't see each other's trauma, so there is no natural resolution. It's manipulated them from the beginning."

"Fear," Eddie whispered.

Jonathan almost wept for joy as his husband understood. It was the one thing that came between father and son and the one thing that threatened the marriage, life, and happiness of the two men. Instead of weeping, Jonathan smiled broadly, proudly, and felt as empowered as a lion, better than he had felt since they'd moved in.

"So both of them are there with it?" Eddie asked, and Jonathan nodded. Eddie moved into Jonathan's arms. "I guess broken hearts can't see each other. So what do we do?" he asked, safely in the arms of the man he loved. "That's heartbreaking. What are we going to do?"

"We're going to try to find a way to help them. Come on," Jonathan said and unlocked the truck. He threw the suitcase in the back, climbed into the driver's seat, and cranked the Durango to life. They hit their own buttons on their doors to lower the windows—the inside of the truck was stifling hot, and beads of sweat were already trickling down their backs.

"Babe, I have to ask: What did you experience while you were…uh…in your trance, so to speak? You said you remembered everything," Eddie said.

Jonathan put the truck into gear and started guiding it out of the parking lot and toward the road. He left the lot, pulled out onto the main road, and started for home. He reached over and turned on the air conditioner full blast, as the windows provided little relief from the heat, and both men rolled their windows up. Once settled into traffic, Jonathan began to tell Eddie about everything he'd seen and what Alan had shown him. His story was intermittently interrupted with gasps and "wows." He reached for his cigarettes and didn't find them.

"Oh. Here," Eddie said. He pulled out Jonathan's pack of Marlboros, took one out, lit it for Jonathan, and handed it over. He reached back into the pack, pulled one out for himself, and then lit the end of it, inhaling deeply. This time his head didn't swim, and he rolled his window down a crack to let the smoke filter out into the Kansas air. Jonathan watched the whole thing happen, looking surprised.

"Who are you and where is my husband?" he asked, laughing.

"It's been a long couple of days. Shut up and drive," Eddie said with a wink, and Jonathan laughed and shook his head as he wove through Manhattan traffic. When they stopped at a red light, Eddie asked. "So, how do we help them? I mean, how do we communicate with them? Do we have to wait for you to go to sleep before we can talk to them or what?"

Jonathan considered what Eddie was asking before he answered. The truth was he didn't know.

"What did you all find out about what was happening to me physically?" Jonathan asked, and Eddie told him about what the fMRI had indicated, along with his vitals and EEG.

"Then I'm acting as some sort of medium?" Jonathan asked, and Eddie shrugged.

"I don't know. This is way out of my pay grade," he said, and then he took another drag on his cigarette.

When the light turned green, they drove in silence for a while until Jonathan saw the red sign of a Target store, and the thought hit him. He signaled to get into the right lane and watched for traffic as he merged and then turned into the parking lot.

"What are we doing?" Eddie asked, surprised at the sudden detour.

"Going shopping," Jonathan said and pulled down the lane of the shopping center. "I've got an idea."

***

"You're serious?" Eddie asked with his hands on his hips, looking at what Jonathan was holding. They were standing in the game aisle of the store as people browsed. One gentleman near them looked at what Jonathan was holding and narrowed his eyes. Whispering something to a woman in a floor-length jean skirt, they quickly walked away. Jonathan shook his head and rolled his eyes.

"Yes. I mean, what else are we going to do? Unless you have a medium or psychic on speed dial, then were at a loss," Jonathan said.

Eddie laughed and slapped Jonathan on the ass as they walked up to the checkout. They waited in line for a few minutes until they got up to the register. The lady at the counter chuckled when she saw what they had.

"I haven't seen one of these in years," she said. "You boys throwing a party?" she said as she scanned the back of it.

"Yes, ma'am, we sure are," Jonathan said with a grin. He reached inside for his wallet and was about to swipe the card when the woman grabbed his hand. Eddie thought she was going to instruct him on the use of the pad but changed his mind when he saw the look in her eyes.

"You gotta be careful with these things, boy. It's like looking through a two-way mirror. Don't get yourself stuck, hear?" she said. The blood drained from Eddie's face. Jonathan and the woman locked gazes. Her brown hand was clamped around his wrist. "People get lost too quickly and too easily in these things and can never be found again. A part of them gets caught up when they open those doors. Tread lightly."

She blinked once, twice, three times before she withdrew her hand, shamefaced, and looked suddenly very embarrassed. "I…I am sorry. I have no idea what came over me," she said, breathing hard.

This time Jonathan reached over the counter and patted her hand. "It's okay. And thank you," he said with a smile. He swiped his card, and she gave him his receipt. As they walked away, Eddie looked back to see her watching them leave.

As soon as they passed through the double sliding doors and out into the oppressive heat, Eddie grabbed Jonathan's arm. "I feel like I am in the twilight fucking zone, babe. What was that?" he asked as they headed for the truck.

"I don't know either. But it's my guess that Alan and I aren't the only ones in the world who have dealt with or gone through what we've been through. I think that's the link. I think he's reached out to me because both of us were abused. Do you remember me seeing that station wagon?" he asked as he opened the truck door.

"Yeah," Eddie said, climbing in.

"Well, when we were at the university I dreamed…eh, if you can call it dreaming…I was shown a scene in Alan's life. He was cycling me through them. And in one in particular, that station wagon pulled up and his father got out," Jonathan said.

"So what?" Eddie said. "I'm not following you."

"The age Alan was when he showed me the scene, that car hadn't been made yet. And to top it off, that was the same exact car my father drove," Jonathan said. He slammed the door shut and started the ignition and put the car back in drive.

"He's using your memories to fill in his gaps," Eddie said.

"Bingo," Jonathan said. "Either that or he's trying to explain to me our mutual…issues," he said, getting onto the freeway.

"That's incredible," Eddie whispered. He leaned against the seat and felt the truck's engine kick as the blue vehicle jumped into high gear. He looked at Jonathan, who was deep in thought as they wound their way back home.

"So why is he stuck here?" Eddie asked, breaking the silence again.

"One of two reasons: Do you remember when we first met? How much of a mess I was?" Jonathan asked.

"You weren't that bad," Eddie said with a smirk.

"No, I was worse. You know my past—the string of love affairs that never lasted, the constant running from one place to another, looking so desperately for stability, which got me into bad spots over and over. I was punishing myself. I longed for something I thought I could never have," he said, looking over at Eddie. Jonathan's eyes were tender, and his smile was genuine and affectionate.

"What happened to you wasn't your fault," Eddie said, reaching over and grabbing his hand.

"I know it. I knew it then too, but still, there was something deep, dark, and lonely in me that wouldn't let that truth sink in. Until you showed up, that is," Jonathan said.

"I love you, Jonathan David."

"I love you, Eddie Dorman," Jonathan said.

There was a pause, and then Eddie spoke. "So, they're trapping themselves. Each feels like they deserve the punishment."

Jonathan nodded. "They both do."

"Yeah?" Eddie asked.

"His father. He was the one who attacked me," Jonathan said, stretching his neck to the right until Eddie could see purple bruises already turning a nasty shade of green.

"But the father was an abusive asshole," Eddie said angrily. "He should be punished."

Jonathan arched an eyebrow. "I am surprised at you, doctor."

"Why? He was a drunk who took his anger out on his kid," Eddie said heatedly.

A truck was taking its sweetass time in front of Jonathan, so when he found the perfect moment, he swung out, hit the gas and passed the old man, then settled back into the lane. Ahead of them were the thunderheads, rising up into the atmosphere like a massive black anvil, angry and foreboding.

Eddie shivered as lightning danced like a drunken ballet dancer upon the earth below. It was still miles away, but to Eddie it looked like the end of the world. They would make it home before it hit, but Lord knew what the night would bring for them or how this would end. He was angry—angry at Alan for doing this to Jonathan, angry at Mark for hurting his son, and angry at himself for his shortfalls as a husband, questioning the man he loved.

"There is no way you could have known, Eddie," Jonathan said. Eddie turned his head to look at him, eyes large, but Jonathan continued. "No, I didn't read your mind. Or, I did, but not because I can connect to you like the woman in the store. I can because I am your husband. In a sense, you're doing what Mark did to himself. You know, I feel sorry for him. I can't imagine what I would do if I were to lose you. You're my everything. Certainly, I wouldn't beat our child or make him run away, but not everyone is capable of holding themselves together. Especially if liquor is involved."

"So what do you plan on doing when we get there?" Eddie asked.

"Force them to see each other," Jonathan said.

"The Ouija board will help?" Eddie asked.

"I think so. But Alan is the least of our problems," Jonathan said.

"What do you mean?" Eddie asked.

"You ever try to talk down a drunk person? "Jonathan asked.

"Yeah. That usually sucks," Eddie said. "Aw, shit. Mark. He's drunk on grief."

"God, you're sexy when you use that brain of yours," Jonathan said with a chuckle.

Eddie laughed at that. This situation was twisting his brain in so many different directions, he didn't know if he could ever sit behind the desk and diagnose patients ever again with the same self-assuredness. He didn't feel smart anymore, but then again, Socrates had said the beginning of wisdom was the realization that one knows nothing. As they drove into the storm—that was what the future felt like to him: a darkness shrouded with bursts of light—he felt his stomach knot up and his nerves start to hum.

Fuck that, he thought as he turned on the radio and cranked up whatever CD was in there. There was a pause in the track, then suddenly rock music floated out of the speakers as Boston began to sing about peace of mind. He turned it up louder and leaned over and kissed Jonathan on the cheek before singing along. The blue Durango, his lover's jukebox on wheels, rocketed forward on the empty highway and into the arms of the waiting storm with both men defiant as the music floated out their windows.

***

Forty-five minutes later, both of them having settled down once they reached the Clay Center City limit sign, they pulled into the driveway off Frederick Street to find lights burning inside the house. Jonathan put the Durango in park and sat there for a moment, staring inside. The black van was still parked out front, and there was activity in the house. He sighed. He had a gnawing feeling in his stomach, and his mind was already being assaulted by energy from the house. He took a deep breath and let it out slowly, every nerve in his body on edge. *Just leave, you dumbass. You can't save everyone,* the annoying voice said, chastising him.

"Shut up," he said aloud.

"What?" Eddie asked, surprised. Jonathan instantly felt embarrassed; he had never actually spoken aloud to that tiny cold and selfish voice in his head.

"Not you, babe. I was talking to myself," he said, killing the engine. *I was talking to fear.*

"Careful, someone might think you're crazy," Eddie said with a wink. He sobered up and reached across the space between them to put his hand on Jonathan's leg. "If you want to leave, if you want to leave this place and never look back, I won't think less of you."

F.E. Feeley Jr.

Jonathan shook his head. "Can't do it, babe."

"I know, I just thought I'd say it anyway. I am very proud of you, by the way," Eddie said.

Jonathan unbuckled his belt and grabbed the back of Eddie's head, and pulled him into a deep kiss. Their lips touched, and instantly they clung to each other, Eddie undoing his belt and pushing back into a kiss so deep that when they parted, their breathing was labored.

"Promise me, if I start sliding too far in, you'll come get me. Don't let me get lost. Promise me," Jonathan said with his eyes closed.

"Never. I'll chase you through if I have to. I'll never let you go," Eddie whispered back.

"I love you," Jonathan said.

"I love you, babe," Eddie replied. They parted, and Jonathan reached behind him for the game he had picked up.

"Here we go," he said, and both of them stepped out into the dramatically cooler air. It hit Jonathan dead-on, whipping his thin, loose cotton shirt against his body and sending chills down his spine. The front door was open, and he could see everyone. The duo walked hand in hand up the sidewalk and up the stairs. Jonathan grabbed the door and held it for Eddie to step through, and came in behind him. It was immediate chaos as soon as the people inside realized they were there. People he didn't know were yammering on about what had happened the night before, and Jonathan was suddenly overwhelmed. It took Maggie yelling and wading through the throng of people with her elbows to get everyone to back up and let them in the door. Apparently she had become the alpha of the group, as people respectfully parted ways and let her walk uninhibited.

Immediately she walked up to Jonathan, stood on her tiptoes, and kissed him on the cheek. "How are you, sweetheart?"

"I'm good, thank you," he said, his face heating. "How are you? I heard you all had some excitement last night," he said, putting the board underneath his right arm.

440

"Oh yeah, I've been here all night. You aren't going to believe the stuff that went on…or maybe you will. I'll let Paul tell you about that. Anyway…" She stopped and looked at Eddie. "How are you, sweetheart?"

He reached in and gave her a big hug and a smack on the cheek. "I'm good. We're good," he said.

Dr. Spencer walked in from the kitchen with a serious look on his face, but he brightened when he saw the two of them standing there. "I just got off the phone with Joey. He said you two were headed here, and that he is on his way as well. Jonathan, do you think that's a good idea?"

"Hey, Doc. Don't really care whether it's a good idea. I just couldn't take being in that observation room any longer. I know we were supposed to be there for three days and be brought in later, but honestly, I don't think my mind can take much more of being under the influence of…whatever this is," Jonathan said.

Paul nodded. "Well, I gotta be quite frank here. My students and I are thrilled to no end with the amount of evidence we have collected in just one night," he said. Jonathan looked over at the youthful faces staring up at him excitedly as they nodded with enthusiasm. "We look forward to being able to keep studying this phenomenon as long as you'll have us."

Eddie spoke up next. "Well, Paul, that's why we're here."

Paul furrowed his brow and gave them a questioning look. "What do you mean?"

"It means this observation is being cut a little short," Jonathan said. "We're putting an end to it."

Paul looked crestfallen. "I don't understand. What do you mean?"

Jonathan walked over to his couch, and one of the students jumped up to let him sit down. "We'll get to that in a second, Paul. You said you had something for us to see?"

Paul motioned for one of the guys to come forward. He looked exhausted and had dark circles under his eyes. Jonathan assumed none of the people in the house had gotten much sleep. The young man, who introduced himself as Byron, brought with him a laptop computer and sat next to Jonathan with Eddie, sitting on the arm of the couch, leaning over.

Byron began to speak so low everyone had to lean in to hear him. "The first thing we did, that you must understand for the record, is when we came in, we used EMF detectors to check the wiring of the house. This is important for one main reason: high levels of electromagnetic field can cause issues in some people. Paranoia, skin rashes, feelings of being watched, so on and so forth. A lot of people don't realize their home can be so flooded with high levels of EMF, it can affect them physically.

"So we took this equipment and did a sweep throughout the whole house, from the top floor to the basement, and although we found a higher than normal concentration down at your power box in the basement, that shouldn't affect anything at all. Unless you're down in the basement doing laundry or something," he said with a chuckle. "The rest of the house is fine.

"The next thing we did was to set up cameras all over the place. Dr. Spencer, as he always does, goes in to each place we investigate to find out where these occurrences go on. Yet, unlike the television shows that do this very same thing, he withholds the information from us to see if what we discover correlates to what the people complain about," he said, turning to each person and making sure both Eddie and Jonathan understood.

"Now, my methodology is to cover a house from stem to stern with cameras to watch the hallways and rooms from various angles. I don't want anything uncovered by a camera, so when and if I see something out of the ordinary, I don't want there to be a doubt that something outside the camera's frame caused it. Like, if you were sitting down at a table and the camera's frame is on the top of the table and suddenly the table jumps. Well, if you were sitting there you could have done it on purpose to make it look scary, or it could happen on its own, but if you have crappy camerawork, then the event is useless. Do you understand?" he asked them.

"Yeah," Eddie and Jonathan said together.

"Okay, good. Now, if you look around, you'll see where I have the cameras set up. They cover this room completely, and when we put it all together on this screen…" he said as he woke the laptop up with his finger on the mouse pad, "…it offers a panoramic view of the entire room. I have one of these laptops set up in every room in the house, and I monitor each laptop individually. The cameras are motion sensitive, so they follow movement, and their autofocus is always on," he said, as he shut down the camera window and opened another window

"What I've done here is collected all the events of last night here in this one video stream. You're about to see some pretty interesting stuff. But I'll walk you through the events as they happen. Okay, let's see here," he said as he adjusted the glare of the screen by tilting it downward and turned the volume up. "All right, here we go. After you all left last night—" Byron was interrupted as a knock came at the door and Joey walked in, followed by his tech, Diane, and her bruised forehead.

"Sorry, didn't mean to disturb anything," Joey said as he came in with a heavy bag. Everyone's gazes went to him when he did so, and then turned to Jonathan and Eddie.

"You're fine, Doc. Come on in. We were having movie time. Think you might want to see this, as well. Byron, can we move this back and make room on the couch or on the floor so everyone can see?" Jonathan asked.

"Sure. Yeah. Here, help me push this back," Byron said.

Eddie leaned forward, and together they pushed the coffee table back and everyone slowly gathered around, taking a seat on the floor. Jonah flanked one end of the couch, with Maggie on the other side, and everyone stared at the screen. Byron leaned over and pressed play. Jonathan reached over and squeezed Diane's shoulder, giving her an apologetic squeeze, and she kindly patted his hand. All had been forgiven.

"As I was saying, after you all left last night, we set everything up as quickly as possible and got to work. Now, right here, you see me putting the cameras together in the kitchen, with Maggie helping me adjust them. Next, the cameras in the rest of the house were set up and this was the last room. If you'll notice, all the cabinets are shut and there we are leaving the room. Watch this," he said, pointing at the screen, and sure enough he and Maggie left the room and the camera angles began to switch from a standing tripod to mounted cameras pointing in all directions.

Suddenly, the camera angles stopped shifting and settled on one feed, which offered a standing view of the room. The image on the screen grew fuzzy and then sharp and then fuzzy again.

"What you're seeing happening here is the autofocus trying to see something," Byron said, and Jonathan concentrated on what he was seeing. And just like he had anticipated, after the camera stopped trying to focus, the cabinet door opened up on its own. First the pop of the magnet disengaging and the creak of the door as it opened all the way, showing the empty cabinet. He was expecting that even though there were murmurs around him, but something else caught his attention.

"Wait, Byron. Go back a couple of frames," Jonathan said. Byron reached over and thumbed the pad, doing as Jonathan asked. "Right there. Stop. Look at the kitchen window."

There, staring at them all, was a brown-haired man in the reflection. He was staring directly into the camera, his body barely visible, see-through, almost, but there.

"Holy shit. I never saw that. Dr. Spencer, get in here and take a look at this," Byron said, motioning for him to come closer. Paul leaned over, then looked at Jonathan.

"Who is that?" he said, his face going white.

"Maggie. Who is this?" Jonathan asked, knowing the answer but wanting her to say his name.

Maggie came closer with the aid of people moving so she could lean forward. Leaning down so she could see the computer screen better, she gasped. "My. God. That's Mark Pemberly," she said, straightening up and rubbing her arms. Jonathan could see the gooseflesh on her skin as she backed off.

Byron's eyes were wide. "That's an apparition?" he asked Paul, who looked over at him with a big grin.

"That's an apparition," Paul said with a nod.

Byron looked like he had wandered into a glen after having spent years chasing the end of a rainbow to find a whole valley of leprechauns playing around pots of gold.

Paul moved away and let the video continue. The image shifted to the living room, where Byron and the two other people Paul had brought with him the night before were talking in the corner of the room. Again the cameras rotated, showing the different angles before settling on a certain angle. This one was a view from the ceiling, and once more, the camera was struggling to focus. When it did, it began to move from a horizontal view to the point where the camera was directed on the floor, where the camera once again struggled to focus. Whatever it had "caught" was walking toward it and forced the camera to shift downward. On the video, you could hear Byron calling for Dr. Spencer and there was a verbal exchange.

The video began to shake and shimmy as if there was an earthquake. The video shifted back and forth, hard right and left, and then stopped and pulled up to face the rest of the group again, who were openly staring at the camera lens. The video shifted to another camera in the room, the free-standing one that showed what the group had seen. Again, the camera moved downward and pointed to the floor, but it didn't show anything underneath it or anyone having a hold on it while it was being shaken. It also showed the swivel of the camera moving upward once more and the group moving to the left, as if getting out of the way for whatever invisible entity was coming toward them.

"When this shot happened," the young blonde girl sitting near them said, "the strangest thing happened. I smelled liquor. Like...heavy in the air right next to me," she said, stifling a yawn. "And then it dissipated." She apologized after shaking her head. "Sorry, it's been a long night."

"No need to apologize at all," Eddie said with sympathy. "I am sure all of you are worn out."

"This here is upstairs. The camera is focused on your bedroom door. We stayed out of there for the most part, except to do some EVP," Byron said.

"Electronic voice phenomenon," Jonathan said, and Byron nodded with a grin. "Yeah, I watch *Ghost Hunters* too."

"It's the best one," Byron said.

"Hell, yeah, it is," Jonathan quipped.

"Anyway, look at this," he said. Again, the camera did its focusing thing and panned right to an empty hallway, and Jonathan could see the stairwell. It was empty, and suddenly the camera moved left and stopped in front of their bedroom door, which swung open and then shut violently.

"We all heard that and came running up. Now, mind you, these cameras had just been placed, so none of us were stationed at any point in the house yet. We were still getting our game plan nailed down when all this started happening," Paul said as the video ended.

"Is that all you have?" Jonathan asked.

Paul bristled. "Isn't that enough?"

Jonathan raised his hands. "I didn't mean it like that. What I meant to say is, did the activity continue?"

Byron shook his head. "No, that's all we got on video. Things seemed to calm down after that. But we got some really nice EVPs, and I think Samantha, here, can let you hear some of those," Byron said, moving his laptop away as the pretty young blonde took his spot. Of course, she had her own computer, and on the screen her program was open. Some type of audio mixer replaced the image of the desktop, and she cranked the volume all the way up.

"Okay. Just like on the show, we went through and did an EVP session. We asked questions such as: Who are you? What is your name? Why are you here? Things like that. Now, it's going to sound like we did these all back-to-back, and that is just because of the editing. I wanted to reduce the time it took between each sound we captured. But what you're going to hear is me and Dr. Spencer asking questions and then you can determine for yourself what *you* hear," she said, leaning forward and pressing play.

There was static at first, and then Paul's voice rang out so loudly, everybody jumped back.

"Sorry," Samantha said and reduced the volume. She restarted the sound bite and let it play.

"Is there anyone here with us?" Paul asked. There was nothing but dead air.

"Why are you here?" Samantha asked next.

There was static, but then Jonathan heard a whisper. "Play that back," he said, sitting forward and turning his right ear to the computer.

"Sure," she said and did so.

"Help us," Eddie said.

Jonathan nodded, and Samantha leaned over and put her hand up to Eddie for a high five. Smiling, Eddie humored her.

"That's what I thought it said too," she said. "This is incredible. Listen to this, and tell me if this doesn't make your skin crawl." She pressed play, and it was Paul again.

"Do you have a name?" he asked. Again static, but then the word was spoken clearly by a voice that seemed very far away. "Jonathan."

"Jesus," Maggie said.

"Your name is Jonathan?" Paul asked.

"No," said the same voice.

"That's Alan," Maggie said as she started to cry. "Oh my God. That poor baby."

Jonah walked around the coffee table and led her into the dining room.

"Okay, that's enough," Jonathan said and stood up. "Babe, can you go check on her?"

Eddie said he would, stood up, and followed the duo into the dining room, where he wrapped his arms around the older woman. Jonah kept his hand on her back the whole time.

"There is plenty more," Samantha said, sounding surprised, but Jonathan shook his head.

"I don't need to hear any more. We've been living it. All this does, as amazing as it is, is just verify that I am not out of my mind, and I thank you for it. Just answer a question for me: did the activity settle down for you as well?" he asked.

"Yeah. We got a few more things, including what sounded like a gunshot, but after that, it was dead air," she said, leaning back and rubbing her eyes.

"Okay. Joey, will you let Paul and the rest of them know what went on last night? I have some things I have to do," Jonathan said and then gingerly made his way through the crowd. He joined Eddie, Maggie, and Jonah in the dining room. Maggie had calmed down quite a bit and was wiping at her eyes and sniffling while Eddie murmured comforting words in her ear.

"Maggie?" Jonathan asked gently, taking her arm.

Her eyes were watery, and she looked at him as if she were shocked he was there. "What?" she asked.

"We're going to help Alan. Eddie and me. Mark too. But I need your help," he said.

"What? How can you help them? They're dead!" she cried, tearing up again.

"I have an idea, but I need you to trust me, as I only have a few in here. If you have any mirrors at your house, I want you to bring them here. I want any and everything you might have of Alan's or Mark's, no matter what it is. Pictures, letters, anything you might have."

She nodded. "I have a few things, and some I wanted to show you anyway. Jonah, can you help me?"

"Sure," he said happily, which caused Jonathan to smile. *Someone is smitten*, he thought. *Good.*

"Can I also borrow one of your helpers?" she asked. "I have lots of mirrors."

"Sure. Go ask Paul," Jonathan instructed, and she and Jonah walked back into the living room.

Jonathan reached out, grabbed Eddie by the arms, and rubbed them. "Hey, babe."

"Hey, babe. What do you plan on doing?" Eddie asked.

"I am going to try and contact them. Awake this time, and see if it doesn't keep me from being a zombie. See if I can control it," Jonathan said.

"Then what?"

"I'm not sure. I'll figure it out when we get there," Jonathan said. Eddie started to protest, but Jonathan put his finger on his lips. "I've got you to hold on to me," he said, lowering his hand. Eddie nodded, leaned up, and kissed Jonathan on the mouth.

When the kiss broke, Eddie asked, "What if Mark gets violent with you again?"

"I'm a big strong man. I'll be waiting for him," Jonathan said. He was more worried about Fear making a cameo, but he didn't say anything about it.

"I love you," Eddie whispered.

"I love you back," Jonathan said and opened his arms for Eddie to slide into them. Jonathan felt anxiety in the pit of his stomach and the annoying voice in his head was screaming for him to reconsider. But there was no turning back. It was time to stop running from the past—his and Alan's.

***

Jonathan sat on the back porch with a cigarette burning between his fingers. The sunlight and the heat of the day had eased with the premature twilight brought about by the dark and ominous clouds bearing down on them. Anxiety tried to surface, along with bile-green fear, but Jonathan breathed in slowly and let it out the same way. Lightning flashed in the distance, illuminating the bruised sky like a spotlight searching in vain for a long-lost someone. When he closed his eyes, he could feel the energy of the house toying at the edges of his mind, and he was actively trying to keep it at bay for the time being.

He didn't know what could happen, and he feared not only for the safety of everyone in the house but also for his mind. How much of this could one person handle before they burned out? How far could this go before his mind broke? And what would Eddie do if he were to fragment and he disappeared between the cracks? Another roll of thunder rumbled, making the ground, the porch, and Jonathan vibrate.

He took another drag on his cigarette, and then exhaled slowly, letting his mind drift back to his childhood, which he had locked away in a box, never to see the light of day again. Mentally, he was sifting through memories as far back as he could remember and cautiously experiencing each one again. Each painful story—rejection, fear, violent tempers, late nights, and crying in his bed when everything was said and done—tore at his heart a little. He felt so deeply for Alan and what he had been through, but he felt for Mark, as well, and he reasoned that would be the only way to resolve this.

The backdoor opened and heavy footfalls walked down the stairs next to him. Jonathan moved over to the side to allow Jonah to pass. He looked up when Jonah laid a heavy hand on his shoulder, giving him a sturdy pat as he made his way through and on to the patio below them. Jonathan rested his head against the railing.

"How ya doin', Jonah?" he asked before taking the final drag on his cigarette and then butting it out.

"Oh, fair to middlin', I guess. This storm is going to be a nasty one," Jonah said, putting his hands in his pockets as he looked up into the black sky. The wind had started to pick up, and dust was flying in the air.

"Yeah," Jonathan said.

"Maggie told me about the goings-on in this house, and about the boy and his father. Nasty business, that," Jonah said.

"Yeah, it really is," he replied, wondering what Jonah was getting at. But a pause had come in the conversation, with Jonah looking slightly uncomfortable and hesitant. He glanced at Jonathan and then down at the ground as he shuffled his big feet. Jonathan couldn't help but smile. That was, until Jonah said what he did and touched his soul.

"I've got four kids, Jonathan. They are all grown and gone now, with only one living near home these days. They all have families and children of their own. But I remember when they were small, and my wife and I were starting out. There were good times and there were times that weren't so good, but our house was filled with love. My wife and I made sure our kids knew we loved them, and even when we disciplined them, we avoided doing it while we were angry. We never wanted to frighten them or make them afraid to come to us for anything. And they weren't." He chuckled as he sat down next to Jonathan. "Sometimes I wish they had been with some things. Sex was an interesting subject. Heh."

Jonah put a big hand on Jonathan's leg and stared him right in the eye with such intensity Jonathan blinked several times. "I don't know what you've been through. I don't know what weight you carry on your shoulders, but let me tell you, as a father, sometimes burdens get misplaced on us from people who mistakenly offloaded their mess onto us."

"What did Eddie tell you?" Jonathan said in a choked whisper.

Jonah shook his head. "Nothin'. I've just been around the block several times in my life, and I've seen enough to know when someone is under a weight they didn't make for themselves. You have a wonderful husband, a great home. You've made an awesome career for yourself, as has Eddie. But I am going to give you some fatherly advice: when this is over, when all this is done, stop looking backward. Life isn't lived in that direction. Your future isn't *in that direction.* It's forward, out into the horizon ahead of you. Stop clinging to dead things—they'll drag you down with them and will destroy everything you two have worked so hard to create. You've got a man in there that loves you. He's in the here and now."

In a trembling voice, Jonathan asked, "What if this thing doesn't go away? What if I am stuck with this?" He placed his palm on his own forehead.

Jonah moved his hand from Jonathan's thigh, put it around his shoulders and pulled him closer. "Then you find a way to deal with it. Hide it away or use it. The choice is yours."

Jonathan nodded and wiped his eyes with the backs of his hand, realizing suddenly that the fear had been replaced with a steely resolve. "Thank you, Jonah."

"Yup," he said as the back door opened. He lowered his arm.

"Babe?" Eddie called.

Jonathan cleared his throat and turned his head. "Yeah?"

"We're ready," Eddie said with his head cocked curiously to the side.

Jonathan stood. "So am I."

Jonah stood up along with him, and they both walked up the steps with Jonah heading into the house. They had moved at just the right time, as big, fat raindrops began to fall, slowly at first, and then the sky opened up. The storm had arrived.

Eddie wrapped his arms around Jonathan's waist. "What were you men talking about?"

Jonathan leaned in and kissed the tip of Eddie's nose. "Oh, the future. You ready?"

"No. I'm scared, Jonathan," Eddie said, putting his head on Jonathan's chest.

Jonathan wrapped his arms around him. "Nothing to be scared of. We're just going to help two people find their way back, is all."

***

"So what are the mirrors for?" Paul asked as everyone began to take seats around the table. Outside, all hell had broken loose, and they had quickly shut windows and turned the air back on to keep the inside from getting soaked. The thunder clamored so loud it made people jump or duck reflexively.

"Jesus," Eddie whispered.

Samantha pulled out her cell phone to check the weather. "This isn't going to end anytime soon either. This is a massive cell."

Jonathan sat down and took a few deep breaths and tried to concentrate on the sound of the rain, the steadiness of it, and the power of it. Joey started attaching fMRI equipment to Jonathan as Diane took his vitals. She didn't seem the least bit worried and even patted his shoulder when she finished. "There are volumes of myths and legends about mirrors being able to reflect the soul, capture the soul, and trap the soul, etcetera. Having seen the reflection of Mark in the window, it made me think that perhaps

I could use the mirrors in some way. I am not sure how yet. We'll have to see," Jonathan said, opening his eyes.

"I brought what you asked for, Jonathan, along with the photo album, a letter Mark wrote to his son that I helped him write when he sobered up, and the letter you two found," Maggie said, handing the stuff over to him. Jonathan took it all and set it in front of him, then started going through it. He opened up the album to a picture of all three of them together and found the letter to God Alan had written, and before he set the last letter down, he read the curled yellow page.

Dear Alan,

I have sat here at my desk on occasion to write you, on several occasions, for the past six months, ever since Wells told me he knew where you were. I have started, stopped, thrown away, and restarted letter after letter, trying to think of what to say to you. The only thing I can say is how sorry I am. I know that doesn't make up for the things I did and said to you. I know I can't take those things back, and as I sit in this empty house, sober for the first time in more than five years, the silence is deafening. So I am not going to try and explain to you why I let myself become the monster that I was. Instead, I hope to explain to you the steps I've taken to get better. First of all, I entered a twelve-step program. I am sober. I go to meetings at the local Methodist church I attend in Clay Center. The minister stopped by the house one day, and he told me about an outpatient program through the hospital in Junction City. I entered rehab and did a three-month stint there. The withdrawal was terrible, and I thought I was going to die. I wanted to. As I sobered up, the realization of what I had done nearly drove me mad and made me want to drink that much more. I should have protected you. I should have been there for you. I lost a wife, but you lost your mother, and I am sorry.

These are my sins against you: I hit you. I screamed at you. I called you names. I blamed you for the death of your mother. I blamed you for my own misery. I made you cry. I made you afraid of me. I made you hate me.

One of my steps is to apologize to those I have wronged, but I plead with you to understand it is more than just that. I want to be your father again. I want to be your dad again. I know I don't deserve it. I know I am not worthy of it. And if that isn't possible, I would like to ask that you forgive me. I am not the man I used to be. I am the man I was before the bottle. I am the man who held you as an infant, who got up in the middle of the night to feed, and change, and burp you. I am the man who taught you how to ride your bicycle. I am the man who dropped you off at school and picked you up. I am the man who held your momma's hand as she held yours, and we walked together as a family. That is who I am now. I am sorry it took you leaving me here alone in my own vomit for me to realize this. You were and always will be my proudest accomplishment.

Your loving father,

Mark Pemberly

P.S. The home number is still the same.

"Hmm. Read that, babe," Jonathan said, handing over the letter to Eddie, who read it quickly.

"He did get better," Eddie said in wonder.

"Yes. He made great progress toward the end," Maggie said sadly.

"Okay, everyone ready?" Jonathan asked. "Joey, are you ready?"

"Yes. Your vitals are normal. Your fMRI readout is as normal as...well...your abnormality. Your frontal lobe is highly active again, just like before."

"Okay. Eddie, hang tight to me. Paul? How are you doing?" Jonathan asked.

"The cameras are all operational and recording," Paul said, adjusting the last one.

"All cameras in the house are working," Byron called from the living room, where he and Samantha were monitoring both visual and audio. Outside, the wind howled and rain slammed against the windows in the dining room, making the scene incredibly creepy given the fact that Jonathan's head was hooked up to electrodes and he had a Ouija board in front of him.

"Jonathan, what are you attempting to do?" Eddie asked nervously.

"Well, every time I've gone into a trance like that, it's been involuntary, either in my sleep or awake. What I am going to try to do is control it this time by seeking them out consciously. I think that maybe, if I go in awake and cognizant of what is going on, I might be able to control the situation better," Jonathan said, leaning over to kiss Eddie on the cheek.

"Wait!" Eddie said when a lightning strike caused the lights to flicker. He stood up, ran over to the cabinet, and retrieved several thick candles and candle holders and placed them on the table. "Just in case," he said.

"Good thinking. Okay. Here we go."

Jonathan said and closed his eyes and took a deep breath. In and out, in and out, slowly, he began to open his mind, seeking out the energy in the house. He reached out for the planchette on the table and let his hands rest loosely over it.

***

Eddie sat worriedly next to Jonathan. If his professors could see him now, they would have thrown him out of class for sure for tossing out everything he had ever known to take part in this… this…witch doctor madness. He would have burst out laughing had this happened a few weeks ago. Now, his stomach clenched as the seconds passed and Jonathan sat there as the rain pelted the window. Everyone was watching Jonathan intently, leaning forward and resting their arms on the table.

Eddie was about to say something when he heard one of the cameras swivel. He jerked his head up. It was the one nearest the kitchen, and he closed his eyes when he heard that damn cabinet open again. Everyone heard it except Jonathan, whose face had crumpled into a frown of concentration. Breathless minutes passed, and everyone began to relax. The camera didn't swivel back into position, however, and everyone's gazes were glued on it.

They all turned back when the planchette slid across the cardboard in circles. Jonathan cocked his head to the side as if listening to something intently. Sweat had begun to form on his forehead and upper lip, although the air in the room had cooled considerably. Jonathan's face relaxed suddenly as well as his body, and the swinging planchette stopped.

"Is he…" Maggie began but stopped when Jonathan's hand shot over the first letter.

"H," Eddie said.

"E," Maggie said.

"L," she and Eddie said together.

"P."

"Help," she said.

Eddie's heart sank.

"U," she said.

"S," Eddie mouthed as Maggie said the letter.

"Help us," Jonathan whispered.

He was there.

All three cameras moved their lenses inward and pointed at the table simultaneously. Dr. Spencer's face went white as a chill cascaded past him to settle over the table. Jonathan's head lowered and his arms slid off the table to rest at his sides. Eddie's heart was thudding so hard, he felt like he was going to be sick.

Jonathan's head came up with a snap and his eyes opened, causing Maggie to shriek and cover her mouth. His eyes were rolled up in their sockets and his jaw went slack with a popping noise that made Eddie cringe and recoil in fear. Jonathan sat up straight as a board, his back painfully erect, and then something incredible happened.

***

Jonathan found himself standing in the dark, like the transition place they went to when Alan had shown him the scenes from his life. He couldn't see a thing in front of him nor in any direction. There was no light, no nothing. Just emptiness.

"Alan?" Jonathan called into the darkness. He could speak, and the sound of his voice startled him. Last time, he couldn't speak, nor could he move. He took a cautious step forward and found solid ground. His confidence grew.

"Alan!" Jonathan called louder.

"W-w-who's there?" cried a timid voice in the void. It was Alan.

Jonathan's heart swelled. "It's me. Jonathan," he called out. "Alan, come see me. You don't have to be afraid, pal. I'm here to help."

"Why did you leave me, then? I was trying to talk to you," he said accusingly.

"Because I didn't know what you were trying to say. I had to put a little distance between us so your words wouldn't be so loud. But it's okay. I'm here now," Jonathan said.

A light illuminated the darkness so brightly that Jonathan had to shield his eyes from it for a moment until he adjusted to it. A figure approached him, the grown-up version of Alan, and the light behind him snuffed out. Alan was illuminated, but he wasn't ghostly. No, he was solid as any other human being Jonathan had ever seen.

"Why are you back here?" Alan asked. "He tried to kill you."

"I came back because you and your father need help," Jonathan said.

Alan shrugged in a noncommittal way. "I don't know how to reach him. I've tried everything, but all I get to see is my whole life repeated over and over again every day, and I can't intercede. And then he dies. Every day. It's the same thing over and over again. I figured I would go mad long ago, but even the blessed release that would bring has been denied me. I'm in hell," he said sadly.

"Then why are you doing it to yourself?" Jonathan asked.

"What?" Alan asked. "I'm not. I have no control over this."

"Yes, you do. Your father isn't doing this to you. You're doing this *to you*. You think you deserve it. You're punishing yourself," Jonathan said, walking forward. Alan took a step back.

"These memories, Alan, they're yours," Jonathan said. "Not your father's. He's here but he's suffering in his own torment. That's why you can't reach him. Broken hearts can't see each other, remember?" Jonathan asked.

"No. No. That can't be true," Alan said angrily, shaking his head.

"Yes, it is, Alan. It's true," Jonathan said, reaching out and taking his hand. Just as he suspected: here Alan was solid.

Alan was shocked at the touch and tried to recoil, but Jonathan wouldn't let him. Instead, he grabbed Alan's other hand and clasped them both in his.

"Why are you doing this to me?" Alan cried out.

"Because it's your turn to see," Jonathan said. And just like that, the darkness melted away. They found themselves in another bedroom, one of the far back bedrooms, the one with the super pink walls. Jonathan walked at Alan's side, but kept hold of one hand. He held it firmly in his own grasp. Eddie had done this with him, figuratively, throughout their entire relationship. Never letting go, never giving him a moment to stumble, solid, secure, and it was the only way he knew how to reach Alan.

Before them, lying in bed reading a book, was a very young Mark. His hair was brown and rich and his face stubbly from his beard starting to grow. He flipped a page and then kept reading, the bedside light sending a rich glow into the otherwise darkened bedroom. Next to Mark, his wife stirred and moaned. She turned over and sat up, her thick brown hair done up in curlers, her nightgown clinging to her shoulders.

"Ugh. Dammit," she said, wincing.

Mark set his book in his lap and sat up straighter, moving to touch her shoulder. "What is it? Are you okay?"

She shook her head. Sweat had begun to pop out on her forehead. Through clenched teeth, she groaned and then her eyes grew wide. She shot her hands underneath the covers, and when she brought them up, her fingers were covered in blood. She quickly pulled the covers back to discover she was bleeding excessively between her legs. Her nightgown was soaked in the front.

"Oh God," Mark muttered. He jumped out of bed and ran around to the other side of the bed to his wife, who had begun to cry.

"It just won't stop, Mark. I can't make it stop. Something's wrong!" she cried.

"I told you to go to the doctor a month ago," he cried, obviously afraid of what he was seeing. "Get dressed. I'll call Maggie over. We're going right now," Mark said, walking her out the door and down the hallway. Jonathan and Alan didn't follow.

"Why are you showing me this?" Alan asked.

But before he could answer another question, the scene shifted. The darkness of the room was replaced by the harsh white light of a doctor's office. Standing in the corner, still holding onto each other, Alan and Jonathan watched as Mark and Beverly received the news from a middle-aged doctor sitting at a mahogany desk. His white lab coat hung open, revealing a plaid shirt and tie. He wore his white hair combed neatly back on his high forehead, and he rested his hands on the desk in front of him.

Mark Pemberly's eyes were wide and his face was almost as gray as steel. His wife's head was bowed and her shoulders slumped. She kept wiping at her eyes with a tissue in one hand and clutched Mark's hand tightly with the other.

"The cancer has metastasized and spread all throughout your abdomen, Mrs. Pemberly. It's aggressive, but we can be aggressive too. I am ordering a very heavy round of chemotherapy and radiation to shrink the tumors. After a few months of weekly treatment, we'll take another look to see if they shrank enough to be operable, and we can then perform a hysterectomy. Hopefully that will get rid of the source of the cancer and let us fight the rest of it off," he said confidently. To Jonathan, it sounded fake, and it must have sounded that way to Beverly as well, as she smirked and raised her head.

"Hey, Doc, let's cut the bullshit, shall we? What's the prognosis if it goes untreated?" she asked, her voice like steel.

The older man nodded once as he leaned forward. "It isn't good. Without the chemo and radiation, I can only see you living another six months. With it, if it responds well, we can do what we have to do. But I have to say, that even with chemo and radiation, maybe a year, possibly a year and a half," he said solemnly. Beverly began to cry and leaned against Mark who was stone-faced but bravely trying to comfort her. The doctor said he would give them a few minutes alone and left the office, shutting the door behind him.

"Momma?" Alan asked, trying to move forward. He was weeping, but like Jonathan had experienced, he couldn't move.

The scene changed yet again, and they found themselves transitioning from the light to the dark. They were standing on the tile floor of the kitchen. The man who'd worn a brave face in the doctor's office was sitting on the cool tile floor in his pajama bottoms, barefoot and bare chested, rocking back and forth. He sobbed so hard, his shoulders shook. His face contorted in pain.

Jonathan looked around, and on the table, bottles upon bottles of prescription pills were displayed, and every time Mark looked up at them, he would break into a fresh bout of crying.

The wretched sound was terrible to hear; it was the sound of a heart that was being broken before their eyes.

***

Eddie's eyes were wide with wonder, as were everyone else's as they looked at the wall of mirrors. Every time a scene changed, a mirror would darken to solid black, no reflection, and then a light would shine through and Eddie could see Alan and Jonathan standing side by side in a mirror as a new scene played out in front of them. It was soundless, but one didn't have to hear anything to understand what was going on. The mirror showed everything.

Instinctively, Eddie looked behind him. Jonathan was still in the same state, with his eyes wide open and his jaw slack. His vitals were elevated but not dangerously high. However, the fMRI was brightly lit as his brain registered activity all over the place.

Jonathan stared blankly at them, and his mouth worked with silent words. Maggie sat next to him, wiping the drool that slid down his chin. Jonathan didn't react to her touch. She looked up at Eddie and nodded, giving him a brief smile, and then she turned her attention to another mirror that had darkened. She pointed at it with her finger, and Eddie turned to see it, tapping Paul on the shoulder as he did so.

"It's another one. This is incredible. Byron, are you getting this?" Paul hissed at him quickly.

"Yeah. It's recording. My God," he said, looking down at the minirecorder in his hands. He was moving it along as each mirror opened up a new scene like a bootlegger in a theater.

Eddie closed his eyes and silently prayed to God to give his husband strength. When he opened his eyes, he saw wonders happen again.

***

It was much later now, perhaps a year or two, but they were back in the bedroom of Mark and Beverly. A nurse brushed past them to change out the IV that was attached to a very frail arm atop the bedcovers. Little Alan was standing in the room with a very young Maggie holding his shoulders. A woman Jonathan didn't recognize but assumed was Maggie's mother stood next to them, and another doctor was leaning over the fragile woman in the bed. She was barely recognizable, as thin as she had become, and as much as her body had curled up as if she were disintegrating from the inside out. The doctor had a stethoscope in his ears and had it down on her chest, listening to different parts of her bosom.

Mark Pemberly was sitting next to the chair with his hands in his shockingly gray hair. He had aged a decade in two years and had put on several pounds, probably from the drinking that had begun in earnest.

The doctor stood up, lowered the stethoscope out from around his ears, and rested it against his chest. He moved over to Mark and placed a hand on his shoulder. Mark raised his gaze to the man, misery awash over his face. The doctor shook his head and held up a hand for the nurse to stop what she was doing.

"Mr. Pemberly, it's almost time," he said sadly. Mark nodded, turned his head to young Alan, and gestured him to come over. Older Alan and Jonathan turned their heads to see a timid boy slowly walk to his father's side and look up at him uncertainly.

"I remember this," older Alan said. Jonathan squeezed his hand, and Alan squeezed back.

"You're not alone," Jonathan said reassuringly.

"I know," Alan replied.

Mark looked down at his son and picked him up in his arms. The boy had grown quite a bit in the past two years, but he was still a little guy.

"What's wrong with Momma?" the boy asked. "Is she going to heaven now?"

Mark tried to speak, couldn't, and turned away for a second. He then nodded with watery eyes. He set the child down beside the bed. Little Alan stood there silently for a moment before reaching out to touch his mother on the forehead. Behind them, Maggie and her mother clung to each other, crying.

"Momma? It's okay. You can go to heaven now. Ms. Maggie said you were going to be going there because that's where angels go. I'll try and take care of Daddy, and I'll talk to you every night before bedtime."

The two women behind them wept openly now, and they clung to each other like two swimmers afraid a shark was going to attack at any moment. The heart monitor's beeping slowed to irregularity and stopped all together.

The darkness returned, and they stood alone in that in-between place with only Alan to light their way.

"Please let me go. Please," Alan pleaded, trying to pull away. "This is worse than what I've been going through. You said you were here to help. This isn't helping!" he cried, trying to jerk free of Jonathan's grip.

"You can't hide from the truth, Alan. It isn't doing you any good. You've been blinded by your own pain," Jonathan said, hanging on to him tightly.

"My *pain*? The son of a bitch beat me! What are you talking about, my *pain*!" Alan screamed as he pulled harder.

Jonathan grew angry. "I'm talking about this!" Jonathan yelled, and suddenly they were in a hospital room. The air was pungent with the smell of sweat and vomit. Alan stopped struggling almost instantly as he looked over Jonathan's shoulder. Jonathan turned to see what he was staring at.

"Dad?" he asked. A much older Mark was lying on the bed, mumbling incoherently and shaking. An IV ran down from a pole next to his bed to a vein in his hand as saline solution was pumped in along with medication to take the edge off.

"What's wrong with him?" Alan cringed.

Mark began to call Alan's name loudly as a large black man in white scrubs leaned over the bed and smoothed back his hair.

"It's gonna be all right, Mr. Pemberly. It's gonna be all right. You just relax now, man. Let that medicine work. You're gonna get through this."

"I want my son! I heard my son speak! Alan? *Alan!*" he cried out. His voice was unbearable in this hospital room, which echoed the words. Alan went to speak again, and Jonathan held up his hand and shook his head.

"Shhh. Mark. Alan will be around when you get better, remember? This is why you're doing it. You told me so when you checked in. You're doin' this for your boy. You hired the detective and everything. Now you just relax, big guy, otherwise you're gonna give yourself a heart attack. Let that medicine work!" the big man said, resting his massive hands on Mark's shoulders. Mark seemed to pay attention to what he said and did begin to relax.

But they never saw the end of it. Suddenly they stood in the middle of a crowded bar. A man had just finished speaking, and people clapped and cheered. At the end of the bar sat a well-composed and nicely dressed Mark Pemberly.

"He's in a bar!" Alan exclaimed. "He…wait…something's not right."

"Noticed that, did you?" Jonathan asked, slightly amused. It was a bar, but there was no alcohol to be seen. There was plenty of soda, coffee, and vending machines with snacks. The next person who came up to the microphone wore a black priest's outfit with a white collar.

"Next up, we have a newcomer. Everyone welcome Mark," the man said.

"Hi, Mark," the room exclaimed at once. Mark looked uncertain as he shuffled up on stage. The priest gestured to the spot for Mark to replace him as he stepped away from the microphone, and Mark reached out for it. It squealed and reverberated through the room, and everyone winced.

He cleared his throat. "Hi. Like Father Tim said, my name is Mark Pemberly. And I…I…I wasn't supposed to give you my last name. Oh, Jesus, sorry. I…I…just say it. I'm an alcoholic," he stuttered.

"It's okay, brother," yelled one man in the crowd, which made Mark jump a bit.

"Uh...thanks...I guess. Several years ago, my wife was diagnosed with terminal cancer, and that's when I started drinking," Mark began.

Jonathan watched Alan's face as he stared at his father in wonder.

"I...uh...got really bad. After she died, my son, my...my Alan... I started b-b-beating him. I did this a lot. I don't know why. I think I somehow blamed him for her being sick. She... Beverly...was my whole world, and so was he, but I lost that somehow. Well, after several years of being hit, the little guy grew up and became a big guy. One evening, after I'd been out at the bar after work, I came home drunk, as usual, and started hitting my son. He did something he had never done before. He fought back. Little shit broke my nose. Heh," he said, absentmindedly touching it and then putting his hand down. He took one deep breath and then another and then another.

"In a rage, I tried to really hurt him. But, thank God, I couldn't get to him fast enough. He ran upstairs to his room and shimmied down a tree and ran away. That night, I drank so much, that I vomited and slept in it. I wanted to die. I had done what I had set out to do: my wife was gone and now my son was as well. The only thing I had left to remember my wife by was no longer in my life. I had been thinking about suicide for a long time, ever since Beverly passed, and the morning I woke up in my own puke, I had every intention of doing it...had Father Tim not come to the door. Now I am four months sober and am starting to look for my son...to apologize... Thank you," he said hurriedly, red-faced, and then he left the microphone and went back to his place at the bar. Several people stood up at once and came over to him to pat him on the shoulder or shake his hand.

"I never knew," Alan whispered in awe.

***

The machine that monitored Jonathan's vitals beeped once, making everyone jump. Joey walked away from the mirrors and looked at it, then turned to Eddie.

465

"His blood pressure is still climbing. He's heading toward dangerous levels. He can't stay like this much longer. He's one fifty over one hundred," he said, taking out his stethoscope. He put it to Jonathan's chest and listened.

"His heart's hammering away in there," Joey said.

Eddie walked over to take a looked at the monitor. "I don't know what to do."

"Remember how you talked to him before to get him to come back? If this goes on much longer, give that a try," Joey said. Eddie nodded and sat down next to Jonathan, taking his hand. It was limp in his, but warm to the touch. Eddie rubbed it with his other hand and prayed this would end soon.

Everyone jumped as they heard a crash upstairs.

Samantha, who had stayed in the living room to monitor the laptop, called, "The three doors upstairs, one of them opened. It's the center one," she said.

"That was Mark and Beverly's room," Maggie whispered. Heavy footfalls started almost at once. *Boom. Boom. Boom. Boom.* They were coming closer to the stairwell, each step determined and angry-sounding. *Boom. Boom. Boom.* Paul hollered for Samantha to come into the dining room. She didn't need much encouragement.

"It's Mark," Maggie whispered fearfully. "I'd know those steps anywhere."

Eddie turned to Jonathan, and in a determined voice said, "Hey, babe. Alan's dad just showed up. You might want to hurry it up in there," he said. "Come on, babe. Listen to me."

Boom. Boom. Boom.

"Oh, God. He's on the landing now. He's coming down the stairs," Maggie said.

Jonah pushed her behind him as another mirror went dark and the smell of liquor flooded the room.

***

Suddenly the two of them shifted back to the darkness, this time without Jonathan piloting them. Something was wrong. In

Jonathan's head, he heard Eddie calling to him. Someone was coming. Someone...

"Jonathan, what is it? What's...oh no," Alan said, his voice rising an octave.

"What is it?" Jonathan asked.

"It's my father. He's here!" Alan said. "Go. Come on. We have to hide."

"It isn't your father," Jonathan said.

"What? I've been hiding from him all these years. I know what he looks like. Come on!" Alan cried.

"No," Jonathan said and pulled Alan back. "No. It isn't your father. Your father is in the same state you are: dead, but lost. It's the same thing that has been keeping you both imprisoned."

"What...what are you talking about?" Alan asked.

"Alan, it's fear. It's a spirit of fear. And you have to stand up to it," Jonathan said.

"What? No! It'll hurt me. It'll hurt me like it did before. It's my father. He'll be drunk. He'll beat me. Let me go!" Alan cried.

"No, Alan. No. Your father can't hurt you. Not anymore. You're both beyond that now. You two have been hurting yourselves because of this guy. But you have to stand up to him. You have to stand your ground or this nightmare will never end!" he said.

"But I'm afraid," Alan cried.

"Don't be. You stood up to it once, remember? You punched it dead in the nose when you were a boy. You faced your fear and found freedom, Alan. You can do it again. This time, I'll be here to—" Jonathan was cut off before he could complete the sentence. The room melted away, and Jonathan now stood alone in the house he'd grown up in.

Well, not actually alone. The blow came before he could register what was happening, and he hit the floor in a daze. His mind swirled and spun as his head hit the hard red-tiled floor. He saw stars. Above him, he could hear people screaming and the sound of slapping and crying out. It took him a second to clear his vision, but when it came back, he looked underneath the counter and saw something that stopped his heart.

Jonathan David saw himself. His five-year-old self, anyway, who had crawled underneath the empty section of counter, nursing his aching head and crying from suffering the same blow Jonathan had suffered long ago. Jonathan was stunned by what he saw as the little boy wailed in both fear and pain—his porcelain baby skin broken by the chicken pox he had begun to get over. It would be the first of two rounds, he thought to himself with a smile that was completely out of place given the situation. He was about to stand up when the little boy looked at him, directly at him, in confusion. Then the room shifted underneath him.

This time he was in the car, in the blue station wagon he'd hated so much. They were on their way home, and Dad was screaming at them. Jonathan was sitting in the backseat between his brothers, watching his thirteen-year-old-self getting punched in the head, but this time something was different. His father hit the brakes when he saw Jonathan in the backseat, staring at him.

"What the hell..."

The scene shifted once more, and there was his fifteen-year-old self, pants down, leaning over a bed getting the bejesus beaten out of him by his father while his mother encouraged him from the dining room. Jonathan knelt to look his young self in the eyes. The fifteen-year-old registered shock at first and didn't cry out in pain as the next swat with the wooden board came down on his back. His ass and back would be bruised for weeks, to the point where he couldn't sit or lie down properly.

"Hey, kid. Hit him." Jonathan showed his younger self his balled-up fist. He planted it in his own hand, and the message registered in the young man, whose eyes had turned from hot pain and fear to cold rage. The old man had to take a breath, he had winded himself, and young Jonathan, fat, pimply faced, timid, and kind, stood up.

He reached down, pulled up his pants and turned.

"Hey, I didn't tell you to—" his incensed father said, but he was cut off as Jonathan landed his fist square on his mouth. Jonathan hit, and he hit hard, sending daddy dearest flying backward into the corner between the closet door and the bedroom window, a look of total shock and disbelief on his face. Older Jonathan jumped in the air and cheered as he clapped, his hands high above his head.

The boy leaned over and asked, "How does it feel, you son of a bitch?" And then he stood up and fixed his pants with his shocked and bloodied father looking at him in fear. That younger Jonathan walked out of the room past his mother as she backed up in fright, and then he limped out of sight.

The room shifted again, and now Jonathan was standing in Alan's room. The window was shut, and Alan was up against the glass, his eyes shut in fear and a very drunk and very angry man standing over him.

"Hey, asshole," Jonathan bellowed loudly. The Mark-looking thing spun around. His face was contorted in a mask of fury, his eyes red and glowing—a demonic presence. Jonathan pulled his fist back as far as he could and then nailed him square in the face. The Mark thing stumbled backward, and Alan dodged out of the way with a look of shock and elation on his face when he saw Jonathan standing there.

"I softened him up for you, kid. Have at him," Jonathan said.

That was all Alan needed. The creature recovered quickly but not soon enough. Alan landed a blow to the side of its head. And then another one on the other side, back and forth, back and forth, he wailed on the thing as it raised its hands, trying to deflect the blows. Suddenly it vanished, and Jonathan reached out to grab Alan before he ran into the wall.

The kid was breathing hard and grinning from ear to ear. "I think it's over."

"Not yet, it isn't," Jonathan said, and his words registered in Alan's eyes.

"Dad," Alan said simply, and the room slid out from underneath them again.

This time they were standing near a pool of vomit on the living-room floor. They heard heavy footfalls upstairs and the sounds of wailing and sobbing.

F.E. FEELEY JR.

"Oh my God. The gun," Alan said as he shot up the stairway. Jonathan was hot on his heels. They'd reached the landing when Alan began to call. "Dad? Dad! I'm home. Don't do it! *Dad!*" he screamed as he made his way down the hallway. He tried the door: it was locked. Alan fought against it hard, then backed up and was getting ready to shoulder it hard when the shot rang out.

"*No!*" he screamed and plowed into the solid structure. It gave with a splintering crack.

Jonathan was right behind him, in time to see the spirit of fear hovering over the body of the dead man. Alan screamed and had started to bend over his father's lifeless body when Jonathan grabbed him and turned him toward himself, holding him close. Jonathan was shocked as well, and dismayed. He'd thought they could beat it and stop this endless cycle. He was horrified and brokenhearted for the young man who wept in his arms.

"Get out of my house," Alan cried.

Jonathan tried to protest, but Alan cut him off. "I'm not talking to you."

The spirit of fear still hovered above them, and Alan turned in Jonathan's arms to face it. "I'm talking to you, you rotten son of a bitch. I know exactly who you are and what you're doing here. You're no longer wanted, do you understand? You're no longer in control of us! *Get out of my goddamn house!*" Alan screamed.

The spirit shimmied and roared in pain and fear and, just like that, winked out of existence. Alan, weak and brokenhearted, wept onto Jonathan's chest.

"Alan?" came a voice behind them. Alan stopped weeping and instantly broke free of Jonathan's hold. The body on the floor was gone as the voice came from behind them.

"Dad?" Alan said, poking his head around Jonathan. "*Dad!*"

"Oh My God! *Alan!*" Mark Pemberly cried, opening his arms and rushing forward. Jonathan stepped back and leaned his head on the doorjamb, and with a smile on his face, he watched the happy reunion.

Mark held his son out to look at him. "I've been looking for you for so long! Where were you?" he asked, confused.

"I was looking for you." Alan replaced Jonathan with his father.

"Oh, son, oh, my son, I never meant to hurt you. I am sorry. I am so, so sorry." Mark wept openly. Jonathan watched the reunion with a smile so big his face hurt.

"It's okay, Dad. It's over. It's all over now. I know everything. It's all over," Alan said, hugging the man once again. "There is nothing to be afraid of anymore. Not anymore."

Mark nodded and for the first time looked at Jonathan. "Are you the one that helped Alan come home? You don't look like the investigator I hired," he said, confused.

"I'm not," Jonathan said, and then he cleared his throat and wiped his face. He was smiling from ear to ear, and his heart felt so full, it was about to burst. "Alan came and asked me for help to find his dad. He helped me out too, by showing me how to find my way back home. You've got a brave young man there," Jonathan said.

"Yeah, he is. Killer right hook too," Mark said, and Jonathan laughed.

"Yeah. Well. You guys should be all right now," Jonathan said.

"Are you going to be able to find your way back?" Alan asked, breaking away from his father to stand in front of him. Jonathan nodded.

"Oh yeah. I can find my way home again. I have someone waiting on me back there," he replied. "Go find your mom. Mr. Pemberly, go find your wife. I think you'll find she has been waiting an awful long time for you two."

Alan nodded, reached for Jonathan, and hugged him. "Thank you so much."

Jonathan began to cry as he wrapped the young man in his embrace. He had never in his life thought things would work out this way, but the kid had saved him and forced him to do what he had never been able to: face his fear. He pushed Alan out the same way his father had. "What are you thanking me for? You helped me too. I'm glad we met, Alan Pemberly. I'll never forget you. Now go on. I've got to get home."

Alan nodded and went back to his father's side. The room shifted to the dark place once more, and the only illumination was the sight of father and son strolling away. Jonathan watched them as long as he could before the sliver of white light opened and they disappeared inside it.

"Good-bye, guys. Good luck," Jonathan said and closed his eyes.

CHAPTER 14

BABY... BAAAABY. COME on, babe. Follow my voice. That's it. That's it. Come on home, Jonathan," Eddie whispered as he rubbed Jonathan's face. Everyone in the room was crowded around them. Jonathan's vitals had spiked very high and then slowly begun to return to normal. Eddie was still worried Jonathan wouldn't come back, but now those fears were starting to subside as Jonathan reacted to the sound of his voice. His face was horribly slack, his jaw still wide open.

"*Baby!*" Jonathan barked.

"That's right, come home," Eddie said soothingly.

"*Home!*" Jonathan repeated.

"That's right, home. Come on home. There you go, there ya go," Eddie said, stroking his face. Jonathan began to blink rapidly as he rolled his beautiful blue peepers back down. He inhaled once, twice, and a heavy third time. His slack jaw clicked shut hard enough to ring Jonathan's bell and bring him back more quickly. He leaned forward, blinked, rubbed his eyes, and blinked some more. He then turned to Eddie.

"Hi, sweetheart," Jonathan said.

"Oh God," Eddie said and leaped up from the chair next to him to wrap his arms around Jonathan's neck. "Hello, baby." He wept.

"Shhhh. It's over. It's all over," Jonathan said, holding on to his anchor, his rock, his lover, and his family. The room burst into applause as everyone hugged each other. Outside, the dark clouds had long since passed, and a fragile evening twilight peeked through the remaining puffs of moisture to cast its waning light upon an old farmhouse in the middle of Clay Center, Kansas. A place where one should always feel at home.

EPILOGUE

T HE SKY WAS pure and the fields were green as Eddie and
Jonathan stood hand in hand over the grave site marked
"Pemberly." Maggie stood with them, along with Jonah, who
had his arm wrapped around her waist. They had cleared off the
brush and debris from around the three graves and planted fresh
flowers in the bed. The cemetery had long since been vacated by
anyone who would bitch about them planting anything there.
The granite stones read "Beverly Lynn," "Mark Alvin," and "Alan
Robert" and gave their dates of birth and the dates they'd passed
beyond the veil.

The days following the event were agonizingly slow. Eddie
had insisted that Jonathan subject himself to a battery of tests,
including another sleep study and fMRI scans. Although his
brain activity still seemed to be more elevated than it should
be, both in the house and in the clinic, his sleep patterns had
returned to normal. No more nightmares plagued his dreams
and no paranormal activity was experienced throughout the
house. Peace had finally come to their abode.

After much consideration, Dr. Paul Spencer decided to put the
tapes in a vault and promised to never unseal them to anyone.
When asked why, he replied, "The world's not ready for this.
And as a professional and as a friend, I can't imagine throwing
you to the media wolves like that. It would make what happened
at Amityville look like a fairy tale," he said and packed up his
belongings. Samantha and Byron agreed with him, but it was the
blonde girl who said, "Hey, you know, there is a way to tell the
story. Write it, Jonathan. Tell the world that way. Even though the

truth is much stranger than fiction, let them have it, and let their imaginations do with it what they will."

Jonathan mulled it over and decided even if he didn't publish it, he ought to write it down for posterity's sake.

"You think they're at peace now?" Eddie asked.

Jonathan nodded. "Yeah. At long last."

"We should come and keep this up every now and then," Maggie said, and everyone agreed. Just because the Pemberlys were gone now, really gone, they shouldn't be forgotten. Perhaps Jonathan would write their story after all.

They said their final good-byes and began to walk back to the road where they had all parked. Maggie and Jonah were laughing and whispering in each other's ears and hightailing it for his truck. "We'll see you guys back at the house," Maggie hollered and waved as she half ran, half walked, chasing Jonah to the truck, leaving both Jonathan and Eddie laughing at the sight of them and waving as they drove off.

As they approached the blue beast and Jonathan hit the key fob to unlock the door, Eddie turned when he heard the rumble of thunder in the distance. Jonathan heard it too and hesitated before he opened the truck door. On the horizon, sure enough, were the bloated black clouds of a midsummer storm. The wind picked up slightly as well, sending a cool breeze over their T-shirt-and-shorts-clad bodies.

"Think we'll make it back to the house in time?" Eddie asked.

Jonathan frowned, looking up at the sky, and then nodded. The frown turned into an easy smile as he lowered his sunglasses to wink at Eddie. "Sure. We have plenty of time," he said before climbing in. They had left the windows down so the inside of the vehicle wouldn't be superheated when they got back in. As they buckled up and Jonathan turned the engine over, he stopped for a second before he put the car in gear, reached across the seat, and put his hand on Eddie's thigh.

"I love you," he said.

"I love you back, my brave man," Eddie said, leaning over and kissing him on the lips. He sat back with a look of pondering on his face.

"What is it?" Jonathan asked.

"Do you…? No! Do you think they're going back to her house to have sex?" he asked.

Jonathan immediately covered his ears. "I am a writer with a very good imagination. Dammit, babe. I'm getting mental visuals. Shush," he said as Eddie laughed. Jonathan laughed as well, threw the truck into gear, and made a U-turn out of the cemetery. Eddie leaned over and turned on the radio, and the intro to "Highway to Hell" began to play. Jonathan drove about fifty feet before he hit the brakes.

"What is it?" Eddie asked.

Jonathan was looking at the rearview mirror at the dark clouds rolling in behind them. He reached up, grabbed hold of both ends of the mirror, and with a firm and powerful tug, pulled the thing off the windshield. Eddie let out a surprised shout.

Jonathan held the mirror in his hands and looked over at his husband. "No more rearview-mirror stuff, babe," he said, and Eddie simply nodded as Jonathan tossed it out of the truck.

Jonathan reached down for his pack of Marlboros, pulled one out, and lit it up. He wanted desperately for things to go back to normal.

"Those things are going to kill you." Bingo. There it was: normal. Jonathan took a big drag and smiled at his husband, who was grinning at him as he let out a stream of bluish-gray smoke.

"Not today," he said, returning a wicked grin as he cranked the radio up and took off for home, leaving the broken rearview mirror where everything else stayed when it needed to be buried.

***

She had watched them depart the cemetery from her hiding spot behind a tree. The ageless woman made her way down to the road and bent over to pick up the busted mirror. As she held it in her hand, she closed her eyes for a moment as the edges of her lips pulled up in a smile. The wind whipped downward from the heavens and tossed her skirts around her legs and her long hair forward to caress her ample bosom. She could feel him, feel his elation and relief like she had felt him miles away.

"He's powerful, that one," she whispered aloud. A crow perched on a tree next to her cawed at her as it tilted its head as if considering her words. She turned and bowed her head to it.

"Go, beloved. Watch them for old Francine. With those abilities, he'll be needin' our help soon enough," she cooed. The bird did the bidding of its master and took to the sky as lightning lit up the world around them. The golden coins that adorned her hair jingled as they were tousled by the breeze.

"Power like that doesn't go unnoticed for too long. Sho 'nuff," she said as she began to make her way out of the boneyard, praying for their safety in the time to come.

AUTHOR'S NOTE

If you or someone you know is the victim of domestic violence, please seek help. Bullying outside the home is bad. Domestic violence inside the home, is Hell.

Your biggest fan,

F.E. Feeley Jr

www.thehotline.org
www.childwelfare.gov/systemwide/domviolence
www.trevorproject.org

STILL WATERS

Promise, Michigan is very much like every other small town across the state. Built on the edge of a lake, the homes sit in neat little rows in cute little neighborhoods. During the summer Promise bustles with tourists who come to spend their vacation dollars and enjoy the lake's refreshingly cold water. But Promise holds a terrible secret. In the center of the lake is an abandoned island where a curse is rumored to wait for victims, unabated and deadly. Most think it's just a story, something used to keep kids out of trouble. Still, everyone gives it a wide berth. Everyone except Bret and Adam. They dare to venture out the night of Bret's birthday. When they declared their love and promise to get married, they believe no one else heard their whispered words—but they are wrong.

Five years later Adam dies, and Bret returns to his family to heal. But someone is killing the people of Promise in random acts of violence. Bret, with the help of FBI agent Jeff McAllister, must discover the identity of a murderer with death on his mind and revenge in his heart.

PROLOGUE

S UMMERTIME HAD COME to the Great Lake State of Michigan and to the little town of Promise. A quaint little burg down I-96, where those considered low-income still earned triple digits, far from the hustle and slums of Detroit, Promise boasted magnificent shops and stretches of beautiful homes with deep yards and nice cars. The high school, home of the Indians, was state of the art, modern, the curriculum tough, and the teachers' salaries kept them happy. The town was truly the land of milk and honey for those wealthy enough to afford it. A picture of the modern Gilded Age, where everything in town was connected by telephone wires and gossip like spindly threads of a spider's web.

When a new family moved in, the lines hummed, and before the family could finish unpacking, several neighbors would show up at their door with baskets, pies, or fresh flowers from their gardens to welcome them to the neighborhood. Which, on the outside, looked pleasant enough, but these little visits were less a welcome wagon and more of an interview, and the people who came, less like neighbors and more like spies. These spies not only assessed the people themselves but their belongings. All the information gathered would be traded via the telephone wires that crisscrossed over their new neighbor's home, without the new family being aware.

It was a test of sorts, given to these new tenants, of whether or not they would be accepted into the social circles of the locals. If you made enough money, voted Republican, and believed Barack Obama was the Antichrist—if you drove the right car, were fashionably religious, and never wore white shoes after Labor Day—you were accepted with open arms. You were automatically welcomed into their circles if you had enough money to purchase a home on Promise Lake, the most expensive of the residential areas, and were dragged into the who's who of the town. All the others—the ones who lived in subdivisions run by associations, where Labrador retrievers and red begonias in copper pots were all the rage this season—had to work just a little bit harder.

The kids, however, were luckier than their triple-digit parents. Promise High School, for whatever reason, always boasted a rebellious streak along with high grades. It was almost fashionable to kick against the pricks as hard as possible there. They longed for the day when they could get out, far away from having to be under their parents' roofs, and silently vowed to themselves to always vote Democrat. The kids sensed something was amiss. They couldn't quite figure it out, but deep down they knew that Promise was unlike most places where what you got was what you saw. Something deeper than greed, envy, and lust ran amuck. Other far more malignant things traversed in the deep shadows between shops and back alleys.

That night the weather was balmy, but the wind blew through the trees so hard that branches whipped and leaves sighed as if pleased to be cooled from the heat of the day. Above, thousands of stars dotted the night sky as the moon shone orange across the surface of the still lake. These same winds forced the clouds to pass overhead quickly as the moon cast its glow on the earth below before being covered once more, like a game of peek-a-boo with the world. The water's surface broke only by the occasional jump of a fish as it surfaced for a mayfly that had strayed too close to the water. The lake rippled out in tiny waves until it settled again, making the surface of the lake a still mirror reflecting the sky once more. Around the shore, houses sat quiet and still that Wednesday night in May. The humidity was thick, floating in the air like strands of ancient memory, wispy and tendril-like. It swirled around street lamps, which dotted the deserted concrete walkway that stretched around the far side of the lake.

In the center of the lake sat an island, dark and quiet. Its many trees reached up toward heaven as if in supplication to some long-dead god. The island was large—big enough at least to build a large home upon it, but no one had ever tried. No one wanted to.

The stories that surrounded this island kept everyone away, except of course for the silly high school kids sent across on a dare. Legends old and urban hovered over that little piece of earth, and the locals whispered about them to their children who were being naughty. Stories of an ancient people who once roamed the lands of Michigan, stories about curses, and stories about what would happen should they not behave themselves and clean their plates. The children listened with wide-eyed fascination.

The heat made its way back now that summer was again upon them, and people were happy to have it. After a long, frozen winter, summer would bring revelers, travelers, and sunbathers to the shore of the spring-fed lake. Soon Memorial Day would be upon them. Barbeques would be held in the small segment of the lake that was a state park, where sand had been trucked in to make a small beach and families would frolic in the shallow, unusually cool water. On the lake, fishermen would take their little boats out and cast lines, and on July Fourth the township would host a fireworks display as it had done for the past twenty years or so.

Promise was a good place to raise a family. Income was high and crime was low.

For the adults, it was still a work night, even if the majority of them made their own schedules. Most of the adults there dealt with the end of the school year, with graduation parties on the weekends and trips to Cedar Point with the younger children. Come September they would be escorting their new college students to university either in Ann Arbor or Lansing, or even down to the biggest football rival, Ohio. It was the kind of night that inspired young lovers to their first kiss and old lovers to wrap an arm around the shoulder of their loved one as they rocked in their front-porch swings. The fragrance of freshly cut grass and evening dew hung so heavy and sweet you could almost taste the nectar of the flowers. On the horizon, far off to the west, heavy clouds brought the promise of a rain shower later in the evening as lightning zigzagged with celestial arcs, illuminating the clouds. It wasn't close enough yet to hear thunder, but it would come, and in the morning the roses, which had just begun to bloom steadily, would drip when the beads of rain they'd collected became too heavy to stay on their tender petals.

That night was also heavily shadowed. As the breeze bent the sturdiest of trees and swung around their leaves, the branches and limbs cast darkness in mysterious and elongated shapes. It was the kind of night that scared children at two in the morning as tree limbs scratched at windows, when the familiar became phantoms that made them crawl into their parents' beds. Being home alone would cause a person to turn on lights and fall asleep watching television just to drown out the sound of the whistling winds. The music of the night was a trade-off—inspiration and fear. Life, the perfect neutral referee, would host both joy and tears. In the ever-spinning lottery that was the world, all one had to do to play was breathe.

Bret Williams wasn't worried about the cost of college that fall or about going to campus to find a job to supplement his income, even though he had acceptance letters from all three schools, two of which were nearly begging him to attend due to his SAT scores. He wasn't thinking about buying books, finding housing, or cleaning out his room, which his mother had begged him to do before he left for school in the fall. She had meekly informed him that she would be turning his bedroom into a sewing room once he vacated.

Bret didn't mind. They didn't really want him back, and to be honest, he didn't want to come back. Not after what they'd done. Not after what they'd said.

Bret's parents had fallen into the snares of those concerned more with wealth and image than family and home. His mother, a former ballet instructor, now stayed home and "took care" of her husband. Bret's father worked to "take care" of his wife and son. They used to be happy, back when they were struggling to make it, but all that had changed when money became the focus of their lives. Bret was able to handle most of it, rolled his eyes about the rest, and ignored the worst—well, that was until it became personal. Mom and Dad became Elle May and Doug, two people he didn't recognize anymore.

That night, Bret's stomach was in terrible knots with those thoughts and with another as he left the police station for the thirteenth time already this week. He braked hard at a stop sign and quickly grabbed hold of the stack of paper on the passenger seat to keep it from flying forward and spilling into the floorboard of the car. As he did so, he caught a glimpse of the photo he had been staring at for the past few days. Adam's face grinned back at him from the black-and-white photo, his eyes dancing with mirth as if he knew a secret—as if he knew where he was and refused to tell Bret. Adam was handsome and kept his blond hair carelessly long though it easily fit underneath his swimmer's cap on the high school team, where they'd met three years ago.

With a sigh, Bret sat back in the driver's seat and whispered, "Where are you, baby?"

"Your breast-stroke needs work" came a voice through the din of slamming lockers and shuffling feet.

Bret, lost in his own stormy thoughts, nearly jumped out of his skin. Looking to the right of where he sat, he continued two feet upward to muscular thighs and the white-towel-clad waist of the person standing next to him. Sitting back, he skipped the muscular abdominals and chest he had admired from afar since the beginning of the semester, straight up to the face of Adam Woolsey, the best swimmer on the team. Adam's piercing blue eyes looked at him sympathetically, unlike everyone else on the team after Bret had brought down their average score.

Bret felt his face heat up for the briefest moment but then dissipate as he cast his eyes back to the floor. "Yeah."

F.E. FEELEY JR.

"Dude, really, don't sweat it. It just takes practice and style. You're new here, right?" Adam asked, sitting next to Bret.

"Yeah. I transferred from Belleville High at the end of last year. My dad got a new job," Bret said with a smirk.

"I'm Adam, nice to meet you." He extended a hand.

Bret swallowed hard. "Bret. Same here," he said, shaking Adam's hand. It was solid and warm despite them having climbed out of the cold pool a few minutes prior when Coach had launched into his tirade at Bret—how he'd better shape up if he planned on staying on the team. Bodies around Bret and Adam shuffled flip-flop-clad feet along, avoiding slick spots, into the waiting steam and soap of the locker room showers.

"You're not a swimmer, are you?" Adam asked.

"Nah, I was a gymnast, but we don't have a program like that here," Bret said, removing his shirt.

"You've got a great body, but I see where the problem is. As a gymnast, you train different, your muscles are more square. Swimmers' muscles tend to be longer and smooth. We can change that, but it's going to take practice, is all," he said with an inviting smile and a welcoming gaze.

Bret nodded. "I'm down for a change."

"Good. We'll meet after school every day for an hour. Do you have wheels of your own?"

"Meh...yeah, but I haven't put the engine back in yet," Bret said, thinking about the 1970 GTO he'd found at a junkyard and was restoring.

"Oh, no sweat, then, you can always hitch a ride with me. Anyway, we'll start today. Come on, let's shower, otherwise we'll be late for fourth period."

And with that, it had begun…

***

A car horn honked behind him, jarring Bret out of the memory. They didn't wait for him to move, just whipped around while someone yelled out their window. In anger Bret flipped them off as they tore through the intersection and down the road. He threw the photo flier back atop the stack and wiped away the tears that came too quickly as of late. Biting his tongue to stave them off, he flipped on the radio and turned it up.

"…search continues tonight for missing high school graduate and three-time state swim champion Adam Woolsey. Authorities have said that its possible Adam has left town and there is no sign of foul play, but there has been no word from him in several days. Stay with…"

Bret drove through the intersection and passed Promise High School before making his way home, listening to the radio as he turned left at the next intersection. He rode up Willis Drive, the road parallel to the lake, and eventually pulled into his parents' driveway. Killing the ignition, he sat back and sighed. He wanted to go into that house as badly as he wanted a bullet hole between his eyes, but it was just for a few more days. The Woolseys had told him to stay with them, but with Adam missing, they were so upset, Bret didn't want to be a burden on them and a constant reminder that Adam was gone.

Angrily he opened the car door and was met by the deep bark of his dog Kaiser. He walked around to the back door, inserted his key, and met the tail-wagging one-hundred-pound German shepherd he and Adam had bought together last year. *At least someone in this house is happy to see me.* Bret reached down and petted the dog's silky fur. Kaiser sat back on his haunches and brought a paw up, and Bret knelt to scratch his neck.

"We're still looking for your Adam." The dog whined and nuzzled his hand.

"Bret, is that you?" his mother called from deeper inside the house.

"No, it's the fucking Boston Strangler, who has a key to the house," he muttered, rolling his eyes.

"Bret?" she called again, obviously not hearing him.

"*Yeah!* It's me, Ma!" he said again. He motioned for Kaiser to move, and the dog backed up enough to allow him to ascend the stairs into the kitchen, but stayed right at his heels, sniffing the backs of his pant legs, trying to figure out where he'd been and who he'd been with. Bret swiped backward with his hand.

"Get out of my butt!" The dog reared his head before Bret could make contact with his nose.

Mrs. Elle May Williams came into the kitchen with hope in her eyes. "Have you heard anything about Aaron?" she asked politely.

"You mean Adam," Bret said, annoyed with the same smile she offered him every time.

"Yes, him. Any word?" She looked at him expectantly.

She loathed Adam. Loathed what Adam meant to him, who they'd been, what they were. Bret felt the anger rise like bile in him, but he just shook his head as Kaiser nudged at his hand, feeling the tension in the room.

"Well, I'm sure he'll turn up just fine," she said. "Your father will be home in a few days. You may want to get a head start finding campus housing. I mean, the fall is coming quickly, and it'll take your mind off your friend."

"Fiancé," Bret replied.

"Excuse me?" she asked, her eyes narrowing.

"Fiancé, Mother. I am not leaving behind someone I love because—"

"Please, don't try to dignify what the both of you do as love."

"Oh, right. Because that's what you and Dad have? Tell me, when Dad had his affair with—what was her name…Jessica?—was that love as well?" Bret fired back with a smile on his lips. His mother's lips puckered, and he watched as her fury grew.

"You little son of a bitch, how dare you—" she said, growing furious, but Bret put up a hand.

"Tell the truth? Look, let's just keep from jumping on the merry-go-round of knives, shall we? Stay out of my way, and I'll stay out of yours. Deal?" he asked.

"Fine. But I will be telling your father when he gets back," she sniffed, putting her hands on her hips and then dropping them in outrage as Bret suddenly burst into laughter.

"Oh no," he said, grabbing his heart. "Oh, please don't tell Daddy. What will I do with his disapproval?"

"Oh, you don't care much about his approval, I know. Your father cheated on me because he couldn't handle having a gay son. It disgusted him," she said venomously.

The statement would have hurt him if he hadn't turned her off a long time ago. He still wanted to slap her. But instead, he decided he'd hit another way.

"Mother, your husband cheated on you because when we moved here, his wife became Queen Ice Bitch of Promise Lake. That, and Jessica was twenty-three. So don't put your Stepford bullshit on me," he fired back.

She took an angry step forward, and Kaiser let out a menacing growl that caused her to hesitate. However, the look of fury on her face was replaced with one of stone calm, something that scared Bret even more than their heated war of words.

She was beginning another "how dare you" statement, which had become common since her discovery of Bret's sexuality, when Kaiser let out a series of very loud barks that caused them both to jump. The reflection of two lights across the kitchen wall caused Bret to turn as a car pulled into the driveway.

"Kaiser, come on," he said, snapping his fingers.

The dog turned from the window and looked at Bret before wagging his tail and following him on his way to the stairs that led up to his room.

"Where are you going?" his mother demanded, and Bret turned and was about to respond when a car door slammed and a voice tore through the night—and right into his heart.

"Bret! Bret!" The voice sobbed and broke the second time.

The tortured sound hit him like a truck. His heart skipped, and the truth he was yet to discover, the hand fate had held, was shown for the first time. Bret's mouth went dry as his throat constricted, and he swore if he were to try to step forward, he would fall flat, but with another shout of "Bret!" he ran forward. He knew the voice, and Kaiser was hot on his heels while his mother complained about the racket they were causing.

Bret hit the door, his heart lodged in his throat and his knees trembling. Kaiser rushed between his legs to the person standing in the light of the car. Bret's view was obscured as the beams from the headlights stole his night vision, but Kaiser knew the newcomer and got out of their way as they came into focus.

It was Timmy, Adam's older brother, and the look on his face screamed through Bret's body like electricity as realization dawned horribly in his mind. The cards were being laid out on the table.

"No." Bret sobbed, shook his head, and brought his hand up to his mouth. As if shaking his head would somehow slay the dragon, he reached out for Timmy as his knees finally gave out on him. Timmy fell too as he gathered Bret in his arms, as Adam's mother and father shrouded both boys in grief.

Kaiser, unsure of what was happening, raised his head toward the sky and let out his own mournful wail as they wept, their tears soaking the parched concrete driveway with the truth.

Adam wouldn't be coming home.

CHAPTER 1

Five years later

H E SAW THE sheriff pull up in his patrol car, open the door and get out, hitch his pants up, and grab a bag before slamming the door shut. Following close behind, they walked up the stairs together, the sheriff unaware of anyone behind him.

The sheriff unlocked the door, opened it, and closed it in his face. However, that did not matter; the ghost simply stepped through into the living room illuminated by the soft glow of a lamp that stood off to the side near a brown recliner.

After laying his bag down, the officer walked into the kitchen, as did his pursuer.

The sheriff opened the fridge, grabbed a beer, and pulled the tab. The beer hissed, and the can opened. While his unseen guest tilted his head to watch, the sheriff took three large gulps and belched before setting the can down. The man turned and walked over to the built-in oven, where he lowered the door.

A large casserole dish sat inside, and the ghost watched the man put on two oven mitts before grabbing the white glass to pull it out. The ghost smirked, reached over, and slid the beer can slowly to the edge of the counter it was set on until it toppled off the side and hit the ground, its contents pumping out onto the floor.

"Aw shit," the sheriff said, sliding the dish onto the same counter. "Dammit." He bent to pick up the can of beer and grabbed the roll of paper towels before lowering again and wiping the mess from the ground. The sheriff did not know how close he was to the source of his beer's demise. The cell phone on his hip began to ring, and he muttered something inaudible as he stood and threw the beer-soaked paper towel in the trashcan before answering it.

"Hello."

A female voice responded.

"I thought I told you not to call me at this number," the sheriff said gently with a smile on his face. He smirked when the voice on the other end replied. "When?" he asked, checking his watch.

The woman responded.

"And where's your husband?" He tugged at his groin.

Again, another response.

"Alright. Let me take a shower, and I'll meet you there."

She responded once more.

"Me too." He hung up and then grinned again.

"Why eat pot roast when you can have a steak?" the sheriff asked the room, thinking no one heard him.

He didn't even bother to put the casserole dish back in the warm oven before he left, walking upstairs to the second floor with the shadow at his heels.

The sheriff grabbed a pair of nice jeans, a button-down shirt, clean underwear, and socks from the dresser drawer before looking out the window of the house onto the lake. Satisfied, he turned and made his way into the bathroom.

The sheriff placed his cell phone and service revolver on the sink before taking off his utility belt, which he laid on the floor. He took two steps away toward the shower, unbuttoned his shirt, and took it off before sliding the expensive glass door open and turning the shower on high.

The unseen one, who had been lusting after the revolver, snapped his head right once he heard running water, nostrils flaring. Suddenly the ghost had a better idea.

Naked, the sheriff entered the spray of water and slid the glass door shut. He reached for a bar of soap and began to lather up, his legs first, his chest, and then his face as he hummed happily, thinking perhaps of what was to come.

If he only knew…

The specter acted quickly, reaching inside the wall and wrapping his fist around the pipe with one hand and placing another on the glass of the shower. The fury and contempt he felt toward this man revealed itself as two things happened at once: first, the glass darkened as the spray stained green around the edges—he began to claw toward the sides of the shower walls, sealing the man in—and second, the water that had been clear and clean turned brackish. Its heat now gone, the man with soap on his face arched his back away from it and tried to open his eyes.

"What the hell...fuck!" he yelled as the burn started immediately. He closed them only to rub them with soapy fingers. In pain, he ran his face under the now cold water.

The specter smiled to himself as he backed off to observe. Water was sloshing around the tub now as the sheriff, who had finally managed to clear his eyes, looked down to see his feet immersed in lake water. Immediately he reached for the faucet to turn it off, but as much as he turned and fought them, they simply spun uselessly. He fumbled behind him for the clasp on the shower door and pulled...nothing. Turning around, startled, he saw for the first time the state of the shower door. He pulled again, angry.

Slightly amused by the spectacle, the phantom quickly grew bored and reached back into the wall as the man struggled. As he wrapped his hand around the pipe, there was a groaning sound and a shudder before the water pressure cranked up. The head of the shower bowed forward before exploding, its fragments tearing into the flesh of a now frantic sheriff as more water rushed unabated. He began to pound on the glass door, begging for help from the woman he had planned to cheat on, whom he'd been cheating on, and who'd made his pot roast before heading over to a girlfriend's house to play cards. The shrillness of the sheriff's cries reached another octave and thrilled the specter as he watched the sheriff pound on the glass.

The water kept rising and soon covered his chin, nose, and head before the specter reached once more and shut the water off completely. The glass had begun to bulge from the pressure, and he did not want it exploding outward. The man was holding his breath and still struggled against the glass, floating helplessly. That was when the specter made himself known. His sudden appearance scared the sheriff so badly he took in a lungful of lake water. The specter smiled at the sheriff's violent realization—as life drained from his eyes and he ceased to struggle.

His rage was only sated for moments as the twitching man ceased to move and his body, now void of air, drifted until it reached the floor and leaned back against the wall. His sightless eyes gazed forward in a horrible, mannequin-like way. With a snarl, the specter turned from the drowned man and paused by the mirror, catching sight of his own reflection…

***

Bret stared into the mirror of the club's bathroom, his face white as a sheet. Outside, the bass thumped so hard he could still feel it in his chest. A man left the sink beside him and smirked, thinking perhaps Bret had snorted a line too many.

David, Bret's best friend, reached for his arm as he saw the color drain from Bret's face, his eyes widened in horror.

"Dude, what's wrong?" He placed a hand on his shoulder.

"Don't come back here," Bret said.

"What?"

"I can't protect you."

"Protect me? Dude, whatya talkin' about?"

Suddenly Bret pitched forward and began to vomit into the sink. Except it was not vomit. It was green and looked like water…

CHAPTER 2

FEDERAL AGENT JEFFERY McAllister stepped up on the porch of a colonial house after showing his badge to the beat cop standing guard at the end of the front walk. When the agent asked where he could find the lead detective, the beat cop nodded and pointed inward with his thumb. He didn't miss the narrowing of the cop's eyes when he showed his federal badge, and McAllister couldn't help but roll his eyes when he crossed the yellow tape that surrounded the property to keep the nosey neighbors from getting too close. It was 2:00 a.m. An urgent phone call from his boss that brought news of the homicide of a police officer—a sheriff of a small town within his field office's district—had dragged him out of sleep. When asked about the circumstances and why Michigan State Police couldn't just handle it, the FBI director from Detroit just told him to get dressed, get down to Promise and report back what he found at the crime scene.

A forty-minute drive, a stop to pick up bad gas station coffee, and he drove right into a picture-perfect town he would never have had the opportunity to visit until now. As he got out of the car, he looked heavenward, and the moon was full, heavy, and the sky cloudless. It bathed the world in silver light that seemed to cast shadows just a little larger and exaggerate their dark visage, creating the air of menace. He shook the thought off and passed through the doorway of the home to see several officers milling about while crime scene investigators went through the entire residence piece by piece.

A couple of uniforms standing at the bottom of the stairs looked pretty shaken up as they themselves were questioned by a man in a suit and a female officer.

As Jeffery approached, a redheaded female officer cleared her throat and cast her eyes in his direction, causing the suited figure to turn and look at him. The man was balding, short, and had jowls where a chin should be, but his eyes were sharp, and when he saw McAllister walking through, his face looked even more like a junkyard dog as he nodded. He muttered to the officers to dismiss them and pulled out a handkerchief to wipe at the sweat on his forehead. It was uncomfortably stuffy in the house, even with all the doors open, and the people milling about did nothing to help, but the man's weight and attire were probably killing him as he stood there. McAllister went to pull his badge again, but the man waved him off.

"You're from the Bureau. Name's Bob Woodward—they said they would be sending someone," he said, putting out his hand.

Jeff took it and was surprised by two things: first, how strong it was, and second, how clammy. The man was sweating like a boar hog.

"Jeff McAllister. I am sorry to hear about you losing one of your own. It's never easy."

"Ahh, shit, Jeff...you mind me calling you Jeff? I've been on the force thirty-five years, worked almost every kind of homicide you can imagine, and I've never seen anything like this. And I reckon you haven't either, but I needed another pair of eyes on this before the media gets ahold of it," he said, leaning close and almost whispering.

"Was the victim married?" Jeff asked, looking around. He noticed picture frames and doilies under knickknacks; the house was delicately run, probably by someone of the gentler gender. Pictures of teenagers at graduations, babies, and one of an older couple outside a church linked arm in arm together sat upon the mantel of a stone fireplace.

"Yeah, Lisa was the one who called 911. She was hysterical. Kept screaming, 'He's drowning, he's drowning' to the operator."

Jeff turned from the mantel to look at him. "I'm sorry, you said drowning. What? In the lake? In the tub? What do you mean by drowning?"

"That's where this is way above my pay grade," Woodward said, nodding toward the staircase and motioning for Jeff to follow.

"No one but Lisa and the officers you saw me talking to downstairs have been in there. I have threatened to take their badges if they speak to anyone about this, and as for Lisa, she's been doped up and sent to the hospital," he said, heading up.

McAllister did everything he could not to stare at the ample butt of the man trudging up the stairs in front of him and instead focused attention to the stairs as they ascended.

They came up to the landing and turned right at the top of the stairs, where another police officer was standing guard at the entrance of a bedroom. The detective motioned for him to scram, and the uniform did as he was told, staring at McAllister curiously as he walked by. When they entered the room, Jeff saw that it looked very well kept, spotless and meticulous.

"Is the vic's wife a housewife or something? There is nothing out of place in the entire house," Jeff observed.

"Yeah, I think she's hired a housekeeper to help her now that the kids are all gone and married, but"—he entered the bathroom and stood by the sink—"this is what she came home to."

Jeff was still confused about everything until he walked into the bathroom, turned his head, and saw what Detective Woodward was staring at with disbelief on his face. Jeff blinked once, twice, and approached the shower slowly, his jaw lowering with each step. The secrecy suddenly made sense, and so did Lisa's madness. What he observed caused the hairs on the back of his neck to stand up and his skin to crawl. There, leaning against the back of the shower, was a naked man. The buoyancy of the water kept him erect, and for him to be leaning just so, the body language saying, "so, come here often?" made Jeff's skin crawl. The dead man's eyes were wide with sightless fear as the strands of hair floated about his head like a halo. His mouth stretched wide in a silent scream, and his arms floating limply beside him.

"Jumpin' Jesus Christ," Jeff whispered.

As he drew closer, Bob warned him to be careful, but Jeff waved him off. *How is that possible?* He neared the dead man in the shower stall. That is when he saw the glass bowed out under the weight of the water pressure—yet that was not the end of it. All along the edges, where the glass met the wall, was a thick line of greenish-black tar-like muck that looked like a sloppy J-B Weld job and prevented the water from escaping. Just like a fish tank, the shower had been sealed shut. Jeff went to reach out a finger and touch the seal.

"Maybe you shouldn't," Bob warned, and Jeff withdrew his hand, thinking that perhaps he was right.

"Who the fuck did this?" he asked.

"Beats the hell out of me." Bob replied.

"Get the medical examiner up here. I want everyone in this house to meet me downstairs in five minutes. I want an entire roster of who has been on these premises since the initial call went in to 911, in case anyone decides they are going to go to the press. I want pictures taken of this before they remove the body, and I want this…this…sealing stuff taken down to the lab to be tested, as well as the water."

"How do you propose we get him out of there?" Bob asked incredulously.

Jeff turned his head and stared at the overworked, overweight, and underpaid officer and felt a pang of sympathy for him. It was going to be a very long night. "Tell 'em to bring a sledgehammer. Until I know what's happening here, this is now a federal investigation."

Bob nodded and disappeared beyond the bedroom door and out into the hall again. Jeff reached into his pocket for his BlackBerry and dialed his boss's number. After the third ring, a very alert voice answered, and Jeff wondered if the son of a bitch ever slept. He doubted it.

"What's the situation?" his boss asked quickly.

"Honest to God, I don't know. But I do know I'm going to need several agents down here with me."

"I can send three right away, and two more on Thursday night. Anything you need in particular?"

McAllister snorted. "Yeah, send me Fox Mulder and Dana Scully."

"I beg your pardon?" Apparently, the director did not get the reference.

"You'll understand when I text you a picture of this, but send me a...shit, Jesus, a biologist, and a medical doctor." Jeff exhaled.

They spoke for a few more minutes before he hung up the phone and shoved it back into his pocket. There, staring at the naked sheriff floating in a sea of what looked like lake water; Jeff wondered what the hell he had stumbled into.

CHAPTER 3

S IX THIRTY CAME quickly, and when the alarm went off, Bret thrust a hand out from under the covers to mash the snooze button and keep the newscaster from screaming in his ear. Kaiser raised his head from his curled-up position and stood up on the bed, stretching his back. He wandered over to the sleeping form and then proceeded to lick Bret's face.

"Uggh…awww…come on, Kaiser, five more minutes," Bret protested, but Kaiser lay down on his chest with a huff and was having none of it as he continued the lick assault. Bret tried to shove him off, but that did not work either. Kaiser thought he wanted to play and jumped up to bark at him.

"Fine! You win," Bret said, sitting up.

The dog spun, jumped down off the bed, and stood at the door, wagging his long tail as Bret swung his legs around. He reached over and shut the alarm off for good, then stood and stretched.

"Alright. Let's go." Bret opened the bedroom door as the dog shot out and down the hallway to the kitchen.

Padding down behind him, wrapping a robe around his body and tying it at the waist, Bret watched the dog get to the door and turn excitedly.

"Alright. Alright," he said, reaching for the door and unlocking it.

Kaiser shot out like a bullet, down the back stairs and into the yard to do his business. Bret shut the door behind him and walked to the bathroom off the kitchen to take care of his own. After he flushed, he stood before the mirror and looked at his face. He leaned over the sink to check out his skin and rub a hand over the scruff he wanted to shave off, when the ring he wore around his neck slid out and hung suspended on its chain.

"What is this?" Bret asked, breathless.

"A promise," Adam said with a smile. He slid it on as they stood on the island the night they had first made love.

"A promise?" Bret asked, his insides trembling hard.

"Yeah. You and me. After college. If you're alright with that," Adam said, standing up. "Forever."

"Forever never came, Adam," Bret said and sighed, sliding the ring back under his robe.

It had been five years since that horrible night—well, almost five years. There were seven days left, and as always, he took a vacation this time of year and went back to Adam's family. It had become a tradition.

The first year was hell. However, it got easier after that, and they kept up with each other all the time. The family had sort of adopted Bret after Adam died, and they became closer as he and his own family drifted apart almost to the point of total silence. So, at around eight, he was going to be loading Kaiser into the back of his GTO to head back down to Promise for a week or so.

He heard scratching at the door and walked out of the bathroom to let Kaiser in just as his cell phone rang. Kaiser was huffing and puffing as if he'd climbed up Everest, and he made a beeline for the water bowl, where he slopped water all over the place as he drank. Reaching for the phone, he saw it was David calling and rolled his eyes, thinking of letting it go to voice mail. David was probably still worried about last night and wanted to make sure Bret was okay, so he slid his finger over the answer button and pressed it.

"Hey," he said, walking over to coffeepot.

"Hey, weirdo, any more visions?" David asked, laughing.

Bret laughed as well, but not as humorously. "Yeah, no. No more visions."

"Dude, you really freaked me out last night," David said anxiously.

Good ol' David. He was a friend because Bret wouldn't let him be anything other than. They had been on a few dates together, and everyone assumed they were a couple, much to David's pleasure, but Bret refused to give in. Bret regretted taking him to bed the times it had happened. It had even caused a few fights between them, and Bret *did* like David, even had feelings for him, but that's where it ended.

"Like I said, I don't remember a thing," he replied as he put a K-Cup in the Keurig and placed his mug underneath it.

"I thought someone had slipped something into your drink. You started vomiting right after and then passed out. Are you making a doctor's appointment?"

"No. No, I think I'm fine. I woke up this morning, no headache, no stomachache, no nothing. Slept like a rock," Bret said as he watched Kaiser eat his breakfast.

"Are you sure? I mean, I think your friends could wait a couple more days…" David let his voice trail off.

"No. Once I've showered, I'll be headed down. I'll be back in a week or so."

"It's morbid."

"What's morbid?"

"Going down there like that. I mean, every year for the anniversary of *his* death."

David resented Adam, Bret knew. He blamed him for being the wall between David and him, and perhaps he was right. Perhaps it was a bit morbid, but as far as he was concerned…

"It isn't any of your business." Bret finished the thought aloud, immediately feeling like a jerk after he said it.

"Fine. Go. I'll see you when you get back," David replied tersely, and the line went dead.

"Davi…ugh." Bret tossed the phone back on the counter. "Come on, Kaiser, let Daddy shower, and then we're gonna go see your PawPaw and GiGi."

Kaiser's big German shepherd ears perked up at this, and he spun around in circles before succumbing to an itch on his hindquarters, which he attacked with fervor. His big teeth gnawed at that spot as he snorted and his eyes burned with fire.

"God help that flea." Bret laughed and took his coffee back down the hallway.

***

The drive was beautiful, and as Bret made his way down the freeway, he did so with both windows down. Winter was long over, as was spring, and summer was in full swing as it marched steadily toward the heart of June. The air was just cool enough to keep both man and man's best friend from sweltering. Not that Kaiser was worried about that. He had his head out the window as the wind blew through his fur, tongue lolling out in pure joy. Occasionally he sneezed, which made Bret laugh, and then he would pull his head in and cock it to the right or left with a quizzical look before sticking it back out.

I-94 was clear for a Thursday morning, and Bret thought about what David had said about calling a doctor, but dismissed it. After Adam's death and the funeral, he had suffered from horrible nightmares and terrible depression. The therapist his mother insisted he go see had assured him this was completely normal and prescribed him a series of antidepressants to help him over it. They had established a good doctor-and-patient relationship, and every six months or so, Bret would make an appointment and update her on how he was doing. She encouraged him in his job as a history professor, and while working on his PhD, she made it a point to clear her schedule for moments when the stress became too much. Now, two years remaining, he was doing quite well for himself and had even managed to purchase his own home, saying good-bye to apartment rentals and sublets. She didn't even mind his becoming close to Adam's family or the separation from his own.

"You have to go and be with people who build you up, not tear you down, Bret. Life, as you have been shown, is very short. Don't waste a moment of it," she said as she sat across from him. But she kept on at him to start dating, which infuriated David, and he ignored it. His little episode at the bar the night before he just shrugged off as anxiety at the proximity of the fifth anniversary of Adam's death. His mood normally downshifted about this time, and Adam's family always managed to level him off. By the time he left the Woolsey's, he was ready for the world again.

And as for dating...

"I'm just not ready," he said aloud as he weaved out of the way of the debris left by an exploded semitruck tire.

After an hour or so on the freeway, Bret made it to the all too familiar exit and pulled off. He knew this route like the back of his hand and could drive it blind, deaf, and dumb. It took another fifteen minutes of winding roads, stop signs, and passing his old high school before the Woolseys' house came into view. Several cars were parked in the driveway, and Bret felt himself smile as he pulled in and killed the ignition. He stepped out of the car and held the door open for Kaiser, who bounded out and ran up the driveway barking. Immediately Timmy came out with a big grin on his face, announcing back over his shoulder that Bret was there.

Bret laughed as Timmy swept him up in a bear hug, his large body engulfed Bret's more slender one. Bret stilled his laughing and wrapped his arms back around him, and the two just held each other for a moment before Timmy cleared his throat and held Bret at arm's length. Bret could see the start of gray hair at Timmy's temples and his laugh lines had deepened since last they saw each other, but Timmy was still handsome.

"You look good," Tim said.

"I feel good. I do. You look great yourself."

They hugged once more, this time shorter than the first because the back door swung open and Margaret bounded out.

"She's gonna yell at you for not eating," Tim mock whispered, letting go as Adam's mom came out.

"Oh, I am not!" she protested, laughing and hugging Bret as well. Kaiser immediately demanded Tim's attention, bumping his hand with his head. "Oh, well, maybe I will. You are too skinny!" she said, laughing and wiping her eyes. A voice from the inside boomed out, "Bret's here?"

"Outside, Mark!" Margaret shouted and stepped to the side as Adam's six-foot-seven father lumbered out the door.

"Hey, Big Daddy," Bret said, using the family's affectionate name for him as the man crushed him in his own embrace.

The man was built like a lumberjack, and his hands could palm a basketball. This was a funny contrast to his shorter and thinner wife. Where Timmy had taken after his father's stocky build, Adam had had a thinner frame like his momma.

"Hey, boy," Big Daddy said. "Still driving that piece of shit, I see."

"Heh…better than that souped-up piece of sh…Chevelle you drive around." That was *their* greeting, and of course, they both laughed before Bret asked Timmy where his girlfriend Molly was.

"Who's callin' my name?" A voice came out of the backyard.

A belly preceded a woman around the corner of the house, and Bret's jaw fell open before he looked over at Timmy.

"Dude! Why didn't you say somethin'?" he said, slapping him in the chest with the back of his hand and rushing forward to hug her.

"Hey, girl!" he said, hugging her gently.

She laughed as they broke the embrace, and Bret put a hand right on her stomach.

"We wanted to surprise you!"

Bret got down on his knees and placed one hand on each side of her swollen stomach. "Is it a boy or a girl?"

"We don't know yet," she said. "I go next week to find out."

"Hello! Hello, baby. This is your uncle Bret. How you doin' in there? Do you need anything?" Bret said very close to the baby.

Everyone laughed, including Molly, whose belly bounced with each chuckle as Bret stood up.

"Right now, it's chocolate ice cream and Doritos," she said, laughing and rubbing her tummy.

"Yeah, but last month it was beef, steak, hamburger, you name it," Margaret said. "I keep telling her it's a boy. Both Timmy and Adam had me craving steak fajitas so bad through the pregnancy; I thought I'd never lose the weight."

Bret kissed Molly on the cheek. "Congrats."

"Thanks," she said and they hugged once more.

"Speaking of food, I think it's lunchtime, Big Daddy, whatdya say?" Margaret asked her husband, who was already headed down the driveway to get Bret's bags.

"I say that's a winner. Hey, Bret, come unlock your trunk!" he boomed, and Bret hightailed it down the driveway as he had when he was in high school while everyone laughed. In this family, you learned to jump when Big Daddy said so. It felt good to be home.

CHAPTER 4

T HE PRELIMINARY REPORT is what you would think. Drowning," Agent Reggie Doucette said as she tossed her red hair over her shoulder.

Reggie stood for Regina, a name she hated, and no one dared use it around her. She didn't make the force because of her good looks, even though they were obvious, and sometimes people mistook her for a wilting flower. They usually regretted it.

"Tell me something I don't know," Jeff said, looking at the folder they had created for this case.

"Well, this is where it gets weirder." She handed him over another piece of paper. Jeff read it with growing interest and confusion.

"Algae?" he asked, and she nodded.

"In an advanced stage of growth, so thick that it acted as a seal between the glass and the wall. And that's not all. Crime scene investigators have analyzed the actual glass itself. Have you ever been inside an old house and noticed that the windows look warped?"

"Yeah, those old lead windows?" Jeff asked, sitting forward.

"Right. Well, glass is not completely solid and those windows you see that look all distorted are due to the glass melting down to the bottom over an extended period. The liquid in this glass was dispersed to areas that would be vulnerable to the pressure of a couple of hundred gallons of water."

"Five hundred twenty-eight gallons of water, to be exact," Jeff said, looking back at the report in his hand. "How is that possible?"

"Beats the hell out of me. They are taking apart the shower stall wall to figure out where that water actually came from. In addition, the report on that says just what you saw. Lake water." Reggie sat back and exhaled.

"No theories?" Jeff asked.

"Couple of the techs are tossing around the idea of a lightning strike, a weird electric current possibly. But they're just grasping at straws."

"Okay, what about the not so creepy facts. What do we have?"

"Well, really nothing out of the ordinary. Except the sheriff had a history of being a low-down dirty shame.

"We pulled his phone records, talked to the last person he called, a Mary Beth Anderson. Seems these two were quite the pair. Both married. When we went to speak with her and told her of his demise, she burst into tears and told us they had been seeing each other for over a year, blah-blah, he was going to leave his wife, blah-blah," Reggie said.

"You don't seem too impressed." Jeff arched his eyebrow, and Reggie rolled her eyes.

"I think we can rule her out as a suspect. She was more concerned about her broker husband finding out about the affair and tossing her out on her can."

"Alright, and what about the wife of the sheriff?"

"Well, this story gets interesting," she said, leaning forward and placing a hand on Jeff's. Surprised, he looked right in her eyes and noted the seriousness of her tone.

"I've never seen anything like that either. After the police arrived, she was naturally beside herself. However, she never got better. Doctors admitted her to the psychiatric ward of Botsford Hospital. They think the incident caused a psychotic break. We had to get a judge's order to be able to see her, and I swear, Jeff, it was chilling. First off, she will not go around water. At all. They have to sponge bathe her. If they try to ask her to shower, she loses her shit."

"My God."

"It gets better. Her hair has gone completely white, and she stares at you, wide-eyed. But to speak to her, she is completely lucid. Has total control of her faculties, and she swears someone else was in the house that night. She went over the entire event as it happened, can recall exactly what she told the operator on the telephone, even apologized for her behavior," Reggie said before sliding another piece of paper to him, and he flipped it over to see a sketch of a young man, early twenties possibly, and very descriptive.

"What's this?" Jeff asked.

"For shits and giggles, I took a sketch artist with me. She began to describe someone she swears was standing behind her when she walked into the bathroom and discovered her husband. She said one second he was there, smiled at her, and then"—she snapped her fingers—"he was gone."

"You believe her," Jeff said. It was a statement, not a question.

"If you had spoken to her, you would have as well," Reggie said, finally taking her hand off his.

Jeff stared at the paper and sighed. "Alright, we'll run it through our database. See what we find."

"Sorry, boss." She gave him a sympathetic smile.

"Not to worry. Hey, what about the media?"

"As far as they are concerned, he fell, hit his head, and drowned in the tub," she replied as her cell began to ring.

"Let's keep it that way," Jeff said, standing up and turning to go.

"Agent Doucette," she said into her phone. "Hold on just a second. And Jeff?"

He turned to see her hand covering the mouthpiece of the cell phone. He arched his eyebrows.

"You look like shit. Why don't you get some sleep?" she said with a smile.

He grinned and nodded. "Yes, boss. Call me when you hear anything."

"Will do," she said and returned to her phone.

CHAPTER 5

O H GOD, I'M stuffed," Bret said, sitting back and rubbing his tummy.

Lunch had consisted of Polish kielbasa, sauerkraut, and fried potatoes, and Bret could not remember a time he had been so full. They had all sat down once they'd moved his belongings inside to the guest room. It was good to see the house hadn't changed much over the year it had been since he'd last seen them.

"Alright, everyone, let's pitch in, and we can get these dishes done quicker," Margaret said as she stood up, but Molly waved her off.

"No. I've got the dishes. With this baby on my bladder the way it is, there is no way I can be outside of a few feet of the bathroom anyway. Why don't you and Big Daddy and the boys go out on the deck? I've got this."

"Molly, are you sure?" Timmy asked.

"Yup. Margaret washed the pans as soon as she was done, so all there really is are some plates to wash and food to put away. Go on." She stood up and waved them away.

So they grabbed their drinks, Timmy kissed her forehead, and they headed out.

Kaiser, who had been napping on the deck, raised his head as soon as they emerged. As they took their places around a new patio set to look out over the lake, they became quiet for a while, lost in their own thoughts as the wind gently brushed past them.

"How's your mama?" Margaret asked, breaking the silence.

"Same. She and Dad are getting along. I called them on Christmas. They called me back before New Year's," Bret said.

"I don't understand that woman." Margaret shook her head.

"Tell me about it."

"How's teaching?" Big Daddy asked.

"Great! I am getting ready to publish my first book and editing it now. It's based upon the 'queer fear' of the mid-to-late 1930s and how masculinity has changed as a result."

They looked impressed, and he laughed. "It's the most boring stuff you'll ever read."

"We expect a signed copy," Margaret replied, and he promised it would happen.

A few moments passed before she spoke again. Bret could feel the pressure that hung in the air between them and waited for it. Finally it came.

"Bret. We've changed Adam's room. We boxed his stuff up, put it in the attic, and gave away his old clothes. But all the important stuff we kept, and Big Daddy will—"

"You had to," Bret said, reaching over with a smile and grabbing her hand with his own. She looked guilty. "You had to. It had to happen eventually. Just like I'll have to eventually date again, and…" He sighed, tightening his hand as his throat constricted. "And life must go on."

It came then, as it needed to. Relief they'd all sought as the year ticked by and brought the earth full circle around the sun. Another cycle, yet another season to fight the good fight, made them come and witness the commonality they all shared. Timmy, who had been listening and watching them both, was wiping his eyes with his shirtsleeves. Big Daddy, who had his arms folded around himself over his ample belly, was red-faced. Margaret, who should have been Bret's mother-in-law, and Bret himself—all reached for each other and wept as they had done in the driveway of his home five years ago.

The weeping was hard. It was not the kind you saw in movies where they cried with perfect makeup or silently into the crook of their arm. No, this was a deep-down body ache. A soul ache born from loneliness and despair. They missed Adam—brother, lover, friend, and son. The unanswered questions, the circumstances, and just the void he'd left filled them. It was poison, and they had to get it out. A tragedy had touched them all, and what they did was not morbid, Bret realized as so many hands and kisses abounded. It was healing. It was why they were there, for the family that was humble enough to cry together, stayed together.

As the tears tapered off and they regained their composure, they spoke about what they missed the most about Adam. Bret kept the most intimate details to himself, for obvious reasons, but the memories were there—they always were. At first, he was afraid the details of their life together, what Adam looked like, what he felt like, would disappear as sandcastles built on beaches, easily swept away. However, as he met men, if just for a roll in the sack to relieve pressure and to touch and be touched, he found himself comparing them to Adam. The way he'd moved, spoken, looked, acted... He knew it wasn't healthy, but late at night, when he was lonely, he conjured up Adam's face and fell asleep clutching a pillow, pretending Adam was just in the next room and would come to bed soon.

Molly came outside once she figured the crying jag was over. "I'm already crying at television commercials. The ASPCA one with Sarah McLachlan comes on, and it's over for me."

Everyone laughed as Timmy pulled out a chair for her before disappearing back into the house. He came out carrying a case of Budweiser longnecks, and Bret thought he was gonna jump up and kiss him for it. In the other hand, he carried a huge glass of lemonade, which he handed off to Molly. Timmy passed out a few bottles to his mom and dad and handed one off to Bret before popping the top on his own.

"How's the fishing been this year?" Bret asked, changing the subject.

"Great, Dad and I were out Sunday. Lots of catfish near the island," he replied before taking a swig of his Bud. He winced as Margaret hit his leg.

"What?" he exclaimed, wiping the beer from his chin.

"I told you two to stay away from that island. It's dangerous," she said, scolding him but only half-serious.

"Oh hush, Ma, it is not," Big Daddy said, laughing.

She looked at him in mock surprise. "You of all people should know better."

She winked at Bret, who winked back.

"Aww, don't give me that shit. The stories are nothing but old legends. They can't hurt nobody," Big Daddy said, snorting. "The only reason folks still tell them is to keep the young people from going over there for some nooky."

Bret laughed aloud but had to turn his face when the blush he was trying to avoid crept up his neck. He hoped no one would notice, but his hopes were dashed when Molly spoke up.

"That's a lovely shade of pink you're wearing, Bret. What's the matter?" she asked in a singsong voice. She grinned at him mischievously over her glass of lemonade.

Timmy caught on and said, "Yeah Bret, what's the matter?"

"Oh come on," Bret said, his eyes getting big, hoping they would stop. He even nodded in Margaret and Big Daddy's direction.

"Why, Bret, what are they talking about?" Margaret asked good-naturedly.

He shook his head, refusing to answer. He didn't have to.

"Adam took Bret over there, and that's where Bret finally turned in his V card," Molly said.

"We did not!" Bret protested, laughing. He wanted to die.

She rolled her eyes. "You did too. Who do you think he commandeered to help him set up that night?"

Bret's jaw hit the floor. He had forgotten about that part, but Margaret reached over and patted him on the shoulder. "Calm down, honey. You look like you are gonna have a stroke. When you refused to have sex with him in the house, it wasn't necessary, even though it was very sweet and considerate of you. Yes, we talked about it. Adam and I had a very open relationship for a mother and son."

Big Daddy chuckled. "Bret, he talked about you nonstop. Bret this, Bret that, Bret, Bret, Bret. When he finally came out, we didn't have to guess who his boyfriend was."

Margaret finally took a drink of her beer, and Bret smiled, thinking a conversation like this would never have taken place in his home. He turned away and looked in the direction of where his home sat, and felt a twinge of...what? Homesickness, loss? He didn't know. But it was there. They were his parents, after all, and there had been better times. But like Adam, those times were long gone.

Timmy raised his beer. "To Adam. Miss ya, bro. Rest in peace."

They all raised their drinks to the toast Timmy gave.

As they watched the sun sinking lower in the sky, their conversation switched to this and that. They talked about the baby, the wedding, Timmy's job, Bret's schedule for the fall, Big Daddy and Margaret's retirement plans, and about them wintering in a cabin up north the winter before. The five of them lounged and talked, each of them relaxed, and what little bit of awkwardness had built up over the year slipped away, each of them silently excited to see what the next several weeks would hold as they hung out together and enjoyed the summer.

***

Whispers...

He followed the two men as they climbed out of their truck. One carried a cooler and fishing poles, and the other carried a tackle box with his poles. Both of them were laughing, but it was the one on the right with the tackle box he was interested in. The man staggered left a little, and then with the help of his equally staggering companion, they made their way down to the heavy stream that fed into the lake. There they placed their gear on the ground and worked to assemble their fishing poles.

"You hear about the sheriff, Jim?" the one on the right said.

The other guy grunted an affirmative as he threaded his pole and opened the tackle box to pull out a bobber and a hook. The sun had set about ten minutes before, and the sky was still aflame on the western horizon as they baited their hooks, sprayed themselves down with mosquito repellant, grabbed their beer to set in the water, and waded out into the creek.

"Heard his wife's gone to the nut house," the other man said, and Jim snapped at him.

"So what?"

"Well, don't you think that's weird, Jim?"

"I don't know, Larry. Why should I care?" the man spat back.

Larry, yes, that was his name. He had forgotten. Larry was the one whose vehicle they had put him in that night. Larry had been waiting in the woods for them while the sheriff had laughed as he struggled.

Fury roared through him, but he was not going to make his move. No, not yet. He would wait. Minutes passed and turned to half an hour before the one named Jim got his line snagged and decided to go back to the truck for a pair of pliers. That was when the specter moved. As Jim came up the embankment, he accidentally stumbled right and passed through him.

"Sweet Jesus," he whispered.

Larry turned his head. "What are you sweet Jesusin' about now, Jim?"

"I...I...could have sworn..."

He stared, but Larry cut him off. "Get the damn pliers, you pussy," he said, lighting a cigarette.

The ghost remembered.

> "Look at this pussy fight. Look at him struggle. Little faggot's got more piss and vinegar in him than you thought, huh, Sherriff?"
>
> "Shut up, Larry, and fucking get out of here. Go on," the sheriff said as he shoved the drunken man out of the way.
>
> "I still get my cut, don't I, boss?" Larry asked, laughing shrilly as he looked down on their prize.
>
> "Yeah, Larry. You'll get what's comin' to ya." He grunted as he landed another punch to the gut of the struggling form at their feet.

Yeah, Larry, you're gonna get what's comin' to ya.

Jim stumbled up toward the truck, and the specter moved past him and into the water, where it moved easier. Within the blink of an eye, it had its hand around the bobber and started pulling.

"Hey, hey, I got a bite, Jimbo!" Larry laughed and tugged, but the line wouldn't move. Instead, the specter pulled it back, causing another shout of happiness from Larry.

"It's a big one! Bet it's a catfish! Hurry up with those pliers, Jimmy, I may need to use 'em to get the hook out this big ol' bitch's mouth." He waded out to where the water grew deeper, a stupid grin on his face.

"Alright, Larry. Don't lose him," his friend said excitedly.

"I won't if you hurry your ass up. Bring the net!" he crowed as he took another few steps into the water until it was up to his waist. The bobber hung suspended on the surface, and to Larry it seemed there was nothing attached.

"Aw fuck, it got away," he said, reaching for the red-and-white plastic ball.

When a white hand grasped him around the wrist, he barely had time to scream before it dragged him under the water. Larry came down hard, screaming as he struggled against him. As they rolled, the specter let himself be seen, and the horror that filled Larry's eyes thrilled him. But he wasn't gonna kill this man right away, oh no. With the sheriff, he had been too quick to act. This time he wouldn't make the same mistake. He eased his grip and let Larry surface.

"Aaaaaiiieee!" Larry screamed as he broke through to the air. "Jim! Help me! It's Ada—"

He didn't finish as the specter pulled him under again, letting him see him completely. See the death, the rot, the bloat, the empty eye sockets, and the smile when he pulled his lips back. Larry's scream was muted by the water, but it was still there.

From above he heard Jimbo splash into the creek, but he wouldn't make it. The life was drifting out of this one quickly, as the years of smoking, cocaine, meth, and whatever else he could get his hands on had weakened the walls of Larry's heart.

It seized in his chest, and the body stiffened before the specter let him go. Two large hands came down into the water and pulled the body up, and he let it go, drifting backward, unseen again, to rest for now.

There was more to do before he would finally be avenged.

***

"Here ya go, dude," Timmy said, handing Bret a beer.

"Thanks, Timmy." Bret adjusted himself in the seat on the deck.

The sun was setting quickly, and supper was finished. The family had gone in. Big Daddy had to work the next day, and Molly and Margaret were watching *American Idol* but promised to come back out when it was over.

"I miss living here. I miss the summertime crowds that gather across the lake and the laughing kids," Bret said as he took a draw from the longneck.

"Not much has changed. Molly and I bought a house down on Grover at the north end. Work's picking back up, and houses are selling again, so…we're doin' pretty good."

"That's great. Really. What's your schedule like this week?" Bret asked.

"I knew you were comin', so I took it off," Timmy said, peeling the label off his beer bottle.

"You do that every year," Bret said, smiling.

"Hey, don't think I won't keep you busy, office dweller. Good hard work this week if you'd like."

"Sounds great." It got quiet again. The wind shifted, and Bret shivered as the sun began to go down. The flesh on his arms stood up. Tim noticed and scooted closer to him, wrapping an arm around his shoulder and bringing him closer until Bret's head was on his shoulder.

"He loved you so much. I remember when you would stay over and the both of you would crash in the living room after a moviethon. Back then, Dad didn't know. I think Mom knew, but I walked in from the other room to see him lying on his side next to you on the floor. He didn't see me, and I was kind of embarrassed to stand there. I knew I was observing something intimate, but you were sound asleep, and he was just watching over you. That's when I figured it out. Figured out why you two were so close. After that I paid attention to your mannerisms, how close you two sat, how much time you spent together, and I knew you loved each other. You two met on the swim team, right?"

"Yup. I knew I was gay. I'd had a few girlfriends but nothing too serious. I didn't know he was. But it just developed. One day we were friends, and soon all that changed," Bret said. "And I loved him."

"I wish they would have found his killer. I know my brother. It wasn't suicide," Timmy said resolutely.

Suddenly Bret stiffened and gripped the beer bottle tightly. Something was wrong. The sun had set ten minutes ago, but now he was freezing and his jaw clenched shut. He began to shake. His grip tightened on the bottle until it snapped and crushed in his hand, spewing beer everywhere.

"Bret? Bret! *Dad!*" Timmy yelled.

There was the sound of running, but everything seemed far away to Bret.

He was suddenly out of the chair. Faces above him as someone forced his mouth open and inserted something cold on his tongue. He reached for the chain around his neck.

Then everything went black.

CHAPTER 6

T HE TELEPHONE BUZZED on the nightstand next to his motel bed, and Jeff's eyes snapped open as he reached for it.

"McAllister," he grunted into it.

"We've got another one," Reggie said.

"Where?"

"Five miles upstream. We've got a screaming drunk right here, saying the vic was drowned on purpose."

"Alright, I'm on my way," Jeff muttered.

***

"What have we got?" Jeff climbed out of his Navigator.

Reggie walked up to him, then led him down to the spot. The ME had the body bag half-zipped as crime scene investigators walked the scene.

"Got a call about thirty minutes ago after a trucker nearly ran this guy's friend over on the highway up there." She indicated the road he'd pulled off.

"What's he saying?" Jeff asked.

He didn't have to wait too long for an answer. A man bellowed it out as he sat on the bumper of an ambulance, its red lights flashing and casting their crimson light over everything.

"It wasn't me! It wasn't! I wasn't even near him when he went under!" the man cried, fighting off the paramedic's attempts to calm him down. A uniform stood there, trying to keep the frantic man from slugging someone.

Jeff and Reggie walked toward the ambulance and the uniform came to meet them.

"Who is he?"

"Jim Person. Town drunk. Came out with Larry Jones, another worthless town junkie, to do some evening fishing. Said he went back to get a pair of pliers when Larry was attacked and drowned," the beat cop said.

Jeff recognized him from the other night at the sheriff's house.

"It's true!" Jim said, his eyes wild.

Jeff walked down the short path to the truck and waved the paramedic off for a moment. "How are you sure he didn't just get caught in an undertow and drown?"

"Not deep enough down here. We ain't had rain in a couple of weeks, creek's low," he said, shaking his head. "No. No! He was drowned. He...he...he was my friend!" The man sobbed.

"*Stop!*" Jeff yelled, causing Reggie to jump, and the man sobered up quickly and looked at him with pitiful eyes.

"Who drowned him, Jim?" Jeff asked.

"I dunno. But before he went down for the last time, he said a name. He said, 'It's him! It's him! It's Adam!' and then he was gone!"

"Adam Woolsey?" Reggie asked.

"Nah! Can't be," Jim said, shaking his head again.

Jeff turned his head and looked at her again curiously. "Who?"

"Got a moment?" she asked, indicating she wanted him to walk to where she could talk to him privately.

Jeff turned to the uniform and motioned for him to come back. "I want a uniform posted outside his hospital room until further notice. Rotate shifts."

The paramedic helped Jim get in the back of the ambulance as the officer spoke into his radio, and only then did Jeff follow her away.

"What is it?" he asked her.

"We ran the image against every database we possibly could and came out with an almost perfect match. Adam Woolsey. Born November 7, 1984."

She handed him another piece of paper. Jeff recoiled; the description of the sheriff's wife had been spot-on.

"Okay, so where is this Adam guy?" Jeff asked.

"Adam died, Jeff. Five years ago this next week."

***

There were voices close to him. Whispered words and mumbling as he came to the surface of consciousness and turned his head. Timmy was asleep in the chair next to him in what looked like an emergency room, while the doctor spoke with Margaret outside the curtain. As soon as they noticed him coming to, they were immediately at his side. Big Daddy, whom he had not noticed on the other side of the bed, stood up and cast a shadow over him.

"What happened?" he asked.

"Oh, thank God," Margaret said as Tim snorted awake and stood. Bret's face burned with embarrassment as he sat up.

"Easy does it, Bret," the doctor, a Middle Eastern man with a Canadian accent, said.

"Where am I?" he asked.

"You're at Botsford Hospital. Do you remember what happened?" Margaret asked.

"I was outside talking to Timmy," Bret said, confused. He tried to think back on what had happened, but it was all murky and didn't make sense.

"You don't remember anything after that?" the doctor asked, using a penlight to look into Bret's eyes.

"No." He had an IV running out of his forearm, and it tweaked him as he moved his arm, reaching for the chain around his neck.

"Mr. Williams, do you have a history of epilepsy in your family?" the doctor asked, and when Bret just stared at him dumbly, clarified, "Seizures. Petit mal, grand mal?"

"Wha...no. Not that I know of."

"Are you on any drugs, prescriptions for any medical condition?"

"No."

"Narcotics?"

"No! What the hell is going on?" he asked, growing angry and increasingly uncomfortable.

"Alright, alright, take it easy," Big Daddy said, putting a hand on his shoulder.

"Mr. Williams, you had some kind of episode on the deck of your friends' home this evening. I have other questions for you. Did you go for a swim earlier this afternoon, stay out in the sun too long, drink too much? Did you ingest any lake water?"

"No," he said sullenly. The doctor sat down next to him on something Bret couldn't see from his position in the bed.

"Bret, Big Daddy rolled you over onto your side this evening when you…seized, for lack of a better term, and Timmy grabbed the bowl Kaiser was using to drink out of to catch the vomit so it wouldn't get all over the deck. You filled it up with what looked like water," Margaret said as she reached for his hand.

"Yeah, dude, you started saying some weird shit," Timmy said.

Bret looked over at the big, hulking man in the corner. Tim had tucked his hands into his jeans, and he looked horribly uncomfortable.

"What did I say?" Bret asked.

"Your face got all funny, and you looked at me and said, 'You're right. I didn't kill myself.'"

Bret's jaw lowered in disbelief.

"Timmy…" Bret started, but words left him.

Tim raised a hand, turned on his heel, and walked out. Bret turned to Margaret with his jaw still on his chest and tears threatening to surface. The thin woman did not seem upset by it at all. Instead, she looked so sympathetically at him that he had to cover his face to keep from sobbing. Perhaps David had been right—he should have gone to a doctor first before showing up there. But what about the water…? He'd been drinking beer. Once he took a calming breath, Bret lowered his arm and looked at the doctor with a very determined expression.

"Alright, what do we need to do?" he said, clearing the frog out of his voice.

"Well, we're going to keep you overnight for observation and for a few tests. If those come back negative, unless there are any other developments during the night, then we can let you go in the morning, with doctor's orders to rest," he said seriously.

When Bret agreed, the doctor informed Big Daddy and Margaret he'd be in again after the techs had wheeled Bret down for his tests and brought him back. They nodded, and the doctor left.

"Hey, why don't you head home? You've gotta be up in the morning," Margaret said to Big Daddy, who looked down at Bret.

"You gonna be alright, kid?" he asked, concern in his voice.

"Yeah. Yeah, I'm fine. Do me a favor, huh? Go find Timmy?" Bret asked.

"Yeah. No problem." Big Daddy kissed Margaret good-bye before he walked out.

"Can this get any worse?" Bret asked, and Margaret winced and patted his hand. "What?"

"Well…your insurance has an emergency contact number. You listed your mother, and they called her."

Bret groaned and pulled the pillow down over his face.

***

Jeff pulled up in front the Washtenaw County sheriff's department and parked. It was nestled between the municipal courthouse and a fire station. He did not like the growing feeling gnawing at his stomach. Something was wrong in this little burb, and he wondered what it was.

He had nearly laughed in Reggie's face when she gave him the dramatic news, but between the riverside and the office, he had to admit he was creeped out. It wasn't unusual for a crime to go unpunished, or for there to be a cover-up in a town as small as Promise, but for someone to be going to the extent they were to take revenge—which was what this was starting to look like—Jeff knew one thing. They were pissed.

"Now we just have to figure out how deep this goes," he said, looking in the rearview mirror and straightening his tie. He noticed the onset of crow's-feet around his eyes, and his handsome face was a little thinner than he'd like, but otherwise he looked awake and alert.

"I'm just afraid we're gonna need a bigger boat." He tilted the mirror back up before he got out of the car.

As he walked up the front steps and through the front entrance, he already had his badge out to show to the deputy before he could say anything.

"How may I help you?" the deputy, named Martin, asked suspiciously.

"I need some old records. The Woolsey case file," Jeff said as plainly as possible. *There, something flickered in the deputy's eyes.*

"Our records department is closed for the evening. If you'd—"

"I think you know where the key is, Deputy Martin," Jeff said sternly, indicating he was not going anywhere.

Martin looked as if he was considering standing there and going back and forth with Jeff, but luckily he grunted and got out from behind the desk and fished the key ring off his hip.

"Right this way, sir," he said as he headed for a long hallway.

"Kind of a strange thing going on, two deaths by drowning," Jeff said as they made their way down the hall.

"Crazy world we live in," Martin said.

"Are you the acting sheriff?"

"Until another one is appointed by the city council, yeah," Martin said with his back still to Jeff.

At a solid metal door labeled Records, they stopped. Martin inserted the key and opened the door, held it open with a doorstop, and walked through. As Jeff turned the corner, Martin flipped the overhead lights on, illuminating a large room. There were a few chairs lining the wall and a counter where the day staff took orders for documents needed for court.

Going around that, they set off toward another closet-looking place, and again Martin used a key to get access, opened the door, and flipped on the light.

"All purged cases are in that filing cabinet," Martin said, then turned, and walked out, leaving Jeff standing alone in the sickly light of the overhead halogen bulbs.

Jeff pulled on the filing cabinet drawer marked U-Z and slid it open all the way. Surprisingly it was full, but then he remembered that southeastern Michigan had a huge Polish community, so there were a lot of Wazniaks, Woloczyks, Yoznicks, and Zanarowskis. As he dug through the Ws, he eventually found the file he was looking for, pulled it, and closed the filing cabinet. Standing up, he placed it on top and began to riffle through it.

The preliminary report had Adam listed as a missing person, his mother having made the report herself after forty-eight hours of him being gone, and it was just like Reggie had alluded to—this all happened five years ago. As a matter of fact, tonight was the fifth anniversary of Adam's mother filing the report.

According to the file, a 911 call had been placed by a woman jogger forty-eight hours after he was reported missing. She had discovered the body in the reeds, when her dog snapped its chain and bounded into the lake, barking and growling. She immediately phoned the police after the dog came back with a piece of a shirt. A squad car was sent out, and an hour later, they pulled the body of Adam Woolsey out of the water and contacted the family.

"A-ha," Jeff murmured. Officer Martin was the one who had informed the family of the deceased and was in charge of the investigation, and it was Martin's notes that interested him—not for notes he wrote, but for the lack of them. It was just the names of Adam's family members—mother, father, etcetera—and then one other name that stood apart. Under the title "Queer Lover" was the name Bret Williams.

As he stood there and read the file, Jeff noticed that all the formality was there, but there was no substance. No in-depth notes, no scribbled phone numbers, no backgrounds on the family or the boyfriend. And sure as shit, there it was, the one thing he'd dreaded seeing: the declaration of suicide as the cause of death. According to the notes, the young man was homosexual and because of that must have filled his pockets with rocks and drowned himself in the style of Virginia Woolf.

Jeff closed the file with a snap and stood there, shaking, as he rubbed the stubble that had begun to grow. He reached into his pocket, pulled out his phone, and dialed Reggie, who picked up after the second ring.

"What's up, boss?" she asked.

"Where you at?"

"I just pulled into a diner. They close in thirty minutes. What do you got?" she asked.

"I think we're dealing with a homicide." He was surprised when Reggie laughed.

"Where you been all evening, handsome?"

"No, no. I am not talking about what is going on right now. I stopped by the police station and pulled the file on Adam Woolsey. I think we may have revenge killings going on." Jeff told her everything he *didn't* see in the file.

"Jesus. They killed the kid because he's gay?" she whispered.

"Looks like it," Jeff answered.

She was silent for a moment.

"You alright?" she asked.

Jeff sighed. Reggie knew about him and his sexuality, and was the closest person in his life. Always on him about dating or seeing someone, she nagged him mercilessly and tried to set him up on blind dates, but he either couldn't make it due to work or flat-out refused to go because she tried setting him up with other agents. His personal motto was "You don't shit where you eat." And he tried to avoid as much drama as possible. Reggie thought he was being picky. He was not. He didn't want someone who knew the job, wanted to talk about the job, or had schedules that would ensure they never saw each other because of the job. He'd been down that road before, and it didn't pan out. At thirty-five, he had a successful career, and being gay in the FBI meant he had to work harder at it than others.

"Yeah. But Reggie, watch your back. We've got dirty cops," Jeff whispered, staring at the door to make sure Martin was nowhere around.

"You too. What are you going to do now?"

Jeff checked his watch. "I'm taking this file with me, and I'm going to head back to the hospital to talk to Jim. If I gave you a list of names, would you do a background check on them for me?"

After he rattled them off, she asked, "I don't know how this is being done, Jeff. But they're passionate about it. Are you leaning toward the boyfriend?"

"That's why you're the best damn agent we have," Jeff said.

"Sweet-talker."

"Thanks, Reg," he said and killed the call.

Jeff reached for his service pistol, took it off safety, mentally counted the rounds in his clip, and placed it back in his holster. Grabbing the folder, he took a deep breath, willing his anger down deep into his insides, and let calm come over him before walking out of the office, making sure he shut the door and turned out all the lights. He did not want it to look like he was rushed or concerned about anything. As he made his way past the man at the front desk, he saw that another deputy had shown up, and they stopped talking as he walked past.

"Find what you were lookin' for?" Martin asked, his face stony. Was he sweating?

"Sure did. Hey, thanks a lot, guy," Jeff said with a smile, holding up the folder. He did not give him a chance to respond as he hit the glass door and stepped out into the night, heart pounding and dry mouthed. He inhaled a lungful of cool damp air as he made his way to the Navigator.

***

Bret was swimming. His powerful strokes cut through the water with ease as the sun shone down bright around him. The water parted as if he were a knife cutting through its placid surface while his muscles warmed with each stroke. One, two, three, breathe, head back down, just as he had been taught. Feel the water, do not fight it, Adam had said. And Bret had followed that advice, winning championship after championship. He followed it now as he joyfully made his way across the lake. Tired, he let up and felt his body immediately slow down as he surfaced, treading water. The lake was empty save for the blond-haired guy in the center with a grin on his face.

"Hurry up, slowpoke!" Adam called out.

"Awww, come on, I'm tired," Bret said back.

"I'll give you a kiss."

"Nope."

"How about two?" Adam said, laughing.

"I deserve at least four," Bret said as his hands and feet worked to keep him afloat.

"How about three and I promise I'll make the fourth one up to you tonight when my parents go to bed?" Adam said with a wink.

"Deal!" Bret cried and dived in.

Again, he pushed, every muscle in his body working. He remembered not to overdo it, but simply treat the water gently as if it were his friend. One, two, three, breathe, and down again as his heart hammered in his ears and he burned off the remaining calories of his large breakfast. He broke the surface again, expecting Adam's arms to come around him immediately, but as he wiped the water from his eyes, he found himself alone.

"Adam?" Wondering if Adam had dived to swim out even farther made Bret roll his eyes. He didn't want to swim anymore.

But Adam didn't resurface.

"Adam!" He called out again, turning himself this way and that. Nothing but the still surface of the water and an empty shoreline greeted him as he felt something in his left hand. He pulled his hand up to look. Adam's ring lay there. A simple golden band, the match to Bret's, glinting brightly in the sunlight.

***

"Adam!?"

With an intake of breath, Bret sat bolt upright in bed, suddenly afraid. He was not familiar with where he was, and just beyond a curtain, a dark shadow loomed. Quickly he looked about, trying to get his bearings. Suddenly the curtains slid back to reveal a man in a suit looking at him. Everything came rushing back to him in an instant, and he relaxed a little. He looked at the clock on the wall and saw he had only been asleep for a few minutes after they had wheeled him back from a series of tests.

"Are you alright?" the man asked.

He was handsome, six foot two, with short, cropped hair and a strong jaw.

"You're not the doctor…" Bret said suspiciously.

"No, Bret. I'm not."

The man closed the curtain behind him. Bret sat up in the bed, suddenly very conscious of himself and of lying down on his back. Bret didn't know who the man was, but from his frame, he looked strong and capable, and given the nightmare he'd just woken from, it made Bret a little uncomfortable.

The man must have sensed this as he raised his hands, palm out, and said, "It's okay. I'm an FBI agent. I know it's late, but I wanted to see if you wouldn't mind talking to me for a few minutes."

"Can I see your badge?" Bret asked.

"Sure." The man reached into his coat pocket, pulled out a wallet, and flipped it open. "FBI" was all Bret needed to see.

"How can I help you?" he asked.

"Do you mind?" he asked, pointing to a chair.

"Please."

The agent spoke as he pulled the chair beside Bret's bed and sat down. "My name is Agent Jeffery McAllister. I hate to barge in on you like this, but like I said, I'd like to ask you a few questions."

"What could the FBI want with me?" Bret asked, cautiously curious. "How did you know I was here?" he continued when Jeff did not respond.

Jeff looked at him seriously for a second, his eyes searching. *For what?* Bret wondered. Finally Jeff spoke.

"I am investigating a series of recent deaths. Drownings."

Bret gave him a confused look. Jeff sat back and watched him for a second.

"I came to talk to you about Adam, Bret," he said seriously.

Bret stared at him for a second, but didn't register the surprise in Jeff's face as Bret suddenly burst into laughter. It was more of a giggle, really, but it was there nonetheless. "You want to talk about Adam? Where the fuck were you five years ago when I contacted your field office in Detroit to help me find him?"

"I'm sorry?"

"Oh, yeah. You guys, the state police, the sheriff's department, everyone. Adam was missing and—"

"You talked to the sheriff's department?"

"Yeah. When Adam went missing, I practically lived there," Bret said, his eyes narrowing.

"Who did you talk to?"

"The cops, Sheriff Townsend, just about everyone up there too. Why?" Bret asked as Jeff exhaled and sat back.

"Where were you tonight, around eight thirty?" Jeff asked.

"I was at Adam's parents' house."

"And you go there frequently?"

Bret felt his face grow hot. "I go there on the anniversary of Adam's death. Every year. Don't believe me, ask them."

"Where were you last night around ten thirty?" Jeff asked.

"At a gay bar in Livingston, where I live. My friend David was with me there and can vouch for that. Oh, yes, that's right. I'm gay. Now what the hell are you bothering me for? And what the hell does this have to do with Adam?" he asked hotly.

Jeff reached into his pocket, pulled out his smartphone, and slid it open. "Do you know who these two men are?"

Bret leaned over, and Jeff readjusted his sitting position on the chair so Bret could see the phone. As he drew closer, Bret was able to smell Jeff's cologne—woodsy, masculine—and something fluttered in his stomach before the images popped up on the screen.

"That's Townsend," Bret said, and Jeff swiped the image to another man. This one Bret didn't recognize at first until he looked harder. It had been a few years, and the man had aged badly, but sure enough, Bret confirmed his identity as well.

"You know him too?" Jeff asked.

"It's a small town." Bret responded, and Jeff sat back to look at him.

"What's this all about, Jeff?" Bret asked.

"These men are dead," Jeff responded plainly.

"Dead? These were the men who drowned?"

"Yes, they drowned."

"Both of them?" Bret asked, feeling confused.

"Yeah."

"I still don't understand what this has to do with Adam or me."

"Can I ask you a personal question?" Jeff asked.

"Sure, why not? I'm lying in bed attached to an IV after having passed out on a deck this evening, and now I wake to find a federal agent here talking to me about drowned men," he said exasperatedly.

Jeff didn't flinch, didn't move, and Bret didn't feel uncomfortable around him, just vaguely annoyed. It had been a strange couple of days. Jeff wasn't backing down.

"Go ahead," he whispered.

"Why do you come back? Really," Jeff asked.

Bret laid his head back into the bed, suddenly feeling very naked, and pulled the sheet up. He reached for the chain around his neck and held it in his hand. The cool metal comforted him.

"Five years ago, I lost someone I loved, who loved me. We were supposed to be married this year. See? But he didn't get cancer, he didn't move away, he didn't die in an accident, and he certainly didn't commit suicide. I don't care what the police say. He loved me, and his family loved him even though he was gay—unlike mine. And they loved me too. Big Daddy and Margaret and Timmy…" Bret had been holding up the ring around his neck for the agent to see, but then he laid it back on his chest.

"Bret, do you know anyone who would want to hurt Adam?" Jeff asked, reaching over and taking his hand.

Bret was startled a bit from the touch, the question, and the look on Jeff's face. He had been shocked to hear the question five years ago after he'd asked it of himself. Instinctively, he curled his fingers around Jeff's and felt their calluses, their hardness, and he closed his eyes. He drew strength from the heat of it crawling up his arm.

"Why are you asking me this?" he asked, opening his eyes.

"There have been two deaths in this town in the past forty-eight hours. I think they're revenge killings," Jeff said.

"What?" Bret sat up. Suddenly he couldn't breathe, and he couldn't believe what he was hearing.

"Bret, I think your boyfriend was murdered. And I think anyone who may have had a hand in it is being murdered as well. Someone is out for revenge."

CHAPTER 7

Y OU DID WHAT?" Reggie asked over coffee the next morning. "I told him," Jeff said, stirring the cream into his own coffee.

They were sitting down for breakfast at a roadside café along the stretch of highway that ran next to the lake. He had been staring out at it most of the morning. Traffic whooshed by, but his gaze stayed fixed on the vast expanse of lake in front of him. His mind was unsettled, and he did not like the direction this case was going. Someone was out there in this sleepy town exacting justice at his or her whim.

"You just told our primary suspect that we're on to him," she said plainly.

Jeff shook his head. He had suspected Bret for these current murders himself before he pulled back that curtain. When he called Reggie about the folder he had taken from the station, she had informed him that not only was Bret in town, he had been taken to the hospital as a result of having a seizure and for, reportedly, throwing up water.

"I don't think he's our suspect. But he is the link between who killed Adam and who is killing those responsible for his death," Jeff said.

Reggie watched Jeff for a while as the server put their meals in front of them and Jeff began to eat.

"What?"

She shrugged.

"Spill it."

"I think I was followed last night," she said and took a sip of her coffee.

Jeff took a bite of food, chewed, and swallowed. "Get a description?"

"A dark sedan. Looked undercover."

She buttered her toast. Jeff watched as she meticulously went through her routine of preparation before she ate, and he couldn't help but grin.

"Radio the other team?" he asked.

"Yup. They're on it."

"Don't get caught out anywhere alone, Reggie. Stay visible," Jeff said.

"I know the drill." She finally took a bite of her toast. He watched the mischief dancing in her eyes. She was enjoying this.

"The huntress on the prowl." He smirked.

"Gotta bag 'em and tag 'em." She winked, which made him laugh. They spent some time eating before Reggie brought *him* up.

"He's adorable," she commented, looking at him from under heavy-lidded eyes.

"He is," Jeff replied.

"He could also be the perp."

"No. His alibis check out," he responded.

"He could have hired out."

"Bret's working on his PhD, and I've already had someone look into his assets. Nothing major has been moved in or out," Jeff replied, pouring syrup on his pancakes.

"How did he take the news when you told him you think Adam was murdered?" she asked.

Jeff sighed. "He looked at me for a long time and then nodded. Then he started to shake. Bad. Then he cried. It was tough. I think he had just started to move on. I mean, he suspected as much, but over the years, I think he was starting to let it go. It was pretty horrible."

What he was leaving out was that he had gotten up and sat on the edge of the bed when Bret started to shake, and the young man reached for him. Jeff didn't know why he'd let it happen, but before he knew it, his arms were around Bret as he whispered nonsense to calm him down.

"It always is," Reggie said, eyeing him.

"So what do we have so far?" he asked, mentally shaking himself.

"Well, I went through the list of names you gave me last night, including Bret's and Adam's families. Everyone checked out, clean records. Timmy has a couple of unpaid parking tickets, but that's it."

"Adam's folks?"

She shrugged as she riffled through the sugar container. "Mom is a Suzy Homemaker type, has worked odd jobs in the past around the holidays, but nothing substantial. Father is a UAW local president at the Chrysler Plant. Clean records, taxes paid, mortgage will be paid off in seven years. They are not poor by any stretch of the imagination, but they are definitely lower on the totem pole when it comes to finances in this area."

"Tell me about Bret's parents."

"Mom and Dad own a real estate company, active in their local church, quite a bit of resources, rental properties. Dad sits on the local school board and Mom is part of the Daughters of the American Revolution."

"Typical cream-cheese American family," Jeff said. "I talked to Bret's doctor, by the way. The hospital called his mother last night, as she's listed as an emergency contact. They never showed up."

"How nice of them. You thinking what I'm thinking?" Reggie asked.

"Keep an eye on the folks," Jeff said, taking a sip of coffee.

While they ate, his mind wandered back to the man he had sat with until he fell asleep, and felt a stirring.

***

"You could have called us," Elle May said as she stood there, arms crossed over her breasts.

Bret just stared at her and his father, who was looking incredibly uncomfortable in the room. He kept shifting his feet, folding, and unfolding his hands as he stood there. It had been two years since he had seen them, and it seemed as if they had not aged a day except for his father looking a little rounder in the middle. His mother, however, was the picture of elegance and grace. Cold beauty, which could only be observed, not touched.

"I didn't want to bother you," Bret said as he waited for the nurse to bring him his discharge papers.

His mother made a disgusted noise in the back of her throat. "No. A phone call in the middle of the night saying you were having a seizure bothered us."

"Why am I not surprised?" Bret said sweetly.

She stared at him and then fiddled with her blouse sleeves. "So...you know...are you sick?"

"The doctors don't know. They think it's stress," he replied.

"It's not AIDS, is it?" she whispered disgustedly, the word AIDS coming out as if the comatose patient in the other bed would suddenly come alive, jump up, and run down the hallway to inform everyone.

Bret's jaw dropped. "AIDS...what? Mom, no!" Bret exclaimed as she made shushing noises.

"Elle. I have that appointment at ten thirty," his father said impatiently.

"What's the matter, Doug? Afraid someone at First Baptist might see you here with your son?" Bret asked and watched as his father's face turned scarlet.

"Listen here, you're a dark stain on our famil—" he started, but was interrupted by a female voice coming in the room.

"The only dark stain I see is the two of you calling yourselves parents," Margaret said as she entered with Timmy in tow. Margaret shoved past Doug to come and plant a kiss on Bret's head.

"Oh well, guess that's my cue." Elle pulled her purse strap back over her shoulder.

"Oh, come on, what's the rush? Oh, that's right. It's uncomfortable to be around the family that you sued after my son died, huh?" Margaret said, mockingly exaggerating 'oh' with lightning flashing in her eyes.

"Well, if your perverted son had kept his hands off my son—"

Elle May too was cut off as Margaret reached over and slapped her face. Elle May's look of shock was priceless as Timmy got between Doug and his mother, expanding his chest as Bret's father seemed to shrivel in his presence. Margaret leaned in close to Elle May's face.

"If I were you, I'd be careful what you say to me. After the judge threw your case out of court, I've been dying for a chance to catch your uptight West End ass out in town for the past five years after the ten thousand you cost me in attorney fees and pain. Now get your tight ballet-trainer behind out of here before I show you what a real mother is capable of."

A look of cold fury passed through Elle's eyes as she cradled her reddened cheek in her hand. Bret watched the whole thing with mouth agape, while Timmy smirked. Elle squeezed past her and grabbed Doug by the arm as she headed toward the door.

"You'll be hearing from us," Elle said as she departed.

"Not if you value your life, bitch," Margaret replied, a little louder than she should have. As she spun back around, the anger in her face replaced with the reddening of her cheeks, and she sighed. "I'm sorry. I shouldn't have done that with you here."

"I...no. I...it's fine," Bret said. He'd never seen his mother back down from anyone before, but he was worried she'd make good on her word. As if reading his mind, Margaret patted his hand.

"Big Daddy gets free legal service now through Chrysler's Union, honey. Don't worry about it."

"She sued you? Why didn't you tell me?" Bret asked, avoiding Timmy's gaze. He was still as embarrassed as he had been last night.

"Why, so you would worry your pretty little head over it? Please. I wouldn't do that to you. Besides, we knew it wouldn't hold up. The judge all but laughed at her."

"Yeah but she had her fun too, Mom," Timmy said, speaking for the first time. Margaret tried to quiet him, but it was too late. When Bret looked at her expectantly, she shook her head and held up her hands.

"There were a few committees I was on. I got turned away after a while. Which is fine, I fired back with an article in the newspaper. They lost fifty percent of their volunteers," she said with satisfaction in her eyes.

A male nurse walked in with discharge papers and some medication to help him sleep, and after explaining the medication and taking back the signed discharge papers, he let Bret know he was free to go.

All three of them were quiet as they left the hospital, got into Timmy's truck, and headed back to the house.

As they drove, Bret's mind drifted back to Jeff—what Jeff had said and Bret agreed not to repeat—and felt guilt right away at the proximity of the two at his left. *Murder.*

"Earth to you," Timmy said, causing Bret to turn his head quickly.

"Nothing."

"Nothing what?" Timmy replied, looking at him strangely.

"I was in my own thoughts," Bret said.

"Alright, but I'd like you to answer my question."

Bret stared at him for a moment. "Which was?"

Margaret laughed, and Timmy rolled his eyes, raising one beefy hand off the steering wheel and patting Bret's head. "Do you want to go fishing, space cadet? Molly is at her mom's tonight."

Bret smiled. "That'd be great."

Timmy smiled back at him and reached over to clap a hand on his shoulder. Bret reached up and held it there for a second. All had been forgiven.

***

Plenty of sunscreen, beer, a cooler, fishing poles, a portable radio, and forty minutes later they were on the family's pontoon, puttering out to the center of the lake with an oldies rock station blaring and Bret tapping his feet as they made their way. The lake was populated today, and the bathers on the public side of the beach were wading, swimming, and laughing as parents cooked and lifeguards watched on.

Bret and Timmy positioned the boat and put down a small anchor to keep them from drifting, and then removed their shirts.

After putting their feet in the water, they baited their hooks with worms and tossed them in. Timmy had been very present in Bret's life since Adam passed, dropping by his school to say hello, having Molly call at least once a week, and cheering the loudest at his graduations...both of them. In return, Bret showed up at birthday parties, went with him to livestock auctions, and the occasionally they went to a concert at Pine Knob.

"Hey, since you two are having a baby, is the wedding still on for the fall?" Bret asked.

"Yeah. You're still my best man, right?" he asked.

Bret looked over and grinned. "Duh."

"Good. Hey, Bret, about last night..."

"Dude, I'm so embarrassed about that, really, I'm sorry."

"No. It freaked me out, not because of what you said but how you said it," Tim replied, taking a swig of Budweiser.

"What...how I said it? I don't understand." Bret was sitting in the sunlight and had to put a hand over his eyes to even see Timmy.

"You sounded just like Adam. I mean *just* like him. Even your face, for a moment...you went totally *What Lies Beneath*. I could have sworn I was looking right at Adam," Timmy said softly, staring out into the water.

Bret was speechless and a little creeped out. A chill caught hold of him, and he shivered despite the heat of the sun. His gaze wandered over to Promise Island, and he watched as the wind blew through the leaves in the trees.

"Maybe I should go home," he said quietly.

"Please don't. We're worried about you," Timmy said, wrapping his arm around Bret's shoulder.

"This wasn't the first time," Bret confessed, looking down at the water.

"This has happened before?" Tim asked.

"The other night at a club I went to—my friend David was with me. We took a bathroom break from dancing and were just getting ready to go. David said I turned white and told him something about a promise and then one down, five to go," Bret replied.

"What promise? What were you talking about?"

"Dude, I don't know," Bret said with a huff, leaning his head on Tim's shoulder. "Maybe something *is* wrong with me."

"I don't know. But whatever it is, you've got Mom, Dad, and us," Tim said. "Hey! *Hey!* I got one!"

Bret scooted back and stood up, grabbing for the net they had brought with them. Sure enough, Timmy reeled in a good-sized catfish, which he took the hook out of and threw in a mesh cage he had tied off the end of the boat. They fished, drank, and swam most of the day until they grew so weary they had a hard time pulling themselves back up on the boat. The tension of the night prior seeped out of his body as exhaustion set in. After a little while longer, they decided to head back to the shore so Timmy could make dinner.

***

Jeff waited in the driveway as he watched the pontoon come in from the lake. It was quarter after six, and he was thankful he had changed into a pair of shorts and a T-shirt instead of the suit he had been in for the past few days. As the boat made its way to the ramp, Jeff checked himself out in the reflection of the window one last time before he could be seen and then watched them come ashore as he leaned against the SUV. Laughing, Bret and a large man—whom Jeff assumed was Adam's older brother Timothy—came up the dock carrying fishing equipment and a cooler. Yet when Bret saw Jeff, he slowed a little, and his smile evaporated, which tugged at Jeff's heart.

The larger man whispered something in Bret's ear as he stared at Jeff. Bret just shook his head, and the smile was back, although the larger man eyed Jeff suspiciously, as they made their way to where he stood. Jeff straightened up.

"Hey, can I help you?" Tim asked.

Before Jeff could reply, Bret spoke up.

"It's alright, Timmy. I can take care of this. Meet you up at the house?"

"You sure?"

"Yeah. Yeah, here take these with you, though." Bret handed off a couple of fishing rods.

Jeff, struck at how handsome Bret was, felt his breath hitch. His blond hair was a little flyaway from being out on the water, but his skin was tanned, and he was well muscled. His jaw was perfectly square, and his lips full. Bret's blue eyes sparkled as he caught Jeff staring, but Jeff played it off quietly, and Bret didn't say anything.

"Okay, see you up at the house."

Timmy trudged off with his load in his hands. Bret and Jeff watched him go and made sure he was out of earshot before either spoke.

"You didn't tell them," Jeff said.

"No. You asked me not to," Bret replied.

"Fair enough."

"Is it?" Bret asked, folding his arms across his chest. The look in his eyes made Jeff second-guess his reason for coming here.

"No, it isn't. But we're working on it."

"Is that why you're here?" Bret asked, standing in front of him.

Jeff looked at him from behind his sunglasses. "Partially. I wanted to talk about Adam. And I wanted to find out how you were doing."

Bret did something that surprised Jeff—he reached up and gently removed the glasses from Jeff's face. He folded them, reached for Jeff's right hand, and slid them in, folding Jeff's fingers around them before looking back up. Jeff felt his touch all the way up the length of his arm.

"I like to look into the eyes of someone talking to me," Bret said.

Timmy had reached the house, and suddenly both turned at the sound of a bark. Kaiser, who must have skirted between Timmy's legs, came bounding down the expanse between the house and where they stood. Jeff stiffened a bit, but Bret put out a hand and placed it on his chest.

"Easy. Just let him sniff you," Bret said, and Jeff felt himself relax.

"Hey, baby!" Bret said as Kaiser slowed down, keeping watchful eyes on the newcomer.

"It's okay. He's okay," Bret said, comforting the huge black-and-tan shepherd.

To Jeff, the eyes said "Make a wrong move and it's you and me, pal." The dog leaned in to sniff Jeff's sandal-clad feet and then up his legs and then—

"Kaiser, *no!*" Bret said, laughing and shoving the large dog away. "We need to talk about your manners."

Jeff, who had instinctively twisted his hips to keep the large dog's nose out of his crotch, couldn't help but laugh.

"He's friendly!" he said, and Bret's handsome face broke into a grin.

"Too friendly sometimes, I think. Kaiser, heel."

The dog immediately sat.

"So, Ada—Wait, not here," Bret started and then stopped, looking up at the house. Margaret had come to the door, and Bret gave a friendly wave. She waved back and then continued on around the porch and into the backyard.

"You got plans for dinner?" Jeff asked.

"No. You like bar food?"

"Sounds good."

"Alright, give me thirty, and I'll be out," Bret said and walked away.

Kaiser stayed, watching Jeff until Bret hollered for him, and then the big black mound of teeth and fur took off on the heels of his master. Jeff watched Bret go, marching toward the house with a purpose, and felt his heart sink a little. Bret was completely business, and Jeff felt a twinge of disappointment. There was something about the way he moved...

Before coming to the Woolseys' to check on Bret, he'd made a point to drive around Promise. The area was certainly well-to-do, from the shops that lined the main street to the town square, and even the Baptist church was resplendent. The homes in town showed off the amount of money that lived there, except for the Woolseys' residence.

No, Jeff thought, this house was older. Not to say it was run-down. Not at all. The yard was huge, shaded by tall elms and oak trees that dotted the property. It must have been an acre between their front porch and the main road. The driveway was graveled and wound along the side of the property up to a carport, where several vehicles sat.

The home itself was built up, no doubt in case of flooding, and the porch sat at the top of a steep set of stairs. It had a rustic look, like a cabin, but everything around him indicated that they took great care of their property, so he assumed the inside was just as well kept. It looked cozy, not sterile like some of the houses in the multiple subdivisions looked. It had character.

While he waited, Jeff wandered to the water's edge and the small dock they had parked the boat on to look out over the water. He inhaled deeply, the woodsy scent relaxing him, and thought he would like to retire somewhere like this one day.

Retire and what…live alone?

With a frown, he reached down and picked up a handful of stones. Repositioning himself, he expertly flicked his wrists as stone after stone skipped over the water only to disappear underneath the placid surface. He sighed at his lonely thoughts and let his mind drift back to Bret and his wild blond hair and big blue—

"Stop it," he said aloud.

He tossed the rocks back angrily. This was a job, this was another job, and like so many jobs before this one, he would finish it and move on. He turned his head back to the door Bret had walked through moments ago.

And yet he wondered…

***

Bret immediately felt ashamed at his attraction to Jeff. The night before had been one thing. But now his face burned as he took each step, walking back to the house, feeling the evening sun and Jeff's eyes on his back.

Jeff had felt warm and wonderful, his cologne a mixture of leather and something Bret couldn't place. His neck had been soft as Bret cried his anger out in the hospital, and his arms had been strong as Bret shook. All these years of being told Adam had died at his own hand, and then for it all to be reversed and set in his lap had overwhelmed him with a bitter triumph that had caused him to shake in anger. Jeff's arms were strong enough to control the spasms that had shaken him, and even though Bret felt foolish for his emotional outburst, somehow it had allowed him to sleep, deep and dreamless. When he woke, though, Jeff had gone.

Now here he was again, and Bret felt his heart race. Sure, he had bedded men since Adam, including David, but none of them had been lasting. Their physical interaction had only been enough to satiate his desire for touch, but he kept the walls of his heart high and the battlements well guarded against unwanted intruders.

Shaking his head, he climbed the front porch with Kaiser and walked through the door. Immediately the smell of fish fry hit Bret's nostrils, and his heart sank a little. Timmy was in the kitchen with Margaret and Molly, cleaning the fish they had caught. As he walked in, all three of them raised their heads with varying expressions between curiosity and caution on their faces. Molly was the first to speak up.

"Who is Mr. Hottie out there?" she asked as she snapped the ends off the green beans in a bowl.

Bret's mouth ran dry, but Margaret spoke up.

"He owes us no explanation, Molly," she chastised, staring at the very pregnant girl, who shot Bret a knowing look.

"Jeff's a friend of mine. Came in from Ohio to visit family," he lied, face burning, making him want to crawl under the table.

"Will he be joining us for dinner?" Timmy asked, throwing something into the trash.

"No, I think we're just going to grab something while we're out. We won't be too long," Bret said, trying not to wince.

Margaret smiled and nudged Timmy in the arm. "Go. Have fun. You've been under too much stress as it is. Take the house key, though. It's hanging up on the nail by the door."

"Are you sure? I can reschedule—" Bret said, but was stopped short by Molly.

"No. Go on."

"Okay," Bret said awkwardly making for his bedroom.

"Bret?" Timmy called out.

Bret turned around and walked back into the kitchen. "Yeah?"

"I'll wait up for you."

Bret relaxed. "Thanks, Timmy. I won't be long. Promise."

Twenty minutes later, he walked out of the house, freshly showered and dressed well enough to make an appearance in public. Wearing a pair of light cotton shorts and a button-down white shirt, the evening breeze felt good on his skin as he made his way down the driveway to find Big Daddy home from work and talking to Jeff. As far as Bret could tell, the conversation was friendly enough as both men stared out over the lake.

"Used to be Indian land. Algonquin tribes owned most of this before the white people rushed them out a long time ago. That's why you'll notice a lot of counties have Indian names: Lenawee, Washtenaw, Wyandotte, and on and—Oh, there he is. Hey, Bret, I didn't know you knew an FBI agent," Big Daddy said.

"Uh, yeah. He's a friend of mine," Bret stammered.

"From Ohio. Wanted to know about the lake."

"Mark was telling me about the Indian tribes that lived in this area a long time ago," Jeff said nonchalantly. Bret relaxed a little.

"Oh yeah. See that island out there? It's cursed," Bret said, adding to the conversation.

"Oh, horseshit," Big Daddy replied. "They only kept that rumor going so high school girls wouldn't get in trouble out there with their boyfriends, if you know what I mean."

"Well, Mr. Woolsey, it was a pleasure." Jeff offered his hand, and the older man shook it.

"You boys headed out?" Big Daddy asked, getting out of the way of the SUV as Jeff made his way around to the driver's side.

"Yeah, Big Daddy. We won't be long, though. Just gonna get a beer or two," Bret said, opening his door.

"Alright. You two be safe now," Big Daddy said and began to lumber up the long driveway to the house as Bret got in the SUV.

"Big Daddy?" Jeff asked, watching the man go. "That's appropriate. That man is huge."

"He's the best man in the world," Bret said as he settled in and guiltily watched as the elder Woolsey made his way up the steps. He hated lying to them.

"We don't have to go if you don't want to," Jeff said.

"You told him you were an FBI agent?" Bret asked, changing the subject.

Jeff put the SUV in gear and turned around in the driveway. "There is no use lying to them about anything. They'll find out soon enough. And I am sorry for the awkwardness of the situation, so I want to apologize ahead of time."

Bret buckled himself in and turned to Jeff, who was looking at him for a response. His blue eyes were almost electric in how light they were. Framed by a tanned complexion with dark hair, which was kept short, but that didn't stop the gray starting to show at the temples. He was handsome, rugged-looking, and the way he gazed at Bret as if searching…

"It's okay."

Jeff favored him with a slight smile before driving down toward the road. "So, where we headed?"

"Uh, you probably eat bar food all the time, right? How about something a little more not gonna kill you in five years?" Bret asked.

Jeff laughed.

"Italian?"

"That'll work. Which way?"

"Take a left and follow this all the way around the lake," Bret instructed, and off they went.

CHAPTER 8

T HE RESTAURANT WAS slow for a Thursday evening, but Bret knew it would be. This restaurant was usually a weekend place that lovers brought dates to on the weekend. It boasted a beautiful deck where patrons could sit and overlook the lake while eating. That night most would be gathered at the sports bar watching the Red Wings take on the Colorado Avalanche in their fight for the Stanley Cup. Which was perfect for Bret—he did not want to see or be seen by any of his parents' friends. Therefore, once inside, they asked to be seated out on the patio.

"Wow, this is really nice," Jeff said as they sat down.

There was another couple out on the deck, but far enough away from them not to hear what they were saying.

"Yeah, their calamari is fantastic," Bret said. "It's been a while, though."

"Well, then, we'll start off with that, and may I have a bourbon on the rocks and a glass of water?" he asked the server, a petite, dark-haired girl with a friendly smile.

"Sure, I'll put that right in for you, and for you, sir?" she asked, looking at Bret.

"Make mine a double Johnnie Walker and Coke, please," he replied.

"Red or Black Label?" she asked with a smile.

"Black, please." He smiled back.

She turned and walked away before Jeff spoke up next.

"How are you feeling?"

Bret turned and looked at him. "After what you told me last night? Odd. Better in a way, worse in others."

"How so?" Jeff asked.

"I'm happy I was right and absolutely pissed off all at the same time. If you're right and someone is taking revenge on people, which by the way would make me the prime suspect in your investigation, then both Townsend and that old drunk were working together?" Bret asked.

"Did you do it?" Jeff asked.

"Did I drown those men? No," Bret responded. "But I'm not sorry they're dead."

They grew quiet as their drinks were brought out to them. Bret sat back as Jeff looked at him seriously. His eyes seemed to be searching Bret's, who stared back without flinching.

The server came out this time, carrying a tray of their calamari, and asked them if they would like to order. Jeff quickly picked up his menu and searched while Bret ordered the lasagna.

"Is it good?" Jeff asked.

"It's the best," Bret replied, and Jeff told the server he'd take that as well. She took their menus and thanked them.

"Timmy's a big guy," Jeff said matter-of-factly.

"And wouldn't hurt anyone," Bret countered, knowing where Jeff was going.

"Are you sure? He seems awful protective of you." Jeff made a plate, squeezing lemon on top of the calamari before trying one.

"The whole family is. Big Daddy, Margaret, Timmy, and his soon-to-be wife, Molly. But you know all of this, don't you?" Bret asked, taking some calamari onto his own plate.

"I do," Jeff admitted. His face registered pleasure as he chewed.

"And you have no leads," Bret said, taking a bite of his own. It was a statement, not a question. Jeff did not reply, and Bret focused on their hors d'oeuvres. The calamari was just as good as he remembered. They ate silently for a few minutes, enjoying the reddening of the western sky and the occasional gull that flew crying out over the surface of the water. Occasionally Bret stole a glance at Jeff, who took frequent sips of his bourbon between bites of seafood. His hands were strong looking, with long fingers and chewed nails.

"That's a bad habit," Bret said.

"Drinking?" Jeff asked, a look of surprise on his face.

Bret snorted and took a sip of his own drink before replying. "No. Chewing your fingernails."

"I...uh...I..." Jeff laughed. "I never noticed I was doing that." He set his hand back down on the table, a smile on his face.

Bret watched him for a little while as Jeff dug back into the calamari. He could feel the liquor clouding his brain, making him feel pleasant. The air was perfect, as the summertime breeze caressed his warm skin and the smell of sun-warmed earth helped to lull him into relaxation.

"So, tell me about yourself."

Jeff emptied his glass and set it on the table. "What do you want to know?"

"Why we're eating out, why you look amazing and relaxed with a murderer on the loose. Also, I want to know more about you. I've seen enough *Law & Order* to understand you have a file with my name on it somewhere on your person and it contains everything I've ever done. Possibly including my macaroni art from kindergarten," Bret said simply. Color rose in Jeff's face, and Bret was pleased with himself for the moment.

"I served six years in the Marines as an MP, went to school while I was in and got a degree in Criminal Justice. After that, I went to train with the FBI in Quantico."

"Married?"

"No."

"Gay?" Bret asked, taking another sip of his drink. It tasted good, and his mouth was dry.

"As far as I can tell. But I haven't dated anyone in a long time. Reggie, my partner, wants me to hook up with another agent," Jeff said.

"That's not unreasonable," Bret said. The server brought out their food and set it down in front of them. The lasagna looked amazing, and Bret's stomach growled in anticipation.

"Can I refill this for you?" the young woman asked Jeff.

"Sure, make it a double, please," he replied, and she was off.

"I'm sure your job puts you in a lot of dangerous situations," Bret said, cutting off a piece of his meal.

"Sometimes."

He was quiet again, and to Bret he looked forlorn and lonesome. Perhaps it was the booze, perhaps it was the sunset—either way, Bret had this incredible desire to reach across the table and touch his hand.

"So, the Marines. Something you wanted to always do, or...?"

Jeff nodded. "Yeah. I was a little hellion when I was a kid. Dad walked out on Mom and me when I was three. She worked a lot, so I was left to my own devices. The Marines offered structure, discipline, something I didn't have, didn't know I wanted either," he said with a mischievous grin.

The way he looked at Bret made him catch his breath. The skies above might have been a deep-set purple and cloudless, but there was a storm in Jeff's eyes. Bret swallowed thickly.

It would not have been anything for Bret to seduce him. The thought of it caused his shorts to grip him in a not so unpleasant way. Instead, he diverted the conversation as best he could.

"Why drown them?" he asked. "Why go through the trouble and not plug them or, I dunno, stab them with something?"

Jeff laughed. "Plug them?"

Bret felt his face color. "Sorry. *Law & Order*, remember?"

Jeff shook his head and finished his drink.

"They want them to be afraid. They want them to fear death, knowing it's coming," Jeff said nonchalantly, and Bret felt his face pale.

"The same way they made Adam afraid," he whispered. "Oh, my God."

Jeff nodded.

"Then I hope you never catch who's doing this," Bret replied and sat back to watch the lake.

"You don't mean that."

"Don't I?" Bret said indignantly, turning back to him. The look of sympathy on Jeff's face made him deflate.

"No. You're right, Bret. I have studied you. I have a file on you. I've read your papers you wrote for school. I know who you associate with, your grade point average, and I know your PhD track is exceptionally fast. You pour passion into everything you do. Everything you write comes alive and...well, I don't think you're the type of person to do this. Nor do I think you're the type to let something like this happen if you could help it," Jeff said.

"You've read all of that?" Bret asked, astounded.

Jeff nodded and looked down at his empty glass.

Bret laughed. "Why not just strip me naked right here? I mean, what's the whole point of questioning me at all?"

"I'm sorry. It's been a long couple of days," Jeff admitted. It was his turn for color to infuse his face. Bret felt a pang of sympathy. He wasn't trying to hurt Jeff or make him uncomfortable. Jeff was being honest, more honest than he had to be. It didn't mean Bret had to like it, however.

"Wow. I've never had my life opened up like this before. Tell me, did you like what you saw?" Bret asked, suddenly not wanting to even touch his meal. He didn't know whether to be disgusted or flattered.

Another family was coming out onto the patio, led by a waiter who walked them past where they sat.

"I do."

Bret chuckled. "I feel like my future, or any hope of a future, hangs on this. I have to let go. Just make me a promise."

Jeff watched him for a moment. "What's that?"

Bret reached across the table and placed a hand over Jeff's. It was warm, and before he knew it, Jeff turned his hand and curled his fingers within Bret's.

"I have a family that hates me. I have a family that loves me. The ones that love me, trust me. I won't put them through any more unnecessary pain. I've spent the past five years rebuilding my life. I loved Adam, and I'll tell you what you need to know. Take it easy on me. I don't know how much I can take," Bret pleaded.

Jeff looked down at their intertwined fingers and nodded. "I'll do the best I can."

***

Jeff liked him. He liked how smart he was. As they ate, the drinks kept coming. They went down easy, and Jeff didn't know if it was the heat of the day, the liquor, the pleasant tug in his shorts, or the way Bret smiled that put him so at ease. The gentle breeze off the lake kept him cool enough to be comfortable, and he'd laughed so much his face hurt. Out of the corner of his eye, he could see people glance over and lean forward to whisper about the two men who were enjoying each other's company. It didn't make him self-conscious, but it did keep him sober enough in case he needed his faculties to react.

"Favorite color?" Bret asked.

"Easy. Blue," Jeff replied with a smile.

Bret's eyes widened, and he nodded as if that was the answer he'd suspected all along. "Ah, cool colors. Calm. Serene. Thoughtful."

Jeff grinned. "Alright, what about you?"

"I like earth colors—browns, reds, yellows," Bret said, stirring his glass.

"Warm colors. Sensitive, passionate, endearing," Jeff said and watched as Bret's face colored again. Jeff wanted to melt through the chair and run off between the boards of the deck upon which they sat. His gaze kept straying to Bret's lips. They were full, sensual, and he wondered if they tasted as good as they looked. Bret cleared his throat, and Jeff glanced up again.

"Okay. Favorite movie."

"What do you think it is?"

Bret cocked his head to the side. "*The Hunt for Red October.*"

Jeff shook his head, laughing. "No. That was a terrible guess."

Bret shrugged. "I tried the whole Marine-slash-FBI thing. Sorry."

"No reason to be sorry. But no, I like the classics. *Bringing Up Baby, North by Northwest, How to Marry a Millionaire...*"

Bret's eyes grew wide with excitement. "*Penny Serenade, Gentlemen Prefer Blondes!*"

Jeff sat forward. "Yes!"

"Cary Grant, Audrey Hepburn, Kathryn Hepburn..." Bret said dreamily.

"Marilyn Monroe, Greta Garbo, Marlon Brando, Humphrey Bogart..." Jeff continued.

"Clark Gable!" they said in unison and snickered.

Bret had leaned forward, and now he and Jeff were leaning close. Bret was grinning, and in his gaze there was something... something playful, sure, but a light in his eyes that was a little hot. Jeff swallowed and felt his heart kick-start a bit. Then just as quickly as it came, it tore Jeff's heart a little when it drifted away and Bret turned his attention from him to the lake behind them.

"Hey, you still with me?" Jeff asked, reaching across the table. Bret's hands were warm to the touch, and Jeff rubbed the top of them with the pad of his thumb. But Bret didn't look back at him. Instead, he gazed out over the water. The longing in his eyes, the sadness had replaced the humor, and Jeff turned his head to figure out exactly what he saw. It was there, off in the distance but still visible in the fading light...Promise Island. It would be a matter of moments before it disappeared on the horizon as the sun sank away. Perhaps once it was gone...

"I think I should be getting back before it gets late," Bret said, and Jeff was glad Bret's head was turned away from the wistful smile Jeff couldn't help.

Bret turned back and found Jeff's blue eyes again, and Jeff simply nodded.

***

As he stood in the driveway, Bret watched the taillights of Jeff's vehicle disappear into the night. He was sad. He could not help it. He felt like he was standing between two worlds: caught within the world of the living—driving away—and the dead. It was a shaded, gray world, and it hurt Bret. He frowned, turned his attention to the lake, and sighed.

"When will it end?" he asked the stars above. Their cold light shone down on him and offered no answer he could hear. Deep in the woods, he heard an owl call its constant question, its lonely sound coupled with the cool evening breeze that chilled his sun-kissed skin, and he shivered involuntarily before trudging up the stairs to the Woolseys' front door. Bret fished the keys out of his pocket and opened the screen just as the big door swung open.

Timmy stood there in a pair of sweats and a T-shirt. Bret let his hand fall away as the front porch light chased the shadows where they stood. He had forgotten that Tim had promised to stay awake until he got home, and when their eyes met, Bret's shoulders slumped. Timmy chuckled, stepped out, and wrapped Bret in his arms. Bret allowed himself to be held.

"What's the matter, buddy?" Timmy asked.

Bret turned his head and verbalized what he'd been feeling for so long. "This trying to live again is killing me."

Timmy did not say anything, and he did not move.

Around them, the summer night was alive and singing. The nocturnal lullaby floated on the scented air like a gospel choir testifying to their struggle for a chance to live. Creatures great and small peeked out from behind the trees and high grasses of the lake to watch the two bathed in artificial light while moths fluttered against the lamps. They stood there while the crickets played their symphony in the place where friendship exists the strongest—in their stark, naked humanity, far from the prying eyes of people, and deep in the heart of the night.

CHAPTER 9

JEFF WOKE UP to an aching back and, even worse, an aching erection. The alarm on the motel's nightstand generated a growl of contempt as his hand slapped down hard on the snooze button. He rolled over, his eyes grainy from too few hours of sleep. His mouth tasted bitter, mirroring his mood as he stared upward at the ceiling of the unfamiliar room.

He'd driven back there the night before after dropping Bret off, and he'd climbed into bed, hoping to hitch a ride into sleep on his crumbling mood. But sleep eluded him. Instead, he tossed and turned as thoughts barreled down the highway of his mind. Thoughts of Bret, his smile, the way he talked or narrowed his eyes when Jeff was speaking, the touch of his hand... All these things led to fantasies, which burned the edges of his nerves with erotic images that crucified him as he lay in bed. He tried chasing those thoughts away with the little bottles of booze he found in his minifridge, but they had only served to lubricate the wheels and bring the fantasies floating above his body, and at one point, he caught himself reaching out, only to wrap his fingers around thin air.

He sat up with a grunt as his head protested and pounded between his ears. He stood, naked, his erection pointing outward like a divining rod leading him to water as he shuffled to the shower. Once in there, he soaped up, ignoring his current state of arousal as he slowly brought the water temperature down. Shivering, he finished up and stepped out. His mind was suddenly free of the cobwebs of too little sleep. He was pissed, and he didn't know why.

He dressed quickly and, while he was doing so, Reggie called. They had to run back to Detroit to brief the director on the goings-on, and she said she would be by in a few minutes. She wanted to brief the agents on the role they would take while she and Jeff were gone. They were staying at another motel across town to avoid all of them being in one place, given the current circumstances.

"I want them on Bret's and Adam's families. Keep out of sight, but be present. Wherever they go, till I get back," he said.

"Think that's a bit much?" she inquired.

"No," he said flatly. He had a bad feeling about leaving, but he had to.

"Alright, boss," she said and hung up.

Jeff slid the phone in his pocket and exhaled to try to steady his thoughts. They drifted to Bret, and he prayed silently that nothing else would happen today.

***

Bret woke up, begrudgingly, when someone came in and sat on the end of his bed. He could feel the weight shift the bed down, and a hand rubbed his side. He opened his eyes to find Molly sitting next to him, smiling down. He smiled back and rolled over, inhaling deeply. He smelled breakfast cooking in the kitchen, and his stomach grumbled at him.

"Hey, sunshine," she said.

"Mornin'."

"You boys watch movies all night?" she asked.

She'd gotten up several times to use the bathroom while he and Timmy shared a bag of popcorn and sodas. Timmy had fallen asleep sitting up, and Bret had turned the TV off and made him go to bed before turning in himself, only to lie there staring up at the ceiling, his thoughts dancing between Adam and Jeff.

"Yeah. Sorry, I didn't mean to commandeer your husband." He sat up.

"Oh, please, he's hovering over me right now. It's driving me bananas," she said, placing her hands on her stomach. "Commandeer away."

Bret snickered and placed his hand on her belly.

"He's being quiet right now. I think he's sleeping," she said.

Bret took his hand away. "Are you hoping for a boy?"

"I think Timmy would be a great daddy to a little girl, but yeah, he's excited for a boy," she said, sitting back, using her hands as a kickstand, and exhaling.

"Which do *you* want?" Bret asked, smiling.

"I just want a healthy baby. Ten fingers, ten toes—I'll love it just the same. That's all I care about." She paused, looking at him.

"What?" he asked, confused by the hesitant look in her eye.

"Can I tell you something without upsetting you?"

Bret nodded, uncertain where this was going.

"I haven't told Timmy, and Lord knows we've gone through baby books looking for names, but..."

She paused, and Bret understood.

"You want to name him Adam if it's a boy." She nodded, and Bret reached for her arm. "I think that's a great idea. I think Timmy will love that," he said.

"He loved Adam so much. It's been hard all the way around. I never thought I'd get him back after...you know...Adam died. But he came around. I just think that it's the right thing to do," she explained.

"Well, what if it's a little girl?" Bret asked.

"Well, Eve, I think. It's still symbolic of new beginnings."

"I think Eve is beautiful," Bret said as a knock sounded on the door. "Hey, come on in!" Bret looked up. Big Daddy was standing there in his work clothes.

"Just checking in before I head out to work. You have a good time last night?" he asked, standing there with his lunch bucket.

"Yeah, it was good," Bret replied.

"Good. He seems like a nice young man. He is welcome here any time he wants to come. But I didn't come down here for that.

Margaret has breakfast on the table. Molly, will you go wake Tim up before she comes down the hallway with a bullhorn?"

Molly nodded, and Big Daddy reached down to help her up before Bret kicked his feet over the edge to stand. They all walked off down the hallway and parted in the living room, going three separate ways.

Bret sat down at the table, set with steaming piles of food.

"Dig in, baby. Tim said he has a whole day planned for you two. I think Molly and I will join you if ya'll don't mind," Margaret said, shutting the refrigerator door.

"No, that'd be great." He grabbed for the scrambled eggs.

Timmy and Molly came into the kitchen a moment later, only for Molly to roll her eyes, claiming the baby was on her bladder. She shuffled back down the hallway as her boyfriend walked over and kissed his mother on the cheek. He opened the fridge and took out the orange juice before sitting across from Bret, whom he winked at. Bret smiled back.

"Hey, you guys are going back on the lake today, right?" Margaret asked, and Timmy shook his head.

"No, Molly has to pee too often, so why don't we hang out lakeside?"

"That sounds good. I think I'll bring down a book," Margaret said, coming to sit at the table.

Kaiser barked somewhere outside, and a second later the sound of a herd of elephants came rushing up the back deck, and Kaiser stood at the door, wagging his tail. Bret got up and let him in.

"Hey, you," he said, kneeling down. "Where were you last night, huh?"

"He slept in the room with me and Daddy," Margaret said. "Took up half the bed before he was shooed off this mornin'." She took a sip of coffee.

"Oh yeah? You traitor." Bret laughed as the dog let his master love on him.

"Speaking of which, Big Daddy said he was acting funny this morning when he let him out to run," Margaret said.

Bret turned his head. "Yeah?"

She nodded. "He was sitting outside of Adam's old room. Big Daddy said he went to let him out and found him whimpering."

Bret's and Timmy's eyes met. "That's strange, he's never done that before."

"I know it. When Big Daddy tried to coax him away from the door, he said he lay down and then rolled over, as if the door was telling him to," Margaret said with a smile before she set her coffee cup down. "Maybe Adam's spirit is hanging around, after all. There are times…"

A shiver ran down Bret's back before he looked back at Kaiser. "You miss your daddy?"

On cue, Kaiser barked and then took off down the hallway toward Adam's room. Bret stayed behind, as did everyone else, but they watched him go. The only one who smiled was Margaret.

Bret stood up and looked out to the lake and the island off in the distance. Absentmindedly he reached up for the ring around his neck and held it.

***

The day was beautiful as Bret lay out in the sun. The lake was placid, as always, like a sheet of green glass stretched across the surface. On the opposite side of the still waters, Bret could hear the children splashing and laughing as the summer revelers came to the beach on the other side, while he lay on the Woolseys' property. The warmth of the sun's rays warmed him. He and Timmy had gone wading into the water to cool off after bringing several coolers and lawn chairs down from the house. They had set up an umbrella as well, and Molly and Margaret talked about baby clothes and her upcoming baby shower while Kaiser, also wet from the water, snoozed at their feet.

Tim had gone back out into the water with his fishing pole and was currently bitching because nothing was biting. Every expletive made the three on the shore laugh as he cast only to recast a few moments later. Bret shook his head and rolled over just as his cell phone, which was underneath his towel, began to ring. He reached for it and sat up to see who was calling.

"Hey," he said as he answered the call.

"Hey back" came Jeff's smooth voice. Bret looked over at the two women, who were now watching him with bemused looks on their faces. Molly elbowed Margaret as they pointedly turned their heads.

"How are you?" Bret asked.

"Good. Reggie and I had to go to Detroit for a couple of hours of brainless paperwork. Everything good on your end?"

Bret smiled as Timmy turned around.

"Is that Jeff?" Timmy asked.

"Yeah," he called back.

Jeff had fallen silent.

"Tell him to come out to the lake. Park behind my truck when he gets here," Timmy said.

"I, uh…" Bret looked over at Margaret, who nodded.

"Yeah, tell him to come out and bring his shorts," Molly said.

"You hearing this?" he asked Jeff. He looked at Margaret with wonder as she looked back at him with an expression of open curiosity.

"I hear. Are you okay with that?" Jeff asked, and Bret looked questioningly back at Timmy, who winked and nodded.

"Yeah. Come on," Bret said.

"Alright, be there in a bit," Jeff said.

"Okay," Bret replied and said bye before hanging up. He felt his face flush.

"Honey, he is a fine piece of real estate. You better get you some land," Molly said with a wink.

"*Mmm*-hmm," Margaret said.

"Hey," Timmy said in protest.

"Not as fine as you," Molly said reassuringly. However, she rolled her eyes, laughing.

"Yeah, well, he ain't got this." Timmy flexed his ample muscles for his wife in several comical poses. Bret and Margaret rolled their eyes.

Molly cheered. "That's right, baby."

Margaret spoke up, looking at Bret. "Oh yeah, that's right. That is right about how it happens, first there's 'Oh baby!' and then it's '*Oh!* A baby!'"

"Oh hush, Mom, you and Big Daddy are so excited for this grandbaby you can't stand yourself." Timmy shouted from the water.

Margaret feigned a look of shock.

"Oh don't even look that way. Bret, between these two, the excitement is cranked to a hundred. They are so damn excited I wish Margaret was getting the stretch marks and Timmy's made to push," Molly said, rolling her eyes. Bret laughed as the three of them went back and forth like that for quite a while.

***

Thirty minutes later a tall and slightly less muscular man showed up in a pair of swim trunks and a T-shirt. Less muscular, perhaps, but the sight of Jeff in the shorts, which rode up his thighs as he walked, made Bret's mouth dry and his heart thump in his ears.

Kaiser got up from his spot and watched as the man made his way down. The dog looked at Bret to see his reaction to the newcomer. When he saw that that everything was okay, he huffed once and laid his head back down.

"Jeff, this is Molly, Margaret, and Timmy," Bret said, introducing them.

Jeff shook their hands and said hello.

"So, Jeff, what brings you to Promise?" Margaret asked.

The heat of the day dissipated with that question.

"Pleasure. I'm here staying with friends," he replied without missing a beat. "Thought Bret and I could catch up."

Bret felt a little awkward. "Would you like something to drink?"

"Sure."

"There's beer in the cooler, dude," Tim said, and Jeff nodded and grabbed one before popping the twist top off.

They made pleasant talk, and before too long Jeff was charming them with tales of his work at the FBI. The stories kept them all riveted and listening with great interest before Molly stood and announced her departure for the house.

"It was nice to meet you, Jeff. Hope to see you again," she said.

"Thanks, Molly. Congrats on the baby, by the way," Jeff said, standing as she stood.

Margaret led her by the elbow to make sure she didn't misstep and also expressed her pleasure at meeting Jeff. Timmy was the one who stayed the longest, and the three of them talked before he too decided to head up.

"Go ahead and leave this stuff here, Bret. I'm probably going to come back out in a bit. See ya later, Jeff," Timmy said, shaking his hand.

"You too, sir," Jeff said.

They watched him go before Jeff turned to Bret. "I hope I didn't chase them away."

Bret shook his head. "Nah. They probably figure we want some time alone. Molly has commented over and over again how handsome you are."

Jeff grinned good-naturedly, hands on his hips, as a blush crept up his face. "Do you agree with her?"

Bret smiled and shrugged. "Yeah, you're all right."

Jeff's mouth opened up in an O of feigned hurt before Bret walked into his arms and gave him a hug. "I'm teasing. How was your night?" Bret asked as they parted.

"It was all right, could have been better. How was yours?"

Bret's eyes flashed when Jeff said "better." Something in his voice suggested a thousand different things, and Bret felt his knees grow weak.

"Uh, it was great. I, uh, wanna go for a swim?" Bret asked. He wanted to diffuse the desire in his own body. Jeff looked out into the water and nodded before reaching down and removing his shirt.

"You're going to burn," Bret said and walked over to where Molly had been sitting to get her sunblock.

He opened the bottle and palmed some into his hand. Jeff had followed him and, when directed, turned around. Bret placed his hands on the hard, muscular back and worked his way downward first before coming back up to Jeff's shoulders. His heart thumped hard as he dug his palms into the flesh there. Jeff groaned and leaned into the massage. He felt pretty knotted up, and Bret took his time working them out.

"Here, now take care of the front, while I wipe my hands off." Bret handed the bottle around his body.

Jeff took it.

Bret kicked off his sandals and began to wade out into the water. He didn't want Jeff to see the obvious erection in his shorts and figured the water would cool his jets long enough for him to come back to his senses. From behind he heard Jeff's sharp intake of breath, and Bret turned to see him thigh-deep as he waded out, holding himself.

"Sweet Jesus," Jeff yelped, rubbing his arms.

Bret laughed. "Come on, tough guy."

"This water is cold!" Jeff called as Bret fell backward, letting the chilly water cascade over him as he went under.

Bret swam a few strokes before he resurfaced to find the water behind him empty. Jeff was nowhere to be found, so he looked left and then right, and then he felt a hand grab his ankle.

"*Aaiiyeee!*" he squealed, jumping back as Jeff came up, grinning and wiping water out of his eyes.

"You're not the only good swimmer, Mr. Williams," Jeff said with a mischievous look.

"You scared the shit outta me," Bret said, laughing. He gave Jeff a playful shove, but Jeff didn't move. Timmy was big, but Jeff was no slouch. He stayed steady on his feet, laughing the whole time, and even caught and held Bret's arm, pulling him close. Their faces were inches apart, and Bret could feel the heat coming off Jeff and smell the sweetness of the lotion he'd applied to Jeff's skin.

"Hey there," Jeff said.

"Hey, back."

Jeff placed his hands on Bret's hips and ran his fingers gently against his skin as Bret placed his hands on Jeff's chest. Bret could feel the beat of Jeff's heart underneath his hand, and desire rocketed through him. He laid his head down on Jeff's shoulder and exhaled. He wanted him. The nerves in his body absolutely hummed with their proximity, but Bret fought hard against it. He liked Jeff, and he didn't want to hurt him.

Jeff pulled back as if sensing his thoughts and used a finger to raise Bret's chin. "Your thoughts are making a cloud over your head."

Bret smiled and touched Jeff's hand. "Trying to be valiant is hard around you, Mr. McAllister."

"Well, then, I guess I'm gonna have to dunk ya," he said softly.

"What?"

Before he knew it, he was up in Jeff's arms. Bret yelped in protest, but it did no good. He went sailing through the air and hit the lake water.

***

Jeff smiled as they trudged out of the water hand in hand and poured themselves onto the dry ground, breathing heavily. They had chased each other and played in the water until they could not stand, both laughing, splashing, and occasionally squealing as one got the upper hand and put the other underneath the green surface of the water. Their bodies came together, and they touched, and the touches lingered a little bit longer and a little bit longer, until their fingers intertwined. Jeff felt his heart thudding hard in his chest, partly from the exertion in the water, partly from the man lying next to him. While Bret lay on his stomach, Jeff lay on his back and closed his eyes to allow the warmth of the sun to kiss his face and take the chill off his body.

"That water is colder than I thought it'd be," Jeff said, putting his hands behind his head for support and turning to look at Bret. He found the younger man staring at him.

"It's always been that way. No one can figure it out. It's deep too, possibly spring fed, but still. It's stumped plenty of people."

"Well, I'm sure 'round August people appreciate it," Jeff replied, looking into his eyes.

"Yeah, I could spend the rest of my life here, if this damn town wasn't attached to it." Bret gave a wistful turn of his lips.

"You like it here? I can see why."

"You're impressed?"

Jeff rolled over onto his stomach and placed his arms under his head. "Yeah. But I don't think the lake or the town has anything to do with it."

Bret smiled and, with a finger, brushed the sand off the side of Jeff's face... He let his fingertips linger a little before he put his hand back on the ground.

Jeff returned the touch and traced Bret's nose down to his lips and chin, before letting go and allowing his hand fall as well. The way Bret's lips looked, so full and inviting, made Jeff want to lunge forward and take his mouth in some Midwestern version of *From Here to Eternity*. As the cool air raced over their bodies, Jeff couldn't help but wax poetic in his thoughts of Bret's straw-colored hair or blue eyes. He understood why Adam might have loved him so much. Jeff liked just looking at him. No, that wasn't right. He liked that, but he liked the timbre of his voice, his movements, his heart, his fierce determination. He wanted to draw him into his arms, hold him there, and shield him from all that was occurring right then. But he knew he couldn't. What must be done, must be done, but that didn't mean he couldn't be a shoulder, maybe as a friend, maybe—

"Hey, space cadet, where are you at?" Bret asked.

"Neverland."

Bret snorted. "Oh yeah? What's happening in neverland?"

"Hmm...you'll have to go to dinner again with me to find out."

"This time I'm buyin'." Bret narrowed his eyes.

"Nope."

"Aww, come on," Bret said, his eyes large.

"Nope. FBI rules." Jeff grinned.

"Heh. I have my own set of rules, double-o hot stuff," Bret said, rolling his eyes.

Jeff rolled on his back and laughed until his side hurt. He'd never heard anything like that before, and when he opened his eyes he saw Bret had joined in the laughing.

"Alright, you can pay," Bret said when he caught his breath.

"Okay."

"Good," Bret said with a mischievous twinkle in his eye. "'Cause the last one in the water has to leave the tip."

***

The pastor of the First Baptist Church of Promise was putting the hymnals back in the pews as the choir filtered out. Thursday night choir practice had ended, and there was plenty of talking as the parishioners made their way out of the sanctuary and into the back, where refreshments awaited them.

Watching silently, the wraith let them pass on either side of him, each person unknowingly skirting around his presence, feeling a chill when they passed, but he didn't care. He didn't care about them. His eyes were on one person only.

The minister whistled "How Great Thou Art" as he quickly finished his work and made his way toward the altar. The wraith moved then, darting unseen, giving him a wide berth so as not to alarm him by his presence. The preacher was older but still looked the same, except that his belly had widened over the years and his pants had to be held up with suspenders. However, the shock of white hair above his brow was combed oh so carefully, and the rings on his fingers were polished gold.

He remembered.

"The homosexual agenda is ruining our children! These kids today think that being bisexual is normal. It's what they're being taught in schools!" Pastor Dennis roared out.

The congregation nodded in approval, as well as the five sitting there, center row, among the other parishioners.

The pastor shook his head sadly. "You know, I gotta tell ya. If God doesn't destroy America, then he'll have to resurrect Sodom and Gomorrah and apologize to it!"

"Amen!" someone shouted.

The crowd was restless. Their future was in question, and mothers hugged their children tighter to them as fathers' faces turned red.

"Someone ought to be angry," the pastor said, looking at the leader of the five, who gave him a curt nod.

Permission had been given.

The wraith sneered at this memory, contributed to the library of this human wraith. Its anger boiled over as it lashed out, knocking one of the microphone stands over.

"What in the…?" the pastor asked, looking up to see the metal shaft on its side. He stared before leaning over and picking it up, right beneath the cross that hung directly behind the pulpit. Once it stood again, the pastor checked to see if the base was broken.

The wraith just grinned in satisfaction.

It had been his message that encouraged them. His fiery resolve to rid the world of the evil that plagued it. They had all heard it. They all understood what he was speaking about and of whom he was speaking. The rumors had flown, and when confirmed, there had been outrage and contempt.

They could not leave well enough alone. Now they had to pay.

Turning his attention to the baptismal pool, the preacher tucked his tie within his shirt and rolled up his sleeves.

"Pastor Dennis?" a woman called suddenly, causing both man and wraith to turn.

"Yes, Judy?" he asked, grinning.

The plump woman was alone. "We're waiting on you to bless the food," she said sweetly.

"Ah. Well, can't let good food go to waste. You make your banana pudding?" he asked, and she grinned proudly.

"Sure did."

"Alright, let me see to this baptistery, and I'll join you all in a moment," he said.

She nodded and walked away, leaving them alone once more. Meanwhile the wraith had made its move. Reaching through the walls of the baptismal pool and down toward the pipe, it released the drain and, with its will, started a backup, but not sewage. No, his power came from the lake, and it was that which filtered into the pool. The pristine water turned green and murky, and when the preacher turned his head back toward it, Pastor Dennis whispered a curse.

"The hell…?"

Sliding on a pair of waders, he climbed up into the pool, which was quickly becoming sludgy water. The pastor grabbed the plunger, which he kept on the side of the pool for good measure, and began to work on the drain, pumping up and down with all his might.

The wraith struck. Grabbing the pastor firmly by the shoulders, he twisted him around and, with all his strength, plunged him underneath, as the pastor had done on so many occasions. The pastor flailed uselessly before the wraith allowed him to surface. He wanted him to see. Just like the others, he wanted him to know, and as the pastor broke surface, the wraith became visible.

The wild horror in Dennis's eyes made the wraith grin mercilessly.

Sputtering and spitting, the man cried out for deliverance. "Oh my God!"

The wraith sent him back under. He went, and as his hands surfaced beneath the sign of the cross, the pastor's life passed beyond the veil.

He would testify no more.

CHAPTER 10

A FTER DINNER, BRET and Jeff left the SUV where it was and went for a walk through the marshes once the lights had come on over the promenade's lamps above them. Crickets played their evening lullaby as the moon rose high and orange in the sky, and while the last bit of daylight bled away, the stars emerged from the depths of the universe. Walking slowly side by side, both deep in thought, both aware of each other's presence, their arms would occasionally brush. It happened once, twice, and on the third time, Jeff reached once more for Bret's hand and held it in his own with nothing more than a glance between them to confirm whether it was all right.

"How long were you two together?" Jeff asked.

"Three years. Well, that's not exactly true. We were inseparable for three years as friends. Dated other people—girls, I mean. Then one night he crashed over at my place when my parents were out of town. It was during the winter of my junior year, and we were filling out college applications together and studying for the SATs. I remember that night perfectly. It was during a thundersnow, and we knew we wouldn't have school the next day, but it ended up shut down for the entire week.

"Our lives were so uncomplicated back then, or so we thought. We were always very close. Always sat close to each other and were very tactile. People noticed and talked," Bret said, looking up into the sky.

"Is that why you dated girls, to keep people from gossiping about you?" Jeff asked, and Bret nodded.

"Looking back, yeah. I mean, we didn't know what we were feeling for each other. There isn't a handbook for anything like this. Anyway, we were in the kitchen working, when suddenly a transformer blew somewhere down the street and all the lights went out. It was so bad outside, the wind was howling, and thunder just boomed as the snow fell. Lightning was everywhere as the sky turned purple and green," Bret said and then laughed.

"What's so funny?" Jeff asked, smiling.

They had made their way farther into the marshes, and the crickets were now joined by the chirping of frogs.

"I was pretty worked up. I'd never seen a thundersnow in my life, and I was oohing and aahing. I had gotten up from the table and walked to the patio door. At one point the thunder rumbled so loud, I leaped back from the door and lost my balance, and suddenly his arms were around me," Bret said softly.

"He held you?" Jeff asked.

"I let him," Bret admitted. "It felt right, right."

Jeff stopped walking and Bret along with him. Bret turned and looked at him. "How long has it been since you've let someone hold you?"

Bret continued. "My parents hated us—together, I mean. When they found out, they did everything short of sending me away to one of those 'pray the gay away' camps. They were constantly inundating me with tracts and literature and Bible verses. When he died, somewhere inside me, I thought that maybe they'd been right all along. Like God was punishing me for being so happy in my sin. After that, outside of the function of sex, the desire for intimacy, I didn't let anyone hold me," he said quietly, holding Jeff's hand. "I'd almost forgotten what this felt like."

Jeff stepped forward and brought Bret into his arms. As Jeff held him, the younger man melted against him.

Bret turned his head and laid it on Jeff's shoulder. Jeff felt his world spinning too fast, and it was nice to close his eyes and hold someone. Bret chuckled. He leaned back, causing Jeff to open his eyes.

"What?" Jeff smiled, tilting his head.

"Is this standard operating procedure for a homicide investigation?" Bret asked, tilting his head to the side.

Jeff shook his head and put his finger underneath Bret's chin. "Nope."

Then he lowered his mouth onto Bret's. It was tender at first, questioning, exploring. Their lips met and grazed each other's before passion and need took over. With a moan, Jeff pulled Bret closer to him and kissed more urgently, and Bret met the passion with his own. Jeff's hands went up to Bret's face to cup it as he broke the kiss and pulled his head back. Bret gazed at him with heavy-lidded eyes. Bret reached up to touch Jeff's face and then down his strong arms, and he placed his hands on Jeff's chest as Jeff pulled him closer to cover his mouth once more. When they broke the kiss, Jeff still had his eyes closed.

"Oh, God," Bret said, and Jeff's eyes shot open, worried they had been busted. Instead, he found Bret white as a sheet and clutching a chain around his neck.

"Bret?" Jeff asked, grasping him. Bret was trembling from head to foot.

"It's happening again. Jeff…Jeff…I…"

If Jeff hadn't seen it for himself, he'd never have believed it. But Bret's whole face changed, as well as the color of his eyes. They turned from blue to green, but Bret's body was as stiff as a board as if in the throes of a seizure. Jeff quickly grabbed him and began to gently lay him down and cradle him in his arms.

"Three down, three to go," he said with a wicked grin. "They broke the promise. They took me away from him. And they must pay."

"Who are you?" Jeff asked.

"I am vengeance."

As quickly as the face had changed, it changed back, and as Bret's eyes came back into focus, he started gagging. Bret turned his head and expelled copious amounts of water onto the dock where he lay.

***

He was walking down the side of the hill toward the lake. Ahead of him stood the only man he had ever loved—naked, no less—staring out over the placid water. Bret smiled as he made his way downward.

"I knew you would come. You never listen," Adam said.

"How could I?" Bret said, placing his hands on Adam's hips and closing his eyes. He knew his body, every inch of him he could recall from memory. Placing his head on Adam's back, he inhaled as Adam brought Bret's arms around his stomach and held them.

"I've missed you," Adam said.

"I tried, Adam, I tried!" Bret cried into his back. "I spent days trying to find you."

"Shh, I know, Bret. I was there. Every step of it. I watched you. I lay with you in your bed and held you when you cried. Even the day they buried me, it was me standing next to you," Adam said in a soothing voice.

"Then why are you here now? How come I am seeing you now?"

"Because of the promise we made. The island is holding me to it. The night we made love, don't you remember?" Adam asked.

Bret raised his head. "It was true, then?"

"It demands the promise be fulfilled."

"Adam, these people can be brought to justice. They can't run—"

"I have no choice, Bret. I am bound to the promise. You should take your friend and leave. I can't protect you," Adam said, turning his head partially. "I like him, by the way."

"Adam, protect me from whom?" Bret asked, ignoring the last part.

"The six—three down, three to go."

"Who's left, Adam?"

Bret cried out. Adam's flesh had suddenly become damp and spongy. He tried to withdraw his hands, but Adam grasped him firmly. His skin lost its healthy luster and was turning grayish blue.

"Adam? What's happening?"

"I'm dying, Bret," Adam said simply.

"Adam, I'm afraid. Let me go!" Bret struggled.

"I have to keep the promise, my love."

Adam began to turn. The horrific sight of Adam's dead face forced a sob out of Bret. Adam's right eye was fine, but his left one was distorted and milky. The beautiful face that he'd once loved was destroyed. The lips he'd kissed were now blue.

"How's about a kiss, just one more?" Adam cried sadly, and the longing in his eyes broke Bret's heart.

His dead lover leaned in.

"Adam, no, Adam!" Bret screamed, turning his head away.

***

"Adam!"

Bret sat bolt upright, and when he felt the restraints on him, he immediately struggled. A hand shot out of nowhere and placed itself on his own, and he cried out in fear.

"Bret, it's okay, you're alright."

Bret whipped his head toward the sound of the voice and discovered Jeff behind the steering wheel of his vehicle. The look on his face was a mixture of curiosity and fear.

Bret was soaking wet, and his shirt clung to his chest. "What happened?" he asked, trying to clear his head.

"You don't remember?" Jeff asked, occasionally glancing at him as they made their way down a freeway.

"No. I was talking to you and—"

Suddenly the dash of the Navigator lit up as Jeff's cell phone rang. Jeff reached over, snatched it up, and held up a finger for Bret to be quiet.

"McAllister," he said into the phone.

Bret could hear a woman speaking but not what was being said. But it probably wasn't too good when Jeff shot him a look.

"Where?" Jeff asked. "Alright, Reggie. I'm on my way." He hung up the phone and placed it back on the cradle on the dashboard.

"What's wrong?" Bret asked, a sinking feeling in his gut.

"That was my partner. There's been another murder," Jeff said quietly. Bret felt a chill cascade through him. "Now would be the time to tell me anything you know."

Bret was silent for a long time as they drove.

"Is it Adam?" Jeff asked, and Bret stared at him.

"How is that possible? Adam's dead," Bret whispered. "Five years, Jeff."

"What does 'the promise' mean? Someone broke the promise, and they have to pay. That's what you said when you...when you...passed out," Jeff asked, turning right.

Ahead of them flashing red and blue lights dotted the road, and it took a second to realize where they were going. They pulled up next to a squad car as an officer tried to block Jeff from entering the driveway. As soon as Jeff pulled out his badge, the officer waved him in, but not before he got a good look at Bret.

"Mind your business, Officer," Jeff said, hitting the brake and stopping the vehicle with a brief squeal of the tires.

The officer backed off real quick with his hands up in surrender, and Jeff shook his head as he continued forward. People were milling about, arms wrapped around each other and weeping. Other officers were busy taking statements, but it was one in particular who caught Bret's attention.

"Hey, you, you son of a bitch," Bret said when he caught sight of Officer Martin.

Martin didn't hear him; he was too busy talking to a redheaded woman who, when she spotted the Navigator, nodded and walked toward them. Martin shrugged and stepped back into the sanctuary.

"Roll your window down," Jeff instructed, and Bret found the control on the armrest.

The window came down, and the redhead looked at Bret and then over at Jeff. Bret was struck by how pretty she was, her hair dyed an unnatural shade of red with black streaks throughout. She was thin, but he could see the muscles in her arms.

"Hey, Reg, this is Bret. Bret, Agent Reggie Doucette," Jeff said, introducing them.

"Hey, sugar. How are you feeling?" Reggie asked Bret with a friendly smile.

"I'm alright," Bret said, feeling his face turn slightly red with her greeting. He could hear her Cajun accent, and it wrapped itself around her words like tendrils of whiskey-drenched smoke.

"Who is it this time?" Jeff asked.

"The pastor...a Reverend..." she said, checking her notes, but Bret finished the name.

"Larry Dennis," he said quietly.

"You're familiar with him?" Jeff asked, and Reggie eyed Bret.

"He's my parents' pastor. They go to church here," Bret replied, looking at Jeff. Something flashed in his eyes, and Bret was about to ask him what he was thinking when he spoke up.

"What happened?" Jeff asked Reggie.

"The congregation heard him shouting and came to see what was the matter. It was choir practice tonight, and they were in the back ready to sit down to supper. When they found him, he was floating faceup in the baptistery. The water was the same as before," Reggie said.

"Lake water," Jeff said, and Bret's eyes grew wide.

"Looks like it."

"Any sign of a struggle?" Jeff asked.

"Sure, there was water splashed everywhere outside of the pool. Like he was struggling to get out. Looks like someone held him under," Reggie replied.

"Oh my God," Bret said.

"Anyone see anyone leaving? A car? Someone on foot?" Jeff asked.

"Same as last time," Reggie replied, and Bret took that as a solid no.

"I've known that man since I was in high school. My parents brought me here, and I attended their youth ministry," Bret said in a whisper before turning his head to Jeff.

"He had something to do with Adam?" Bret asked.

"We don't know yet. But...given the circumstances, I'd say yes."

"We have to tell his parents. This has gone on too long," Bret said, looking at Reggie.

"I dunno, boss, what d'ya think?" she said, giving Bret a sympathetic look. Both of them turned to look at Jeff, who was staring straight ahead as if in thought.

"They have a right to know," Bret said, but turned and saw what Jeff was staring at.

Martin was coming down the church steps, watching the vehicle. Bret sat back to hide his face in the shadow and whispered, "Especially if the cops are dirty."

"Who's here with you?" Jeff asked.

"I have two agents inside. Martin was pissed when I showed up with our backup. Tony Shaffer and Mark Hill are both inside, watching over the shoulders of their people on the crime scene. Our forensics are on their way as well, that doctor and biologist you ordered," Reggie said, and Jeff grinned.

"Clever girl."

"Yeah, I arrived first and then Martin and right behind him were our boys, so...I will be alright tonight. Ah, there they are. Forensics."

A blue Econoline van with FBI written over the seal pulled up and parked between Martin and their SUV. Because of that, Bret was able to relax a little.

A large black man got out of the driver's side, and Reggie waved him over. He and a woman with mousy brown hair walked up. They were dressed in khakis and polo shirts and had blue windbreakers on.

"You gonna be okay here?" Jeff asked, and Reggie turned her head and nodded, giving him an "are you kidding me" look as the other two made their way over to her.

"Alright, I'm gonna take him home, talk to Adam's parents," Jeff replied.

"Who's in charge here?" came a voice from behind their car, and instantly Bret's blood froze.

Reggie turned and answered. "I am. Who are you?"

"I'm Doug Williams. I represent Pastor...what the hell are you doing here?" Bret's father asked, staring in the rearview mirror.

"That's our cue, Reggie," Jeff said, putting the car in reverse.

Reggie held a hand up, trying to guide Doug away, but he wasn't having any of it. He leaned his head in the window although Jeff hadn't let off the gas yet.

"What the hell is going on?" he asked as Reggie tried shoving him back.

"Dad, back up," Bret shouted as his dad reached for the collar of his shirt.

"Do you have anything to do with this, you goddamn troublemaker? Who the hell is in the truck with you?" he yelled as Reggie started pushing him back. Jeff slammed the car into park, and leapt out of the SUV. Feeling like he could defuse the situation, Bret got out just in time to see Jeff circle the back of the black vehicle.

"Hey! You were ordered by a federal agent to back the fuck off!" Jeff shouted. "You wanna know who the hell I am, my name is Special Agent Jeffery McAllister."

Reggie backed up just in time for Jeff to grab ahold of Doug's shirt collar, spin him around, and pin him up against the truck while pulling out his badge with the other hand. "You, sir, are interfering with a police investigation into three deaths. Now, if you don't want me to arrest your ass, I suggest you do as the lady says and back the fuck off...*now!*"

Doug sputtered. "I...I...I'll have your badge."

"You won't have shit, you two-bit ambulance chaser," Jeff growled. "Now if you don't want me to cart your ass in for obstructing a police investigation, I suggest you move it out of here, do you understand me?" He let go of the man.

"Wha...what are you doing with my son?" Doug asked, his face red and appearing on the verge of tears.

"Like you give a damn." Bret smirked and nodded toward the church. "Go. Those people need you."

A cluster of people had gathered on the porch to witness the altercation, and to Bret's chagrin, Martin stood there silently watching. There was something in his eyes that Bret did not like. Disdain, fear, hate, or all the above, it was hard to tell. But it didn't make Bret afraid. Quite the opposite. If he was somehow involved in Adam's death, then Bret wanted nothing more than for him to come after Bret. Alone.

Through the fog of the years, a rage settled in Bret's gut as the two stared at each other. A smile crept slowly over his face as Bret stood there, hands on his hips, and he moved forward. Jeff called his name, but he didn't listen. Doug moved, the parishioners moved, but Martin stayed put as Bret climbed the steps. When he was within reaching distance of the officer, Bret, who still had his hands on his hips, grinned even wider.

"What are you smiling at?" Martin asked as he loomed over him. Bret motioned for him to come closer, and Martin, surprisingly, leaned in as Bret whispered in his ear.

"I know what you did. I know. And someone else knows too. Your time's running out. Enjoy the rest of your evening," Bret said and backed up.

Martin's face drained of color as Bret turned and walked down the steps. Jeff had a smirk on his face and his arms crossed over his chest. Everyone was watching Bret, and he knew all these people hated him, hated who he was, and hated whom Adam and he had been together. Bret knew he was alive not out of the goodness of anyone's heart. He watched their silent condemnation.

"Agent McAllister, I'm ready to go. God has abandoned this place," Bret said loud enough for everyone to hear. Murmurs rippled through the crowd as Jeff and Bret climbed back in the Navigator.

"I'm sorry," Bret said.

"For what?" Jeff asked. Bret looked over at him and was about to open his mouth, but Jeff cut him off.

"I didn't hear what you said to him, but I could tell by his expression you basically told him you knew what he'd done. Which, in fact, makes my job easier. If I can get him to come forward and dump on the rest of those involved, we may be able to stop this before it gets worse. You did pretty good," Jeff said proudly.

"Then why do I feel like all hell is about to break loose?" Bret asked, buckling himself in.

***

Whispers were all around him as he sank slowly into his rest. Three down, three to go, three down, three to go, they whispered, like a promise of encouragement. Weary, exhausted, the words were kinder to him than they had been previously, when they had called his soul back from its eternal rest. At first, he had been scared and had no idea what was happening. Light, noises, all these things had slipped past him when he closed his eyes for the final time. He did not care about them after that, but he must again. They demanded it.

As he closed his eyes and felt his soul become one with the vast expanse of the water, its greenish hue nursing him like a mother nurses a babe, he rested. But no matter how deep his exhaustion, there was a deeper thing still that rattled his bones in their grave.

Anger.

But he knew he couldn't do anything about it now. He must rest.

In respite, as he moved across the face of the deep lake, he went to the place where it all began. His ethereal form, invisible to the naked eye, crossed the distance from the shore to the island in the blink of an eye. Death made these things possible. Time and distance were all relative now as he climbed the banks of the island and found the spot where it had happened.

He heard laughter and turned his face, a sad smile crossing his lips as two young lovers crept upward near him. Despite the late hour, the sun began to shine, and the solemnness of this place changed. They were showing him something, and he had no choice but to watch.

"Adam, where are we going?" a young blonde-haired man asked, a blindfold over his eyes. He had one arm wrapped around the arm of another young man the same age. His other hand was placed on the chest of the blond who was leading him.

The intimacy of it warmed his soul, and if they had been anything more than a memory, he would have become visible to them.

"Shh. It's a surprise. Keep that blindfold on, Bret." Adam let go and tied the little rowboat to a tree stump while Bret stood there smiling. He walked back over and took his lover again by the arms, wrapped one around himself, and held him close.

"Okay, you bring me to this creepy little island for what? To crucify me in some weirdo ceremony because I'm a virgin?" Bret asked, laughing.

Adam grinned, but Bret couldn't see it, which caused Adam to slow down and Bret's face to fall.

"Come on, stupid. No, I am not here to kill you. That's so 1980s. Come *on*." Adam rolled his eyes and led Bret away from the shore and up an incline to a clearing in the trees.

"Better not. I have a final in the morning," Bret replied, his fear assuaged.

He remembered everything.

Adam walked over and lit two tiki torches, and finally turned back around and told Bret to remove the blindfold.

His throat closed when Bret's face first reacted to what was in front of him, as it had the evening this happened.

"Oh, my God," Bret whispered.

His heart soared at this moment.

"Babe, I love it," Bret said, stepping forward.

He felt like it would burst. The wraith and Adam spoke at the same time:

"I love you, babe. Happy birthday."

Adam's lithe, tan, muscular body in the firelight was enticing. But it was the face of the handsome man that Adam was concentrating on.

Where they stood had been mowed down the night before Adam brought Bret over. It took him three hours to clear enough space for a tent to be erected and a table with chairs to be set up. Timmy and Molly had helped him bring everything over on the pontoon and set up a couple of hours before. They had also helped get a bottle of cheap wine and ice as well as dinner, picnic-style, waiting for them in the cooler.

"You did this for me?" Bret asked, his chin trembling a little.

"Yeah, you said your mom and dad never really gave you a happy birthday. I thought I would. It's not too *Dawson's Creek*, is it?" Adam and the wraith said together.

Bret lowered his head and walked into Adam's waiting arms. As they kissed, the wraith brought his hands to his lips, longing to feel that once more.

Adam stepped back, lowered himself to one knee, and then pulled something out of his pocket. Bret, who was crying now, stepped back in shock while Adam chuckled. The wraith and he spoke together.

"I have to do this again in front of Mom and Dad, so act surprised when I do it there. But I wanted you alone with me for the first time. Bret, I love you. I want to live the rest of my life with you. With school coming up in the fall, everything is going to change, but we won't. Marry me," they said.

"When?" Bret asked, wiping his eyes with the backs of his hands.

"Five years. You and me, after school. We'll bust out of this old town, our middle fingers in the air, anywhere you want to go," they said.

Bret nodded, his eyes flashing in defiance. "Okay. Yes. Yes, Adam, I will marry you."

Adam reached for Bret's hand—as did the wraith, but only one could touch—and slipped the golden ring on his hand.

"Promise?" they asked as Adam secured the ring.

"I promise," Bret said.

The light faded as the memory disappeared into thin air, leaving the wraith sobbing in the night.

Promise, promise, promise, the gentle whispers insisted, and Adam nodded.

He must rest now. They had broken the promise, and now they had to pay.

CHAPTER 11

JEFF SLOWED DOWN just short of the driveway and turned off the lights before he pulled over. They sat there in the quiet for a moment, windows down, listening to the night birds and crickets.

"How do you feel?" Jeff asked as Bret stared out the window.

"I feel crazy. Ten days ago my life was shit, but it was manageable shit. Today I'm passing out all over the place. Impressive for a first date, huh?"

"So this was a first date?" Jeff grinned, and Bret narrowed his eyes.

"You bought me dinner twice and then kissed me," Bret replied. Jeff laughed. "You've never seen anything like this before, have you?"

Jeff shook his head. "No. I've been doing this for years. I've seen just about anything you can imagine, and I can't figure this one out. Bret, you looked just like Adam did from the photo I saw. It was like you were possessed," he said quietly.

"This place. These people. Adam was murdered by these people in this town, and you know, I've always heard that phrase, 'still waters run deep...' I just never got it until now."

"Bret, do you think your parents may have had something to do with it?" Jeff asked simply, and Bret shook his head.

"Why? They knew we were supposed to leave. I told them I was never coming back before it happened. We were just to be married—" Bret started and then sat up all of a sudden.

"What is it?" Jeff asked.

"They never found his ring," he whispered.

"What ring?"

Bret pulled out the chain from around his neck and handed it over to Jeff. "Before he proposed to me, he went out and bought the both of us matching rings. I have mine, but when they recovered his body, he wasn't wearing his."

"Do you think that maybe we're wrong and he was simply robbed?"

Bret shook his head fervently. "He had just gotten paid, it was a Friday night, and none of the cash was taken out of his wallet. His car was recovered a few miles away from the lake and all the contents—radio, cell phone, wallet, all of that—were still in the car. Everything was there, except for his ring."

"Okay. May I keep this? I'll be sure to give it back."

"Sure. Yeah. That's fine. Look, if we're gonna do this, we need to go do it," Bret said, nodding toward the house.

"Are you sure? We could wait till the morning."

Bret shook his head. "No, we've waited too long already."

"Alright. I'll take the lead on this—only speak when I give you direction. Don't indicate that you know who the killer or killers may be. I don't need his brother or father going off half-cocked, do you understand me?" Jeff said, suddenly authoritative and serious.

"I understand," Bret said with a nod, and Jeff turned the lights back on, put the truck in gear, and followed the road down to the Woolseys' driveway, where he turned in.

Big Daddy and Timmy were sitting out on the porch smoking when they got out of the truck and walked up.

"Evenin', gentlemen," Big Daddy said as he rocked on the swing.

"Hey, Big Daddy. Hey, Timmy. Is Margaret up?" Bret asked solemnly.

Timmy perked up right away, and Big Daddy leaned forward in the swing.

"She just went in for a minute, bud. What's wrong? Did you get sick again?" he asked just as Margaret was coming out the door, wiping her hands on a dishtowel.

"Hey, guys, what's—Bret, what's wrong?" she asked, her expression turning from a smile to a look of concern.

"Mr. and Mrs. Woolsey, I need to have a moment of your time, please," Jeff said, and for the second time that night, he pulled out his badge.

***

The porch was silent and tension hung over the house so thick, Bret thought he would suffocate. Big Daddy was stone-faced, and Margaret had her hand over her mouth in shock. It was Timmy who moved first, his large body graceful as he walked around his mother and headed down the stairs. Bret swallowed down his fear as he watched him come down.

"What are you doing, son?" Big Daddy asked as he stood up, but it was too late. Timmy grabbed Bret by the arms and held him fast, his hands digging into Bret's biceps as his jaw worked.

"We were right all along, Bret," he said, nodding as tears surfaced on his handsome face.

"Timmy..." Bret said, but the big man shook his head and wandered past them before he turned and screamed to everyone and no one.

"*We were right!*" he sobbed.

Molly, who had been in the house before, had stepped out halfway through the conversation and now waddled down the steps, calling for her boyfriend. Timmy turned away from her, but she went around him and wrapped her arms around his big frame as he wept.

Margaret and Big Daddy just stood there holding each other on the porch.

Bret looked at Jeff, who stared at the ground in uncomfortable silence, then walked over to him and placed a hand on his arm. Jeff favored him with a sorrowful gaze that spoke a thousand words. He hated doing this, and Bret simply nodded and rubbed his back to give the messenger comfort.

Timmy cried for a good while but eventually returned with his Molly on his arm, and the two sat in front of Bret and Jeff like parishioners hearing the words of a prophet.

"You knew about this, Bret? I mean, you always suspected, but why didn't you tell us?" Molly asked, her eyes puffy and red rimmed. Bret's heart broke for her, and he shook his head.

"Not until after the first episode I had on the porch. After you left the hospital, that is when Jeff walked into my room and we met," Bret replied, shamefaced, and Margaret turned her attention from Bret to Jeff.

"What do you need, Agent McAllister?" she whispered.

"This doesn't have to happen tonight, ma'am. I can come back in the morning if it would be better," Jeff said, but Big Daddy was already shaking his head no.

"No one will sleep tonight anyway, Jeff. You may as well get this over with," he said, lighting the end of his pipe.

"We've told you about Adam to lead into more news," Bret said, and Jeff's eyes widened.

Everyone's attention shifted to him.

Bret figured Jeff had already taken enough heat. "Three people have been murdered here in Promise. Sherriff Townsend, the drunk who used to hang out at Moe's liquor, and tonight it was the pastor of First Baptist," Bret said.

"Pastor Dennis?" Margaret gasped.

Bret nodded.

"I don't understand," Molly said, speaking up.

Bret's mouth worked, but no sound came out. He felt like he was suddenly struck dumb.

"Adam was murdered by more than one person," Big Daddy said calmly.

The gravity of it being said made Bret's stomach clench in rage and queasiness as his mind raced through possible scenarios of how it was done.

"We think someone is avenging Adam's death," Jeff finally said. "All three victims were drowned under, shall we say, suspicious circumstances."

Timmy didn't miss a beat. "Good."

"Hush," Margaret hissed.

"Why? Whoever it is, they're right. Adam wouldn't ever have hurt anyone, and the only reason anyone hated him was because he was gay, Mom. He was a hell of a swimmer, took the school to state with Bret. You two were the goddamn dynamic duo!" he said, turning to Bret as Molly rubbed his arm.

"Yeah," Bret muttered, remembering the win.

"You two were popular, then?" Jeff asked, and Bret shrugged.

"We were in high school, yeah. We were always busy going off to one party or another. Even when everyone figured out we were together. I mean, sure, some people beefed about it, but after state champs, no one gave a damn." Bret smirked. The night was growing cooler, and he shivered. Jeff reached out his arm and rubbed his back this time.

It did not go unnoticed.

"Nobody except the west end," Big Daddy said.

"The west end?" Jeff asked, and Molly nodded.

"That's where all the money is in this town. All the who's who of Promise lives there. Lawyers, judges, old and new money. They have the biggest grocery store, the biggest churches…" Her voice trailed off.

"The biggest egos," Bret finished.

"And the best intentions," Margaret whispered finally, and everyone grew quiet.

"Mrs. Woolsey—" Jeff started.

"Margaret, please," she corrected.

"Okay, Margaret. When the police conducted the investigation and his things were returned to you, was everything there? Was anything missing?" he asked.

"Bret's ring," Big Daddy said, and Bret nodded.

"That's it?" Jeff asked.

Everyone looked at each other for confirmation.

"Okay. Alright. We're going to find who is responsible for your son's death. Will you all please excuse me for a moment? I have a phone call to make." Jeff walked away.

Big Daddy came down the stairs toward Bret and motioned for Margaret to do the same. "Come here, Mama. Tim, Molly, you too."

Timmy stood up and helped Molly to her feet as the family walked up to Bret. "Now, Bret, I want you to listen to me. You walked into our lives what, eight years ago has it been, Margaret?" Big Daddy asked.

His wife nodded. "Yeah, it's been about that," she said.

"Thought so. I didn't know much about the gay life. Still don't. But I knew my boy as a levelheaded, compassionate, and tender child who grew up a fine young man. When he came out to his mother and me, there were tough times, tough conversations, because his mother and I feared for his safety. We were afraid about AIDS, about how he would be treated in life, worried about whether or not he'd be happy. When he told us it was you he loved, I had no reservations whatsoever. We loved you the moment we laid eyes on you."

Bret, who'd had his eyes downcast, nodded and folded his arms as Big Daddy continued.

"Our greatest fear was realized five years ago, and Bret, I was born at night, but it wasn't last night. I knew our Adam didn't commit suicide. I knew he wouldn't do that to us, and most importantly, I knew he wouldn't leave you."

He paused, and Margaret finished for him. "You never got to be our son-in-law. But that's okay. You're our son now, you hear me? We will get through this as a family. No more secrets," she said, lifting up Bret's face to look her in the eyes. "We love you, Bret. No more secrets."

"Okay. Good. No more secrets," Bret said, looking out on the lake. The moon reflected on the still water as his gaze fell upon the island in the center of it. He loved them, and their determination to keep him safe touched his heart. However, there was one secret he just was not ready to tell yet. He had to know the truth first.

**

"Hey, handsome," Reggie said, and Jeff jerked awake.

590

She laughed as she got in the SUV and motioned with her hand at the vehicle that had dropped her off. She sat, eased down a carrier with two large Styrofoam cups, and handed one to him. His annoyance at falling asleep and then being startled awake quickly abated at the smell of the coffee.

"Reg, you're a lifesaver." He took a sip. It was hot, it was sugar-free, and it tasted like bitter relationships, but it would do the job.

"All in the day's work for Wonder Woman," she said, sitting back with her own after she placed the carrier on the floorboard of the passenger seat.

"How did the church go?" Jeff asked, staring out of his SUV and toward the house where Bret and his family slept.

"What? After you announced our entire mission statement to the congregation?" She laughed.

"That bad, huh?" The coffee was starting to perk him up, and he felt the caffeine cause his blood to hum.

"Nah. Except the cops shut up real fast. Martin left right after you did, and the rest of them cleared out of the way. We have Dennis being autopsied right now, as we speak." She turned her head toward him with a smile. He sat back and stared at her.

"You wanna take lead on this?" he asked.

She arched a manicured eyebrow as the side of her mouth went up. "I would say yes, since I think you're becoming emotionally involved with Bret. But then I gotta say no, because of how the final report is going to read."

"And how is it going to read?" Jeff sat up. The interior of the car was getting a little warm, so he reached over and turned the fan on.

"You're serious?" When he just looked at her, she sighed. "Look, I took the same classes you took at Quantico. I hold a degree in Chemistry and am a board-certified medical doctor. But I am not Dana Scully. I come from backwoods Louisiana, Cajun, Creole country. Growing up west of New Orleans, there is a lot of superstition in my blood, and during the daytime, it is less prominent. But at night…"

"Go on," Jeff said.

"There was this old woman who lived not far from us. And when I say old, I mean Methuselah old. Anyway, the family had been in that area for generations and nobody messed with them. The Decoundreaus... Anyway, the old crow would scare people into crossing the street whenever she came hobbling down with her nephew Pierre or her granddaughter Francine. Unlike her, they were beautiful. Creole, half-white, half-black, all gorgeous. Parents would scare their kids and tell them the old Basil woman would come whisk them away in the night if they didn't behave. Everyone said she was into voodoo, and she had these milky white eyes. You'd think she was blind...

"We didn't have a lot of money growing up. Daddy ran off after Charlie, the youngest, was born. So I started trying to find ways to help Momma, and we had this beat-up old lawnmower I went back and forth through the neighborhood with, and one day I went by this old house and saw that old woman rockin' on her porch. I remember stopping in my tracks as soon as I came around the corner and saw her. And she stopped too and raised her head. She looked right at me. And before I could move, she said, 'You mow my lawn, baby. You come on over here and see old Celine. Ain't nothing but white folk got you scared. I'll pay ya good.'"

Reggie stopped to take a drink as Jeff listened with rapt attention.

"Mamma threw a fit that I mowed her lawn, but even back then I was pigheaded. The woman had paid me fifty dollars and told me to tell my momma that I was to come back twice a month, three times if we got good rain. Which, being down there, we did, so I was over there more than that. That summer I bought my first dress for freshman year homecoming."

"So what does this have to do with what we're doing here?" Jeff asked, confused.

"Shut up and drink your coffee, I ain't there yet," Reggie said, letting her accent slip back in.

"Okay, okay."

"One day she and Pierre were out on the porch when I came haulin' my lawnmower and gas can. But that day I was upset. Momma had lost her job as a secretary. They thought she was stealin' from the boss. Well, she wasn't, but no matter how much she protested, they walked her out the door. I hadn't even said hello to them when Celine leaned forward and said, 'Chère, what's got you so upset on a day like today?' Well, I burst into tears and told her everything, and she sat back, listening, those white eyes just starin' at me as she gummed her toothless mouth. I'll never forget that day. Pierre started laughing all of a sudden, and so did Celine, and it scared me. They both had funny looks on their faces. But she said, 'Don' be scared, baby, nah, yo' mamma didn't steal that money sure as I'm one hundred and two,'" Reggie said, smiling down into her coffee cup.

"She motioned with her finger and had me lean in and whispered something in my ear, and then told me to run home right away and tell my momma. I did. The Decoundreaus were so infamous, but their abilities were legendary, and Momma tore right off to her job. She came back thirty minutes later just dancin' up the driveway." Reggie snorted.

Jeff couldn't believe what he was hearing. However, Reggie was not only his partner but his best friend. "What did she tell you?"

"She told me who had taken the money, how it was done, and where the money was stashed. Momma not only got her job back, the woman was fired and Momma got her job with a pay raise and dental!" Reggie said, pointing her finger toward the roof of the cab, and Jeff grinned, assuming that was exactly how her mother put it.

"That's incredible," he said.

Reggie finally looked at him with a sad smile on her face. "There is a whole lot of crazy out in this world and not just in New Orleans. There is stuff we can't explain, and I gotta tell you, this place gives me the creeps. Still waters run deep here."

"You don't think we're dealing with a flesh-and-blood perp?" Jeff asked, watching her face.

"No, *mon ami.* That boy is back. Adam, yeah…he's back here. And he's pissed as hell."

Jeff shivered, reached over, and turned off the vent. He sat back quietly. His thoughts went to Bret, who he hoped was sleeping well tonight as Jeff stood guard over their home. Bret's admission to Martin had been enough to spark fear in Jeff's heart that they would try to shut him up. Their kiss earlier still lingered on his lips, and he could still smell him on his clothes.

"Whatcha thinkin', boss?" she asked quietly.

Jeff pulled out the chain he had in his front shirt pocket and reached for Reggie's hand. He placed the chain in it, and she tilted her head to see it by what little light came in the window.

"For me? You shouldn't have," she said, smiling.

"I didn't." He snorted, and she elbowed him. "That's Bret's ring Adam gave him. He bought a matching set at a specialty jeweler in Ann Arbor—I have the address right here on this card. I want you to go down there, see if the other one has been sold back, then I want you to get a crew out to all the pawn shops in the local area and within a fifty-mile radius to find it. If we don't find it there, I'll ask a judge for a warrant to go search inside our three victims' houses for it."

"You think whoever has the ring is the leader of this whole thing," she said, putting it in her shirt pocket and closing the button. "And if we don't find it there?"

"Then we need to start putting the squeeze on Martin."

"What about Bret's folks?" she asked cautiously.

Jeff shook his head. "Yeah, them too. But we'll wait to do them last. He said there were three left. Three down, three to go."

"Who said that?" Reggie asked, and Jeff looked at her.

"Adam."

***

Bret woke slowly from the best night's sleep he'd had in ages to the sound of his phone ringing. Sleepily he reached for it and stared at its face. It was Jeff, so he answered on the fourth ring.

"Hey."

"Good morning, Bret. How did you sleep?" came the too awake voice.

Bret smiled, picturing him back in his suit. "Good. What about you?"

"Just fine—the sound of the forest lulled me like a baby," Jeff said, and Bret could hear the smile in his voice.

"Sound of the forest? Are you high?" Bret asked, sitting up and wiping his eyes.

"I've had so much caffeine, I'm shaking like a leaf." He laughed. "I was just wondering, before I go crash, if you'd like to get some breakfast with me. My treat."

"Are you standing outside?" Bret asked, getting out of bed.

"Uh...yeah?"

Bret looked out of his window. Jeff's SUV was in the driveway, and Jeff wore the same clothes he'd had on yesterday.

"You didn't," Bret said.

"Kind of."

"Alright, give me five minutes to brush my teeth and put some clothes on. But I'm driving."

"I'm glad you said that," Jeff replied.

Bret killed the line. He quickly made his way into the bathroom with a small smile. He washed his face, brushed his teeth, and was riffling through the drawers for something to wear when a knock came on his bedroom door. He had just finished putting a pair of shorts on.

"Yeah?" he called out.

The door opened slightly. "You decent?"

It was Timmy. "Yeah, dude, I'm good," he replied, and the door swung open.

"Your friend slept out in the driveway all night," Timmy said with a smile.

Molly poked her head around the corner, her hair disheveled.

"How do you know? I could hear you snoring like a log all night." Bret shot him a look. He put a hooded shirt on and reached for a baseball cap, then put it on backward before sliding his feet into a pair of sandals.

"Because I have to pee every two hours, and I looked." Molly said, grinning.

"And she woke me up every two hours to update me on the fact the Navigator was still there. Where ya headed?" Timmy asked.

"To breakfast, Nosy Rosy." Bret said, grinning.

"I like him." Timmy said quietly.

"Ooh, gotta pee again. Have fun, Bret!" she said, disappearing behind her boyfriend.

Bret could hear her slippered feet shuffling down toward the bathroom.

Bret nodded and smiled. "Me too."

After kissing everyone good-bye, Bret made his way out to the driveway. Big Daddy had already gone to work and Margaret was in the laundry room when he left, so when he discovered Jeff snoring lightly in the passenger seat of his Navigator, arms crossed over his chest, Bret stood there watching him doze for a moment. Jeff's mouth was slightly open, his breathing slow. Bret quietly opened the door and climbed in, but before he started the truck, he did something that surprised even him—he leaned over and kissed Jeff on the side of the mouth. When he pulled back, Jeff had a smile on his face, yet his eyes remained closed.

"Well, hey there," Jeff said.

"Hey, crazy. Why'd you stay out here all night?"

Jeff chuckled. "'Cause I don't think they would have appreciated me sneaking through your bedroom window to sleep with you," he said matter-of-factly, and Bret was a little shocked. This was as forward as he'd been since they met. "I've offended," Jeff said worriedly, sitting up.

"No. Not at all. But yeah, I think Big Daddy would have come in with a shotgun, given all that's been going on lately," Bret admitted.

"I wouldn't blame him," Jeff said, buckling himself in.

"You were worried too."

"A little. That's why I didn't hide my truck. If they drove by—and I'm sure they did at some point—they knew where I was and what I wasn't going to allow to happen," Jeff said.

"Should we leave them here alone, then?" Bret asked.

"They aren't alone." Jeff pointed back over his shoulder. A dark sedan sat across from the driveway. He looked at Bret with a brief smile. "Neither is…Big Daddy?"

Bret shook his head. "This is professional courtesy, I'm sure."

"Totally." Jeff straightened his pants and ran a hand through his hair.

Bret looked back over his shoulder, then at the house, and back over his shoulder once more before kissing Jeff. At first Jeff seemed shocked and stiffened a bit, causing Bret to pull back. But he relaxed, and Jeff reached for him for one more tender, slow kiss.

"That was a professional thank-you," Bret said, sitting back and turning the ignition over. He backed out of the driveway and onto the main road as Jeff waved at the two men in the dark sedan. They pulled away, both quiet as Bret drove. He saw Jeff struggling to stay awake and reached over with one hand and grabbed his hand.

Twenty minutes later they pulled in to a farmer's restaurant in the next little burg over, and Bret killed the engine. Jeff perked up, and they stepped out of the SUV into a warming summer morning. Jeff stretched and yawned, and Bret shot him a sympathetic gaze, which Jeff caught.

"Don't worry about me, I've done this more times than I can count," he said as they made for the door.

"All-nighters?" Bret asked, opening the door.

"Yeah, once I get some more coffee in me, I'll be alright," Jeff said as Bret held open the door. The smell of food wafted out, and Bret took an involuntary inhale. Fried potatoes, omelets, bacon, and sausage caused his stomach to growl with anticipation. A lady at the counter told them to take a spot anywhere they wanted in the surprisingly sparse café. They chose a corner booth and sat down.

"Hey, I'm Elizabeth. You boys want coffee?" said another woman, who set two coffee cups down.

"Please, and keep it coming," Jeff said, pulling his cell phone out of his pocket and setting it on the table.

"Alright. Your menus are right behind the napkin dispenser, but we have the farmer's special, which is a real hit here. It's a three-egg omelet with onions, green pepper, mushrooms, cheese, and hash browns and comes with a side of biscuits and gravy," she said as she poured coffee into their cups.

Both men looked at each other and nodded. "Yeah, that sounds good," Bret said, and she winked at him before turning away. He blushed a little, and Jeff grinned. "What?" he asked, reaching for the bowl of creamers and sugar.

"She has good taste," Jeff said. That made Bret blush harder. "Yeah well, she couldn't have had too good taste—I got the wink, you didn't." He pulled off the top of the liquid container and dumped its contents inside his coffee cup.

"I'm an old man compared to you," Jeff said.

Bret raised his eyes and looked at him while he considered that statement. There was some salt and pepper in Jeff's hair and worry lines around his eyes, but his face was handsome, and the morning stubble that shadowed his chin made Bret wonder what it would feel like against his face.

"Well, don't feel too bad, unless you had plans of picking up the waitress. I think you're handsome," Bret said, and it was Jeff's turn to become a little red, which made Bret grin bigger. "When was the last time someone said that to you?" he asked, curious.

Jeff raised his tired eyes and gave him a brief smile. "It's been a while."

"Why is that?"

Jeff shrugged.

"It's the truth." Bret reached across the table.

Jeff placed his warm hand on Bret's and gave it a squeeze. "Any more...episodes?" Jeff asked, and Bret withdrew his hand and stirred his coffee.

"No. Any more dead people?" he asked.

"No."

"This shit is so fucking crazy," Bret said, putting his hands over his eyes.

"Hey...hey...we'll figure it out," Jeff said. "I've got my best people on it."

Bret lowered his hands and leaned forward. "Oh yeah? You're so tired you just put salt in your coffee, mister."

"Huh? Aw, fuck," Jeff said, putting the saltshaker down. He picked up the coffee, sipped it, and shrugged.

"How is it?"

"I've had worse." Jeff took another sip and set it back down.

Bret laughed as Elizabeth came back and set steaming plates of cholesterol heaven in front of them. They ate quietly for a while, mumbling about how good the food was, and spoke about pleasant things. At one point Bret got tired of Jeff wincing every time he took a drink of coffee and asked for a fresh cup for him.

After receiving the new cup, Bret took it, making sure to add sugar, and placed it back in front of Jeff.

"Not sweet enough." Jeff slid it back.

Bret shrugged and placed his finger in it for a second, made a quick stirring motion, and then pulled it back out and placed it in his mouth. It was hot. "Try it now."

Jeff took another sip and grinned. "Perfect."

"You must tell all the guys being haunted by their dead boyfriends that," Bret said with a smirk.

"You think it's him?"

Bret shrugged. "I'd rather think that this is all a horrible nightmare, my dead lover's family isn't being tortured five years later, that dead bodies aren't turning up, and I am not doing a Linda Blair impression every time he strikes."

"It could still be a flesh-and-blood—" Jeff started, but stopped when Bret gave him a withering look. "—or not."

"I'm sorry. I never thought the legends were true," Bret said, running his hand through his hair.

"What legends?" Jeff said, sitting forward.

"Weren't you and Big Daddy talking about this?" Bret asked. When Jeff shook his head slightly, Bret continued. "It's the island."

He sat back and rolled his eyes. "When I was in high school, the kids had this urban legend about the island in the middle of the lake. They said it was cursed and no one ever went there, right? Some went, on dares, and usually scared themselves stupid, then ran back to tell us all the 'horrible' things they had heard, yada yada. Anyway, Adam took me out there for my birthday and proposed to me there."

"He took you to the cursed island?" Jeff asked, smiling.

"It wasn't cursed. When the Algonquin Indians, Chippewa, I think, lived here, they blessed the island. When people settled disputes, when they made treaties with other Native Americans, they would go over to this island to do it. It was this huge deal." Bret set his fork down and pushed his plate away from him.

"How do you know all that?" Jeff asked, sitting forward.

"Adam looked it up one night on his way back from some swim meet. He stopped by U of M's library. That is where he got the idea. He had bought our rings already, and he wanted to make the night extra special. It was the first time we made love. We stayed the whole night," he said, his voice low. Then he laughed. "We thought the legend was a way the adults kept kids from going out there to do what we did." The mirth left Bret's face, and he said, "If we'd only known."

Jeff yawned deeply, and Bret said, "Come on, Jeff. Let's get you back to your room."

Jeff, bleary-eyed and tired, nodded. "Sounds like a plan."

He motioned for the server to bring the receipt and laid a few tens down, and then they stood up. Waving good-bye, they stepped out into the sunlight just as the first shot rang out.

CHAPTER 12

B RET WAS ON the ground so fast, he had no idea what was going on until he heard the second shot and a squeal of tires. There was pandemonium as people came running, and Bret was rolled over by Jeff.

"Are you hit? *Are you hit?*" Jeff screamed in his face.

"No! No. I don't think so," Bret said as he was brought roughly to his feet, his knees quaking. Jeff's hands were all over him when Bret noticed the blood running down Jeff's face.

"Jeff, you're bleeding!" Bret cried, reaching for his face.

Jeff hissed as Bret touched him and fragments of what felt like small rocks fell out of a small gash on his cheek. Bret's gaze strayed to the brick surface of the building and saw a huge chunk had been blown off, millimeters from where he had been standing.

"What the hell?" the server asked.

"Call the police. Tell them there was a drive-by shooting! Tell them to contact Special Agent McAllister by cell phone. Come on, Bret, we have to get you out of here," Jeff said, pulling him to the car.

"Someone tried to kill us."

"I'm sorry, Bret. I am so sorry. Get in the car. Folks, check for anyone injured, the police should be right here," Jeff called as he threw Bret in the Navigator and ran around to the other side, leaving people looking confused and scared.

He turned the ignition and slammed the car into gear. The Navigator shot forward, and the transmission complained from the abuse.

"Jesus Christ, Jeff, who was it?" Bret was shaking in the passenger seat. The Navigator swung a wide right on a side street, and Jeff kept looking in the rearview mirror. Satisfied they were not being followed, he got on the phone, dialed a number, and placed it to his ear.

"Hey Reg, it's McAllister. You all bein' followed?"

Bret couldn't hear what Reggie said in reply as they drove up the entrance ramp to the freeway.

"We were just shot at. ...Nothin'. Saw the sedan, though. Dark blue. Tinted windows," he replied.

"He's fine. Little shaken up. ...Got it. Tell whomever you send there to watch their six—they need to watch their backs. They almost got us, Reg. Someone had good aim. ...Alright, you too." He hung up the phone.

"The glove compartment, Bret. Reach in there, grab my pistol, and hand it to me."

Bret did what he was told. He found the pistol in a holster, took it out, and handed it over to Jeff. "What about Adam's family?" he asked.

"Reggie just got off the phone with them. They are still there and said all was quiet. She's sending a team over to the restaurant," Jeff said while changing lanes and cursing to himself. The phone rang, and he picked it up. "McAllister." His eyes narrowed. "Yeah, they missed us. It's alright, though. ...I slipped up; it won't happen again. ...Oh, yeah, this world's getting crazier by the minute, Martin. It's alright, though. I'll be packin' and waiting for them when they come back," he said coldly and nonchalantly.

Bret felt sick to his stomach.

"I'm sorry, what was that?" Jeff asked. "Ah. Right. Well, ballistics will trace it. And my people are already—" He stopped and laughed. "Oh sure, they're already on their way." With his sleeve, he wiped off the blood running down his face.

"Oh no, he's fine. I'll tell him you said hello." Jeff hung up the phone, tossing it onto the dashboard. "Son of a bitch."

"He knew about it," Bret said.

"Yeah, he called too soon," Jeff said.

"We need to get you cleaned up, Jeff. You're bleeding all over the place."

"My hotel is right up here. I've got a first aid kit in the back," he said, taking the next exit.

As soon as they got through the light, Jeff turned into the parking lot of a hotel where all the rooms were reached from the lot or up the stairs on the balcony. Thankfully, no one was around as he parked his car and picked up his weapon. Bret dived in the back for the first aid kit, and then they got out.

They walked quickly through the lot and up the stairs, Jeff looking around the entire time. At room 204, Jeff used his key to unlock the door but pulled his weapon out first and checked the room while Bret waited by the open door.

"Come on. It's fine," Jeff said, and Bret entered, shutting and locking the door behind him.

The room was nothing but a typical hotel room. Bed, dresser, mirror, and a bathroom off to the side, as plain Jane as all other hotels of its kind. Jeff had already taken off his shirt when Bret set the box down on the table and opened the kit. He fished out the antiseptic ointment and a roll of bandages and gauze, then followed Jeff into the bathroom.

"Here, turn around," Bret said, setting the stuff down. "I got this."

"No."

"Jeff..." Bret started.

"I should have expected that! You could have been killed!" Jeff said angrily.

Bret shook his head and stared at him in the mirror. He stepped closer and gently turned him around. Jeff was looking at the ground. "I wasn't hurt. I wasn't killed. I'm right here because you went all Kevin Costner for me," Bret said, smiling, even though his hands shook when he placed them on Jeff's chest. Jeff's pectorals were firm and felt warm under his hands.

"I'm sorry," Jeff murmured.

"You're a man. Just a man. Who would have thought the police department would be this corrupt? How could you know? I'm from here, and I didn't know. If I were them, I'd want the troublemakers shut up too," Bret said, reaching for the iodine swabs. Jeff had washed his face already, and Bret gave it a once-over to make sure no fragments of brick lingered in the four cuts on the right side. Satisfied, he opened up the package and gingerly applied iodine to each wound. Jeff didn't hiss or move; he stood there as Bret worked.

"Well, you won't need stitches, and all this looks like it's just a bad shaving job," Bret said, wiping the excess iodine away from around the wounds. He tried like hell to hold his hand steady even though he was shaking on the inside.

Jeff watched him work. "You're trembling." Jeff reached up and took hold of Bret's hand.

"Sorry, I've never been shot at before." Bret closed his eyes.

"I guess you really pissed him off. Martin, I mean," Jeff said.

"Fuck him. Adam or us, he's going down," Bret said with firm determination.

Jeff's eyes widened a bit, and he placed his hands on Bret's hip.

"Do you still love him?" Jeff asked.

"Who, Adam?"

Jeff nodded.

"Of course, I'll always love him," Bret said, opening his eyes.

"I like you, Bret," Jeff said.

"I know."

"And I won't push..."

"Which is fair." When Jeff went to say something else, Bret kissed him. It wasn't gentle. It was urgent, and Jeff responded in kind. Their lips met, and they embraced, their hands running up the lengths of each other's backs. They stumbled back toward the bed, tongues colliding, hands exploring. Bret shook, his whole body trembling in Jeff's hands, and then he broke the kiss. He laid his head on Jeff's shoulder.

"Are you okay?" Jeff panted.

Bret nodded and then nestled his head in the cleft between Jeff's neck and his shoulders.

Jeff's arms came up, and Bret felt them circle his back and hold him tight. Bret eased his body against him.

"I'm sorry. I know all of this is overwhelming."

Bret smiled but didn't raise his head and instead placed a hand on Jeff's chest to feel the warmth of him. "These past five years have been insane. I feel like one day my life stopped and picked up somewhere in someone else's. It's like I buried me when we buried Adam, like a part of me went with him. And I suppose that's the case," he said, eyes closed, feeling Jeff's heart beat under his palm.

"So where do you go from here?" Jeff mumbled, then kissed the top of his head.

"I don't know. But I feel like I'm trying to claw my way back up to the surface, like that girl in *Kill Bill*. I'm going to emerge covered in dust, and I'm going to scare the shit out of some poor old bastard who's been working in the graveyard," he said, laughing.

Jeff chuckled and pulled him closer. Bret reveled in it and rubbed the spot where his hand lay. It felt so good to feel someone under his palm, flat, hard, strong. Bret's body ached, and desire was present. He could feel his own desire burning against his leg, but he felt something else stir from a chamber that had been abandoned for so long.

"What if I wait above your gra—can we use another analogy? Given what's been going on, I mean," Jeff said, and Bret eased his head back to look him in the eyes.

"I get what you mean. I'd like that," Bret said, smiling, and then kissed him once more on the side of the mouth before letting go and stepping away.

"I, uh, think maybe we should get you back," Jeff said as Bret moved closer to the bed.

"No." Bret scooted back instead and pulled the covers down before kicking his sandals off, removing his shirt, and sliding himself in.

"What are you doing?" Jeff asked.

"You need sleep."

"I—"

"No. Come here. It's alright. I'll be fine, you're right here. You said your friends are at the cabin watching over Margaret and Big

Daddy. Come on, tough guy. You're no use to me exhausted." Bret patted the pillow.

Instead of scooting back, Jeff walked around to his side of the bed. Bret watched the relief flood Jeff's face at not having to go out again, and he felt his heart tremor a little. Jeff was beautiful, well muscled, and capable. Compassionate and tender. He was trained to do harm if needed, strong and protective. But underneath that Broadway show, Bret saw something else. Something gentler, kinder, that needed attention as well.

Jeff slid between the cool sheets next to Bret and settled himself as Bret did something he hadn't done in years. He moved forward and without asking, placed his head on Jeff's chest. His stomach had butterflies, and when he felt Jeff's hesitation, he almost moved back over.

"Are you sure?" Jeff asked as if this were a risky sex position instead of a lover's embrace.

The tenderness in his voice melted Bret. "Yeah. Yeah, I'm sure," he said and closed his eyes as he felt Jeff's arms come around him. Bret listened to him breathe and felt Jeff's heart beat as his own eyes grew heavy. He thought he saw something move in the shadows of the room, but as his eyes fluttered back open and he raised his head, he saw nothing there but shadow and wall. He laid his head back and closed his eyes. It didn't take Jeff long at all before his breathing slowed down and his hold on Bret loosened a little. When Jeff gave a little jerk, Bret's eyes opened back up, and he smiled as he felt sleep gnawing at the edges of his mind as well. The adrenaline that had pumped through him suddenly dissipated and left him drained.

Jeff's chest slowed even more until his breathing was slow and even, and before Bret fell off the edge of oblivion, he realized the slumbering man had saved him from certain death and would help him put an end to all this wandering. Bret wondered what it would be like to get familiar with this chest and the heart that beat steadily beneath him. He pondered these things as sleep reached up and claimed him.

***

He had been angry at Bret. He told him he could not help him. He could not protect him. But as he stood in the shadow of the hotel room, watching, he felt a sad smile tug at his face. He did appreciate the care this new one paid Bret, but he longed for what he saw displayed in front of him. Through the years, Bret had stayed true and had not let anyone hold him, even when they brought him to the climax of desire. Jealous at first, green with envy of the nameless faces that touched Bret the way he had, he had been furious with him. However, that fury turned to wonder and then to heartbreak as Bret would struggle with putting his clothes on, head bowed, while the lovers would beg him to stay. He would not. Not even once. He would turn and walk out, head hung low. In the beginning, he would cry in the driver's seat of his car, and Adam would silently scream at him as if he'd walked in and caught him in the act. That was until he had cried out Adam's name and wrapped his arms around himself as he wept.

That was before the whispers began. Before his soul was pulled back to the lake to do their bidding. To do what must be done. The promise had to be fulfilled.

He'd tried to warn him off, but Adam had assumed too much. He figured Bret would be safe from the effects of the blessing. He'd been wrong. Perhaps Bret needed this to end as much as Adam did. Receding into the shadows, he changed his plans. He had planned to go after the one responsible, the promise breaker next, but no. His sights were now set on another.

In darkness he came and in darkness he left…disappearing among the shadows like a thief in the night.

Three down, three to go.

***

Bret woke a little after one in the afternoon to the sound of his cell phone ringing. Jeff shifted and murmured in his sleep as Bret lifted his head and rolled over. His eyes were bleary as he reached for the phone on the floor and answered it.

"Hello."

"You don't sound like Jeff. Is this Bret?" a female voice asked. Suddenly Bret was very much awake, and he groaned.

"I answered the wrong phone. Uh, hi, Reggie, I'll get him," he said apologetically. He heard her laughing on the other end.

Wincing, he rolled back over and shook Jeff, who was snoring, head buried in his pillow, hair tousled, and lips slightly parted.

"Jeff, Jeff, wake up. It's Reggie." Bret shook his shoulder.

"Wuzzat? Here?" Jeff asked, rolling over and opening his eyes.

Bret couldn't help but smile. "No. Here. Sorry, I thought it was mine." He winced again and handed him the phone.

Jeff took it and sat up, the blanket falling down past his stomach. Bret felt horribly awkward and decided quickly to shower while Jeff was on the phone, to give him some privacy. As he padded toward the bathroom, he stepped in a wet spot on the carpet, which caused him to raise his foot involuntarily before looking around him for a leak somewhere. Not finding one, he shrugged and carried on.

Once in the bathroom, he wandered over to the shower and turned it on. The hot water began to steam the room up almost immediately as he adjusted the temperature and stepped in. The shower felt great and did the job of washing away the sleep and the smell of sweat from their entangled bodies. Bret stood there underneath the spray and let it sluice over him as he raised his hand to his sore lips, where the phantom of Jeff's kiss remained. They were tender to the touch.

The shower ran over him and dragged away the confusion of sleep as he washed his face and body. He heard the door of the bathroom opening and Jeff saying good-bye to Reggie on the phone. He bit his lower lip as he washed his hair, hoping he hadn't started a mess.

"I'm sorry about answering your phone," Bret said with a wince, pulling the curtain back. Jeff was leaning against the sink with his arms crossed over his chest, smiling.

"It's alright. I spent three minutes going over the details of the shooting and the rest talking about you."

"Oh." Bret's face burned with embarrassment, and he ducked back into the shower and rinsed his hair.

"She's excited. She's always on my ass to date. She says until I do, she'll be there 'fussin' and cussin'" at me," he said.

Bret smiled as the lather worked its way out and down his body. Satisfied and squeaky-clean, he bent over and turned off the water, then poked his head back out of the shower.

"Can you hand me a towel?" he asked, wiping water from his face.

Jeff turned around and grabbed the towel off the steel rack attached to the wall and handed it over to Bret, who took it with a wink and disappeared back behind the curtain.

"So, Agent McAllister, tell me why someone as handsome and as great a guy as you hasn't found someone to fuss and cuss over you. Seriously, no bullshit," Bret said as he wrapped the towel around his waist and pulled the curtain back.

Bret saw desire and surprise pass through Jeff's eyes. He was a little bashful and felt his face heat up a bit as he stepped out and prayed he didn't slip and bust his ass. He didn't, although his knees trembled a little.

Jeff put his gaze to the ground. "I did everything I could do to rid myself of being gay. I joined the Marines, figured they would beat it out me. Literally. That didn't work. There were gay people in the Marines who did their jobs just as well as anyone else. I was raised in a pretty conservative family, and I felt like they would never accept me. So I hid."

Bret felt his heart break a little as he understood what Jeff was saying, but he didn't respond and just let him continue.

"From my politics to my job working at the federal level to serve and protect…I figured somehow these hero things would *somehow* make up for my *shortfalls* in life," he said thickly, shamefaced. "I had lovers, plenty of them. I even had some relationships, but they all had a shelf life attached to them from the first hello. I knew our first kiss was already the first kiss good-bye."

Jeff looked up, his eyes misted over and his jaw clenched. "I'm getting older. Time is slipping away a little more each day, and when I look around me, I see all *my* stuff. My work. My job. My responsibilities. And I just want someone to miss me. I see what you and Adam had, and I just...I...just want someone inside of all of it. In my life. Heh, sorry."

He wiped his face and dropped his arms to the side. Bret stepped forward, picked them up, and wrapped them around his own waist. Then moved his own to be placed on either side of Jeff's face and brought his red-rimmed eyes up to meet his own. Bret leaned up and kissed Jeff's forehead and his nose, then brought their lips together gently before drawing Jeff closer to cradle his head to his shoulder. Jeff let out a shuddered sigh, and turned his head, laying it down.

Another fissure appeared in the wall surrounding Bret's quickly beating heart.

CHAPTER 13

I T WAS QUARTER past two when they pulled back into the driveway. The agents' car was not in the spot it had been, and Jeff urgently scanned the area until he saw their car pulled up to the house. Fearing the worst, they leapt out and started up the porch.

Margaret came storming out of the house. Everyone else, including the two agents, were hot on her heels.

"You were shot at!" she exclaimed, making her way down the stairs for Bret.

"I'm fine. Really. Jeff made sure of it," Bret said as she hugged him.

"How the hell did they find out?" Jeff barked at the two agents holding cups of coffee.

They looked slightly stricken, but it was Big Daddy who held up a hand.

"We got a phone call from someone who recognized Bret. Your guys didn't say anything. In fact, they already got the riot act when Margaret called me out of work," he said sternly, and Jeff calmed down.

"Why are you two not posted?" he growled.

"I told them to come up to the house," Margaret said defiantly. "If there are people shooting now, we want them closer to us."

"She stormed over to the vehicle. We were not about to make her a target that far off the road, so we did what she asked," one of the agents said indignantly.

Jeff opened his mouth to respond and then shut it with a click, as she had deflated his argument.

F.E. Feeley Jr.

"Alright. The shifts are being extended. I want twenty-four hour surveillance on this home. I'll have your relief here by ten thirty. I want you fresh. Alert. This wasn't gang violence. This was a hit. Do you understand?" Jeff asked.

"Yes sir," the tall blond man said.

"Roger that," the shorter black one replied.

"I want one of you down by the driveway to watch the road. Switch out every couple of hours. No one comes in or goes out unescorted until this is over," Jeff ordered.

He turned to the family next. "Mark, we will be notifying your employer that you're being sequestered until this is over. Guys, just relax. I know that sounds a little nuts, but I don't see a problem with maybe going for a swim or taking the boat out on the lake. If you do, take one of the agents with you," he said.

Everyone nodded.

"What about you?" Bret asked, feeling his anxiety mount.

"I am going to meet with Reggie. The guilty ones are starting to panic and act irrationally. We're going to find out who they are," Jeff replied calmly. He placed a hand on Bret's arm and rubbed it.

"Be careful, huh?" Bret asked, reaching for his hand.

"You got it. I'll have my phone on me if you need anything."

Bret watched him walk away with trepidation fluttering around in his chest. Jeff got in his SUV, turned the engine over, and began to pull away, but put the brakes on when Bret bolted toward him. As Bret ran around to the driver's side, Jeff brought the window down.

"Come back. Okay? Promise," Bret said, and Jeff reached for his hand and held it.

His expression turned from surprise to stern resolve as he kissed the knuckles on Bret's hand. "I'm coming back, Bret. I promise."

Bret nodded and backed off as Margaret came up and wrapped her arm around his waist. Jeff rolled the window up and backed out of the driveway, giving them one more wave before putting the vehicle in drive and disappearing from their view after he turned onto the road. The sun came through the leaves overhead to dapple the world around them as they watched him go.

***

Jeff got out of the vehicle at the designated rally point. There were five cars, two state police vehicles, and a K-9 unit. He had stopped quickly to change into a pair of khaki pants and a polo shirt. Everyone nodded as he made his way around the vehicle and opened the hatch to the back, where he kept his vest and blue jacket with the yellow letters FBI on the back. Reggie spotted him and ended her conversation with two of the state troopers, then headed toward him.

"The preliminary report on the pistol says the bullet came from a standard Glock nine millimeter," she said, looking him in the eye as he put his vest on.

"How did they know where we were, Reg?" he asked.

"They waited till you sent us out on the fishing expedition. The only agents that were in the vicinity were the ones following Mark Woolsey to work and the other two in front of their residence," she admitted.

Angry, Jeff strapped his vest on securely. "Speaking of which, what did you find?"

"Not a damn thing. The owner of the jewelry shop remembered Adam, and you were right—those rings were specially made and engraved for the both of them. He was surprised at Adam's openness about who he was marrying. I didn't get a vibe of homophobia from the owner, but the more we hear about these two, the more I see their relationship. They didn't hide anything," she said, adjusting her own vest.

"They shouldn't have had to. From what I understand, Adam was the most out of the two and Bret trusted him. When he made up his mind to do something, he did it. No asking permission, no questions asked. Sounds like a hell of a kid," Jeff said.

"And now?"

"With what's going on? Sounds like the exact same person," Jeff admitted.

Reggie smirked. "So what are we going to do about it?"

"Someone kept a token of their handiwork," Jeff said.

"The ring," she said, and he nodded.

"Yup."

"We find the ring, we may put a stop to this," Reggie said.

"Yes. But for now, I want the bastard who shot at us brought in. I think if we nab him, question him, scare him a little, he'll go running to the person who arranged this whole thing. And I'll put my badge on it that that's where we'll find the ring."

"We have the warrant to search the premises of the three victims as well as the one to arrest Martin," she said.

"Alright."

"Just one more thing, Jeff," she said.

"What is it?" He didn't like the look on her face.

"Jeff, it's Bret's parents," she said cautiously.

Jeff felt his blood pressure spike. "What about them?" he said, concentrating on keeping his voice calm.

"They just booked two tickets to Mexico."

He closed the hatch of the SUV. "So what? Second honeymoon? How do you know that, by the way?"

"Our tail followed them to a travel agency. Watched them go in and waited for them to leave. Posed as a frustrated banker, waved some cash around, and booked a whole trip to find out where they were going. She said the travel agent didn't think anything of it," she replied.

"Wow, good job on his part."

Reggie snorted. "Her."

Jeff grinned. "Her. Alright. We'll go visit Bret's parents when we're done."

Reggie, his best friend, winked at him before they made their way around to where everyone else was standing.

"Alright, Reg—Agent Doucette and I will be leading on this. We are going to offer Officer Martin professional courtesy. He should be waking soon to go on shift at the station. Remember, he's one of ours regardless of what he's done, so you'll be present, but hang back until Reg and I signal you to advance. Understood?"

There were nods and murmurs of approval, and Reggie spoke next. "Don't let your guard down, though. He's one of us, sure, but he's also dirty. I am not cutting into what Agent McAllister said, but I want you to stay on your guard."

More nods.

"Alright, teams one and two, you have your orders. Go through the residences with a fine-tooth comb. I want reports every hour on the hour and if you find something, call either Reggie or myself directly. Watch your six, watch your partner," Jeff said.

"Teams three and four, you're with us. Okay, let's go," Reggie said, and everyone moved out.

They jumped in their vehicles and, after they separated underneath the cover of trees, broke into two groups, one headed left and one headed right. Jeff's group took the highway leading from their rally point to the point located on the GPS that guided him. Reggie held in her hand the photo of Martin's front door and reassured Jeff she'd briefed all their people on the entrances and exits of the house before Jeff showed up.

"How's Bret?" she asked as they quickly made their way along the winding freeway.

"A trooper. He's tough," Jeff said.

"He seems like it."

"What else did you find out?" he asked.

"Adam was right. In the early days of the country, the Algonquin dealt with people on that island. It was a huge deal to them to go there. There was this whole ceremony before they talked. It consisted of lighting a fire and breaking bread together before they bothered to talk about the business at hand," she replied.

"Okay, so what if we're right? What if Adam is back whacking people who had something to do with his death? What's his role besides killing people?"

"Maybe to bear witness, maybe to protect Bret. This isn't going to end well for anyone. Especially Bret. If his parents are involved, he loses again," she replied.

Her words hit Jeff hard. He wanted nothing more than to shield Bret from anything. Even though they were new, he was worried that their affections would be overshadowed by it all.

"We're cops, we're supposed to bring the bad guys in so justice can be served. Not stand back to watch the bad guys be annihilated," he said as he expertly weaved through traffic.

"What do you suggest we do?" Reggie asked as Jeff's phone began to ring. Reggie pulled it off the dash and was about to hand it over to him. Instead she read the ID of the person calling. "It's Martin."

"Open it up and put it on speaker."

***

The wraith watched him as he paced through the living room with the cell phone attached to his head. The room stank of fear, sweat, and booze and the whispers pleaded, urged, and demanded his action. With a shout of disgust, the man hung up and slammed the phone down on the table before walking past him to head back into the kitchen.

He followed.

The man opened up the refrigerator, took out another beer, popped the tab, and took three hard swallows before closing the door. He wiped his mouth with the back of his hand and leaned his head against the fridge, closing his eyes. His handsome face screwed up in a grimace as anxiety poured out of him in waves. The scent of it was like blood in the water for sharks, the whispers feeding on it.

Adam was about to seize the opportunity of the moment when he was surprised by Martin's next action. Tearfully Martin reached up on top of the refrigerator and pulled down a pistol sheathed in a holster. His hands trembled as he pulled it out of its holster and looked at it in the palm of his hand. He opened his mouth slightly and brought the pistol up...

With a gagging sob, he dropped his hands and wept. "The preacher told us to do it! He said the Bible said it was okay! Oh God!"

He watched this with a measure of futile sympathy. At no time in his life had he been violent. But his life was over. This… this was something else. Even though Martin's reaction was the first sign of regret any one of them had shown, the whispers were unaffected. They steadily climbed louder and louder around him. But he hesitated once more as the man took his gun, put it in the waistband of his jeans, grabbed his car keys, and ran out the door.

Adam was waiting for him in the backseat of his patrol car before he could even get out of his door. When Martin got in and turned the ignition on, Adam sat back and watched as they pulled away and headed toward the lake. At the first red light, Martin grabbed his cell phone, dialed a number, and waited for it to ring.

The light turned green, and they continued on.

"It's Martin. Look, I want to meet somewhere. I want to confess everything," he said, piloting the car with one hand and holding his cell phone in the other. He listened for a minute to the voice on the other end of the phone.

"Yeah. I'm at Salisbury getting ready to turn onto Lakefront. I'll meet you halfway. …Yeah, I know who did it all. There are three of us left. …No, I have no idea who's behind the new kill. …Yeah, yeah. Give me three minutes." Martin hung up, tossed the phone down on the passenger seat, and pulled out his pistol.

"If I am going out, motherfucker, so are you," he said, taking the safety off his pistol. "You're with that little queer boy. We should have taken him out too."

Adam closed his eyes and, in rage, shifted forward.

***

Bret slowly chewed his late lunch. Everyone was quietly eating and only the occasional, "could you pass the" and "can you hand me one of those" questions cut through the silence. When they did, everyone jumped and reached for whatever was asked for. The mayonnaise jar almost became a football, so many people grabbed for it. It would have been funny if everyone wasn't so damn jumpy with one of the agents sitting with them at the table. Margaret had made hamburgers and french fries, and the only one eating with any enthusiasm was the agent. Occasionally he would moan and grunt his approval after a couple of bites.

"Don't they feed you poor boys in the FBI, Agent Sams?" Margaret asked with a slightly amused look on her face.

"No, we eat out. A lot. It comes with the job. I have to say, though, I've eaten a lot of hamburgers in my life, but this…this is amazing," he said happily.

Molly grinned and winked at Bret, who tried to manage a return smile. She was about to say something when her mouth made an O shape and she grabbed Bret's hand. First he was scared she was going into labor early, but he was put at ease almost immediately.

"Want to feel your nephew kick?" she asked and placed his hand on her belly. Her distended stomach felt weird under his hand, and he tried to gingerly press down even though he was afraid he was going to hurt her. As soon as he felt the kick, Bret jerked his hand away, and she laughed.

"Strong little shit," she said as Bret put his hand back.

Shock ran all through him, and he looked over at Timmy.

"Hey, that's our little shit," Timmy said, before taking a bite of a french fry.

"He's a Woolsey," Big Daddy replied.

Sure enough, the little guy was going to town, and every time Bret was filled with wonder.

"Maybe he'll be a swimmer like his uncles Adam and Bret were," Margaret said, and Bret grinned.

"Heck, yeah. Adam would love that," Bret said. He should have been happy, but something happened suddenly. He turned his head—he'd heard someone speaking. Turning in his seat, he looked behind him.

"Bret, you've just gone white as a sheet." Margaret sounded far away, like she was in a tunnel.

"Don't you hear that?" Bret asked.

"Hear what?" Timmy asked, starting to rise from his seat.

"Whispering." Bret came up off his chair as well.

Molly looked worriedly at Big Daddy, who had stopped eating and grabbed the agent's arm.

"Bret, we don't hear anything," Big Daddy said.

The agent stood up immediately and walked behind where Bret was.

"Oh no," Bret said. "Timmy, take me outside."

The whispering was something new, and he couldn't identify any of the words. It sounded like gibberish. It came faster and faster, making his head swim and his stomach lurch. His heart pounded so hard it felt like it was going to bust free, and sweat started to drip down the back of his neck.

Suddenly the dining room table wasn't there anymore. Bret was in the backseat of a car heading fast down the road beside the lake. He was watching the back of someone's head as they drove at a high rate of speed. Bret tried to move forward but couldn't, and then suddenly he pitched forward, through the front seat, through the windshield, and out onto a far point in the road as if time, space, and physics didn't exist.

It happened so quickly that Bret was just recovering when his head was turned by an unseen force. The whispers he had heard earlier hadn't abated either—they were chanting in unison now, loud like a drumbeat.

Coming in the other direction was a familiar SUV, bearing down on them. It was Jeff's Navigator, making its way up Lakeside Road, followed by what looked like two squad cars. Bret's head swiveled right as the car they had been in bore down on him even faster now, and as the vehicle drew closer, Bret was able to make out the face of Officer Martin as he drove recklessly toward them. Panic struck Bret as he tried to move, but his body didn't cooperate. Caught in the center of these two vehicles, he knew his death would come quickly.

Then something happened. When the car was but a few feet from where he stood, Bret felt himself being pulled forward as if the air around him was giving birth to his presence, like being yanked from a vacuum. The look of fierce determination on

Martin's face turned to a mixture of horror and surprise as he jerked the wheel hard to the right. Tires squealed and smoked as the squad car left the road and hit the guardrail, tearing through it like a hot knife through butter. It sailed for a moment before crashing hood first into the lake water. Bret wanted to scream, wanted to close his eyes and turn his head from the sight of the disaster, but couldn't. Instead, the vacuum feeling came over him again, but this time instead of being pushed out, he was being pulled back in as the unintelligible whispers turned into a full-on shout.

He moved again, going forward out and above the lake, and suddenly reappeared in the backseat of the squad car as water began to fill it. The driver was shaking his head, apparently dazed by the force of the impact and the discharge of the airbag that, now deflated, filled the interior of the car with a powdery smoke. Water poured in through the doors and was coming through Martin's open window. The coolness of it, something Bret realized in passing that he couldn't feel either, must have jarred the officer back to reality as he struggled with the seat belt. The car was sinking fast.

Bret felt himself look down at the seat in front of him and watched as Martin reached out and grabbed the belt taut.

"Son of a bitch. Why won't you let go! *Help! Help!*" Martin cried as he fought the restraints. The water was up to his chest now. Bret saw movement out of the corner of his eye and felt his head turn to see Jeff swimming up. Jeff fought with the driver's side door and swung it open.

"Here, unbuckle yourself," Jeff yelled.

"I can't! It's stuck!" Martin cried frantically, jerking the belt with all his might.

"No it isn't. It's loose. I'm looking right at it. You're not buckled in. You're not—what the hell?"

The same whooshing vacuum feeling, and Bret realized what was happening. He could tell by the expression on Jeff's face that he had become visible once again. He wanted to cry out to Jeff he was sorry, or that it wasn't him, or any number of nonsensical things, but what Jeff said next surprised him.

"Adam, you don't have to do this," he said calmly.

"What?" Martin asked and looked up into the rearview mirror. Bret felt his head move from Jeff until he met Martin's eyes.

"Oh my God! Oh my God! Get me out of here! Get me out of here!"

The man was clawing now, screaming as if he had seen death personified. Bret wouldn't, couldn't let go as the whispers now sounded like a hurricane in his ears, the drumming of the words like explosions all around him. The man bounced, pulled, tried to crawl, and finally reached out to Jeff, screaming and begging him and God for help. The water rushed up to his chin, to his nose, and he tilted his head back, shaking it back and forth as if in denial before the water slipped over. Bret's head turned once more to lock eyes with Jeff.

"Four down, two to go," Bret said in Adam's voice.

Jeff pulled back, the car went under, and Bret knew no more.

CHAPTER 14

THERE WERE FIVE of them present in the shadow of an oak tree that jutted out over the lake. They stood there silently now that the deed was done, each of them staring at their handiwork. Each one of them looked at it with varying thoughts and emotions, bound together in the silence of their evil deed. In front of them, the lake was still, its waters placid, the ripples they had caused now calm, the way they preferred life in towns like these. Smooth as glass. They knew it would be discovered. They counted on it, actually. It would serve as a warning to any of those who tried to do what had been done.

"We shouldn't have done it here," one of them said.

They all looked at him.

"Why is that?" asked another.

"I don't know, we should have done it elsewhere," he replied nervously.

"You worried about that old legend? You worried those old Indians are gonna getcha?" another snickered, drawing his hands up in claws. A ripple of mocking laughter skirted through the gathering.

"What? No. Fuck you."

"What about the other one? He's been asking questions."

"So what? He'll never figure it out, and if he knows what's good for him, he'll leave" came the growled reply.

"God said we could kill them. That's what the preacher said," one of the others said as if their deed needed an affirmation.

Murmurs of approval now rippled through the men present. However, as they comforted themselves with those words, a moan of chilly wind blew in from across the surface of the glassy water.

The moon chose that moment to come out from behind passing clouds to cast them in cold light, and the island in the center of the lake became illuminated. From far across the lake, on the shores of that island, tendrils of fog began to creep forward, swirling and dancing about as its thin, wispy fingers rose above the surface of the rolling water.

"Jesus," one of the silent five finally whispered.

"Come on, you goddamn pansies," the leader said. "Let's get out of here before someone sees us. Remember, anyone speaks, you'll meet the same fate. You were paid to do a job."

No one spoke this time. They only nodded and backed off. They would remain quiet.

As they made their way up the embankment, their mood lifted the farther they got from the body, which floated facedown and lifeless. The tendrils of fog stretched forth like reaching hands, making their way across the lake as the five drove off, the beams of their headlights casting themselves over the body once more for them to see their handiwork.

In the silence, the fog rolled still as if given a life of its own. Pushed by an unseen hand, it spread out, thicker. The insects and chirping frogs became silent as the whispers started. The bank of fog stopped short of the body for a moment as if considering what lay there before mounting up like a wave. The whispers grew louder, more insistent, a language that had existed almost as long as the lake had. The fog rolled upward, wrapping itself around as faces emerged, twisting and boiling before it came crashing down hard beside the body, turning it over.

It twisted underneath, on both sides, surrounding the body and covering it like a funeral shroud. The man's sightless eyes stared heavenward, his lifeless hands spread open, fingers curled inward, and mud underneath his fingernails. The fog whispered incessantly as it swirled, moving the body with cold, damp fingers before plunging into the lungs, expanding the chest, causing it to bow outward as it filled him, as his sightless eyes stared on. Yet, he didn't stay that way.

The mouth, which had been shut, now opened wide as the fog exited outward and upward. It carried something with it, something golden like the sun, a tiny star that illuminated the world briefly as the fog held it firmly, yet tenderly, in its grasp. The whispers crescendoed before a name was whispered. One name. *Adam.*

Once said, the fog whisked the light away, back across the glassy surface toward the dark island, leaving the body as lifeless as it had found it, staring upward with sightless eyes open wide. Just staring, heavenward, with those empty, unseeing eyes.

***

Jeff nursed a glass of whiskey as he sat in the heavily shadowed room lit only by a lamp in the far corner opposite him. In the bed lay Bret, mouth open, eyes shut, his breathing regular and steady. The sound of silence only broke by the occasional mumble as Bret called out Adam's name. Jeff raised the glass to his mouth once more, the ice cubes clinking against the side because his hands still shook. The amber liquid burned on its way down as he took a sip. Alcohol raced through his bloodstream, aided by a heartbeat that was still faster than it should be since what he'd seen toyed at the edges of his mind, but competing thoughts kept the alcohol at bay and his blood pressure up. The face of Adam and "Four down, two to go" as Martin was murdered right in front of him, gasping for mercy, screaming for relief. Was that how Adam had died? Both things made him want to take a bottle full of Valium and sleep for a week.

After the car was pulled out of the lake and Martin's body was put in a body bag and on a stretcher, his sightless eyes staring up into the night sky while his mouth remained open in a silent scream, the memory burned behind Jeff's eyes. He lowered the glass and set it on his stomach while he slouched in a high wing-back chair, silently wondering if he would ever sleep again. Jeff was angry at himself for leaving Bret alone, angry that he couldn't save Martin, and angry that he had wandered into an impossible case where he felt as useless as a screen door on a submarine.

The door behind him opened gently, and he tilted his head to the left in a halfhearted attempt to see who had come in. It was Reggie. She gave him a brief smile, pulled up another smaller chair, and sat down next to him. She reached over for his hand, and he took it, glad for the contact as their fingers intertwined. She squeezed gently in a silent promise that she was right there, and not simply in the flesh, a touch he had gotten to know very well in his years working with her. It was a silent discussion of the mutual respect and love they had forged together over the years. He smiled at her and squeezed back his appreciation, a wordless thank-you. Sometimes words were not enough…

"He hasn't come around yet?" she asked, and Jeff shook his head.

"He's been mumbling in his sleep, but no, he hasn't woken up yet," he replied.

"I checked him over, Jeff. He's going to be sore tomorrow, but Timmy saved his life. You know, as big as he is, I was expecting at least a few cracked ribs, but everyone said he handled this like a pro and was very careful with him. Although, this is getting worse. This time he nearly drowned."

Jeff nodded, feeling sick to his stomach. "They seem to be an awesome family. Bret's lucky to have them."

"He's lucky to have you too," she replied.

Jeff gave a sarcastic snort. "Is that right?"

"Stop feeling sorry for yourself right now, *mon ami*," she whispered, her Cajun accent creeping in. "There was no way you could have done anything to prevent all that's happening around you right now. Nothing. That badge of yours only deals with the law as we know it. There are older things than this country. Other laws in a metaphysical sense that, under certain circumstances, drown rational thought. Case in point," she said, pointing at Bret.

"Why were you more willing and able to accept it in the beginning?" he asked, looking at her.

"So you think I was right?" she asked.

He nodded, and she raised her free hand and ran it down the side of his face.

"I come from a different world than you do. Where I come from, things like this are talked about openly, we celebrate them. Well, not people dying, but the thought of life after death is not just for the superreligious," she said in a matter-of-fact tone.

He regarded her for a moment, mulling it over and taking another sip of the whiskey Big Daddy had poured.

"The media is reporting on a serial suicide epidemic. They haven't been able to connect the dots yet, although one of our agents was questioned as to yesterday's shoot-out. He told the press it was unrelated gang violence." She snorted.

Jeff almost choked with laughter. Reggie snickered next to him.

"When in doubt resort to gang violence." She shrugged.

"Tricks of the trade."

After they calmed down, Jeff asked, "Ballistics report come back?"

"Yup."

"Was it Martin's weapon?"

"*Oui.*"

"With everything going on—the murder and the cover-up—that's all they are, really: a gang. We went over so many different definitions of terror organizations the world over, including right here in the good ol' US of A. What happened here is no different. But you know, I have to respect gangs a little more now," he said, rubbing his forehead.

"Why's that?"

"They don't hide behind God to do their evil deeds."

It was Reggie's turn to snort.

"So, what's the next step?" Jeff asked before he tilted the glass up for his final drink. He was beginning to calm down again. It was amazing what a friend's presence and good booze would do for you.

"Oh, shit, Jeff. Let's go all Earl Warren with this. I think we should go find someone who knows what the fuck we're dealing with."

He grinned at the Brown v. Board reference. It was appropriate. That was the first time the high court had gone outside the law to seek answers to the questions before them, which is what she was asking him to do.

"Alright, I'll take your lead on this. I have nothing. As this continues, whatever force is at work here has ahold of Bret as well. I am afraid it gets worse every time. I don't think he can survive much more. Adam or this curse is killing him as well. And…I, uh," he said, feeling his face flush.

"You like him."

"I am thinking about long walks on the beach and puppies, yeah. But I want him safe. I'd turn my badge in right now if I thought that throwing him in the truck and just getting him away from Ground Zero would fix the problem," he said sadly.

She squeezed his hand again. "Yeah, I know. But we have a family in there now who've also been pretty shaken up. They claim Bret's face changed right in front of them. That he looked like Adam and even spoke in his voice."

"I know." Jeff sighed. "I'll take your lead on this, whatever you want to do. We'll run it by Bret when he wakes up and—"

"I'm awake," Bret said softly, startling them.

They turned to look at him and saw him starting to sit up. Bret grabbed for his chest with a grunt, and Jeff was immediately on his feet and rushing to the side of the bed to help him. Bret's face was drawn and he looked haggard as he struggled to right himself. Jeff sat next to him, reached out, and pulled him into a hug, partly to add pressure to his chest and support his back, and partly to wrap his arms around him. Breathless, Bret leaned against him as Jeff adjusted the pillows.

"Easy. Easy does it," Jeff said tenderly. "It's alright."

"It's not alright. It's not alright!" Bret sobbed into Jeff's shoulder. He was shaking his head back and forth. Hot tears soaked through Jeff's shirt as the younger man trembled and cried, gasping for breath.

"What's happening to me? I was there… I…I killed Officer Martin. I saw him die! You were there too!" Bret wept.

Jeff pulled him away as Reggie came over to the other side of the bed and sat down. He was stunned to hear those words.

"Bret, what do you mean?" he asked calmly. His voice lied to Bret. Inside, a hurricane was raging. Winds howled, trees bent, roofs flew off. Usually this meant someone was in trouble when Jeff was able to direct it toward a criminal. Right then, the perpetrator of these deaths was beyond his grasp and the storm couldn't continue forward in any direction, so the only victim it was taking was Jeff, and he knew that.

"I saw it all happening. I was in the car with him, in the backseat. Except it wasn't me. Not entirely. You called me Adam," Bret said, wiping his face. He took a shuddering breath and then clutched his chest again.

The door behind them opened once more, and Timmy and Margaret stepped in. Both looked ashen and tired as well as worried. Bret lowered his head and buried his face in his hands. Jeff was going to say something else when Margaret walked forward and motioned for him to scoot over. He complied, but made sure he was close by just in case.

Margaret reached for Bret's hands and lowered them from his face. His look of sheer misery made Jeff's heart skip. He also saw the fear in Bret's eyes.

Margaret stared at Bret for a minute and then grabbed him and pulled him to her. She rocked him back and forth when the tears came again.

"Shh, my precious boy. Shh. It's alright. Cry it out. It's okay," she mumbled.

"I'm so sorry," he cried.

"There is nothing in the world to be sorry over, Bret. This isn't your fault. This isn't Adam's fault either. Shh," she said, rocking him back and forth. After a moment or two, she put Bret at arm's length and looked in his face.

"Big Daddy was raised on this lake. He was raised with all the folklore and the legends. We built the house here because we thought it was romantic and that those stories would bring us luck. We passed these down to Adam and Timmy. But Bi—"

She stopped short. "Your father and I never thought anything like this would happen. When we saw your face change, Bret, all those old superstitions became real."

She turned halfway around to look at Jeff. "Call whoever you will. Someone has to know how to resolve this before we lose Bret as well."

Jeff looked over at Reggie and nodded. She winked at Bret and stood to go.

"That isn't Adam. That isn't my Adam. He was gentle, caring, that...that *thing*...is cold-blooded...a killer," Bret stammered, shaking his head.

Jeff watched the chaos going on behind his eyes as the truth of what Bret had known fought with the truth of what now was.

"Adam wasn't mean, you're right, Bret. But he was tough. He was a man of his word. And he didn't put up with no shit," Timmy said. "He was a man of his word. Maybe this is the curse or the blessing or whatever we're calling it now. But it's Adam, Bret, as he is now."

Everyone was silent, including Bret, who looked stricken. He eventually nodded and closed his eyes.

"How about we let him have a little bit of rest, shall we?" Jeff asked, and everyone began to file out of the room.

"Jeff, will you stay?" Bret asked.

Jeff had been the last one to walk to the door, but he turned back. "Are you sure?" he asked, and Bret nodded, so Jeff closed the door. He walked over to the edge of the bed and sat down.

Bret opened his eyes and looked up at him. "Don't feel bad about Officer Martin. He was on his way to kill you," he said.

Jeff's eyes widened, not from the news of Martin's objective, but that Adam had either purposefully or inadvertently saved his life.

"It's fine. He's gone and you're still here. We just have to find the last two people before Adam gets ahold of them."

"I am going to die, aren't I?" Bret asked.

Jeff emphatically shook his head before leaning forward and kissing Bret on the forehead. "No. As long as there is breath inside my body, you'll be safe."

Bret raised a hand and ran it down Jeff's face, and Jeff turned into his touch. He grasped Bret's hand and held it there.

"It was Coach Polanski. He's your fifth one."

Jeff's eyes shot open. "How do you know?"

Bret smirked. "Adam's in my head, and I am in his apparently. I saw the night he was murdered. They took his ring. Wherever that is, is where you'll find the one who ordered the hit." He looked away and out the window.

Jeff kissed his forehead.

"What are you thinking?" Jeff asked.

Bret lowered his head, a look of sheer anguish on his face. "I think it was my mom and dad. Or one of them," he said, his chin trembling.

Jeff was surprised. But out of all the suspects, including Adam's family, Bret's revelation was the only one that made sense. "I'm sorry, Bret."

"I don't know how much more of this I can take."

Jeff didn't say anything this time. In moments like these, when the truth is so dry words freeze, it's better to remain silent. So Jeff stood up and climbed into bed next to Bret and pulled the man closer to his side. Bret came willingly, resting his head on Jeff's chest, and Jeff slid his arms around Bret's back to hold him close. It wasn't long before Bret's breathing slowed down and he stilled.

Jeff pulled out his cell phone and sent a text to Reggie, updating her on what Bret had told him. After an exchange of orders, questions, and confirmations, Jeff placed his cell phone on the nightstand next to the bed with the intention of only staying for a little while. He yawned and closed his eyes.

He woke himself once snoring, but it didn't last.

***

Bret didn't know what woke him, but suddenly he lay there staring up at the ceiling as the fan blades spun around and around. He turned his head to the side and saw Jeff lying beside him, still clothed in his uniform. The vest, crammed upward, and Jeff's head tilted at an odd angle made him look so young Bret couldn't help but smile. He sat up, wincing at the pain in his chest. Timmy had done a number on him as he'd pumped water out of his lungs, but Bret was able to manage his way up the headboard and to turn his legs to get out of the bed. Standing, he felt better, stretched cautiously, made his way around the bed, and stared at Jeff's impossibly adorable sleeping position.

Snickering, Bret reached down for his feet and began to untie his shoes, sliding one off, then the other, followed by his socks.

Jeff stirred and sat up. "What are you doing?" he asked sleepily.

"Here, sit up," Bret said, and Jeff did, his hair sticking up and his eyes sleepy.

Bret reached around Jeff's sides, undid the Velcro, and pulled the vest up and over Jeff's head. He placed it on the floor next to his shoes and came back for his shirt. Jeff closed his eyes and raised his arms so Bret could take it off. As soon as it was discarded, Bret made to turn when Jeff grabbed his waist and laid his head on his stomach. Bret laid the shirt on the bed, wrapped his arms around Jeff's head, and held him. He ran his hands through Jeff's brown hair, dragging his fingertips over Jeff's scalp as Jeff reached his hands down and squeezed Bret's butt. Emotion soared through Bret's heart as his blood turned hot and seared through his veins. It was the middle of the night, and everyone was asleep, but Bret felt an overwhelming need to hold and be held.

Bret let go of him and reached down for Jeff's undershirt. Jeff raised his arms to allow it to come off. Bret reached down again as Jeff lowered his arms, while Bret ran his hands over Jeff's muscular shoulders. He had heard Jeff's words to Reggie about wanting to keep him safe. And while that might be futile, the intention was pure. Jeff believed he could, and Bret felt that in the strength in his muscles as they grew taut under his hands. Nothing was normal anymore, nothing felt solid, and Jeff seemed like the only thing standing still, while the world rocked back

F.E. FEELEY JR.

and forth and spun Bret with it. Jeff pulled him forward gently until Bret crawled up and straddled his hips.

Bret watched as passion ignited in Jeff's eyes when he placed his hands on Jeff's firm pecs and ran a thumb over each nipple. Jeff's full lips parted slightly as his heart beat furiously under Bret's touch. Jeff groaned in pleasure as Bret took Jeff's top lip between his lips for a slow and drawn-out kiss. It always amazed Bret that kissing another man would be as soft as it was. You'd expect it to be hard, like their bodies, but it never was. They were gentle, soft, and the flesh was like the flesh of a rose. The kiss deepened, their tongues touched, tasting and teasing as Bret bore down on the hips of the man he straddled. Jeff's hands rose to his ass and squeezed, causing Bret to break the kiss and let out a low moan, leaning his head against Jeff's shoulder. Jeff took the opportunity to gently pull Bret's shirt up, and Bret tried to assist him by raising his arms, but pain shot through his chest, causing him to hiss in discomfort.

"Are you okay?" Jeff growled low.

"Yeah. Just...I'm sore," Bret whispered.

Jeff was still for a moment, perhaps considering their predicament. "Do you favor this shirt?" he asked, looking Bret directly in the eye.

"It's just a shirt," Bret said simply, and that was all the permission Jeff needed.

He grabbed the hem of the shirt and with a quick flex of muscle tore it open, revealing Bret's bruised and muscular chest.

"Jesus." Jeff moaned as he raised a hand and ran it down the angry, purple bruising.

Bret gave an involuntary shiver. "How bad is it?" he asked, refusing to look down.

"We should be careful," Jeff whispered, his hands trembling.

"That's the last thing I need."

"What *do* you need?" Jeff asked.

"To feel."

Their mouths collided again as Jeff sat forward, wrapped his arms around him, and with a strength that surprised even Bret, rolled them over gently until he was on top. Jeff gave him what he asked as he feasted, hungry and unyielding, on Bret's mouth. Not being a wilting flower, Bret gave as good as he got, the stubble of Jeff's mouth bruising his lips as Jeff's hands wandered up the length of his side to seize his hands and put them over his head, holding him down. Jeff broke the kiss, both of them breathing hard, to stare longingly into Bret's eyes. Bret found a wild wind, a storm raging, with the sound of a legion of horses' hooves and lightning flashing there that made him catch his breath. But there was something else that softened them. There was Jeff walking alone in the maelstrom...searching...searching... Bret decided to wander into the storm to find him, in hopes of being found himself.

Bret raised his head and kissed him again, flinging himself forward into the storm and praying to be washed away. Jeff didn't disappoint as he covered him with his body and weight, their naked chests touching. Bret met passion with passion as he reached between them to the waistband of Jeff's pants. Jeff raised his hips to give him access and he fumbled with his belt and buttons before they gave way, allowing Bret to slide his hands inside his pants and underwear and guide them down. Jeff's erection caught briefly in the shorts but broke free to slap against his belly, but quickly disappeared as Jeff lay back down. Bret brought his legs around Jeff's waist and hooked his big toes in the pants to pull them down the rest of the way. Jeff kicked the remains of the clothing away and now lay naked on top of him.

Bret ran his hands down Jeff's back to his waist and the muscular globes of his ass, then squeezed as Jeff arched his back and grunted his approval. Jeff reached between them to the waistband of Bret's shorts and undid them, sitting up and pulling them down, exposing Bret to the cool air. Jeff reared back on his haunches, his chest heaving as he drank in Bret's body. His eyes flitted everywhere the skin was exposed, and Bret felt his face flush with his nakedness.

"Don't. You're beautiful, Bret," Jeff said. His naked maleness was thick, heavy, and swollen in agreement.

Bret had tried to cover himself, to hide not only his naked skin but to hide his exposed soul, but he stopped short at the command.

The sight of Jeff's lithe, muscular body, the way his chest, as broad as it was, narrowed down to his hips, the way he sat on his haunches, his thighs strung tight like cords of thick rope made Bret's mouth dry. And when he leaned forward and crawled up over Bret's body to cover him, to anchor him, Bret rose to meet him. The passion ignited once again as they reached for each other's touch, whispered words and called each other's name. The sweat and shaking limbs, the tossing of the insanity of the world around them into the ether as they clung together, grounded them in the here and now.

Jeff reached between them and with one hand joined their swollen sexes together as they made love with their mouths. He worked them over steadily and firmly.

Bret could feel the power of his climax roaring upward from the base of his spine as he whimpered and gave a grunt, his sore chest protesting the contraction of muscle, and then his whole body clenched and he erupted in a shattering crescendo that caused his eyes to roll back in his head. Above him he heard Jeff's words of encouragement, grunted and shuddered above Bret, before he too succumbed to their lovemaking.

In whispered words they found each other again, not in passion, but in the fragile dawning of a new beginning for both of them. They had made the night burn as bright as the day at three thirty in the morning, and it left them breathless and sated.

As if reading Bret's mind, Jeff said, "I'll do everything I can to hold you here."

Bret didn't say a word. He just nodded as Jeff held him. He didn't know if Jeff could do anything at all, if those words were in vain. But it didn't matter. Not right now, then. What mattered was that they both clung to that hope as they clung to each other, their exhausted, tangled bodies sweaty and spent, still holding each other in defiance of the world that spun around them.

***

Heartbroken, Adam wept as he watched them slip into unconsciousness. He wept not for the love they made, or the tenderness of it, he wept for what the screaming voices demanded of him. He had tried to hold them off as long as he could, but they were insistent now, and he was bound to the promise he had made. As he stood there and gazed upon the sight of Bret's bruised lips, which he had once turned that angry red color, he brought his hands up to his own mouth in a longing so deep, the trees outside sighed as the wind tousled their leaves.

He wept for the injustice of it all.

Bret didn't belong to Adam now. He belonged to the promise he'd made in the years prior. Adam had tried in vain to make him stay away, but even distance wouldn't save Bret now. The promise would not only claim the lives of those he was taking, it would claim Bret as well.

The promise had to be kept. But the promise was a double-edged sword.

Four down, two to go.

The promise had to be kept.

Adam turned to go, but before he did, he gave Bret and his lover one last look over his shoulder. He didn't want to do what must be done. For when it was complete, Bret Williams would die.

The promise had to be kept.

CHAPTER 15

T HE MORNING DAWNED bright and early, and both men were
awakened by the sound of birds chirping and the sunlight
tossing its golden rays onto their brows. Jeff was the first to wake
and found Bret sprawled across his chest. He closed his eyes and
took a few moments to soak in the sunlight and the warmth of
the body on top of him. Looking down, Jeff brushed the hair back
from Bret's eyes and smiled at the pursed lips and the sleep lines
across Bret's face. He brought his arm up and placed it on Bret's
back, then tenderly rubbed his smooth skin, going from his neck
down his spine to his backside.

Jeff's phone chirped at him, and he reached over to pick it up.
It was Reggie. He grunted and laid his head back on the pillow,
the glow of the night before steadily replaced by the gravitas
of what the day presented. He set the phone back down on the
nightstand, kissed Bret gently on top of his head, and slowly and
carefully rolled him over. Bret shifted and murmured, sighing
deeply. Jeff had been afraid of waking him, yet although he
stirred, his eyes never opened. He lingered for a moment more,
hating the thought of leaving the warm bed and Bret's naked
body. Jeff placed a kiss on his forehead and, with another sigh,
rolled himself up and tossed his legs over the side before picking
his phone back up.

It was seven thirty in the morning, and as he stood up, he
stretched, reaching for the ceiling. Usually, sleeping with someone
new made for a long and restless night. After their lovemaking,
Jeff had slept like…well, like the dead. He winced at that thought.

"I slept like someone who was really sleepy," he corrected
himself. There had been too much death lately.

Jeff quickly dressed in his discarded clothes from yesterday, clipped his phone on the waist of his dress pants, kissed Bret's disheveled head once more, and walked out. He carried his vest on his arm as he made his way down the hallway. When he entered the kitchen, Margaret was pouring Reggie a cup of coffee. Jeff's face flushed a little when Margaret smiled at him and pointed suggestively to the coffeepot. He nodded, and she grabbed a coffee cup from the cupboard and poured until his cup steamed with black gold.

"Cream and sugar are right here. Did you sleep good?" she asked, sliding the containers over to him.

"Uh, yeah. Thank you," he said bashfully. "I didn't mean to stay in there all night. I just fell asleep and…"

Margaret held up a hand. "You don't have to apologize. We're just glad you're here for Bret."

Jeff gave a brief smile, and Margaret turned to Reggie.

"Can I get you anything else?" she asked.

"No, ma'am. Coffee is great," Reggie said.

Margaret nodded. She looked like she was going to say something, then stopped, started to again, and stopped once more.

"Margaret, if—" Jeff started.

"Look, I'm a mother. Two boys, one very pregnant soon-to-be daughter-in-law, and Bret. I'm not his real mom, but I am his mom. He spent days, weeks, months, years of his life in this house. I know you're a little older, and I know you have the best of intentions, and I understand he needs someone in his life and to move on, although I don't think any of what is going on here is helping… All I am saying—" She stopped short as a voice behind him spoke up.

"I'm going to be fine. I'm not made of glass."

Jeff turned around and saw Bret standing there, fully dressed.

"Honey, I wasn't saying that you are, it's just these past few days—" she started.

"I spent five years saying 'these past few days' as I described my life. I said I was letting go, moving on, but I didn't, I couldn't.

I wouldn't. I've run from everything. From the truth. I always wondered who killed Adam. I always tried to put it in some kind of context, and right afterward I hated walking around town, staring at faces, wondering, 'Did she do it? Did he do it?'"

He leaned against the wall and wrapped an arm around his bruised ribs.

"I've known all along, deep down in my gut and in the dark places in my heart who was responsible for Adam's death, and I wouldn't—couldn't—accept it. So I ran away from it. I've been in school for the last five years! Stationed at one place in my life, the very place Adam and I were supposed to go. And now I have to face it, whether I like it or not, because it's killing me." He moved his arm to expose his chest.

"So if you're going to feel bad or protective of anyone, perhaps you should feel bad for Jeff, because I may not make it through the next one. Or maybe you should feel bad for you, but don't feel bad for me. I made a promise. We were two foolish boys who didn't know shit about life or what we were doing that night out on the island, and who knows what might have happened over the years? We might have ended up breaking our own promise to each other, then what?"

Jeff spoke next. "You couldn't have known—"

"It doesn't matter now," Bret said wearily. "Ignorance of the law is no excuse, right? What matters is we get to the bottom of this, and I am not sitting by waiting for Adam to come and claim me. You're a Marine, right? Well, let's go get these last two bastards. I want them to know I know. Especially him," he said, stone-faced.

"Especially who?" Margaret asked.

Jeff winced but kept his eyes on Bret, whose face flushed. Bret's jaws clenched, and he jumped as Big Daddy walked up from behind him and made his way into the kitchen.

"What's going on?" he asked, walking into the room.

Margaret put a hand up to silence him. "Bret, who?"

Jeff saw her come around the island, but he kept his eyes locked on Bret. Bret's eyes filled with tears as his jaw clenched, a look of torture on his face. Jeff was about to tell her when Bret let it all out in a whoosh.

"My father. I think my father had your son murdered because we were together," he said.

Margaret's hand went to her mouth.

"Wait. Wait. Hold on, Bret. How can you know that?" Big Daddy asked.

Bret was shaking his head. Timmy and Molly made their way into the room, and by the looks on their faces, they'd heard the conversation. A phone rang in the background—Reggie's, possibly, but Jeff didn't break eye contact with Bret to find out. It was confirmed, however, when he heard the ringing retreat as she took the call outside.

"Who else would have been that invested in us besides all of you?" Bret asked, his voice cracking. Jeff wanted more than anything to reach out to him to make it stop, but he needed Bret to cement the idea in his head, especially since they were about to move on that assumption.

"I'm not hearing this. I'm not hearing this!" Margaret screamed as her husband tried to grab hold of her. She shook him off. "How could you, how could you after all these years of knowing...?" she cried.

Big Daddy finally had his arms around her when Jeff finally spoke up. "That's the whole point—he considered it. But he didn't know. Not till Adam showed up," he said, finally turning from Bret to regard her.

"But he suspected!" she screamed at him.

"And what was he going to do with that, Mom? You heard him. He suspected everyone, and so far he's been right!" Timmy said. "The drunk, the preacher, a cop, and the sheriff? How many other people could possibly have been tied up in this thing?"

"The swim coach," Bret said, loud enough for everyone to hear.

Molly was the one to gasp this time.

"Coach Polanski?" Timmy asked, and Bret nodded.

Pandemonium broke out, first with Big Daddy, who started yelling and cursing, and then Margaret, who broke into a fresh round of sobbing.

"Jeff, we have him in custody," Reggie said, opening the door. Everyone turned to look at her, and silence reigned.

"When?" Jeff asked.

"Right now. Our agents knocked on the door this morning. He admitted everything to them right on the spot. Said he'd been hearing noises in his house all night long, like someone had been following him around. Agent Fessenden said he looks like he's on the verge of a heart attack he's so freaked out."

"I want him taken immediately down to the station, I want two agents here at the house and the rest inside the police building keeping an eye out for any of the other cops in there who may feel some sympathy for their buddy or old swim coach," he said sternly, sliding the vest over his chest.

"Roger that," she replied, turning to go.

"And Reggie?" he asked.

She turned her head to look at him. "Yeah?"

"I want a confession from him, including who hired him. I don't want to give Adam an opportunity to deal with him before we get the truth out of him and lay this whole thing to rest. I also don't want any dead agents, so tell them to avoid driving by the lake, tell them to take the long way to the station."

She nodded once more and walked out.

"I'm going with you," Bret said.

Jeff felt a brief twitch, a sad smile, and he nodded. "Alright."

"Take your stuff with you," Margaret said, cool and distant.

"Mom, stop!" Timmy shouted.

Bret stared at her, and she returned his gaze. "No, it's okay, Timmy. I have to do this. Might as well be on my own," Bret said. She cast her gaze to the floor. "I'm sorry. I just need you to keep Kaiser until I can come get him again."

With that, he turned on his heel, shoulders slumped and head down, and went back to retrieve his things.

*** *

They took the quick way to the police station, Jeff silent on the driver's side with Bret riding shotgun and Reggie in the back.

Bret's heart hurt, his chest hurt, but a fiery determination to see this through was burning a hole in his gut. He watched the little town out of his window as they drove. Occasionally, he felt Jeff's gaze on him. Bret wanted to touch him, wanted to reach over the center console and place his hand on his leg. He was nervous. Anxiety climbed up his spine and down through his fingertips, causing his heart to race and his palms to sweat.

They pulled up to the station fifteen minutes later, and Bret was the first out of the car. He stared at the building he had known so intimately back when Adam was a missing person. He had worked with them, thinking he was doing the right thing, but now he knew he should have gone out on his own to look for Adam. With Martin and the sheriff now dead, having been accomplices in the whole thing...it made Bret's skin crawl. Jeff and Reggie got out of the car and flanked him as they ascended the concrete stairs. Reggie went in first, followed by Bret, and Jeff brought up the rear. Yet once inside, they took their roles at his side once more.

An agent was waiting and made her way up to them as they entered.

"Denise," the awaiting woman said, shaking Jeff's hand.

"Nice to meet you," he replied.

"We have the suspect in the interrogation room with two guards, as you requested. He seems like he's on the verge of a massive meltdown."

"Did you find anything at the scene?" he asked as they all made their way down a long corridor. Bret could feel the patrol officers' gazes on him as they passed, and he grinned when Reggie put a hand on his back and spoke up.

"Not the ring you described," she said. "However, we found a great deal of gay porn videos under his television."

Jeff snorted.

"Do we have a sight problem, gentlemen?" Reggie barked at the staring officers. "Because I'm sure we can have it adjusted for you."

Low grumbles of "No" were the only reply as they headed in the opposite direction with Denise leading the way. They came upon a set of doors.

"The first rooms are for observation with a two-way mirror. The other side is the interview room," she explained.

"Okay, Denise. Bret will be observing—do me a favor and stay with him till we're finished? Have you found the location of Mr. and Mrs. Williams?" Jeff asked.

Bret was startled by the question and felt his heart race again. So this was actually going to happen.

"Yes, we have agents at their home now. They haven't come or gone at all in the past twenty-four hours. They have had a visitor, and we checked the plates. It's a lawyer from Detroit," she said disgustedly.

"Thank you. Ladies, if you can give us a minute?" he asked.

Reggie and Denise walked into the room and shut the door.

Jeff wasted no time putting Bret at arm's length and staring into his eyes. "You don't have to do this. I can have the agents take you back to my room to wait if you want."

Bret shook his head and gave him a weak smile. "No."

"I didn't think so," Jeff said, his eyes full of concern.

Bret took the opportunity to hug him and bury his head in the crook of Jeff's neck.

Jeff immediately held him close and kissed the top of his head. "You're very brave, Bret."

Bret nodded and backed away, taking a deep breath and exhaling it. "Okay, I'm ready."

Jeff kissed his forehead once more and opened the door to the interrogation side of the room. Denise stepped to the side, as did Bret, to allow them passage. Jeff and Reggie entered while two other suits left to make room for them. Bret kept his eyes on the window, walking right over to it.

The coach, who had given Bret such a hard time before he'd met Adam, sat there, looking pale and shaken through the two-way mirror. He'd gained weight since the last time Bret had seen him, and what little hair he'd had when he first transferred in was long gone. He was fidgeting, shaky, and rocking back and forth.

***

Adam walked in, unseen, with Jeff and laid his eyes again on the man he was after next. He had followed the man when the agents had interrupted his plans. Out of curiosity, he allowed the arrest of the man, of course, following very closely until they brought him here. He'd waited outside until Bret and his new lover pulled up and made their way in. Now he stood behind the coach, watching over his head and back through the glass, awaiting the moment to strike as Bret watched.

As soon as Jeff walked into the room, the man began confessing.

"It was us! It was us! We did it. I helped. I killed that kid. Now they're all dead!" he cried, sobbing.

"Slow down, sir. I need to get this on record," Jeff said, pulling out his cell phone.

The man shook his head emphatically. "No. No. There's no time. He has come for me like he did the others. He's come to kill me and take me to hell! Please help me!"

Reggie and Jeff looked at each other. It was the woman who spoke next.

"Who has come for you, Mr. Polanski?" she asked, scooting the phone with a recording app closer to him.

"Adam Woolsey." He sniffed.

"Why would he do that?" she asked.

The man swallowed thickly, understanding what she was doing, and leaned forward in his chair to speak into the microphone. "I, along with four others—Larry, Officer Martin, Reverend Dennis, and the sheriff—murdered Adam Woolsey."

Jeff asked, "Why?"

"We were hired," the man replied.

"By whom?"

The man hesitated.

Reggie prompted, "By whom?"

"Elle May Williams," he said quickly.

Although no one else in the room could hear and see what he saw, Adam heard Bret gasp and raised his head. He saw the hurt in Bret's eyes and the agent named Denise reached out a hand comfortingly and placed it around his shoulders. Bret wiped the tear from his eye and with a grave nod of affirmation confirmed what he believed to be the truth. Adam longed to touch him, to comfort him, but that would never be. The whispers grew louder.

"How did this come about?" Jeff asked stonily.

Adam could feel the contempt radiating off him and smiled to himself as the whispers began to gain momentum.

"Adam and Bret were very close. They were always together, they switched classes to be near each other, swam together, they were always together. People talked, and we heard rumors in the teacher's lounge about them being queer for each other. One day his mother appeared in my office and asked me to keep an eye on them for her, saying that she thought Adam was a bad influence on her son."

"And you agreed?" Reggie asked.

The man looked at her in misery and nodded.

"Mr. Polanski, why? My agents found a great deal of gay pornography at your residence," Jeff asked, his jaw clenching.

Polanski's face turned beet red. "Because I hated them! I hated them for being so free about who they were. For living a life I could never live. We were always taught that que—gay people were an abomination. I tried to fight it off, I did!"

"Then what happened, Mr. Polanski?" Jeff asked, interrupting Polanski's self-loathing tirade.

"Well, at first I tried to tear them apart. To make things difficult for Bret, I really rode him on his performance. But the harder I tried to wedge myself between the two, the more Adam pushed Bret in performance, eventually their work paid off. They went on to be the best swimmers this school ever had. They started winning competitions, and no matter what I did, their popularity grew. Then it became known that they were a couple. I figured all hell was about to break loose," he said, shaking his head.

"But everything is different now, isn't it?" Reggie asked.

He nodded, bitter tears rolling down his cheeks. "There were some kids who gave them shit, but the majority of the others silenced them. They even went to prom together."

Jeff sat forward. "When did she hire you all?"

"It was before graduation. She approached the minister first and put up the sum of money. He really hated gay people. Preached against them all the time, so she knew where to go. He called us all individually and had us meet him at the church one Wednesday night after services."

"So he just said 'Hey, let's knock off some queer kid'?" Jeff asked, folding his arms over his chest.

Polanski shook his head emphatically. "No. He wouldn't dare be that direct. He started off with a speech, then pulled out the Bible and read some passages in Romans and Leviticus about how gay people should be put to death and how they won't inherit the Kingdom of Heaven."

"So, he let you all come to your own conclusions?" Reggie asked.

"Adam and Bret were a big deal in this little town. People either loved them or hated them, but they were extremely popular. As soon as he spoke, it was like a chain reaction."

"Who mentioned them first?" Jeff asked.

"The sheriff."

"And then?"

"I jumped in and told him about being asked to watch them."

"And it went from there?" Reggie asked.

He nodded.

"Say it," she prompted.

"Yes."

"What happened after that?" she asked. The man hesitated. "Mr. Polanski?"

"We planned to kidnap him. Take him to an old abandoned warehouse in the next county over. Kill him and bury his body out in a field," he said, his face turning green.

"Why did you murder him at the lake?" Jeff uncrossed his arms.

"Adam had come to me one evening before graduation and asked if he could come and swim in the evenings. I agreed. It was perfect, actually. But something screwed up. The night we all planned to do it, he didn't show up to swim. Officer Martin put out the word over the radio asking for any patrol cars to call in if they spotted his car in town. Twenty minutes later, we caught up to him coming out of a florist."

"You just grabbed him off the street?" Jeff asked, sitting forward.

"We pretended there had been an accident at home. Made up some bullshit story about his dad getting hurt at work, so he got in the car with Officer Martin. We followed behind him. Then I guess Adam started to suspect something, and suddenly Martin's car started to swerve. I think Martin must have let him know. The kid was pretty strong and managed to kick out the area between the front of the patrol car and the backseat, he managed to kick out the back window right behind the driver side, attacked the Sheriff, and made a run for it."

"Wait, wait, Adam was missing for a couple of days before he was discovered," Reggie said.

"The sheriff told us to put him pretty far back in the reeds and let the elements sort of...cover up the bruising...when we...uh, when we..." he said sickly.

"Beat him," Jeff said.

"Yes."

"You weren't afraid of someone coming upon you?" Reggie asked disgustedly.

Polanski shrugged. "Have you looked at YouTube lately? Or the Internet? There are videos all over the place of cops using excessive force thanks to today's Supreme Court. Nobody stops them. No one dares interrupt—what are you going to do, use foul language? Besides, it was a secluded area that nobody but old-timers went down to fish at."

Reggie looked like she was going to slug him.

Jeff put a calming hand on her arm and continued. "So who did you give the ring to that was removed from the body?" he asked.

The color drained from Polanski's face. "How do you know that?"

"Just answer the question, sir."

"Elle May. She wanted it. She was disgusted that they'd become 'engaged.'" He made quotation marks in the air.

"Did her husband know anything about this?" Jeff asked. "Was he involved?"

He shook his head. "Who, Doug? No. Doug didn't know, and she wanted it kept that way."

"Why is that?" Reggie asked.

Polanski shrugged. "Doug was always screwin' around. That was no secret. Everyone knew, even though Elle May played them off like the perfect family. Adam threatened that image. She'd been holding that image together for a long time, but if the truth came out, it would be too much. Doug's screwin' around she could manipulate to get sympathy. But Bret being gay *and* her husband screwing around, would put the ol' red eye of this town on her as the failure. She couldn't have that."

"Why not kill Bret too?" Jeff asked.

Adam was watching Bret.

"She said she would if he didn't leave for school, but she wanted time between just in case someone got suspicious. But since he left, she said he'd never end up being a problem. Image is important in this town."

Reggie looked over at Jeff. "What a sick bitch."

He nodded and stood up. "Mr. Polanski, you're under arrest for the murder of Adam Woolsey. You have the right to remain silent. Anything you say can—"

"I know the deal. I'm glad to be under arrest. I don't want to end up like the others," Polanski replied sadly.

"You deserve it," Jeff replied.

"I know that too. Just...before you put me in my cell, may I use the restroom?"

Jeff nodded, walked over to the window, and knocked. Denise came to the door, and then Jeff motioned for Polanski to come with him.

Adam let them all file out before him and slipped through the door as they were shutting it. There Bret and Mr. Polanski met face-to-face.

"Oh my God!" the coach cried before lowering his head.

"Oh your God? Is that it? You took the one happy thing I had in life away from me and... Oh your God? Your God has abandoned you, Mr. Polanski," Bret said and continued in a singsong voice, "But don't worry, Adam hasn't. My boyfriend's back, and you're gonna be in trouble..."

Adam smirked.

***

"I am so sorry!" Coach Polanski cried in horror as the agent Jeff had ordered took Mr. Polanski by the arm. Denise followed them out.

"You should be" was all Bret could reply as the man left, leaving Jeff and Reggie in the room with him.

Reggie walked over and wrapped her arms around Bret in a hug. He returned it fiercely before turning her loose as Jeff looked on.

"What happens now?" Bret asked as she backed away and Jeff took her place.

"We have enough for an arrest warrant. Elle May will be going to jail for a long time," Jeff replied, reaching out to take his hand.

"Which reminds me, I need to call this in," Reggie said. "Please excuse me, gentlemen, I am going to step out into the hallway." She patted Jeff on his back.

He watched her walk out the door and turned his head back to Bret to speak. Bret had lowered his head and closed his eyes. Jeff's heart went out to him.

"It's going to be alright. We are going to make sure she's in protective custody after her arrest, and she'll go far away from this place," he said soothingly while rubbing Bret's arms.

Bret suddenly felt cold to the touch and sort of damp. "It's not going to be alright" came the reply.

Jeff's heart sank as the hairs on his arms stood up. Bret raised his head and looked at him through Adam's eyes.

"The promise has to be kept."

"Adam, you're killing him," Jeff said, his mouth going dry.

Adam looked at him painfully. To Jeff's surprise, the eyes were filled with sympathy and pain as if he knew how far-reaching his actions were. The look was so tender, it tightened Jeff's throat.

"Then it is me who is sorry. I never wanted this."

"Then stop."

"I can't!" he cried. "The promise must be kept!"

As Adam's face melted back into Bret's, Bret began to tremble and he bent over, coughing up lungful after lungful of water. Jeff grabbed him and screamed with all the power he could, "Reggie!"

That was when the popping noises and the shouting began.

***

The agent waited outside after instructing the man to do his business and come right back. Mr. Polanski nodded and continued through the push door and into the men's bathroom. The door shut in his face, but Adam simply passed through it, taking the time to seal it shut as he had done to the sheriff's shower stall.

Four sinks ran the length of the counter in front of the mirror, and along the other side of the wall were two toilet stalls and two urinals. Polanski chose the center sink, walked over, and turned the faucet on. He leaned over, cupped the water with his hands, and splashed it on his face. When he stood up, he looked at himself in the mirror, then gasped in horror as Adam revealed himself.

With a shout, Polanski turned and came face-to-face with him.

Adam sneered in anger as the whispers rose, demanding and pleading. The ground beneath them shuddered and rumbled before the farthest faucet exploded, spewing out green water. Then the next, its silver-plated handle hitting the ceiling before skittering across the bathroom, and then the next.

Shouting from the agent outside the door broke Polanski's wordless stare. He immediately began to scream for help when Adam seized him and dragged him into the middle stall. Polanski kicked and pleaded but to no avail as Adam forced him to his knees. The water inside the bowl had turned the same green color, and Adam plunged him face-first into it.

It amused Adam slightly that the man pedaled his arms like a swimmer as he tried to break free. He kicked his legs. The whispers had turned into a roar. It took only a minute or two before Polanski ceased to struggle and fell limp.

Adam let go. It was over.

Exhaustion took him as the voices were once again sated. "Five down, one to go."

Before he drifted into an oblivion of darkness, his heart broke for Bret and the screams of his new lover as he pleaded with God to show mercy.

Then all was black.

***

Jeff reclined in the backseat of the Navigator, holding Bret close to him as Reggie sped down the freeway. Bret clutched onto him, his hands ice-cold and his body shivering. Jeff kept rubbing his back and murmuring nonsense into his ear, alternating between this and placing kisses on his cool forehead. Tears leaked from Bret's eyes and began to soak the front of Jeff's shirt. With a grimace of pain, Bret buried his head farther into Jeff's chest as the occasional bump in the road wreaked havoc on his already sore body. Jeff did everything he could to absorb it, using his body as a buffer and a heating pad.

"How we doin', Reg?" he called out.

"ETA thirty-five minutes. I told them to meet us in the parking lot," she replied, guiding the vehicle over into the next lane.

Jeff knew she was speeding, and he would have been nervous if they hadn't gotten a police escort with a squad car in front and one behind, flashing lights and wailing sirens.

"I'm going to die, Jeff," Bret sobbed.

Jeff reached for Bret's hand and kissed his cool fingers, wondering if Bret was right. But he forced those thoughts out with a shake of his head. "No, sir. You're not going anywhere. I need you to take it easy, try to relax as much as possible."

Bret didn't respond vocally, but he did cling tighter to Jeff and Jeff to him.

Jeff was amazed at the strength of the younger man in his arms. He thought for sure Bret's body would have given out with the last attack, but Bret fought to remain conscious, clutching onto Jeff as gusher after gusher of lake water was deposited on the floor. His back arched, his neck bulged, and the force of it turned his face from red to purple, which didn't help matters much and caused him to faint once it had passed, but he came back around quickly.

The police in the station were so beside themselves, Reggie had to take command momentarily. They managed to bust through the door that had become oddly sealed while Adam took care of his latest victim, whom they found lying beside the toilet. The bathroom was flooded, and water was spraying everywhere, adding to the chaos they found as it ran out onto the hallway carpet. They were shocked at what they discovered, unnerved by it, and as they clustered around the door to peer in, Reggie jabbed at them.

"What's the matter, boys? Don't like your boss's handiwork?" she asked, walking through the water to check the pulse of Coach Polanski. Of course he was dead, but she had to do her job.

"What the hell do you mean, our boss's handiwork?" one of the officers asked.

She stood up from the recently deceased and walked over to him. "I know little towns like this can keep terrible secrets.

That still waters run deep. But this"—she motioned behind her—"is what happens when what you bury rises again. Your boss conspired with another officer and several town people to murder Adam Woolsey, and it happened right under your noses. Why? Because he was gay."

The officer snorted. "Right, and some ghost is taking revenge on them."

Reggie got nose-to-nose with him. "How would you explain it, then?"

The man's mouth moved, but no words came out as he turned to look for support from his comrades. They had nothing either.

"Or what about him?" she asked angrily, pointing to a collapsed Bret.

She waited for a second and then shook her head. "You all let a murder happen in your town, and all the information was right here the whole time. I want to ask, how is it you all can sleep at night? Nothing? You, nothing?

"I want all of this documented and added to a file I have placed on the good sheriff's desk, and so help me *God*, should the file go missing, you'll wish to trade places with the victim in there, do I make myself clear?" she growled.

There were murmurs of yeah, yes, and uh-huh.

"Good. Get started, and someone shut off the goddamn water!" she barked. Jeff had never seen people move so quickly in his life.

"Reggie, how many agents did you send to Bret's parents' house?" Jeff asked as Bret's breathing slowed and his grip loosened.

"All of them. How is he?" she asked.

"Asleep."

"We'll be there soon, bud. You two hang tight."

She reached behind her to grasp Jeff's hand. He squeezed before she took it back.

"Hey, Reg, you said you grew up around stuff like this. Was there any mention of miracles?"

"There's always room for miracles, baby, no matter where you're from."

Jeff looked down at Bret, closed his eyes, and prayed. He wondered if anyone heard him.

***

Bret walked down the hillside again, toward the figure he'd know anywhere. Night was all around them, silent, as the stars shone like diamonds in the inky blackness of the heavens. Adam stared out onto the lake, his naked back to Bret. Bret didn't hurt here, the pain in his chest and throughout his body miraculously gone.

He trudged through the high grasses as he made his way to the man he'd loved in life and whom he still loved, even in death. As he came upon him, just as before, he slipped his arms around Adam's waist and rested his head against his back. Adam clasped Bret's hands in his, and they were silent for a little while.

"You're not angry with me?" Adam asked.

"No, Adam. No. How can I be? This isn't your fault. You loved me when no else would." He felt Adam sigh in his arms as his hands rubbed against his own.

"I still do, ya know?"

"You still what?" Bret asked.

"I still love you," Adam replied sadly.

"I know. I love you too, Adam. I always will. No matter how things end."

"Could you be happy here, with me?" Adam asked.

Bret's thoughts wandered to Jeff's face, and he was silent.

"You'll miss him, won't you?" Adam asked.

Bret said nothing.

"Do you love him?"

"Adam..."

"It's okay, you can tell me," he replied softly.

"He's in my heart," Bret said, and it was true. Bret would miss him, and that made him sad.

Adam's flesh, which had been warm and inviting a moment before, was turning cold and damp under Bret's touch.

Bret tried to let go.

"The promise must be kept," Adam said as his skin turned blue.

"Adam…"

"Five down. One to go."

"Adam!"

"I love you, Bret!" Adam cried and turned.

His face was still the horrible mask of drowned death. Bret tried to fight him off.

"Kiss me, Bret. Like you kiss your new love," Adam said sadly.

"No, Adam. Please."

Adam leaned forward, and Bret turned, fought harder. Adam's hands were like cold vise grips on his own. He pulled Bret closer to him.

"No, Adam, stop! No!"

***

Bret shook himself awake, and suddenly he realized two things: they were still in the back of the Navigator, and the pain that had been gone was now red-hot once more. He woke grabbing hold of Jeff, who immediately held him close.

"It's okay," Jeff murmured.

Bret sighed and relaxed against him.

"Were you dreaming?" Jeff asked.

"Yeah."

"About Adam?"

"How did you know?"

"We heard you say his name a couple of times, sugar," Reggie said from the front seat.

Bret nodded. God, he was tired. His insides felt like they had tried to come outside of his body. Everything hurt.

"Alright, we're pulling into the driveway. There they are. Hang tight, guys," Reggie said as the vehicle turned right up and over a bump that made Bret grimace.

From where he lay, Bret heard Reggie's window roll down and her voice as she asked, "Mr. Shaw?"

"I'm Mr. Shaw's assistant, David. This is Mr. Shaw. We understand that you said you had some questions about Promise Island. I still don't understand why you had us come out here instead of you coming inside to greet us," he said curiously.

"Well, you two hang tight right there. I'll show you why," she said.

Bret could hear the vehicle's transmission shift as she put it into park. Her door opened and shut, and a second later the back door opened, casting him and Jeff in the sunlight. Bret hid his eyes from it.

"A drunk? Is he high? What is the meaning of this?" came the same voice.

Bret couldn't raise his head or his voice.

"Mr. Shaw?" Reggie asked.

Bret heard them move, and suddenly felt his leg grabbed by a warm hand.

"You go and bring us a wheelchair, David. Move quickly" came another voice, older, raspier, but commanding nonetheless. "Here, sit him up," he commanded.

"Okay, Bret. We're gonna do this nice and slow," Jeff said. "Use my body as a pillow, and we'll get you sat up."

It took a few times, and Bret thought he was going to pass out from the pain that flashed across his abdomen and chest. Tears formed in his eyes, blurring his vision, and he had to bite down on his lip to keep from crying out. Once up, he leaned his head forward on the seat in front of him to catch his breath.

"Easy, young man." The voice that had commanded David to grab the wheelchair had turned gentle when speaking to Bret.

Bret turned his face to him, and the glare of the sunshine and tears made a halo around a face he couldn't quite see. Bret raised a hand and wiped his eyes, letting them focus, and placed a hand above his brow to block out the sun.

Finally the face swam into vision. The man was old, and his face looked weatherworn and deeply lined. But the eyes, a deeper brown than his skin, were very much alert and searching Bret's. His face was framed by white and gray hair, which was tucked behind his ears.

"Are you an Ind…uh, a Native American?" Bret asked simply, and the man stared at him for a second before his lips parted in a wide and happy grin.

"That I am, Bret. I am Chippewa, my given name is Annawon. But my friends call me Chief."

"I'm Bret."

"You're two-souled, my friend. Both Bret and another," Chief said. "You can say his name out loud. He won't hurt you here."

"Adam," Bret replied.

"Adam," Chief said as if tasting the word for the first time. He stared at Bret, then back to Jeff, and then to Bret again.

"Who told you to come to me?" he asked.

Bret wasn't sure who he was speaking to, but Jeff replied.

"My partner, Reggie."

"Ah, you're the one I talked to on the phone?" he asked, giving her a smile.

"Yes, sir."

"Hmmm. What is your name, your given name?" he asked.

"Regg—Regina Doucette," she said.

"That explains the Cajun accent. I thought so. Pleased to meet you," Chief said.

A voice from behind him announced someone's presence, and Chief got out of the way for his assistant, who had returned with a wheelchair. Chief motioned for Bret to be put in the seat, and his assistant came forward so Bret could get a good look at him. He was huge, a tower of a man, who had the same dark skin and dark brown eyes as Chief. He reached in for Bret's hand, and while he gently pulled, Jeff gently pushed, keeping himself right behind Bret in case he fell back. Together, along with what little help Bret managed to give, they sat him in the wheelchair.

"U of M? I'm on campus," Bret said, looking around.

"Welcome home, then, Bret," Chief replied.

CHAPTER 16

T HE ROOM THEY sat in was dark, and it was made darker still when Chief instructed David to pull the shades of his office to block the sun. Reggie, Jeff, and Bret sat in front of his desk in a large room. They were in a part of campus Bret had never been to before. The room was large, with a set of drums on a table and artifacts all over the walls—bows and arrows and paintings of Native American scenes decorated the room.

"I never in my life thought I would hear about that island in this context," Chief said, sitting forward. "Tell me everything, Bret. Start from the beginning. Don't worry about being judged here."

Bret shifted in his chair and looked over at Jeff, who gave him a wink and a nod. "Adam and I were boyfriends in high school. I was a transfer midsemester, when my dad got a new job in this area. I signed up for swim class, and that's where we met. We became friends and stayed that way for a long time. Then things changed."

"As they often do," Chief said with a smile.

Bret relaxed a little. "Yeah. Well, we were always together. Pretty well-known and, I guess, kind of popular. Rumors abounded concerning us, sure, so when the relationship actually did change and we became a couple, people just accepted it."

"This isn't the sixties anymore," Chief grinned. "Tell me about the island."

"It was a place no one went to, except on dares, and then they came back telling horrible stories of ghosts or dead bodies. Urban legend stuff. We heard there was an old Native American curse on the island and so people just stayed off of it. But Adam was older and he never believed in any of that stuff.

"My birthday was coming up, and he wanted to do something really special. So he looked up the island here on campus and found out that it wasn't cursed…it was blessed. And that it was a place where promises were made, hence the island's name. He looked up the blessing, and on the night of my birthday, he took me over there. He lit the torches. We ate together, talked together, and promised to marry each other after graduation from college. We planned it out five years from that night."

Chief watched him like a hawk and listened to every word he said.

"Graduation for spring is tomorrow night, Bret," he said gently.

"I know," Bret said.

"What's going on tomorrow night?" Jeff asked.

"The promise will be kept, one way or another," Chief said.

"I don't understand," Reggie replied.

Chief stood up and scooted his chair back. He turned his back to them and opened up something. Bret could hear liquid being poured, and then Chief turned, walked over to Bret, and handed him a glass tumbler with an amber liquid in it.

"There seems to be a duality that's repeated here. Adam was right, and so were the kids at school, Bret. It is called Promise Island, but it should also be called Cursed Island as well, as that is what happens when the promise is broken." Chief sat down on his desk and folded his arms.

"They were innocent kids," Jeff protested.

"Ignorance of the law is no excuse, right, Agent?" he asked, looking at Jeff, who opened his mouth to respond, but Chief continued. "When a promise is made on that island, the two parties trade a part of their soul for the one they made the promise to and vice versa. It was a way to keep the promiser honest.

"A long time ago, long before even the Algonquin tribes, there was an old tribe in this region. They were the ones who made up the rules and blessed the island. It was a big to-do, then, to take canoes to that place and make treaties, to form alliances with other tribes, and to make war. When the Algonquin nations came, the old tribe was already thinned out and disappearing, so we took them and made them a part of us. But over time, even we forgot the dangers, and some of our own people fell victim to the power of that little piece of earth. Legend became myth, and things that should have been remembered, disappeared.

"Why don't you have a couple sips of that? It'll help with the pain you're in. Jeff, explain to me what brought you here today," Chief said.

"I was investigating a bizarre death, which became more than one. They looked like crazy revenge killings, which led us to investigate further. Come to find out, not everyone was happy with Adam and Bret's relationship." He paused and looked over at Bret, who lowered his glass and nodded. "Bret's mother hired five men to kill Adam. They drowned him in the lake," Jeff said finally.

"The rash of suicide deaths we've heard about," Chief whispered, his brow furrowed.

Jeff nodded. "Yeah. I met up with Bret, and I didn't believe it was anything more than some very skilled killer, until I saw it for myself. Bret changed right in front of me, became Adam, before he started to convulse and vomit lake water."

"My God," Chief whispered. "So the sheriff and a whole gaggle of people decided to drown him? Just when I thought humanity would right itself…"

"Yeah, it's pretty shitty. I loved him, and he loved me," Bret said.

"It's a terrible thing that was done to you, but the island will seek its own justice now, as it has been. The promise must be kept."

"I know."

"So you know what you must do," Chief said.

"Yeah, I know."

"Whoa, wait a minute. What do you mean?" Jeff sat up straight and looked over at Bret with confusion and fear in his eyes.

Bret looked at him sadly. "The promise must be kept. I'm sorry. I really did like you."

"Bullshit!" Jeff bellowed. "We came here with…with…with—"

"With what, Mr. McAllister? In hopes that I, as an Indian, can magically wave my hands and this can be undone? It doesn't work that way," Chief said, shaking his head sadly.

Jeff stood. "They didn't know."

"Then perhaps you'll think about that the next time you decide to go after some youth or some unsuspecting person concerning your own laws, Jeff," he countered.

"Come on, Bret, we're leaving," Jeff said, reaching down for him. Bret reached up and wrapped his arms around Jeff's neck as he leaned in.

Reggie got up and walked in front of them, opening the door for them as they went.

"Take care, Bret," Chief said as they were leaving.

"Yeah, thanks for nothing, Chief," Jeff responded.

***

Forty minutes later, they were back in Jeff's hotel room. Bret had fallen into an exhausted sleep, and Jeff paced the floor like an angry tiger as Reggie looked on. He was furious. Disgusted. His mind raced a mile a minute with thought after thought of what he could do.

"This isn't right, Reg," he said, clenching and unclenching his fists. His gaze kept turning to the clock. The minutes were flying too fast for him, and as the hand ticked by, his heart sank farther and farther into his chest.

"I know," she replied.

"He's going to die," Jeff said.

"I know."

"I'm powerless!" he hissed.

"I know."

"So what do I do about it?"

"I don't know," she replied.

"He's alone," Jeff whispered, stopping in his tracks. It finally hit him.

"No, he has you. He has you, Jeff."

In disgust, Jeff grabbed his keys off the table and ran out of the motel room. Jumping back into the Navigator, he squealed the tires, taking off out of the parking lot. In his mind's eye, he could still see the blond-haired guy he'd met in the hospital who had cautiously probed him about his life, who sought his touch in the middle of the night. Like waves gently lapping at the shore of his senses, Bret's smiling face over dinner came back to Jeff, and the thought of that face no longer smiling made him sick.

Fifteen minutes later he pulled into the driveway of the Woolseys' cabin and blew the horn three times in protracted bursts before getting out and slamming the door shut. He saw people coming to the door as he approached.

"*Hey!*" he bellowed. "*Heeeey!*"

First out the door was Big Daddy, followed by Margaret.

"You know, I've gotta tell ya. I've worked law enforcement now for over six years and never have I ever had a perpetrator that I couldn't catch. Or let alone see," Jeff started as a way of greeting.

"But now I do. And it's your son, Adam. Some sweet kid who fucked up and got himself and his boyfriend in over their heads. The boyfriend, who by the way not only will lose his fiancé, but his mother—"

"Agent McAllister"—Margaret cut him off—"if you're trying to make me feel bad for kicking Bret out of our house—"

"You know, why don't you shut your mouth?" Jeff bellowed.

Timmy took a warning step downward.

"All this talk about family, about love, and how you're sticking by Bret," Jeff said, advancing on the big man. "You're all full of shit."

Timmy clenched his hands, and Jeff laughed.

"What the hell do you want?" Big Daddy asked, coming down the porch to his son's side.

"I want you to keep your goddamn promise to him," Jeff said as his vision began to blur. "Tomorrow Bret is going to die. Adam will take Bret's mother like he's taken each of his other victims, the ones who made a victim out of him. And there isn't fucking shit I can do about it." His voice hitched.

"Now I've sent people to the gas chamber, or to lethal injections. People who did horrible, horrible things to others, and to tell you the truth, I slept fine those nights. But this—I don't blame Adam for his role in all of this, but Bret? *He's fucking innocent!*" he screamed. "All he did was love your son!"

Jeff put his head in his hands as the outrageousness of it hit him all at once. The insanity of it, the pressure from having the power of the federal government at his disposal, and all of it falling far short of anything that could come close to being Bret's salvation. He wept bitterly.

"Jeff…"

He jerked his head up and saw through blurred vision that Margaret had advanced on him. He stuck a hand out. "No. No Sunday school answer from you. No, I'll go mad. So this is what you're going to do. Tomorrow morning we're going after the one who gave the order to kill your son. We're going in so Bret can confront the woman face-to-face. The one who signed not only your boy's death warrant, but the one who signed Bret's as well. Then Adam will come."

He wiped his face, his voice hoarse and his mind spent. They all looked at him.

"He loves you. And the funny thing is he loves his mother as well. That's why he never turned her in, you silly woman. Ask yourself, would Adam have done the same?" he said to her tear-streaked face.

"You'll be there to witness him being taken by your son, either voluntarily or at gunpoint. I swear to God, I'm not kidding," Jeff said and turned on his heel. He marched to the SUV, climbed in, and peeled out of the driveway backward, too disgusted to look at them anymore as he rolled down the driveway and out to the road.

***

Bret woke up slowly and found himself sitting up in bed, his middle wrapped with an Ace bandage snug enough to keep him breathing shallowly. It was dark in the hotel room save for a light on the wall that cast a dull, sickly glow. Reggie's head was bent down as she gazed at her cell phone, which illuminated her pretty face. Bret felt bad that he wouldn't have much time to get to know her. She seemed like a cool person.

"I think Regina is a pretty name," he said.

She startled and looked up with a grin. "Well, hey there, handsome. You think so?" She took her legs down off the little table, the sort they always stick in motel rooms.

"Yeah, I think it's great," he replied.

"You know, you're the only one who's ever dared call me that. Even the boss." She winked, sitting forward.

"I get a feeling you're the boss and Jeff is just around for the ride." Bret smiled.

"And he's a charmer, ladies and gentlemen. No wonder Jeff likes you so damn much." She grinned, putting her phone up. Her smile faded with Bret's.

"I like him too, a lot. Maybe even love him a little. I know that's fast, but it's kind of been a crazy couple of days." Bret laughed weakly, although he didn't feel too much humor at all. His heart hurt in ways he'd never thought anyone could survive.

"Honey, don't you give up hope," she said, standing up and walking over to his side of the bed. "Can I sit down without rattling your insides too bad?"

Bret nodded.

She sat down and reached out a hand, brushing back his blond curls from his face. "Don't give up hope. You'll be able to get to know Jeff so well, he'll get on your nerves just like he gets on mine," she said, laughing, but stopped when she saw Bret just give her a courtesy smile.

"Are you afraid?" she asked.

Bret shook his head. "No. Adam will be there, I think. I think we'll be together, at least. I mean, how many others can say the same when they die? How many know for sure?"

"You have a point," Reggie said, taking his hand.

"Besides, you two will be there too. So, I mean, I could do a lot worse than the FBI watching out for me." He chuckled weakly.

Reggie sat forward, wrapped her arms around him, and pulled herself to him as gently as possible. "You sweet man, you damn well better be sure we'll be right there. All the way."

Bret hugged her back, even though it hurt him. He didn't care. He embraced the pain of it.

The door of the motel room opened and a disheveled Jeff walked in. He looked worn-out, and his eyes were red rimmed. His hair was a mess, and Bret wanted more than anything to run his hands through it, to straighten it out.

"Hey, you're awake," he said, grinning. The door shut behind him as Reggie stood up.

"Please excuse me, gentlemen, I am headed back to my room. Sleep well," she said awkwardly before she stopped to hug Jeff.

He hugged her back fiercely, and then she walked out.

"Can I get you something to drink? Something to eat?" Jeff asked, taking off his jacket. He took off his handcuffs, pistol, and phone, then laid them down on the table where Reggie had been sitting.

"Some water and a handsome FBI agent, if you please," Bret said smiling.

"I can do the water, but I'm not sure where there'd be a handsome FBI agent. I mean, I may have to do," he said, reaching into the minifridge. He pulled out two bottles of water and brought them over to the bed. He handed Bret his and gently climbed into bed next to him.

"I think you'll do just fine," Bret said, looking over at him.

"Yeah? Think so?" Jeff asked.

Bret leaned in and kissed him on the side of his mouth.

Jeff tossed his water bottle to the side and took Bret's mouth in his own, kissing him back passionately. The kiss broke, leaving them breathlessly staring into each other's eyes. Bret reached up and ran his hands through Jeff's hair, smiling the entire time.

"What are you doing?" he asked, his soulful eyes gazing into Bret's.

"Fixing this mess you have goin' on up here." Bret ran his fingers through Jeff's hair again, feeling this silky smoothness of it.

"Is it all better?" Jeff asked, smiling sweetly as Bret's hands slid down and held his face. Jeff closed his eyes and brought a hand up to Bret's to hold his fingers there as he leaned into his touch.

"It will be better soon," Bret whispered.

Jeff's face crumpled and pain flashed in his eyes. Bret's heart broke for him, for this Superman who suddenly found himself without the ability to fly.

"I don't want you to go," Jeff whispered, his words so stripped-down of pretense, of any hint of strength, just raw emotion.

Bret leaned in and kissed him again, his chest reminding him that he was hurt. Yet Bret ignored it. When Jeff responded, Bret scooted himself forward until he straddled his hips. Outside, thunder rumbled low, mimicking the sounds coming from Jeff as he reached for Bret and pulled him closer.

"We'll have tonight, Jeff. You and me. The world will be ours until the sun comes back up," Bret whispered into his ear once the kiss broke.

"What do you want me to do? Anything, just say it," Jeff begged.

"Love me like you would if you were in love with me."

"I am in love with you."

"Then this shouldn't be hard for you."

"Won't I hurt you?" Jeff asked, his eyes betraying his caution.

"It'll hurt if you don't. I'm tough. I can handle this," Bret said.

Their mouths came together, and Jeff's hands found his ass and squeezed, making Bret groan. Jeff broke the kiss and looked at him worriedly, afraid he was hurting him. Bret smiled reassuringly and kissed the end of his nose before returning to his mouth. He reached up and began to untie Jeff's tie and slide it out from around the collar, then his fingers found the top button as the rain began a slow pitter-patter against the motel window.

The buttons came undone as their tongues touched and their kiss deepened. Sliding his hands inside the shirt, Bret felt Jeff's large shoulders and muscled arms as he slid the shirt back, then returned to reach for the bottom of Jeff's T-shirt.

The kiss was broken once more as Jeff raised his arms over his head to let Bret slide the undershirt off and cast it on the floor. Bret looked down at Jeff's chest, soaking him into his memory—the mounds of his pecs, the pinkish hue of his nipples, the way his body filled out. Each breath etched it in his mind.

Jeff reached for where the bandage was clasped and gently unrolled it, leaving Bret's bruised body bare for the briefest of moments before he pulled him into his arms and their mouths came together once more. With an oh-so-gentle motion, Jeff gathered his muscular arms beneath Bret and picked him up, then lay gently back on the bed before he kissed his way down from Bret's chin to his chest and belly. His large callused hands, as gentle as an angel's feather, caressed Bret's skin. Bret gathered the sheets in his fists and held on as Jeff found the button of his shorts and unclasped them. He raised his hips to allow Jeff to pull them down his legs and off, leaving him exposed, his manhood filled to the limits of its length and girth.

Jeff stood and unbuckled his belt and trousers, then slid them down along with his underwear until he stood naked before Bret, who was in the same condition. Their gazes were locked together until this moment, till Bret drank in the sight of him. Jeff slid back in over him, skin to skin, their hands roaming each other's bodies. Whispers of pleasure could be heard, along with the beat of their hearts and the steady rhythm of the falling rain.

With effort, Bret turned over underneath him and arched his back in wordless invitation. He felt Jeff reach up to his shoulders with firm hands and then back down, before he felt the insistence of Jeff's erection push gently. He heard him quietly spit in his palm. There was pain at first, as with all things, but as it subsided, and with a shiver that shook Bret, Jeff filled him. Bret lay back down, his own erection pinned between himself and the mattress as he willed Jeff to give him everything.

As thunder rolled outside and lightning streaked across the sky, as the rain came down in torrents, cleansing the world, both men found safety and each other's souls in the darkness. As Bret willed Jeff to give him his fear, love, pain, and fragile hope, Jeff's desire was to give comfort and make Bret feel his love for him. As their moans turned to shouts, as their bodies arched, receded, and came together again, as skin heated and sweat pooled between them, the fever broke in a final shout of defiance against the fate the morning would bring.

Collapsing in exhaustion, they held each other and drifted in momentary peace.

***

Bret had fallen asleep, leaving Jeff wide-awake, lying in the darkness beside him.

The rain began to taper off as Jeff lay there in misery. The only light that filtered inside was from the neon sign that cast a yellow glow on the carpet. But his eyes were fixed on the darkness at the corner of the room, upon a shadow that seemed too dark.

"I know you're there," he said aloud. "You may as well show yourself."

Adam stepped forward into the light far enough to confirm Jeff's suspicions but not far enough to expose his face. Bret murmured in his sleep, saying Adam's name.

"I'm always with him," Adam said simply.

"Because you're bound to him?" Jeff asked, looking down at the sleeping Bret.

"Because I love him."

"I love him too."

"I know."

"He loves me back," Jeff said as he reached out a shaking hand to rest on Bret's side.

"He is bound to me," Adam said sadly.

"Because he loves you?"

"No. Because of fate." Those words hung heavily between them, and Jeff could swear he heard whispers in the room.

"I'll be there, you know. I'll be there at the end of this. I won't leave him," Jeff said.

"I rather hoped you would be. He shouldn't have to do this alone."

"Will you take care of him?"

"If I say yes, will that bring you comfort?"

"Do you really care about my comfort?"

"You brought him ease in his last days, so yes, I do care for your comfort, Jeff. It isn't the same, but in a way, I've fallen in love with you as well."

Jeff tore his eyes away from Bret to look at Adam. He stepped farther into the light, and Jeff saw the horror that had befallen all his victims. He saw what they saw in their last moments on earth.

"I am sorry for what they did to you," Jeff whispered.

"And I am sorry for what I must do to you," he replied.

With that, Jeff turned his head to look out the window into the darkness that lay beyond. Eventually he heard a sigh as Adam made his way back into the darkness to keep watch over his charge. Time refused to stand still, no matter how much Jeff willed it to do so, and as the morning dawned gray and drizzly, Jeff swore he could hear the sound of his own heart breaking.

CHAPTER 17

T HE DRIVE TO the lake was like a funeral procession. Several cars all in a row, their lights on and sirens silent, made their way down the highway. As Reggie drove, Bret held Jeff's hand the entire way, his heart hammering in his chest and his mouth as dry as desert sand. He wanted to speak, but his tongue felt cleaved to the roof of his mouth, and his mind was barren of any thought. The occasional *thump* of the windshield wipers cleared away the drops of rain as if heaven wept openly for them. A steady fog had crept out of the lake, as the air was cooler than the water, which made the drive slower than usual.

They had dressed in silence, unspoken words heavy between them as they gathered themselves together as best they could. At one point they held each other tightly until the sound of a knock came to the door. It had been Reggie, who looked as upset as they felt. Jeff had given his five agents, who had been waiting for them in the parking lot, explicit instructions on how the morning was to be run. His temper was foul, and Bret's heart went out to them. The agents couldn't possibly understand the gravitas of the situation they faced. But by their acknowledgment of his orders, Bret hoped what they had planned would go off without a hitch.

However, when they grew close to the house he'd grown up in, the Woolseys' vehicle, parked alongside the road, made his heart leap into his throat.

"It's okay. I told them to be here," Jeff said as they drove past it and pulled into the driveway. The entire situation was extraordinary, as one of the agents had pointed out earlier before they left. It wasn't standard operating procedure to bring along civilians during an investigation. And Jeff had begun to growl at him before Bret laid a calm hand on his arm. Gathering himself, Jeff explained that it was well within the purview of the FBI, in certain cases, to bring out psychics to help in the solving of a case when everything else failed. The agent looked from Jeff to Bret, his eyes wide. He didn't say anything else.

Immediately Bret's father came bounding out of the house, followed by Elle May, who stood in the doorway. Jeff made his move to get out, but Bret held him back for a second.

"He's a shit. He's a dick. He doesn't deserve the term 'father,' but he is innocent in all of this. Everything she did, she did for him. He doesn't love her and never has. Squeeze him and he'll fold like a cheap hat, and that'll give him the out he needs," Bret said.

"What do I say to him?" Jeff asked.

"Threaten his money."

Jeff nodded and got out of the vehicle, followed by Bret, who stood on trembling legs. Once Bret's father caught a glimpse of Jeff, his stern walk toward them faltered. Bret was sure his father remembered their last encounter. Behind them, the other vehicles pulled in, and by the sound of slamming doors, Bret assumed the party was all present and accounted for. Doug looked like he was going to throw up when Jeff pulled out his badge and flashed it.

"What is this all about? You've kept us under surveillance for days, have cut off our trip—I demand an explanation," Doug said.

"You are not in a position to demand anything, Mr. Williams. Now, you have two choices: you can get caught up in this murder investigation of Adam Woolsey and be named an accessory to it, or you can get in your car and simply drive away," Jeff said sternly.

"Murder investi—what are you talking about? That boy drowned. This is you," he said, pointing in Bret's direction.

"You're more right than you can ever know, you worthless son of a bitch! Your wife, to impress you and keep our little world looking as pristine and flawless as possible, hired five men to beat up and murder Adam," Bret said, clenching his fists.

The color drained from Doug's face. "What?"

"All these deaths lately? One by one we've uncovered the truth, and one by one they took their own lives," Jeff lied.

"You have no proof," Doug said breathlessly.

Jeff pulled out his phone.

"I have the confession of Coach Polanski right here. I can play it for you. Now, Mr. Williams, if you don't want every red penny you have ever earned to go to pay for expensive lawyers in a surefire open-and-shut case, then I suggest you get your ass in a car and hit the road," Jeff said in a matter-of-fact tone.

Doug looked back at his wife, then at Bret, and then back to Elle May. "Is this true?"

She came out the door, a look of devastation on her face. "No, of course not. It's Bret. He's making all this up."

"I can play it for you if you'd like," Jeff suggested.

"I won't be tied to any of this?" Doug asked.

"Doug!" she screamed in disbelief.

A smile crept across Bret's face.

"Not if you leave now," Jeff said.

"Man, screw this," he said and headed for the garage, leaving his wife of twenty-eight years standing alone on her porch screaming his name.

"How do I get my car out of the garage?" Doug asked, halfway there.

"Drive across the fucking grass!" Jeff barked at him.

Doug jumped and half walked, half ran the rest of the way.

Bret walked forward, flanked by a crowd of federal agents including Reggie and Jeff. Off in the distance, the Woolseys began to walk forward, led by Margaret. Bret gave them a brief look before settling his eyes on his mother.

"Where's the ring?" he asked.

"I don't know what you're talking about," she said, her voice shaking as she reached to clasp the sweater around her shoulders.

Always the lady.

"Where is Adam's ring, Mother? We know you have it," Bret said, advancing on her.

She backed up, blocking the doorway.

"You little son of a bitch, you little faggot. You disgraced this family. *You!* You are why he fucked Jessica. He was disgusted with you!" she said, her voice rising several octaves.

"No. I wasn't," Bret replied simply. "You wasted your life with him, and now he's gone."

"Step out of the way, ma'am, we have to search the premises," Jeff said as she blocked the door.

"Are you fucking him? Does he give it up to you like he gave it up to that other faggot? Is this what this is all about? You're disgusting," she spat.

"Ma'am, I have to ask you to move," he said again.

"Fuck you, show me a warrant!" she screamed.

"Let them in, you rotten bitch or you can deal with me outside here," Margaret spoke up.

Bret turned and saw Adam's entire family standing there. Reggie walked up and pulled Elle May out of the doorway as the rest of the agents came up the front porch. She pulled out Bret's ring, attached to a chain, and showed it to them.

"This is what we're looking for," she said, her voice stone cold.

"Hey, look across the lake," Timmy said.

Bret walked over to the edge of the porch, followed closely by Jeff.

The fog had burned off where they were, but across the lake it was rolling, seemingly boiling, and had steadily begun to drift across the wide expanse of still water. Adam was coming.

"Jeff…"

"I see it. I want everyone in the house. Woolseys, that means you too," he said.

Reggie had already taken the screaming Elle May back through the door and into the house. As Bret made his way toward the door, he was stopped by Margaret.

"We're sorry," she said, reaching out a hand to touch him.

"Me too," he replied sadly. "We need your help, please."

***

Everyone filed into the house, and before much longer, agents were going through everything. Drawers were being opened, shelves searched, cabinets thrown open and their contents laid out on the floor.

Elle May sat on the couch, indignantly cursing everyone for everything they touched as they spread their search out.

"Where is the ring, Mom?" Bret yelled, coming out of his parents' bedroom.

"You'll have to arrest me." She sniffed.

"Oh, there are by far worse things waiting for you than prison. You're going to die," Reggie said simply.

"You people can't kill me." She laughed maniacally.

"No, we can't, you are right, but Adam can," Reggie said.

"Adam's dead."

"Not dead enough," Jeff replied.

The sound of crashing came from upstairs, and Elle May screamed and stood up, walking toward the back stairs.

"Where's the ring, Mom?" Bret screamed.

"Agent McAllister, we found this," Denise said as she bounded down the stairs. In her hands was a small safe.

"You put that back. You people don't have a right!" Elle May screamed, reaching for it.

A knock sounded at the door, and everyone turned to see who it was. Bret was surprised to see Chief Shaw standing at the door, along with his assistant, David. Jeff motioned for them to come in.

"Who the hell is that?" Elle May shrieked.

"Give us the combination," Reggie exclaimed.

"Go to hell!" Elle May screamed, and Margaret rushed her, grabbing her by the hair and forcing her head back.

"Tell it to them!" she said as she rained slaps on her face. "You murderous bitch! *Tell them!*"

Elle May shrieked with each blow. Agent Doucette grabbed Margaret and pulled her back, but not before a fistful of Elle May's hair came with her.

"Okay! *Okay!*" she sobbed finally.

Margaret let go, and Big Daddy pulled her back into the cluster where Adam's family stood.

"Four, thirty-seven, two, twenty-two," she sobbed, stumbling farther into the back of the house.

"Jesus, look at that," Timmy said his voice a mixture of awe, fear, and shock.

The whole back of the house was being overtaken by the fog that arched past. The house gave a shudder under their feet, followed by the loud cracks and groans of bursting pipes. All at once the sound of running water filled the room.

"What is that?" Denise asked, her voice shaking.

Jeff took the safe from Denise and set it down on the dining room table as everyone huddled around it, and proceeded to input the number. The house had darkened further now that the fog had consumed it.

"Jeff…"

"I know."

"Hurry, babe."

"I know!" he said again. But his hands were shaking so badly he must have missed a number. As he went to open the safe, it wouldn't give.

"This better be the right number!" he screamed at Elle May.

"It is!" she cried, looking around her.

Water started flowing out of the kitchen and into the dining room where they all stood. It was still clear. The sound of whispers grew louder and louder, distracting Bret.

Jeff zeroed the safe out again and was on his second attempt to make it through when someone screamed. It was Margaret.

"*Adam!*" She pointed behind Elle May.

Bret's mother stopped her own crying.

"Look at what your money bought you, Elle May," Reggie said tremulously. Several agents pulled their weapons at once, but Reggie held up her hands and instructed them not to open fire.

Elle May's eyes grew large as she slowly turned to look. There, standing in the kitchen, his ruined face bloated and discolored, the iris of his right eye blown, was a soaking-wet Adam.

"The promise must be kept. Five down, one to go," he said as he grabbed a handful of Elle May's blouse.

The horrific scream that came from Bret's mother chilled him to his core as Adam grabbed her, spun her around, grasped her shoulders in his hands, and stared into her eyes. The whispers that had started quietly now sounded like a great hurricane where they stood. Elle May was reduced to sobbing now, her head shaking back and forth as if trying to clear the image from in front of her. Then, as if bending space and time itself, Adam withdrew with her, heading back out of the house.

"I got it!" Jeff cried and opened the safe.

"Is it in there?" Bret asked.

Jeff pulled out a single gold ring.

"Give it to me," Bret said.

"Bret…" Jeff hesitated.

"Jeff, we're out of time," Bret said, choking up.

Jeff handed him the ring. Reggie gave him the other one. Elle May's screams faded in the background. She was being dragged to the lake.

Bret took off through the back of the house, his eyes blurred with tears. As he cleared the house and made his way across the deck, he saw that Adam was already near the lake.

He heard shouts behind him as he ran as fast as his injured limbs would allow. Yet he stumbled when Adam pulled Elle May out into the water and shoved her head under. Bret felt himself choke and begin to vomit water as he fell to his knees. As soon as his body painfully exuded one lungful, another wave hit him, and then another. He felt a rib snap with the force of it.

Suddenly he was up in the air. Jeff had picked him up and was running with him. As his head swam, he heard Jeff screaming Adam's name over and over again while they made their way down to the water's edge. Elle May screamed again and Bret was somehow able to take in a lungful of air. They reached the water's edge, and Jeff began to walk them out.

"Adam, stop!" Jeff cried.

"The promise must be kept" came the reply as Jeff set Bret back on his feet.

"It will be," Bret panted, clutching his sides.

Elle May was on her knees, her hair wrapped in Adam's fist as Adam stared longingly at Bret's extended palm. She was fighting futilely with his grip on her.

"Adam, it's okay. Let her go. Come here," Bret said. "It's okay. I'm here to take her place. I am here to keep my promise."

Adam looked down at the woman and released her. Elle May scrambled out of his reach and back toward the shore, where the crowd of agents, family, and Chief stood watching, openmouthed and still. She tried to run past them, but Reggie grabbed her.

"Oh, no, you don't. You're going to watch all of this," Reggie said, grabbing her and turning her attention back to the lake.

Bret turned his attention back to Jeff. "You won't leave?"

"No. I'll be right here."

"I love you," Bret said and reached for him.

Jeff's arms wrapped around him as they held each other close, shaking and crying.

"I love you," Jeff managed to say before Bret broke their embrace.

Bret looked back at the crowd and locked eyes on Chief.

"Five years ago, Adam and I made a promise to marry. We pledged to each other our lives. Now the promise has to be fulfilled. Chief, would you do the honors?" he asked.

Chief nodded and reached for his assistant, who helped him out into the thigh-deep water. It was then Bret realized the fog had shrouded them from the onlookers.

Bret turned and made his way out to Adam, who stood there looking at him, the familiar look of longing on his distorted face. Bret smiled at him and almost slipped, falling forward, but Adam stopped it from happening by reaching out and steadying him.

On the shore, Bret could hear whispered words of disbelief mingled with the whispers on the wind that whipped around them. As soon as Chief was in his place between them and David stepped to the side, the old man cleared his throat.

Bret reached forward, grabbed Adam's hands, and held them in his own. That which had repulsed and scared him before ran fleeing from his mind, and although physically the ruined Adam remained the same, the Adam that existed before was now the only thing Bret could see.

If he were to die, it would be with his end of the bargain kept.

***

Jeff watched with a mixture of horror and wonder. Standing next to Reggie, he glanced over to the Woolsey family, who openly wept and clung to each other. At their feet, Elle May had finally shut up to watch as well.

"We are gathered here today in the presence of the Great Spirit to see a promise between these two men fulfilled. The ties they secured five years ago have now tugged taut and pulled them back together by laws long forgotten by humankind. So, before you now, they seek to make their vows."

Bret smiled, his beautiful face lighting up, and to Jeff's shock, Adam smiled back.

"Do you, Adam, take Bret, to love him, till the end of all things?"

Silence. Then "I do."

Chief turned to Bret.

"Do you, Bret, take Adam, to love him, till the end of all things?"

"I do."

"Do you have the rings?" Chief asked.

Bret nodded and broke the chain off his, tossing it into the water.

"Please, Bret, take Adam's ring and place it on his hand."

Bret took Adam's left hand and slid the ring on before handing Adam the other ring.

"Adam, please take Bret's ring and place it on his hand," Chief instructed. Oh-so-carefully, Adam did.

"With the power vested in me, by Bret and the Great Spirit, I now pronounce you married before your families, friends, and the foundations of this earth."

Jeff watched the miraculous. As the shroud of fog surrounded them, he bore witness to Adam and Bret's marriage. And all the while, Jeff could think of nothing but a face. The mask of death that replaced the once beautiful visage and the blown-out eye that regarded Bret as if he was the single most precious thing in the world. Everyone stood transfixed as Bret smiled, his living hands wrapped in the cold blue of Adam's drowned ones, their fingers intertwined. What surprised Jeff even more and drew a collective gasp from the onlookers was when Bret reached up and cupped Adam's face and drew him down for the kiss. Jeff watched Adam's face, the disbelief, the elation, and emotion all rolling through him. The longing and adoration.

But that wasn't the miraculous part. No. At first Jeff didn't notice, but something drew his attention out over the lake. He realized the bank of fog that had rolled so thick and heavy was now no longer there, and the whispering that had accompanied it was replaced with the constant sound of the beating of his heart. When a sob broke through the crowd, Jeff cursed himself for taking his eyes off Bret, even for just a second, but what he saw made up for it.

The ruined face had become a living one. The horrible gray-blue of the skin turned flesh-colored and vibrant. The ruined eye now repaired. Jeff saw the man Adam used to be, restored and shrouded in a golden light. Adam broke his gaze with Bret, who still grasped his hands, to look over at his family with one final grin of happiness before he slowly faded into the golden shafts of sunlight.

And Bret collapsed.

EPILOGUE

One year later

J EFF WATCHED THE video again. It was from a closed-circuit monitor of the mental health facility that had housed Elle May Williams, now deceased. He'd seen it a thousand times—the FBI had had it sent to his office with a note from the director:

I think you were right, this one should be labeled X Files. *It's too bad we don't have a branch for this particular thing. So I am sending this and your files to storage for later analysis. Perhaps somewhere down the road we can figure out what actually happened.*

Brightmore Mental Health Care Facility in Jackson, Michigan, was a state-of-the-art hospital that worked with the criminally insane. All residents were kept, not behind steel doors or bars, but behind observable glass walls similar to the room in which Hannibal Lecter had been kept.

After the "wedding," Elle May snapped. Ranted and raved about what had happened to her in court, while everyone present who was called upon to testify denied what she was saying. The court saw her as unfit to stand trial until such a time as she could be declared competent. That had been enough for Jeff, and it had been enough for Margaret as well. To see Elle May trapped in a prison of manmade structure or in her own mind, neither of them cared much. Just as long as she was somewhere she couldn't hurt anyone.

They thought the curse was over, the promise kept. However, even though Adam was released from his part of it, the spirits of the island still resented her for breaking the promise and meant to have justice done.

The video contained several CCTV images edited together to show the entire scope of what had occurred shortly after her incarceration. A steady stream of events that left many scratching their heads and caused several meetings with Reggie, Jeff, and their director, who wanted a blow-by-blow account of what had happened in the town of Promise the previous year. Off the record, of course.

They told him three times. The director forbade them to put any of it in their reports. They didn't have a problem with that.

In the first frames, Elle May was led down a long corridor, flanked by security personnel and medical doctors in white coats. The black-and-white CCTV image first showed her walking in one direction down the corridor and then coming from the opposite angle. Through the speakers, the security guard called for each segment of the hallway they walked through to be opened individually, through various checkpoints. This was no doubt an added layer of protection placed in case of a riot among the inmates.

Along with the shouts of the security guard were the shouts, shrieks, and laughter from the other inmates, who lined up against their various cell walls to watch her being taken down the hallway. The sound of it chilled Jeff to the bone, and he shivered upon hearing it once more.

Elle May's shoulders were slumped, her slipper-clad feet shuffling, a possible result of the amount of drugs they'd pumped into her system to keep her "sane." Her once well-kept hair was a disheveled mess, and Jeff shook his head for the hundredth time as he watched her go, remembering Bret's final words to her.

Look what your money bought.

"Bret," Jeff whispered, closing his eyes with a wince.

He reopened them to observe her being led down to her own cell, where the security guard called out the cell number. Elle May was taken into it, sat down on a simple bed, and uncuffed. She didn't move as a doctor appeared to talk to her before leaving once again. She sat there for an hour or so before a nurse made rounds and delivered medication to her, again flanked by security.

She took her medication without a problem.

The time-lapse video started at 7:00 p.m., and thanks to editing skipped through the mundaneness of security making their rounds. The shrieks and cries settled down once the patients were sufficiently medicated. That was until 10:05 p.m.

The first thing that could be heard were the whispers, faint at first, and then, as the CCTV monitor focused on her cell, they grew louder and more insistent. Then the shrieks began again, this time coming from inside Elle May's cell. She was at the glass, pounding away, begging for help. A chunk of ceiling caved in, and a pipe burst into her cell, and water began to fill it. Chaos erupted as the CCTV showed security trying to reach her, but the security doors refused to open.

The camera flashed in and out as if an electrical surge was shorting it. Each time it flashed back on, it showed the water even higher. But that wasn't the most disturbing point. Several figures could be seen inside the cell with her. The sheriff, the drunk, Martin, Pastor Dennis, and finally, Coach Polanski. All dead. All drowned the way Adam had been. She saw them too, as she kept turning her head back to see them grow closer to her. The water was up to her chest when they reached for her and pulled her away from the glass. The video cut out once more for an extended period of time and then cut back in one final time as the security guards managed to get inside the block, only to find her floating in the center of the cell, her lifeless body suspended, her sightless eyes staring, and her mouth left open in an eternal scream.

Jeff reached forward and turned the monitor of his computer off for the final time. He sat back, sighed, and rubbed his eyes.

A knock on the door sounded, and knowing who it was, he called "come in" before even lowering his hands.

"Hey, boss," Reggie said, and he smiled.

She stood there, arms crossed over her breasts, looking at him with a sad smile on her face.

"Not anymore, Reg—congrats on the promotion," he said with a grin that matched hers.

She came into the room.

"I've come one last time to beg you to stay. This place won't be the same without you," she said, taking a seat in front of him.

He regarded her for a moment and sighed. They'd been over this a thousand times since he'd handed in his resignation.

"I think it'll be just fine with you at the helm. You're a good agent, Reg," he said.

"Only because I learned what I know from you."

"Nah. You have gut instinct. You follow leads I would hesitate to follow. That I *did* hesitate to follow."

"You followed your heart."

"Yeah."

"So what's next?" she asked.

"I go where my heart tells me to go. I was nothing but the job. Everything was the job. I'd forgotten how to live. I think I'll do a bit of that for a while," he said.

"He did that for you," Reg conceded.

"He still does." Jeff held a hand over his heart.

"You'll keep in touch?" she asked, and Jeff nodded, standing up.

Over the past few months, he'd slowly packed up his belongings in the office, tied up loose ends with other cases to make sure they all were completed, and he reached for the single box that contained his life, and then picked it up.

"Of course I'll keep in touch. I'm not that far away, you know," he said, picking it up and walking around the desk.

Reggie stood up and hugged him as he came to the other side, and he held the box out, his belongings light enough to hold in one hand. She kissed his cheek as she let go.

"I know you won't be far. I'll drop by every now and then to see how you're getting on."

"You'd better."

They broke their embrace. Reggie walked him out and escorted him down to the end of the corridor. It wasn't for nostalgia's sake, or not completely anyway. She had to, now that he was no longer an agent. He didn't have the clearance any longer to travel the hallways of the Detroit field office.

After kissing her good-bye one final time, Jeff took the elevator down and walked out to the parking lot, where his black Navigator sat awaiting him. After throwing his box in the backseat, which had of late become covered in dog hair thanks to Kaiser, Bret's German shepherd, he shut the door. He took off his jacket and tossed that into the front seat, which he determined at least be kept clean. Jeff loosened his tie, rolled up his sleeves, and unbuttoned the top button before opening the driver's side door.

Jeff got in, pulled out of the garage in downtown Detroit, passing through several lights before he made his way to I-69 and drove west. The wind was warm, the sun was high, and the roads were pretty empty at 10:00 a.m. as he made his way down the stretch of highway that was now very familiar to him.

As he drove, his mind filtered back to the past year since the day he first laid his eyes on Bret. So much had changed to show Jeff that he was not in control of anything. The curse had shown him that, and as he drove down the highway, his thoughts wandered back to what Reggie had said about old laws, old rules long forgotten. It made him wonder about how everything he thought of as solid in the world had been covered in concrete and glass. That realization had been the primary reason for him turning in his badge. Too many variables now existed, too many what-ifs that now made him uncomfortable with the idea of trying to go on with his life as it had been. He glanced back once more to the skyline of the city he'd departed, and with a flip of his wrist, turned the mirror up and away from his gaze.

Twenty minutes later he got off on the exit that led to Promise. Jeff had been making this trek now for the past six months since the Woolseys sold their house to him. They'd had enough of the town and enough of the lake that claimed their son's life. Jeff passed the high school Adam and Bret had attended and smiled to himself as he turned down the lake road. His worries of the day and of the future seemed to lift from his shoulders as his home came into view and he saw Timmy and Molly's vehicle parked out front.

Jeff pulled up alongside, killed the engine, and sat there, because he knew the inside of his house was chaotic now that baby Adam was toddling.

He got out of the SUV and purposefully slammed the door shut. He made his way around it and up the driveway.

"Hey! Jeff's home!"

Through the screen door, he heard Timmy call out from inside the living room, before the big man walked out with a huge grin on his face. Kaiser came barking happily in front of him. The dog stopped by Jeff long enough to get a scratch behind the ears and then bounded off, tail wagging, to the shore of the lake to do whatever dogs do when they're alone.

"Hey, Timmy," Jeff said, walking up.

"Hey back. How's it feel to be just another unemployed drag on society?" he asked, coming down the stairs.

The two men embraced, and Jeff could swear this man gave the best hugs in the world.

"It feels great," Jeff said, trying to sound convincing. He did feel better about it, but it too, just like the world, had become full of unknowns.

Timmy let go and stepped to the side, grinning. "Good. We'll have to celebrate with some fishing poles and beer later."

"Sounds like a plan."

Molly came to the door next, carrying Adam, who currently had a fist full of her hair that he was happily chewing on.

"Look, Adam, it's your Uncle Jeff," she said, and the toddler squealed.

"Wanna go say hi?" she asked, opening the door. Her body had thinned out since she was no longer being led by a baby bump.

She walked down the stairs, and when she got down to the ground, she placed Adam on his feet. The blond-haired boy navigated the ground with a look of fierce determination as he stumbled his way toward Jeff, who crouched down and opened his arms. The boy's face, which had been tight in concentration, lightened up as he reached Jeff and opened his own arms. Jeff scooped him up, much to their mutual delight.

"Hey there, big guy. You been good for your momma and dad?"

Everyone laughed when Adam responded in baby talk.

Timmy and Molly had become Jeff's lifesaver after the events on the lake that day. They'd taken him in when his world had been rocked, when everything he'd been so sure of evaporated right in front of him. He loved them now like family, which was appropriate for who the Woolseys had always been. Big Daddy and Margaret also made it a habit to come down every now and then to see them, and they loved on Jeff as if he too were one of their own.

"Now that is the sexiest thing I've ever seen" came another voice from inside the screen door, and Jeff's eyes found the one thing that still managed to make his words stumble out of his mouth.

Bret stood there, leaning just inside the doorway, arms crossed over his chest and a grin on his face. Jeff felt his eyes tear up at the sight of him, and he did everything he could to keep from crying.

He'd thought he'd lost him.

When the rings were exchanged, and the "I dos" said, once Chief had announced the completion of the union, he'd also announced that the curse had been lifted. The promise fulfilled.

At least their part of it had been.

What happened to Elle May in her cell was beyond them, and as Chief explained later on, was part and parcel of the dangers of breaking a promise on this lake.

The following months had been tough. Bret, who had been severely hurt, made a full recovery physically but remained a little distant, a little cool, and Jeff had done the noble thing and backed away. He poured himself into his work, as Bret poured himself into his.

Meanwhile, change had come to Promise. The house Bret grew up in had been sold, and apparently, the affair Bret's father had been having with Jessica had never actually ended. He remarried, and she stole every last dime he had before running off with another man, leaving him broke. The police force had been replaced and each of the remaining officers either fired or put on permanent layoffs, pending an ongoing investigation into the death of Adam Woolsey. That had been a gift from Reggie herself.

The five deaths that occurred in Promise had all been ruled suicides at Jeff's insistence. Because of the nature of the investigation and to keep suspicion at a dull roar, his boss had agreed to it. The sixth death, Elle May's, had been ruled a freak accident. Afterward, when Jeff brought the video and a copy of the files to Bret, the man shed a single tear, and then they talked. And talked. And talked until the sun came up.

They'd been through a lot, and it took a little patience and navigating to bring them back together.

They'd taken it slow, dated, made love over and over again to make sure that they weren't together simply because life had thrown a wrench in their machine, until they uncovered the love they'd first felt for each other that night in the motel room, when they had been convinced Bret would die. And Bret had needed time to mourn the man who was now really gone. Although sometimes at night, he stared at the shadows a little harder.

Now Jeff couldn't bear the idea of his life being taken away by some criminal's bullet, to leave Bret alone in the world once more. Jeff couldn't bear the thought of making him a widower again.

Bret came outside and walked down the porch steps to make his way up to him. Jeff handed Adam back to Timmy, who took the babbling baby. He grinned and opened his arms again for the man who'd shaken his whole world. Bret walked into them willingly, and they held each other before Bret leaned his head back and looked him in the eyes.

"You are sure about this?"

"When you're nowhere to be seen, I have my doubts. Reggie thinks I'm crazy. My boss threw a fit on me. But every time I lay eyes on you, I've never been surer of anything in my life."

"We'll make a good life together, Jeff," Bret said. Jeff had plenty of money saved up, and they'd talked about him going back to school to teach criminology at U of M, where Bret taught. His interview was scheduled for next week, and from the sounds of it, he'd already gotten the job.

"I love you, Bret," he whispered.

"Do you mean it?" Bret asked, smiling back at him as Timmy and Molly looked on. Adam was squealing now to be let down.

Jeff cupped Bret's face in his hands. What he held there was more precious to him now than anything had ever been in his life. In death, they found hope; in fear, they found solace; and it would be in uncertainty, he would find peace. Because Jeff knew one thing, just one thing now his whole life had been uprooted—he knew he loved Bret. In addition, he knew Bret loved him. He could live with that.

Jeff kissed him once more out in the midst of the forest, in eyeshot of the lake, and in the shadow of the island's power. Jeff thought he heard a sigh of contentment. Maybe it was his imagination, maybe it was the whispering voices, or perhaps it was Jeff's own spirit. Either way, it was a sigh of a weary soul now at peace.

When their lips parted, Jeff leaned forward to whisper in his ear. "I promise."

ABOUT THE AUTHOR

F.E. Feeley Jr. is a poet and the author of six published works — four full-length novels, two short stories featured in anthologies, and a good deal of poetry.

Married to the love of his life, John, he came to the writing world about four years ago where he fell in love, again, with the written word.

Website: https://fefeeleyjr.blog

BY THE AUTHOR

The Scarecrow

Memoirs of the Human Wraiths
The Haunting of Timber Manor (Book #1)
Objects in the Rearview Mirror (Book #2)
Still Waters (Book #3)

Indigent

Contact (Gothika, #5)

Between Us

When Heaven Strikes

LOVE IS LOVE Poetry Anthology:
In aid of Orlando's Pulse victims and survivors

Closer

BEATEN TRACK PUBLISHING

For more titles from Beaten Track Publishing,
please visit our website:

http://www.beatentrackpublishing.com

Thanks for reading!